The Cloud
Pine View County Trilogy
Book Two

Lee W. Payne

Dedication

For my dad, Joe Payne. I wish you were here. I miss you and I love you.

Acknowledgments

I would like to thank my niece Amanda Schneider-Martinez. Amanda read every chapter of The Cloud as I wrote it and provided feedback and the encouragement I needed to complete it. I love you more than words can express.

I would also like to thank my friend, Anne Kimmel-Scamardo. Anne read The Cloud after I finished it and provided critical feedback needed by all authors to polish our work. Anne was my beta reader and found mistakes I missed. Thank you, Anne.

Finally, I'd like to thank my editor, Amanda Armstrong for providing positive feedback. My proofreader, Arlo Young, for finding inconsistencies and wording issues that needed my attention. And I would like to thank Genene Valleau for creating The Cloud's cover art. Genene created The Pack's cover art and I couldn't wait to work with her again. As before, Genene nailed it.

Prologue

A dense fog rolled into the Port of Houston shortly before midnight on December 23, 2015. A few minutes later, the bow of the eight hundred foot, trans-Atlantic, cargo vessel Constanţa Catarg emerged from the fog like a ghost ship and docked at the Woodhouse Terminal in the Houston Ship Channel at twelve-thirteen a.m. It was Christmas Eve, but the mood aboard the vessel was anything but festive. Of the thirty-six crewmen who left Constanţa, Romania, only twenty-nine survived the crossing.

~ * ~

The twenty-one-day voyage began with every sailor's dream conditions—clear skies and calm seas. But this wasn't to last. One day into the voyage, a persistent fog enveloped the vessel like a cocoon. With the technology aboard the Constanţa Catarg, the fog was less a hindrance to navigation than it was to morale aboard the vessel.

The first crewmember who went missing, Marku Bălan, the ship's boatswain, disappeared before the vessel exited the Black Sea through the Bosphorus Strait. His body was found two days later in a forward cargo hold. The ship's doctor, Anton Zaharia, performed the postmortem examination. Cause of death was easy to diagnose. Marku's head faced backwards as if twisted violently. What wasn't easy to explain was the complete lack of blood in Marku's body. It had been drained. Although rats feasted on his remains for two days, a wound on Marku's upper, inner, right thigh was especially grievous and large. Whether it resulted from one massive bite or a particularly enticing area that many rats had nibbled at since Marku's death, Dr. Zaharia could not tell. Dr. Zaharia, conditionally, ruled Marku's death accidental and his body was placed in the ship's freezer.

As the vessel sailed the Aegean Sea, south of Greece, a second crewmember died under mysterious circumstances. Nicolæ Şerban, the ship's chief engineer, left the mess hall after enjoying a meal of *slănina afumată, sarmale, cartofi copţi*, and *mămăligă cu brânză şi smântnă*— smoked bacon, cabbage rolls, baked potatoes, and corn meal with salty cheese topped with sour cream. Six hours later, his body was discovered behind one of the ship's boilers. Like Marku's body, Nicolæ's head faced backwards, his body was drained of blood, and there was a grievous wound on his upper, inner, right thigh. Because Nicolæ's body was discovered shortly after he went missing, rats hadn't had time to nibble at his remains. This gave Anton an opportunity to examine the undisturbed thigh wound. Aside from being larger than expected, the wound resembled a human bite. Nicolæ's death was ruled non-accidental, Dr. Zaharia lacked the forensic training necessary to rule it a homicide, and his body was placed in the ship's freezer with Marku's body.

News, and the circumstances, of the second crewman's death traveled throughout the ship's remaining crew quickly. Rumors circulated that the vessel and voyage were cursed. Whispers of '*vampir*' were exchanged in secret and crosses hung from chains around crewmen's necks migrated from beneath their shirts to be displayed on top of their shirts.

Like clockwork, every three days, another crewmember went missing. The third crewmember to succumb to the phantom menace was Dr. Anton Zaharia. As it turned out, they would not need his services for future deaths. They found no more bodies. They simply disappeared. As if they never existed.

The remaining crewmen took it upon themselves to search the ship in groups of three or more for the unseen evil, but to no avail. The bowels of the ship were bathed in perpetual darkness with only artificial light to chase away the shadows. The lack of sunlight created perfect hunting conditions for the unseen presence. All the crew members ever saw of their hunter was a shadow blacker than the ever-present surrounding darkness. All the crew members ever heard of their hunter was the faint flutter of leathery wings.

They heard the screams, though. Suddenly, and without warning, one of the roving group members would vanish in the blink of an eye. Within seconds of the disappearance, a startled scream would emanate from what seemed an impossibly long distance from where they were taken. The screams always ended abruptly; as if they were swallowed by whatever unseen evil haunted them.

Toward the end of the twenty-one-day voyage, the remaining crewmen remained huddled in their sleeping quarters. Regular maintenance on the Constanța Catarg went undone, and the ship fell into disrepair. Except for the captain, Costel Alexandrescu, who remained steadfast at the ship's helm and seemed immune to the surrounding horrors. This led more than a few crewmen to speculate Captain Alexandrescu had purposefully cursed the ship, but mutiny wasn't an option. The unseen evil had systematically eliminated the chief, second, and third mates. Captain Alexandrescu was the only person alive who could navigate the Constanța Catarg.

~ * ~

The unseen evil that feasted on crewmen every three days since the voyage began wasn't, as many suspected, a stowaway. Its passage was paid in full, and in cash, in Constanța a day before the vessel departed for America.

The man who secured the passage, a tall, slender man in his early fifties with thinning blond hair and piercing blue eyes, introduced himself to Captain Alexandrescu as Dănuț Roșca. He had very specific instructions about how the crates being shipped were to be handled. The four-foot wide by eight foot long by three-foot-deep wooden crate was to be secured, along with three smaller crates, in a large shipping container. Dănuț paid extra for the unused portion of the shipping container without complaint. He insisted the shipping container be placed at the bottom of a stack in the middle of the cargo hold. Captain Alexandrescu agreed to Dănuț's shipping terms and oversaw the loading of the shipping container, number 5261897, himself.

After securing passage for the precious cargo, Dănuț Roșca boarded a plane at Constanța Mihail Kogălniceanu International Airport bound for Houston George Bush Intercontinental Airport. After landing in Houston, Dănuț got into his 2015 black Cadillac Escalade and made the two-and-a-half-hour drive to Pine View, Texas. Dănuț had three weeks to prepare for the Master's arrival and much work still needed to be done.

~ * ~

Captain Alexandrescu remained unmolested by the unseen evil for the same reason the remaining crew refrained from mutiny. It needed him to navigate the Constanța Catarg safely to its destination. Once the Constanța Catarg docked at the Woodhouse Terminal in the Houston Ship Channel, the captain and remaining crew disembarked the vessel quickly. A final headcount revealed a seventh crewman taken since the previous headcount twenty-four hours earlier.

Flaviu Grigorescu was last seen entering the forward head earlier that evening. Captain Alexandrescu and two brave crewmen boarded the Constanța Catarg to search for Flaviu. The head was locked from the inside. Captain Alexandrescu used his key to unlock the head door. It was empty, except for a single drop of blood in the sink basin. The captain and two crewmen disembarked from the Constanța Catarg for the last time. None of the crew would ever board the cursed vessel again.

~ * ~

Captain and crew secured plane tickets and landed safely at Constanța Mihail Kogălniceanu International Airport on Christmas day. Black Sea Crown Shipping, owner of the Constanța Catarg, sent a replacement crew to navigate the vessel back to its home port in Constanța. The return voyage was uneventful.

Shortly after the successful return of the Constanța Catarg, Captain Alexandrescu was charged under maritime law with a lack of basic seamanship and dereliction of duty. All but three of the remaining crew were eager to point an accusatory finger at their former captain. When the guilty verdict was announced, Captain Alexandrescu didn't protest, nor did he appeal.

He accepted the verdict because he knew he was guilty of the charges. He negotiated the shipping arrangements with Dănuț Roșca and he pocketed the substantial fee. Although tempted to reveal the off the books deal with Dǎnuţ Roşca to his prosecutors, Costel Alexandrescu withheld the information. He didn't withhold the dealing out of judicial self-preservation. Costel accepted his culpability in the murdered and missing crewmen. He did it out of fear. There was something about Dǎnuţ Roşca's strong, cold handshake and piercing blue eyes that unnerved him. The man scared him.

In his twenty-six years as a captain, he had never accepted an off the books shipping arrangement, but he did so willingly when Dǎnuţ Roşca requested it. It was as if Dǎnuţ Roşca entered his mind and overpowered it. If it hadn't been Dǎnuţ Roşca overpowering his mind, it had been whatever was in the secretive crate, and that thought unnerved Costel Alexandrescu even more.

To further Costel's internal guilt, he knew in his heart that whatever was in the crate had been responsible for the murdered and missing crew. He had also been secure knowing, as long as the Constanţa Catarg was at sea, he was safe. Whatever was in the crate needed him to deliver it to America. Re-boarding the Constanţa Catarg after docking to search for the missing crewman took all his courage. He knew he was no longer needed and now expendable. But he owed it to the missing crewman to investigate.

When the guilty verdict was rendered, and the magistrate sentenced him to eight years in Aiud Prison, former Captain Costel Alexandrescu nodded at the magistrate. He nodded once more at his wife of thirty-one years, Oana, as they led him away in chains.

~ * ~

The longshoremen who unloaded the Constanţa Catarg witnessed none of the horrors the ship's crew relayed in broken English as they scattered from the ship. By eight a.m. on Christmas Eve morning, the Constanţa Catarg's cargo hold was empty.

Trucking company, freight train company, and destination of cargo determined shipping containers' positions throughout the Woodhouse Terminal docks. Per the stevedore's instruction, one blue shipping container, number 5261897, was set apart from the other containers. Also, per the stevedore's instruction, the container was oriented with the doors facing north, so the back end faced the southern sunlight.

This container had not been on the Constanţa Catarg manifest. Chuck Kowalski, the stevedore, pocketed a substantial sum of money from Dănuţ Roşca to navigate the rogue shipping container through customs without raising alarm. Like Captain Costel Alexandrescu, Stevedore Chuck Kowalski had never accepted a bribe to facilitate illegal activities. He was a dedicated longshoreman who began as a casual worker and, once he was added to the union books, worked his way up the union ladder from dock worker to foreperson. After several years as a foreperson, he was promoted to stevedore. Every step earned with hard work and honesty, but something about Dănuţ Roşca had him nodding and holding out his hand for the stack of bills before he knew he'd agreed to help him.

Before leaving the docks, after a long night of work, Chuck approached shipping container 5261897. The morning was cool and clear as the rising sun chased the night chill away. The shipping container seemed colder than the surrounding air, though. And it looked like the container was vibrating, too. It had a blur to its edges. Chuck put his ear against the cold metal and heard a slight humming sound from within. He listened closer, blocking out the surrounding sounds by plugging a finger in his other ear. The humming was rhythmic and soothing. He closed his eyes and let the hum lull him. He could feel the hum. It was around him and in him.

Then a whispered thought, in a foreign tongue, entered his mind, *Intraţi înăuntru.*

Somehow, Chuck knew what the words meant, "Come inside."

Chuck moved, as if in a trance, to the shipping container doors. A padlock he didn't have a key to secured the doors. As he looked at the lock, dumbfounded by its presence, it clicked open and fell to the ground. Chuck opened the doors. It was dark inside the container, but Chuck saw a large wooden crate and three smaller crates. He moved inside and closed the doors behind him. As soon as the doors closed, he heard nails screeching as they extracted from wood. Then he heard a hiss. He wasn't alone.

A whispered thought, more powerful than the previous one, echoed in his brain as if it were echoing off the container's metal walls, *Întoarce-te și vezi-mă*.

Again, Chuck knew what the words meant, "Turn around and see me."

Not wanting to, but unable to resist the command, Chuck turned around. The interior of the shipping container was ink black. He strained his eyes, trying desperately to see the source of the command. Narrow, silver eyes flashed in the darkness.

~ * ~

On any other Thursday morning, Luke Matthews would have been behind the wheel of his delivery truck and well on route to his first destination by nine a.m. It was Christmas Eve and his boss, AJ Davenport, graciously closed Port City Trucking to allow his employees an extended Christmas weekend. Although not driving his truck, a truck was involved with his current activities. A Tonka truck.

Luke sat on the living room floor, beside a decked-out Christmas tree, with his three-year-old son, Aiden. Aiden pushed a Tonka truck, while Luke made all the necessary rumbling sounds. Aiden giggled at his dad's truck sounds while he pushed the Tonka truck around and tried, unsuccessfully, to imitate the rumbling sounds his dad made. Luke's wife, Rachel, sat on the couch watching the two men in her life play and laughed along with Aiden.

"Come play with us, Mommy," Aiden squealed.

"Yeah. Come play with us," Luke said playfully. "It's twenty-fifteen. Girls can play with boy toys now."

"It's more fun watchin' you two goofballs," Rachel giggled.

"I'm not a gooball." Aiden giggled. "Daddy's a gooball," he added and fell into a fit of laughter.

Luke began to respond when his cellphone rang on the nearby coffee table. After picking it up, he saw the source of the call.

"It's AJ," Luke told Rachel.

Rachel shook her head. "No. Whatever it is, the answer is no."

Luke answered the call. "No. Whatever it is, the answer is no. This comes from my boss."

"I'm your boss," AJ replied.

"Not when I'm home and not on my day off. Rachel's my home boss."

AJ chuckled. "Just hear me out."

"I'm listenin'."

"I have a delivery that needs to be made today. Pickup is at the Woodhouse Terminal and delivery is Pine View, Texas. Four crates. Six hour round trip."

"C'mon, AJ," Luke said. "Ya gave us the day off. I'm enjoyin' my morning playin' with Aiden."

"You can continue enjoyin' your mornin' playing with Aiden," AJ said. "The client specified delivery for after six o'clock this evenin'. Head north by three and you'll be home by nine, ten at the latest."

"Ya got seven other drivers. Why me?"

"You're my best driver, Luke."

"In other words, everyone else turned ya down," Luke said.

"No. I'm bein' serious, Luke," AJ said. "The best part is that you get paid five thousand bucks."

"Five thousand for six hours' work?" Luke said intrigued. "What's the catch?"

Upon hearing this, Rachel, who sat on the couch shaking her head disapprovingly since the conversation began, stopped shaking her head.

"No catch," AJ said. "I just need someone I can trust to make the delivery after six o'clock."

"Hold on a sec," Luke said as he tapped the mute icon.

"What do you think?" Luke asked Rachel.

"I think five thousand dollars is a *lot* of money and that we can use it."

"So, I should deliver the crate?"

Rachel nodded.

Luke tapped the mute icon again. "I'll do it."

Clearly relieved, AJ said, "Great. You'll need a small box truck, and I have the Woodhouse Terminal contact for you. You'll be dealin' with Chuck Kowalski."

"I know Chuck," Luke said. "I'll let him know to expect me about three."

Luke ended the call and put in a few more hours of quality time with Aiden and Rachel before leaving to make the delivery.

~ * ~

A little after three o'clock, Luke drove into the Woodhouse Terminal and parked beside the small building that served as the stevedore's office. Before he could get out of the truck, the passenger door opened, and Chuck Kowalski climbed into the cab.

Chuck was an imposing man. He'd spent his entire adult life as a longshoreman on the Houston Ship Channel docks, and it showed. He wasn't tall, but he was thick. Not fat, thick. He had massive shoulders, arms, and hands. Luke thought Chuck would make a good dwarf in one of those Hollywood movies that kept coming out, but Chuck didn't look himself that afternoon. To Luke, Chuck looked drained. His tan skin appeared ashen, and he had dark bags under his eyes. Luke chalked it up to overwork and followed Chuck's directions to the lone shipping container.

After arriving at the container, Luke let Chuck open it. They stepped inside and the smell of decay overwhelmed Luke. As quickly as the putrid smell hit him, it was gone. And Luke didn't find that the least bit strange.

With the use of two pallet jacks, Luke and Chuck maneuvered the large crate to the back of the box truck and onto the hydraulic lift. After the short ride up the lift, they used the pallet jacks to position the crate over the rear axles, where Luke secured it with two ratchet straps. Then they moved the three smaller crates inside the truck and secured one on each side of the large crate and one in front of it. The pallet jacks belonged to PCT and Luke secured these as well. With the cargo loaded, he and Chuck climbed out of the truck into fresh air Luke hadn't been aware he had missed.

Once the back of the box truck was closed, Luke and Chuck

stepped away and into the afternoon sunlight. It felt good to Luke, but he noticed Chuck wince and squint his eyes. He also noticed a few drops of blood on Chuck's shirt collar, but he chalked this up to a messy shave.

After several seconds of awkward silence, and nothing forthcoming from Chuck, Luke said, "Don't I have to sign somethin' sayin' I'm takin' this outta here?"

Chuck shook his head slowly. "Not on this one. This one's a special delivery."

He smiled and Luke saw blood on his teeth.

"You okay, Chuck?" Luke said. "Ya look…tired. And there's blood on your teeth."

"I am tired, and I got bad gums," Chuck said angrily. "Any other shit ya wanna point out?"

"Whoa there, Chuck," Luke said and took a step back. "Just a little concerned. Point taken. Strictly business now. Ya got the delivery slip?"

Chuck winced again, as if his own words assaulted him.

His features softened. "Sorry, Luke. I don't know where that came from. I must be tired. I lost about three hours earlier today. I woke up in that damn shippin' container with no memory or clue why I was in it. Here's the delivery slip."

Luke took the pink paper that had a yellow sheet behind it and looked it over quickly. He knew how to get to Pine View, but not where in Pine View to deliver the crates. He spotted the address and the establishment's name. Eternal Rest Funeral Home, care of Dănuţ Roşca. Suddenly, the size of the crate made perfect sense.

"It's goin' to a funeral home," Luke said. "Ya figure there's a coffin in that crate?"

"If it is a coffin, it ain't empty," Chuck said. "That's a heavy crate."

"Better not be a fuckin' body in there," Luke said. "That shit gives me the heebie-jeebies."

Chuck chuckled. "Whatever it is, it's your problem now. Safe travels, Luke."

Luke checked his watch and saw it was almost three-thirty. "Yeah, I better get goin'. I wanna be back in time to put my son's Santa gift together. I got him one of those drivable, battery powered Tonka dump trucks. I doubt the furniture will survive, but he'll have fun wreckin' the place."

The two men shook hands. Chuck's large hand felt cold in Luke's. They parted company and Luke headed north to Pine View.

Before Luke left in the truck, Chuck received a last whispered thought, *Ucide-te.*

Chuck went home and, following the foreign tongue command he understood perfectly, put the barrel of his single-shot shotgun in his mouth.

Chuck translated the whisper thought aloud, "Kill yourself."

He pulled the trigger, and his world went dark. No narrow, silver eyes flashed in the dead dark.

~ * ~

It was almost seven o'clock when Luke pulled into the Eternal Rest Funeral Home parking lot. Houston traffic, even on Christmas Eve, had been a bitch on Highway Fifty-Nine North. Once north of Cleveland and clear of the traffic, he pushed it on the speed limit. Not because he was running late with the delivery. It was to be delivered after six o'clock, not at six o'clock. He was in a hurry because he wanted to get home and put Aiden's Christmas present together.

There was a late model, black Cadillac Escalade in the parking lot and a black hearse, also a Cadillac, parked beside the building under a covered area. As Luke brought the truck to a stop, a tall, slender man emerged from a door behind the hearse and motioned for Luke to drive around back. When he got to the back of the funeral home, he saw two large garage doors. He backed the truck in front of the one on the right, secured the parking brake, and killed the engine.

As Luke stepped out of the truck, the tall, thin man appeared, as if out of nowhere, and startled him so badly his boot slipped off the truck step. Luke thought he was headed for an embarrassing tumble to the asphalt, but the tall, thin man grabbed him by the arm, strongly but not roughly, and easily righted him.

"Thanks," Like said appreciatively. "I thought I was gonna end up on my ass."

"You are most welcome," Dănuţ said with a skeletal smile in an accent Luke couldn't place. "I am just pleased that you are here."

"I'll be pleased when I'm headed south again. Are you…Dannut Rosca?"

The tall, thin man chuckled. "I am he. You can address me as Dan. I think that would be…easier. Yes?"

"Dan it is, then," Luke said. "Ya got anyone here to help me unload the crates?"

"I will help you unload the crates."

Luke eyeballed the tall, thin man and had reservations. Then he remembered how easily Dan had righted his fall and how strong his grip was. The reservations evaporated.

"Okay, then. I'll get the crates unstrapped and we'll kick this pig."

"Kick this pig?" Dănuţ asked with a grin.

"It's an expression," Luke said. "Means we'll get it done."

Dănuţ smiled, which made his face look skeletal. "By all means, then. Let us kick this pig."

While Luke opened the box truck, removed the ratchet straps, retrieved the pallet jacks, and unfolded the lift gate, Dănuţ opened the large garage door.

"I can lower the lift and give you a ride up," Luke offered.

"No need," Dănuţ said as he effortlessly and gracefully leapt into the back of the box truck.

Luke began to explain how to use the pallet jack, but Dănuţ took one, rammed it under the large crate, and pumped the handle to lift it. Impressed, and realizing first impressions are often deceiving, Luke did the same at the other end of the crate. A few minutes later, the large crate and three smaller crates were inside the building.

The room was large and full of equipment Luke recognized from movies as tools used in the embalming process. But the embalming jugs were empty, and Luke didn't smell chemicals he associated with the embalming process. Not that he'd know what they smelled like, but the lack of any smells struck him as odd.

Luke inadvertently shuddered. Dănuţ saw this and chuckled.

"You are uncomfortable here?" Dănuţ asked.

"Yeah," Luke said nervously. "This crap gives me the heebie-jeebies."

"Heebie-jeebies?"

"It means…uncomfortable."

"I have so much to learn about your language," Dănuţ said. "You have educated me with the kicking of pigs and the heebie-jeebies, though. For this, I thank you.

"Young man, you have nothing to fear from the dead," Dănuţ continued with a shrewd grin. "They are no more and no longer a concern for this world."

Luke shuddered again. "I know you're right, but I'd like to get your signature and payment so I can get back on the road."

Dănuţ smiled his skeletal smile again. "Of course. You have fulfilled your obligations splendidly. I will sign your paper and pay you for a job well done."

Dănuţ produced a bundle of cash from the inside pocket of his jacket and handed it to Luke. When Luke handed Dan the paperwork, he placed it on top of the crate, quickly scribbled an unreadable signature, and handed it back to Luke. Luke separated the pink copy from the yellow copy and handed the pink copy to Dănuţ.

"Come," Dănuţ said as he extended his long arm toward the large garage door. "I will show you out and help you load the pallet jacks,"

Luke hesitated briefly. "None of my business, unless there's somethin' illegal in those crates, but…is there a coffin in the large crate?"

Dănuţ smiled wider than he previously had, which made him look even more skeletal. "Yes. An ancient, ornate, and very special coffin. It was constructed in the year twelve hundred and fifteen. It is eight hundred years old and priceless. Would you like to see it?"

Part of Luke wanted to see the ancient coffin, but a bigger part of him wanted to get out of the death house and home to his family. He politely declined the offer. Fifteen minutes later, Luke merged onto Highway Sixty-Nine South, headed for Highway Fifty-Nine South and home.

~ * ~

Once the large garage doors were securely closed, and Luke on his way home, Dănuț removed the crate lid. No tools were needed. The nail holes had widened by many removals during the voyage. The large crate contained a large, ornate coffin and the three smaller crates contained Romanian soil. Dănuț reached into the crate and easily lifted the large, ornate coffin. He placed it delicately on the concrete floor and stepped back.

The coffin was a work of art. It had been constructed of solid black walnut and engraved with intricate scenes and images. The scenes were dark and disturbing. They displayed plagues, pestilence, beheadings, hangings, war, slaughter, death, and destruction. They included many winged monstrosities, snarling wolves, demons, ghouls, and undead creatures. The hardware that adorned the coffin, handles, hinges, and corner caps, were made of solid gold that shone under the harsh, florescent light.

"*Sunteți acasă, Maestre. Rise,* Dragoş Văduva." Dănuț shouted, which translated to "You are home, Master. Rise, Dragoş Văduva."

The ornate coffin lid slowly opened and Dragoş Văduva stepped from the Romanian, home soil lining the bottom of the coffin onto American ground for the first time in his more than eight hundred years of existence.

Chapter One

A shadow, blacker than the surrounding darkness, drifted soundlessly through the dense East Texas forest south of Pine View. The sound of a woman laughing penetrated the otherwise silent night. The shadow shifted and turned in the direction from which the laughter came. Narrow, silver eyes flashed in the blacker darkness. With the faint flutter of leathery wings, the shadow dissolved into the mist and disappeared.

~ * ~

Melanie Zane started to get in her car after Midnight Mass when Paige Lambert came running up to her. Like Paige, Melanie was one of the MRB Massacre, as it was referred to afterwards, survivors. Because of their shared experience, faith, and singing, Melanie and Paige had become close friends in the recent months. As it did with anyone who shared that horrible night with her, interacting with survivors, Paige included, always triggered memories. Terrible memories.

Melanie's therapist said she suffered from post-traumatic stress syndrome. Her therapist also said she needed to power through these memories and find the joy of having survived what so many of her classmates had not. Her therapist also said there were no such things as werewolves and Melanie's brain was playing tricks on her to cover up what really happened at the Mill Road Barn. So, what the hell did her therapist know?

In the seconds it took Paige to close the distance between them, Melanie's mind transported her back to that horrible night. The sights, the sounds, and the smells came back to her in crystal clarity. She was just outside the MRB's only working door when the nightmare creatures attacked.

~ * ~

Two of them came out of the surrounding woods, and the screams followed. Melanie watched in horror as one werewolf dragged Maggie Crawford from a car parked close to the bonfire and tossed her into the flames. She saw Maggie's long, blonde hair burst into flames and swallow her head in an orange ball of fire. Maggie's screams of pain and horror were like nothing Melanie had ever heard. She watched as Maggie, clothes on fire too, crawled out of the fire. Her bald head looked like a black canvas with rivers of blood-red lava bubbling up between the cracks. Then the werewolf picked Maggie up by the head with one large hand. The blackened skin on her head cracked and peeled away as the beast's clawed fingers dug into her skull. Blood gushed over her face. The beast rammed its left hand into Maggie's chest, extracted her heart, and woofed it down in a single bite. Maggie finally stopped screaming. When the werewolf tossed Maggie's lifeless body into the fire, it moved toward Melanie. With nowhere to go, Melanie backed into the MRB.

Once inside, Melanie realized she was trapped. The werewolf that murdered Maggie entered the building and a second one joined the first seconds later. Melanie huddled with the other frightened students as the two werewolves paced back and forth, almost nervously, in front of the only exit, as if they waited for something to happen.

Several minutes into the ordeal, a crashing sound came from inside the upstairs Wood Room—the room where horny teens went to release sexual energy. One werewolf leapt up the stairs with incredible speed and agility. It crashed through the door.

Melanie heard a girl scream in horror and then a boy screamed, "Don't fuckin' touch her."

She recognized the boy's voice. It belonged to Freddy Colburn. Seconds later, Freddy's body crashed through one of the Wood Room's windows in a shower of glass. He hit the concrete floor with a thud and blood immediately begin spreading around the back of his head like a halo. Then the werewolf leapt from the Wood Room with a battered and bruised girl under one of its arms. The girl was Ella Patterson, who was the late Freddy Colburn's girlfriend.

Melanie and the other trapped classmates remained huddled

around Freddy's body for what seemed like hours, but had only been minutes, while the two werewolves continued to pace in front of the exit. Then a yelp came from outside the barn and everyone, including the two werewolves, turned that way. A spilt second later, a piece of lumber sliced through the metal siding and skittered across the concrete floor. Murmurs and surprised shouts erupted from the students. The two werewolves growled loudly and advanced toward the piece of lumber that unexpectedly arrived. This was when Ella took off toward the opened door at a dead run, or as quickly as her battered body would carry her.

It was an ill-advised escape attempt and Melanie knew it wouldn't work. Within a few steps of her run for freedom, Ella doubled over at the waist and Melanie and the remaining students got an eyeful of her exposed lady parts. Unluckily for Ella, the view was brief. One werewolf pounced on her, lifted her into the air by her head, and flung her across the building where the second werewolf waited. Ella let out a tortured scream when she hit the concrete floor, but the scream was cut off when the waiting werewolf plunged its clawed hand through her chest, ripped out her still beating heart, and woofed it down in one bite. Then the werewolf gave Ella's body a tremendous kick that sent it flying. Her body landed face up on top of Freddy's body with a sickening thud and blood sprayed up out of the ragged chest wound into Quincy Wiseman's face. Quincy vomited beer and bile all over Freddy and Ella's bodies.

It was too much for Melanie. After seeing her second heart extraction and consumption of the night, hearing Quincy retch was all it took to trigger her vomit reflux. Melanie doubled over. Seconds later she vomited supper and alcohol, three beers from Freddy's keg, onto the concrete floor. Of all the horrific sounds the night had presented, the splat of her vomit hitting the concrete was the one that most haunted Melanie. It was her sound.

Seconds after killing Ella, the two werewolves jerked their heads toward the direction the yelp and piece of lumber came from. They looked at each other briefly and took off through the opened door at breakneck speed. Melanie, Quincy, and the others remained silent for several seconds, unsure as to their fate. Then, in unison, and as if unable to stop themselves, they moved toward the opened MRB door. Once outside, they headed left, toward the direction the werewolves had exited.

That was when Melanie saw Paige standing alone just inside the tree line of the surrounding woods. She was naked and covered in blood. Melanie saw Paige and Justin walk towards the woods earlier that night. That Justin was no longer with Paige led Melanie to believe he had met a similar fate to those of Maggie, Freddy, Ella, and several others whose disfigured bodies were strewn around the MRB grounds. And to Paige's benefit, Melanie assumed, since Paige was alive, the blood covering her belonged to Justin.

~ * ~

These thoughts raced through Melanie's mind in the short time it took Paige to close the distance between them. For all the horrors that night had created, Melanie was glad Paige survived. Although they had become good friends in the aftermath, Melanie never asked Paige why she was naked when she first saw her that night. She had a pretty good idea why, though. Adolescent love had run its course.

"Your singin' was beautiful tonight, Paige," Melanie said when the two were close enough to talk without shouting.

"Thanks. I was so nervous."

"It didn't show at all," Melanie said and smiled. "Well…maybe at first, but ya powered through. Where's Lindsey? I thought she might be here tonight."

Lindsey had been Paige's best friend since kindergarten and sister of Paige's boyfriend, Justin, who was killed by the alpha werewolf the night of the MRB Massacre. Since Lindsey had usually been at Paige's side, she didn't find the question odd.

"Her folks prefer Christmas Mornin' Mass," Paige explained. "She was gonna come with me tonight, but…after everything that happened, her folks wanted her with 'em Christmas Mornin'."

Melanie nodded. "Yeah, that makes sense."

"As for my nerves," Paige continued with a smile. "My grandpa has a sayin' that fits. I was puckered so tight ya couldn't drive a needle up my butt with a sledgehammer."

At hearing this saying, Melanie laughed loudly, and the laugh seemed amplified in the otherwise silent night.

Just as Melanie laughed, Paige's dad, and county sheriff, Garrett Lambert, pulled up in his personal truck.

When Paige opened the door to get in, Melanie said, "Merry Christmas, Mister Garrett. You too, Miss Mandy."

Garrett waved and together, he and Mandy said, "Merry Christmas to you too, Melanie."

A big smile spread across Melanie's pretty face. "I think it will be. Now that...ya know."

Garrett knew.

Garrett gave Melanie a reassuring smile. "I think you're right. Want me to wait until you get in and get started?"

Melanie shook her head. "No, sir. Thank you, though. I like to sit in my car and reflect a little after Mass."

"Ya sure?" Garrett asked.

Melanie nodded. "I'm sure. Thank you, though."

Paige chimed in with, "She'll be okay, Daddy."

Somewhat reluctantly, Garrett nodded and gave Melanie a wave.

"I'll call ya tomorrow," Paige said and shut the truck door.

As Garrett idled away at a snail's pace, Melanie got into her car and started the engine. She turned on and up the heater and waited for the engine to warm up enough to warm the air blowing on her feet. She looked in her review mirror and saw Mr. Garrett slowly driving on the gravel road that led to County Road Five Eighty-Eight, which was the only exit from St. Joseph's Catholic Church.

Melanie knew Mr. Garrett hadn't liked leaving her alone after midnight in the deserted church parking lot. She wasn't worried. The "you know," werewolves, were behind them. The church parking lot was so peaceful late at night, and the heater had finally warmed up.

She looked out the windshield at the church graveyard. A mist was forming on the ground, but she could still clearly see the granite markers for her paternal family plot. At the center of plot stood an eight-foot-tall obelisk with 'ZANE' written vertically on all four sides. Smaller markers designated the resting place of several Zanes going back four generations.

Her mom and dad would be buried there in the future, too.

~ * ~

A shadow stood just inside the tree line that surrounded the cursed, hallowed ground of the small church and watched as the people in the parking lot dispersed and left. Except for a young woman who remained alone sitting in her car. The vampire had fed well on the hardy stevedore, Chuck Kowalski, earlier that day, so hunger wasn't what drew him to the woman's laughter. He had much more elaborate plans for the young woman. She would become the first of his American *nor*. His American cloud.

Before seeping out of the woods for the, hopefully, unconsecrated ground of the parking lot, Dragoş sent Dǎnuţ a telepathic command to come to him. Then he placed a barefoot, with gnarled, long, yellowed toenails, onto the gravel that covered the church parking lot. No burning discomfort came. Dragoş smiled and revealed needle-sharp upper fangs.

Had the parking lot been consecrated ground, Dragoş would have had to wait for Dǎnuţ to arrive and bring the young woman to him. Because the church parking lot had not been consecrated ground, Dragoş could enjoy giving the gift of eternal undead life to the young woman without an audience. He found the one-on-one method much more intimate. Dragoş eased out of the woods and melted into the mist covering the parking lot.

~ * ~

Lost in thought, and mesmerized by the beautiful, full moon in the cloudless sky that turned the graveyard mist into a moving silver blanket, Melanie was unaware another nightmare closed in on her. A scratching sound that seemed to come from under the car pulled Melanie from her thoughts. The sound reminded her of when she ran over a metal band that had fallen off a big-rig's load of lumber. It scrapped and screeched the length of her car's undercarriage while she passed over it. She wasn't moving, though.

Somethin's under my car, Melanie thought.

With that thought, Melanie decided it was time to head for home. Just as she put her hand on the gearshift to put her car in reverse, a thunk issued from somewhere under the hood and her car died.

"Not now." Melanie shouted as she tried, unsuccessfully, to restart her car.

At first, she heard the starter grinding under the hood. Then there was another thunk and it died, too. After that, all she got were helpless clicks when she turned the key.

Frightened, Melanie reached for her handbag on the seat that had her cellphone tucked safely inside. She relaxed a bit when she felt the familiar object in her trembling hand. She relaxed even more when she pulled the cellphone free of the handbag and had it in front of her. Then she couldn't remember why she'd been frightened or why she wanted to call her parents to come help her. She looked out at the beautiful, silvery blanketed cemetery and exhaled a deep, calm breath that fogged the windshield in front of her. She wasn't the least bit startled when a large, black shadow rose in front of her car.

~ * ~

Dragoş looked down at the beautiful young woman who sat calmly in the car. Although not as powerful a link as Dragoş had with Dănuţ, who had been his familiar for decades, Dragoş reached out telepathically to calm the young woman. That she was lost in deep thought seconds before he reached out made it all the easier for him to invade the calm part of her mind. Now that he had direct eye contact with her, she was mesmerized to his every will.

Come to me, Dragoş willed her.

~ * ~

Melanie saw two silver slits that looked like eyes materialize in the large, black shadow in front of the car and they replaced the calm feeling she experienced with a need to serve the shadow. When the command to come to it echoed in her mind, she didn't question or resist it. She stepped out of her car and into a night that was no longer cold, although she could still see her warm breath plume in front of her face. As she neared the large, black shadow, it extended impossibly long arms to each side and blacked out the cemetery behind it. Melanie stepped into the shadowy blackness. It closed its arms and engulfed her.

A raspy voice whispered, "You will be the first of my cloud in this new land. It is a great honor."

"Yes, Master," Melanie whispered. "I am yours."

Melanie looked up into the penetrating, silver eyes that seemed to illuminate the darkness within the shadows. A beautiful face looked down at her. He had a firm chin and high cheekbones. His skin was almost the color of ivory and appeared translucent. His lips were a deep shade of red, made deeper by the contrast with his flawless ivory skin. The hair falling from under the cowl was long, light brown, and curly. It framed his handsome face perfectly. The silver in his eyes was replaced with a deep, crystal blue that Melanie felt she could dive into and never hit bottom.

He looked like a prince, and she was eager to serve him. Melanie tilted her head to the right and exposed her slender neck. When she felt his soft, cold lips close on her neck, she shuddered as she experienced her first orgasm. Her knees buckled, but the powerful prince held her tightly. When his needle, sharp fangs penetrated the soft flesh of her neck, Melanie moaned and held the prince tighter as he consumed her life blood.

Even as Melanie faded, and she realized the prince would consume her completely, she didn't struggle. If her life was the cost of serving him, she would gladly give it. She felt weaker, and the cold came back to her. It wasn't an external cold, though. The cold emanated from within her weakened body. The cold and the prince consumed her together, like an erotic dance between two new lovers.

Her vision closed in, and a blinding whiteness that threatened to consume her as well replaced the blackness. She fell into the comforting whiteness and drew her last breath.

~ * ~

Dragoş had eight hundred years' experience of creating undead for his many clouds over the centuries. Although he didn't have to show the young woman his younger visage, the way he looked when he was turned at twenty-two seasons eight hundred years ago, he still enjoyed the way women melted when they looked upon his youthful, princely beauty. Masquerading his true appearance took concentration, though. As he eagerly drank the young woman's virgin blood, he removed the masked deception. It wouldn't have mattered if he'd never put the princely mask on. He had her mesmerized. She would worship his true appearance after the transformation.

~ * ~

Dragoş was the oldest vampire in existence. There were others that had been older, but they had all been hunted down and killed. In life, Dragoş was a young prince of a fiefdom in Transylvania. Had he lived, he would have become king on his father's passing. In death, Dragoş was the king of vampires, but he was more than that. He was godly. A God of the undead realm. His realm spread much farther than a fiefdom in Transylvania. The world was his realm, and America his new playground.

~ * ~

As Dragoş fed on the virgin blood, he remained vigilant of her heartbeat. What began strong and rapid slowed to a few beats per minute. Dragoş stopped feeding seconds before he felt her strong, young heart stop. She exhaled a chilly breath and expired. It was time to bring her back. It was time to make her one of his undead cloud.

Dragoş extended his right arm and easily cradled the young woman's dead body in the crook of his elbow. With his left hand he pealed back the black cloak and ran a long, gnarled thumbnail across his right nipple. Thick black blood oozed from the wound. He pressed the young woman's face against his bleeding nipple and forced his blood into her slack mouth. Within a few seconds, he felt her tongue move. A few seconds later and the young woman greedily suckled his nipple, like a newborn baby.

In a way, she was just that. Creating members of a cloud required a lot of patience and teaching. Dragoş was ready for this challenge. Young cloud members, never children, were so much more eager and willing to learn. Never children because they were impatient and became sexually frustrated as they aged in prepubescent bodies. Dragoş learned this lesson when he turned a nine-year-old girl. At the time, he was a young vampire. Only two-hundred and twenty-three years old. He dispatched the young vampire fifteen years into her undead existence, and never made that mistake again. Dragoş looked down at the beautiful, young, undead creature suckling at his nipple and smiled, which revealed his needle fangs. Although he wore his real, ancient face, the young beauty with translucent skin smiled back. Black blood leaked from the corner of her mouth and two perfect fangs protruded from beneath her upper lip. Dragoş would have fun with this one.

~ * ~

Melanie forgot about her beautiful prince and the cold that consumed her. The comforting whiteness was everywhere. It was around her and in her. She heard the familiar voices of her long-dead grandparents on her mother's side and dead friends from the MRB Massacre, calling her name. She tried to go to the voices, but something held her back. A cold, coppery awareness filled her senses, and the whiteness dimmed. Melanie wanted the whiteness and the voices, but the copper sensation was so sweet. She had to have more of the copper nectar. She let the copper take her and the whiteness disappeared.

She opened her eyes and looked up at her Master while she hungrily suckled the wonderful, copper nectar from his stiff bleeding nipple. He looked ancient and weathered. Wrinkled and leathery skin, which was no longer ivory but still translucent, obscured his firm chin and high cheekbones. His lips were still a deep shade of red, but they sagged on either end, which gave him a perpetual frown. Unless he smiled. His long, light brown, and curly hair was replaced with wisps of long, stringy white hair that looked like spun cotton candy. He still had his deep, crystal blue eyes, which were locked on her now deep, crystal blue eyes. Melanie found her aged Master more beautiful than the young prince. The young woman who had been Melanie Zane in life had never felt more content than she felt while feeding from her Master.

~ * ~

Dragoş let his young fledgling feed for several minutes. He had plenty of blood to offer and she would need her strength. When he sensed Dănuţ was near, long before he heard the approaching hearse, he pulled the fledgling's face away from his bleeding nipple. She hissed, but a stern look from Dragoş quieted her quickly. She stood there beside him, licking the blood from her lips and chin with an impossibly long tongue, and waited for further instructions.

When Dănuţ pulled into the church parking lot, he, instinctively, because he'd served the Master for several decades, backed the Cadillac hearse alongside of the car his master, and new cloud member, stood in front of. As he got out of the car, he was prepared for what came next. The fledgling hissed and lunged toward him, intent on drinking him dry. Without a spoken word, the fledgling immediately fell to the ground at the Master's feet. Dănuţ knew he was off-limits to feed on and the new cloud would learn this quickly enough.

"What took you so long?" Dragoş hissed.

Dragoş didn't think Dănuţ took any longer than it should have, but it was in the ancient vampire's nature to inflict fear in people. Even his trusted familiar.

"I-I-I'm sorry, Master," Dănuţ stammered. "I have not yet learned about the rural roads. It will not happen again."

"See that it does not," Dragoş said harshly. "You have work to do while I teach my new fledgling. Do you find her attractive?"

Dănuţ knew this was a trick question. If he said she was attractive, which she was, Dragoş would threaten him with loss of life for looking at her. If he said she wasn't attractive, he would insult the Master's taste, which could cause loss of life as well.

He answered as he always did. "She is of no interest to your human servant, Master. Dănuț will do as he is ordered. No more. No less."

Dragoş smiled, revealing his long, needle fangs. "There is a reason I have kept you around for such a long time, Dănuț. Do you know what that reason is?"

The tall, slender man with thinning blond hair averted the Master's stare and shook his head.

Dragoş looked down at the cowering man and laughed loudly. He wasn't concerned anyone in the rural area would hear him. He'd used his substantial powers as an ancient vampire to blanket them from view and sound.

"I have kept you around because you are a loyal servant, Dănuț. Do not fear me."

Dănuț looked up at his master and smiled a weak smile.

Dragoş ignored the human servant's smile. "You have work to do. You must secure my new fledgling with proper accommodations and soil. I would help you, and make quick work of it, but I fear the cemetery is consecrated soil. I leave you to your work now."

With that, Dragoş touched the fledgling on her face. With the faint flutter of leathery wings, they dissolved into black mist and disappeared.

Dănuț knew his job. He had done it hundreds of times before. Consecrated ground or not, the Master never helped him. Dănuț retrieved a shovel from the back of the hearse and headed into the cemetery. He hoped there were a recent burial. They were easier to dig. Within a few minutes, he found a few recent graves. He picked one, stabbed the shovel into the consecrated ground, and began digging.

~ * ~

Dănuț returned to the Eternal Rest Funeral Home shortly before dawn and found the Master and fledgling waiting for him. The fledgling's face and dress were covered in blood. Dănuț knew what that meant. She'd had her first kill and feeding. Still, the stuffed fledgling eyed him like a tasty snack.

Dănuț easily removed the fledgling's new accommodations. A nice wood-grain coffin with plush, silk cushioning on the inside. The young man inside the coffin hadn't decomposed to where his exposed flesh adhered to the silk, which made Dănuț's job easier. He placed it next to the master's ancient, ornate coffin. Then he brought out several large bags of cool, wet soil he collected from outside the cemetery. He couldn't risk killing the Master's new fledgling by putting consecrated soil in her coffin. Dănuț covered the plush, silk cushioning completely.

Satisfied with his work, Dănuț stepped back and let the Master inspect it. Without saying a word, the Master held his long-fingered hand out to the fledgling. She took his hand, and he guided her into the soil-packed coffin. After she laid down, the Master stepped away and then into his coffin. Dănuț closed both lids and readied himself for a busy day.

The last item on the Master's list had almost been completed. Dănuț walked to the side of the large, embalming room and moved a heavy metal table and cabinet from the wall. On the concrete floor behind the cabinet was a large, ragged hole. Dănuț moved to the top of the hole and stepped into it. He landed in an enormous cavern he'd been excavating since he arrived in Pine View. The cavern would be the ultimate resting place for the Master's coffin, and the coffins of his cloud. It would be his throne room. Dănuț began digging again.

Chapter Two

A soft, warm sensation on a sensitive part of his body pulled Garrett from a deep sleep. He knew the touch well and what it portended. Mandy was awake and 'in the mood.' Garrett rolled over and looked into her beautiful eyes. It was early, but enough morning light filtered through the blinds for Garrett to see her. When she smiled, he smiled back.

"Merry Christmas," Mandy whispered.

"It's certainly startin' out that way," Garrett whispered back.

"Ya want your first present?"

Garrett nodded.

Mandy smiled and rolled on top of Garrett.

~ * ~

After all the years of being single, he and his first wife Lacy divorced within three years of getting married, Garrett wasn't sure he would find someone to share his life with again. Mandy changed all of that.

Oddly, Garrett had the werewolf incident of the previous summer to thank for this change. Garrett and Mandy had dated for three years, but he drug his feet on committing to anything more serious or permanent. Then the alpha werewolf sent Garrett a message. It had marked Mandy's scent, and she was no longer safe. After this, Mandy moved in with Garrett temporarily—until the werewolf situation was taken care of. Mandy's temporary move into Garrett's house during the werewolf scare turned into a permanent living arrangement. So permanent that, one evening in October, while they walked through the woods on his property admiring the multi-colored autumn leaves, Garrett took a knee and proposed to Mandy. She said yes, and they set the wedding date for Saturday, April 30th, 2016.

Living with someone again was a bit of a change for Garrett. Not that he didn't enjoy having Mandy living with him. He did. He especially enjoyed mornings that started as Christmas morning began with early lovemaking. That always put a bounce in his step for the rest of the day. Garrett didn't like bringing work-related issues home for Mandy to deal with, but sometimes this was unavoidable. The most recent of these occurrences happened at the end of November.

~ * ~

The pack of werewolves that terrorized Pine View County during the previous May and June had murdered many people—twenty-two in all. The alpha had also passed the curse to three people, two of whom were very special to Garrett. Paige and Ty were the two who were very special. The third was Trowa Raintree, who Garrett came to consider a friend. To break the curse, they had to kill the alpha. Doing so required an elaborate plan.

With the help of James Huff, a Stephen F. Austin State University English professor who specialized in the occult, mythology, and folklore, and Lola Laveau, a clairvoyant seer, Garrett had devised such a plan. Using Paige, Ty, and Trowa as bait on the full moon after they were cursed and would transform for the first time, Garrett lured the alpha to a clearing he prepared on land owned by Trent Stucky where Garrett and his dad used to hunt deer. Garrett was safely perched fifty feet up a pine tree, out of reach of the werewolf that couldn't climb trees, on a folding tree stand armed with a shotgun loaded with silver, double-ought, buckshot, supplied by Deputy Mike Middleton, his nine-millimeter pistol loaded with silver bullets, also supplied by Deputy Mike Middleton, a laser scope on his pistol, purchased at Walmart, and night-vision goggles, supplied by the Pine View Sheriff Department. As often is the case with best-laid plans, things didn't go as expected.

Just as the alpha entered the clearing, and Garrett was leveling the shotgun on it, a massive, and unexpected, werewolf slammed into the tree Garrett was perched in. His shot went high, missing the alpha completely. To make matters worse, the massive werewolf's impact with the tree broke the metal loop that secured the folding tree blind to the tree and it, along with Garrett, fell fifty feet to the ground. The only thing that saved Garrett's life was that the tree blind safety straps were still in place and the fall was more of a quick decent until the straps broke about fifteen feet above the ground. After which Garrett fell and had the wind knocked out of him on impact. To further complicate matters, Garrett lost his pistol in the fall, and the shotgun was rendered unusable because the barrel sank into the dirt, which clogged it. Killing the alpha that cursed Paige, Ty, and Trowa wouldn't be Garrett's problem. The massive werewolf took care of that by biting the alpha in half at the waist.

Unfortunately, killing the alpha didn't release the three fledgling werewolves from the curse. Because the massive werewolf had created their alpha, it became their new alpha as they were of its curseline. All seemed lost, until Lola communicated with Garrett through a totem she'd given him. The totem resembled Lola's cat-like, seeing eye. Lola instructed Garrett to remove the silver necklace and crucifix Paige wore to keep the curse from transforming her. Ty and Trowa were wearing silver for the same purpose.

Prior to setting the alpha's trap, Garrett met with Lola, hoping to understand a recurring nightmare he'd had annually for fourteen years. In the nightmare a monstrous werewolf Paige, that aged as she did, Monster-Paige aged in the nightmare as she aged in life, clawed and chewed its way out of Lacy's distended belly, as if being born. Then Monster-Paige and another larger werewolf would leave together, and each time, Monster-Paige would wave bye-bye to Garrett.

After seeing Garrett's palm and identifying a faint pentagram in the lines on it, Lola explained that Garrett and Paige, by extension, had an ancestral werewolf in their family lineage. This meant the werewolf curse had already been dormant within them, like a recessive gene. She told him since a werewolf had bitten Paige and the curse was no longer dormant, she had a fighting chance at controlling the curse. It was a long shot, but when Lola told Garrett to remove Paige's silver and let her transform, he did.

What Paige transformed into was nothing like the monsters that terrorized Pine View County. Where they were covered in coarse, black hair with burning, red eyes, Paige's werewolf was covered in silky, silver hair with glowing, green eyes. Paige's silver werewolf had also been taller and more muscular than the other werewolves. Excluding the unexpected, massive werewolf that, at ten feet tall, was a foot taller than Paige's werewolf.

Size wasn't an issue when Paige's werewolf engaged the massive werewolf. Speed and agility won the battle. After Paige's werewolf killed the massive werewolf by tearing the top of its head off, it released Ty and Trowa from the curse. Paige had not been released from the curse. This wasn't an issue either. Paige had complete control over her silver werewolf. So much control that she wasn't a threat to man or beast. Paige would remain a werewolf for the rest of her life.

After they killed the alpha and massive werewolf, Garrett, Paige, Ty, and Trowa left what remained of their human bodies in the Stucky clearing and went home to resume their normal lives. Then, towards the end of November, Garrett was called out to the Stucky property.

Trent Stucky's son, Brent, was four years younger than Garrett. He knew him from the years he and his dad deer hunted on their property, though. Brent was quail hunting when he discovered what he thought were three bodies. Garrett knew there were only two bodies and one of them was bitten in half. He also knew the identity of the two-part body. Her name was Alexis Jordan.

She was a student at Stephen F. Austin State University who was reported missing by her father, Alex Jordan, the Monday after the massive werewolf killed her when she failed to appear in Houston for a scuba diving trip to Barbados. The identity of the second body, that of the massive Mexican werewolf, had still been a mystery to Garrett. All he had to work with was the Monterrey Produce box truck parked next to Mike Middleton's faceless body on Highway Sixty-Nine. There were no prints to be found in the truck. Just a lot of course, black hairs. It was almost as if the man had driven with werewolf hands to mask his identity.

Dental records provided the proof of what Garrett already knew. The two-part body was Alexis Jordan. No such luck with the other body. His teeth were rotten to where it was clear he'd never seen a dentist. Decomposition was so extensive that fingerprints were out as a means of identification, too. Thinking it was a shot in the dark, but wanting to cover all available bases, Garrett ordered a DNA profile on the unidentified remains. They got a hit.

The remains belonged to a nasty Mexican national by the name of Juan Escobar, who went by *El Lobo*. The Wolf. Juan Escobar was wanted in Mexico and Texas for a long list of transgressions that included twenty-three murders, seventeen in Mexico and six in Texas. Eight counts of kidnapping, all in Mexico. Eleven rapes, six in Mexico and five in Texas. Drug trafficking, distribution of controlled substances, many assaults, robberies, and thefts. But Juan Escobar had an uncanny aptitude for escaping inescapable law enforcement task forces on both sides of the border.

Garrett thought the fact that Juan Escobar could transform into a massive werewolf had more than a little to do with his avoidance of law enforcement. He wasn't wrong. Juan Escobar got out of many situations by transforming and using his wolf's abilities to avoid arrest. Garrett also thought Juan Escobar's list of transgressions was much larger than those listed on various warrants. He wasn't wrong here either. Juan Escobar's, as a human and as a werewolf, murders and rapes numbered in the hundreds, if not the thousands. He had planned to let his wolf rape Alexis the night he bit her, but she escaped after he killed Alexis' drug purchasing associate, Carlos Garza, that night.

What wasn't easy to explain was why Alexis Jordan and Juan Escobar were in the Stucky clearing together or how they were killed. There were canine tooth marks on both sides of Alexis' lower spine where she was bitten in half, but Dr. Emily Yost accredited these to postmortem animal activity.

Yost was a biologist who specialized in zoology at Stephen F. Austin State University. She also consulted for the Pine View County Sheriff Department when animal activity was part of a crime scene. Emily was Garrett's first contact after the strange killings began in early May. She had identified hairs collected by Garrett and Ty from Carla Weaver's slaughtered pigs, the morning of the werewolves' first kill of Russ Lomax, as being *Canis lupus* in nature. She couldn't speculate as to the actual species without DNA analysis of the hairs, which was done, but the results were inconclusive because the hairs were contaminated with human DNA.

She recommended Garrett meet with Dr. James Huff for information about werewolves.

When Emily told Garrett the teeth marks were postmortem, and canine, she threw a wink in at the end. Although she hadn't been privy to all the information James had regarding the extent of werewolf activity that had gone on, she didn't know Paige, Ty, and Trowa were bitten, she wasn't close-minded to the idea of werewolves existing. She had examined the human remains of two werewolves, Seth Daniels and Cole Duncan. That wink told Garrett the werewolf secret was safe.

Through insect activity and decomposition, time of death for the unlikely couple was placed at late May or early June. Since this timeline roughly matched up with all the other strange murders that occurred during the werewolf threat, Alexis and Juan's deaths were attributed to whatever had committed the other murders and mutilations.

That this was the presumed explanation was fine with Garrett. He couldn't provide the actual explanation. That Alexis and her pack had committed the Mill Road Barn and other murders as werewolves. Or thar Juan Escobar was the Mexican werewolf that cursed Alexis and came to Pine View County to kill her. He was an elected official and talk like that got folks a long stay in a padded room in the Rusk State Hospital, which was one of the state facilities for the insane.

The worry concerning the outcome of the Alexis Jordan and Juan Escobar investigation, and his elected future, were the work-related issues Garrett brought home toward the end of November. He was concerned the publicly, unsolved murders would cost him his job, but something unexpected happened that made both issues moot.

Over the course of the one-month werewolf horror, many folks who witnessed the attacks and lived through them saw the beasts. Information like this is impossible to keep isolated. Especially in the social media age. First-hand accounts, and rumors, spread like wildfire through the rural East Texas area. Within weeks of the first murders, folks who were nowhere near any of the incidents swore they'd seen the werewolves. National tabloid media converged on Pine View County and reported many eyewitness accounts. Sketch artists produced varying likeness portraits of the beasts, none of which resembled the actual monsters perfectly. This led Garrett to believe actual witnesses were keeping quiet about what they saw. This was mostly true.

The result of all this activity was that the community had been saturated with the werewolf explanation, and most folks were inclined to believe it. There were vocal naysayers who didn't mind telling the believers they were full of shit, which resulted in several bar fights and other altercations Garrett's deputies had to respond to. But most folks believed it. So, when the killings stopped after the first full moon in June, folks assumed, correctly, that Garrett had ended the nightmare. When Alexis and Juan's bodies were discovered by Brent, along with some silver, double-ought, buckshot pellets found by the state police in the woods surrounding the clearing, rumors circulated that Alexis and Juan were the werewolves that terrorized Pine View County. People assumed Sheriff Garrett Lambert had contributed to their demise, which was true, too.

In the end, and without confirmation from Garrett, they hailed him as a silent hero. Everywhere he went, folks would offer their hand or pat him on the back or throw a wink his way. Comments like, "Good job with the, you know whats," or, "I don't know how ya did it, but I'm glad ya did," were issued regularly. Most importantly for Garrett was the fact that Paige being a werewolf had remained secret.

He allowed her to run her wolf, but only on his and his parent's adjacent property or if he was with her elsewhere at the old Wiseman barn that had been Alexis' den. Paige was smart enough to avoid human contact. With her werewolf senses, she could smell, see, and hear humans long before they could get a glimpse of her.

It all worked out. Ty and Trowa were free of the curse. Paige's werewolf was safe, and Garrett's reelection in November 2017 was inevitable. No one had even considered running against him. Then Melanie went missing.

~ * ~

A soft moan escaped Mandy's lips as she lowered herself onto

Garrett. He pulled her close and kissed her. They began, as they always did, slowly. As they fell into the familiar rhythm of each other's bodies, the pace quickened. Without slowing, Garrett rolled over and pinned Mandy beneath him. They were so lost in the moment, and in each other, they didn't hear the bedroom door open.

~ * ~

Being a werewolf came with a plethora of advantages. Increased metabolism, Paige could eat as much of anything she wanted and never put on weight. Better health, she didn't get sick anymore. Heightened senses, more so in wolf form but heightened in human form, too. Also, the ability to operate with little sleep. To name a few. The latter two of these advantages led to the embarrassing encounter Christmas morning.

Christmas had always been Paige's favorite holiday. She loved the crispness of colder weather and bundling up to keep warm. Paige loved watching her warm breath plume when she exhaled. She, of course, loved giving and receiving gifts, too. As her religious beliefs and faith grew, she loved the meaning of Christmas more than ever.

As she had, for as far back as she could remember, Paige woke up early Christmas morning. She laid in bed, full of nervous energy, and waited for a sign someone else was awake, too. She didn't want to wake them, but she would if her daddy and Mandy didn't wake up soon.

After what seemed to Paige an eternity, but had been less than twenty minutes, her heightened sense of hearing picked up Mandy whisper, "Merry Christmas." Unfortunately for all concerned, Paige didn't bother to take in the conversation's context between her daddy and Mandy. She was so excited to get Christmas morning started, she didn't pick up on the prevalent but subtle clues. She could smell sexual arousal and hear rapid heartbeats. She'd gotten pretty good at blocking out her daddy and Mandy's sexual arousal. Knowing when they were horny gave Paige the shivers, but Paige was single-minded that morning. Gift time.

Paige got out of bed, put on her puffy green robe, and left her room. When she got to the living room, she turned on the Christmas tree lights. They sparkled in the early morning light, and she headed for her daddy's bedroom door.

Paige threw open the door and shouted, "Merry Chris…" but the words joked in her throat.

Luckily, for all concerned, Paige was spared a visual. The covers were halfway up her daddy's back and his body blocked Mandy from view. Paige immediately understood what she'd walked in on. The musky smell of sex almost knocked her over.

Calmer than Paige expected, her daddy said, "Ya gotta knock, Paige-Turner."

"Um, yeah," Paige said. "Sorry 'bout that. I'm just gonna close the door and let y'all…do your thing."

As the door closed, so did the mood. Frustrated, Garrett rolled off Mandy and stared up at the ceiling.

"There goes my first Christmas present," he whispered.

Mandy giggled.

"Really?" Paige said from beyond the closed door. "That's a Christmas present? Y'all realize this is baby Jesus' birthday, right?"

"That damn hearin' of hers," Garrett whispered more quietly.

"I heard that," Paige said and suppressed a giggle.

Mandy giggled again.

"Of course ya did," Garrett huffed. "Mind givin' us a couple of minutes to get dressed so we can open presents?"

"Not at all. I'll be out here shakin' my presents and tryin' to figure out what I'm gettin'."

Paige moved away from the door, knowing her daddy and Mandy wouldn't be continuing what she interrupted. The sex musk smell had dissipated, and their heartbeats had slowed considerably. She sat down cross-legged at the base of the Christmas tree. Paige picked up a book-sized present with her name on it and gauged its heft. It was too heavy and thin to be a book. She had an idea what it might be. She'd left enough hints, but she wasn't positive. Her increased senses didn't help her see through wrapping.

As she inspected another smaller gift, her daddy's bedroom door opened, and Mandy and her daddy stepped out. Mandy wore a robe like Paige's, but blue, and her daddy had on an old T-shirt and gray sweatpants.

He had his cellphone in his hand. Paige knew he would take videos of her opening presents. That was a tradition.

"Want some hot chocolate?" Mandy asked.

"Yes, please," Paige said and added. "With marshmallows."

"Sweet tea for me," Garrett chimed in.

"Don't open presents without me," Mandy said before heading into the kitchen.

Garrett 'popped a squat,' one of his dad's many colorful sayings, next to Paige, and took the small present she shook from her.

"What are ya, five years old?" He playfully scolded.

Paige grinned. "On Christmas mornin'? Yeah. I'm always a kid."

"Yeah, well. Did ya consider that this might be breakable?"

"Is it?"

"You'll just have to wait a little longer to find out."

Paige ignored him and picked the hefty, book-sized gift up again. "I'm openin' this one first."

"I figured ya would," Garrett said as he picked up a gift with his name on it and gave it a quick shake.

"Hey," Paige said with a laugh. "Weren't you just givin' me a hard time for doin' that?"

Garrett grinned. "I guess we're all kids on Christmas."

Mandy came out of the kitchen with two steaming mugs and one glass of tea. "What're you two goin' on about?"

"Daddy got on me for shakin' my gifts and then he did the same thing."

Mandy looked at the gift Garrett held. "Garrett. Don't shake that. It might be breakable."

Garrett and Paige glanced at each other and then burst into shared laughter. Mandy, who didn't know Garrett had just scolded Paige for the same thing, smiled down at them.

Mandy handed out the drinks and took a seat on the floor next to Garrett.

"Who's first?" Garrett asked, even though he knew the answer.

"Me." Paige shouted as she tore at the wrapping paper on the book-sized gift.

"Hang on, Paige-Turner," Garrett said. "You know the rules. I gotta record this."

Paige stopped tearing at the paper and, with a hint of frustration, said, "Hurry, Daddy."

Garrett placed his sweet tea on the coffee table, picked up his cellphone, opened the camera app, set it to Video, and tapped the red button. "Tear away."

The wrapping paper disappeared in a flurry of rips and Paige looked down at the gift she'd been, not so subtly, hinting at wanting. A rose-gold and white iPad Air 2.

"Thank you, Daddy," Paige squealed. "Thank you, thank you, thank you."

Garrett grinned. "You're welcome, sweet girl."

"Open mine next, Paige," Mandy prompted.

Paige's gift from Mandy was the smaller one she'd shook. Paige didn't have a clue what Mandy might've gotten her and shaking it hadn't helped. She picked up the smaller gift and quickly unwrapped it. There was a plain cardboard box beneath the wrapping paper. She opened the box and looked inside. There was a small, ring sized, black velvet box and a card inside. Paige took the velvet ring box out and flipped it open. Inside was a gold ring with a beautiful emerald stone set with small diamonds encircling it. It was beautiful.

"Oh, Mandy," Paige said in a hushed voice. "This is so beautiful. Thank you so much. I love it."

"You're very welcome, Paige. When I saw it, it reminded me of your beautiful eyes, and I had to get it for ya. Try it on."

Paige removed the ring from the box and slipped it on her right ring finger. It fit perfectly and looked more beautiful on her than it did in the box. She held out her hand so her daddy could get a closeup.

After getting a good closeup of the ring, Garrett said, "Don't forget the card."

Lost in the excitement of getting the ring, Paige had forgotten the card. She took the card out, opened it, and read it. Tears streamed down her checks before she finished reading it. When she finished reading it, she turned to Mandy, who had also been crying, and they embraced each other.

Garrett knew what was inside the card and did not know why two of the three women he loved most in the world, his mom the third, held each other, sobbing. To his reckoning, it was a happy request. He kept taking video of the strange reaction.

After several seconds of hugging and crying, Paige sniffed. "Yes. Of course I'll be your maid of honor."

Mandy sniffed, too. "I wouldn't want anyone else."

After this exchange, a fresh round of tears flowed.

Garrett waited patiently while they hugged and cried for several more moments. When they were finally composed, it was Mandy's turn to open her gifts.

From Paige, Mandy received a silver necklace and crucifix exactly like Paige's. Mandy had often commented on how pretty Paige's was and it thrilled her to have a matching one. Mandy lifted her blonde hair out of the way so Paige could fasten the necklace. That left Garrett's gift to Mandy. It was in a large box, the box Garrett's last printer came in, and weighted with a few bricks for deception.

Mandy carefully removed the wrapping paper. "A printer?"

"Not a printer," Garrett assured her. "Look inside."

Mandy opened the box and looked inside. "Bricks?"

"Not bricks. Look under the bricks."

Mandy removed bricks and saw a blue folder underneath. When she'd removed enough bricks, she took the folder out and opened it. As she took in what was inside the folder, a big smile spread across her beautiful face.

"Really?" Mandy said excitedly.

"Really," Garrett said and smiled.

Mandy squealed, threw her arms around Garrett, and began kissing his face. "I love you. I love you. I love you."

"What am I missin' out on?" Paige asked.

Mandy stopped kissing Garrett and showed the contents of the folder to Paige. There were lots of brochures and tickets in the folder, but a highlighted map of Europe pulled the content together nicely. Her daddy and Mandy would honeymoon in London, Paris, Berlin, and Rome with lots of stops between these destinations.

"Wow. I wanna go," Paige said.

"Not this time, kiddo. When we're not seein' the sights, we'll be seein' each other."

Paige thought about that for a few seconds. "Ew. Forget I asked."

"I already have," Garrett said with a chuckle.

"Okay, enough grossin' your daughter out with aspects of our love life," Mandy said. "Open your present, Garrett. It's from me and Paige."

Garrett handed his cellphone to Mandy so she could video his gift opening and picked up the box he'd shook. It had a little heft to it, but it wasn't too heavy. He pealed the wrapping paper away and saw a picture on the box of something he'd wanted since the werewolf scare. Night-vision goggles. He quickly tore the rest of the paper away and saw Mandy and Paige gave him Pulsar Edge GS Night-Vision goggles.

The night of the alpha trap, he'd borrowed night-vision goggles from the Pine View County Sheriff Department. Since then, he'd talked about getting one for himself, but he wasn't the kind of guy who spent money on himself for what he considered a luxury item. Mandy and Paige had relieved him of that problem.

"Thanks, ladies. How'd y'all know I wanted this?"

"Please, Daddy," Paige said and rolled her eyes. "Ya talked about wantin' this more than I talked about wantin' an iPad."

Paige wasn't wrong, but Garrett played it off.

"Whatever, or as y'all say, whatevs," Garrett said. "Well, I wanted this. Thank ya both. I can't wait to try 'em out tonight."

"We don't say whatevs, Daddy," Paige said with another eye roll.

Garrett turned the box to look at the specs. Mandy continued to video him. Then his cellphone rang.

"It's Trowa," Mandy said as she handed the phone back to Garrett.

Garrett took the phone and tapped the answer icon. "Merry Christmas, Deputy Raintree."

~ * ~

Trowa Raintree's life as a logger, an exceptional logger, had changed as much, if not more, than the others' by the werewolf incidents. Prior to the werewolf attacks, Trowa's services as a logger were in high demand. Not only could he fell a tree on a nickel, Indian Head or otherwise, Trowa could climb trees, without gear, as quick as a cat. As a subcontractor, these abilities kept Trowa consistently employed, and it was his tree climbing ability that saved his life.

The night after the MRB Massacre, which is what the local media called the murders of fifteen students at the Mill Road Barn, Trowa, unaware of the murders, went to Knucklehead's Icehouse to drink a portion of his week's pay away. Knucklehead's Icehouse was a local biker bar and as a biker, Trowa fit right in. It was there Trowa, and the others, heard about the murders from Norm Hoyt, who was cousins with a Pine View County Deputy Sheriff Billy Hoyt. It had also been there that a young man, who said his name was Eddie Quist, told the Knucklehead's patrons he was a MRB Massacre survivor, and he'd seen what did the killings. Werewolves.

The young man who said his name was Eddie Quist had been Cole Duncan. Cole was a member of Alexis' werewolf pack and a troublemaker. After Alexis' werewolf was badly injured when Paige crammed her silver necklace and crucifix down its throat, Cole's werewolf challenged the alpha. Even injured, the alpha put Cole's werewolf in its place. This didn't sit well with Cole.

That was how he found his way to Knucklehead's Icehouse that night and using the name of the main werewolf from the movie *The Howling*. His plan was to create his own rival pack by luring some of the burly bikers into the woods, turning them, and then taking out Alexis' werewolf. It almost worked.

Against Trowa's better judgment, he left Knucklehead's with Mont and Jack Lee, twin brothers who stood six foot eight inches tall and tipped the scales at three hundred and sixty-ish pounds, Lewis "Bear" Campton, a short in stature, barrel-chested, man with tree trunk arms, and Eddie Quist. The plan was to load up on firepower at the Lee's house, head out to the MRB, and without his knowledge, possibly use Eddie as bait to draw a werewolf in for the kill. It was an ill-advised plan that went tits up when Eddie, Cole, transformed into a werewolf and attacked the four bikers. Things got worse when the alpha showed up.

Alexis had her own evil plans that night. She intended to turn Paige, not kill her, the previous night when Paige hurt her wolf with the necklace and crucifix. By doing so, Paige unintentionally fulfilled the alpha's wishes because it bit her, but the defiant act enraged the alpha. Her evil plan the next night was to infect Paige's daddy, Garrett, so she could force his wolf to do unspeakable things to Paige's wolf. She hadn't planned on Garrett having silver bullets, though.

Garrett's aim was true, but the bullet deflected off the metal frame of the sliding back door as the werewolf crashed through and hit the alpha's left ear. Although the contact was minimal, it was enough for the alpha to know the bullet that hit it had been silver. Further enraged by having its plans thwarted, and fearing for its life, the alpha fled from Garrett's house to the safety of the deep, East Texas woods. After running for several miles, the alpha stopped to rest and fume. While resting, the alpha realized her beta's intentions to create a rival pack through the mental connection it shared with those it had created. This could not stand. The alpha sprinted away, intent on ridding itself of troublesome beta once and for all.

Bear was the first to be attacked. Cole's wolf ambushed him from behind, bit his shoulder, and flung the heavy man thirty feet through the air, where he slammed into a tree and crumpled to the ground, unconscious. After Bear regained consciousness, Mont and Jack helped him to his feet and followed Trowa to the truck, Beast, with guns at the ready. The hunt was over, but they needed to be cautious. That was when the werewolf attacked Mont.

Jack saw the werewolf on Mont, and because shooting at it might hit Mont, did the only thing he could. Jack tackled the massive werewolf and put it in a stranglehold. It worked to the degree that he got the werewolf off Mont, but it was on top of Jack and its substantial weight made it difficult for him to breathe. It was Mont's turn to help Jack. Unfortunately, this resulted in the werewolf removing Mont's left leg with a single, bone-crushing bite. To further complicate matters for Jack, the werewolf grabbed Mont and pulled him on top of it. The weight of the werewolf and Mont was too much for Jack. He fell unconscious, and the stranglehold released. The werewolf had the upper hand again. Briefly.

Trowa watched all of this play out in a matter of seconds. He wanted to help his friends but didn't have a safe shot. The opportunity arrived shortly after Jack's arms slipped limply from the werewolf's neck. Free from Jack's stranglehold, the werewolf tossed Mont's three-hundred-and-sixty-pound body ten feet away. Then it turned to deliver a curse-infecting bite to Jack. Trowa raised his gun to shoot it but, before he could pull the trigger, a second werewolf, the alpha, slammed into the beta with enough force to send it flying. Then the alpha reached down and ripped Jack's throat out with its deadly claws.

The alpha turned toward Trowa but, before it could attack, the beta got its attention with an angry growl. The alpha turned its attention to the beta. As the two werewolves came together with a crash, Trowa assessed the situation. He knew Jack was dead and Mont would likely bleed out and be dead soon. That only left Bear to rescue, but Trowa knew he couldn't support Bear's weight by himself, which meant Bear would soon be dead, too.

Trowa had two options. Try to get to the Lee brother's truck, aptly named Beast, and drive out on the slowly traveled log roads. Or use his climbing ability to seek safety in the treetops. He opted for the treetops.

Trowa quickly scaled a tall pine tree, called 911 and waited for help. While he waited, he heard the epic battle going on between the two werewolves. It sounded like hell had opened and released a hoard of demons. When the battle was over, only one werewolf remained. Trowa couldn't be sure which one it was, but he thought it was the second one that arrived.

The angered werewolf made several attempts at removing Trowa from the tree, one of which almost succeeded, but when it heard the approaching sirens, it sprinted away. Unfortunately for Trowa, it had marked his scent and wasn't done with him. This was the night Trowa met Garret.

Two nights later, while Trowa enjoyed a late supper of Wolf Brand Chili and watched *Street Outlaws* on the Discovery Channel, the alpha came for him. It slammed into his Airstream travel trailer with enough force to knock it onto its side. Although Trowa had expected the attack and secured an escape plan, the toppled Airstream presented a problem. Exits from the trailer, front door, skylight, and floor door, were no longer where they belonged. Trowa escaped through the floor door and stabbed a butcher knife into the werewolf's right eye. The werewolf bit Trowa's right foot in the process and infected him with the curse.

Once Trowa was safe, high in a pine tree behind his battered Airstream, he called 911. Unfortunately, the responding deputy had been Foster Timpson. Foster was the only Pine View County deputy sheriff who, stubbornly, refused a clip of silver bullets from Mike Middleton. He didn't believe in werewolves. That disbelief ended seconds before the werewolf removed his head.

Garrett showed up shortly after Foster's murder, but the werewolf had gone. It recognized Garrett's scent before he arrived and knowing he had silver bullets, retreated to the woods behind the CP Sawmill where Trowa's Airstream was parked. After coaxing Trowa down from the safety of the pine tree, Garrett, knowing Trowa had been bitten, explained what the bite meant. It was then that Trowa stayed in Pine View County. He'd planned to head to Arkansas where he could find logging work. After being bitten, he stayed to help Garrett kill the alpha. It was that night Garrett deputized Trowa.

After they dealt with the werewolf problem, Garrett was short two deputies—Foster Timpson and Mike Middleton. It was then Garrett offered to make the deputizing permanent and official. To put Trowa on the county payroll.

Trowa had never done anything other than logging and he wasn't very fond of law enforcement. He liked Garrett and Ty, though. After living through what should have killed him or made a killer out of him, he thought working on the other side of the law might make up for some of his past transgressions. Make a karma down payment. Plus, Garrett gave Trowa a reassuring wink and told him there wouldn't be piss tests for marijuana. That sealed the deal. Trowa accepted the offer and dedicated himself to becoming as good a deputy as he was a logger. It turned out he had an aptitude for law enforcement.

So, it was Trowa who received the call early Christmas morning that Melanie Zane hadn't returned home from Midnight Mass. Her parents didn't realize she hadn't come home until they woke up Christmas morning and found her bed hadn't been slept in and her car wasn't in the driveway. Since St. Joseph's Catholic Church was her last known location, Trowa drove to the small church. He found her car, with the driver's side door open, and something even more disturbing. An open grave. He called Garrett.

~ * ~

"Mornin', Chief," Trowa replied.

"Not even a Merry Christmas?" Garrett asked.

"I forget about the white man's silly holidays," Trowa said. "I wish you much fertility instead. How's that?"

"Um, no," Garrett said in a whisper so Mandy wouldn't hear. "I'm not interested in more…fertility."

"Ah, Big Chief whispers when turnin' down a fertility wish," Trowa said with a laugh. "Mandy must be within earshot."

Garrett had a bad habit of sharing a little too much when he drank, and he drank with Ty and Trowa regularly. It was during one of these get-togethers Garrett shared Mandy's wish to have a baby. Garrett also shared he wasn't committed to the idea.

Garrett walked away from Mandy and Paige. "I'm sure ya didn't call me on Christmas mornin' to wish me much fertility. What's up?"

"Yeah, sorry," Trowa said. "I got lost in the moment there. We got a missin' girl."

Garrett swallowed hard. He knew who it was before he asked.

"Who?"

"Melanie Zane. Her folks called in that she didn't come home last night after…"

"Midnight Mass," Garrett interrupted.

"How'd ya know that, Chief?"

Garrett walked further away from Mandy and Paige, into the kitchen, and in a low voice, said, "I was there. I left her in the parkin' lot, alone, after Mass. I offered to stay until she was ready to leave, but she told me she wanted to be alone after Mass. I fuckin' knew I should'a stayed. Where are ya?"

"I'm at Saint Joseph's Catholic Church. Her car's here. The door was open when I got here, but no sign of her."

"I'm on my way."

"Slow your roll, Chief," Trowa said. "There's somethin' else ya need to know."

"What?"

"A grave was…disturbed, too."

"Disturbed?" Garrett said. "How?"

"Dug up."

"Someone took a fuckin' body?"

"Um…no," Trowa said. "The body's here. They took the coffin."

"Are you fuckin' kiddin' me?"

"I wish I was. Garrett, it's Justin."

"What d'ya mean it's Justin?" Garrett said with a sinking feeling in his gut.

"It's Justin's coffin. They took his coffin and left his body."

"Fuck me," Garrett whispered.

"Sideways," Trowa added.

"I'll be right there," Garrett said and ended the call.

Garrett put on a cheerful face as he walked back into the living room, but Paige looked at him and tears were gathering in her eyes. Then he remembered her enhanced hearing. He would have had to drive to the main road to keep her from hearing the conversation.

Fuck that hearin' of hers, Garrett thought.

"I'm goin' with ya, Daddy."

"Sweetheart, that's not a good idea," Garrett told her.

"She's my friend, and Justin was my boyfriend," Paige insisted as tears ran down her cheeks. "I'm goin' with ya."

Mandy, not possessing werewolf hearing and therefore unaware of what happened, looked from Paige to Garrett with a very confused look on her face.

"What's goin' on?" Mandy asked.

Garrett looked at his feet. The guilt he felt over not staying with Melanie weighed heavily on him.

Before he could answer Mandy, Paige did it for him. "Melanie didn't go home last night. She's missin' and someone dug up Justin's coffin, took it, and left his body."

Mandy looked positively scandalized by the news. Her eyes turned into saucer-sized orbs and her mouth formed a perfect 'O.' She covered her mouth with shaking hands and looked at Garrett. After several seconds, she regained her composure and dropped her hands. Her eyes were still large, though.

"It's not your fault, Garrett," Mandy said.

Still looking at his feet, Garrett said, "I shouldn't have left her there alone."

"We thought she was safe," Mandy said. "We all did."

"Yeah, Daddy," Paige said. "I told ya she'd be okay, too."

Garrett looked up and surveyed the two girls in his living room. He knew they were right, but he couldn't shake the guilt.

"Who could do such a thing?" Mandy asked.

"*What* could do such a thing?" Paige added.

They were all thinking it could be a what and not a who. James and Lola had warned them that trouble, supernatural trouble, sometimes follows supernatural occurrences like a werewolf outbreak, but Paige, being supernatural, was the only one of them willing to give voice to the thought.

"I don't know, but I'm gonna find out," Garrett said as he headed for his bedroom to get dressed.

"I'm goin' with you," Paige shouted after him.

"No." Garrett replied.

"Paige can help, Garrett," Mandy said. "She might catch a scent and be able to track it."

Garrett stuck his head out of the bedroom. "My daughter is not a bloodhound."

"You're right, she's not a bloodhound," Mandy said. "She's better. She's a werewolf. Paige can help ya, Garrett."

"Yeah, Daddy," Paige said. "I can help. Glinda can help."

Glinda was the name Paige gave her wolf. Named for Glinda, the good witch in *The Wizard of Oz*. It made sense, because her wolf, like

Glinda, was good.

Garrett looked from Mandy to Paige and thought about a time, not so long ago, when they were never in his house at the same time. It wasn't because Paige didn't like Mandy. She'd always liked Mandy. It was a self-imposed policy of Garrett's making so he could devote one hundred percent of his attention to each of them when they were with him. Now they were together and ganging up on him.

"Okay," Garrett relented. "But you're only involved in the Melanie part of this. I don't want ya seein' Justin like this. No arguments. Understood?"

Paige offered a weak smile, she still had tears on her cheeks. "Yes, Daddy."

Fifteen minutes later, Garrett and Paige pulled out of the driveway headed for St. Joseph's Catholic Church. They had no way of knowing the depths of the fresh nightmare Pine View County was about to endure.

Chapter Three

Garrett and Paige pulled into the St. Joseph Catholic Church parking lot about forty minutes after receiving the call from Trowa. Melanie's car was where Garrett had last seen it, but now there was crime scene tape stretched from the chain-link fence that surrounded the graveyard on either side of the car and anchored to Trowa's patrol SUV parked sideways behind it. Outside of the taped off area, Trowa talked with Fr. Mike, who looked very upset. Garrett parked, facing the graveyard, a few spaces to the right of Melanie's abandoned car.

"Remember, you and Glinda are only here for Melanie," Garrett told Paige. "Use your senses to pick up on anything that might help us find her."

She heard him, but her eyes were locked on the pile of dirt beside Justin's grave. Worse, the yellow plastic sheet that covered something slumped beside the freshly dug hole. She didn't need Glinda to know it was covering Justin's body.

"Understand?" Garrett said.

Paige averted her eyes from the horror of Justin's disturbed grave and looked at her daddy. "I understand. We're here for Mel."

Like Paige, Garrett saw Justin's grave and knew she'd seen it. His heart broke for her at that moment.

He took her small hand in his. "I knew this was a bad idea."

Paige stiffened. "I'm okay, Daddy."

He knew she wasn't.

He gave her hand a squeeze. "That's not Justin, Paige-Turner. He's safe in heaven with God, watchin' over you."

Paige wasn't used to hearing her daddy speak of God and heaven, but he'd been doing so more often of late. It comforted her.

She offered a weak but genuine, smile. "I know, Daddy. Let's see if Glinda and I can help find Mel."

They got out of the SUV.

Garrett, unaware of what Paige was experiencing, immediately headed toward Trowa and Fr. Mike on the far side of Melanie's car. A putrid smell immediately assaulted Paige.

Since being turned and finding out about the ancestral werewolf connection, Paige saw Lola Laveau regularly. Lola was her supernatural therapist. With Lola's guidance, Paige had learned how to, for lack of a better description, adjust Glinda's input while in human form. While dialed to low mode, as it was earlier that morning, her senses were still enhanced, but only slightly. When she dialed Glinda up to high mode, as she had when she stepped out of the SUV, they were almost, but not quite, as strong as when she transformed. Lola called this mode, "Almost Glinda." It took Paige many attempts, and several sets of clothing, she shredded her clothes when she'd inadvertently bring on the full transformation, to get the hang of it, but she'd learned to control it.

As the putrid smell assaulted her, she wished she'd dialed Glinda back a bit. She shook her head, causing her long, dark brown hair to fly wildly around her head, and concentrated. The putrid smell was death, old death, ancient death. Mixed with the ancient death smell were two more death smells. One was chemical. She knew that was Justin's remains and the embalming process meant to slow the natural process of decay. The other was recent death. Very new death, and she knew the scent of whom the recent death belonged. It was Mel's scent. Fighting back tears for Justin and Mel, Paige dialed back Glinda mode to about fifty percent, collected herself, and went to join her daddy, Trowa, and Fr. Mike.

"Go over it again," her daddy said as Paige joined the three men.

"I told you everything I remember, Garrett," Mike said. "I told Deputy Raintree before you arrived."

Garrett put a reassuring hand on Fr. Mike's shoulder. "I know; but maybe you'll remember somethin' else as ya go over it again."

Garrett didn't think he would, but he wanted Paige to hear it from Fr. Mike, not him. He didn't know if Glinda could pick up on anything missing from Fr. Mike's recount. Probably not, but it was worth a try.

"Okay," Mike began, "After Midnight Mass, I made a quick check of the pews to make sure everything was in order and went to lock the front doors. I saw you slowly pulling out of the parking lot, and Melanie sitting in her car. I know it was late, but I also know Melanie likes to sit in her car after Mass and...contemplate the readings and homily. I know this because I asked about it after seeing her do it several times. So, I thought nothing was out of sorts. I wish to God I had, but I didn't. I locked the front doors, exited the back of the church, and went to the rectory. I didn't hear or see anything."

"Was it unusually quiet?" Garrett asked.

Paige knew what her daddy was asking. When the werewolves were in an area, everything was silent. Like they scared the sound out of everything in the area, which they did. Glinda didn't have that affect, though. Because Glinda wasn't evil, she wasn't something to be feared. The forest critters had instinctively known it.

"No," Mike said shaking his head. "Just normal, late night quiet."

Garrett looked toward Paige to see if she had gleaned anything from Fr. Mike's recollection of events, but she was looking toward the front of Mel's car.

Paige had listened to Fr. Mike's retelling of events. She couldn't tell if he'd seen or sensed something out of the ordinary. That was beyond Glinda's abilities. That was more in Lola's wheelhouse of abilities. She would suggest Lola talk with Fr. Mike later. As Fr. Mike told her daddy the night was normally quiet, she picked up on a nearby scent. She dialed Glinda up a bit and knew there was something in front of Mel's car that might be important. Blood. She turned and sniffed her way to the source.

Because he'd been looking at her, only Garrett noticed Paige's slow move toward the car. He could hear her sniffing. He followed her.

Paige stopped outside the crime scene tape at the front of Mel's car and looked at the gravel. Looked for the source of the scent. Her vision was enhanced too, and she saw the source. A couple of drops of bright red blood, Mel's, and one drop of thick, black blood.

Garrett followed Paige to the front of the car. "What'cha got, kiddo?"

"Blood," Paige whispered.

Garrett looked and saw nothing. "Where?"

"About a foot in front of Mel's car. Just a couple of drops."

"Mel's blood?"

Paige nodded.

"Well. If it's just a couple of drops, that's a good thing."

Paige shook her head. "Mel's dead, and there's more."

"More what?"

"More blood," Paige said and crinkled her nose. "It's not Mel's."

"That's great. We might get some DNA."

Paige shook her head slowly, fighting back tears again.

"I don't understand," Garrett said. "What's goin' on?"

"Mel's blood is fresh. She was alive when it fell."

"But she's dead now?"

Paige nodded.

Confused, Garrett asked, "How can ya tell she's dead?"

"I...we can smell her death," Paige said. "It's faint. Fresh."

Garrett didn't want to ask, but he had to. "Couldn't that be..."

Paige spared him from having to say Justin's name. "No. His has a chemical smell to it. Mel's is new, but the other blood. That blood's black. It's fowl. Evil. It's ancient. That's why ya won't get DNA from it. It's been dead for a long time."

"What're we dealin' with, Paige?"

Paige shook her head. "I don't know, Daddy. But it's bad."

"Can ya track it?"

Paige shook her head again. "No. it's like it, they just... melted away."

Garrett put his arm around Paige and held her close. "Ya did good, Paige-Turner. We *will* figure this out."

Garrett turned to where Trowa and Fr. Mike were still talking and said, "Bring me some gloves and evidence bags, Deputy Raintree."

"Ya got somethin'?" Trowa asked.

"I think I see some blood."

"I looked and didn't see anything. How'd ya..." Trowa didn't finish because he knew.

Paige had found it. "Okay. Be right with ya."

Upon hearing all this, Fr. Mike walked toward Garrett and Paige.

Paige whispered, "Stay close to the fence and watch me. I'll let ya know when you're close. Mel's will be easier to see. There are a few drops and they're still bright red. The others will be harder. It's a single drop and looks like a black pebble. It's closer to the fence."

Garrett nodded.

Fr. Mike joined them and looked at the gravel. "I don't see anything."

Thankfully, Trowa joined them with the items Garrett requested and kept Garrett from having to answer Fr. Mike. He put the gloves on, took the evidence bags, lifted the crime scene tape, stepped under it, put his back to the fence, and began slowly making his way toward the front of Mel's car. All the while with one eye on Paige.

When he saw her nod slightly, he stopped inching his way along the fence and looked at the mix of multi-colored gravel. He couldn't see anything resembling blood. Red or otherwise. He wished he could share the connection werewolves had. Then, as if he could, he saw some bright red pebbles, but the black one eluded him. There were several blackish pebbles. Remembering Paige had said it was closer to the fence than the red ones, he got down on his knees and studied several that might be the one.

Monitoring Paige, he pointed toward one. Paige shook her head. He pointed at another. Paige shook her head again. He was getting frustrated, but when he pointed at a third black pebble, Paige nodded. He picked it up carefully and studied it. It was black on top and reddish-brown on the bottom. The black blood looked thick. Garrett brought it up to his nose and sniffed it. He didn't have Paige's enhanced abilities, but it smelled...off. He put it in one of the evidence bags and then gathered the three pebbles that had Mel's bright red blood on them.

He gave Paige a quick glance to see if he'd gathered everything needed. She gave him a reassuring nod, and he joined Paige, Trowa and Fr. Mike on the other side of the crime scene tape.

Garrett handed the bag containing the single, black pebble to Trowa. "Possible perp."

Then he handed the other one to him. "Potential victim."

Fr. Mike seemed interested in the black pebble.

He held out his hand. "May I see the black one?"

Trowa looked to Garrett. He nodded. Trowa handed it to Fr. Mike.

Paige watched closely as Fr. Mike brought the evidence bag containing the black, blood-stained pebble up close to his face to inspect it. She saw it move. To the others, it probably looked as though it simply shifted by a tilt in the evidence bag, but she knew better. It had moved away from Fr. Mike. Paige knew something else. Something Glinda sensed. The black blood was afraid of Fr. Mike. That was good to know, and she thought she knew something else. Fr. Mike sensed it, too.

Fr. Mike handed the evidence bag back to Trowa, who put both evidence bags in the forensic kit in the back of his SUV and closed the back door.

He turned to Garrett. "What now, Chief?"

Garrett knew; but he hated to make the call.

~ * ~

The Pine View Sheriff Department didn't have a forensics unit. Forensics was Mike Middleton's job on minor cases. Bigger cases were handed off to the Department of Public Safety. For obvious reasons, Garrett, once again, found himself in a situation when leaving the DPS out of the investigation was the prudent thing to do. This was the case with the werewolf situation, too. Then, keeping them completely out of the loop was impossible. Fifteen mutilated teenagers weren't something he could hide. He kept them out of his private investigation. One missing girl in Pine View County wouldn't be a blip on their radar. For now, at least. Forever, if he could keep it contained.

Unfortunately, for many reasons, Mike was killed by the massive Mexican werewolf. That left Pine View County without a forensics deputy. So, Garrett turned to his best friend, and best deputy, Ty Jackson. Ty attended a DPS, two-week crash course on forensics in Austin, Texas in August. Garrett added a little to the per diem so Ty could take his wife, Jasmine, and son, Derrick named after Ty's deceased father and called Little D, with him. When not in forensics classes, Ty and his family made a vacation of the experience. That meant Garrett had to interrupt Ty's Christmas morning with his family.

To Trowa, Garrett said, "I'll call Ty. You call Brent Simmons to have the car towed back to the department, but not before Ty gets everything he needs here. Then, y'all go over the car with a fine-toothed comb."

"Got it, Chief," Trowa said.

Mike said, "May I speak with you, Sheriff Lambert?" He cut his eyes towards Paige and added, "Alone."

"Sure," Garrett said as he and Fr. Mike put some distance between themselves and Paige.

Garrett knew moving away wouldn't help. Depending on how dialed up Paige had Glinda, they couldn't get far enough away to keep their conversation private from her.

Fr. Mike stopped walking after they'd covered about twenty feet and in a low voice, said, "About Justin Anderson. I assume you're planning to tell his parents. I think they might better receive news like this coming from me."

That was fine with Garrett. He had planned to let them know about the desecration of their son's grave. If Fr. Mike was volunteering, all the better. Garrett nodded.

Fr. Mike exhaled heavily. "Okay, then. I should probably head that way."

Paige, who was listening, said, "What about the ten o'clock Christmas Mass?"

Fr. Mike looked at his watch. It was five past nine. Given the circumstances, he didn't question how Paige could've heard their conversation.

Frustrated, he shouted, "Crap."

Paige, who had never heard Fr. Mike use a cross word, and regardless of the horrors surrounding her, had to suppress a giggle.

Fr. Mike took his cell phone from the inside pocket of his jacket. "It's okay. I have an app most of my parishioners have, except for the older folks who don't use cellphones. I can send a message letting them know the ten o'clock service has been canceled and to attend the noon Mass instead."

Garrett, baffled by the technology, said, "A little church in deep East Texas has an app?"

Fr. Mike's thumbs typed away.

Without looking up, Mike said, "A little church connected with the biggest church on the planet has an app."

That made Garrett feel foolish.

Fr. Mike tapped the 'Send' icon. "Done."

Seconds later, Paige's cell phone dinged.

"Got it," Paige said.

"Great," Mike said. "That still leaves the older folks and those who may not bother to check their phones before coming. Would it be possible for Deputy Raintree to tape off the two entrances and inform those who come of the delay?"

"I can do that," Trowa put in.

"You'll have to," Garrett said. "Until Ty gets here and documents everything, and Brent tows the car, this is an active crime scene."

Then, looking almost ill, Mike said, "What about…Justin's body? My parishioners can't see that. Especially the children."

"About that," Trowa said. "I called Digger, but didn't get an answer."

It was Garrett's turn to be frustrated, and he shouted, "Crap."

Given this conversation, Paige didn't feel like giggling.

Trowa patted the air with his hands in a calming gesture. "Slow your roll, Chief. I had Erica look up the number for that new place north of town, the Eternal Rest Funeral Home, and I called it. It isn't open for business yet, but a man answered the phone. He has an accent I can't place. After I explained what happened, he said he'd come. Even said, under the circumstances, he'd comp the family a mid-range coffin. If they want somethin' better, he'd deducted fifteen hundred dollars from the upgrade. Called it a gesture of good will."

"That's damn nice of him," Garrett said.

"Very," Mike added.

As if on cue, a late model black Cadillac hearse cruised slowly up County Road Five Eighty-Eight, turned into the church parking lot, and parked behind Trowa's patrol SUV. The door opened and a tall, slender man in his early fifties with thinning blond hair and piercing blue eyes stepped out.

He approached Garrett, Trowa, and Fr. Mike, and gave a curt bow. "Dănuţ Roşca. At your service, gentlemen."

"Mister Ros…" Garrett began.

"Dan. Please call me Dan," Dănuţ said as he held his bony hand out to Garrett. "It much easier to pronounce. Yes?"

Garrett shook the strange man's hand. His grip was deceivingly strong, considering his thin appearance, and heavily calloused. Garrett introduced himself and then Deputy Raintree and Fr. Mike, who shook hands with him.

With the introductions completed, Garrett said, "Deputy Raintree told ya why we need your help?"

Dănuţ gave a quick nod of his skeletal head. "Yes. This is most…unfortunate. Especially on Christmas."

"And thank you for offering to help the family with the coffin," Mike said. "Paying for another one is the last thing they need to worry about right now."

"Have they been informed of the…incident?" Dănuţ asked.

"No. Not yet," Mike said. "I was about to go do that now. But I can help with…Justin before I leave."

"Nonsense. This is no job for a priest," Dănuţ insisted. "You must go to the family. They are more in need of your attention than we are. Besides, the dead, they do not weigh so much."

Fr. Mike looked from Trowa to Garrett.

"Go," Garrett said. "We can handle this."

Before Fr. Mike turned to leave, Dănuţ produced a business card, as if from thin air, like a magic trick, and handed it to Fr. Mike. "Please. Give them my card and assure them their loved one is in expert hands. They can contact me when they are ready."

Fr. Mike took the card, thanked him, and walked away.

"Shall we…kick this pig?" Dănuţ asked.

Garrett and Trowa looked shocked by Dănuţ's expression.

"If I offend, it is not my intention," Dănuţ said. "I am still learning the nuances of English. I was told by a delivery man that this phrase means to get it done. Yes?"

Shocked or not, Garrett couldn't help but smile at the turn of phrase. "Yes, it means that. In this context, probably not the best way to put it."

"My sincere apology," Dănuţ said with a curt bow.

"No harm, no foul," Garrett said.

Then he turned to Paige. "In the SUV. I don't want you watchin' this."

Following Garrett's head turn, Dănuţ's piercing blue eyes flickered toward Paige. It was a very brief glance, but he took her in.

"Don't worry," Paige said as she headed for her daddy's SUV. "I don't wanna see this."

Even with Glinda on alert, she didn't feel Dănuţ's eyes on her.

Oh, how my Master would love to have you in his cloud to play with, Dănuţ thought.

The Sheriff's daughter might not be a risk worth taking. He would, of course, tell Dragoş about her, though. That was his duty. If the Master wanted her, the Master would have her.

~ * ~

Paige really had no intention of watching them put Justin in the new coffin. She didn't want to see that, and the tall, thin man named Dănuţ, Dan, gave her the heebie-jeebies. A phrase he had become familiar with. But she, and Glinda, got no sense of danger from Dan. In fact, they got nothing from him, which was strange. It was almost like he existed on a different plane. Or between two planes of existence. Neither here nor there. Which, Paige thought a little strange. Dan was new in town. He was foreign, and he had, what most folks would consider, a creepy job. Bottom line, he was an enigma. Paige decided she and Glinda should be on high alert around him, but she couldn't foresee a circumstance that would warrant their paths crossing again. That was Paige's first error in judgment. It wouldn't be her last.

Paige got back into her daddy's patrol SUV. The engine hadn't been running, but a residual warmth lingered. It was warmish. Certainly, warmer than the chill outside. She watched as her daddy and Trowa opened the double gates that lead into the cemetery and the black hearse, driven by the man with the funny name who went by Dan, drove into the hallowed place. Her daddy and Trowa left the gates open and walked behind the hearse until it reached its destination.

She really didn't want to watch them put Justin's body into the new coffin, but she couldn't have if she did. The hearse blocked her view. She saw Dan get out and join her daddy and Trowa at the back of the hearse. The back end opened, and Dan slid a wood grain, whether actual wood or metal painted to look like actual wood, she couldn't tell, with brass hardware coffin from the hearse and all three men carried it to the far side where she couldn't see. She took out her cellphone.

~ * ~

As Garrett and Trowa walked behind the hearse, to a destination he dreaded, Garrett said, "Did ya take pictures of all this?"

"Yeah," Trowa said. "A lot. I knew you'd want to go over 'em. No footprints, no tire marks, no nothin'. It's like his coffin just popped up out of the ground."

What the fuck? Garrett thought.

"Justin looks better than I thought he would. But…" Trowa said.

"But what?"

"He was discarded," Trowa said. "Like trash. Just thrown aside in a crumpled heap. Who would do somethin' like this? What the hell would they want with his coffin?"

"I don't know," Garrett said. "I plan to call James Huff later and see if he has any ideas."

"Good idea," Trowa said. "Someone else gettin' a fucked-up Christmas present."

Garrett didn't know if James was a religious man. In fact, he knew little about his personal life, other than he made muscadine wine, liked to read, and was gay. He'd been meaning to get to know him better but hadn't. James didn't volunteer personal information except if something relevant came up in casual conversation. That was how he found out James was gay. Garrett made an offhand remark about how James' English Bulldog, Winston, was a chick magnet. That was it.

~ * ~

The hearse stopped in front of Justin's desecrated grave and Dănuț got out. He used the key fob to open the back end of the hearse. A wooden coffin was inside.

"It is metal painted to look like wood," Dănuț explained. "It is nice, yes?"

"You're very generous," Garrett said.

Dănuț pushed a button on the inside left of the hearse's back end. There was an audible thunk as the clamps holding the coffin in place retracted into the floor. He grabbed the brass handle on the end and effortlessly slid the coffin about halfway out. Little rollers on the hearse's floor spun quietly as he did.

"It is not so heavy," Dănuț said. "Please. Take hold of the side handles."

Garrett and Trowa did as instructed and the three of them walked the coffin over to where Justin's body lay beneath the yellow plastic sheet Trowa had used to cover it. Trowa had placed clumps of dirt on the corners to keep it from blowing off.

Dănuț looked at the grave marker. "Pity when someone so young is taken, and so recently. Did you know the young man, Sheriff Lambert?"

Garrett sighed. "I did. In fact, he was my daughter's boyfriend when he died."

Dănuț's piercing blue eyes flickered quickly towards the SUV Paige sat in. She intrigued him. Garrett and Trowa didn't see this. They were looking at the yellow plastic sheet.

"I am sorry for her loss," Dănuț said in what passed for empathy.

"Thanks," Garrett said. "Let's get this over with."

Trowa removed the sheet, exposing Justin's discarded remains. He was face down with his right arm under his body and his left arm outstretched toward the hole in the ground, as if pointing toward where his body belonged. His legs were bent at the knees, but the right one was caught under his body, elevating his butt in an unnatural and undignified position.

"Fuck me," Garrett whispered.

Dănuț was all business. He opened the coffin and, without requesting help, turned Justin's body onto its back and straightened his sprawled limbs.

When this was done, Dănuț said, "I will take the shoulders. Each of you take a leg."

Again, Garrett and Trowa did as instructed. Dănuț had said the dead weigh little, and he was right. Garrett couldn't believe how light Justin's remains were. A couple of seconds later, Justin's body was in its new coffin. Dănuț gently folded Justin's arms across his chest.

Garrett looked down at the boy, who had been his daughter's boyfriend. The boy who would've taken her virginity if the bitch werewolf hadn't viciously murdered him that night. His face looked thin with protruding cheekbones and his eyes were sunk deeply into his skull. Justin's lips were drawn back, exposing impossibly white teeth. His cuticles had withdrawn, making his fingernails look like long, yellow claws. Garrett felt sick. If he'd looked at Justin any longer, he probably would've vomited. He and Trowa had different ideas of what looks better than expected meant. Mercifully, Dănuț closed both lids.

Without speaking, the three men loaded the coffin back into the hearse. Dănuț positioned it, pushed the inside button again. The clamps thudded back out of the floor to secure the coffin in place. Dănuț pushed a button on the inside of the back of the hearse and the backend closed silently.

With the dirty work done, Garrett walked back and looked into the ragged hole that was Justin's eternal resting place. By law, coffins weren't just buried in the ground as they had in the past. They required a burial vault. Modern ones, like Justin's, were made of concrete. The vault lid was tilted up against the left side of the hole.

"How long have you been in this business, Dan?" Garrett asked.

"Almost fifty years," Dănuț replied.

That took Garrett aback, because Dan looked to be in his early fifties. "You must've been very young when you started."

"You could say I was *made* for this," Dănuț replied with an unsettling grin.

The wording of his answer seemed odd to Garrett. He assumed it was a language barrier issue, and what Dănuţ meant was he was *born* into the business. As in his father had been a mortician and his father's father had been a mortician, and so on, through several generations.

"How much would you say that vault lid weighs?" Garrett asked.

"Several hundred pounds," Dănuţ said. "Why do you ask?"

"Then it would stand to reason that several people were involved," Garrett said.

"Most assuredly," Dănuţ agreed. "Unless it was the giant, green Hunk who did this."

Garrett chuckled. "I think you mean the Hulk."

"Ah, yes," Dănuţ said. "I am not so knowledgeable about American pop-culture yet. I will learn."

Without further conversation, Dănuţ got back in the hearse and backed out of the cemetery. Garrett and Trowa followed.

As they walked, Garrett took out his cellphone. "Time to fuck someone else's Christmas."

He quick-dialed Ty.

~ * ~

Ty and Jasmine watched and videoed Little D push around the living room on his new truck Santa had left in the middle of the night. Nothing was safe. Little D made rumbling truck sounds with his lips, producing an ample amount of drool, and bounced the little truck off of just about everything in the area. Including the Christmas Tree, which almost brought it down on top of him. Luckily, Ty grabbed it before it crashed on top of Little D. That was when his cellphone rang.

Ty looked at the screen. "It's Garrett."

"Take it," Jasmine said as Little D rammed the truck into the coffee table for, perhaps, the fourth time. "I'll keep recordin' Little D. You won't miss anything."

Ty stepped into the kitchen and answered the call. "Merry Christmas, Garrett."

"It was," Garrett replied flatly.

"What happened?" Ty asked.

Ty listened as Garrett quickly filled him in on all that had transpired since Midnight Mass ended and he left Melanie alone in the church parking lot. His merry Christmas mood evaporated.

"Fuck me," Ty whispered when Garrett finished.

"My words exactly," Garrett replied. "I hate to do this to ya, but you're the only one with forensics trainin'. Trowa took pics, but I need ya out here when Brent comes to tow her car to the department. Then I need ya to go over it and collect everything ya can."

"Yeah. Of course. I'll be right out."

"Thank you, Ty. I really hate to do this to ya on Christmas, but…"

"Is it startin' again, Garrett?" Ty interrupted.

Garrett sighed. "Accordin' to Paige, somethin's not…right."

"Fuck me twice," Ty said.

"Sideways," Garrett added and hung up.

When Ty came back into the living room, Little D seemed to have run out of gas. He pushed slower and drool induced rumbles sputtered from his mouth. Jasmine turned to Ty with a smile on her face. One look at Ty erased it.

"What?" Jasmine asked.

"Missin' girl, missin' coffin," Ty said. "You know. The usual for Pine View County."

Jasmine wasn't privy to the true nature of the previous summer's murder outbreak. Since Ty was one of the three bitten and cursed, he had purposefully kept her in the dark, but she wasn't stupid and had figured the perp or perps weren't your average murderers.

"Okay. You go do your deputy thing, honey."

"Of all the days. I'm sorry, darlin'."

Jasmine smiled a smile that made Ty love her even more, and cocked her head toward Little D. "He'll be out before long. When ya get home, I'll be wearin' the Christmas gift ya gave me."

Despite the bad news, that brought a smile to Ty's face. The Christmas gift she alluded to was a sexy blue lace teddy.

"I'll be back as quick as I can," Ty said.

"Don't make me start without ya," Jasmine teased.

"If ya do, video that for me, too," Ty said with a wink.

Jasmine smiled a wicked little smile.

Ty kissed her, and she kissed back.

"Gross," Little D chimed from the stationary truck.

"I love ya both," Ty said and left.

~ * ~

Paige entered her passcode, Justin's birthday, tapped the 'Messages' icon, and looked at the string of text messages. At the top of the list, the most recent text exchange was Lindsey Anderson's name. Lin had texted Paige at two that morning to see how her solo at Midnight Mass had gone. Paige tapped on Lin's name and then her thumbs hovered over the electronic keyboard. She didn't know what to say. If she should say anything or let Fr. Mike handle it. Finally, she began typing.

"Father Mike is on his way to your house."

The little, blue, rippling dots appeared immediately, followed by Lindsey's reply, "Why"

"I can't be the one to tell u," Paige texted.

"Why? What happened?"

"I can't say."

"Does this have something to do with text about mass being canceled?" Lindsey texted.

"Yes."

"Why is he coming here? Is it bad?"

"Yes. It's bad," Paige texted.

"Why won't u tell me."

"I can't Lin. We can talk after he sees y'all. I luv you. ♥"

Lindsey sent back two heart emojis, signifying she loved Paige more. Paige sent back three. Lindsey sent back four. Sometimes this would go on until the number of hearts filled the screen. Then one of them would surrender with a kissy face emoji. Paige had just sent seven, but the rippling dots didn't immediately appear. She looked at her phone's screen, waiting. It dimmed. Then, just before it went black, the dots appeared. Paige tapped the screen, bringing it back to life.

"He's here," Lindsey texted.

"I luv u Lin ♥," Paige texted back.

There was no reply. Her heart ached for Lin and her parents.

When she looked back up, and toward Justin's grave, the hearse was already backing out. She watched it, and the strange man driving it, back into the church parking lot, then slowly exit the parking lot, and turn left onto County Road Five Eighty-Eight. She was glad he had gone, but she didn't know why she was glad.

After her daddy and Trowa closed the cemetery gates, they headed to the back of Trowa's SUV. When they reemerged, each carried a roll of yellow crime scene tape. Trowa headed toward the front entrance the hearse had just exited, and her daddy headed her way. She turned Glinda down all the way, to avoid the stench of the ancient death, and got out of her daddy's SUV, intending to help him tape off the back entrance. Then things went from bad to worse.

~ * ~

Trowa was almost at the front entrance when an older model, tan Ford pickup raced up County Road Five Eighty-Eight. It turned into the gravel parking lot too fast and fishtailed wildly, spraying gravel everywhere. Trowa leaped out of the way, but the fishtailing back end of the pickup missed him by only an inch. Had it been any other deputy, they would've been hit. Hit hard. Bone breaking hard, but Trowa wasn't any other deputy. He was thin, fit, and light on his feet. Like this world's version of a J. R. R. Tolkien elf, Legolas. Quickness aside, he still caught a face full of stinging gravel that opened several minor cuts.

The trucked raced toward where Garrett and Paige stood. Garrett protectively pushed Paige behind his body. The truck skidded to a stop, kicking up dust and gravel a few feet in front of them. Zack Zane, Melanie's dad, leaped from the truck.

"Is that her?" Zack screamed. "Is she in that hearse, Garrett?"

"No, Zack," Garrett replied as calmly as he could. "She's not."

Zack Zane was a big man, about six feet, four inches tall, with a ruddy, pock-marked face and thick, soup strainer mustache. The kind Sam

Elliott wore, but Zack's was brown, not gray. His hair was a wild, uncombed tumble of brown with gray on the sides. Despite the chilly morning, his face was slick with sweat, making it look oily. He had a square jaw and a flat nose. His shoulders were broad, and his arms were long and thick. They ended in huge, calloused hands. He was a logger since before Garrett and Trowa's logging careers and both men knew him from that work.

Zack looked over Garrett at where Melanie's crime scene tape encased car was parked with the driver's door open.

His watery brown eyes drifted to Garrett's face. Tears streamed down his oily looking, ruddy cheeks and thick, yellow runners of snot were on his soup strainer mustache. It unsettled Garrett to see the big man so shaken.

"Where is she?" Zack pleaded.

"We're lookin' into it, Zack."

To Paige, Garrett said, "Grab some tissues from my SUV."
Paige knew exactly where to look. Her dad kept several travel-packs of tissues in the center console between the front seats. She did not know why. He wasn't prone to colds, he didn't have allergies, and thanks to Mandy, he'd finally stopped part-time smoking. Hacking up smoke-induced phlegm wasn't likely. In that moment, she thought travel-pack tissue mystery was solved. They were for other people. People like Mel's dad, who needed tissues.

Under the prior sheriff, Oliver Henry, reporting deaths to family members, was left to the responding deputy. Like when, as a deputy, Garrett had to inform Arleen Crawford her husband Ben Crawford was killed in a single vehicle roll-over accident. After Garrett became sheriff, he took that responsibility upon himself, sparing his deputies the horrible task. It was as sheriff that he revisited Arleen to inform her that her only daughter, Maggie, was killed at the MRB that fateful night.

~ * ~

Paige returned quickly and handed a travel-pack of tissues to her daddy. Trowa was there by then, too. Several trickles of blood pocked

Trowa's bronze face where gravel had peppered him when Zack came fishtailing into the parking lot.

Zack staggered and then he went down hard on his right knee. Trowa and Garrett helped the big man to his feet. Garrett handed him a few tissues. Zack wiped his eyes first and then ran one under his nose. It helped a little, removing the top layer of snot, but it was still caked in his thick Sam Elliot mustache.

After wiping his face, he sobbed, "I can't, Garrett. I can't lose her. Not after what happened at the MRB. I could'a lost her then. You gotta find her, Garrett. Please find her."

Garett believed Paige when she told him Melanie was dead, but he couldn't tell Zack this. Not without proof. He'd gotten good at telling partial truths during the werewolf incidents. He was going to have to dust off that ability again. Before he could say anything, the passenger door opened and Kathy 'Kat' Zane, Melanie's mom, stepped out of the truck.

Unlike Zack, Kat appeared calm. Too calm. She slow-walked, shuffling her slipper covered feet through the gravel, to the front of the truck. She wore what looked like one of Zack's large, T-shirts, as a nightshirt. Her blue eyes looked forward, but it didn't look like she was focused on anything. Couldn't focus on anything. Her eyes looked like little frosted over windshields.

Then, to no one in particular, Kat said, "She came to see me last night."

"Don't start that crap, Kat," Zack shouted. "It was a dream. Had to be a dream."

Garrett ignored Zack and turned his attention to Kat. "What do ya mean she came to visit ya last night?"

"She's in shock, Garrett," Zack insisted.

Ignoring her distraught husband, Kat, in a flat voice, said, "I woke up 'bout two thirty and went to check on her. She wasn't in her bed. It was still made. I got worried and turned to let Zack know she wasn't home. Then I heard it."

"Heard what?" Garrett asked.

"Tappin' on her window," Kat said. "I turned, and there she was. Standin' outside her window."

"Her bedroom's on the second floor, Garrett," Zack said. "It was a dream."

"Go on," Garrett said to Kat

Zack threw up his arms in frustration.

"I opened the window and said, 'What are ya doin' out there?'," Kat said. "She said she was cold and asked if she could come in. I said, 'Of course ya can.'"

"Then what?" Garrett asked.

"I don't remember," Kat said flatly. "I woke up on her bed this mornin'."

Because of the putrid smells surrounding Mel's car, Paige had dialed Glinda way back. Even way back, some smells were inescapable. Like blood. While Paige listened to Missus Kat tell about her encounter, she smelled blood on her. Then she saw it. A dried trickle on Missus Kat's inner left thigh, just above her knee. She smelled something else on her, too. She smelled the fresh death she associated with Mel.

"You're bleedin', Missus Kat," Paige said.

Garrett, Trowa, and Zack looked from Kat to Paige, and back to Kat again.

"I am?" Kat said flatly again.

"Yes, ma'am," Paige said. "There's blood just above your left knee."

All three men bent lower to see, and all three saw it.

"Must be my monthly visitor," Kat said.

All three men straightened up and looked anywhere but at Kat.

Really? Paige thought angrily. *Grown men reactin' like that to a woman's period? Teenage boys, I can understand. But grown men?*

Garrett regained his composure. "Are ya sure ya can't remember anything else?"

"I can't," Kat said and looked at her husband. "But I know it *wasn't* a dream,"

The inference on "wasn't" had been the only time Kat's voice broke from the flat tone she'd been speaking in.

"But..." Kat trailed off.

"What?" Garrett asked.

Kat's eyes lost that frosted over windshield appearance.

She looked at Garrett. "I think she's…not okay. Ya have to find her, Garrett. Please find her."

Then she broke down and sobbed. Garrett handed her several tissues, which she took with trembling hands and pressed to her face.

Just then, Ty pulled into the church parking lot through the back entrance and parked beside Garrett's SUV. He got out and joined the others. Paige gave him a big hug, and he hugged back. A strong hug Paige loved.

To the Zanes, Garrett said, "Deputy Jackson's gonna go over every inch of Melanie's car. If there's somethin' to find, he'll find it. When he's finished with her car, I'll have him out to your place to check Melanie's room. I know this is hard, but it's best for y'all to go on back home and wait for Deputy Jackson."

Zack and Kat looked at Melanie's car and then back at Garrett in unison.

"Okay," Zack said.

"Please find her," Kat pleaded.

Garrett handed them the travel-pack of tissues. Kat took it with a look of gratitude. Then they got into their truck and drove slowly away. Kat looked out the back window at her daughter's abandoned car until the truck was out of sight.

"Fill me in," Ty said.

Since Ty and Trowa knew about Glinda, Paige told them everything she had sensed about the ancient and new death she'd smelled. She left out Justin's chemical death smell she'd told her daddy about, though. She also told them how she couldn't track Mel and the other's scents. That the smells had vanished, not trailed off.

"What the hell are we dealin' with now?" Ty said.

"No idea," Garrett said.

"Oh yeah," Paige added. "That blood on Missus Kat's leg wasn't menstrual blood."

All three men looked shocked.

"Grow up." Paige said angrily.

"Y-you can tell the difference?" Garrett asked.

"Of course I can. Would y'all like to know how they smell different?" Paige asked out of spite.

In unison, all three men said, "No."

Paige took a moment to enjoy their horror at hearing the offer. "It was regular blood. Missus Kat's blood. And it was dry. It was there for some time."

"Like, since two thirty this mornin' dry?" Ty asked.

Paige nodded.

They heard a rumbling sound coming up County Road Five Eighty-Eight. Seconds later, Brent Simmons' tow truck pulled into the church parking lot through the back entrance.

Before he got out, Garrett said, "Okay. We still need to tape off the entrances."

"We who, Chief?" Trowa said. "I got the front one taped off after Zack showered me with gravel."

Garrett glanced toward the front entrance, saw the crime scene tape, and continued, "Good job. I'm gonna drop Paige off at home and go see James Huff to see if he has any idea what we're dealin' with. Ty…"

"I think Miss Lola should talk with Father Mike and Missus Kat," Paige cut him off. "She might get 'em to remember more than they do now."

Garrett, irritated with the interruptions, none the less, smiled at Paige. "That's an excellent idea, kiddo. Now, where the hell was I? Oh yeah. Ty, when ya go to the Zane's house, get her folk's fingerprints and somethin' of Melanie's you can pull prints off of so we can eliminate theirs from any found on the car. Trowa, tape off the back entrance after Brent gets Melanie's car out'a here and stay here to deal with anyone who didn't get Father Mike's text and shows up for the ten o'clock Mass. When Father Mike gets back, take the tape down and head back to the department to help Ty. I think that 'bout covers it. Questions?"

Ty and Trowa shook their heads as Brent walked up.

"What'cha got here, Sheriff Lambert?" Brent asked.

"Abandoned car," Garrett said. "Possible crime scene, though. Glove up when ya hook it up."

"My hands are too damn big for those rubber gloves," Brent said.

"Remember how they kept rippin' when I tried to get that Honda outta the woods last summer? One'a your deputies will have to glove up and hook it up."

Garrett remembered finding Cole Duncan's Honda at Alexis' den and how the gloves tore when Brent tried to put them on his large hands.

Before he asked for a volunteer, Trowa said, "I'll hook it up, Chief."

"Thanks, Trowa."

"Gonna need that patrol SUV outta the way afore I can winch it onto my truck," Brent said.

"Got it," Ty said as he headed that way to remove the crime scene tape and move the SUV.

Satisfied that everything there was as under control as it could be, Garrett said, "Let's go, Paige-Turner. I gotta get ya home and go see James."

They got into his patrol SUV and buckled up.

Before Garrett started it, the two-way radio crackled and Erica Harris, the dispatcher on duty Christmas morning, said, "Sheriff Lambert?"

Garrett keyed the mic. "Go for Garrett."

"I just got a call about a missin' boy," Erica replied.

This just keeps gettin' better and better, Garrett thought.

"Where?" Garrett asked.

"Way north," Erica said. "Almost to Smith County."

"Names?"

"Troy and Penny Henderson. Son's name is Trevor."

"What're the parents sayin'?"

"Got up early this mornin' to put his tricycle together," Erica said. "When they went to wake him up, the window in his room was open. He was gone. He's only three years old, Sheriff."

"Okay, shoot the address to my cell and I'll head that way."

"Hell of a Christmas mornin'," Erica said before the mic went dead.

Garrett looked at Paige. "You and Glinda up for helpin' find a lost boy?"

Paige smiled. "Heck yeah."

Garrett pulled out of the church parking lot onto County Road Five Eighty-Eight. By then Erica had sent the address and the map app had charted their destination. They headed north.

Chapter Four

Fr. Mike tried hard to focus on the task at hand. Informing the Andersons someone had desecrated Justin's grave. His mind kept getting pulled back to the little, black, blood covered pebble. When he'd seen it in the evidence bag, he'd felt *compelled* to look at it.

The power of Christ compels you, he thought, remembering the famous line from *The Exorcist*.

Compelled was the right word. He'd felt it in his spiritual soul. He had to look at it, and as he brought the bag up to his face to inspect it, it had moved. Not a simple shift in the bag that caused it to settle in a different position. It had moved. It had moved away from him, as if an invisible string had tugged it gently. He doubted if any of the others had noticed, but he had. He sensed an evil presence associated with the black blood. If a single drop of whoever, whatever, it came from had reacted that way, he couldn't imagine how the source would react.

That he had these thoughts at all surprised him. He was a man of God. A staunch believer in his Lord and Savior, Jesus Christ, who was the Son of God, who had suffered and died on the cross for his, and everyone else's, sins. As a believer in God, he, of course, believed in the fallen angel, Lucifer, who reigned in hell as God reigned in heaven. As an extension, he believed in evil, but he considered himself a 'new school' priest. Which meant, unlike the 'old school' priests who were quick to assign demonic possession as the cause of those exhibiting abhorrent behavior, he was more likely to consider psychological or psychiatric reasons for their behavior. He knew evil was real, though. That black, blood covered pebble, and its reaction at being close to him, as if it needed to be away from him, as if it was afraid of him, had him second guessing his 'new school' beliefs. If evil could manifest in a single drop of blood, anything seemed possible.

As he drove and contemplated these thoughts instead of how he would break the news to the Andersons, he found himself at their driveway. He pulled into their driveway, parked, got out of his car, and walked to the front door, realizing he'd have to wing it. He rang the doorbell.

~ * ~

Lindsey, who was looking out of her upstairs bedroom window for Fr. Mike's car since Paige's texts, saw it turn onto their street and drive slowly toward their house. Given Paige's elusive texts, she wasn't exactly happy to see him arrive, but she had to know the reason for his visit. She turned, sprinted out of her room, down the stairs, and opened the front door before he rang the doorbell.

~ * ~

The front door opened before he pressed the doorbell, and Fr. Mike looked at Lindsey. She wore a blue dress with little red wrapped gifts in a scattered pattern on the blue; it was a Christmas dress. Her blonde hair was pulled back in a ponytail. She looked beautiful, but anxious. He had a pretty good idea why she looked anxious.

"Did Paige tell you I was coming?" Mike asked.

Lindsey nodded, causing her ponytail to bounce up and down behind her.

"Did she tell you why?"

"No," Lindsey said. "She just said it was bad."

Bad doesn't exactly cover it, Mike thought.

"Do your parents know I'm coming?"

"No. I didn't wanna worry 'em."

Fr. Mike found Lindsey's response touching and sweet.

"May I come in?" he asked.

"Yes," Lindsey said as she stepped aside. "Of course."

Then Lindsey said, "Mom. Dad. Father Mike is here."

Fr. Mike stepped inside the warm house. It smelled of wintergreen and he looked to his right and saw a real Christmas tree in the corner. They had decorated it with assorted ornaments, twinkling white lights, icicles, and red stencil. Beneath the tree were shredded paper wrappings, empty boxes, and one unopened gift. He knew whose name was on the card. Justin's.

Her husband, Andrew, followed Gloria Anderson who had entered the room while Fr. Mike looked at the Christmas tree.

"That one's for Justin," Gloria said. "Not havin' a present under the tree for him felt...wrong."

Fr. Mike turned and looked at Gloria and Andrew. Gloria wore a red dress with little green bows in a scattered pattern on the red. It was so much like Lindsey's dress; he knew it wasn't a coincidence. They matched. Andrew wore brown slacks, a button-down, white shirt, tan sports coat, and a bolo tie that had a red cord, green tips, and a Christmas tree slide. His heart broke for them.

"What a surprise," Gloria said.

"Does this have somethin' to do with the ten o'clock Mass bein' canceled?" Andrew asked.

"I'm afraid it does," Mike confirmed.

He saw Lindsey take her mom's hand in hers.

This was it. Time to ruin what had already been an emotional Christmas morning. He didn't need to see Justin's unopened gift to know it was tough on the beautiful family standing in front of him.

"I have some...unsettling information I need to tell you guys. Please have a seat on the sofa."

As Lindsey, Gloria, and Andrew took a seat on the sofa, Fr. Mike bowed his head and asked God for the words he needed to tell them the unthinkable truth of what happened. His hands were clasped in front of him, and he saw his rosary in his right hand. The cross hung over his palm and rested on the back of his hand, Jesus side out. He didn't remember taking it from his pocket, but there it was. It gave him strength. It gave him resolve. He told them what happened.

Gloria's mouth fell open, and she quickly covered it with her trembling hands. Tears and sobs quickly followed. Lindsey sat, stoic, with tears streaming down her cheeks. Andrew's eyes leaked tears, too. His expression was a mix of anger, disgust, and sadness. When Fr. Mike finished, questions followed. Some he could answer, some he could not.

"Why?" Gloria moaned.

"I don't know," Mike answered.

"Who?" Andrew asked through gritted teeth.

"I don't know that either," Mike said. "Sheriff Lambert was at the church when I left. Melanie's disappearance and what happened to…Justin are likely connected. He has her car and they're looking for evidence. Hopefully, they'll find something that leads to the who."

"Where's my boy?" Gloria sobbed.

"That, I know," Mike said. "Before I left, a gentleman from the Eternal Rest Funeral Home arrived. He is taking care of Justin. He even offered to give you guys the new coffin at no price."

He took the card Dănuţ gave him from his coat pocket and handed it to Andrew. "Here's his card. He said to contact him when you're ready."

Andrew took the card and studied it. "How is his name pronounced?"

"Not sure," Mike said. "He said to call him Dan."

"And he's givin' us a new coffin?" Andrew asked.

"Yes."

Andrew stiffened and put the card in his jacket pocket. "Damn nice of him. Pardon my language, Father."

"No need," Mike said. "Perfectly normal response. Now, shall we pray?"

The Andersons stood and the four of them joined hands.

Fr. Mike bowed his head and began. "Our Father, Who art in heaven…"

The Andersons joined in. A Hail Mary followed this and concluded with a Glory Be.

With the prayers finished, Mike said, "I apologize, but I need to get back to the church to prepare for the noon Mass. But I am here for all of you. Whatever you may need, whenever you need it. Under the circumstances, I certainly dispensed you guys from attending Mass today."

"It's Christmas," Gloria said. "We're comin' to Mass."

Fr. Mike smiled. "Good. I will see you guys in a little while."

As he turned to leave, he took another look at Justin's unopened

Christmas gift. He thought of his stolen coffin and the black, blood covered pebble. Fr. Mike resolved to confront this evil. He did not know the extent of the evil he would battle.

~ * ~

Garrett and Paige had neared their destination when his cell rang. Even though the phone was mounted on a vent holder so he could see the map directions, he always tried to set a good example of not messing with phones while driving, an example Paige rarely heeded, so Garrett asked her to answer the call on speaker. He saw it was Ty on the caller ID.

"Hey, Ty," Paige said. "You're on speaker with me and Daddy."

"Garrett?" Ty asked anyway, which annoyed Paige.

"Right here. What'cha got?"

"Not much yet," Ty said. "But I found a receipt from Sparkles Auto Detailers in the console dated December twenty-third. Detail cleanin', inside and out."

"Why is that important?" Paige asked.

"Because that will narrow the fingerprints and DNA that *should* be there for Melanie, probably her parents and some workers at Sparkles," Garrett explained. "Any other fingerprints and DNA will have to be investigated, and any others might belong to the perps."

"Perps?" Paige asked.

"Yeah," Garrett said. "Dan said one person couldn't have lifted the vault lid to…Justin's coffin."

"I didn't smell anything out of the ordinary except Mel's and the ancient's scents," Paige said. "So, it might take more than one person to lift it. But what if we're not dealin' with a person?"

That hadn't crossed Garrett's mind since the conversation with Dan.

Ty broke in. "I found three long hairs on the driver's seat back. Probably Melanie's, but I'll send 'em off for testin'. Then we'll swab for DNA and fingerprint it."

"Good. Don't forget to get her folk's prints and somethin' of Melanie's for comparison, too," Garrett said. "Sparkles won't be open today, but I'll call Harvey tomorrow and see if he'll let us get prints and DNA from his workers."

"If he won't?" Ty asked.

"Slam dunk search warrant. But I think he will."

"Okay. Anything else?" Ty asked.

Garrett thought for a moment. "Have ya tried to start her car?"

"No," Ty admitted.

"Are ya close to it?"

"Standin' next to it."

"Try to start it," Garrett said.

"Okay."

There was a brief pause and then Ty said, "Dead as a doornail."

"It was runin' when we left and when Father Mike saw her," Garrett said. "Look under the hood and if nothin' stands out, look underneath it."

"Will do," Ty said, and ended the call.

When the call ended, the map app came up again. They were close; less than a mile from the address Erica had sent. As they got closer, Garrett saw a pristine, green mailbox mounted on a rustic cedar post on the left. He turned into the driveway. It was long and cut through dense woods.

"Stop here," Paige said.

"Why here?" Garrett asked.

"Duh," Paige said and rolled her eyes. "So, I can slip into the woods, outta my clothes, and let Glinda do her thing."

Garrett pulled to a stop. "Okay. But, if ya find him, you'll scare the crap outta him."

"Glinda's not scary," Paige insisted.

"To a three-year-old? Hell yes, she will be."

"Okay," Paige said. "When I find him, I'll find you and lead ya to him."

"Alright. I'll see ya in a bit."

Paige opened the door and stepped out of the SUV. The scents hit her like a brick in the face.

She turned back to her daddy. "They were here."

"Who?"

78

"Mel and the ancient."

"That's not good," Garrett said.

"No, Daddy. It's not."

She closed the door and Garrett spun the tires in the gravel driveway as he took off fast for whatever was at the end of the wooded lane.

~ * ~

Paige walked about fifty feet into the dense woods, found a large oak to hide behind, stripped, and brought on the full transformation. Glinda's silvery hair glistened in the sunlight, filtering through the leafless hardwood tree branches and always green pine tree branches. And she smelled it. Recent death. Young death. A child's death. Tears ran from Glinda's bright green eyes.

~ * ~

Garrett sped up the driveway fast. Too fast. Before entering the clearing at the end of the driveway, he purposefully slowed down. The missing boy's parents would be frantic enough without him being over emotional. The news Paige gave him gave him every reason to be worried. For the parents' sake, he needed to be calm and professional.

As he entered the clearing, he saw a well-kept, double-wide trailer house. It had skirting along the bottom, manicured landscaping, and a new looking, large front porch with latticed railings. Beside the opening to the steps leading down from the porch leaned a baby gate that could be put in place to keep Trevor from taking a nasty fall down the steps. To the left of the double-wide was a carport with two vehicles parked under it. One a late model, blue Ram pickup the other a late model, green Dodge minivan. Both were clean and sparkled in the early morning sunlight slanting in from the back side of the carport.

In Garrett's experience, most off-the-road trailer houses weren't kept in such good condition. In fact, they were usually run-down crap heaps used for cooking meth or housing, what he considered, the backwoods poor of Pine View County. He didn't think the Hendersons fell into either of those categories.

As Garrett pulled to a stop, a nice-looking man with short, brown hair, who couldn't have been over thirty years old, wearing pajama bottoms and no shirt, rushed out of the front door, leapt off the porch, not bothering with the steps, and was at Garrett's door before he could kill the engine and step out.

When he stepped out, Troy said, "Thank God you're here, Sheriff. My boy's been taken."

"Taken?" Garrett asked. "The call said he was missin'."

"I called before I saw the footprints in the frost," Troy explained.

"Footprints…" Garrett began, but a wail from Troy's wife, Penny, interrupted him.

He looked toward the house just in time to see Penny, an attractive young woman with long auburn hair, dressed in a pink housecoat, collapse on the deck. Troy ran to her and Garrett followed quickly. Troy had her back on her feet before Garrett got to her. Her pretty face was a mess of tears and snot, and the sclera of her green eyes were a roadmap of red veins.

"Find him, Sheriff," Penny wailed. "Please, please, please, find him."

"Let's go inside and y'all can tell me everything that happened this mornin'," Garett said.

Troy helped Penny in, and Garrett followed, pulling the front door shut behind him. The inside of the house was warm, and every bit as nice as the outside. This had not been the norm in Garrett's experience, either. There was a fake Christmas tree in front of the back, living room window with lots of unopened gifts and a shiny, new, red tricycle with a red bow on the handlebars parked prominently in front of it.

Troy led Penny to a blue couch that she collapsed, not sat, on and Troy sat beside her with a supportive and protective arm around her shoulder. Garrett saw a recliner near the couch and sat down, too.

Troy did the talking while Penny slumped against him, sobbing. He told Garrett they had gotten up early to put Trevor's new tricycle together. Once they finished, he went to get another cup of coffee and

Penny went to wake up Trevor. That was when he heard her scream. He rushed into Trevor's room and saw his empty bed and the bedroom window opened. That was when he called 911.

Garrett took all this information in. "Did y'all touch the window or windowsill?"

Troy looked horrified. "Oh, shit. I did. I leaned out the window and called his name. I think I put my hands on the sill when I did. Because of the cold, I closed the window, too. Did I screw up, Sheriff?"

"No," Garrett assured him. "We would expect both of your fingerprints to be in those places. I was just hopin' to get a look at it the way it was when y'all found it. Anything missin'?"

"His stuffed dragon. He slept with it every night," Penny sobbed.

"May I look at his room?" Garrett asked.

"Of course," Troy said and got up.

"Stay with your wife," Garrett said. "Just point me in the right direction."

Troy settled back onto the couch. "Down the hall to your right, second door on the left."

Garrett got up. "I'll be back in a few minutes."

"Find my Trevor," Penny sobbed as Garrett started down the hall.

The second door on the left was open and Garrett stepped into Trevor's room. The walls were painted a mint green and there was a dragon print wallpaper border across the top of the walls. They weren't scary dragons, like in *The Game of Thrones* HBO series. They were playful dragons, like the ones in an animated movie of which the name escaped him. His little bed had a dragon print comforter on it too, with the same playful dragons. There was a bookshelf full of children's books, a little desk with a coloring book on it, an assortment of stuffed dragons that matched the ones on the border and comforter in one corner, a table with a slot-car racing track set up on it, a toy-box too full with toys to close all the way, and a ceiling fan with different colored crayons for blades. Just by looking at Trevor's room, Garrett could tell Troy and Penny Henderson were wonderful parents. His heart hurt for them.

Garrett went to the boy's bed and examined it. He couldn't see any signs of a struggle. The comforter and sheet were folded back neatly, as if

Trevor had simply gotten out of bed in the middle of the night to pee, or spy to see if he could catch Santa leaving his gift.

He pulled two latex cloves from his shirt pocket, put them on, opened the window, and looked out. He put the distance from the bottom of the windowsill to the ground at about eight feet. If Trevor had fallen from that height, he most likely would have injured himself. Perhaps not badly, but a broken arm, or leg, or some kind of cut was a certainty. But there was no sign of anything like that. Then he remembered Troy saying he'd seen footprints in the frost. He couldn't see them. The sun had melted the frost away. That, coupled with Paige telling him Mel and the ancient had been in the area, made his stomach turn. He headed back to the living room.

"You said ya saw footprints in the frost, Mister Henderson. Where?"

"After I called 911 I went to look for him," Troy explained. "That's when I saw 'em. Under Trev's window."

"Show me," Garrett said.

Troy got up slowly from the couch. When he did, Penny slumped over onto the spot he'd been occupying and continued to sob uncontrollably.

"I'll be right back, darlin'," he told her.

"Please find him," Penny said between hitching sobs.

Troy led Garrett around to the back of the house to Trevor's window. "They were right here. Two sets comin' outta the woods. A small set and a larger set. The larger footprints looked like the person was barefooted. I saw toe marks in the frost. Funny thing, though."

"What?" Garrett asked.

"Well, they came outta the woods, but they didn't go back into the woods. Just stopped under Trev's window."

"They're gone now. Melted away by the sun," Garrett said, more to himself than to Troy.

"I took a video of 'em with my phone," Troy said. "I can show ya."

Smart man, Garrett thought.

"That'd be very helpful."

Troy pulled his phone from his front pajama pocket and showed

Garrett the video.

Troy talked in the background about how odd the footprints were, but Garrett was more interested in the actual footprints. They were as Troy described them. Two sets coming from the woods, about twenty feet behind the house, and stopped under Trevor's window. Troy had even gotten closeups of the footprints and, as he said, the larger of the two had definitely been barefoot. Garrett could clearly see five toe imprints on each of the larger feet.

When the video was over, Garrett handed Troy one of his business cards. "Email that video to me."

"Of course. Will it help?" Troy asked hopefully.

"I think it will. Ya did good, Mister Henderson," Garrett told him. "Go on back inside with your wife while I take a look-see."

"Okay, but I looked everywhere," Troy replied.

"I'm sure ya did. But I might catch somethin' ya missed."

"Of course. You're the expert. I'll email the video right away," Troy said before leaving Garrett alone.

When Troy left, Garrett headed into the woods behind the house. He wasn't looking for more clues. He was looking for Paige, and he found her right away.

~ * ~

After the transformation, things were different for Paige. Dialing her wolf between 'almost Paige,' she would never be 'just Paige' again, and 'almost Glinda,' lessened or heightened her senses. But they still registered in her human form. As Glinda, she lost that part of her, to a degree. As she would never be 'just Paige' again, she would never be 'just Glinda' either.

This was because, as Lola had explained, Paige had tamed her ancestral werewolf. As Glinda, the putridness of the ancient's death wasn't as nauseating. That was because animals lived with the smell of death all the time. A human who stumbled upon the rotting carcass of a deer might vomit from the smell. For animals that lived and died in the forest all the time, those smells were natural. Although there was nothing natural about the ancient's death smell, as Glinda, it was less offensive. Glinda dropped to all four feet and sprinted toward where she didn't want to go. She sprinted to the dead child.

Although the mission was one of dread, Paige felt good being Glinda again. It had been a while since she'd fully transformed. Studying for finals at the end of the Fall semester and the business of the Christmas season had preoccupied Paige and left little time to run Glinda.

She marveled, as she always did, at the power and grace Glinda possessed, and how the chill in the air evaporated when in her wolf. The way she dodged trees at full speed, leaped over deadfalls and small ravines with ease still made Paige feel like she was on some fantastic ride, but this ride was ending. She had reached her destination.

Up ahead, about fifty feet away, the trees cleared, and she smelled and heard water running. It was a small stream and where she would find the boy's body. Her daddy was right about Glinda possibly scaring the child, but he was beyond being scared now. Not that he hadn't been, though. Even in death, Glinda could smell fear oozing from the pores of his small body. She instinctively knew something else. Whatever did this to the boy wanted him terrified in the last moments of his young life, as if it fed off fear, too. An angry growl rumbled from deep within Glinda.

Even though the boy was beyond being scared ever again, Paige didn't want to see him through Glinda's eyes. For his sake, she needed a human connection. No more monsters for Trevor. She brought on the transformation. The chill in the morning air nipped at her naked body, but she didn't care. She made her way carefully to the little stream and saw him. And what she saw horrified her.

The boy, Trevor, had curly, light red hair that fluttered in the slight breeze. His face was turned toward Paige and vacant, dead, blue eyes looked at her, as if asking for help. His exposed skin was white. Too white. Like porcelain. Almost translucent, and no veins were visible beneath his almost translucent skin. There should've been. But this didn't register with Paige.

He was dressed in footy pajamas with dragons from the animated movie *How to Train Your Dragon* on them. From the knees down, his legs were in the stream and the gentle current pulled on them, making his little body move slightly. His right arm stretched out beside him and his little hand was open. Just out of reach of his hand was a stuffed dragon. It was Toothless from the movie. His left arm was out of sight, twisted beneath his small body.

All of this was sad beyond comprehension. What horrified Paige was the bite on little Trevor's neck. It was impossibly large, almost half his small neck was missing, and ragged, like something had ripped away at it. And there was no blood on the ground beside the wound.

Paige's knees felt weak, and she sat down hard on the edge of the stream a few feet away from Trevor. A rock bit into her left butt cheek and the cold ground was enough to make her hitch in a quick breath, but she didn't really register either sensations. All of her hurt for Trevor. Tears flowed down her chill induced, pink cheeks.

She knew she shouldn't do it, but she had to. Paige could picture Trevor in her mind, scared beyond anything a child should ever endure, clinging to Toothless as whatever monster did this to him, clinging to Toothless with all his might, until he was murdered and Toothless fell from his little hand. She reached down, picked up Toothless, and put him in Trevor's cold, dead hand. She cried some more.

After a minute or two, Paige stood, looked at Trevor one more time, walked into the woods, and transformed. Glinda's ears twitched to the left, and she heard her daddy and another man, who she knew was Trevor's dad, talking about footprints. She was, perhaps, a little more than a mile from them and from that distance, even Glinda couldn't make out everything they said.

Glinda dropped to all fours and sprinted toward the voices. She arrived quickly and lingered about a hundred feet in the woods behind the well-kept trailer house. Glinda had no concern Trevor's dad might see her, even if he looked her way. She was on all fours and her silver hair blended well with the gray tree trunks and underbrush. She waited.

A moment later, after more conversation about the footprints and the video Trevor's dad took of them, she heard her daddy say, "I think it will. Ya did good, Mister Henderson. Go on back inside with your wife while I take a look-see around."

They exchanged a few more words, but Glinda wasn't listening anymore. She found a large pine tree, ducked behind it, transformed back into her human form, and waited.

~ * ~

Garrett made his way slowly into the woods. He didn't know where Paige would be, but he hoped she'd be there with good news, that she'd found Trevor unharmed. Garrett didn't really believe there would be good news, though. He didn't need Glinda's senses or Ty's 'tunch' to tell him this hadn't ended well for Trevor.

When he heard the front door close, he, in a low voice that wasn't quite a whisper, said, "Paige?"

From behind a large pine tree about twenty feet in front and to his left, he heard Paige say, "He's dead, Daddy."

Then he heard her crying.

He made his way quickly to the tree. When he was near it, he asked her where Trevor was. Paige stepped out from behind the tree, wrapped him in a tight hug, buried her face in his shoulder, and sobbed. Garrett put his right hand against the back of her head, cradling it and wrapped his left arm over her cold shoulders. Uncomfortable as the situation was for him, he held her tight and let her cry.

~ * ~

Since inheriting her ancestral werewolf, Paige had become much less modest. She had to undress to become Glinda. Not undressing shredded her clothes. She'd lost several outfits while being taught by Lola how to regulate Glinda's input when she, inadvertently, brought on the full change. When Lola suggested she practice naked, Paige agreed without hesitation. It wasn't just because Lola was a woman. Glinda was always naked. As were all the other animals in the wild. Men and women were the only animals who covered their nakedness. The more Paige associated with Glinda and the other animals, the less she cared about nakedness in her human form.

Of course, there were situations when wearing clothes were

necessary. Anywhere in public, for example. In her private life, she avoided the restrictive sensation of clothing whenever she could. She didn't know it but, Alexis, the werewolf who infected her, had felt the same way about clothing. Although Alexis had never been as modest as Paige before becoming a werewolf.

Regardless, after several awkward encounters for him, Paige and her daddy came to an understanding concerning her lack of modesty. It was to be avoided in his presence. After finding Trevor, she needed his strength. She was profoundly grateful he wrapped her in a tight hug and let her cry instead of turning away and scolding her, as he usually did when, for whatever reason, their understanding was breached.

~ * ~

Garrett held Paige and let her cry because he knew she needed to. She'd said Trevor was dead, but it must have been bad for Paige to so willingly break protocol and expose her nakedness in front of him. The strange thing about their 'agreement,' concerning Paige's immodesty, was that Garrett knew it was his problem, not hers. Even Mandy had told him his reluctance to accept Paige's new "freedom," as Mandy described it, bordered on the ridiculous. But he wasn't alone in this problem. Garrett and Al Sanders, Paige's stepdad, shared this discomfort.

Al and Paige's mom, Lacy, knew nothing about Glinda, but Paige's immodesty was on display at their house too, which was where she lived during the week and every other holiday.

Al, uncomfortably, broached the topic one evening when they were at a Woodpecker's home football game. He told Garrett Paige frequently came downstairs from her bedroom not wearing clothes, as if she'd simply forgotten to put anything on. Garrett got the distinct impression Al was avoiding the word "naked." Al also clarified that he would immediately avert his eyes and tell her to put some clothes on. Garrett believed him. Al was a good man. Unlike Lacy's second and third husbands, who Garrett thought wouldn't have averted their eyes. With Lacy's third husband, David Richmond, Garrett thought he wouldn't have had a problem with seeing Paige naked at all. That he would've probably invited Paige to sit on his lap. That was the kind of dirtbag David was. Not Al.

Garrett explained to Al he was having the same issue with Paige. This seemed to put Al a little at ease. Garrett told Al it was a phase that would run its course and peter out. He lied. But Paige would only live with her mom and Al for another year and a half. She wanted to attend Stephen F. Austin State University in Nacogdoches and had told Garrett she wanted to live with him and Mandy after she turned eighteen, which thrilled Garrett to hear. He knew it wasn't a matter of loving him more than she loved her mom; he and Mandy knew about Glinda, which would make Paige's life easier. When the time came, Lacy wouldn't like it, but Paige would be an adult and Lacy couldn't stop her. Garrett told Al he'd talk with Paige about it, which he did. Paige agreed to control her instinct to go without clothes in front of Al. Since Al hadn't brought it up again, Garrett believed Paige had kept her word.

~ * ~

Garrett held Paige tight as she sobbed uncontrollably. At one point, her knees went weak, and Garrett had to move his left arm from her shoulders to her lower back to support her. A moment later, Paige's knees stiffened, but he continued to hold her lower back, just in case it happened again. Her skin was so cold from the chilly morning, but just as he began to insist she put his jacket on, Paige composed herself. The sobs trickled to a hitching cry. She pulled her face from his shoulder and looked up at him. Tears flowed down her pink cheeks, her eyelids were red and puffy, and her green eyes were bloodshot.

"What happened?" Garrett asked.

"I-I can't tell you," Paige said. "I'm tryin' so hard to forget what I saw. If I tell ya, I'll have to picture it all over again."

"Where is he?"

Paige removed her right arm from his waist and pointed back behind her. The move exposed her right breast, but Garrett kept his eyes focused on her face. He had become quite good at avoiding her lapses into immodesty.

"He's a little over a mile back that way, beside a stream," Paige told him.

"Can ya show me?"

"Yeah. But it'll take some time to get there," Paige said. "There's a lot of underbrush and deadfalls to deal with."

"Take my jacket and show me."

"No," Paige said. "My feet are freezin'. It'll be easier if Glinda shows you."

"Okay. I'll turn around and you can transform and let Glinda show me."

"Actually, it'd be easier if you rode Glinda there."

"I'm not...ridin' my daughter," Garrett insisted.

"You wouldn't be ridin' *me*," Paige said with an eyeroll. "You'd be ridin' *Glinda*, and she can get ya there much faster. Walkin' would take half an hour or more. Even at a slow run, Glinda can get ya there in a couple of minutes."

Garrett was surprised when he realized he'd never asked Paige how fast Glinda could run. Now he was curious, and he asked.

"It's difficult to put in miles per hour but, on long runs, twenty or thirty miles, about fifty miles per hour," Paige said. "On short runs, under ten miles, probably close to eighty miles per hour, dependin' on the terrain."

Garrett was awestruck. He did not know Glinda had that kind of speed, or that Paige took her on twenty to thirty-mile runs.

"Don't worry," Paige said. "I'll keep her at a safe speed when you're on her back."

Not believing he was even considering it, Garrett asked, "How would I hang on?"

"Just grab fistfuls of hair on her shoulders."

"Won't that hurt?"

Paige smiled. "Not at all."

It was the first time he'd seen her smile since she stepped out from behind the tree, and that sealed the deal. Garrett was going to ride Glinda.

"Okay. Just don't throw your old man off."

"I won't, Daddy."

With that said, Paige let go of Garrett and backed away a few feet; her immodesty on full display. Garrett quickly looked down and the bill on his Pine View County Sheriff Department cap blocked out everything but her grimy feet. There was a kind of shudder in the air, like reality being disturbed, and less than a second later, he saw Glinda's large, silver-haired hind feet.

He looked up, way up, at Glinda towering over him, and into Paige's deep green eyes. Glinda winked at him and lowered to all fours. On all fours, Glinda was the size of an enormous bear and Garrett had to jump up onto her broad, powerful back. He grabbed two big fistfuls of Glinda's silky silver hair, and they were off.

Paige was right. It was difficult to gauge just how fast they traveled, but he figured it was close to thirty miles per hour. It was exhilarating. Garrett had ridden plenty of horses in his life; some bareback. Glinda's gait was smoother than any horse he'd ever ridden. Even when she dodged a tree, it was more like she glided past it, and he never felt off balance. Up ahead, he saw a large, downed hardwood tree. The roots came up with it and at the direction Glinda headed, Garrett put the height at about fifteen feet. Glinda stayed the course and Garrett held tight to her silky fur as she leapt, effortlessly, up and over it. The landing was as smooth as if they'd never left the ground. Garrett marveled at her dexterity and gracefulness. He enjoyed the ride much more than he thought he would. Garrett could only imagine what it was like for Paige, inside Glinda, doing this at much faster speeds. He even envied her.

Just as Garrett wished the ride would never end, and the reason for the ride momentarily forgotten, Glinda slowed and then stopped. Garrett looked up and saw a break in the trees about twenty feet in front of him. It was the stream. It was where he would find Trevor's body. He released the death grip he had on Glinda's silky fur and slid off her. Glinda stepped behind a large pine tree to his right. A second later, Paige's arm came out from behind the thick trunk, and she pointed.

"He's there," Paige said, fighting back tears again.

Garrett walked toward the stream. His boots crunched loudly in the dried leaves and twigs littering the forest floor. Only then did he realize Glinda's footfalls made no such noise. Even when they'd been running.

He marveled again at the supernatural creature's abilities.

As he neared the stream, he could hear its gentle babble. A large hardwood blocked his path. He stepped around it and saw Trevor. The sight caused his stomach to cramp, and bile filled his throat. He covered his mouth and swallowed hard. The bile burned as he forced it back down. He gagged and fell into a coughing fit. Tears blurred his eyes, and he had to turn away from the sight of the little boy.

Paige had made her way from the pine she'd transformed behind to the large hardwood her daddy had stepped around before seeing Trevor. When she had found him, she'd come in from the boy's right and the savage bite mark had been one of the last things she saw. She had purposefully let her daddy off so he would see Trevor from his right, so the bite mark would be the first thing he saw. She thought it best he saw the cause of death first. Seeing her daddy's reaction had Paige second guessing her strategy.

Garrett regained his composure and turned back to look at the little dead boy. To look at the bite mark. It was impossibly large and vicious.

What the fuck could do that? How do I explain this to his folks? Garrett thought.

"Daddy," Paige said

Garrett could tell she was closer, and she'd moved to behind the hardwood close to the stream.

"I'm so sorry ya had to see this, sweetheart," Garrett said.

"Me too," Paige said with a sniff. "I have to tell ya somethin' and you might be mad at me 'cause I kinda messed with the crime scene."

"I won't be mad," Garrett assured her.

"After I found him, I put Toothless back in his hand."

"Toothless?"

"The stuffed dragon," Paige said. "It's from that animated movie *How to Train Your Dragon*. It was right by his left hand. Like he'd dropped it when they killed him, and I thought he needed it."

All the playful dragons in Trevor's room finally made sense. He hadn't seen the movie, but he'd seen the trailers for it.

"That's okay, Paige-Turner. Ya did the right thing. I think he needed it, too. His mom said it was his favorite stuffed animal."

"Okay," Paige said weakly from behind the tree.

"This is them? Melanie and the ancient?" Garrett asked.

"Yes."

"Can ya track 'em from here?"

"No, here and at the trailer is like at the church," Paige said, sounding close to tears again. "Their scent was at the trailer and here. Nothin' between here and there. Not even Trevor's scent is between here and there. It's like…they just vanished from one spot and reappeared at another. Then they're gone again."

"Damn it." Garrett shouted.

"Somethin' else too, Daddy."

"What?"

"There's no blood. Not that I could smell. I didn't come to him as Glinda. It didn't feel right."

"Maybe the stream was higher last night and washed it away?" Garrett reasoned allowed.

"No. That can't be what happened," Paige told her daddy.

"Why not?"

"Well Toothless was right beside his hand and dry," Paige said. "If the water was up, it would've carried Toothless downstream. For another, the top of his PJs and hair are dry. They'd be wet, too."

Garrett took in what Paige said. She was right. Right about everything.

"Damn, Paige," Garrett said. "You want a job as a deputy when ya graduate? I missed all of that."

"Well, I had some help from Glinda. I'm sure you would'a figured it out, eventually."

Garrett thought he might have, but he knew Paige was being kind.

"One more thing," Paige added

"What's that, Paige?"

"Mel did this. Not the ancient," Paige said, and began to cry.

"Are ya sure Mel killed him?"

Paige sniffed. "Yeah. Their scents are slightly separated here. The ancient was standin' 'bout where you are. Only Mel's scent is on Trevor."

"Ya think Mel killed and…drank Trevor's blood?"

"I do."

"What the hell are we dealin' with here?"

"Vampires," Paige said.

"Vampires? You can't be serious?"

"Doctor James and Miss Lola told us that supernatural events, like werewolves, attract more supernatural events. Remember?"

"Yeah. But what the hell would a vampire find interestin' 'bout Pine View County?"

"I think ya need to talk with Doctor James about this."

"On my list of things to do today, sweetheart," Garrett said. "On my list."

A moment or two of awkward silence passed between them.

Then Garrett said, "I can't call this in yet. Everyone except Ty and Trowa would wonder how I found the body so quickly. And you can't stand around naked any longer. You'll catch a cold or somethin'. Change back into Glinda, go get your clothes back on, and wait for me to leave."

Paige wouldn't catch a cold ever again. She had Glinda's supernatural immune system in her DNA. But she was cold, and she didn't want to hide in the woods for what could take hours before her daddy finished.

"I have a better idea," Paige said.

"What's that?" Garrett asked.

"I'll change into Glinda, get my clothes, and run Glinda home," Paige explained.

"Are you crazy? You can't get Glinda from here to home, in broad daylight, without bein' seen," Garrett said. "You'll have to cross Highway Sixty-Nine. No way."

"I've traveled this far in daylight before," Paige said. "You forget Glinda can see, hear, and smell humans long before they can her. She can avoid 'em. There are ways under Sixty-Nine. Don't worry. I'll be fine."

Garrett remembered Paige telling him Glinda could maintain a speed of about fifty miles per hour for twenty or thirty miles. He hadn't thought to ask her how she knew that. Garrett thought Glinda's runs had never ventured beyond their property. He felt foolish. She was a teenager. Of course, she had pushed the boundaries. Now he knew.

"I don't think it's a good idea," Garrett said. "I don't think it's safe."

"I'll see ya at home, Daddy. I love you."

The air shuddered and Glinda stepped out from behind the hardwood tree. She came down to the stream, to Trevor, lowered her massive muzzle to the ragged wound, and sniffed deeply. She had mastered how to speak while in werewolf form, but she didn't like it. It sounded too much like a snarl and that seemed, somehow, wrong. She made an exception.

Glinda turned toward Garrett and snarled, "There is a little blood under Trevor's neck. You'll have to turn him over to see it."

Hearing Glinda's snarling voice unnerved Garrett, too. It just didn't fit with Paige's gentle nature.

"Okay. Thank you. Be careful."

"I will, Daddy," Glinda's deadly muzzle snarled.

Glinda dropped to all fours and sprinted into the woods. She vanished from Garrett's sight in a blink. He walked over to the stream bank and sat down. Garrett figured he'd have to wait at least an hour before calling it in. He wished he had a cigarette, but he had quit smoking. Garrett sat and looked at the small, dead boy. He wondered if vampires were as real as werewolves. It seemed anything was possible.

~ * ~

Glinda made it from the stream where the dead boy had been to Paige's neatly stacked clothes quickly. She gently picked them up with her mouth. Her deadly, pointed fangs didn't so much as snag on the clothing. Then she quickly leaped the driveway of the dead boy's home and disappeared into the thick woods.

For Paige, the sensation of tasting herself on her clothing was odd. Especially her underwear. Glinda didn't seem to mind. Glinda enjoyed the taste. It was more of being the animal Paige was learning to be. Kind of how the ancient's death smelled so putrid to Paige in 'almost Glinda' mode, but not so offensive to Glinda, even though the stench was stronger for Glinda. It also reminded her of her second stepdad's beagle, Barky.

Paige loved dogs and Barky was the best part about David, who she never liked. He looked at her in a way that made her uncomfortable. But, as great as Barky was, he grossed her out frequently. If she wasn't careful to close her bedroom door completely, Barky would push his way in and make himself at home among her things. Specifically, he would knock her dirty clothes hamper over, find her panties, and chew on them. More than a few were beyond saving when he finished with them. She would scold him but, if being Glinda had taught her anything, Barky had just been being a dog. She was learning.

Glinda made her way deeper into the woods, always on alert for human activity, which she easily avoided. Paige didn't have to worry about Glinda's moves. Glinda had a built in GPS system. She always knew where she was in relation to where Paige wanted to go. The little voice she'd heard in the earlier days of being Glinda, the one she thought of as her guide, was no longer there. She and Glinda were one, and Paige trusted Glinda's instincts completely.

After several minutes of running through the woods, Glinda jumped a small river and followed it east to a bridge on Highway Sixty-Nine that crossed it. The area around the river under Sixty-Nine was cleared and asphalt roads led down from either side of the highway for access to the river for fishing. No one was fishing Christmas morning, but this area was where Glinda would be most exposed.

She crouched in the thick underbrush and listened. A big rig truck came from the left, heading south. As soon as it passed, Glinda leaped from the brush, clearing the thirty exposed feet easily, and stopped under the bridge. Three cars came from the right, headed north. As soon as they passed, Glinda leaped the thirty exposed feet on that side and disappeared into the woods on the east side of Sixty-Nine. From there to home, Glinda would have to cross Highway Twenty-One, again under a bridge, and a few county roads. These were less traveled and twenty minutes later, Glinda emerged from the woods behind her daddy's house.

~ * ~

Mandy sat on the couch with her back to the sliding back doors when she heard a soft tap on them. She turned her head and saw Glinda standing there. Even after all the times she'd seen Glinda, it still gave her a start and she let out a startled cry. She immediately regretted the reaction. Glinda's large shoulders were slumped, and she looked sad. Her startled cry didn't help. Mandy saw Glinda drop what she recognized as Paige's clothes from her mouth and then Glinda dissolved into Paige, who was dirty and crying. Mandy got to the back door quickly, unlocked it, opened it, and wrapped Paige in a tight, protective hug. She held her for several moments before ushering her inside.

Mandy quickly guided Paige to the couch and sat her down. Paige's nakedness didn't bother Mandy, but her skin was cold to the touch, and she was trembling. She wrapped Paige in the throw that rested on the back of the couch and sat down on the coffee table in front of her.

"I should've listened to your dad. It wasn't a good idea for you to go. Especially since it involved Justin," Mandy said as she put a hand on one of Paige's cold, dirty knees and squeezed it.

Paige sniffed. "It wasn't Justin. That was bad, but…"

"But what?" Mandy prodded.

Paige shook her head slowly as more tears leaked from her eyes.

"Hot chocolate," Mandy said, as if that was the remedy for everything bad, as she got up and went into the kitchen.

Paige sat on the couch trembling and listened to the familiar sounds of Mandy making hot chocolate. The water running, the tear of the Swiss Miss hot coco package, the clinking of the spoon against the cup as she stirred the powder, the microwave being opened and closed, the beeps of the timer being set, the hum of the microwave, the ding when the timer finished, and the microwave door being opened and closed again.

Everything since she and her daddy had arrived at the church was so abnormal. The normal sounds of Mandy making her hot chocolate had a calming effect.

Mandy sat down on the coffee table again and handed the warm cup to Paige. She took it, blew into it a few times, causing the sweet smell to waft up with the ripples on the sweet, brown liquid, and took a small sip to test the heat. This wasn't necessary, and Paige knew it. Mandy was the Goldilocks of hot chocolate. Never too hot, never too cold, always just right. Paige did it out of habit.

It was the perfect warmth and Paige took several deep drinks. It warmed her insides and made her feel better. The way Mandy looked at her made her feel better, too. She was worried and Paige loved her for that.

"Better?" Mandy asked with a smile that equaled the warmth of the coco.

"Yes. Thank you," Paige said with a weak but real smile.

"Okay, then. You don't have to tell me anything. I hope ya know ya can, though," Mandy said as she placed her hand on Paige's dirty knee again.

Paige took another sip of coco. "I know. I can tell you more than I can my mom."

Mandy smiled and gave Paige's knee a reassuring squeeze.

"When Daddy and I were about to leave the church, he got a call about a missin' three-year-old boy in north Pine View County," Paige said. "We thought Glinda could make quick work of findin' him, so Daddy took me along. I really need to start with what happened at the church."

As Paige recounted everything that happened since arriving at the church, Mandy reacted in predictable fashion. Shock, interest, horror, and sadness. Expressed verbally and non-verbally with gasps, wide eyes, opened mouth, hands covering her mouth, and tears.

When Paige finished, Mandy said, "I'm so sorry, sweetheart. You shouldn't have had to see...smell any of that."

Paige swallowed the last of the hot chocolate. "The worst thing is...I know it was Mel who killed Trevor."

Mandy's eyes went wide again, and she said, "How can ya be sure of that?"

"It was her smell on Trevor," Paige said matter-of-factly. "The ancient's smell was away. Like he was watchin' her do it. Instructin' her *how* to do it."

Mandy didn't doubt Paige's, or Glinda's, knowledge of this.

She gathered herself as much as she could. "What's doin' this? What are...they?"

"I think they're vampires."

"Surely not?" Mandy replied.

"If werewolves are real, why not vampires?" Paige said.

Mandy considered this briefly and decided Paige was probably right, but she hoped she wasn't.

"Well," Mandy said. "There's nothin' we can do about that now. But ya know what?"

"What?"

"I can run ya a warm bath. Let ya get cleaned up. That might make ya feel a little better. Would ya like that?"

"I would. Thank you."

"I'll run it in your daddy's tub," Mandy said with a smile.

That brought a needed smile to Paige's face. Her bathroom had a regular tub with a shower head. Her daddy's bathroom had a shower stall and a large tub with water jets.

Mandy got up and said, "I'll throw in a green bath ball. I'll let ya know when it's ready."

Paige watched Mandy disappear into her daddy and now, Mandy's bedroom. She relaxed a bit. Mandy was right. There wasn't anything they could do about it then. But Paige knew she and Glinda would be busy that night, and every night until she had answers. The problem was, as she'd discovered at the church and at Trevor's, their scent vanished when they did. That would make tracking them difficult, like trying to grab smoke.

She came out of these thoughts when Mandy said, "It's ready."

Paige got up, letting the throw slip off her body onto the couch, and walked into her daddy's bathroom. She could smell the sweet bath ball bubbling in the turbulent water. It looked so inviting. She tested the water's warmth with her toe. It was perfect. Mandy was the Goldilocks of bath water, too. She sank into the warm, turbulent, bubbling water and felt her whole body relax.

"Better?" Mandy asked.

"Perfect. Thank you, Mandy."

"You're welcome, sweetheart. I'll leave ya to it." Mandy said and turned to leave.

"Please stay," Paige said.

Mandy's heart swelled. She and Paige had become very close, but this was a new level of intimacy. Something she might have expected if she'd been in Paige's life when she was much younger. Not as a teenage girl, when friends replaced parental figures.

Mandy turned. "Of course I will," and took a seat on the side of the tub.

Paige smiled. "If it's not too weird, will ya help me wash my hair? It's full of twigs and leaves."

"Not weird at all," Mandy said.

Paige was right about her hair. Mandy picked several twigs and leaves from it and then put her hand on top of Paige's head and dunked her under the swirling green water. Then she lathered her long, brown hair thoroughly, and used several pitchers of water to rinse it completely. After washing it, she worked conditioner in and repeated the rinsing process. After Paige's hair was taken care of, Mandy sat on the side of the tub while Paige scrubbed the forest grime from her body. Their talk turned to a happier subject. The wedding, all the planning Mandy and her maid of honor, Paige, would have to do.

~ * ~

Garrett couldn't stand to look at the dead boy's body any longer. He knew he'd need to take pictures, eventually. He also had to wait a reasonable amount of time before doing so. The pictures were dated and time marked, and he had to give himself enough time to find the boy without Glinda's help. He estimated a little over an hour would be sufficient.

He left the creek bed and walked about twenty feet into the woods where he found a downed tree that was the perfect sitting height. He sat down and pondered how he would tell the Henderson's their three-year-old boy was dead. Dead on Christmas morning. Worse. Killed on Christmas morning. He thought about all the half-truths he'd told so easily during the werewolf killings. Now he would half-truth about Trevor's death to the Hendersons. Hypothermia with postmortem animal activity was the easiest explanation. He would need the County Coroner, George Krats, to back his story. George had worked with Garrett on keeping the werewolf killings under wraps. Would he do it again if Garrett told him it was probably vampires this time? He could only hope.

He was so deep in thought he didn't notice the movement in front of him until it was close. He looked up slowly and saw a beautiful, twelve-point buck not ten feet in front of him. It was rooting for acorns under a large oak tree; its antlers gently and quietly moved through the underbrush concealing the delicious treat. For a quick moment, Garrett wished he was on his lease with the buck in the crosshairs of his Winchester. The antlers would look good on his wall. As he watched the strong, graceful creature live its life, he was glad he didn't have his rifle. The buck was too beautiful to kill, and Garrett realized it had a right to live. Finally, he realized he would never shoot another deer again.

Just as these realizations were solidifying in his mind, a breeze kicked up from the stream and ruffled the back of Garrett's jacket. A split-second later, the buck's head and tail shot up simultaneously. The buck stamped his left hoof on the ground several times and snorted loudly. As a hunter, and someone who lived in the woods and saw white-tailed deer all the time, Garrett recognized this behavior. Something had spooked the buck.

At first, Garrett thought the breeze had carried his human scent to the buck, but it looked to Garrett's left. It was looking where the dead boy's body was. The buck snorted and stamped its left hoof several more times. Then it turned and sprinted away, its white tail bobbing as it did. It was as graceful as Glinda, but noisy. Its hooves trampled through the underbrush and its antlers slapped through low-hanging branches. Within a few seconds, it disappeared.

With certainty, Garrett knew the buck had smelled what Paige called the ancient's death. A shiver went up Garrett's spine. Then his phone rang and startled him so badly he almost fell off the downed tree. He took it from his chest pocket and without looking to see who it was, because the ring was just too damn loud in the quiet woods and he didn't want it going off again, answered it. It was Mandy.

"Paige is home," Mandy said. "She told me what was goin' on and took a bath. She's settin' up her new iPad now. Paige was pretty shaken up but doin' better now. Are you okay?"

I was, until your call scared the shit outta me, Garrett thought.

Garrett said, "Yeah. Just waitin' a bit before I call it in."

"How much longer before ya call it in?"

Garrett looked at his watch and was surprised to see almost an hour had passed since Paige left.

"Ten or fifteen minutes. Then I gotta walk back to the Henderson's house and tell 'em about their son."

"Oh, Garrett. I'm so sorry. I know ya hate this. Have ya thought about what you'll tell 'em?"

"Yeah. But I gotta get George to play along," Garrett said. "He helped last time. So, I think he'll help again."

"Is it really... Is it really vampires? That's what Paige thinks?"

"Hell if I know. Given what she's sayin' 'bout their scents vanishin' and what she calls the ancient and the lack of blood, she could be right."

"When will you be home?"

"It'll be a while. After we finish here, I'm gonna give James a call and see if I can go talk with him."

"Okay. Please be home before dark."

She thinks it is vampires, too, Garrett thought.

"I will. I love you," Garrett told her.

"I love you too," Mandy said and ended the call.

Garrett sat there, looking at his watch for ten minutes. It was time to call it in. Just as he began to call Ty, his phone rang again. Again, the harsh loudness in the serine quiet of the woods startled him. It was Ty. He answered it.

"I swabbed for DNA in all the right places and lifted prints from the car, too," Ty said without a hello. "Several partials and a few full prints. I'll get the swabs sent out with the blood from the parkin' lot and get prints from the Zanes when I head out there. Oh yeah. I know why her car wouldn't start."

"Good job. Why won't her car start?" Garrett asked.

"I checked under the hood. It's a good thing it's an older car or I wouldn't have known what to look for. Three wires from the distributer cap look like they were...chewed through."

"Not cut?" Garrett asked, confused.

"Nope. Definitely chewed. Like rats did it."

"That's impossible. Her car was runnin' when we left her," Garrett said.

"Well, that's not the strangest thing. Her car should crank even with those wires not workin'. Not start, but crank. So, I looked under the car."

"And?" Garrett asked.

"The starter was...ripped off. Shredded the grooves on the bolts. It's just hangin' there by the cable."

"How the hell could that happen?"

"Beats the hell outta me," Ty said.

Garrett pondered how strange everything about this, these cases, were. He knew one thing, though. It would take substantial strength to shred bolts. Chewed through distributer wires were an even deeper mystery. Whatever chewed through them had done it quickly. He didn't know of any critter capable of that.

As he came out of these thoughts, he remembered why he'd been about to call Ty.

He swallowed hard. "I've got worse news."

"What?" Ty asked apprehensively.

"You'll have to put off goin' to the Zane's until later. The three-year-old missin' boy I came out here to find is dead."

"Fuck," Ty said, quietly.

"That's not the worst of it."

"What is?" Ty asked.

Garrett explained everything that happened, leaving out only the buck. And he told him about Paige's vampire theory. Ty listened without interruption.

Then Garrett said, "I'll send ya the address. I'm gonna take some evidence pictures and head back to the Henderson's house to tell 'em the awful news. I'll meet you and Trowa there. Give George a call and ruin his Christmas. We'll need him to back up our interpretation of events."

"Got it, Garrett. I'll see ya there in a bit."

After the call ended, Garrett took several pictures of Trevor's body. Taking a closeup of the ragged wound that took half of his small neck made him choke back bile again. Then he headed back to the Henderson's house. He dreaded every step.

~ * ~

Before Garrett cleared the woods behind their house, Troy, who had dressed in blue jeans, boots, a sweatshirt, and goose down jacket, came running up to him.

"Did ya find him? Did ya find Trevor?" Troy shouted.

Garrett looked at him. "Let's go inside, Mister Henderson."

"No." Troy screamed as his knees gave out and he began to fall.

Garrett caught him and got an arm under Troy's right shoulder. "I'm sorry. Let's go inside."

Garrett had to support most of Troy's weight; his boots drug across the brown grass behind him. Luckily, Troy could help with the porch steps. When Garrett opened the door, he saw Penny, still in her housecoat, slumped on the couch. She looked up, hopefully. One look at her husband told her what she didn't want to know. She sobbed loudly as Garrett helped Troy to the couch. Once Troy was on the couch, they clung to each other, sobbing uncontrollably. As Garrett turned to sit in the recliner, he saw Trevor's shiny, red tricycle and choked back tears, too. He sat and looked at the grieving young couple. He'd never hated this part of his job more.

He cleared his throat. "There's no easy way to say this…"

"Then don't." Penny screamed in a spray of snot that had run down from her nose over her lips.

"I found Trevor 'bout a mile back in the woods by a stream."

"Oh, God," Troy wailed. "I used to take 'em there to float his boats. It's my fault."

"It's not your fault, Mister Henderson," Garrett explained. "I think he got out, for whatever reason, and got lost in the woods. He found the stream. It was just too cold last night."

"What about the footprints?" Troy asked with a little composure.

"I got your video and I'm gonna look into it. I'm not speculatin' on the cause of…death. That'll be up to the County Coroner. I've got a team on the way, and we'll leave no clue uninvestigated. I promise y'all that."

They all heard the sirens coming and getting closer.

"That'll be my team," Garrett said as he stood. "I need to meet with 'em and take 'em to…the spot,"

"Can I see him?" Penny sobbed. "Can I see my baby before y'all take 'em away?"

"That's not a good idea, Missus Henderson," Garrett said sternly.

"Why not?" Troy asked.

Garrett cleared his throat again. "There was some…animal activity after he passed."

They both wailed. Garrett stepped out onto the deck and into the welcomed chill. He closed the door, but it did little to shut out their painful cries. Garrett stepped off the deck as Ty and Trowa turned into the far end of the driveway. He waited, with the crying couple's wails still echoing in his head.

~ * ~

The single patrol SUV, Trowa riding shotgun, came to a stop behind Garrett's. Ty and Trowa got out. They approached Garrett.

Ty had filled Trowa in on the ride and Trowa said, "Vampires?"

"That's Paige's theory. And there's no blood by the body," Garrett said.

"Could'a been killed somewhere else," Trowa said.

"Naw. Glinda would'a picked up on that," Garrett replied.

"Maybe the stream was higher last night and washed it away," Ty offered as an explanation.

"I thought the same thing, but Paige pointed out that the tops of Trevor's PJs and hair weren't wet. And his stuffed dragon hadn't floated away from the body," Garrett told them.

"Damn. She's good," Trowa replied.

Changing the subject, Garret said, "Did ya get a hold of George?"

"Yeah. He wasn't too happy, but he's on his way," Ty said.

As if on cue, Garrett saw George's van pull into the driveway and head toward them.

After George parked and joined Garrett, Ty, and Trowa, Garrett said, "Thanks for comin', George. Hate to break up your Christmas mornin' with this."

George shrugged. "The dead don't care what day it is. Just part of the job."

"Yeah, about your job," Garrett began. "I might need ya to keep a few things under wraps again."

George looked stunned. His mouth opened and closed a few times, making him look like a fish out of water.

When he composed himself, George said, "Not more of what happened last May."

"Not quite. This is different. If ya find what I think you'll find when ya do the autopsy, it'll be hard to explain."

"What do ya think I'll find?"

"That there's no blood in his body," Garrett said. "Drained completely."

"Well, dependin' on the size and placement of a wound, and the position of the body at time of death, there are many causes of near complete exsanguination," George explained.

"The boy's neck is bit almost in half and there's no blood anywhere. I just need ya to work with me on this. George," Garrett said, "I told his folks he probably died of hyperthermia and that some critters got to him after he was dead. And high water could'a washed the blood away. Understand?"

He hated talking to George that way. Hated putting him in this situation again.

George nodded his head slowly. "I understand."

"Okay," Garrett said. "There's no need for you to make the mile walk through the woods, George. Just give us a bag and we'll bring him out."

George looked relieved. He got a body bag from the back of the van and gave it to Garrett. Then he got back in his van, started it, and cranked up the heat. He felt colder inside than it was outside.

~ * ~

Garrett, Ty, and Trowa made their way through the woods without talking. There wasn't much to be said that hadn't been said already. And none of them looked forward to their destination.

About thirty minutes into their trek through the woods, Garrett pointed to a large hardwood tree. "He's on the creek bed just beyond that tree. Ty, given that Little D's about the same age as this boy, if ya wanna wait here, I'll understand. Trowa and I can handle this."

Ty, thinking back to the day he met Garrett when he witnessed a Camry get its top sheared off under a log truck, and the bloody mess of the decapitated husband and wife in the front seat and the gore covered little girl named June who he pulled from the back seat and the eyeball looking at him from the mess that was her dad's head, said, "I'll be okay."

The three men walked past the tree and looked at Trevor's little body and the ragged, savage wound on his neck. Ty turned away.

"We can handle this," Garrett said again.

Ty took a deep breath and turned around to face Trevor again. "I'm okay. But…that wound. It's too big to be human. Too big to be Melanie."

"I thought vampires just bit with fangs and sucked the blood out. Not…this," Trowa added.

"Yeah, well. That's why I'm gonna ruin James' Christmas once we get Trevor loaded in George's van," Garrett said. "Maybe he'll have some answers."

"Ya took pictures already?" Trowa asked.

"I did. Paige said there's some blood under his neck," Garrett explained. "We gotta roll him over so I can take pictures and collect what's there."

Trowa started toward Trevor's body. "Let's get this shit over with and this little guy in the bag so we don't have to look at him any longer than we have to."

Garrett and Ty followed Trowa to Trevor's body.

Trowa put on latex gloves, took hold of Trevor's left shoulder, and gently rolled him onto his side so Garrett could get a look under the neck wound. The boy's body was stiff with rigor mortis and his whole body rolled like a stiff board. Garrett hunkered down and looked. Paige had been right. There was a little blood on sand under the wound. Garrett took a few pictures. When he stood to get an evidence bag, Ty was ready and took his place. He found a piece of tree bark on the stream bank and used it to scoop the bloody sand into an evidence bag. When that was done, they placed Trevor's little body gently into the body bag, zipped it, picked it up, and headed back to George's van. They thought the worst of this situation was over. They were wrong.

~ * ~

When they emerged from the woods behind the Henderson's house a short time later, Trevor's parents were waiting. Penny ran toward them and threw herself on to the body bag. Trevor weighed next to nothing, so they weren't gripping the bag tightly. Penny's weight dislodged the bag from their hands and mother and dead son hit the ground. Worse yet, before they could gather their wits and stop her, Penny unzipped the bag and looked at her dead son's face and his half missing neck. She screamed and threw herself backwards, crab walking away from the horror she'd seen.

"What did that to him?" Penny screamed. "What did that to my Trev?"

Garrett quickly zipped the bag up again and motioned for Ty and Trowa to take it to George quickly. Seconds later, they were gone, and Garrett was left with Trevor's parents. He hadn't wanted them to see Trevor for a reason, and it wasn't because the cause of death was probably supernatural. He hadn't wanted them to see the body because the last thoughts of seeing their son should be happy ones; like how excited he would have been when they put him to bed on Christmas Eve. Penny had robbed herself of that. For the rest of her life, Trevor's dead face and half eaten neck would haunt her.

"I'm sorry, Sheriff," Troy said.

"No. Not you. I'm sorry," Garrett said. "We shouldn't have let that happen."

Penny was on the cold ground with her arms wrapped around Troy's legs, sobbing hysterically. With Garrett's help, he and Troy got

Penny back inside the well-kept, double-wide and deposited her, that was the right word, on the couch where she continued to sob in deep, heaving breaths. Garrett thought she might pass out, which, he thought, would be a blessing for her.

He turned to Troy. "I'm very sorry for your loss, Mister Henderson. I promise I'll do everything I can to get y'all answers."

He looked at Penny again and asked, "Do y'all have family comin' to help?"

"Yes, sir. I've already called our folks. Mine are in Denton, north of Dallas, and on their way. Penny's are in Sealy, west of Houston, and are comin' too."

Garrett was glad to hear this. They'd need help. Lots of help. He figured Penny was going to need a lot of therapy, too. Garrett excused himself and left the grieving parents to salvage a life without Trevor. As he closed the door, he took a last look at the red tricycle Trevor would never ride.

~ * ~

George's van left, but Ty and Trowa waited for Garrett by his SUV. Both looked shaken.

"That was a real shit show," Trowa said.

"I should'a been holdin' the fuckin' bag tighter," Ty said through clenched teeth.

Garrett put a hand on Ty's broad shoulder and squeezed it. "That's not on you. She told me she wanted to see him, and I told her it wasn't a good idea. I should'a expected she'd try to, anyway. This is all on me."

Ty shook his head. "I just keep thinkin'. What if that was Little D? I wouldn't want that to be my last memory of him. We gotta catch this...*these* fuckers, Garrett."

"We will. But this ain't gonna be the last of whatever this is does. It's just startin'. We gotta do our jobs, the three of us," Garrett glanced at Trowa. "Because we've been here before. Are ya up for goin' to the Zane's, or should Trowa go?"

"I got it," Ty said.

"Okay," Garrett said. "Remember the blood on Kat's leg, and her story, or dream, about Melanie comin' to their house?"

Both men nodded.

"Paige thinks it might be a good idea for Lola to talk with Kat and Father Mike to find out if she can...*see* anything they're forgettin'. Father Mike can wait. What Kat's sayin' is more important. If Lola's agreeable, you up for takin' her with ya?"

"If she can get some information, hell yeah," Ty said.

"Okay, then," Garrett said. "Let me call Lola and James. Fuck up two more Christmas mornin's."

"I doubt Lola is a Christmas person," Trowa said.

Garrett laughed. He couldn't help himself. Garrett didn't really know if James was a Christmas person, either. He made the calls. Because Trowa had probably been right, he called Lola first.

Chapter Five

Trowa was right. Lola Laveau wasn't a Christmas person, but she had celebrated the Winter Solstice on December Twenty-First in New Orleans with some of her sisters, her coven. Christmas morning, she walked her property bare footed looking for twigs and sticks to construct totems with. She, like Glinda, was impervious to the cold.

She gave Garrett a small totem with a green leaf in the middle that resembled her seeing cat-like right eye during the werewolf troubles. That totem connected her to Garrett so she could communicate with him, aid him. But there were many uses for her totems beyond communication and seeing.

Depending on the situation, the totems, along with an assortment of salves and brews she made could cure ailments like migraine headaches, appendicitis, anemia, gout, arthritis, anxiety, irritable bowel syndrome, glaucoma, and any other medical issue modern doctors treated. The only catch to Lola's remedies was the ailing person had to believe the treatment would work. This wasn't a placebo effect; the recipient had to have faith in the treatment. If they had faith in the treatment, it worked.

Lola and her kind had been curing people with non-traditional treatments for millennia. Even at the risk of their own lives during the dark period of witch trials and burnings at the stake, which usually resulted in a non-witch being murdered. That's not to say many of her ancestral sisters weren't persecuted. They had been. Healing and helping were their nature. They were nature.

Lola had just spotted a twisted twig that would work nicely in a totem to treat and cure insomnia, when her cellphone rang. The ring tone was *Magic* by Olivia Newton-John.

Without looking at the caller ID, she didn't need to, she answered and said, in her warm honey voice, "Good mornin', Garrett."

Garrett, as always, felt lulled by Lola's warm, honey voice. It was a mix of Cajun and East Texas, and it was so soothing and comfortable.

Like a worn easy chair. One you could sit in forever.

He cleared his head. "Merry Christmas, Lola."

"And a happy post, Winter Solstice to you, Garrett," Lola said. "But that's not why you called me. What has happened and how may I help?"

Garrett told Lola a condensed version of all that happened that morning, only including what he thought was relevant. He wasn't trying to hide anything from Lola; he doubted he could, but he thought it best for time reasons, it got dark early in December, to leave out some irrelevant information.

When he finished, Lola said, "Vampires. I hope that's not the case. They are soulless. Pure evil. My kind have been at odds with those foul demons since the beginnin'. It wouldn't surprise me, though. James and I tol' y'all somethin' like this was likely to happen."

"I remember," Garrett said. "Anyway, Paige thought it might be a good idea for you to talk with Father Mike and Kat Zane. Especially Kat, since she says Melanie came to visit her last night and she had blood on her inner thigh. Paige thinks you might see more than Kat's rememberin'."

Lola smiled. "Paige-Turner is somethin' else. That chil's aura shines so bright and true. Yes. I will see Kat's story. Will I be in your company?"

"Um, no," Garrett said. "I need to talk to James about all this. Ty and Trowa are pickin' ya up."

"Well, that *is* a shame, Garrett. I do so enjoy your company. They are beautiful men, too. I enjoy the company of all beautiful men. I'll be ready when they arrive."

"Thank you," Garrett said, and the call ended.

~ * ~

James Huff sat in his well-worn, leather, wingback chair in his study reading *To Kill a Mockingbird* on his iPad. His English Bulldog, Winston, had worn himself out playing with the stuffed, squeaker hedgehog he'd gotten for Christmas and snored on the couch with his large head resting on the hedgehog, like a pillow. It was a good morning, and

James looked forward to a quiet afternoon of reading.

A cozy fire crackled and popped in a stone fireplace to James' right. The mantle was empty, but a print of Edvard Munch's *Der Schrei der Natur*—*The Scream of Nature*—hung above it. In front of James stood a large Cherrywood desk. Behind James' wingback chair were three highly polished Cherrywood bookcases, with glass doors that had shiny brass hinges and pull handles. Beside the wingback chair was a brass floor lamp with a round, wooden table encircling the stand on which was a decanter set with a crystal bottle of scotch that had a stag head stopper and spots for four crystal, lowball classes, three of which were still in place. The fourth crystal, lowball glass sat on the table close to James and was one finger shy of two fingers of scotch. In front of the sofa on which Winston slept and snored, was a redwood coffee table with an assortment of scrimshaw pieces carved in elephant tusk ivory, walrus tusk, and whale bone neatly arranged. On either side of the stone fireplace were built-in oak bookshelves. The shelves on the left contained a collection of books on the occult, folklore, mythology, and all matters of ghouls, apparitions, werewolves, vampires, witches, warlocks, zombies, etcetera. These were James' work-related readings. The shelves on the right contained readable copies of classic works from Socrates, Dante, Augustine, Marx, Locke, Hobbes, and more recent writers like Fitzgerald, Salinger, Steinbeck, Nabokov, Heller, Lee, Capote, Orwell, and Huxley. These were James' leisure time readings.

The current classic novel he read was one of James' favorites and he'd lost count of how many times he'd read it. The iPad, e-book edition replaced a truly worn-out paperback edition several years back. The glass-enclosed bookshelves lining the walls of his study held the real treasure. A first edition, first print of *To Kill a Mockingbird*. It was the first book of his rare book collection, which had grown to over a hundred books since.

He purchased it shortly after receiving his Ph.D. at a book auction, for fifteen hundred dollars. At that point in his life, it was an exorbitant amount of money, but he had to have it. The book's condition was rated at excellent, which was second only to fine. This meant there were minor flaws in the dust jacket and slight toning of the pages. It was worth at least ten times what he'd paid for it now, which made it an excellent investment.

He had never read it and only took it out with gloved hands to show it off occasionally. He had shown it to Mandy the evening she stayed with him while Garrett, Paige, Ty, and Trowa confronted the alpha. That was the last time it left the case.

Most people didn't understand James not actually reading his rare book collection. Even a colleague, an English Professor no less, had compared James not reading the books to having a classic car and not driving it. Mandy understood, though. She marveled at his collection and told him she wouldn't read them for fear of damaging them and devaluing them. The same argument could be made for damaging a classic car, but James didn't care. The valuable books remained locked away and James read them repeatedly on his iPad. E-books were easy to replace, if accidentally deleted.

He was deep into the book when his cellphone rang. He checked the caller ID and saw it was Garrett. There were many people who called James who he would've let go to voicemail, but not Garrett. Especially since he was calling on Christmas and his gut told him it wasn't a social call. He answered.

"Hello, Garrett." James said. "Is somethin' wrong?"

Feeling guilty that James wouldn't expect a Merry Christmas call from him, Garrett said, "I'm sorry to bother ya on Christmas, James. Some things have happened this mornin' that I can't explain. I thought ya might offer some insight on all this."

"Of course. Happy to help. Should we do this over the phone?"

"I'd prefer comin' to see ya, if that's okay?"

"That'll be fine," James said.

"I'm about an hour away. I'll get there as quick as I can."

"Okay. I'll see ya when you get here."

James looked over at Winston. His brown eyes were half open, brought out of his slumber by the ringing phone and hearing his person talk.

"We've got company comin', Winston. But I think I can get through a few more chapters before he gets here."

Winston closed his eyes. James brought his iPad back to life and continued reading. An hour later, reading *To Kill a Mockingbird* would be the last thing on his mind.

~ * ~

Ty and Trowa arrived at Lola's house within a few minutes of leaving the Henderson's house. Lola sat on the front porch swing, waiting for them. As they stopped, she got up and glided, not walked, down the steps toward the SUV. Lola, dressed in the only thing any of them had ever seen her wear, a long white dress that hugged her curvaceous body seductively and the fabric was sheer; her milk chocolate areolas and perky nipples were pronounced in the morning chill. As usual, her long black hair was braided in cornrows with pink and white beads adorning the tip of each braid.

"I bet she's somethin' in the bedroom," Trowa said.

"I bet she's somethin' anywhere," Ty added.

"You're a married man," Trowa teased. "Get your mind outta the gutter."

"A man can wonder without strayin'," Ty said with a laugh.

They got out of the SUV and met Lola about halfway between her house and their SUV. Lola greeted each of them with a warm hug neither man wanted to end.

"Well, gentlemen. Shall we go see what Kat has to say?"

"Yes ma'am," Ty said, "But I gotta drop Trowa off at the department to get the latest evidence booked in. So, it'll just be you and me goin' to the Zane's."

"Well, that's a shame," Lola said in her warm, honey voice. "I prefer the company of two beautiful men,"

Trowa blushed, which made Ty want to laugh. He refrained. They got into the SUV with Lola riding shotgun and Trowa in the back. After dropping Trowa off, Ty and Lola headed to the Zane's. Ty was curious to see Lola do her thing. He wasn't disappointed.

~ * ~

Not ten minutes after dropping off Trowa, Ty and Lola pulled into the Zane's driveway. The house was an older, two-story ranch. At one time, someone had nicely painted it brown with tan trim, but the brown paint was pealing in places revealing the light blue it was before. Zack parked the old Ford pickup at a slant across the driveway, taking up both spaces. Ty parked on the road in front of the house.

"Ya ready for this?" Ty asked.

"Always," Lola said with a smile that made Ty feel tingly inside.

"Okay," Ty said. "I need to get prints and DNA from her folks and find somethin' of Melanie's with prints and DNA. Her toothbrush'll have DNA. That's the easy one. Findin' good prints might take a little longer."

Lola looked at the house, toward an upstairs window. "Mel has an iPad in her desk drawer with all the fingerprints you'll need."

Like when Lola had addressed Paige as Paige-Turner, with no one mentioning Paige's nickname, Lola knew Melanie's friends and parents called her Mel.

Shocked, Ty said, "How? Never mind. You see it, don't ya?"

"I do, and I see a lot of grief, too. I'll need some time with Kat. You're welcome to watch, though."

"Not a problem. I'll deal with Zack."

"No. I will deal with Zack," Lola insisted.

Ty nodded. He understood Lola would handle Zack differently. One would be easier. Ty grabbed a black nylon bag, about the size of a large book, from the center console. They got out of the SUV and walked to the front door. There was no doorbell, so Ty rapped hard on the door several times. A moment later, Zack opened it.

"Took ya long enough," Zack said with no genuine anger.

"Yeah. Sorry 'bout that." Ty said. "We had another call."

Zack looked at Lola, seeing her for the first time. "Who's this?"

"I'm Lola Laveau, Zack. May I call you Zack?" Lola said as she reached out her hand.

Zack took her small hand in his large one, and Ty saw an instant calm come over him. As if all the tension in his body evaporated.

"Yes, ma'am," Zack said dreamily.

Lola smiled; it brightened not just her face but everything around them. "Then you must call me Lola."

"Okay, Lola. Y'all come on in," Zack said in the same dreamy voice as he stepped aside and let them in.

The inside of the house was in better repair than the outside. It had been decorated like a hunting lodge. Several taxidermy deer head trophies hung on the walls; a full-size bobcat was on the fireplace mantle. Above the bobcat, mounted to the fireplace, was a large elk head, and a large, wild boar with long, deadly tusks stood in the front, right corner.

The sofa and loveseat had rustic pine frames with a green and white checked pattern on the upholstery. The coffee table was a large tree stump, no doubt cut down by Zack, the top of which was sanded smooth and covered with so many layers of lacquer and varnish it shined like a mirror. In the left, front corner, was a decorated Christmas tree; the still wrapped presents below it would remain so for some time.

"Kat," Zack shouted. "Ty and Lola are here."

From upstairs, Kat shouted back, "Who the hell is Lola?"

"Come down and meet her," Zack said. "She's here to help."

Ty realized neither he nor Lola had said anything about her being there to help. He knew Lola had somehow conveyed the sentiment to him.

Kat came down the stairs, still wearing Zack's big T-shirt, on wobbly legs. Ty thought she might fall, and he rushed over to catch her if she did. Zack showed no such concern. When Kat got close to Ty, he understood two things. She was drunk and, by Zack's non-reaction, she was often drunk. Given what she'd been through, Ty couldn't blame her for tying one on that Christmas morning.

Ty hadn't seen Lola move, but there she was, right beside him. She reached out for Kat's hand. Kat took it and Ty witnessed the effect of Lola's touch again. Kat didn't appear drunk anymore. She traversed the last few steps with what might pass for grace. Lola's abilities amazed Ty.

"Hi, Kat," Lola said soothingly. "I'm Lola Laveau. Like Zack said, I'm here to help y'all,"

Kat made it to the bottom of the steps. "Thank you. You're very kind."

Lola led Kat to the rustic sofa and, without saying a word, Zack joined Kat. They sat down simultaneously; composed, calm, and attentive.

"I've pulled several partial prints and a few full prints from

Melanie's car," Ty told them. "Luckily, she had it detailed two days ago, so that cuts down on the prints that should be there and those that shouldn't."

"She wanted it pretty for Christmas," Kat said mellowly.

"That's a good thing," Ty continued. "I also swabbed for DNA. And, for the same reason as the prints, the detail helps us out there, too. As Sheriff Lambert told y'all, I need your prints and DNA to exclude yours from the others. I'll need to take somethin' of Melanie's for prints and DNA, too. Understand?"

They both nodded in unison.

Kat said, "Are our fingers gonna be all inky?"

"No, ma'am," Ty said as he opened the black case and pulled something that looked like a large game pad out. "It's done electronically these days."

He turned on the machine, and the screen lit up a dull white. Then he carefully placed each of their hands on the device, cleaning the screen between each use and typing in each of their names and the hand scanned.

"That's it for the fingerprints," Ty said.

"That was easy," Zack said calmly.

"Now I need a sample of your DNA. I'm gonna use a swab, like a long Q-Tip, to rub the insides of your cheeks. Understand?

They both nodded and opened their mouths like baby birds waiting to be fed.

Ty put on latex gloves and removed the DNA test kits from a pocket inside the black bag. Then he carefully swabbed the inside of Zack's cheek and wrote his name on a label on the side of the tube. He put the swab in and repeated the procedure on Kat.

"All done with y'all," Ty said. "Now I'll need Melanie's toothbrush for DNA and her iPad for fingerprints. May I go upstairs and get these items?"

They nodded in unison again.

Lola said, "Will you join Deputy Jackson and me in Mel's room, Kat? I'd like to ask you a few questions."

Kat nodded and got up. Zack didn't move.

"We'll be back in a jiffy, Zack," Lola said.

Zack nodded.

Ty, Lola, and Kat headed upstairs to Melanie's room. At the top of the stairs, they turned left. Melanie's bedroom was at the end of the hall, facing out the front of the house.

Right where Lola was lookin' when she told me 'bout Melanie's iPad, Ty thought, and got goosebumps.

Melanie's room was what Ty thought would be a typical teenage girl's room. The walls were painted a light shade of purple. If he'd been a woman, he would have known it was Lilac, but men see everything in shades of primary colors. All the furniture had been painted white, which included a four-poster bed covered with a purple floral print and an assortment of purple and white pillows placed neatly against the headboard. Nightstands on each side of the bed with a lamp, purple shade, on one and an alarm clock with purple, glowing numbers on the other; dresser containing an assortment of 'girl' items with a large mirror; a desk with a laptop, notepad, purple cover, and cellphone charger that offered a view out the front window; and a bookcase with some books on the shelves but more stuffed animals. Most of which were different shades of purple or white. Across the top of all four walls was a stapled string of lights, the color of the bulbs alternated between purple and white, and posters of people Ty didn't know on the walls.

Lola led Kat over to the bed and sat her gently down. She sat down beside Kat and took Kat's left hand in her right hand.

Ty said, "I'm gonna step into the bathroom and get her toothbrush."

"We'll wait," Lola said in her warm, honey voice.

The bathroom carried on the purple theme with a purple shower curtain, purple shower rug, fuzzy, purple toilet lid cover, but it was a mess. There were makeup and hair styling equipment, hair dryer, curling iron, soaps, and creams everywhere. What mattered was the purple toothbrush in the purple toothbrush holder. Ty gloved up again, collected the toothbrush, and bagged it.

When he returned to Melanie's room, he went to the desk, opened the drawer, and found the iPad exactly where Lola said it would be. He wasn't surprised. Ty bagged the iPad, carried the desk chair over to where

Kat and Lola sat on the bed, and sat down in front of them. Ty didn't know what Lola would do, but he could hardly wait to see.

Lola rubbed her thumb on the back of Kat's hand in a little circle. "Tell me 'bout Mel's visit last night, Kat."

Kat repeated the same story she'd told in the church parking lot. Checking on Mel, not seeing her home, turning to tell Zack, hearing tapping on the window, seeing Mel floating outside the window, opening the window, Mel asking if she could come in, Kat telling her she could, and then waking up on Mel's bed in the morning.

When she finished retelling what happened, Kat said, "Zack thinks it was a dream. But it didn't feel like no dream. I just wish I could remember what happened after I let her in."

"That's why I'm here, Kat. To help you remember. Feel my thumb, listen to my voice, and look into my right eye," Lola said as the circle she traced on the back of Kat's hand got larger, as if Lola's thumb was getting longer.

Kat looked at Lola's right eye as if she'd just noticed it. "Your right eye is so…beautiful."

"Thank you, Kat. Now look into my seein' eye. You're driftin' back, back in time. Back before you woke up this mornin', but after ya let Mel in. Can ya see Mel?"

Kat nodded.

"Is she in this room with you?"

"Yes," Kat said hypnotically. "We're on the bed together."

"What is Mel doin'?"

"She's kissin' me on the neck. It feels…strange. Her lips and tongue are so cold. Outside cold, but good, too. I feel somethin' sharp, like two needles, on my neck."

"What does Mel do next, Kat?" Lola asked.

Kat shrank back a little, but Lola held her trance, and whispered, "He's outside the window tellin' Mel, 'Not on the neck'."

"Who's outside the window, Kat? See him in my eye."

Kat began shaking, but Lola compelled her to see him.

"Oh, God. He's…hideous. Old. *Ancient*. White stringy hair, translucent skin. I can see black veins in his saggin' cheeks, and his eyes.

Oh, God. They're silver. Glowin' silver slits."

"What's he tellin' Mel to do now?"

"Oh, God. His voice is like wet gravel. He's tellin' Mel to do it on my inner thigh. High up. Near my…womanhood."

"Do what?" Lola prodded.

"Feed."

"What does Mel do next, Kat?"

Kat shuddered. "She's kissin' my inner thigh. Up…there where she shouldn't kiss her momma. A place only Zack has kissed me before. It feels wrong, but it also feels good, too. It feels good 'cause I know she needs me. Needs to feed. Needs my nourishment. Almost like breast feedin' her when she was a baby."

Kat jumped.

"What happened, Kat?" Lola whispered.

"I feel a sharp pain. She's bitin' me. Her teeth are long and pointed. Like snake fangs."

"Then what?" Lola pressed.

"Mel's drinkin'. She's drinkin' my blood. She's so hungry. I can feel myself bein' consumed by her. I'm fallin' into darkness. But the man. The retched man tells her to stop. I can tell she doesn't wanna stop. She's still hungry. She stops because he commanded her to."

"May I see where Mel was feedin'?"

Without hesitation or modesty, Kat bent her left knee to the side and pulled up the oversized T-shirt. She wasn't wearing underwear. Ty wasn't interested in her womanhood. It embarrassed Ty for Kat, but he had a feeling, a correct feeling, she wouldn't remember exposing herself when Lola finished. He was interested in the two small puncture wounds about an inch apart. It looked like a snakebite.

Movement from Lola pulled Ty's attention away from the puncture wounds; her left hand moved toward her mouth. Lola licked the tips of her middle and index fingers. Then she placed the fingers tips on each of the puncture wounds and pressed hard into Kat's milky flesh. After a few seconds, Lola removed her fingers, and the puncture marks were gone. Where they had been were two light pink indentions, the color of skin after a scab falls off. Ty had a feeling, again correct, there'd be no trace of the puncture wounds soon.

With that done, Lola whispered, "What does Mel do next?"

"I'm still fallin' into darkness, and I see her float out to that horrible man. No. He's not a man at all. He's a monster. A spawn of somethin' evil. Then…"

"Then what?"

"They…vanished. No. That's not quite right. They…dissolved into the night. But I can hear…"

"Hear what?"

"The flappin' of leathery wings, and they're gone," Kat said as tears filled her eyes. "My Mel left with that monster,"

"Okay, Kat. Ya did real good. Feel my thumb, listen to my voice, and look into my left eye."

Ty saw Kat's eyes focus on Lola's normal eye, and then he looked down at Lola's thumb. The circles got smaller. Her thumb shrank back to normal size.

"You're comin' back to the here and now. You won't remember any of the things you tol' me. Even though you'll never see Mel again, you'll know that she loved you and her daddy with all her beautiful heart. Because you know how much she loved y'all, missin' her won't hurt as much. Do you understand me?"

Kat nodded.

Lola took her thumb off Kat's hand.

Kat blinked a few times, as if noticing her surroundings for the first time. "I'm sorry I can't remember anything after I let her in."

Lola smiled. "That's okay, Kat. I bet ya remember somethin' else, though"

Kat smiled. "Mel loved me and her daddy with all her beautiful heart."

"That's right, Kat. Now, if y'all will excuse me for a minute or two, I need to talk with Zack," Lola said as she got up and left Ty and Kat in the bedroom.

Ty didn't need to follow Lola to know what she was going to do. She was going to put Zack's troubled mind at peace, too.

A couple of minutes later, Lola and Zack entered Melanie's

bedroom. Lola sat Zack down on the bed next to Kat, and they immediately joined hands. They looked at each other. There were tears in their eyes, but Ty thought they were happier tears. Tears for the love their daughter had for them.

Lola turned to Ty. "We can go now."

With that said, Lola turned and left Melanie's bedroom. Ty followed her out of the house and to the SUV. He opened the door for Lola, and she got inside. Then he, feeling as if he'd just witnessed a miracle, got into the driver's seat and started the SUV. He sat there for several moments, trying to comprehend all that happened.

Ty said, "I get that ya…hypnotized 'em so they wouldn't hurt as much now. But what did ya do when we first got there to calm 'em down just by touchin' their hands?"

"Grief, grief that profound, comes from the soul and radiates out," Lola explained. "A dark gray aura surrounded both of 'em, like a thundercloud 'bout to rain. The rain is their tears. When I touched 'em, I absorbed a good bit of their aura, their grief. Just enough to calm 'em down a bit. Of course, it'll stay with 'em for a while, probably forever. Because of what I tol' 'em while they were under, the love they know Mel had for 'em tampers their grief."

"What color were their auras when we left?" Ty asked.

"A grayer shade of their actual aura. Kat's was a grayish green. Green signifies a neuterin' soul. Zack's was a grayish light brown. Light brown signifies a protective soul."

Ty hesitated and then asked, "What color is my aura?"

Lola smiled. "Yours is pure gold."

"What's gold mean?"

"Bravery, honesty, loyalty, and carin'. You're a good man, Tyrone Jackson. You and Garrett have the same color auras. He's a good man, too."

That made Ty feel good about himself, but he couldn't ponder on it.

Getting back to business, Ty said, "So, Paige was right. It's a vampire."

"Not just a vampire," Lola said. "An ancient, powerful, and vile vampire. Not just one vampire anymore. Mel's a vampire now, too. She won't be the last he creates. He's creatin' a *nor*, a cloud."

"A what?"

"A cloud. Ya know. Pack of wolves, pride of lions, cloud of bats."

"Why?"

"Strength in numbers," Lola said matter-of-factly. "And of course, sex."

"Sex?" Ty asked, baffled and repulsed. "Vampires have sex?"

"Vampires drink blood to survive," Lola explained. "They crave the pleasures of flesh, too. Their clouds may contain men and women. Vampires are neither homosexual nor heterosexual. They're sexual. Hyper-sexual to a degree. That said, male vampires usually create female clouds and vise-verse for female vampires. I'd say *this* vampire has a taste for young women, which means he was probably young when he became a vampire."

The thought of the creature Kat described having sex with a young, beautiful girl like Melanie made Ty want to vomit.

"Okay. That's disgustin'. Why'd he stop Mel from killin' Kat, and why on the thigh instead of the neck? Movie vampires always bite their victims on the neck."

"My theory is that she needed strength after he made her. His blood reanimated her dead body but couldn't sustain her. Because home is a welcomin' place, they came here; a vampire has to be invited in."

"Why do they have to be invited in?" Ty asked.

"That's a question for James. Where was I? Oh yeah. He stopped Mel from killin' Kat 'cause vampires can't drink dead blood. Drinkin' dead blood would make an old vampire very weak and vulnerable. It would probably destroy a fledglin' like Mel. Mel didn't know that yet. She's learnin' from her maker. So, he stopped her before Kat died."

"How do you know so much about vampires?" Ty asked.

"I'm a seer," Lola said. "I'm from Louisiana, and Louisiana has a lot of vampires."

"It does? Why does Louisiana have a lot of vampires, but Texas doesn't? We're neighborin' states."

"Texas has vampires. Just not as many as Louisiana."

"Texas has vampires?"

"Yes."

"Why don't we have as many as Louisiana?"

Frustrated with this line of questioning, Lola said, "Remember when James and I tol' y'all that supernatural events can follow supernatural events?"

Ty nodded.

"Louisiana is swamp, neck deep in the supernatural. Witches, voodoo, shapeshifters, and more. That's why vampires and other supernatural apparitions gather there. But the Louisiana and Texas vampires are nothin' like this…creature."

"Why not?"

Lola sighed. "Mostly 'cause they're younger. They're separated from the ol' world ways. They try to fit in with normal night life by goin' to clubs and bars to find food. They feed instead of kill, and they group together instead of makin' clouds of their own. That way, they go unnoticed. This way of life is safer for 'em. Understand?"

Ty nodded again.

"As for why he stopped Mel from bitin' Kat's neck, a bite there would be too conspicuous. A wound on the upper thigh would go unnoticed. Because of the placement, victims might be reluctant to discuss it. As Kat was at the church when she lied and said she had her period. This is how the younger vampires around here go unnoticed. And the femoral artery is larger than the carotid artery, makin' for a quicker meal. Mel probably went for the neck because, like you, that was all she knew from her previous life. Like I said, she's learnin' from her maker. Kat's blood gave Mel the strength she needed to feed on the boy y'all found by the stream this mornin'."

"Trevor's throat was ripped out," Ty said. "How could that not've killed him immediately?"

"She fed until he was almost dead and then bit out his throat to hide the puncture marks from her fangs," Lola explained. "When vampires kill, they always try to hide the puncture marks by removin' a large chuck of flesh, whether on the neck, arm, thigh, or anywhere else. Like the chil', they usually leave kills in remote places where no one will find the body quickly. It's self-preservation.

"Without Glinda, it might've taken days to find Trevor," Lola continued. "By then, there would'a been all kinds of things that had nibbled on his body and the throat wound might've been dismissed as normal, postmortem, animal activity. Vampires are intelligent, but this one doesn't know 'bout Glinda. He's in for a surprise."

"Yeah, he is," Ty agreed.

"I need to call James to let him, and Garrett, know what we learned."

They didn't know it yet, but Glinda was the reason Dragoş Văduva had made the treacherous journey from his homeland to America.

~ * ~

About the time Lola put Kat into a trance, Garrett pulled into James' driveway and parked next to his Chevy truck. James' house was a nice, little, contemporary place on a nice, little, contemporary street in Nacogdoches. It was constructed of gray bricks with white shutters and white trim and a dark gray composite shingle roof. There was a small front porch containing a white, wicker chair. Garrett could picture James sitting in the chair on cool Spring and Fall evenings reading, with Winston sleeping on the cool concrete beside the chair.

Garrett had only been to James' house once before to pick up Mandy the night they had killed two werewolves. So, he hadn't gotten a good look at it. After seeing it in the daylight, he thought it fit James well. Small and nondescript. Garrett got out of his SUV, walked down the sidewalk to the front porch, and rang the doorbell. He heard Winston's muffled bark seconds before James opened the door. A broad smile was on his chubby face.

"Come in. Come in," James said as Winston waddled up behind him, with a stuffed toy in his mouth, which explained his muffled bark, to see who had disturbed his sleep.

"Thanks," Garrett said as he stepped through the door and into James' quaint living room.

This was the only room in James' house Garrett had seen before.

The walls were painted a light gray and the crown molding, trim, and the doors he saw were white with black doorknobs and hinges. There was a black fabric sofa and matching recliner and an oak coffee table with a set of coasters on it, all on a gray area rug. The flooring was large, offset tiles the color of his roof with light gray grout.

James' house was neat and clean, almost compulsively so. And so different from his dark, claustrophobic mess of an office at Stephen F. Austin State University. Garrett felt comfortable in James' house, unlike how he felt in James' office.

"Let me take your coat," James said after closing the door.

Garrett handed James his coat and watched as he hung it on a coatrack beside the door. He didn't see a Christmas tree. That didn't surprise him.

"I'm sorry to bother ya on Christmas, James..." Garrett began.

"No apology needed," James interrupted. "It's just me and Winston, and we already exchanged gifts. I gave him the hedgehog he's currently chewin' on and he gave me a twenty-dollar Apple gift card. I've already used it to purchase two new e-books."

Garrett smiled. "I wasn't sure if ya celebrated Christmas. You don't have a Christmas tree."

"Of course, I celebrate Christmas," James said. "December twenty-fifth isn't Christ's birthday. And of course, Easter's date changes every year. Christians picked holidays to correspond with heathen, solstice celebrations to overshadow 'em. Steal their thunder, so to speak. A man like me, one who studies the occult, folklore, and mythology, can't very well believe in evil without believin' in good and a higher power that drives all the good in humanity. I just don't see a need to decorate with a tree. Besides, Winston would probably pee on it."

Garrett laughed. "Okay. I just wasn't sure. Don't shoot me over it."

"You're the only one packin' heat. So...what's so important that ya felt the need to drive all this way?"

"I think it's startin' again," Garrett said.

James motioned toward an opened door to Garrett's right. "Come into my study and tell me what's goin' on."

Once in the study, James sat in the leather wingback chair and motioned for Garrett to take a seat on the sofa. He did. An instant later, Winston waddled up a set of steps at the other end of the sofa and plopped down. When he did, the hedgehog in his mouth gave out a little squeak. Winston's ears perked, and he began chomping rapidly on the hedgehog, which issued rapid squeaks with each chomp. James and Garrett watched Winston entertain himself and laughed.

After Winston tired of the chomping, which didn't take long, he deposited the drool covered hedgehog on the sofa and rested his large head on it. He closed his brown eyes and began snoring within a few seconds. Garrett envied Winston's untroubled life.

Garrett looked from Winston to James. "It started this mornin' with a call about a missin' girl named Melanie Zane."

Then he told James everything that had transpired since he and Paige arrived at St. Joseph's Catholic Church. He showed James the video of the footprints and the pictures of Trevor's wound.

James didn't interrupt; not once. He nodded during different parts of the events, furrowed his brow at others, and covered his mouth, stifling a gag, when he saw the picture of Trevor's ravaged neck.

When Garrett finished filling James in, he said, "Paige thinks this…ancient is a vampire. What are your thoughts on the matter?"

James drained the remaining finger of scotch from his glass, refilled it with a double, and offered Garrett a drink, which he gladly accepted.

After filling Garrett's glass equally full and handing it to him, he sat back down. "I think Paige is spot on."

"What do we…" Garrett said but, just then, James' cellphone rang.

James looked at the phone. "It's Lola. I'll put her on speaker."

Garrett was eager to hear what she had to say and nodded.

"Lola, my dear. You're on speaker and Garrett is here. What did ya learn from the girl's mother?"

Lola's warm, honey voice drifted out of the iPhone speaker, but it sounded like she was in the room with them. "Good. I'm glad Garrett is here to hear this."

It wasn't lost on Garrett that Lola had said "here to hear this" and not "there to hear this." It was like she was actually in the room with them.

"I'm here, too," Ty said from the other end of the call.

His voice sounded like it came from the speaker. Like it was distant.

"Well," Lola began, and she told them everything she had retrieved from Kat's memory after letting Melanie into her room and what she and Ty had discussed concerning her knowledge of vampires afterward.

This time, Garrett and James sat uninterrupted and shared facial expressions throughout the horrific recall and subsequent conversation.

Lola finished with, "This is a true ancient, James. The likes of which I've never encountered. But we're in this together. With Glinda, I think we'll have the upper hand. Now, if I can borrow Ty for a little longer, Garrett, I'd like to help ease Trevor's folk's grief, too."

Without hesitation, Garrett said, "Please do. They're hurtin' somethin' awful."

"Bye, boys," Lola said as the call ended and her voice seemed to suck back into the cellphone speaker rather than end.

"Well, James?" Garrett asked.

James downed his scotch in two big gulps and refilled his glass. He offered Garrett more, but he shook his head and politely placed a hand over the top of his glass.

Then James did something he'd never done before. He got up and opened the glass doors to the middle bookshelf, and, without putting on his white cloth gloves, removed a book from the middle of the bottom shelf and handed it to Garrett, who took it in his ungloved hands and looked at it. It had a yellow cover and across the top in red letters was the title, *Dracula* by Bram Stoker.

"What you're holdin' is a first edition published on May sixteenth, eighteen-ninety-seven," James said. "It's rare but not in the best of conditions. Its condition is rated as good, which sounds contradictory to my sayin' it's not in the best of condition. That's the ratin' system for rare books. A near fine edition would cost upwards of forty thousand dollars. I paid seventy-five hundred for that copy."

Upon hearing how much James paid for the book, Garrett quickly handed it back to him. James took it, placed it gently back into the bookcase, closed the glass doors, sat down, and took another gulp of scotch.

"Have you read *Dracula*, Garrett?"

"No. But I've seen the old, Bela Lugosi black and white one, and the one that came out in the nineties with Wynona what's-her-face in it."

"There were a few vampire stories written before Dracula, such as John Polidori's, *Vampyre*, written in eighteen-nineteen, and the Penny Dreadfuls series, *Feast of Blood*, by James Malcolm Rymer and Thomas Peckett Prest from eighteen-forty-five to eighteen-forty-seven. But Stoker popularized the vampire genre."

"Does he get it right? Killin' 'em with stakes through the heart and sunlight? And no reflection in mirrors?" Garrett asked.

"As you learned from our first conversation concernin' werewolves, literature and movies get some things right," James said. "They get a lot of things wrong, too. Or simply just don't know enough about the subject to get it right."

"But you do. Right?" Garrett asked.

"Unfortunately, I do," answered James; his chubby cheeks were pink from the scotch.

"Unfortunately?" Garrett asked, confused. "This is a good thing. Isn't it?"

"Yes," James said. "But vampires are another thing, apart, and worse, than werewolves."

"Worse than werewolves? After seein' werewolves, and what they can do, that sounds impossible."

"Yes," James said. "Each has their strengths, and each has their weaknesses. Vampires, like the one Paige sensed and Lola described from Kat's memories, ancient vampires, are powerful and very dangerous. This vampire could be several hundred years old. Older even.

"Vampires don't survive that long without amassin' great intelligence, wealth, and power," James leaned forward and continued. "This sets an ancient vampire apart from werewolves, even old werewolves like *El Lobo*. Remember, besides Paige and the few other werewolves Lola described who have tamed their ancestral werewolf, they are, mostly, mindless, killin', beasts. But werewolves only kill when

129

they've transformed. A vampire is always a vampire. They are always feedin'. They are always dangerous."

"Okay, James," Garrett said. "Step me through it. Just like ya did with the werewolves. Where did they come from? Who was the first? What *are* their weaknesses? How *are* they created, and how do we *kill* the fucker? Tell me everything ya know on the subject."

James chuckled, making his rosy cheeks jiggle. "Okay. This could take a while, though."

Garrett took a big drink of scotch and handed the glass to James. "I told Mandy I'd be home late. I'll take that refill now."

James laughed, making his belly jiggle too, and refilled Garrett's drink. "Okay. Just like with the werewolves, the lore differs in places. When it does, I'll tell ya which side I believe holds more merit."

"Okay," Garrett agreed.

"From the beginnin' then," James began. "As it so happens, this is where the folklore first diverges. Some say vampires have been here from the beginnin' of time. As God created Adam and Eve, the fallen angel, Lucifer, created the first vampire. In this version, it wasn't a serpent that tempted Eve, but a vampire. It wasn't a forbidden apple that created original sin, but forbidden sins of the flesh. Vampires are all about sins of the flesh. It's what sustains 'em. As the story goes, this is when Eve started menstruatin'. Blood...nourishment for the vampire. Women have carried the sin of Eve's flesh to this very day.

"Another version of how vampires came into existence is through a deal brokered with Satan by a mortal man who renounced God after a significant loss; some say it was the death of his beloved wife and others say it was after a defeat in battle and others say the man was dyin'," James took a breath and continued. "Whatever the reason, they struck a deal. The lost beloved is the version Coppola used in the movie *Bram Stoker's Dracula*. Then, of course, there was Vlad the Impaler, named Vlad Dracul. It's unlikely Vlad was a vampire, but his last name is where Stoker came up with the name Dracula. Regardless of when and how vampires came into existence, the origin of the creature is the same, as Lucifer and Satan are the same.

"Here, I must admit that I'm not entirely certain which version is the truer version," James admitted. "Both have merit. If pushed, I lean toward the latter explanation."

"Why?" Garrett asked.

"Science, for one," James said. "We know there's a biological reason for menstruation. Of course, perhaps Eve's sin with the vampire started this biological process and had she not given into temptation, women's uteruses wouldn't need to shed every twenty-eight days, which corresponds with the moon's cycle. The moon, like vampires, is nocturnal, too. Thus, my confliction. Why I lean toward the latter version is because of the restrictions put upon vampires and their specific, and purposeful, affront to Christ, the son of God. Because of the slight to Christ, it stands to reason vampires first appeared after Christ, and not in the Garden of Eden."

"Ya lost me, James," Garrett said. "What slight to Christ?"

"Paige and Mandy are both Catholic, yes?" James asked

Garrett nodded.

"You attend Mass with 'em sometimes, I assume?" James quarried.

"Every Sunday," Garrett said. "In fact, I'm convertin'. I'm goin' through the Rite of Christian Initiation for Adults, RCIA classes, right now. Father Mike is my sponsor. I'll receive First Communion and Confirmation this Easter. Don't tell Mandy or Paige. It's a surprise."

James smiled. "They will be very pleased. Since you're goin' through the classes and attendin' Mass, this will be easier for you to understand.

"The Catholic Church is the first of the Christian religions," James explained. "We know this because we can trace the Papal lineage back to Saint Peter, one of Christ's twelve apostles. Although ya can't receive communion yet, you've witnessed the Liturgy of the Eucharist and heard the priest's Lord's Supper prayer. This is the commemoration of Christ's last supper with his apostles when he gave them bread to eat and said, 'This is my body, eat of it' wine to drink and said, 'This is my blood, drink of it.' Durin' the Liturgy of the Eucharist, Catholics believe, the communion wafer and chalice of wine *become* the body and blood of Christ. Here's the key part, and why I believe vampires came *after* Christ.

Jesus said that whoever eats of his body and drinks of his blood will live forever. But he wasn't talkin' 'bout mortal life. He was talkin' about eternal life, after death, in heaven. Now, do ya see the slight?"

Garrett thought for a moment. "Not really. What am I missin'?"

"Lucifer, Satan, the devil, whatever ya want to call the Fallen One, made the same deal with the original vampire to partake of *his* body and blood," James said. "Instead of eternal life after death in heaven, vampires receive eternal, undead existence on Earth. To sustain their undead existence, they must…"

Finally, understanding what James tried to explain, Garrett interrupted him and shouted, "Partake of the body and blood of God's image on Earth."

James smiled so big that his ears moved. "Exactly. A vampire's existence is a direct and purposeful affront to the message of Christ. Its existence is blasphemous from its creation. Therefore, that is why I'm more inclined to believe this origin over the Eve's temptation origin. Besides, women put up with enough crap without havin' to take responsibility for the proliferation of vampires, too."

Both men laughed and their classes tinked together in a wordless toast.

"Okay," Garrett said. "What are their weaknesses?"

"They are few, but they are important," James said. "First, a moment ago, I said that there were restrictions placed upon vampires as part of the affront to Christ. The first, and most important restriction, was that vampires could never again view the beauty of God's creation in the light of day; they are relegated to darkness for eternity. Unlike werewolves after their first transformation on the first full moon after being cursed, that can transform, and kill, at will. Vampires can only feed, kill, and create at night. This leaves 'em vulnerable durin' the daylight hours. That's why vampires, especially older ones like the one we're certainly dealin' with, always have a familiar."

"What's a familiar?" Garrett asked.

"A familiar is a human servant who guards the vampire while it rests durin' the day," James explained. "They serve 'em in other ways too, like findin' 'em a safe place to rest, bringin' 'em food if they're too weak, or unable, to hunt for themselves. Things like that. I assure you it was this vampire's familiar who dug up Justin and took his coffin for Melanie's new restin' place."

"How do ya know that?"

"Because of another weakness vampires have, which is an aversion to all things holy," James said. "The cemetery at Saint Joseph's Catholic Church is consecrated ground, as is the church. That means this vampire couldn't have dug up Justin's coffin, because he couldn't set foot in the consecrated cemetery. It had to be his familiar who did it."

"Does that mean, since it took Melanie in the parkin' lot, that it's not consecrated ground?"

"Couldn't be," James said. "If it was, the familiar would'a had to bring Melanie to its master. That's what I meant when I said familiars bring 'em food when they're too weak or *unable* to hunt for themselves. Since Melanie's blood, and the black blood that Paige associates with the ancient, were found in the parkin' lot, the vampire took her in the parkin' lot. So, it can't be consecrated ground."

"Are familiars…human?" Garrett asked.

"Yes and no," James replied. "This is a good segue into some basic info ya need to know about vampire behavior. Bites, kills, creation, and familiars. All, of course, include blood; the victim's and or the vampire's, dependin' on the situation, but for different purposes. First, bites. Unlike werewolves, bein' bitten by a vampire doesn't turn someone into one of 'em."

"So, Kat won't become a vampire just 'cause she was bit?" Garrett asked.

"No," James said. "She's safe. But if the older vampire hadn't stopped Melanie when he did, she'd be dead.

"Okay, bites," James continued in a professorial tone. "Lola touched on this in her call. Vampires rarely kill or change their victims. If they did that, their food source would eventually run low. Younger vampires, like we have around here, are feeders. They blend in with the local night life at bars and clubs, find someone to feed on, drink, and let 'em live. Before ya ask, vampires have a sort of telepathy, but it's called mezmery; they mesmerize their victims to do their will. That's why Kat couldn't remember anything after lettin' Melanie in last night. Melanie wouldn't know how to mesmerize yet, so the older vampire, the ancient, would've mesmerized Kat for Melanie. That happened when Kat saw his silver eyes. After they mesmerize their victims, they'll feed on one of the major arteries in the neck, inner arm, or inner thigh. Usually not the neck, though, because the bite marks would be visible. The arms and thighs have bigger arteries, too. Makes for a quicker meal. Afterwards, the victim wakes up with no memory of what happened. Pretty efficient, actually.

"Then there are blood banks where they feed, too," James said.

"Like from a bag of blood?" Garrett interrupted.

"Some might feed that way," James began. "They'd be vegan vampires. I'm talkin' 'bout human blood banks."

"They hold folks hostage and feed on 'em?" Garrett interrupted again.

"That certainly happens, but that's not what I'm talkin' 'bout, either," James said. "Remember, most young vampires just wanna blend in and feed. Missin' people, like murdered people, attract law enforcement. They don't want that. They want to stay unnoticed. The blood banks I'm talkin' 'bout are places, usually some out of the way, underground club, where humans go voluntarily to let vampires feed on 'em."

"Why the hell would anyone do that?" Garrett asked disgustedly.

"Call 'em vampire groupies," James said with a chuckle. "They enjoy bein' around vampires."

"Why?"

"Well, there's a certain allure to it," James began. "Also, they're treated well…"

"Treated well?" Garrett interrupted again. "They're gettin' bit and havin' their blood sucked by fuckin' vampires."

Ignoring this, James continued, "Yes. They're treated very well. Not to equate a milk cow with a human, but it's as good an analogy as any. Dairy farmers treat their milk cows very well. They feed 'em, rub 'em down, keep 'em healthy, keep their utters moisturized, etcetera. If they didn't, their milk cows wouldn't produce milk, and they'd go outta business. It's the same with vampire groupies. They're well taken care of and compensated. This could be a monetary compensation; vampires accumulate substantial wealth over their long lives. Or it could be the promise of makin' 'em a familiar or even a vampire."

Shocked by this, Garett said, "Why the hell would anyone *want* to be a vampire?"

"We had this same conversation about why anyone would want to be a werewolf," James reminded Garrett. "I told ya then that some folks would find the power, increased senses, etcetera, appealin'. Same things apply to vampires with the bonus of eternal youth. A lot of folks would find that very appealin'."

Garrett mulled it over and decided James was right about some folks. Just that morning, he had envied Glinda's abilities. He nodded.

"Vampire kills, at least around here, are rare," James said. "That's not to say that they don't happen. As some humans kill for the thrill, so do some vampires, but this is rare. Rarer, I dare say, than among humans. Kills, like with the Trevor boy, are usually associated with older vampires, like the one we're dealin' with. Part of this is arrogance; they're so old and powerful that they think they're invincible. Part of it is that killin' is the old-world way of doin' things.

"They were vampires long before modern forensics and AMBER Alert and such," James took a sip of scotch and continued. "Quite to the contrary, in the old-world, they wanted the locals to know there was a vampire in the area to instill fear in 'em. They killed with abandon and with little concern of bein' caught. Then, when the food source ran low, they'd move to another area and start all over again. Another part of it, like with serial killers, is the thrill of killin'. When they kill, they release their victim from the trance before doin' it."

"Why would they do that?" Garrett asked.

"Because," James explained, "they feed off of fear, too. Blood is the source that sustains their existence, but fear sustains their superiority over humans. They drink it in like mana from hell."

"Is that why Paige said she could smell the fear comin' outta Trevor's pores?" Garrett asked.

James nodded. "Yes. I suspect the ancient mesmerized Trevor to get him out of the house but, before he had Melanie feed and kill him, he released the trance. They terrorized Trevor in the last moments of his young life. This vampire, the ancient, thrives on that terror. He is trainin' Melanie to be an old-world vampire."

The thought of what Trevor must have gone through before being murdered made Garrett's stomach turn and tears stung his eyes.

James took notice of Garrett's demeanor. "I'm sorry, Garrett. I know this is hard to hear. Should we stop for now and talk again later?"

Garrett stiffened; pure resolve coursed through his body. "No. I need to know what you know in order to stop this fucker. I'm alright. Keep goin'."

"Good," James said. "I've mentioned familiars several times, so I'll tell ya about 'em before explainin' how vampires create new vampires. Ya asked if they were human, and my response was yes and no. They *are* human in that they *aren't* undead."

"You keep sayin' undead. What, exactly, is undead?" Garrett asked.

"Good question, Garrett. Do you remember when Ty killed the first werewolf by plungin' his Silver Star commendation into its chest?"

Garrett nodded. "Yeah. That was Seth Daniels, Alexis' boyfriend. He's how we connected him with Cole Duncan, who tried to turn Trowa, Mont, Jack, and Bear, but was killed by Alexis before he could do it."

"Correct. Do you remember what ya asked me when George was doin' the postmortem on him?" James asked.

Garrett thought for a moment and then it came to him. "Yeah. I asked ya if removin' the Silver Star would bring him back to life."

"Exactly. I told ya it wouldn't because werewolves aren't undead, like vampires and zombies," James said. "Creatin' werewolves and vampires are exactly the opposite. If a werewolf kills its victim, they're dead. But, as you learned with Paige, Ty, and Trowa, if a werewolf bites its victim and they live, they become werewolves. To become a vampire, the victim has to die, and the vampire reanimates them."

"You said they can't drink dead blood. So, how do they do that?" Garrett asked.

"Okay," James said and took another sip of scotch. "We'll get back to familiars soon. It takes practice and I imagine the ancient we're dealin' with has had plenty. They drink their victims to where they've lost too much blood to live. They can tell by hearin' the victim's heartbeat and feelin' the pulse of blood runnin' through their arteries as they drink. Just before the victim dies, they quit drinkin' and let 'em pass. As ya know, dead people don't bleed because the heart has to be pumpin' for that to happen. That's why Paige only found a few drops of Melanie's blood in the parkin' lot. Those drops were, literally, the last second of Melanie's life.

"Now, once the victim is dead, the vampire reanimates the corpse by forcin' its blood into the victim's mouth," James explained. "In a lot of the movies and TV shows, they do this by bitin' their wrists and puttin' it over the victim's mouth. This is certainly a more practical approach, and one probably used by younger vampires when they create a new vampire. Folklore on older vampires has 'em, male or female, cuttin' one of their nipples with a fingernail, and for lack of a better description, breast feedin' their new creation into undead existence."

Garrett's mouth turned down at the edges. "That's damn disgustin'. Why the hell wouldn't they just do it the easy way on their wrist?"

"Well, when ya think about it, and the times when the ancients were created, they were bringin' a new creature into existence, like givin' birth to a baby, and breast feedin' was the natural order of things," James explained.

"So, your tellin' me that after this…ancient drank Melanie to the point of death, he breast fed her back into…undeadness?" Garrett asked before taking a sip of scotch, too.

"That's my educated hypothesis," James said. "Creatin' a new vampire takes commitment from the creator. The fledglin' vampire is very much like a baby. They have to be *taught* how to be a vampire. A fledglin' vampire, left on its own, wouldn't make it past the first dawn. The commitment it takes to create a new cloud is, I dare say, why younger vampires don't do it. A hundred-year-old vampire is like a teenager, and teenagers rarely make wonderful parents.

"Here's another point Lola brought up," James continued with a sly grin. "Vampires are sexual creatures. They crave all pleasures of the flesh, not just feedin' on blood. Much like humans, their attractions differ. Also, like humans, their attractions are *usually* to their age group at the time of their creation. Since Melanie was young, I expect this vampire was relatively young when he was created. Believe it or not, vampires have a sort of code against creatin' child vampires."

"Why?" Garrett asked.

"Well, it's certainly not because they have an affinity for children," James said. "The murder of Trevor is evidence of that. In fact, children are easy targets for vampires."

"Then why don't they change 'em?"

"Have you read Anne Rice's, Interview with the Vampire?" James asked.

"No. But I saw the movie."

"Anne Rice got this one right. Children vampires need constant supervision. Simply put, they're too much trouble. As I've pointed out, and Rice wrote, children vampires grow increasingly frustrated as they age in a prepubescent body. They mature mentally and want the pleasures that adults engage in, but their prepubescent bodies prevent 'em from partakin' in these pleasures. The only vampires that would purposefully create children vampires would be those who were pedophiles when they were human."

"That's fuckin' disgustin'," Garrett spat.

"Yes. Yes, it is," James said. "Like I said, vampires are usually attracted to whoever attracted 'em before they became vampires. Since I agree with Lola that this vampire is creatin' a cloud, he'll go after more victims in Melanie's age group. Young, females."

"How many vampires are in a cloud?" Garrett asked.

"It depends on the age and power of the vampire," James said. "Remember, each new fledglin' vampire must be nurtured and taught by its creator. Younger vampires might just create one for companionship. Given what we suspect about this one's age, I'd say around five at a minimum."

"Fuck. I can't have four or five more young girls go missin'," Garrett said somberly.

"No. We can't have that," James agreed. "Especially since this vampire is trainin' his creations in the old-world ways. The murder count of five or six vampires in Pine View County would dwarf that of the werewolf murders.

"Back to what started us on this conversation, how undead vampires differ from alive werewolves," James continued as if teaching a class on vampires. "The more important point here, and why I brought up Ty's kill, is, unlike werewolves that were never dead to begin with, a vampire that people think they destroyed, can, under certain circumstances, reanimate. Usually with the help of their familiar."

"How do I actually kill it?" Garrett asked impatiently.

Ignoring Garrett's impatience, James said, "Let's get back to killin' 'em in a minute. Ya need to know about familiars and for a very important reason that I'll explain after everything else. Okay?"

Frustrated, Garrett nodded.

"Familiars *are* human, but not human, like you and me," James said. "I told ya that vampires create new vampires by forcin' their blood into the dead victim's mouth and this reanimates 'em. Vampires have another use of their blood, and that use is to create familiars.

"This is usually voluntary by the human who becomes a vampire's familiar; like the vampire groupies I was tellin' ya about before," James explained. "Vampires don't need consent, 'cause they could mesmerize someone into becomin' their familiar. Vampires are narcissistic creatures and appreciate the loyalty of a human who *wants* to be their familiar, though. They usually promise the familiar that they will eventually become a vampire. But, because vampires have no shortage of familiar wannabes, the joke is usually on the familiar, though. After years, or even decades, of service, vampires usually create a new familiar and kill the old one. You'd think they'd learn," James said with a chuckle.

"Anyway," James explained. "Familiars are created by willingly drinkin' small amounts of their vampire's blood and drinkin' it often. So, they are not undead, but drinkin' their vampire's blood makes 'em more than human. Like the werewolf connection Paige discovered she had with the alpha, a vampire and its familiar are connected telepathically. If I haven't already mentioned this, a vampire is telepathically connected with its cloud, too. Where the familiars are concerned, this is so the familiar always knows what its master needs and when it needs it. Also, they have increased strength and senses. Their immune systems are impervious to viruses, infection, cancer, etcetera, and they age slower than you and I do. A familiar could be nearin' a hundred and look middle age, or younger."

"Damn," Garrett said, quietly.

"More like damned," James clarified. "The moment a human partakes of vampire blood, their will is forfeited to the vampire and their soul is forfeited to Lucifer."

"Does that cover all the feedin', creatin', and familiar stuff?" Garrett asked.

"It does," James replied.

"Okay, then," Garrett said. "Let's get back to their weaknesses and what'll kill the fucker. What other holy things, besides crosses, will keep 'em away?"

"We need to talk about more of their strengths, too," James said.

"Okay," Garrett said. "Weaknesses first. I need some good news."

"Alright," James relented. "Weaknesses first. Where crosses are concerned, there is a caveat. A cross will only work if it has been blessed or the person brandishin' it is a staunch believer in God. A staunch believer could pick up two sticks, form 'em into a cross, and it would work. A non-believer could hold up a blessed cross and it would work. Besides crosses, a consecrated communion host and holy water will ward off a vampire, too."

"What about garlic? I see that used in movies, too."

James chuckled. "That one's nonsense. The garlic misnomer roots come from misguided intentions. I told ya that vampires can't drink dead blood. Folks thought, since garlic kinda smells like decay, that wearin' it around their necks would trick vampires into believin' they were dead and protect 'em. Vampires can sense a livin' human by heat and they can hear their heartbeat and the blood pumpin' through their bodies from a substantial distance, though. Kinda like how sharks can pick up on small quantities of blood in the water.

"Aside from holy objects, vampires cannot enter the home of a human without an invitation," James elaborated. "Lola touched on this too, when she said Melanie went home to feed for the strength needed to kill because home was a welcomin' place. The ancient knew that Melanie's mother or father would let her in."

"Why do they need an invitation?" Garrett asked.

"There are different schools of thought on this one, too," James said. "Some say it's livin' magic. A built-in threshold incantation, so to speak, that protects the livin'. Some say that no supernatural creature can enter without an invitation. As ya learned, when the alpha crashed through your back door without an invitation, this one can't be true. Still, others believe that evil only has power over those who let it. By lettin' a vampire in, they're givin' into evil."

"Which do you believe?" Garrett asked.

"Even though this one lends credence to the Eve succumbin' to the vampire creation theory, I'm inclined to believe the latter argument over the former arguments."

"If it contradicts the Eve creation theory, why do you believe this one?" Garrett asked.

"Because I can make a flimsy argument that it fits with the affront to Christ creation argument, too," James said.

"How so?"

"That it's a restriction because God's Son suffered and died for humanity," James said. "This gives humans a natural barrier against evil. I told ya it was flimsy."

"I don't think it's flimsy at all," Garrett said. "I believe God and good are more powerful than Satan and evil. It makes perfect sense to me."

James smiled. "I like your thoughts on that, Garrett. You've convinced me, at least."

Garrett smiled, too. "Happy to help. Heaven knows you've helped me enough."

The smile disappeared from James' face. "I must warn you, though, that crosses, and bein' invited in are the weakest of a vampire's weaknesses."

"How so?"

"Because of a vampire's power to mesmerize," James said. "If the person holdin' the cross or openin' the door looks into the vampire's eyes, it can mesmerize 'em to drop the cross or open the door."

"Well, that sucks," Garrett agreed.

"Y'all need to keep that in mind while dealin' with this vampire. Even when dealin' with the ones it creates. Their powers will be weak at first, but they'll learn quickly from this one."

"Okay," Garrett said. "I'll pass that along. What about vampires not havin' a reflection in mirrors?"

James laughed. "That's nonsense. They're undead, but they are corporal. They live in a body. Alive, dead, or undead, a body has a reflection. Like the garlic myth, this one has some merit in that vampires avoid mirrors."

"If it's nonsense, why do they avoid mirrors?"

James took another sip of scotch and continued. "Well, much like werewolves, vampires can be killed with silver; we'll get to killin' the fuckers after we discuss their strengths. In the old days, mirrors were made by placin' highly polished silver behind glass, or just usin' the polished silver. Naturally, vampires avoided mirrors, and this led to the ridiculous notion that vampires don't cast a reflection.

"There was a movie in the eighties called Fright Night. Not the remake a few years ago with Colin Farrell. The original had Amanda Bearse from *Married with Children* and Roddy McDowell from *Planet of the Apes,* and a lot of other movies, in it. Have ya seen it?"

Garrett shook his head. "I don't think I've seen it. But I know Amanda Bearse from *Married with Children*. I had the biggest crush on Christina Applegate. By the time I started watchin' reruns, she was a lot older than me, but Kelly Bundy was damn hot."

James chuckled. "Yeah. I think every heterosexual adolescent boy shared your infatuation with Kelly Bundy. I, though, had a crush on Ted McGinley. He played Marcy's second husband, Jefferson D'Arcy. Damn good-lookin' man."

Garrett laughed. "I remember him. Seems like that guy was in just about every TV show at some point."

"About the movie, though," James said. "Overall, it was a pretty decent vampire flick. The vampire had a familiar. And like Coppola's adaptation of Stoker's novel in the nineties where Dracula sees a resemblance between Mina and his beloved Elizabeth who died, the vampire in *Fright Night* sees a resemblance in Bearse's character, Amy, and his long-lost love. Anyway, the vampire mesmerizes Amy into bein' infatuated with him. There's a scene where they're dancin' in a club and Amy looks into a mirror on the wall and she's dancin' alone. No vampire. Not even his damn clothes. I mean. C'mon. His clothes don't cast a reflection either. Ruined the whole damn movie for me.

"Silver backed or not, I believe vampires still avoid mirrors."

"Why?" Garrett asked.

James smiled. "I'm glad ya asked. Mind you, this is my theory. I could be wrong, but here's what I think. I think vampires continue to age after they become vampires. Not like humans age, though. Much slower. Like dog years in reverse, but I can't even guess at the ratio. I think they use their power, a unique power from mezmery, to *project* their younger self to the public when they're out and about at night.

"For younger vampires, this wouldn't take much concentration," James explained. "Hell, dependin' on how long they've been a vampire, they might not need to project at all. Like Melanie. She wouldn't need to worry about this for decades. An older vampire, an ancient, would. It's my theory that vampires avoid mirrors because they can't hide their true appearance in a mirror. It reflects their true appearance. Their true vampire self.

"Durin' the werewolf ordeal, I learned two new things I didn't know before," James admitted. "First, the connection between the alpha and its pack. Second, the ancestral werewolf. I'd love to publish these theories but, because of Paige, I won't. I wouldn't want my peers challengin' me on where I came up with 'em. Before we've handled this vampire ordeal, perhaps my theory of vampires and mirrors can be confirmed, too."

"Are you suggestin' we carry mirrors around, lookin' over our shoulders, while huntin' this thing down?" Garrett asked.

"As a matter of fact, that's not a bad idea," James said. "If my theory is correct, I don't think they can mesmerize through a mirror either."

"Mirrors it is," Garrett replied.

"Now, then," James said. "About their strengths. We've already discussed their power to mesmerize, but strength is one of their strengths, too. An ancient, powerful vampire could easily possess the strength of ten or more powerful men. Even Melanie, in her fledglin' state, could easily overpower you or Trowa or, even Ty. They're strong, Garrett."

"Understood."

"They're shapeshifters too."

"Shapeshifters? Like turnin' into a bat?" Garrett asked.

"Yes," James said. "They can assume *any* animal form, not just a bat. Unlike the Bela Lugosi vampire, that turned into a rather large, but not man-sized bat, true vampires can only shape-shift into somethin' equal to their body mass. For instance, a two-hundred-pound vampire could shape-shift into a bat or wolf or rat of the same size. Hollywood usually ignores this part. They can also shape-shift into an equal mass of many creatures. Coppola got this right when Van Helsing, Jonathan, and the others cornered Dracula in the wardrobe in the room where they put Mina at the asylum after they desecrated Dracula's soil. Dracula went from bein' a large bat-like creature to bein' a lot of rats."

"I remember that scene. So, that's true?"

"It is," James said. "They could also become a lot of bats, or two wolves, or a lot of rats, like in the movie. As long as what they shape-shift into equals their body mass, they can shape-shift into it. Coppola got somethin' else right, too. Vampires can turn into mist and vanish. This is why Paige and Glinda couldn't track the ancient and Melanie. She, they, could smell 'em in the parkin' lot and at Trevor's house and at the stream, but not between those places."

"Well, that sucks," Garrett said. "I don't want to put Paige in danger, but I was hopin' she could help find 'em somehow."

"About Paige and Glinda. I said I'd wait until the end to tell…" James began.

"Wait," Garrett interrupted. "If that's it for their strengths, tell me how we kill the fucker."

"You keep askin' how to kill the fucker. What ya need to know is how to *destroy* the fuckers," James corrected Garrett.

Confused, Garrett said, "Fuckers? As in plural? I figured if we took out the ancient, it'd be over."

"Unfortunately, it doesn't work that way with vampires," James said. "Unlike with Ty and Trowa, who were released from the werewolf curse when their alpha's maker was killed, there's no happy endin' for the vampires the ancient creates."

"Why not?"

"Because," James said in the voice that made Garrett feel like a stupid student in one of his classes, "they're already dead. Ty and Trowa weren't killed to become a werewolf, so they could be saved. Melanie, and any others the ancient creates for his cloud, will have to be destroyed, too."

Dejected, Garrett said, "Damn. I was hopin' we'd get her back when we killed the ancient."

"I'm afraid not, Garrett," James said softly. "And I'm sorry. This time, the sheriff doesn't get to rescue the damsel in destress."

"Me too. But, if it has to be done, it has to be done. So…how *do* we destroy these fuckers? Stake through the heart?"

"Yes. With a couple of caveats. First, it must be a silver tipped steak through the heart. Second, their familiar can undo this."

Frustrated, Garrett yelled, "C'mon. These fuckers are harder to kill than cockroaches."

"I told ya this would be more challengin' than the werewolves," James said. "This all ties back to you askin' 'bout Ty's Silver Star bein' removed from Seth's chest. Unlike werewolves, the undead, unless utterly destroyed, can reanimate. All his familiar would have to do is remove the stake, cut him or herself, bleed into the wound, and the vampire would reanimate. It would be weak and need its familiar to find food for it while it recovered but recover it would. The familiar would do the same for any of its master's cloud."

Still frustrated, Garrett asked, "So, how do we utterly destroy the fuckers?"

"While vampires can be immobilized with a silver tipped stake, fire, and decapitation, sunlight is the only actual means of completely destroyin' a vampire," James said. "Sunlight will turn a vampire to dust and even then, the dust must be scattered, most effectively in runnin' water, so it can't be collected and reanimated. For instance, if you stake a vampire, remove its head, take it far from the body, expose it to sunlight, and scatter the head's ashes in a river where they'll be washed away forever. Then it can never be reanimated."

"Well, that sounds easy enough," Garrett said sarcastically.

"You have other weapons to make this less challengin'," James said.

"What?" Garrett asked hopefully.

"Vampires must rest durin' the day," James explained. "Because they're undead, they don't actually sleep, but they rest in their coffin. And the coffin must contain a layer of soil from their homeland. The soil kinda regenerates 'em. If ya can find where they're restin' durin' the day, you can go back at night, while they're out feedin', and put consecrated communion hosts or holy water in the soil. You'd most likely have to get past the familiar to do it. If you're successful, the vampires wouldn't be able to use their coffins when they returned before dawn. Without the aid of its familiar, they'd be very vulnerable."

"You said a familiar is human, but *not* human. Does that mean conventional means can kill 'em? Like with a gun?" Garrett asked.

"Yes," James said. "But remember, they have enhanced abilities because of the vampire blood they routinely drink. Instead of two shots to the chest, ya might have to empty your gun into him or her to stop 'em."

"I'll bring extra clips," Garrett said with a smile.

"Okay. Now we're at the end of everything I know 'bout vampire folklore. Before I tell ya what I've been dreadin' tellin' ya, I have two suggestions. And I hesitate to mention either," James said earnestly.

"Just tell me, James."

"First, you're gonna need Father Mike's help," James said. "I haven't met him, but I know, from Paige and Mandy, that he's a young man. That tells me he's probably a contemporary priest."

"He is young, but what's that got to do with it. And what do ya mean by contemporary?" Garrett asked.

"I mean that he's not likely to believe a word of this and will need proof of the supernatural."

"What proof?" Garrett asked but somehow knew what James would say.

"Show him Glinda."

"No way in hell that's happenin', James."

"It's the only way to make him believe and enlist his help. You'll need his help, Garrett."

Garrett shook his head, but he said, "I'll discuss it with Paige, but it'll be her decision."

This was the response James hoped for. He had a feeling Paige would do everything in her power to stop the ancient. Even if it meant exposing her wolf to Fr. Mike.

"What's the second thing?" Garrett asked.

"They can shift at night to keep Glinda off their scent and the coffins they rest in conceal their scent too, if they want to conceal it," James said. "If you're successful at findin' the vampire's lair, killin' the familiar, and desecratin' their coffins with consecrated communion host and or holy water, that will be Glinda's best chance to track 'em."

"That's great news, James. Why do ya look so damn worried?" Garrett replied.

James downed the rest of his scotch. "Because of what I must tell you now. Have ya wondered why an ancient vampire would show up in Pine View County, Garrett?"

"Well, it's like you and Lola said last June when y'all ruined my celebratory toast. Y'all said supernatural events can follow supernatural events. Y'all as much said we should expect somethin' like this. Lola said it on the phone again today. Right?"

"We did," James sighed. "And she did again today. It's rare that I disagree with Lola, but I strongly disagree with somethin' she said today."

"What's that?" Garrett asked.

"Lola said that vampires are intelligent. On that, we agree. She also said this one doesn't know 'bout Glinda and that he's in for a surprise. On this point, I very much disagree with Lola."

"What're ya sayin', James?"

"I think the only reason an ancient vampire would show up in Pine View County, Texas is *because* of Glinda."

Afraid to ask, but needing to know, Garrett said, "For what purpose? What would an ancient vampire want with my little girl, James?"

James shrugged a helpless shrug. "I'm not sure. Could be for the challenge of killin' her. Could be to create the mythical werewolf vampire hybrid. Or it could be to make her his familiar. A werewolf familiar would be a vampire's dream; to have total control over a werewolf. What I think… No, what I know in my gut is that the ancient bein' here isn't a coincidence. If my gut is right, Paige is in a *lot* of danger."

Garrett shivered uncontrollably and downed the rest of his scotch. It did not warm the chill in his soul.

Chapter Six

Sunset on December 25, 2015, in Pine View County, Texas came at five twenty-one p.m. and a flurry of activity took place as the sun turned into an orange ball in the low western sky.

After logging in the blood evidence collected from beneath Trevor's neck, Trowa went home to the first house he'd ever lived in. As a logger, he was nomadic. Traveling wherever work took him and living in a 1966, Airstream Globetrotter travel trailer. The alpha destroyed the trailer the night it came for him. He had escaped with his life, but not before being bitten on the foot. After that, for a short time, he lived in a cramped camper shell mounted on the bed of his 1972, Ford, F-150 pickup truck. But the deputy job gave him the security he needed to set down roots. Not deep roots, though. Not deep enough to buy a house; he could still get a hankering to pick up and travel. Deep enough to rent, though. Garrett even vouched for him with the rental agent, who was Garrett's ex-wife, Lacy.

The house was a two-room, log cabin on the outskirts of Pine View proper and was on two, wooded acres. He couldn't have lived in town surrounded by other houses. The back-property line ended at dense, untouched forest miles deep. As far as décor went, Trowa had salvaged his fifty-inch, Panasonic, plasma TV from the Airstream and it sat on a wooden crate against the left side living room wall. In the living room was a green plastic patio table and matching chair. The bedroom had a sleeping bag on the floor and a pillow. That was it. That was enough for Trowa who spent most of his off time in the woods behind the log cabin climbing the tall pines, smoking pot, and enjoying nature.

As the orange sun set Christmas night, Trowa was perched in the crook of two thick pine branches about seventy feet high with a joint tucked behind his right ear. From there, he could see rolling treetops for miles. The air was chilly, and the view was beautiful. Trowa took the joint from behind his ear, sparked his lighter into flame, touched the flame to the end of the joint, inhaled deeply, held the smoke for several seconds, and exhaled through his nose. It gave him the appearance of an angry bull snorting in chilly air. But Trowa wasn't angry. He was concerned. Concerned for Paige. He didn't have Lola's seeing eye or James' knowledge, but he had good intuitions about nature and when it was out of balance. Everything that happened that day led him to the conclusion what had happened wasn't a coincidence.

Trowa was proud of his Caddo, Native American heritage, and he knew about many legends from many tribes; like werewolves, what the Navajo called Yee Naaldlooshii, or skin-walkers. He also knew about the Native American version of a vampire. It was an evil spirt called the Jumlin that fed on blood, and it was rumored the Jumlin searched for a Yee Naaldlooshii to enslave as its daytime protector. To Trowa, it only stood to reason if an ancient Jumlin came to Pine View County, it was there for a Yee Naaldlooshii. It was there for Paige.

Trowa looked at the beautiful sunset and took another deep drag on the joint. He hoped it would settle his nerves. It didn't.

~ * ~

After talking with James and Garrett on the phone, Ty took Lola out to the Henderson's house and watched her work her magic on the six-grieving people. Trevor's grandparents had arrived by the time they got there. Instead of one-on-one sessions, Lola had the six people join hands with her in a circle in the middle of the living room. Then she began rubbing the thumbs of both hands on each hand she held, and the others did the same with their thumbs on the hands they held, while they all looked into her seeing right eye.

Lola told the grieving parents and grandparents the same thing Ty heard her tell Kat. Before she released them from the trance, she told Troy to delete the video of the footprints outside Trevor's bedroom and instructed all of them to forget the video and footprints existed. As soon as she released them from the hypnotic trance, Troy took out his phone and deleted the video. When Ty and Lola left, all six people were talking about happy memories of Trevor.

Once outside, Lola stumbled while going down the steps and Ty had to catch her.

Concerned, Ty asked, "Are you okay?"

Lola shook her head lightly, making the pink and white beads at the end of her cornrows click together. "Kat and Zack were difficult. But these six grievers were very difficult."

"Difficult how?" Ty asked.

"To do what I do to take their grief away, I have to take it inside me," Lola explained. "Absorb it. I've never taken on this much grief in such a short period. If you could see my aura now, you'd see the angriest storm clouds ever. Like a tornado is about to whisk me away."

"I'm so sorry, Lola," Ty said as he helped her to his patrol SUV. "I didn't know you were takin' their grief into you. But I guess it has to go somewhere,"

"Yes, it does," Lola said as Ty helped her into the passenger seat.

After getting Lola into the SUV and buckling her seatbelt for her, he asked, "What color is your aura?"

Lola offered a weak smile. "It's pink, silly man. Pink is for peace, tranquility, and healin'."

"Of course it's pink," Ty said with a smile of his own.

Lola looked better by the time Ty parked in front of her house, but he still had to help her inside, into her dark living room with assorted totems on the dark, red walls and a large, ornate curio cabinet, made of dark hardwood, containing glass jars, ceramic canisters, and small wooden boxes. Aside from the curio cabinet, there was a small, round table made of the same dark hardwood as the curio cabinet in the middle of the room. Surrounding the table were four chairs made of the same dark wood. The chair on the far side of the table had a high back, the other three had low backs.

Once inside, Lola said, "Thank you, Ty. I'll be okay after I meditate for a while."

"Ya sure? I can stay awhile, if ya want me to."

Lola smiled. This time it wasn't as weak, and it lit up her beautiful face. "You're sweet, Ty. But I'll be okay after a bit. Then, I'm gonna commune with some of my sisters 'bout this…vile creature for advice.

You go on home to your lovely wife and beautiful chil'.'"

"Okay. If you're sure."

"I am. Go home and hold Little D close."

That was exactly what Ty planned to do. They said their goodbyes and Ty left.

~ * ~

About thirty minutes later, as the orange sun sank in the western sky, Ty was home. Jasmine wasn't wearing the Christmas gift he'd given her. She and Little D were at the dining room table eating supper.

"Took ya long enough," Jasmine said, but with no anger in her voice. "I put a plate in the microwave for ya, but it's probably still warm. Come join us."

"Yeah, Daddy. Oin us," Little D echoed.

But food was the last thing on Ty's mind. He walked up to Jasmine, bent over, and planted a kiss on her lips. She had a fork full of ham halfway to her mouth when he kissed her. Her hand stopped moving, and she kissed him back.

They held the kiss for several seconds and only parted when Little D said, "Get a vroom."

They couldn't hold the kiss after that because they both began laughing.

Still laughing, Ty said, "Get a what?"

"A vroom, Daddy" Little D said, giggling.

Ty reached over, picked up Little D, and held him tightly. "I'll get you a vroom."

Then Ty held Little D over his head and twisted him in loops and circles while he shouted, "Vroom. Vroom. Vroom."

Little D's giggles turned into roaring laughter as his dad vroomed him around the dining room.

After vrooming Little D around the living room for several minutes, Ty stopped and hugged him close again. He thought about Trevor, who was Little D's age, and he cried.

Jasmine saw the tears on Ty's face, got up, and wrapped her arms around both of her men. "What's the matter, sugar?"

Ty let go of Little D with his left arm and wrapped it tightly around Jasmine. "Right now, nothin'. If I have to stand here with my arms wrapped around both of y'all for the rest of my life to keep y'all safe, I will."

"Bad case?" Jasmine asked.

Ty nodded as more tears leaked from his eyes.

"It'll be okay," Jasmine whispered.

Ty held them tighter.

Jasmine wouldn't get a chance to wear her Christmas gift that night, either. Ty insisted Little D sleep in their bed with them, and Jasmine didn't object. The Christmas gift could wait.

~ * ~

Garrett raced the setting sun home. Not because he feared for his own safety after the sunset, but because James had told him the ancient vampire was probably in Pine View County for Paige. No matter how much he thought Glinda might help with the investigation, he couldn't risk her involvement. At least not at night. If he let Glinda help during the day, it could only be with him. He would ride Glinda everywhere she went, if he had to. He knew Paige was stubborn and head-strong enough to argue the point. Then there was Fr. Mike, too. Garrett couldn't deny having a priest on their team would help. If he was contemporary, as James suspected, the thought of letting him see Glinda to convince him was unthinkable.

There was only a tinge of orange in the western sky, and the near full moon was already hovering over Garrett's house, as he pulled into the driveway and parked his patrol SUV next to his personal truck.

As Garrett got out of the SUV, Paige ran out the front door to meet him. "What'd Doctor James have to say? Is it a vampire? I'm right, aren't I? It *is* a vampire."

Garrett wrapped her in a tight, protective hug. "Slow your roll there, Paige-Turner. I'll tell you and Mandy what James had to say after I kick off my boots and get a beer."

In a muffled voice, Paige said, "Okay, Daddy. But you're kinda suffocatin' me here."

Garrett released the hug, but he kept his left arm wrapped tightly around her shoulder, like he expected something to swoop out of the sky and fly away with her as they walked toward the house.

Mandy appeared in the doorway, looking cute as hell in her blue footed pajamas and her dirty blonde hair in a ponytail. Garrett thought Mandy had never been more beautiful than when she was trying not to be. Mandy opened her arms as Garrett and Paige neared the doorway and Garrett hugged her tightly with his right arm. Like Ty, he never wanted to let go of either of them again. Unlike Ty, having Paige sleep with him and Mandy would be awkward, at the least.

"Paige told me about the cases. Are you okay?" Mandy asked.

"Now that I'm huggin' the two most beautiful girls in the world, I am," Garrett said as they squeezed through the door and into the living room, in a rugby like scrum.

"Kinda weird, Daddy," Paige said as she pried herself from the tangle of arms and shut the door.

Garrett barked out a loud laugh. "Says the girl who hugged me while she was naked this mornin'. Which is against the rules, and ya know it."

"That was different," Paige retorted. "And for your information, huggin' you while I'm naked is *less* weird for me. Naked is an animal's natural state. Until Eve went and screwed that up."

Hearing Paige mention Eve, after the conversation with James concerning the origin of vampires, made Garrett stop in his tracks.

Paige saw her daddy halt. "Okay. I know it's against the rules. I won't do it again. Stupid Eve."

"No. It's not the naked thing," Garrett said. "I mean, it is. Don't do that again. It's what ya said about Eve. James and I were talkin' 'bout her earlier today."

Confused, Mandy said, "Eve had somethin' to do with vampires?"

"Maybe. It's one theory," Garrett said.

"Oh. This sounds good," Paige said excitedly. "Take off your boots, Daddy, and sit down. I'll get your beer."

Garrett took off his boots and eased into his comfy recliner just as Paige returned with an opened Miller Lite. It was a little light.

"Did ya take a drink of my beer?"

"Just to clear the foam," Paige lied; she'd taken a pretty big drink.

"Okay. But leave the foam on the next one."

Paige grinned. "Okay, Daddy. Now spill it. Tell us everything."

Paige and Mandy sat huddled together on the end of the couch closest to Garrett's recliner and listened intently. Three beers later, each with the foam syphoned off, Garrett had told them everything he intended to let Paige know, which meant he left out the part about James' fears regarding why the ancient was there.

There was stern disagreement between Paige and Mandy when the subject of letting Fr. Mike meet Glinda was mentioned. Paige was all for it; Garrett knew she would be. Mandy was convinced Glinda would get Paige excommunicated from the Catholic faith. Paige fervently believed Fr. Mike wouldn't be closed-minded on the topic. Garrett leaned toward Mandy's side but stayed out of it. In the end, Paige and Mandy agreed, if there was no other way to convince Fr. Mike of the supernatural, Glinda would be the last resort.

Garrett told Mandy the rest of it later that night in very hushed whispers to keep Paige from hearing. The thought horrified Mandy and she held Garrett tight. This led to Garrett unzipping Mandy's footed PJs. Which led to quiet love making. They did not know Paige was far from home by that time, hunting for the ancient. In hindsight, telling her everything would've been better.

~ * ~

Dănuț Roșca felt filthy to his very bones. He was covered in reddish dirt from head to toe, and he hadn't slept in days, but that didn't bother him. His Master's blood gave him the ability to work hard, without rest, for days and nights at a time. That is what he had been doing. Except for brief interludes to secure shipment of the Master's crate from the Houston Ship Channel to Pine View, take delivery of the Master's crate, secure a coffin for the Master's new fledgling, and pick up the boy's body that had recently rested in the fledgling's new resting place, Dănuţ had done nothing but excavate the Master's new throne room beneath the Eternal Rest Funeral Home. His instructions were clear. The throne room had to be large enough for the master's ancient, ornate, enormous coffin, his throne, and six more coffins for his *nor*. Three on either side.

Dănuţ completed the throne room at five sixteen p.m. Christmas day, just five minutes before sunset, and waited proudly at the foot of his Master's coffin, eager to tell him his throne room was finished. Not that the Master would praise Dănuţ for a job well done. That was never the case. And Dănuţ didn't expect praise. Serving the Master was all the reward Dănuţ required.

Dănuţ watched as the second hand on his filthy wristwatch ticked toward five twenty-one p.m. The instant the second hand hit the twelve at five twenty-one p.m., the lid of the ornate coffin opened and Dragoş Văduva floated into a standing position, towering over Dănuţ. He looked down at him with his silver eyes.

Dănuţ averted his Master's gaze by looking at his dirty shoes. "Your throne room is complete, Master. Once you and the fledgling are off, I will move your throne and her coffin below. Then, if it pleases you, I will visit some other cemeteries to procure resting accommodations for your new cloud. I should be able to retrieve at least three more tonight and the remaining two tomorrow night. I think a cluster of coffin thefts might confuse the local law enforcement."

"Do *not* think," Dragoş said cruelly. "Thinking is not yours to do. I think for you. What is that retched, chemical smell?"

"It is the remains of the boy who rested in your fledging's coffin, Master."

"Why is *it* here?" Dragoş hissed.

"The other mortuary was closed for Christmas, Master," Dănuţ said. "When the telephone rang, I stupidly answered it."

"Do not talk of the Christ child's birth celebration." Dragoş roared.

Dănuţ shrank into a low bow. "I apologize, Master. His father has already called, and they will come for him tomorrow. He will be back in the ground before you rise tomorrow night."

Dragoş chuckled, which sounded more like a growl. "Stupid

humans. Their bodies rot after death. It is the natural order of things. They are food and nothing more. Would they embalm a cow or a pig or a chicken after they feast on their carcasses? Certainly not. They just do not know their place in the predator hierarchy…yet. They *will* learn."

Still bowing, Dănuţ said, "Yes, Master."

Dragoş floated from his throne and alighted directly in front of his cowering familiar. "Bring no more chemical death into this place, slave."

"I will not," Dănuţ promised. "The other mortuary can deal with the next five remains,"

"Wake the fledgling," Dragoş instructed. "They are so lazy in their youth,"

"Yes, Master."

Dănuţ scurried from the shadow of his Master, like a rat scurries from a cat, and opened the lid of the fledgling's coffin. Her silver eyes opened suddenly, and she sprang at Dănuţ the same way a cat sprang upon a scurrying rat. Before her claw-like fingernails could close around Dănuţ's neck, Dragoş flung out his left arm and an invisible force propelled her across the room. She crashed hard into a cinderblock wall, but quickly crouched and hissed at Dănuţ. He saw the thirst in her silver eyes, but she was powerless to attack him again. The Master wouldn't allow her.

"Thank you, Master," Dănuţ said.

"Thank me again and I *will* let her rip your throat out," Dragoş said coldly.

"Yes, Master."

Then, in a softer voice that he rarely used with Dănuţ, Dragoş said, "By the grace of Lucifer, I got lucky with this one. She was there the night the werewolves feasted upon young flesh. I witnessed her horror through her blood memory. She will take me to the place it happened. With Lucifer's grace, I will discover more about the magnificent, silver-haired werewolf that is rumored to exist. First, she must feed."

Dragoş held out his left hand to the fledgling, the same one he had used to toss her effortlessly across the room, and she scurried to his side. She took his ancient, translucent hand in her small, translucent hand. Then they dissolved into black mist.

Before they had completely dissipated, Dănuț dared to say, "Master?"

Dragoş rematerialized, the fledgling remained suspended between there and not there, like a specter. "Yes, slave."

Sheepishly, in something that wasn't quite a whisper, Dănuț said, "My constitution is waning. May I please feed, Master?"

"You may, slave," Dragoş said as he cut a slit across his right nipple with one of his claw-like thumbnails.

Dănuț saw the black nectar flow from his Master's nipple and locked his lips around its stiffness and sucked greedily while he could; the Master never let him feed for long. He felt his constitution returning as soon as the thick, coppery liquid touched his tongue. After a few mouthfuls, Dragoş mentally instructed Dănuț to stop. He immediately obeyed.

On the few occasions he hadn't stopped upon hearing Dragos' mental command, the Master had telekinetically thrown him across the room, as the fledgling had been moments before. Unlike the fledgling, who was a vampire and impervious to most corporal pain, Dănuț was seriously wounded on those occasions. Even though it wasn't his place to think, he had learned.

Dănuț stepped back, licked at the precious, black nectar around his lips and on his chin, and found himself alone in the embalming room. His Master and the fledgling were gone. They were off to feed and look for the silver-haired werewolf. Dănuț knew his Master would likely return with more fledglings for his cloud. He had work to do.

Dănuț loaded shovels and pickaxes into the back of the hearse. With his constitution restored by his Master's succulent blood, Dănuț resolved to have four new coffins by sunrise. He drove out of the Eternal Rest Funeral Home and the black hearse seemed to dissolve into the night. It was a cloaking glamor placed upon the hearse and Dănuț by the Master to aid him in his nocturnal activities. Dănuț's Master was benevolent when it suited his purposes.

~ * ~

After Ty left, Lola sat cross-legged in the middle of her dark living room. Her elbows rested on her thighs and her hands were outstretched to either side. She rhythmically touched the thumbs of each hand to each of the other four fingers, starting with the index, then the middle, then the ring, then the little finger. She repeated this several times until the movements slowed and then stopped with her thumbs on each index finger. Her head slumped until her chin rested on her chest. She had reached a deep, meditative state and would remain that way, unmoving for quite some time. Anyone with the gift of sight would have seen her angry, dark, gray aura slowly return to its dazzling, almost hot, pink, natural color as she communed with nature.

By the time Lola was refreshed and came out of her meditative trance, almost two hours had passed. The sun had gone down and the room that was dark during the daylight hours was ink black at night. Lola could see in the dark as well as any nocturnal creature, including vampires.

She got up, went around the table, pulled out the high-backed chair, and sat down. There was a drawer on that side of the table that contained more items than a drawer larger than the entire table could hold. She opened it, reached in, and brought out a large, blood red candle. Lola placed it in the center of the table, put the wick between the thumb and index finger of her right hand, snapped her fingers over the wick, and an impossibly large, red flame materialized, engulfing her right hand when it did. She withdrew her hand from the flame slowly. It was unmolested. Not even the delicate hairs on her smooth, brown arms were singed.

Lola held her arms out toward the empty chairs on either side of her. "Sisters. I seek your counsel on a matter of grave importance. An ancient vampire is roostin' in East Texas. He has already claimed a young girl for his *nor* and the girl has taken the life of an innocent chil'. Come to me with your wisdom, fearlessness, and cleverness in my time of need. Come to me, sisters."

The air on either side of Lola shimmered in the bright red candlelight. Shapes materialized in the two empty chairs on either side of Lola. The shapes had features, but they weren't corporal. As the two shimmering shapes placed their hands in Lola's, a third shimmering shape appeared in the seat across from Lola. This shape held the hands of the other two shimmering shapes. Lola's council was arriving.

As the fourth linked hands with the other three, the shimmering lessened, and their features became more distinct. When they had materialized to the extent they could, they looked like slightly blurred versions of their true appearances surrounded by their brilliant auras. Specters of their living selves.

The woman to Lola's right looked incredibly old, and indeed, she was. At over two hundred years old, she was the eldest of Lola's council and probably the oldest seer alive. Her name was Mamma Deupree. Her loose, wrinkled skin was the color of dark chocolate and she had long, white, matted dreadlocks that hung to the floor. Mamma's regular left eye was cloudy gray from the cataract that was there since the late 1800s, but her seeing cat-like right eye was crystal blue. She wore a loose-fitting moo-moo splashed with all the colors of the rainbow, no shoes on her leathery feet, and a rat-skull necklace. Her aura was deep purple, which signified wisdom. When she smiled at Lola, no teeth showed. When she spoke, she had a deep French accent. Mamma Deupree sat in a dirt floor hut at a table, much like Lola's, projecting her spectral form from Haiti.

The woman to Lola's left was young in appearance. She looked like she could be in her twenties but, like Lola, who appeared to be in her thirties but was in her seventies, she was in her forties and one of the youngest of Lola's coven. Her name was Angelica Freemont. Angelica's smooth, brown skin glistened with salt water and smelled of sun. Her jet-black hair was pulled back in a ponytail that hung loosely to the middle of her back, and she had a diamond studded, pierced, left nostril. Angelica's regular left eye was light green, almost the color of key-lime pie, but her seeing, cat-like, right eye was bright yellow, like the sun. Her ample breasts were covered with a deep blue bikini top and from the midriff down, she wore a loose fitting, white skirt and blue flip-flops. Her aura was bright red, which signified fearlessness. When she smiled at Lola, impossibly white teeth showed. When she spoke, she had a cheerful Jamaican accent that made everything she said sound hopeful. Angelica Freemont sat in a seaside bungalow at a table, much like Lola's, projecting her spectral form from Jamaica.

The woman who sat across from Lola looked middle-aged, which, of course, put her actual age at over one hundred. Her name was Rosa Chavez. Rosa's light brown skin had begun to show its age and hung loosely in places on her arms. Her graying hair was parted in the middle and hung in ringlets to her shoulders, and she wore large, silver, hoop earrings that tugged her earlobes down. Her regular left eye was dark brown, but her seeing cat-like right eye was onyx; so dark it was difficult to tell where the iris ended and the slit of a pupil began. She wore a sleeveless beige top, light green skirt that ended at her knees, and sandals. Her aura was midnight blue, which signified cleverness. When she smiled at Lola, several gold-capped teeth showed. When she spoke, she had a thick Hispanic accent. Rosa Chavez sat in a run-down, third-floor apartment at a table, much like Lola's, projecting her spectral form from Cuba.

With the council convened, Lola said, "Thank you, sisters. Thank y'all for answerin' my summons so quickly. As I tol' y'all in the summonin', a vile, ancient vampire has taken roost in East Texas. He has taken one young woman for his *nor*, and there will be more. The cruelty with which the innocent chil' was slain makes me think he is teachin' his fledglin' vampires in the old-world ways. He must be stopped."

In a voice that crackled, Mamma Deupree said, "Tell us all you know of this…beast."

Lola did. She included information about the werewolf attacks earlier that year. She told them about Paige and Glinda. As she told them, their auras shifted between shades of their original color; growing darker when they were angry and lighter when they were saddened or concerned by what Lola told them.

When Lola finished, Mamma Deupree, in her crackled voice, said, "I must disagree with you on an important point, Lola. I do *not* believe this magnificent, silver-haired werewolf, Glinda, is safe. My wisdom tells me that the vampire has taken roost there *because* of Glinda."

This hadn't crossed Lola's mind, and the thought horrified her. Her bright pink aura turned dark pink instantly.

In her beautiful Jamaican tongue, Angelica Freemont said, "I agree with Mamma. But…this could be an advantage, too. The girl, Paige, and her ancestral werewolf, Glinda, have already proven their fearlessness in battle by taking on, and killing, the powerful alpha that created her alpha. As you told it, Lola, once she was released from the silver that confined her to her human form, she did not hesitate to engage the powerful alpha. This kind of fearlessness, especially in one who has undergone their first transformation, is rare for all, supernatural or not.

"Again, I agree with Mamma that the ancient is there for Glinda," Angelica continued. "His kind are not used to being challenged. This could work in Glinda's favor."

It was Rosa Chavez's turn to offer advice. Her voice, like Lola's, had a warm honey quality to it but with a Hispanic accent, instead of Lola's mix of Cajun and East Texan.

"I too agree with Mamma *and* Angelica," Rosa said. "Paige and Glinda are clearly fearless, but they are also clever. From the battle you described, Glinda tricked the powerful alpha into thinking she would do one thing and once he bit, pardon the pun, she took advantage by reversing course and injuring the alpha grievously before killing it. This cleverness is also rare in one so new to their powers. This girl is fearless *and* clever. The ancient will, likely, never have encountered the likes of Glinda, even if he has walked in darkness for hundreds of years."

"Yes, yes, yes," crackled Mamma Deupree. "But does she have the wisdom to know when to be fearless and when to be clever? She is remarkable. That is certain. She has shown that she comes by fearlessness and cleverness naturally, and that *is* rare. But I am at this table for a reason.

"Wisdom, true wisdom, can *only* come with age," Mamma continued. "As remarkable as she is, she is *still* a child. Children who lack wisdom can act irrationally. The strengths that Angelica and Rosa find so admirable, without wisdom, will probably be her unfortunate undoing.

"Do not dismiss the ancient vampire so carelessly, sisters," Mamma cautioned. "I am old and with my age has come much wisdom. As much as it pains me to admit this, he is much older and likely, much wiser than I."

Lola considered the advice she had received. Angelica and Rosa had confidence in Glinda's natural fearlessness and cleverness. They believed these qualities would be an advantage against the ancient. Lola believed as they did, but Mama's concerns could not be dismissed. And

Mamma was right about abilities that came naturally and the accumulation of wisdom over a long life, as the vampire surely had.

To Mamma, Lola said, "If you are correct about the ancient bein' here *because* of Glinda, for what purpose would he want her?'

Mamma smiled an eerie, toothless smile and crackled, "He wants her to be his familiar."

Horrified, Lola said, "Surely not."

The smile dropped from Mamma's face, and she said, in a less crackled voice, "Most assuredly so, Lola. A werewolf familiar is a vampire's dead spunk, wet dream. Especially one of Glinda's abilities. A young, beautiful girl to play with is a bonus. That is a prize itself. He would have much fun with her and do vile things to her, I fear. Yes, he wants, *needs*, Glinda as his familiar."

Defensively, Lola said, "Glinda's aura is the purest of silver I have ever seen. She would never succumb to that…evil."

Mamma shook her head slowly, causing the long, gray, matted dreadlocks to brush across the dirt floor in her Haitian hut. "Lest you forget, all the ancient need do is mesmerize the child and feed her his foul blood. If he can do this, her will is forfeit to him and her soul is forfeit to the dark one. This is how her fearlessness and cleverness can work to *his* advantage."

"Okay. I'll tell Paige to be careful," Lola said.

"She has not the wisdom to outsmart this vampire." Mamma exclaimed in a loud, crackling voice.

"So, all is lost?" Lola blurted. "I refuse to accept this. I love Paige more than I can say."

Mamma's spectral hand squeezed Lola's corporal one. "I know you love her. I can see it in your aura. I did not say all is lost, Lola. Paige and Glinda are naturally fearless and clever. This is true. It is also correct that true wisdom can only come with age. I can share my wisdom with this girl you love, though. It will not be deep, all-knowing wisdom, but I will be with her and guide her. With the traits she shares with sisters Angelica and Rosa, it just might be enough to defeat this evil."

"How?" Lola pleaded.

Mamma Deupree removed her right hand from Rosa Chavez's left hand, which caused all three of the spectral apparitions to shimmer again, as if fading away, plucked one of the rat skulls from her necklace, and placed it on Lola's table, where it shimmered, too. Then Mamma took Rosa's hand in hers again and the shimmering stopped; their spectral forms and auras were back. And the rat skull was there, on Lola's table. Not spectral. It was really there. Lola picked it up and felt the realness of it.

As Lola inspected the rat skull, Mamma crackled, "Grind that skull to dust and put it in a protection potion. Then Paige must drink half of it and Glinda must drink the other half. This will give each of them needed wisdom, in either form they take, to deal with the vampire's evil plans."

"Thank you, Mamma," Lola said as tears streamed down her light brown cheeks.

"Do not thank me yet," Mamma said. "I pray to the Elements that this will be enough. Even with my gift of wisdom, it will not be an effortless task to destroy an ancient vampire."

"Yes. But Paige has others on her side besides me," Lola said. "They are humans, and they love her as I do. Where Paige is concerned, they are fearless and clever, too. One is even quite wise, for a human. We are a formidable group."

"For the sake of all that is good, I hope this is true," Mamma crackled.

"May the Elements be with you, Lola," Angelica said.

"Yes. Don't hesitate to summon us again if you need our council," Rosa added.

Lola thanked each of her sisters for their advice and support. Then she released Mamma's and Angelica's hands. They shimmered into nothingness. The candle's large, red flame extinguished.

Lola sat in the dark holding the rat skull. The potion would take three days to brew. She had work to do. She got up from the table, went to the curio cabinet, and removed the ingredients she would need. As she worked, she radiated her love for Paige through her pink aura with all her power. She hoped Paige would feel it wash over her like a warm embrace.

~ * ~

164

A moving, black mist seeped out of the woods surrounding the Mill Road Barn and made its way to the opening where the missing door had been. Faded, yellow crime scene tape hung loosely across the opening. The black mist floated under the tape and into the dark interior. An instant later, Dragoş Văduva and what had been Melanie Zane materialized from the black mist.

Dragoş surveyed the building's interior with eyes that could see as well in the dark as human eyes can see in the light. It wasn't the view he took in; it was the accumulated fear of all that happened over six months ago in the building he absorbed.

Anyone who has ever felt a chill run up their spine for no apparent reason or felt a sudden cold spot in an otherwise warm environment, or thought they'd seen a ghost, or heard a sound where no sound should be, has experienced a small example of what Dragoş experienced then. Fear from the living remained long after they left a plane, and Dragoş fed off all the fear. He drank it in and found it intoxicating. Even though the blood in the building and surrounding area was thoroughly cleaned and bleached, there had also been the smell of blood everywhere for Dragoş to take in and enjoy.

While the smell of so much young fear and blood excited Dragoş, they were not the reason he had brought his fledgling vampire to the MRB. It was the memory of that night he absorbed from her blood that excited him most—a specific incident. Dragoş settled into the part of himself that had been Melanie Zane, as he was an accumulation of all the humans he had ever drank from or turned and saw through her memories what she had experienced. Only one specific incident interested him.

Melanie and the other trapped classmates remained huddled around Freddy's body for what seemed like hours, but had only been minutes, while the two werewolves continued to pace in front of the exit. Then there was a yelp from outside the barn and everyone, including the two werewolves, turned that way. A spilt second later, a piece of lumber sliced through the metal siding and skittered across the concrete floor. Murmurs and surprised shouts erupted from the students. The two werewolves growled loudly and advanced toward the piece of lumber that had unexpectedly arrived.

The two werewolves jerked their heads toward the direction the yelp and piece of lumber had come from. They looked at each other briefly and then took off through the opened door at breakneck speed. Melanie, Quincy, and the others remained silent for several seconds, unsure as to their fate. Then, in unison, and as if unable to stop themselves, they moved toward the missing MRB door. Once outside, they headed left, toward the direction the werewolves had exited.

That was when Melanie saw Paige standing alone just inside the tree line of the surrounding woods. She was naked and covered in blood. Melanie saw Paige and Justin walk towards the woods earlier that night. That Justin was no longer with Paige led Melanie to believe he had met a similar fate to those of Maggie, Freddy, Ella, and several others whose bodies were strewn around the MRB grounds. To Paige's benefit, Melanie assumed, since Paige was alive, the blood covering her was Justin's.

Dragoş had what he needed before the memory ended. *A spilt second later, a piece of lumber sliced through the metal siding and skittered across the concrete floor.* He continued through the end of the blood memory because the girl, Paige, interested him in one of two ways. First, she was beautiful and would make for a fun plaything in his cloud. Second, and more importantly, Dragoş thought she might be the one he wanted to find. To, hopefully, confirm the latter interest, he needed blood from the girl. That was why the piece of lumber interested him.

Even through the fledgling's blood memory, Dragoş could smell blood on the piece of lumber. Deductive reasoning, something the old, wise vampire was quite good at, told him, since the piece of lumber pierced the outside of the building where the fledgling had later seen a blood covered Paige, the blood belonged to Paige.

Dragoş came back from the blood memory to find the fledgling tugging on his cape. She was hungry and impatient. Dragoş could go for days, even weeks without feeding. Young vampires have an insatiable thirst for blood; an addiction to blood, not unlike a heroin or meth addict who is always looking for their next fix. Dragoş glared at her, and she fell to her knees, whimpering.

Will it still be here? Dragoş thought.

Dragoş followed the path the piece of lumber took from the hole in the building on his right to where it had skittered to a stop against the inside of the building to his left. There were many discarded items along the wall. Dragoş inhaled deeply, not because he breathed to survive, but to pick up minute traces of unmolested blood, unlike the blood cleaned away with chemicals, and found it. A wicked smile spread across his ancient face and revealed his pointed fangs.

He left the fledgling cowering on her knees; she dared not follow unless instructed to, and quickly pulled the piece of lumber swept up with other debris and missed by law enforcement.

"Foolish humans," Dragoş hissed, but their ineptitude pleased him.

Dragoş studied the piece of wood closely. That humans called this piece of wood a two-by-four was of no interest to him; wood was wood. What interested him were the blood-stained nails protruding from one side. His impossibly long tongue snaked out and encircled one nail. The remnants of the coppery substance soaked into his tongue like raindrops on parched dirt. His wrinkled face drew tight, like he had tasted something bitter. He quickly removed his tongue from the nail. That nail had contained only werewolf blood, which tasted vile to vampires. He spat the vile tasting blood out where it landed, with a splat, in a red blob on the concrete floor. Undeterred, he wrapped his long tongue around another nail. This time, he smiled and savored the taste of Paige's virgin blood.

Because it was such a small amount, and deteriorated by time, Dragoş couldn't absorb all of Paige's blood memories, but several bits of memory remained. He could discern losing her boyfriend, who the werewolf had killed, saddened her. That she was frightened, but also fearless as she battled with the werewolf he had tasted. To his disappointment, her blood was human, with no trace of the werewolf curse that would have been there had the werewolf bitten her.

Dragoş' hope this girl, Paige, might be the silver-haired werewolf, diminished. Even though she wasn't, he still wanted to have her in his cloud.

He returned to the cowering fledgling. "Do you know where the girl named Paige lives?"

Melanie averted his sliver eyes and nodded her head. "Yes,

Master."

Dragoş smiled so big the smaller, fanged teeth on either side of his prominent fangs showed. "Take me to her."

Dragoş and Melanie dematerialized into black mist and floated quickly and quietly away, on a breeze that wasn't there, from the MRB and into the moonlit night.

~ * ~

Paige waited until she was sure her daddy and Mandy wouldn't come looking for her before she snuck out. While she hadn't dialed Glinda's acute sense of hearing up, she didn't feel comfortable eavesdropping on their private conversations; she had a feeling they might engage in some sort of amorous activities that night, so she had dialed up Glinda's acute sense of smell. In just about every way, smelling her daddy and Mandy's sexual arousal disgusted Paige more than eavesdropping on their private conversations bothered her. After all, love making was much more private than any conversation she might hear. From experience on nights before when she could not so easily control Glinda's senses, Paige knew, after her daddy and Mandy were through, they fell into a deep, satisfied sleep Paige could only hope to enjoy some day.

At the first hint of Mandy's arousal, girls were easier to smell than boys; Paige lifted the side window in her room and stepped, naked, into the chilly night. The last thing she did before transforming into Glinda was remove her silver necklace and silver crucifix. She undid the clasps and left it on the outer windowsill, so it would be the first thing she put back on after returning to human form. Her naked body was chilled, but she wasn't cold for long. An instant later, she was insulated from the cold as Glinda. She sniffed the night air, hoping for a hint of the ancient's vile rot, stench, and got nothing. But that was okay. Glinda could cover a lot of ground before morning, and that was what she intended to do.

Glinda dropped to all fours and began to bound into the forest, but before she took a single step, she felt a sensation like a warm embrace encompass her. Glinda and Paige knew the sensation came from Lola. Curious why Lola would pick that moment to embrace her, Glinda changed course and headed for Lola's house. Ten minutes later, Glinda walked up Lola's steps to her front door; the wooden steps groaned in protest under Glinda's weight. Paige transformed back into herself and softly knocked on Lola's door.

~ * ~

Albert "Al" Sanders was home alone Christmas night. His wife, Lacy, was at her parent's house. They celebrated Christmas by opening gifts and having a big family supper late on Christmas day. His stepdaughter, Paige, was at her dad's house. When they first married, Al found their late day Christmas celebration odd. Over the years of their marriage, he came to enjoy it. He liked Lacy's parents, Larry and Lynn, a lot, and had grown to tolerate her brothers, Lance and Lane, who were often off-putting. Both had mellowed to a degree since getting married and having children. Lance had twin, nine-year-old boys and Lane had a seven-year-old daughter.

Al wasn't home by choice, though. He came down with a cold and Lacy's mom had become a germaphobe in recent years. She told him to stay home and rest. He made the best of a bad situation, though. Al was stretched out on the sofa with his pillow under his head and snuggled up under a warm goose down comforter. He wore a robe with nothing on underneath, which was something he never would have done if Paige were there. On the coffee table were his supplies: Vicks VapoRub, a box of tissues, a glass of bourbon, and the remote control. On the flat screen TV, his favorite Christmas movie, one Lacy didn't consider a Christmas movie at all, *Lethal Weapon* played.

It was early in the movie, the part when Riggs, played by Mel Gibson, considered eating a bullet over the loss of his wife, when he heard a light knock on the front door. It was so light, and improbable on Christmas night, he almost dismissed it. But he grabbed the remote, paused the movie, and listened closely. It came again.

Somewhat irritated, he grabbed a tissue to wipe his nose and answered the door with the tissue still pressed under his running nose. He saw a girl standing in the front porch light, but the state of her dress caught his attention before her face did. It was a pretty, green dress, but the front of it was covered in a mess so red it looked almost black in the porch light. It wasn't until she spoke that he looked at her face.

"Hi, Mister Al. Is Paige home?"

Al looked up and saw it was Melanie Zane. He was so shocked to see her he didn't register how white and translucent her skin was.

"Melanie? Are you okay?" Al said with deep concern. "Your folks have been lookin' everywhere for you."

"I went for a walk last night and got lost in the woods," Melanie said softly. "I lost my cellphone, too. When I finally found my way out, I recognized this was Paige's street, and I came here for help,"

"Paige is at her dad's," Al said. "We need to call your folks right away."

"Thank you, Mister Al. May *we* come in?"

Al was so surprised to see Melanie, and so happy she was okay, he missed the plural "we" in her question.

"Of course," Al said as he opened the door to let her in. "Come in and warm up while I call your folks. They're gonna be so happy to know you're okay,"

"Thank you for the invitation, Mister Al," Melanie said as she crossed the threshold into the Sanders' home.

Al closed the door behind her, but, as he was closing it, a dark figure stepped out of the shadows and pushed the door back open.

Shocked by the sudden intruder's presences, Al said, "Who the hell are…"

Before he could finish the sentence, he looked into the shadowy figure's silver eyes and got lost in them. He was mesmerized.

Dragoş Văduva grinned, which exposed his deadly fangs, and said to the fledgling, "Do you know where Paige's father lives?"

"Yes, Master."

"Good," Dragoş hissed. "We shall feast on this one and then you will take me to Paige."

"Here?" the fledgling asked greedily.

"No," Dragoş replied. "Not here,"

The fledgling vampire bared her fangs. "I can see blood pumpin' in his neck. Just one quick bite. Please, Master."

Dragoş chuckled, which sounded more like a growl. "Patience, little one. You must learn to control your thirst."

"Yes, Master."

"Come with me, little one," Dragoş said. "We shall dine on this one together, but not here,"

Dragoş stepped outside, and Al and Melanie followed him. Once outside, and away from the glare of the porch light, Dragoş wrapped his impossibly long arms around Al and the fledgling. He held them tightly and transformed.

To Melanie, it was beautiful to behold. To Al, in the smallest part of his brain where some consciousness still lived, it was horrific to behold. He wanted to scream, tried to scream, but just stood there, slack-jawed in the hideous monster's trance and embrace, with snot leaking from his nose and drool dribbling down his chin.

Dragoş' facial features changed. His forehead broadened, his nose flattened, and his ears became pointed, almost like horns, and migrated upwards until they settled on either side of his broadened skull. Black hair sprouted from everywhere but his eyes, nose, and mouth. Then, his long, black cape spread out on either side of his body as large, leathery, bat-like wings unfolded.

The wings flapped once and propelled all three quickly into the air. A second flap and they were at least a hundred feet in the air. Dragoş tilted his left wing down and flapped his right wing again, but with less force. He turned toward the miles of forest that separated Pine View from Nacogdoches. Once pointed in the direction he wanted to go, Dragoş leaned forward and flapped his wings again. Up and to the east, they flew. When Dragoş had reached the altitude he needed, he spread his large, leathery wings and glided effortlessly for miles, until he spotted a small clearing to land in. He folded his wings back, and they rocketed toward the ground. At the last moment, he spread his wings, flapped once, and lightly touched down. When he did, he released Al from the trance and embrace he'd held him in.

Al came out of the trance, saw the large bat-like creature standing in front of him, and screamed so hard he felt something inside his throat tear.

Dragoş smiled, revealing his fangs that were even larger in bat form. "Scream, human. No one can hear you. No one can help you. Even if there was someone near, I have cloaked our appearance and sounds. They would not see us feed on you or hear your screams, and your screams are music to my ears. Scream, human. Scream."

Al did. Even though the inside of his throat felt like broken glass, he screamed.

"Now, Master?" the hungry fledgling asked.

"Yes now," Dragoş hissed.

Melanie ripped Al's robe off, leaving him naked, cold, and terrified. Then she went for Al's neck.

"No," Dragoş said. "You feed from where you drank of your mother. I will feed from his inner arm. You must stop feeding when I command you to. Do you understand, fledgling?"

"Yes, Master," Melanie said as her long tongue snaked hungrily out of her mouth between her fangs.

Then, without touching Al, Dragoş forced him to the cold, wet ground on his back with his arms and legs spread wide.

Melanie complied, and as soon as Al was on the ground, she attacked his inner thigh savagely. So savagely she didn't notice her right fang pierced Al's left scrotum. Not that she would have cared if she'd bitten through his dick and both balls to get to his life's blood. She was hungry.

Al noticed, though, and let out another terrified and pain filled scream, but only a weak, interrupted sound issued from his mouth. Whatever it was in his throat that allowed him to scream broke. Then the bat creature bit into his inner right arm. It hurt badly, but Al couldn't scream. He laid there, looking up at the almost full moon's whiteness in the black sky. Al felt them feeding. He felt himself fading. Soon, the white of the moon was all he could see. Then, blackness in his peripheral vision closed until all Al saw was a pinpoint of bright white light. From very far away, he heard the bat creature tell the girl he thought was Melanie to stop feeding. He felt his heart take a final, slow beat, and then darkness took the pain away.

When Al was dead, Dragoş and Melanie took large, ragged bites of flesh from the puncture wound areas. Melanie removed Al's left testicle and half his penis, but she didn't care. She spit it out on the weeds next to Al's body without a thought. Al was her good friend's stepdad. Now he was food and nothing more.

After Dragoş had removed almost half of Al's upper arm in one large bite, he spit it out, and looked proudly at his fledgling. "Take me to Paige."

"Yes, Master," she complied.

Dragoş opened his arms and Melanie wrapped hers around the hairy man-bat that was her Master. Dragoş flapped his large leathery wings, and they soared into the air.

~ * ~

Lola began working on the protection potion the minute she gathered the needed ingredients from the curio cabinet. Besides the needed bottles and jars of witchy brews, she had a mortar, pestle, and cauldron on the table. She had just picked up the rat skull to pulverize it when she heard a knock on her door. Lola didn't have a movie playing on the TV, she didn't own a TV, as Al had when he heard a knock on his door, but, as Al had, Lola found it odd someone would pay her a visit Christmas night. She put the rat skull back on the table, opened the door, and saw Paige, very naked, standing there.

Surprised, Lola said, "Get in here, chil' before ya catch your death in the cold."

Paige smiled. "You know I don't get sick anymore."

Lola put her arm around Paige's cold shoulders, ushered her inside, and shut the door. "Not the point, chil'. Why are you here? What are ya doin' out?

The room was dark, but Paige dialed up Glinda's night vision and saw everything clearly. The items on Lola's table, especially the rodent skull and cauldron, interested her.

"I took Glinda out to look for the vampire but, before I started, I felt your aura's warm embrace," Paige said. "So, I came here first."

Lola smiled a knowing smile. "Of course you're out lookin' for the vampire. Does your daddy know you're out?"

"Heck, no. I snuck out while he and Mandy were…you know."

Lola knew what the "you know" was, as sure as she knew Garrett didn't know Paige was out vampire hunting before she asked the question.

"Pretty sneaky, Paige-Turner. And *not* safe. How 'bout some warm, spice tea?"

"That sounds great," Paige said.

Lola's large living room was in the center of her house and went from the front of her house to the back. On the left, next to the curio cabinet, was a door that led to Lola's dining room and kitchen. On the right was a door that went to Lola's bedroom and bathroom. Paige had never been through the door on the right, but she had spent time in the dining room and kitchen while Lola taught her how to adjust Glinda's level of senses without fully transforming. It was toward the left door Lola led Paige.

The dining room and kitchen were in stark contrast to her dark living room. The dining room was well lit and had contemporary furniture. White table and chairs and a white China cabinet filled with light, pink, China dishes, bowls, cups, serving platters, etcetera. Her kitchen was spacious, with white cabinets and pinkish granite countertops. Lola's appliances were brushed stainless steel and there was a small, white table with four white chairs under a window on the back side of her house.

Lola, with her arm still around Paige's cold shoulders, led Paige through the dining room into the kitchen. "Take a seat and I'll put the kettle on."

"Do you have a towel?" Paige asked.

"For what?" Lola asked.

"To put on the chair before I sit on it."

Lola laughed her warm honey laugh. "I don't care if ya leave a booty print on my chair, chil'."

"Ya sure?"

"I am. Have a seat and let Lola take care of you, chil'."

"Okay. If you're sure," Paige said as she pulled out one of the four chairs and sat down.

A couple of minutes later, Lola joined Paige at the small table with two cups of warm spice tea. Paige took the cup, blew into it, and took a small sip to see if it was too hot to drink. It was the perfect temperature. Mandy might be the Goldilocks of hot chocolate and bath water, but Lola was the Goldilocks of warm, spice tea.

Paige took a big gulp of the spicy liquid and felt her insides instantly warm. She thought Lola might have put a little more than regular tea in the kettle.

"What's with the stuff on your table?" Paige said. "Especially what looks like a rat skull?"

"Ingredients for a protection potion," Lola explained. "A protection potion for you and Glinda,"

"Protection potion from what?"

Lola shook her head slightly, which caused the pink and white beads on the ends of her cornrows to click together. "From the ancient vampire that roosts here, of course."

Paige laughed. "Glinda doesn't need protection. I bet she can bite his head off in one chomp."

Lola shook her head again, but more vigorously. "No, Paige. Glinda can't. Not without what the protection position can give y'all. Even then, it won't be easy. Ya see, you and Glinda are fearless and clever, but y'all lack wisdom. Evident by you bein' out vampire huntin' on your own tonight. Wisdom is what the potion will help y'all with."

"Are ya sayin' I'm stupid?" Paige said defensively. "*We're* stupid?"

Lola took hold of Paige's free hand, the one not holding her special brew of spice tea. "Of course not, Paige-Turner. But wisdom isn't the same thing as intelligence. True wisdom can *only* come with age, and you are very young. Especially compared to an ancient vampire's wisdom, like the one we're dealin' with here."

"Okay," Paige said, less defensively. "I still think Glinda can take him."

Lola smiled. "Not alone and not without the protection potion I'm makin' for y'all."

Paige thought about this for a moment. "Wait a sec. Is that rat skull goin' in the protection potion?"

"It is," Lola told her.

Paige's face crinkled up. "That's disgustin'. Uh-huh. No way am I drinkin' somethin' with a rat skull in it."

"The rest of the potion will taste so nasty that ya won't even notice the rat skull in it, chil'."

Sarcastically, Paige said, "Thanks for the pep talk, Lola."

Lola laughed and squeezed Paige's hand. "Glinda will probably like it."

"That's a relief. I thought I'd have to drink it."

"Sorry, Paige-Turner. You drink half, and Glinda drinks the other half. That's how the potion works."

"But-but, I *am* Glinda, and she *is* me," Paige stammered. "Why can't Glinda drink the whole thing?"

"Y'all are *parts* of each other," Lola said. "When you were learnin' how to control Glinda's input without transformin', I tol' ya you would never be all Glinda in human form and Glinda would never be all you when in werewolf form. That's why each of y'all must drink half. To protect the human you, and the werewolf Glinda. Each of y'all will have increased wisdom separate and apart from one another. You'll need the wisdom in case you encounter the vampire while you're in human form."

"Yeah. But I can transform into Glinda really quick," Paige argued.

"An ancient vampire can mesmerize you quicker than you can transform. He can mesmerize Glinda, too," Lola counter argued.

"He can?" Paige asked, dumfounded by what Lola said.

"Yes, chil'," Lola said. "You didn't know that and that's my point about wisdom. That, Paige-Turner, is why *both* of y'all must drink half of the potion."

Still dumbfounded, Paige said, "I thought nothin' could beat Glinda."

Lola smiled. "Thank ya for makin' my point...a*gain*. The ancient is not invincible and nether is Glinda. This potion will give y'all the wisdom to know these things."

Paige's mood brightened.

She smiled. "Will we be all knowin'? Will it help me in school?

Rat skull aside, this could be pretty cool."

"It doesn't work like that," Lola said. "It'll diminish slowly after we deal with the vampire. It'll take me three days to brew. So, no more vampire huntin' until after y'all drink it. I can't stress this enough, Paige-Turner. *Y'all* can't do it alone. Y'all *will* need help with this one. Understand?"

Paige nodded. "Doctor James told Daddy the same thing. He said we'll need Father Mike, too. Also, if Father Mike doesn't believe in the supernatural, I should show him Glinda."

Lola let out a loud smoky laugh. "I wanna be there when ya do. Oh, that'll be priceless to behold."

"Mandy thinks I'll be excommunicated from the Catholic faith if I show him Glinda," Paige said. "I think he can handle it."

Lola had dealt with many Catholic priests, on many issues, over her life. Some, especially the old-school priest, were very open to aspects of the supernatural, like demon possession and demonic mischief. Like James, who had never met Fr. Mike, but heard about him from Paige and Mandy, she too thought Fr. Mike a contemporary priest. She agreed with James that it would probably take showing him Glinda to convince him.

"Well...I think he might not take it well at first," Lola said. "Once he gets to know Glinda like we do, he'll see how pure she is. He'll see that there's no evil in your beautiful Glinda. And...I might help him see that, if needed."

Paige's eyes went wide, and she said, "You can put an incantation on a Catholic priest?"

"I have before," Lola said with a sly smile. "Many times, but I wouldn't call it an incantation. It's more like a nudge in the direction I need 'em to go. My point is, Father Mike *will* see Glinda's pureness one way or the other,"

Still awestruck, Paige said, "Will ya let me know if he accepts Glinda on his own or needs to be nudged?"

Lola smiled warmly. "I will. But here's what we're gonna do now. I'm gonna complete the potion, start it brewin', and then I'm gonna take you home."

"I can get home by myself," Paige said. "I mean, Glinda can get me home."

Lola's brow furrowed. "Have ya listened to nothin' I tol' you tonight? You and Glinda are *not* safe until the protection potion is brewed and you and Glinda have each drank half of it. Out of the question, chil'."

"Are ya gonna tell Daddy I snuck out tonight?" Paige asked.

"Not if ya let me take ya home tonight and promise not to sneak out *alone* at night again until *after* y'all drink the protection potion," Lola said.

"I promise," Paige lied.

Lola looked at Paige hard with her seeing eye. "I'm tellin' your daddy. He can lock you up in the county jail, if that's what it takes. Do you understand me, Paige-Turner?"

Paige felt foolish for thinking she could lie to Lola. Lola's seeing eye saw everything.

Defeated, Paige said, "Okay. I promise."

Lola looked hard at Paige again and relaxed.

"Satisfied?" Paige asked.

Lola smiled. "Very much. Now, do ya wanna help me make the potion?"

Astounded, Paige said, "Really? I can help?"

"Ya sure can. Come on."

Paige followed Lola back into the dark living room, adjusting Glinda's vision as she did, and then followed Lola's directions. Lola told Paige to empty a jar of something that looked like puss, but smelled like vinegar, into the cauldron. Then Lola told her to pour half of another jar into the cauldron. This liquid was amber, like whiskey, but smelled like wet grass. Lola had Paige put a pinch or dash of different herbs from clay pots into the brew, watching as she did to make sure the pinch or dash was just the right amount. While Paige followed these instructions, Lola ground the rat skull into a fine powder with the mortar and pestle. When Lola finished grinding, she poured the fine white powder into the cauldron. The potion was complete. It just needed to brew for three days before Paige and Glinda could drink it, and gain protection and wisdom from it.

Lola opened the drawer and took something from it. "Stand back a little, Paige-Turner."

Paige did and watched to see what Lola did next. Two things happened. First, Lola muttered something in a low voice. Paige dialed up Glinda's hearing to listen to what Lola said. Paige could clearly hear Lola, but she couldn't understand the words. It was a chant she repeated that sounded something like French, but not quite French. On the third chant, the cauldron floated from the table about a foot and turned slowly. Paige's jaw dropped open.

Then Lola changed the chant. It was still in what Paige considered *almost* French, and on the third chant, Lola tossed a green powder onto the dark tabletop. A green flame burst into life under the cauldron. The flame was so bright Paige had to look away. When she looked back, the flame had shrunk and licked at the bottom of the slowly turning cauldron.

"Won't that burn your table?" Paige asked.

"No. Conjured flames only heat what they're created to heat. Here, the cauldron containin' the protection potion of wisdom."

Paige walked closer. She could feel no heat from the magical green flame, but the potion was already bubbling.

"In case you're wonderin', that'll reduce over the next three days," Lola said. "What you and Glinda end up drinkin' will be about a shot glass of it each."

Paige smiled. "That's a relief. I thought we'd have to drink all of that."

"Nope. Just the *essence* of what it started out as. Now, let's get ya home. Ya want a coat, Paige-Tuner?"

Paige laughed. "You worried 'bout my booty print on your pink Cadillac seats?"

"Nope. Just thought ya might get cold."

"I like the cold, and I hate wearin' clothes," Paige said. "Daddy and Al don't understand. Did ya know Al complained to Daddy 'bout me bein' naked and Daddy had a talk with me 'bout wearin' clothes around Mom's house? They just don't understand that naked is natural."

Lola laughed. "I prefer naked, too. A lot of my coven's rituals are performed while we're naked, but nobody wants to see an old witch like me naked anymore."

Baffled, Paige said, "Are you kiddin' me? You're beautiful, Lola."

Lola smiled, but there was no genuine joy behind it. "You're sweet to say that, but you're not seein' the real me."

Confused, Paige said, "I'm not?"

Lola held up her right hand and showed Paige the ring on her middle finger. Paige saw it before. It was gold and the stone in the setting looked identical to Lola's seeing eye.

"If I remove this ring, as all seein' witches do while performin' our rituals, you'd see my true self," Lola explained.

"May I see your true self?" Paige asked quietly.

Lola, nor any of her seeing sisters, had ever revealed their true selves to anyone outside their coven. From the onset of puberty, they are given a ring that matched their seeing eye and the ring slowed the appearance of aging, because seers live long lives and need to blend in with the surrounding people. Removing the ring had only been done while they performed their nature rituals. On that point, Paige was right. Naked was natural. As far as Lola knew, there was no code against a seer revealing their true self to a non-seer. It just wasn't done. James Huff only knew her true age because she told him, not shown him. Since Lola knew Paige's transformation secret, she decided to show her.

"You may," Lola said as she slipped the ring from her finger.

The transformation wasn't sudden, like when Paige transformed into Glinda. Paige watched Lola age. It took almost a minute for Lola to age completely. When she had, Paige looked at a much older version of Lola; older than any of her grandparents.

Lola's dreadlocks were gray, her face wrinkled, and her cheeks sagged a little. She had a slight turkey neck, too. The most noticeable difference was her breasts that sagged halfway down her abdomen. Lola was smaller and darker, too. By Paige's estimation, Lola looked to be close to eighty years old.

Paige smiled a warm, genuine smile. "Oh, Lola. You're still beautiful."

Lola knew instantly Paige was being truthful. She opened her somewhat, sagging arms, and Paige embraced her.

Lola hugged her back and in an older sounding voice that had lost most of its warm honey sound, said, "You're sweet enough to eat, Paige-

Turner. Ya truly are."

It wasn't until the hugging stopped that Paige saw the tears on Lola's wrinkled cheeks.

Lola wiped her cheeks and pointed at Paige's breasts. "Enjoy those before gravity gets ahold of 'em. Mine look like worn out, empty saddlebags now."

Paige laughed. "I will. And yours don't look like that."

Lola smiled. "Thank you, sweet girl. I'm gonna put my ring back on now."

When Lola did, Paige watched the reverse transformation take place. It took about the same time for Lola to grow young again. Paige's gaze fixated on Lola's breasts. It was amazing to watch them shorten and grow plump again.

After the transformation was complete, Lola cupped her breasts. "I got my perky girls back."

Upon hearing this, Paige fell into a fit of laughter. Doubled over fit of laughter. After everything that happened that day, she needed it. Lola laughed, too.

With a final laugh, Lola said, "C'mon. Let's get ya home. They might not sleep as well after they have sex as ya think."

Paige crinkled her nose. "Gross. I said, 'you know' earlier specifically to *avoid* sayin' that."

Lola grinned. "I know ya did. That's *why* I said it."

Paige gave Lola a cross look. "You can be a mean witch sometimes, Lola Laveau."

"Sex is a natural as bein' naked, Paige-Turner," Lola teased.

"Not when it's your daddy and his girlfriend havin' it," Paige insisted.

"Oh, I bet your daddy makes Mandy feel *really* good when they're havin' sex," Lola continued to tease.

Paige clamped her hands over her ears and loudly said, "I'm not listenin'. La, la, la, la, la."

Lola laughed and opened the door. Paige walked outside with her hands still covering her ears, and keeping up her "La, la, la." chant. Lola had had her fun and didn't bring up the topic again. Paige knew Lola had stopped teasing her, but she kept up the act until they got to Lola's 1956, pink Cadillac. When Paige sat on the cold, vinyl seat, she almost wished she'd taken the coat when offered. But her booty warmed the seat quickly and the Cadillac's heater was quick to warm the inside of the car. Lola took Paige home.

~ * ~

Dragoş had his large wings spread wide as he glided high above Pine View County, taking mental directions to the father of Paige's house from his fledgling. The sky was clear and the moon, only one night removed from full, lit up the landscape a beautiful shade of silver. Of course, Dragoş didn't need the moon to see, and he wasn't concerned anyone would see him and his fledgling. He had cloaked them in invisibility.

During the journey, Dragoş saw a strange site. A man sat high in a tree looking out over the same silvery landscape. Had he and the fledgling not just fed on the man the fledgling called Al, Dragoş would have paid the man in the tree a visit. But he was full and eager to add Paige to his cloud, so he flew on.

Not long after flying over the man in the tree, the fledgling pointed and thought, *There's her dad's house.*

Dragoş didn't need the point. He knew their destination as soon as the fledgling saw it. He folded his large wings back and descended quickly but two things stopped him from landing. Not that he was frightened, nothing frightened Dragoş Văduva, but he was interested. First, there was a car on the road next to his destination. That wasn't interesting. What happened next was unexpected. The car's headlights went out, and it turned into the driveway of their destination. Dragoş unfolded his wings, slowly flapped them to decrease their descent, and hovered about fifty feet above where the pink car stopped, secure he and the fledgling would be unnoticed and unheard.

As Dragoş watched, the passenger door of the pink car opened, and a naked girl stepped out.

The fledgling whispered, "That's Paige, Master."

Dragoş didn't need this information from the fledgling either. He had clearly seen Paige in the fledging's blood memory, and what a sight she was. Perfect in her young flesh. Dragoş' long tongue snaked out, and he licked his bright, red lips. He couldn't wait to taste Paige. He couldn't wait to enjoy her flesh.

Whoever drove the car was of no concern to Dragoş. He would let the fledgling dispatch the driver while he fed on Paige, felt of her youthful, naked flesh, and then turn her. She would be the prize of his cloud. Just as Dragoş began to drop from the sky and carry out his unholy plans, a woman stepped out of the driver's side door.

Dragoş took one look at the woman who looked at him, flapped his wings hard enough to propel himself and the fledgling two hundred feet higher into the air, and hissed, *"Vrăjitoare."*

Melanie didn't speak Romanian, but she understood everything her Master said in any language he spoke. He had hissed, "Witch."

~ * ~

As soon as Lola stepped out of her 56, pink Cadillac, she sensed the ancient's evil presence. She looked up and with her seeing eye saw him in his bat-like form, with Melanie in his arms, hovering about fifty feet above them.

"Where's your cross?" Lola shouted at Paige.

Surprised by Lola's sudden outburst, Paige said, "On my windowsill."

"Put in on now. Hurry." Lola shouted.

Because she had felt safe riding home with Lola, Paige had Glinda's input dialed as low as it would go while in human form. As she rushed to her crucifix, she dialed Glinda's input to as high as it would go without bringing on the transformation. The ancient's rotting stench overwhelmed her, and she almost stumbled from the strength of it, but she made it to her silver crucifix. Paige grabbed it and quickly clasped it around her neck.

~ * ~

Dragoş watched all of this happen from where he hovered high above the witch and his prize. He had dealt with *vrăjitoare* many times over his eight hundred undead years. He had even formed alliances with those who practiced the dark powers occasionally, but this one did not practice the dark powers. She was an elemental *vrăjitoare* and a powerful one to so easily see through his cloaking incantation. And his prize was a true believer who had put on a silver crucifix. Alone, Dragoş could have taken one of them easily. Together, he could not. His fledgling would be no match for the powerful *vrăjitoare*, which would not allow him to collect Paige for his cloud. With the *vrăjitoare's* help, he could not place either in a trance.

Frustrated by being so close to the perfection that was Paige, but powerless to have her, Dragoş flapped his powerful wings and disappeared into the night. He would have Paige in his cloud, and he would enjoy her young flesh in many degrading ways. But he would have to wait. At over eight-hundred years of age, Dragoş was good at waiting.

~ * ~

Lola watched the vile, ancient creature fly quickly away, and her heart ached. Whether it was there because it knew Paige was the werewolf it sought as a familiar, or because it simply wanted her in its cloud, made no difference. What mattered was it wanted Paige. With Melanie's help, it knew where to find Paige. And the protection potion wouldn't be ready for another three days.

Paige still stood beside her bedroom window, wearing nothing but the silver cross. The ancient's scent was getting farther away with each breath she took, and so was Melanie's newer death smell. Even with Glinda's senses at full capacity in her human form, Paige couldn't see either of them before they left. She even followed Lola's gaze upward but saw nothing.

Lola came up to Paige. "Go inside and put somethin' on, Paige. We have to wake up your daddy."

"You promised ya wouldn't tell him," Paige whined.

Lola took Paige's face in her hands and forced Paige to look her in the face. "We're beyond that now. Don't ya get it, chil'?"

Confused, Paige said, "Get what?"

"That...thing was here for *you*."

"Me? Why me?"

"Go get dressed," Lola said with sadness in her warm, honey voice. "It's time ya know the truth,"

Chapter Seven

Paige climbed inside her bedroom and got dressed slowly in the clothes she'd left behind before sneaking out. She was buying time while Lola waited outside. The thought of her daddy finding out she'd snuck out again made her stomach hurt. She knew he'd be mad and probably ground her. More than once, while getting dressed, she pleaded with Lola to not tell her daddy, but Lola held fast to telling him the truth. Lola said it was important he knew everything, and she knew everything, too. Paige thought she already knew everything but resigned herself to the lecture and grounding surely to follow.

Once dressed, Paige said, "Do ya wanna come in through my window or should I go open the front door for ya?"

Lola smiled. "I think I'll come in through your window. It's been a long time since I was a young seer sneakin' out and gettin' into all kinds of mischief."

As Lola was climbing through the window, Paige said, "You used to sneak out, too?"

Once inside Paige's cozy bedroom, Lola said, "Of course I did, chil'. All youngin's push the limits of their folks' authority."

"Did ya ever get caught?" Paige asked.

Lola laughed. "All the time. My mamma was a seer too. I bet she knew *before* I snuck out and let me just to tan my hide when I got back."

Confused, Paige said, "And ya still did it?"

Lola nodded. "Yep. Just like you."

Paige blushed. After the night at the MRB, the first time she'd ever snuck out, she'd done it plenty of times since. Of course, she had the reverse of Lola's problem. She could tell when it was safe and hadn't gotten caught once. Until that night.

"Now," Lola said, "are you gonna wake your daddy and Mandy, or shall I have the honor."

Dejected, Paige said, "I'll do it."

"Okay, then," Lola said. "Best get to it."

Paige began to open her bedroom door, but she paused. "By the way, how old are you?"

"I'm seventy-eight years old. Now get your perky tits movin' or I'll go wake 'em up myself."

Despite the predicament she was in, Paige smiled. "Follow me."

They made their way through the dark living room to her daddy's bedroom door. Paige hesitated a moment, gathered her nerves, and then knocked, hard, on the door three times.

From behind the door, Garrett's sleepy voice said, "Paige? Is everything okay?"

"Everything's okay, Daddy. Miss Lola's here, though."

Sounding more awake, Garrett said, "Lola's here? At this hour?"

"Yes, Garrett," Lola said to help clear his head. "I'm here. You, Mandy, Paige, and I need to talk,"

"Okay," Garrett said, sounding fully awake. "We'll be right out. Just need a sec to…get ready,"

Lola grinned at Paige and whispered, "He means they need to get dressed. They're naked after all that pleasurin' they gave each other earlier."

"You're bein' a mean witch again, Miss Lola," Paige said.

Lola laughed quietly as Paige went to turn on the living room light. After the light was on, Paige took a seat on the sofa and Lola sat down next to her.

Lola took Paige's hand in hers and gave it a gentle squeeze. "It'll be okay, Paige-Turner. I'll make sure he doesn't get too mad."

Her spirits lifted and Paige smiled. "Really?"

"Really," Lola assured her. "I promised you I wouldn't tell if ya promised not to sneak out again until *after* the protection potion was ready. You were truthful the *second* time ya answered. It's not your fault that vile creature found ya so quickly. I will ease your daddy and Mandy's anger."

A moment later, Garrett and Mandy came out of the bedroom. Garrett wore the same old T-shirt and gray sweatpants he'd been wearing on Christmas morning and Mandy wore the same blue robe she'd been wearing. That was less than twenty-four hours ago, but it seemed like an eternity to all of them.

Mandy took a seat on the sofa with Paige and Lola, and Garrett plopped down in his comfortable recliner.

When everyone was in place, Garrett, fully awake but with tussled hair, said, "What's goin' on?"

"Paige has somethin' to tell y'all," Lola said.

Nervously, Paige said, "I…um, snuck out tonight to hunt for the vampire."

Garrett and Mandy reacted simultaneously.

Garrett sat bolt upright in the recliner. "What the hell, Paige?"

Mandy looked cross with her and said, "What were ya thinkin'?"

Paige felt Lola's hand lightly squeeze hers and then she felt something radiate from Lola. She didn't know what the something was, but its affect was immediate. Her daddy and Mandy's facial expressions softened, the anger and concern melted away. Her daddy even leaned back in the recliner. While Paige didn't know exactly what Lola had done, she assumed she'd just witnessed one of Lola's nudges.

When everyone had calmed down, Lola said, "What all did James have to say about *this* vampire, Garrett?"

"A lot," Garrett replied.

"Not about vampires. About *this* vampire," Lola clarified. "Does he have a theory why an ancient vampire would come to roost in East Texas now?"

Garrett looked from Lola to Mandy to Paige back to Lola. "He has three theories."

"What are they?" Lola asked in her warm, honey voice.

"First, he thinks it might be here for the challenge of killin' Glinda," Garrett said. "Second, he thinks it might be here to create a hybrid vampire-werewolf. Finally, he thinks it might be here to make Glinda its familiar."

Paige listened closely and realized her daddy had purposefully left this information out of their earlier conversation about what Dr. James had told him. She understood, and the first two theories horrified her. The third theory wasn't something she was familiar with, though.

When her daddy finished, Paige asked, "What's a familiar?"

"I'll explain it in a bit," Lola told Paige.

Then, to Garrett and Mandy, Lola said, "I summoned three sisters from my coven earlier tonight and convened with 'em for advice 'bout why an ancient is here and how to deal with it. My coven comprises thirteen elemental, seein' witches, and each has their strengths. Given our situation, and what we already know about Glinda, the sisters I summoned have strengths in fearlessness, cleverness, and wisdom.

"Mamma Deupree, from Haiti, is the oldest witch in my coven and has the most wisdom," Lola explained. "Angelica Freemont, from Jamaica, is one of the youngest witches in my coven and is the most fearless. Rosa Garza, from Cuba, is a little older than me and is the cleverest of my coven."

"Sorry to interrupt," Mandy said. "If all of y'all are in different countries, how did y'all convene?"

"Their spectral forms convened in my home while their bodies remained in their foreign homes," Lola explained.

"Right," Mandy said, very impressed with what she was learning of Lola's powers.

"Anyway," Lola smiled and continued, "Mamma is convinced that the ancient is here to make Glinda his familiar. A werewolf familiar would be quite the prize for an ancient vampire. Unfortunately, this means he would have Paige in human form to…play with, too."

Frustrated, because everyone except her seemed to know what a familiar was, Paige said, "What the heck's a familiar?"

Lola squeezed Paige's hand a little harder. "A familiar is a vampire's slave. They protect the vampire durin' the day while it's restin' and get 'em things they need, like victims and coffins for new members of their cloud. Basically, anything the vampire needs, the familiar complies. They have no will of their own."

"Glinda would never be a vampire's slave," Paige insisted.

"Remember when I tol' ya a vampire can mesmerize you or Glinda?" Lola asked.

Paige nodded.

"Once you are mesmerized, all the vampire would have to do is feed ya its black blood, and you'd be its slave for as long as it wanted ya,"

Lola explained.

"That can't happen." Mandy shouted.

"It won't," Lola said. "My sisters and I agree that Paige and Glinda are naturally fearless and clever, but wisdom, *true* wisdom, can only come with age. This is Paige and Glinda's only weakness against an ancient, who will have gained much wisdom over its long life. Mamma has generously given me some of her wisdom to include in a protection potion that I have already started brewin'."

"I helped put the ingredients in the potion," Paige said proudly. "It has a ground up rat skull in it, too."

"A ground up what?" Mandy asked with a sour look on her face.

"The rat skull was a gift from Mamma's neckless and contains the wisdom portion of the potion," Lola said.

"I'm confused." Mandy said. "If they visited your house in spectral form, how did Mamma give ya the rat skull?"

"She plucked it from her neckless, placed it on my table, and it materialized," Lola said with a wink. "We're witches, Mandy. We can do all kinds of cool things."

Mandy went from being impressed with Lola's powers to outright awe.

Garrett finally engaged in the conversation. "You told us what the other witch's strengths were. What's yours, Lola?"

Lola smiled a smile that lit up the room. "Why, I'm the prettiest, of course."

None of them doubted that.

Without denying her previous statement, which was true, Lola said, "My strength is healin'. Y'all must understand that all witches, elemental witches, have the same powers. It's just that strengths emerge as we age. No different than humans, who have strengths in the sciences or mathematics or arts. Although all members of my coven are seers, not all witches are seers. This is a special gift that some of us are born with. Other witches are not born with the gift of sight, but they are powerful in their own way. Unfortunately, there are witches who practice dark powers. They are in league with the dark one. What y'all call Satan or Lucifer."

"Are the witches who practice dark magic dangerous?" Mandy

asked.

"Very," Lola said. "But they are not our concern...now. The protection potion Paige and I started this evenin' will take three days to complete. Until that time, she is in great danger."

"See," Garrett said. "This is why ya can't sneak out at night, Paige-Turner. Don't think I forgot about that."

"Actually," Lola said, "it's a *good* thing she snuck out tonight."

"Why? To help ya with the potion," Garrett said sarcastically.

"No," Lola calmly retorted. "Not to help with the potion. It's a good thing she snuck out tonight because the ancient was here when I brought her home."

Shocked, Garrett said, "He was here?"

Mandy let out an audible gasp.

"Yes," Lola told Garrett and Mandy. "When I got outta my car, I sensed him immediately. I looked up, and there he was hoverin' about fifty feet above your driveway. The ancient and Mel. He was in the form of a large bat and had cloaked himself and Mel in invisibility, but he couldn't cloak himself from my seein' eye. That I could see him startled him and he flew off. Vampires don't like elemental witches."

"Holy fu... shit," Garrett shouted. "Does that mean he's already figured out that Paige is Glinda?"

Despite the seriousness, Paige had to suppress a giggle at her daddy, almost dropping the F-bomb.

"I don't believe he knows Paige is Glinda," Lola said. "It's a well-guarded secret. He couldn't have found out this soon. Had Paige *not* snuck out, he would've caught y'all off guard, though. You and Mandy would likely be dead, and he *would* know Paige is the werewolf he seeks."

"How would he know?" Garrett asked.

"Her blood," Lola said. "Vampires despise the taste of werewolf blood. The instant he tasted Paige, he would've known she was a werewolf. Then, instead of turnin' her, he would've fed her some of his vile blood and he'd have his werewolf familiar. Game over."

"Then what *would* bring him here?" Mandy asked.

"This ancient has an eye for young, pretty girls," Lola said. "I think he came here to make Paige part of his cloud."

"How would he even know to look for her here?" Garrett asked.

"Mel's blood memory," Lola said.

"Come again?" Garrett asked.

"James didn't tell ya 'bout blood memory?" Lol said.

Garrett shook his head.

Lola smiled. "I'll have to educate our learned friend on this. When vampires feed, they absorb memories from their victims. We call this blood memory. When he drank from Mel, he fed on her memories as well. Paige and Mel were friends. Paige was one of the last people Mel saw before he took her. If I'm correct, Mel was at the MRB the night the werewolves attacked."

Paige nodded. "Mel was there that night."

"Paige is young and beautiful," Lola said. "It stands to reason she would attract his attention."

"Then, she's not safe," Garrett said.

"Not here or at her mom's house," Lola said. "That's why I must insist Paige stay with me until the potion is ready."

"Oh. That'll be fun," Paige said. "I won't even have to wear clothes."

"Yeah," Garrett said. "That's a good idea, but you're packin' clothes. Whether ya wear 'em is between you and Lola. But you're packin' some damn clothes, Paige."

"I'll pack some clothes," Paige said as she got up to go to her bedroom.

Paige only took two steps before what Lola had said about her not being safe at her mom's house either sunk in.

"If he came here, he probably went to Mom's house, too," Paige said.

As soon as Paige said this, Garrett's cell rang. It was Lacy.

~ * ~

Lacy returned home from her parent's house a little before eleven o'clock Christmas night to find the front door open. She entered cautiously and called out for Al. He did not respond. She ventured into the living room and saw Al's soup, pillow and comforter on the couch, Vicks, tissues, and bourbon on the coffee table, and the menu screen for *Lethal Weapon*, the movie had un-paused and reset on the menu, on the TV screen.

She called out his name again. Again, there was no response. Frightened, because Al wasn't exactly healthy, not that he had any known medical issues, but since he was middle-age and slightly overweight, Lacy ran upstairs to check their bedroom. It was empty and undisturbed. She checked the bathroom. It had also been empty. Really frightened, she called out Al's name several times as she quickly checked the rest of the house. Al did not respond, and the house was empty. With shaking hands, she took out her cellphone and called Garrett.

~ * ~

Before her daddy could answer the call, which he did quickly, Paige dialed Glinda's hearing up to where she began to transform. Quickly, before her clothes shredded, Paige adjusted Glinda's input slightly down and saved what would have been for her daddy the embarrassment of ending up naked in the living room while he talked to her mom.

Garrett answered on the first ring. "What's wrong?"

"Al's missin'," Lacy screamed.

Neither Lola nor Mandy needed Glinda's enhanced hearing to hear Lacy's scream. It was so loud Garrett had to hold the phone away from his ear.

Garrett put the phone back to his ear and, calmly, said, "Tell me what happened."

Lacy took several deep breaths, Paige and her daddy could hear these, Lola and Mandy could not, and Lacy gathered her wits as best she could. "Al has a cold. Ya know how Mom is about germs these days. So, he stayed home while I went to our traditional Christmas evenin' celebration. When I got home, the front door was open, and Al was gone. I've looked everywhere for him, Garrett. He's not here.

"It's just a cold," Lacy said defending her decision to leave Al home. "It's not like he had a high fever and wondered off in some fever-induced stupor. I never would've left him alone if he'd been that sick."

"I know ya wouldn't have done that, Lacy," Garrett said. "Did ya shut the front door?"

"No."

"Shut it now and don't open it for anyone but me," Garret told her. "Not anyone else. Understand?"

Lacy cried. "I understand. Please come quick."

"I'm on my way," Garrett said before ending the call.

"I can help her," Lola said.

"Yeah," Garrett said. "That'd be great, Lola. Paige, pack your clothes and essentials quickly while Mandy and I get dressed. I'm not leavin' ya here alone, Mandy."

"I wasn't *stayin'* here alone," Mandy clarified.

Garrett and Mandy started for their bedroom, but Paige stopped them in their tracks when she said, "I think it's time Mom knows about Glinda."

Garrett shook his head. "No way. The fewer people who know about this, the better."

"I think Paige is right," Lola said.

"What if she freaks the fu…hell out?" Garrett replied.

"I can nudge Lacy into seein' Glinda for what she is," Lola said.

"Yeah," Paige said. "Lola's gonna nudge Father Mike, too. But only if he needs it."

"You can put an incantation on a Catholic priest?" Mandy asked, somewhat appalled.

"Yes," Lola said. "But this is a nudge, not an incantation."

When the idea of what a nudge might be hit Garrett, he said, "Have ya ever nudged me, Lola?"

"Only once," Lola calmly replied.

"When?" Garrett asked with a hint of anger in his voice.

"Just now when Paige tol' y'all she snuck out tonight to hunt for the vampire."

"You nudged me, too," Mandy said. "That's why my anger and concern, when I heard Paige snuck out tonight, just…melted away."

Lola nodded.

Angered, Garrett said, "You had *no* right to alter our emotions like that."

"I *had* to alter *both* of your emotions," Lola said. "Had I not, your anger and concern would've interfered with the importance of what Paige and I had to tell y'all 'bout the ancient bein' here and what had to be done. Do *not* deny this, Garrett. Nor you, Mandy."

Paige watched this play out with fascination. She thought the nudge was to get her out of trouble. She could see the bigger picture once Lola had explained it. Paige saw something else, too. After Lola finished explaining why she nudged them, her daddy and Mandy's anger subsided. She knew it was real because she'd felt the something that was the nudge before but hadn't felt it then.

More calmly, Garrett said, "Okay. I get it. But promise me ya won't nudge me again."

"Or me," Mandy added.

"I promise on the Elements that I will never nudge either of you again, unless y'all need it," Lola said. "I can't make that promise where Lacy or Father Mike are concerned, though. You're right 'bout keepin' the people who know 'bout Glinda small, Garrett. Aside from an incantation to make 'em completely forget about Glinda, a nudge is the only way to keep Glinda a secret. Up 'til now, no one who knows 'bout Glinda, aside from James whose integrity is beyond reproach and doesn't need a nudge, and has had a personal stake in Glinda's existence. Lacy and Father Mike do not. I will *not*, for Paige and Glinda's protection, hesitate, for a single second, to nudge either of 'em, if needed. Are we in agreement on this?"

Garrett and Mandy nodded, but not like the Zane's hypnotic nods. Theirs were free will nods of understanding.

Satisfied, Lola said, "Good. Then we should go to Lacy immediately."

After Garrett and Mandy were in their room, Paige said, "I don't have to wear clothes at your house, do I?"

Lola smiled warmly. "Of course not. For your daddy's sake, pack 'em anyway."

Paige smiled back and then retreated to her room, where she threw some clothes in her backpack. Then she got her toothbrush, toothpaste, she didn't know if witches needed to brush their teeth, and deodorant from her bathroom. She was back in the living room a moment before her daddy and Mandy came out of their bedroom dressed and ready to go.

"Paige, you ride with Lola. Mandy will ride with me," Garrett instructed.

Everyone agreed. A minute later, they pulled out of Garrett's driveway on their way to what had been Al and Lacy's house. Lacy had become the sole owner of the house, though. She just didn't know it yet.

~ * ~

Lacy had shut and locked the front door as soon as the call with Garrett ended. Then she checked the other doors and all the windows. She was locked in, and nervous, concerned, and scared. To calm her nerves, she downed the bourbon Al had on the coffee table. It didn't help. She sat on the sofa for several minutes and then paced between the front door and living room and wondered what took Garrett so long to get there.

After what seemed like an eternity, but was less than thirty minutes, there was a hard knock on the front door. Lacy jumped and let out a startled yelp. She took a second or two to regain her composure and then hurried to the front door.

"Is that you, Garrett?" Lacy asked nervously.

"It's me, Lacy," Garrett said. "And I've brought some people with me."

Without unlocking the door, Lacy said, "Are they deputies?"

"No. I brought Paige, Mandy, and someone ya haven't met," Garrett said. "Her name is Lola, and she's here to help you."

"Why is *she* here?" Lacy almost hissed.

The 'she' Lacy referenced was Mandy. Even though Garrett had moved on and wasn't particularly fond of Lacy's second and third husbands, he was pleasant with all of them, especially her fourth husband Al, who he genuinely liked. Lacy had never extended the same courtesy to Mandy, though.

"For the same reason Al's missin'," Garrett said. "She's not safe at home alone. Now, let us in."

Lacy unlocked the deadbolt, opened the door, and saw Garrett, *her*, Paige, and a beautiful African American woman standing outside under the porch light.

Somewhat reluctantly, Lacy said, "Come on in."

Lacy led them to the living room where the four women sat on the sofa, Mandy and Lacy on each end with Paige next to her mom and Lola next to Mandy. Garrett grabbed a dining room chair on his way past the dining room table, placed it on the other side of the coffee table directly in front of the three women and his little girl. He still couldn't bring himself to think of Paige as a woman, or even a young woman, and sat down.

To say the atmosphere was uncomfortable would be an understatement. Aside from the irrational hatred Lacy had for Mandy, Al was missing and everyone, except Lacy, knew why. They, except for Lacy, had also known Al was dead. Lacy had a tissue in her hand. Paige, who had just registered the ugly truth of it all, cried and grabbed a tissue, too.

Lacy saw Paige grab a tissue, start crying, and even though she didn't quite believe it herself, said, "It's okay, sweetheart. Your daddy'll find Al. He probably had too much bourbon and cold medicine and wondered off."

Paige wiped her tears. "That's not what happened, Mom. I smelled the ancient and Mel as soon as we turned onto your street. They were here, and they took Al 'cause I *wasn't* here."

Confused, Lacy said, "Smelled what and who? Who was here? Why were they lookin' for you? Why would they take Al?"

"Al's dead, Mommy," Paige blurted out and then broke into hard, deep sobs.

Lola took Paige's hand gently in hers, but she didn't take any of her grief. It wasn't because Lola had already taken in so much grief that day already. Lola loved Paige as she would her own daughter and she'd take on the world's grief to help her. Lola knew what people instinctively know, even when experiencing profound grief, that grief is needed. Grief is soul cleansing. It's needed after a significant loss. Grief is needed for the one lost. It's needed to move on. The Zanes and Hendersons had been grieving for hours before Lola helped them. She would help Paige if, or when, she needed it. But not then.

Garrett's heart broke for Paige at that moment. She always called him Daddy, but he hadn't heard her call Lacy mommy since she was a little girl. Not unless she was joking around or trying to garner sympathy from Lacy to get her way. Garrett knew Paige loved Al, but it wasn't until that moment he realized just how much she loved him. Worse, he was powerless to help her.

"No, sweetheart. We *don't* know that. Tell her, Garrett," Lacy pleaded. "Tell her we'll find Al and that he's okay."

Garrett took a deep breath. "I can't tell her that, Lacy. If anyone here knows the truth of what's happened to Al, it's Paige."

"I-I-I, I don't understand," Lacy stammered. "How can Paige *know* that? Who are these people she's talkin' 'bout?"

Garrett leaned forward in the chair. "We need to tell ya some things that are gonna sound impossible to believe. *Crazy* to believe. It's all true, though. Understand?"

"No. I don't understand," Lacy shouted. "Call some deputies and go *find* Al."

Garrett took the ripping the Band-Aid off quickly approach to filling Lacy in and blurted out, "I'm sorry, Lacy, but Al's gone. He's dead. The ancient Paige said she smelled when we got here is a vampire. The Mel she smelled is Melanie Zane, who went missin' this mornin'. The ancient vampire *turned* Melanie into a vampire last night, and they came *here* lookin' for Paige.

"They took Al and killed him after drinkin' his blood. Then they came to *my* house lookin' for Paige," Garrett quickly continued. "Luckily, Lola was there and scared 'em off. If she hadn't been there, Mandy and I'd be dead, and Paige would be his familiar. If ya hadn't been with your folks tonight, when they came lookin' for Paige here, *you'd* be dead, too. We know all of this because Lola is a *witch* and Paige is a *werewolf*."

Lacy sat, slack-jawed, looking at Garrett as if he'd lost his mind. Then she looked at Paige, who was still sobbing, and the beautiful African American woman, who she decided must be the Lola Garrett spoke of.

She looked back at Garrett and blinked a few times as if seeing him for the first time in her life. "Are you outta your fuckin' mind? What kind of bullshit is this? Is it that ya just don't wanna go lookin' for Al, so ya concocted this fuckin'…fairytale to get out of it? And you bring Paige into it with some ridiculous shit 'bout her bein' a fuckin' werewolf. I want all of y'all, except Paige, outta my fuckin' house. You're all fuckin' crazy. I'm callin' the Pine View Police Department, which I should'a done in the first place. *Get the fuck out.*"

Garrett shook his head slowly. "I was hopin' it wouldn't come to this. Show her, Paige."

When Paige stood, Garrett turned around. He still wasn't comfortable seeing Paige naked and probably never would be, or so he thought.

"I'm sorry, Mom," Paige sniffed as she undressed.

"Why are ya takin' your clothes off, Paige?" Lacy asked.

"You'll see," Paige said.

Lacy sat there, unable to think of anything else to say, as Paige slipped her panties off. An instant later, Lacy saw Glinda for the first time. She screamed in horror.

Knowing, from the scream, it was safe to turn around, Garrett did. Lacy's living room had vaulted ceilings, so, unlike at his house where Glinda had to stoop under his eight-foot-high ceiling, Paige's nine-foot-tall werewolf, Glinda, towered over the three women on the sofa. Mandy and Lola, who were used to seeing Glinda, sat calmly. Lacy screamed and tried, unsuccessfully, to crawdad walk up and over the back of the couch, but the sofa back cushions weren't attached to the sofa back, so they just kept compressing down under the weight of her hands, which hindered her escape.

Lola caught Garrett's attention, and he nodded. Instead of a nudge, which would come later, Lola took one of Lacy's hands in hers, absorbing as much fear as she could from Lacy, and Lacy immediately sank back onto the sofa; still slightly afraid, but calm.

"It's *not* bullshit, Lacy," Garrett said. "This *is* Paige. She *is* a werewolf. An ancient vampire *is* lookin' for her. An*yone*, like Al, who he encounters while lookin' for her, he *will* kill."

"How-how?" Lacy asked in a trance-like voice. "How did this

happen to Paige?"

"It happened last summer when those kids were killed at the MRB," Garrett explained.

"Are ya sayin' a werewolf killed those kids?" Lacy asked.

"Werewolves," Garrett clarified. "There were three of 'em. The alpha bit Paige and...infected her. Two others were bitten and infected, too. But..."

"Who? Who else was infected?" Lacy interrupted.

"That's not important," Garrett said. "The important thing is, Glinda, that's the name Paige gave her wolf, after killin' the alpha's creator. This should'a lifted the curse. It did for the other two. Because there's an ancestral werewolf on my side of the family, the..."

"Ancestral what?" Lacy interrupted again.

"That's not important now either," Garrett continued with a dismissive hand wave. "I'll tell ya all the details later. Stop interruptin' me. Anyway, because of the ancestral werewolf, the curse wasn't lifted from Paige. But it's not a curse for Paige. It's a gift. She's nothin' like the werewolves that were killin' people. Glinda is good to her soul. Pure goodness. No evil in her at all. That's how she smelled the ancient and Melanie. All her senses are enhanced. Hell, she's like a superhero. Like Spider-Man, but instead of bein' bitten by a radioactive spider, a werewolf bit Paige to give her supernatural powers."

Lacy looked from Garrett to Glinda to Garrett again. "How can that...*thing* not be evil. How can it be my Paige?"

Garrett nodded to Lola and Lola nudged Lacy hard. No one, except Glinda, felt the nudge. Not even Lacy, who Lola directed it to. Its effect was immediate. All the tension drained from Lacy.

Lacy smiled. "You are my little girl, aren't you?"

Glinda nodded her enormous head and, without warning her daddy, transformed back into Paige and wrapped her mom in a big hug. Lacy hugged back with happy tears in her eyes and rained kisses on Paige's beautiful face.

Beautiful moment or not, Garrett turned away quickly. "Damn it, Paige. Do ya even care about our understandin'?"

"Not right now, Daddy," Paige said.

"Get over it already, Garrett," Mandy said.

Then things went a little south and naked Paige or not, Garrett tried to fend off one of Lacy's irrational attacks on Mandy.

"Wait, a second," Lacy spat. "Did *she* know 'bout Paige and Glinda before I did? Before her own mother knew?"

"Yes. But…" Garrett began.

"I can't believe ya let *her* know before I knew." Lacy shouted.

Garrett turned around to confront Lacy. "Get dressed, Paige. Mandy knew because the alpha that infected Paige knew about Mandy, and she was in danger. This is *when* Mandy moved in with me and *why* she moved in with me."

Paige moved away from her feuding parents and got dressed quickly.

Mandy looked like she wanted to say something, but she didn't.

Lola looked amused by the whole situation.

"And *she* stayed," Lacy shouted.

Mandy had heard enough.

She held up her left hand and pointed at the engagement ring. "I stayed 'cause we're gettin' married. Get over it already, Lacy."

Garrett looked at the amused Lola, while Lacy and Mandy were still arguing. "A little help would be nice, Lola."

Lola smiled. "Well, I promised not to nudge Mandy again, unless needed."

"Then nudge Lacy again," Garrett said. "She's the one bein' irrational."

"Sounds like they're both a little, no, a lot, Garrett crazy right now," Lola teased. "Ya sure you're not enjoyin' them cat-fightin' over you?"

Paige laughed at this, which caused Garrett to turn her way. It was safe. Paige had her sweatpants and bra on and was pulling her SFA sweatshirt over her head.

"I'm *not*," Garrett insisted, "If you *nudge* the crazy outta Lacy, Mandy will be fine."

"What're the magic words?" Lola asked, still having fun at his expense.

"Please," Garrett said.

"I said magic *words*," Lola pointed out.

Confused, Garrett said, "I don't know. Tell me and I'll say 'em."

"Promise?"

"I swear. Just make this stop."

"Okay, then," Lola said. "The magic words are *you'll* get over *your* irrational problem with Paige's natural form."

"I love you, Lola," Paige said from off to the side.

Garrett looked from Lola to Paige back to Lola. "I'll *try*. I promise I'll *try*."

Lola looked at Paige. "What d'ya think? Good enough for a start."

Paige thought for a moment. She was having fun at her daddy's expense too, while her mom and Mandy continued to argue.

"Yeah. If he reneges, you can always give him a little nudge," Paige said.

"What's it gonna be, Garrett?" Lola said. "You promise me you'll try to accept Paige for who she is, and I promise you I won't nudge ya into it. If ya break your promise, I can break mine. Do we have a deal?"

Garrett swallowed hard. "Deal. But just nudge Lacy. Not Mandy."

Paige felt something radiate from Lola again and her mom fell silent. Mandy kept arguing for a few seconds before she realized Lacy had quit arguing with her.

To Lola, Mandy said, "Did ya...you know Lacy?"

Lola nodded.

"But not me, right?" Mandy asked.

Lola shook her head lightly, which caused the beads on the ends of her cornrows to click together.

Confused, Lacy said, "Did she, ya know what, to me?"

Lola took Lacy's hand in hers and rubbed her thumb in a small circle on Lacy's hand. "Feel my thumb on your hand, hear my voice, and look into my right, seein' eye, Lacy."

Garrett, Mandy, and Paige watched, fascinated, as Ty had been earlier that long day ago, as Lola's thumb grew in length, which made the circles on Lacy's hand larger.

In a dreamy voice, Lacy said, "Your eye is so beautiful."

"Thank you, Lacy," Lola said. "Now, listen to me carefully."

Lacy nodded.

"From this moment forward, you will *not* have a problem with Mandy," Lola instructed. "In fact, you'll be nothin' but happy for Garrett and Mandy. Do you understand me?"

Lacy nodded again.

"Good," Lola continued in her warm honey voice. "This is very important. You will *miss* Al. You will *mourn* for Al. But your missin' and mournin' will be tempered because he was the best husband ya ever had and, ya know, he loved you with all his beautiful heart. Do ya understand?"

Lacy nodded yet again.

Garrett was a little hurt by Lola telling Lacy Al was the best husband she'd ever had. In his heart, he knew it had been the truth.

"Good," Lola cooed in her warm, honey voice. "Now, feel my thumb on your hand, listen to my voice, and look into my left eye."

Lacy's gaze shifted from Lola's green, cat-like, right, seeing eye to her normal, light brown, left eye.

Still using her softest, warmest, honey voice, Lola said, "When I remove my thumb from your hand, ya won't remember this happened. You'll only feel the things I tol' ya 'bout bein' happy for Garrett and Mandy and how much Al loved ya. Understand?"

Lacy nodded for a fourth time.

When she did, Lola removed her thumb from Lacy's hand.

Lacy looked around the room and at everyone for several seconds and said, "Okay. What do we do now?"

Amazed, Garrett said, "It's not safe for you here. Can ya stay with your folks until we get this under control?"

"Of course," Lacy said calmly.

"What about us?" Mandy said. "We're not safe at home either."

Before Garrett could answer, Lacy said, "That's right, Garrett. You protect Mandy. Aside from Paige, Mandy's the best thing that ever came into your life."

Everyone, except Lola, went slack jawed upon hearing this come from Lacy. Lola, proud of herself, just grinned.

It took Garrett several seconds to comprehend the power of whatever Lola had done to Lacy.

When he did, Garrett said, "Mandy and I will stay with my folks."

"What about Paige?" Lacy asked.

"Paige is stayin' with me until the protection potion I'm brewin' is ready in three days," Lola told Lacy.

To everyone's, except Lola's, surprise, Lacy said, "Excellent idea."

"We'll wait while ya gather your things," Garrett said.

Lacy took a few steps toward the stairs and stopped. "What about Al?"

"Until the protection potion is ready, it's too dangerous for Glinda to be out at night," Garrett said. "We'll find him first thing tomorrow mornin'. I promise we will."

Lacy looked at Paige. "Glinda's beautiful. Just like you, sweetheart."

"Thank you, Mom," Paige said.

When Lacy had gone upstairs, Garrett turned to Lola. "That was more than a nudge. What d'ya do with your thumb and seein' eye?"

"Acceptin' Glinda for who she is was just a nudge," Lola said. "That's all she needed 'cause, even though she was denyin' it, she could see, in her heart, that Glinda was pure and without evil intent. Lacy's hatred for Mandy was, as ya said, completely irrational. I had to go deeper to get rid of that and to ease her heart 'bout Al. I had to hypnotize her."

"Is that what ya did for the Zanes and Hendersons this mornin'?" Garrett asked.

"It was," Lola said. "Takin' in that much grief took a powerful toll on me. Ty had to help me to the SUV and into my house after I did a group session with Trevor's parents and both sets of grandparents."

Mandy put a hand on Lola's warm, smooth arm. "I'm sorry. I hope doin' this for me hasn't caused ya harm."

Lola smiled her brilliant smile. "Anger and hatred aren't as taxin' as grief. Mostly 'cause anger and hatred are superficial. Grief goes to a person's very soul. That's why takin' on grief is so much more harmful to me."

"What about Lacy's grief for Al?" Garrett asked.

"Oh, it's real. She loves him very much," Lola said. "As I tol' Lacy, I didn't take it all away. I just…muted it a little. She'll carry it with her for the rest of her life, though. As she should. Al deserves that. As does Lacy. It's a balancin' act. One I'm very good at. Remember, my strength is healin'."

"Thank you, Lola," Garrett said.

"Don't you forget our deal, Garrett," Lola reminded him.

"What deal?" Mandy asked.

"Before Lola agreed to make Mom like you, she made Daddu promise to get used to my feelin' more natural, naked, at home," Paige said with a wide smile on her face.

Mandy smiled, and then giggled. "This is gonna be amusin'."

Not amused, Garrett said, "I promised I'd *try*."

"If he doesn't, Lola gets to nudge him into acceptin' it," Paige told Mandy.

Mandy laughed. "You are in quite a pickle, Garrett Lambert."

Garrett looked at his boots in a pouty way. "I did it for you, Mandy. Instead of laughin', ya could thank me."

Mandy moved to Garrett and took his scruffy checks in her hands. "You're right. I won't tease ya anymore. Thank you. I know ya hate this, and it won't be easy. Paige will ease into this slowly. Right, Paige."

"Of course," Paige said with a playful grin. "I promise I won't flop down on your lap naked the next time I see ya in your recliner."

"Take it easy on your daddy, Paige-Turner," Lola warned Paige. "Or I might just have to give you a little nudge in the other direction."

Aghast, Paige said, "You wouldn't?"

"Don't try me, chil'," Lola said.

"Can you even nudge a werewolf?" Paige asked.

Lola smiled. "We're 'bout to find out."

It was the closest thing to an argument Paige and Lola had ever been in. Paige didn't like it. Not one bit.

"Okay," Paige relented. "I'll stop teasin' Daddy and I will be respectful of his feelin's. Jeeze. Y'all grownups are too serious. I was only playin'."

"And," Mandy said, "I'll help with Garrett's side of the deal."

About that time, Lacy came down the stairs with two suitcases and a makeup bag. Garrett wasn't surprised. Everyone looked at her.

"What?" Lacy said. "I don't know how long I'll be gone."

Paige, who had everything she needed in her backpack, giggled, which spread to Mandy, which spread to Garrett, and then even Lola joined in. Then, to everyone's surprise, Lacy giggled, too.

Still giggling, Lacy said, "I need my beauty supplies. I'm not naturally beautiful like Paige, Mandy, and Lola are."

This statement touched Mandy profoundly. Partly because she thought this might have been one reason Lacy had hated her so much and partly because she knew it wasn't true.

Mandy walked up to Lacy and put a hand lightly on Lacy's check. "That's not even close to bein' true, Lacy. I know ya didn't know me in high school, but I knew who you were. I thought you were the prettiest girl in Pine View High School."

Lacy blushed. "Thanks, but that's not sayin' much. Pine View High School had, what, about fifty girls in the entire school. Not a lot of competition."

"Oh, Lacy," Mandy said. "You're still one of the most beautiful women I know. Don't cut yourself down like that."

Lacy smiled. "Thank you, Mandy. That means a lot comin' from you."

Then Paige felt something radiate from Lola again, that something she knew was a nudge.

"What d'ya just do?" Paige whispered in Lola's ear.

"I nudged away your mom's insecurities," Lola whispered. "If I'd known that was the root of her anger and hatred for Mandy, I wouldn't have had to hypnotize it out of her. I had to hypnotize her anyway, for her grief over Al, but no harm done either way."

"I hate to break up this beautiful moment, but we need to get gone," Garrett announced.

"What am I supposed to tell my folks 'bout Al, Garrett?" Lacy asked as tears leaked from her eyes again.

Then Garrett did something he hadn't done since the day Lacy moved out of their trailer when they were inside, alone, looking through their broken home. He stepped up to Lacy and wrapped her in a tight hug. Lacy dropped her suitcases and hugged him back.

"You tell 'em that Al was missin' when ya got home," Garrett said. "Tell 'em ya called me, and I came over. Tell 'em we're out lookin' for Al. And tell 'em I said it wasn't safe for you to stay here alone. Can ya do those things?"

Lacy sobbed and nodded her head against Garrett's still strong shoulder.

Garrett held Lacy until she stopped crying. "You're gonna be okay, Lacy. You've got your folks, your brothers, and me and Paige. We'll get ya through this."

"You've got me too, Lacy," Mandy said.

"And me," Lola added.

Lacy looked at the people in her living room. "I do, don't I?"

"Of course, ya do, Mom," Paige said. "You're part of the Glinda family now. We look out for each other."

"That's right," Lola and Mandy said together.

"Just don't tell anyone about Glinda or the vampire," Garrett reminded Lacy.

"Of course, not," Lacy said. "I'm not stupid, Garrett."

That sounds more like the old Lacy, Garrett thought.

"Okay. Okay," Garrett said with his hands up in a surrender posture. "I was just checkin',"

Without saying another word, five of the Glinda family members, with Ty, Trowa, and James, the family had grown to eight and Fr. Mike would be the ninth, left Lacy's, no longer Al and Lacy's, house. Lacy locked the door. The five of them got into three different vehicles and went their separate ways. It was going to be a long three days waiting for the protection potion to reduce to full potency.

~ * ~

Dănuţ was having a good night. As with Justin's grave, fresher graves are easier to dig than older graves. Thanks to the werewolf killings, roughly six months prior to Dănuț and the Master's arrival, there were plenty of somewhat fresh graves to excavate.

Dănuț's first stop that evening was the Pine View First Baptist Church. He found a fairly recent grave and dug. Aside from the recency of the grave, digging graves was a good bit easier than excavating the Master's lair under the funeral home had been. A bonus was he was outside, not underground, in the cool, crisp night air. He made quick work of it.

Upon hitting the vault lid, Dănuț cleared dirt from all four corners and, using his considerable, vampire blood induced strength, easily pulled the three-hundred-pound vault lid open. Inside was a shiny black coffin with chrome handles and hardware. Dănuț thought it was beautiful and would please the Master greatly, not that he'd show any appreciations. Dănuț didn't need praise from the Master. All he needed was to serve.

Dănuț lifted the coffin out of what was its final resting place, opened it, and was delighted at what he saw. Inside, instead of a body, was a body bag. From his years in the mortuary business, Dănuț knew the contents of the body bag would be in a pressure sealed bag. This was done when the remains were not only not fit for viewing, but when they were in pieces, which made embalming imposable.

"Must have been a gruesome death for you," Dănuț said to the body bag.

He dumped the body bag, which contained what was left of Russ Lomax after the alpha and its pack had ripped him to shreds, onto the ground next to the freshly dug hole, and loaded the pristine coffin into the back of the hearse, which was equipped to carry two coffins at once, and locked it in place. On the way out, Dănuț stopped on unconsecrated ground and lined the coffin with dirt. Then he was off to find another coffin.

Dănuț's next stop was at the Pine View Presbyterian Church. It didn't take him long to find another recent werewolf victim's grave, and he began digging. As with Justin and Russ' graves, the digging wasn't difficult. When he hit the vault lid, he again removed the dirt from the corners pulled the lid free. Inside was a gold coffin with chrome handles and hardware.

Dănuț lifted the coffin out of the hole, opened it, and couldn't believe his luck. This coffin contained a body bag, too. Unlike the previous body bag, this one had a chemical smell to it. While the body hadn't been fit for viewing, it was in one piece and had been embalmed. Either way, body bags made for cleaner coffins. Not that the vampires who would eventually inhabit them particularly cared. But it made Dănuţ's job a little easier.

Dănuţ dumped the body bag containing the burned and mutilated remains of Maggie "Magpie" Crawford beside the freshly dug hole. He loaded it into the hearse beside the black coffin, locked it down, drove to a safe place to gather dirt to line the coffin, and got back into the hearse.

His plan was to secure four coffins for the Master that night and he was on pace to do so. Because the hearse could only securely hold two coffins at once, he needed to return to the Eternal Rest Funeral Home, off load these, and head back out. He pointed the hearse in the funeral home's direction and headed that way. Not two minutes into his return trip, things changed.

I need you here now, Dragoş' mental scream came to Dănuţ's.

Yes, Master. I am on my way there now, Dănuţ thought back.

Quickly, Dănuţ. Or there will be hell to pay, Dragoş' hissed.

Yes, Master, Dănuţ mentally responded.

Because the Master had cloaked the hearse in invisibility to aid Dănuţ in his nightly mission, what had begun as a leisurely drive back to the funeral home became a harrowing, breakneck speed race down the winding, and sometimes narrow, East Texas roads. More than a few times, Dănuţ almost collided with an oncoming truck or car. The cloaking incantation wouldn't save him from a head on collision at the speeds he traveled, but Dănuţ didn't care for his safety. All that mattered was obeying the Master and arriving quickly. The logic of not arriving at all, should he wreck, didn't enter Dănuţ's mind. It had not been his place to think; only to serve. He made the, what should have been, forty-minute drive back in under twenty minutes.

~ * ~

After the encounter with the *vrăjitoare*, Dragoş was angry and frustrated beyond anything he had experienced in his eight hundred year, undead, existence. Why the Paige girl would be in the company of a *vrăjitoare*, and a vile, elemental seer, was beyond his comprehension. With the wisdom he had accumulated over his long, undead existence, that was perplexing.

After putting several miles between himself, and the *vrăjitoare*, Dragoş slowed and hovered high above Pine View County, which stretched out for miles beneath him and the fledgling. He knew Paige was lost to him that night, and because of the company Paige kept, he knew it would probably fall to Dănuţ to collect his prize. This further angered and frustrated him, but he couldn't let the night become a total waste of his time. They had fed and fed well on the man the fledgling called Mr. Al, but that wasn't enough. He needed another young woman for his cloud.

Take me to one of your pretty friends, Dragoş mentally instructed the fledgling.

The fledgling didn't need to respond. The moment she thought of a friend who fit her Master's request, Megan Williams, he had it. Dragoş turned south and quickly flew to their destination.

Not two minutes later, Dragoş and the fledgling lightly landed in Megan's front yard. The house was a small, one-story brick and mortar structure with a large porch that ran the entire length of its front. Smoke rose from a chimney on the backside of the house. Lights were on throughout the house and Dragoş could hear several people talking inside, as well as electronic voices coming from their television.

None of this disturbed Dragoş in the least. He had several options where securing his new fledgling was concerned. His current fledgling knew the girl named Megan and could easily lure her from the house and into his waiting arms. Or he could simply kill everyone inside, after they invited him and the fledgling in, and take the new fledgling. Or he could mesmerize everyone and take the girl. Considering the troublesome *vrăjitoare*, who could see through any glamor he placed on the others, mezmery was out. She would, of course, know whatever action he decided on was at his hands. He wouldn't give her the satisfaction of seeing his work. Angry and frustrated at not getting the beauty named Paige, he decided to kill everyone inside and take his prize.

Dragoş looked at his young, beautiful fledgling. "We need an invitation to enter."

The fledgling smiled, showing her pointed fangs. "Yes, Master."

As he had done at Al's, Dragoş cloaked himself in invisibility and followed the fledgling to the front door, and he watched.

The girl who had been Melanie knocked on the door.

There was a brief commotion of voices wondering who would visit at that hour on Christmas night.

The voice of an adolescent boy said, "I'll get it."

A moment later, Megan's fourteen-year-old twin brother, Mitchel, opened the door.

Mitchel stood there and looked at Melanie, like he wasn't sure if she was real, for several seconds. Her skin was pallid, and her dress was covered in, what looked like, lots of blood. He couldn't quite register what he saw. Especially since everyone knew Melanie was missing. News, especially bad news, travels fast in small towns.

He came out of his stupor. "Mel?"

"It's me," the fledgling said in her best teenage girl, carefree voice.

"Are ya okay?" Mitchel asked. "Is that blood?"

"Actually, I'm not okay," the girl who had been Melanie said. "This is my blood. I've been pukin' up blood since I woke up, lost, in the forest this mornin'. I only just now found my way out, and I saw your house. I need an ambulance. May we come in?"

Like Al, the plural "we" didn't register with Mitchel. "Yes, of course."

He turned his head and shouted, "Mom. Dad. It's Mel. She needs he…"

Before Mitchel could finish the sentence, Dragoş seized the boy by the throat, cutting off his voice, and stormed into the house, holding the squirming boy above his head as he did. In the living room, gathered around the TV, Dragoş saw the boy's parents, a very young girl, and his prize.

The girl named Megan was petite and looked younger than her fourteen years of age. But she had developed the body parts Dragoş craved the most. Small, firm breasts and he could smell she was currently menstruating. She had long, blonde hair and big green eyes, made bigger by the terror of seeing Dragoş in his ancient hideousness. She was perfect. Dragoş' long tongue snaked out from between his long fangs and licked his too red lips.

"Hold her," Dragoş told his current fledgling.

The fledgling grabbed Megan forcefully and held her tightly.

"Why are ya doin' this, Mel?" Megan cried.

The fledgling bared her fangs and hissed in reply.

Dragoş, still holding the boy named Mitchel by the throat above his head, brought his fingers quickly together. His long, yellow, claw-like fingernails ripped the boy's throat out in a spray of blood and a final gurgling sound from Mitchel. Dragoş dropped the boy's dead body to the floor in a crumpled, bleeding heap.

The remaining humans screamed in horror. Dragoş drank it in and advanced on the man, who had grabbed a fireplace poker to defend himself and his remaining family with.

He was a big man, and he brought the poker down on Dragoş with all his considerable human strength. Dragoş easily took the poker from the man's large hand and rammed it up through his chin and out of the top of his skull. The man slumped to the floor and his fireplace poker skewered head fell into the fire burning in the fireplace.

Dragoş turned and saw the woman backed into a corner; the little girl hid behind her and cried.

The woman screamed, "Leave us alone."

Calmly, Dragoş said, "I cannot do that, madam."

"Why?" the woman screamed.

Dragoş pointed a gnarled finger at the girl named Megan. "Because I want her as my new plaything."

"Oh, God. Please, no." the woman screamed.

Dragoş chuckled, which sounded like wet gravel. "God is not here, madam."

"Take me instead," the woman screamed. "Please. Just leave my girls alone."

"My dear lady." Dragoş said. "I am eight hundred years old, and you are too old for me. I like my playthings young and pretty."

"Please," the woman screamed.

"Enough," Dragoş hissed.

Without really moving, Dragoş was suddenly very close to the screaming woman. He plunged his right hand up under her ribcage, grabbed her frantically beating heart, and crushed it. Blood jetted out of the dead woman's mouth. When Dragoş removed his blood covered hand, the woman crumpled to the floor. The little girl who had been hiding behind her shrank back into the corner as far as she could. She wasn't screaming, but her face was a mess of tears and snot. She trembled in fear, and she soiled herself with urine.

Dragoş bent down so his face was level with the little girl's face. "How old are you, little one?"

"Ni-Ni-Nine," the little girl stammered.

"What a pity," Dragoş said. "If you were three or four years older, you could join your sister in my cloud,"

"Leave her alone." Megan screamed.

Dragoş looked at the girl named Megan. "I will leave her alone. She will be your first meal. You will kill her yourself."

"Never." Megan screamed.

"Bring her to me, fledgling," Dragoş hissed.

Dragoş could have mesmerized this one, as he had the fledgling, but he didn't want to. The anger he experienced being denied the girl named Paige was still hot in his black blood and he wanted this one scared and squirming as he drank her life's blood away.

The fledgling brought the screaming and squirming Megan to her Master.

Dragoş grabbed the girl named Megan from the fledgling. "Hold the little one, but do not harm her. I want her fresh for this one's first feeding."

The fledgling did as instructed. She gently took the little girl's shoulders in her cold, undead hands and held her in the corner.

Dragoş looked at the screaming, squirming girl in his arms, and took a deep breath. "I can smell your woman's blood. It smells…delicious. When I am finished with you, you will never again be cursed with the monthly flow, and you will be immortal. Forever young and beautiful."

"I'd rather be dead." Megan screamed.

Dragoş chuckled his wet gravel chuckle. "You will be. But only for a moment."

Dragoş forced her head to one side, which exposed the young, perfect flesh of her neck. He saw blood pumping rapidly through her carotid artery. He exposed his impossibly long, pointed fangs and slowly punctured her neck.

Megan screamed in pain, but that only further fed Dragoş' hunger. He wrapped his cold, too red lips around the girl's neck and drank. Her heart pumped so hard with fear his mouth filled quickly with her virgin blood, and he had to swallow quickly to keep up at first. As her life blood left her body, so did her struggling. She fell limp in Dragoş' arms and still he fed. Her heart slowed to a few beats per minute. Dragoş still fed. At last, Dragoş felt her heart flutter rapidly. He removed his fangs and watched the last of the girl named Megan's life blood bubbled up out of the puncture marks. It was time to reanimate her; time to bring her into the forever realm of the undead.

Dragoş slit his left nipple and pressed the young, beautiful, dead girl's lips to his chest. A moment later, Dragoş felt her tongue move. Then her cold lips locked onto his stiff, bleeding nipple. She fed on his black, undead blood hungrily.

~ * ~

Megan struggled against the vile penetration of the monster's fangs. She had never been raped, but she could relate to the unwanted violation those women must experience. She felt his cold lips pressed securely against her neck and his cold tongue lap eagerly at the blood she quickly lost.

Megan knew she was dying. Worse, she knew she would become whatever Mel had become when the monster finished with her. She fought against the thought of killing her little sister, as the monster had said she'd do. But the fight was leaving her. She forced her eyelids open and saw the ceiling of her once safe living room. As she looked at the ceiling, clinging desperately to life, a consuming whiteness enclosed her vision. The dingy white of the ceiling disappeared completely and the bright whiteness of death washed over her.

For a moment, she was with her family again. Everyone except her little sister was there. They were together in their living room, but the living room was shades of white, not as it was in life. Then she tasted the sweetest coppery liquid. Her family and the living room faded as she drank eagerly of the sweet nectar.

Just before her family and living room faded completely, she heard her dad, in a faraway voice, say, "Stay with us, Megan."

She couldn't. The nectar was too sweet, and she couldn't stop. Her vision came back, and she looked into the eyes of her beautiful Master.

~ * ~

Dragoş looked down into the new fledgling's crystal blue eyes and smiled. Still sucking hungrily on his stiff nipple and the sweet nectar flowing from it, she smiled back, and his black, undead blood leaked from the corners of her mouth. He let her feed a while longer, but not as long as he had let his first fledgling feed. The first fledgling needed strength to travel and feed from her mother. This fledgling's first meal had urinated herself. She whimpered and trembled in the corner.

"That is enough," Dragoş said as he pulled the new fledgling's lips away from his nipple.

"I'm hungry, Master," she pleaded.

"You shall eat, my sweet," Dragoş said as he swept his incredibly long right arm to the side and pointed at the little girl.

The new fledgling lunged for the little girl, but Dragoş mentally stopped her. "Do not attack. Savor this meal."

"Yes, Master," the new fledgling said and drifted toward the frightened little girl.

"No, Megan. It's me. McKenzie," the little girl pleaded. "Don't hurt me, Megan. Please don't hurt me."

"Feed from her inner thigh," Dragoş instructed his new fledgling. "High on her inner thigh, and stop feeding when I command you to stop,"

"Yes, Master," she said.

"Megan don't," McKenzie screamed.

The girl who had been Megan, and a loving big sister in life, paid no attention to the little girl's pleas. She grabbed her, forced her to the floor, pulled up her nightshirt, and saw blood pumping hard in her femoral artery.

Following her Master's command, she sank her fangs up high into the little girl's thigh, just below her urine soaked, SpongeBob SquarePants underwear, and drank. The little girl screamed and tried to fight, but to no avail. The new fledgling drank and drank. As she did, the little girl stopped struggling and then she stopped screaming.

"Stop," Dragoş commanded.

The new fledgling stopped immediately and stood beside the first fledgling. Her face, neck, and nightshirt were covered in blood. The little girl on the floor spasmed once and then stilled.

"Should she remove the fang marks, Master?" the fledgling who had been Melanie Zane in life asked

"No. The only reason we did so with the boy and the man was to conceal our presences here," Dragoş said. "This is no longer necessary because the *vrăjitoare* knows we are here. This is better, though. This is the old-world way, the better way. Now that they know, they will be in constant fear as soon as darkness falls, and we are free to feed."

"Yes, Master," the first fledgling said as she moved to the new fledgling and took her hand.

Dragoş stood and looked at the first two members of his American cloud. Both young, both beautiful, and both virgins. They were perfect. They were almost enough to make him forget about the perfection that was the girl named Paige. Almost.

"It is time that I gave you names," Dragoş told them. "Fledgling One and Fledgling Two will not do. It is fitting that, in life, you both had names that started with the letter M. For I have selected your undead names that both start with the letter A. For my first fledgling, I have selected the name Agrapina, which is a Romanian name for the first-born girl. For my second fledgling, I have selected the name Antanasia, which is a Romanian name for one who will be reborn, immortal. These are nice names, yes?"

"Yes, Master. It is a beautiful and fitting name," said Agrapina.

"Mine too, Master," said Antanasia.

Just then, there was a pop and a sizzle from the fireplace. The three vampires looked that way. The pop was one of the man's eyeballs exploding in the heat and the sizzle came from the fireplace poker protruding from his head, which glowed red hot and slowly melted its way through the man's skull.

Dragoş laughed. Agrapina and Antanasia joined in his laughter. The three of them laughing made an unholy sound in the otherwise quiet house. When Dragoş stopped laughing, Agrapina and Antanasia stopped laughing immediately. They didn't have to be told to stop; they had instinctively known they should.

Dragoş held out his hand. "Come, my beautiful daughters. It is early yet, but we must return to our home. I have business to discuss with Dănuţ."

They came to him willingly and followed him into what had been the girl named Megan's front yard. Dănuţ transformed into the man-sized, bat-like creature and held a hand out to each of his daughters. When they took his hands, he folded them in close to his hairy body, flapped his large, leathery wings, and disappeared into the night sky.

~ * ~

Dănuţ pushed the button on the visor to automatically open the left large garage door. Because of the urgent command he'd received from the Master, he wasn't surprised to see him standing in the mortuary's dark interior. Nor had he been surprised to see the Master had selected another exquisite young woman for his cloud. The new member appeared to be younger than his usual taste. If Dănuţ had learned anything over the decades he had served the Master, he had learned looks can be deceiving. All Dănuţ could hope for, at that point, was the Master's urgent command had involved nothing he might have done wrong. The Master's punishments could be harsh. He was about to find out.

Dănuţ pulled the hearse inside the dark room, pressed the button on the visor to close the door, and stepped out of the hearse.

"What took you so long?" Dragoş said, but with no genuine anger.

"I am sorry, Master," Dănuţ said sheepishly, while looking at his dirty shoes. "I was on the other side of the county collecting coffins for your cloud. I thought to get four, but only got two before you summoned me. I will do better tomorrow night, Master,"

"You did well, Dănuţ," Dragoş said. "I am pleased with two, which is one more than is needed this night. I have other business for you to attend to tomorrow. Day and night, if that is what it takes."

Dănuţ, not used to what might come close to passing as praise for his labor, looked up at his Master. The Master smiled at him. Dănuţ actually swooned a little before clearing his head.

"It would please me for you to move the two coffins you acquired tonight into my throne room so that I might tuck my daughters in for the duration," Dragoş told him. "Then come and speak with me about an urgent matter for which I need your assistance."

"Yes, Master. Right away," Dănuţ said as he turned to unload the coffins.

"Wait," Dragoş commanded.

Dănuţ stopped dead in his tracks. All he could think was the Master's kindness had been a ruse, and he was about to be punished severely for something he had not done to his liking. He thought this while forgetting his mind was an open book to the Master.

"You are not in trouble, Dănuţ," Dragoş said. "I only want to introduce you to my daughters properly. The one you know is now Agrapina. The one you have not yet met is Antanasia."

Dănuţ, who, of course, knew the meanings of the girl's names, bowed to his Master. "Most beautiful and fitting names, Master."

"Do not worry, Dănuţ," Dragoş told him. "Antanasia knows you are my faithful, familiar, and off limits. Now, please see to my wishes so that we may talk."

"Yes, Master," Dănuţ said before scurrying off to do his Master's bidding.

Dănuţ made quick work of it. He was more than intrigued. He was so used to stern disapproval from the Master and being called slave, not familiar, he couldn't help but wonder what was so important as to deserve a discussion with the Master.

Dănuţ had the new coffins in the Master's throne room in a matter of minutes. He watched the Master and his two daughters slip behind the table and shelves that, when in place, concealed the entrance to the Master's throne room and waited.

Urgent matter or not, Dănuţ knew what his Master meant by "tuck my daughters in." It was convenient, in English, tuck rhymed with fuck and that meant he intended to have carnal relations with both. Dănuţ was forced to watch his Master tuck his daughters in frequently throughout his long service. Doing so wasn't a reward. It was a punishment to make Dănuţ long for pleasure of the flesh he had foregone for life when he willingly became the master's familiar. That he was not forced to watch his Master enjoy their young flesh was further evidence his Master was pleased with him. He waited.

Sometime later and looking much refreshed by the activities that took place below, Dragoş emerged from behind the table and shelves and joined Dănuţ at the embalming table where he sat.

"They have so much energy at that age," Dragoş said casually, as if he hadn't just taken the maidenhead of two exquisite young women, one of whom looked more like a prepubescent girl.

"Yes, Master," Dănuţ dutifully replied.

Reading Dănuţ's thoughts, Dragoş smiled, which revealed his deadly fangs. "Not that it is of your concern. Antanasia is young, but older than she looks. She is fourteen and has flowered. In my day, a flowered twelve-year-old was ready for bedding. Age restrictions in these modern times are so...arbitrary. Don't you agree, Dănuţ?"

"Yes, Master," Dănuţ immediately agreed.

"Good," Dragoş said. "Now, on to the important issue we must discuss. There is a girl named Paige Lambert who I must have. I saw her in Agrapina's blood memory. I thought she might be the one I came here to collect, the silver-haired werewolf. I have tasted her blood and sadly, she is not the one. But she is magnificent. Through what little blood memories I could get from her degraded blood, I saw her put up a fight against the werewolf. I *must* have her. When I do, I will name her Vanda, a warrior.

"I saw her tonight," Dragoş continued with a lustful grin. "She was naked in the moonlight and perfect in every way. When I was ready to take her, a *vrăjitoare* stepped out of the car she arrived in. Not just any *vrăjitoare*, an elemental seer. To complicate matters further, this girl named Paige is a true believer. The moment the *vrăjitoare* saw through my cloaking incantation, she had the girl put on a silver necklace and crucifix. The vile seer is a powerful *vrăjitoare* and most certainly has help from her coven.

"Thus, my loyal familiar, you must find this amazing creature and bring her to me," Dragoş instructed. "I am afraid this will not be a simple task. Agrapina took me to this girl, Paige's mother's house, and she was not there; she was at her father's house. Agrapina and I fed on the girl's stepfather, so it is unlikely she will return there. The seer saw us at her father's house, so it is unlikely she will return there, either. I believe she will stay with the cursed *vrăjitoare*. You must find this magnificent girl and bring her to me, Dănuţ. This is the task I give you. Do not fail me."

"I will not fail you, Master," Dănuţ vowed.

"I know you will not," Dragoş said. "Now, I believe my daughters might be ready for another tucking. I'll leave you to it, Dănuţ,"

Dănuţ saw his Master to the opening and sealed it behind him. He had work to do. If the Master was correct, as he surely was, it would not be simple work. He had tussled with *vrăjitoare* before, but never an elemental seer. He would need to be careful and regardless of the Master's warnings to the contrary, he would have to think.

Chapter Eight

Sunrise on December 26, 2015 in Pine View County, Texas came at seven sixteen a.m. and Garrett was up, dressed, and ready to leave an hour earlier. His mom, Mary, was up too and asked him questions like, "Where's Paige?" and "You and Mandy can stay as long as y'all need to, but what's goin' on?" Garrett was elusive with his answers as he sipped the sweet tea his mom had made and tried to stretch the cramp out of his body. He and Mandy had slept in his old room in his old twin bed. It was cozy, but not very comfortable. He knew the drive to Lola's house took about thirty minutes. At six forty a.m., he thanked his mom for the sweet tea and left. He and Paige had to find Al's body before someone else stumbled upon it.

~ * ~

By the clock on Garrett's radio, it was seven eighteen when he pulled up in front of Lola's house and parked. It did not surprise him to see Lola sitting on her front porch swing enjoying the rising sun. Traffic wasn't an issue in Pine View County but, as luck would have it, he got held up for a few minutes at the only railroad tracks between his and Lola's house. It was a southbound freight full of new automobiles and tanker cars, which were probably headed to Houston.

When Garrett got out of his truck, Lola said, "You're late. Sun's already on the rise."

What struck Garrett in that brief statement was they were shouting distance apart, but Lola had simply said the words and it was like she was standing right beside him. Not for the first time, he wondered just how powerful Lola Laveau was.

"Two minutes," Garrett shouted as he walked towards her.

"I figured you'd be here *before* sunrise," she replied.

Mounting the steps, Garrett said, "I would'a been but for the damn train."

Lola smiled that smile that made men's knees weak and patted the spot next to her on the swing. "Have a seat and some of my spice tea."

"I believe I will," Garrett said. "Is Paige awake?"

What Garrett saw next gave him the same feeling he got when he was a kid, and his folks took him to a carnival. He saw a guy hammer a sixteen-penny nail into his nose. Revulsion and amazement.

Lola's right, seeing eye, and only that eye, looked toward her house, while her left eye remained locked on him. "She is. She heard your truck pull up, but she'll need a few minutes. You've got time for some tea and conversation."

Garrett took a seat on the other side of the swing from Lola. It wasn't a big swing, so there were less than two feet between them. Try as he may, he couldn't help but notice her stiff nipples protruding from the sheer fabric of the white, flowing dress she always wore. He noticed she wasn't wearing shoes. The temperature reading in his truck said it was twenty-seven degrees when he pulled up, and he could feel the sting of it on his cheeks.

"Aren't ya cold?" Garrett asked.

"Not in the least. I'm an elemental seer, Garrett," Lola said. "Nature is part of me. I am nature. I adjust to the surroundin' environment."

"Must be nice," Garrett half joked. "I'm gonna freeze my nuggets off ridin' around on Glinda lookin' for Al."

"Have some tea, Garrett."

Lola's single moving eye, her perky nipples, and bare feet had distracted Garrett, so he had failed to notice something even more amazing than all those things combined. To Lola's right was a small white table. On top of the table was a yellow fire, that wasn't burning the table, and a brass teapot hovering about two inches above the flame. Lola took the teapot from the flame, grabbed one of two cups on the porch railing, poured a golden, brown liquid into the cup, which she handed to Garrett. Then she placed the teapot back above the yellow flame where it continued to hover.

Before taking a drink, Garrett said, "You are one amazin' woman,

Lola Laveau."

Lola smiled. "I know."

Garrett knew she wasn't bragging, just as she hadn't been the night before when she teased she was the prettiest seer in her coven. Lola stated the obvious.

Garrett took a drink of the golden-brown tea and blew on it a few times. He preferred his liquid intake, sweet tea, cold but the tea was the perfect temperature and spicy. More than that, though, he felt his insides warm, and the warmth radiated out. He took another drink, and the warmth intensified.

"This is good, Lola. But, there's more in this than spices and tea, isn't there?"

Lola grinned. "I don't think Mandy would be too happy if ya froze your nuggets off. So, I added a little of this and that to the tea to warm ya up."

"How long will it last?" Garrett asked.

"As long as it needs to," Lola said. "But ya gotta empty the cup."

Garrett didn't have a problem with that. The tea was delicious, and the cup was empty after several more heavenly gulps.

"Is that cup for Paige?" Garrett asked with a flick of his eyes to the other cup on the porch rail.

"It is. She doesn't need it like you do. She has Glinda to keep her warm, but she likes it."

"I can see why. It's delicious," Garrett said as he removed the heavy coat he no longer needed and laid it across the porch swing arm rest.

"How is she?"

"She's remarkable," Lola said with a smile that showed most of her impossibly white teeth.

"I'm not talkin' 'bout the Glinda stuff," Garrett clarified. "I mean, how is she holdin' up?"

"I know what you're askin', Garrett," Lola said. "My answer is that she's remarkable. She still mourns Justin and the other friends she lost that night at the MRB. She's sad about Mel, and the Trevor boy's murder wounded her profoundly. And losin' Al last night has taken a considerable toll on her. Considerin' her age and all she's been through since last May, she is remarkable. Truly, I've never had the privilege of knowin' someone as special as our Paige-Turner."

That Lola had said "our Paige-Turner" warmed Garrett's heart as much as the magical brew.

"Speakin' of remarkable," Garrett said. "May I ask about your powers? With your seein' eye lookin' like that, how is it I never heard about you before James told me? I've lived here my whole life, and that's not somethin' that would stay a secret in a small town. I mean, I know ya go into town because I told ya when we first met that I'd seen your pink Cadillac around town."

Lola looked at Garrett, blinked her eyes, and when she opened them, her right, seeing eye looked identical to her left, normal eye. Garrett's jaw dropped open. She blinked again and her seeing eye came back. Garrett's jaw remained slack.

Lola smiled a troubled smile. "You understand that they have persecuted my kind for as long as humans and witches have existed. I, we, have to have defenses against further persecution. Even in these so-called enlightened days. To live in harmony, which, as elemental seers, we must, deception is our greatest defense."

"But people come to you with problems and troubles," Garrett said. "You said as long as they believe the treatments will work, they do. Surely, they must know you're a witch?"

"They come to me, but usually as a last resort," Lola said. "By then, they're desperate and want to believe. If their treatment requires somethin' that needs more than a totem, salve, potion, or brew, I will reveal my true nature, cast the needed incantations, and then make 'em forget. To most folks 'round here, even those I've helped, I'm just some crackpot palm reader. That was your first impression of me, was it not?"

Garrett felt deeply ashamed. That was exactly what he thought when she called him the day he'd found Cole Duncan's car at what turned out to be Alexis' den and told him she needed to see him; that they couldn't conduct their business over the phone. The injustice of it all, even from his first meeting with Lola, made him feel so bad for the amazing woman he, Paige, and Mandy had grown to love deeply, as she loved them. He felt like crying.

As if reading his thoughts, and Garrett knew she could, Lola took his large, rough, right hand in her small, warm left hand, and gave it a gentle squeeze. "It's okay, Garrett. You were right to be skeptical."

The tears came and Garrett said, "I'm so sorry for that. I'm sorry on behalf of everyone who thinks of ya that way. It's not fair to you, Lola. All you do is help people, and you can't even be your true self for fear of bein' run out of town."

Lola pulled Garrett to her and wrapped him in a hug. "It is no different for our Paige. She must hide her true self as well. Neither of us mind. Our reward is helping others regardless of the consequence. Paige truly wants to help ya find Al, and she dreads it as well. She will find him because she can. It is no different for me and the things I do. I'm a seer and a healer. To not use these abilities for betterment would be an affront to who I am. I know it sounds like I'm ramblin'. I hope ya understand what I'm sayin'."

He understood. He also suddenly realized his right check was pressed tightly against Lola's firm left breast. Just as suddenly, he felt awkward. Trying to disguise his awkwardness, he sat up slowly instead of quickly as he wanted to, but he might as well have been trying to hide an elephant in a small room.

Lola sighed. "You really have some deep-rooted issues with the female body, Garrett."

"Are you readin' my mind?" Garrett asked.

"No. I don't have to," Lola said. "It's written all over your face. Any woman could see it, not just a seer. Ya sure you wouldn't like a little nudge to take the edge off?"

For a moment, Garrett considered letting Lola nudge him. He knew it would make his life a lot easier and less awkward.

He shook his head. "Let me try on my own. I think I can get there. I just need time."

"Okay. If ya change your mind, it'd only take a second to get there."

"I know," Garrett said. "To be truthful, I might end up needin' it."

Lola smiled a smile as warm as the spice tea. "Just let me know and all that awkwardness you're livin' with will melt away."

225

Garrett nodded.

"That aside, I need ya to know somethin', Garrett. About what we were talkin' 'bout before. I've never been happier than I am now. You said it's not fair that I can't be myself, but, for the first time, outside of my coven, I *can* be myself with you, Paige, Mandy, Ty, Trowa, James, and now, Lacy. Y'all are the only people I've revealed my seein' eye to without makin' you forget. It feels good to have people I can trust and who trust me."

Garrett smiled. "These are the same people who know about, and love, Glinda. Well, everyone except Lacy. I doubt she loves ya."

"That's okay," Lola said. "I don't love her either. Because of the love we share for Paige, I trust her, and she trusts me. That'll have to do."

"But...all of us, except James, know 'bout you 'cause of the werewolf problem," Garrett said. "And now, the vampire problem. James told me 'bout you. How did James come to know about your true self?"

Lola sat back and smiled. "Oh, that sweet little man. Of course, given his area of academic interest, he heard about the mysterious palm reader and had to investigate. He showed up here one day 'bout ten years ago. No false pretense either. When I opened the door, he said, 'My name is James Huff. I'm a professor at SFA and I study the occult, folklore, mythology, etcetera. Are you a witch?' I trusted him immediately. I invited him in, and we talked for hours. I answered all his questions and revealed my true self to him."

"How'd ya know you could trust him so quickly?"

"His aura is pure white. That's rare. Not as rare as Paige's pure silver. His was the whitest I've ever seen; most are off white or dingy. Not James', though."

"What'd that color mean?"

"Honesty, intellect, trustworthiness, and innocence," Lola explained.

"Well, I'm glad," Garrett said. "Without James, I wouldn't have found you, learned about the ancestral werewolf, and been able to save my little girl."

"Me too," Lola said with a sweet smile.

"So, gettin' back to somethin' I asked earlier. May I ask about your powers?"

Lola grinned. "I could give ya a tail."

Garrett laughed. "I'm bein' serious."

"So am I," Lola said.

"What would I want, or need, a tail for?"

"I think Mandy might enjoy an extra appendage in the bedroom," Lola said with a wink of her seeing eye.

Garrett blushed. "Would it be permanent?"

"Nope. Just like the tea, you'd have it for as long as ya needed it."

Garrett grinned. "Ya know what? I'll ask Mandy 'bout it."

"Don't be surprised when she says yes."

Garrett blushed again or continued blushing.

After he felt like the heat in his cheeks was the tea again, Garrett said, "What I'm askin' is, could ya take out the ancient, if it came to that?"

Lola shook her head, which made the pink and white beads on the end of her cornrows click together. "Not alone. I took out an arrogant, evil young vampire about forty years ago. Actually, I didn't do it alone. I had the help of a Catholic Priest named Father Sinclair."

"How'd y'all do it?"

"As an elemental witch, I can create earth, wind, fire, and water elementals. I'm a little ashamed to admit it, but I used a young boy to lure her to a jetty on Lake Pontchartrain. Believe me when I tell ya that I never would've let the boy get hurt, Garrett. He was in a trance, so he never knew what was goin' on around him.

"Anyway, I had cloaked myself in invisibility and was between the vampire and the boy," Lola looked at Garrett and continued. "She took the bait. She had a thirst for young boys. As she approached the jetty, I conjured a water elemental between myself and the vampire and materialized. She was so arrogant that my appearance didn't surprise her, and she wasn't threatened by the water elemental. She didn't notice that my hands were behind my back.

"She hissed, bared her fangs, and threw herself into the elemental, thinkin' she could power her way through it. When she did, I threw the bucket of water I had behind my back, which was blessed by Father Sinclair, into the water elemental. I can still see the look on her face when the holy water dispersed within the elemental and trapped her," Lola said with a grin. "Complete horror. It was a fleeting look, though, because the holy water immediately boiled her flesh. Within a few seconds, the water elemental turned from green to black as the holy water ripped her dead blood from her dead bones.

"I sent the water elemental far out into Lake Pontchartrain and released it. It collapsed with a splash and what was left of her dispersed into the lake where she could never be resurrected."

"That was clever," Garrett told her.

"Yes. She was young and arrogant," Lola said. "For an ancient, it'd take my entire coven, and Mamma Deupree's too old to travel. She'd be there spectrally, though. Even then, it'd be a hard-pressed battle. One I'm not sure we'd win."

"Damn. He's that powerful?"

"He is."

"How old is Mamma?" Garrett asked.

"She was a slave in the colonies when John Hancock scribbled his large signature on the Declaration of Independence. She fled to Haiti after the Civil War."

"Holy shit. Since she's the oldest, is she, like, your coven's head honcho?"

"No. Light covens don't have a leader," Lola said. "We're all equal. Dark covens have a high priestess or priest. She or he wields power over their members."

"That doesn't sound fun," Garrett said.

"It's not. Dark, high priestess and priest are cruel and punish coven members often and severely."

"Why do the witches stay?"

"To please the Dark Lord, who you know as Lucifer. They actually enjoy the pain."

"That's fucked up."

"Very. Dark covens are savage."

Full of more questions, Garrett asked, "How long do y'all live?"

"Mamma's the oldest witch I've ever known," Lola said "Maybe the oldest witch ever. It's hard to say. Her age makes her contribution to

Paige's protection potion so important. Witches don't live our long lives learnin' 'bout mathematics, philosophy, or politics. We gain wisdom in the balance of nature and how to right imbalances like the vile, ancient that has come here to make the silver-haired werewolf his familiar. When Paige and Glinda drink the potion, they'll have that wisdom, too. It's their only chance against the ancient."

"How long will the potion last?" Garrett asked.

"Like the tea and tail, as long as she needs it."

"Do werewolves and vampires fight often?" Garrett asked.

"More so in the old-world. These days, they avoid each other," Lola explained.

"When they do fight, which usually wins?"

Lola gave Garrett a worried look. "Honestly?"

Garrett nodded.

"Werewolves are pretty evenly matched against young vampires. That said, I've never heard of a werewolf beatin' an ancient. Paige is different though."

"Because of the potion?"

"Yes, but because she's Glinda, too," Lola said. "She's fearless and clever. And because of the ancestral werewolf, she has had the wolf in her genes for several generations. This strengthens her more than your average werewolf. As *El Lobo* learned the hard way. He had never encountered the likes of Glinda either. She caught him off guard. She has that goin' for her against the ancient, too.

"Although Paige will never get sick, never get cancer, never have heart problems, etcetera and she'll heal quickly, because she not undead, she *will* age," Lola explained. "Someday, far in the future, she will pass from this world of old age. Therefore, I've never heard of a werewolf defeatin' an ancient. They don't live long enough to gain the wisdom to outsmart an ancient. Paige will have this gift from Mamma, and…perhaps more."

"More what?" Garrett asked.

"I don't want to say anything until after they've had the potion," Lola answered.

"Superstitious?"

"Yes. It's kinda in my DNA."

Garrett chuckled. "I have more questions."

Lola's right eye flicked toward her house. "Ask. But be quick. Paige is almost ready."

"Okay. How many witches are in a coven?"

"Three or more witches can form a coven, but the ideal number is thirteen. There are thirteen witches in my coven."

"Why is thirteen the ideal number?"

"The calendar," Lola said.

"But…there are twelve months in a calendar year," Garrett pointed out.

"That's the Gregorian solar calendar," Lola said. "Witches use the thirteen-month lunar calendar."

"What's the difference?"

"Four weeks. The Gregorian calendar has fifty-two weeks, but only twelve months. The moon's phase is roughly twenty-eight days, so the moon cycles the Earth thirteen times a year."

"Oh. I see," Garrett said. "If thirteen is the ideal number, what happens to your coven if one of y'all, like Mamma, passes?"

"We'll bring a new witch into the coven as soon as possible," Lola said "Some witches prefer a solitary life and aren't interested in bein' in a coven. Many more want the protection and power that comes with bein' in a coven. Because every witch, like humans, could meet an untimely end, we all have a successor named. Our successor brings the same strength to the coven as the lost witch. When I pass, my successor is a healer too and will take my place in the coven. Mamma is on her third successor because she outlived the first two."

Garrett wanted to ask about Lola's successor. Two reasons, time and he doubted a superstitious witch would speak about their successor, kept him from asking. He was right about the latter. Successor names were never uttered. Not even to the other members of the coven. They were written on parchment and kept in an incantation guarded secret place that only revealed itself to members of the coven when one of the coven's, or a successor, was lost.

"How come ya never talk about wizards?"

Lola laughed her warm, honey laugh. "There are no wizards."

"What?" Garrett said. "Harry Potter is full of shit?"

Lola chuckled. "I have read the Harry Potter books and enjoyed 'em greatly. I am in awe, and jealous, of Rowling's imagination. I've even wondered if *she's* a witch, but I don't think she is. If she were, she'd be riskin' bein' exposed. She gets some things right, though."

"Like what?" Garrett asked.

"As we were just discussin', witches hide from non-witches, and for good reasons," Lola said. "As Snape teaches, we learn about potions, but not from a school. Our learnin' comes from our elders. Light witches, which includes elemental witches, learn defense against dark witches, too. We don't need wands to cast incantations. Our powers are innate. No conduit, like a wand, is needed to use our powers.

"Notice that I referred to light and dark witch's powers, not white and black magic," Lola smiled and continued. "I do so because white and black magic doesn't exist. What we do without incantations, totems, potions, brews, and conjurin' isn't magic. It's part of who we are, which is why we don't need wands. Witches do not differ from humans, in that, just as there are good and evil humans, there are good and evil witches. The same abilities light witches have and use for good, dark witches have and use for evil.

"Somethin' else that I love about the Harry Potter books, and that Rowling got right, in every one of 'em, whether it comes from Dumbledore, Harry, Hermione, or even Dobby the elf, is the message that love, and goodness win out over hate and evil. That's because love and good are elements of light and hate and evil are elements of dark. Since the first earthly inhabitants learned to create and control fire, they have been usin' it to defeat the darkness. Light always defeats dark.

"This is another reason I believe Paige and Glinda can defeat the ancient," Lola said. "A vampire, by design, is a creature of darkness, evil, and hate. Glinda is a creature of light, goodness, and love. If there was ever a werewolf with the ability to defeat an ancient, it's Glinda. With Mamma's wisdom and what I added, if what I added works, Glinda will be, almost, invincible."

"You're not gonna tell me what ya added?" Garrett asked.

"No. I don't want to speak of it until I know if it worked," Lola said. "I will say that, to my knowledge, it has never worked before. We have not tried it on a creature like Glinda, so I'm hopeful."

"Okay. I'll stop askin' 'bout what ya added. Do y'all call us muggles?" Garrett said with a laugh.

"We do," Lola told him.

Shocked, Garrett said, "Really?"

"No. Of course, not. We call y'all humans. To answer your wizard's question, wizards are in the realm of fairytales, fiction, and games. There are warlocks, though. They are few and usually solitary. Also, they gravitate to the dark crafts. In all my years, I've only encountered one warlock, and he was rude."

Garrett found new questions for every one Lola answered, but they would have to wait. Lola had been correct; Paige was ready. The front door opened, and Paige stepped outside onto the front porch.

~ * ~

Paige woke when Lola slid out of the bed around four in the morning. She briefly considered joining her, but she was exhausted, physically, emotionally, and mentally, from the long, eventful Christmas day. She closed her eyes and was asleep again within seconds. The sound of her daddy's truck approaching woke her again, and she knew more sleep wasn't an option. They had to find Al. She opened her eyes, looked up, saw her reflection looking back at her, and smiled as the bizarre and wonderful events that happened when they returned to Lola's house came back to her.

~ * ~

The first thing Lola did, after they were safely inside her house, was to take a large, rectangular totem from the wall to the right of the front door and hang on the door. Its proximity to the door led Paige to believe this was a totem Lola needed quick access to under dire circumstances.

The outer frame of the totem was constructed of tree limbs,

perhaps an inch in diameter. The inner structure was a spiderweb of tangled smaller branches that converged to an open center that held a delicate, green leaf in the shape of Lola's house. That it was green in the dead of winter amazed Paige.

"What's that do?" Paige asked.

"It cloaks my house from those who would do me, us, harm," Lola explained. "If someone, or something, of ill intent should look upon my house, all they would see is a rundown, dilapidated structure. If they entered, all they would see was an unsafe, condemned interior with rotting floorboards, caved in ceiling, holes in the walls, etcetera. If we were standing in front of the trespasser, they wouldn't *see* us. If they walked *through* us, they wouldn't *feel* us. Any vehicles on the property, my Cadillac and your dad's truck tomorrow will appear as rusted hulks with broken glass, spiderwebs throughout, flattened tires, and winter dead weeds growin' around and through 'em."

"Wow," was all Paige managed as a response.

"Let's get you settled in," Lola said as she headed to the door on the right side of the living room that Paige had never been through.

When Lola opened the door and ushered Paige inside, the lights came on without the use of a switch, and she found herself at a loss for words again.

Lola's bedroom was a wonderland of pink. Everything, the carpet, the furniture, the walls, the trim, the doors, the ceiling fan, the lamps, the window treatments, and the bedding, were different shades of pink. It was like being inside a giant ball of pink cotton candy. As far as furniture went, there was a dresser with a large, oval mirror, a roll-top desk, a nightstand on either side of the bed, and a queen-size bed with an ornate, four-poster head and footboards, and an equally ornate, wooden canopy above the bed. To Paige's right were two pink doors.

Lola opened the left one. "This is the bathroom. You can freshen up before we go to bed. The other is my closet. You can put your backpack in there."

Finally finding some words, Paige headed toward the bathroom. "Thank you, Lola. Thank ya for everything."

"You're very welcome, sweet girl," Lola said. "If ya don't mind,

I'm gonna climb on in bed."

"Of course, not," Paige said. "It's your house. Don't let my bein' here alter your normal routine."

Lola wrapped Paige in a tight hug. "For now, it's *our* home. You do as ya please as well."

Paige thanked Lola again and went into the bathroom. It, too, was all shades of pink, even the toilet and tub. Paige undressed and put her dirty clothes in a different pouch inside her backpack from the clean clothes. Then she peed, washed her face and hands, brushed her teeth, put her hair in a ponytail, and exited the bathroom.

Lola was on the right side of her bed with the pink comforter pulled up mid-belly, which exposed her full, firm breasts. Paige could only hope her small, firm breasts would fill in nicely someday. Then she remembered how Lola's breasts looked when she revealed her true age and thought hers staying small might not be a bad thing.

From the bed, Lola said, "Yours stayin' small will keep 'em from lookin' like deflated saddle bags when you're my age, Paige-Turner."

Paige blushed with shame. "I'm sorry. I didn't mean any disrespect."

Lola smiled. "You never need to apologize for honest thoughts, chil'."

"I know, but I didn't mean to hurt your feelins'," Paige said.

Lola patted the bed beside her. "My feelin's are not hurt. Now get under the covers."

Paige hurried to the enormous bed, slid under the covers onto satin sheets, and left her breasts exposed too; it was nice to feel comfortable in her skin around someone else. Then she looked up and saw the mirror and her mouth fell open. Before she could say anything, Lola clapped her hands twice, and the lights went out.

Surprised, Paige said, "You have a Clapper?"

Lola giggled. "Of course not, silly girl. That was a joke."

Paige thought for a second and began laughing. It was a good joke. Lola laughed, too.

When they finished laughing, Paige adjusted Glinda's eyesight so she could see clearly in the dark. "I suppose there's a reason for the mirror?"

"You suppose correctly, Paige-Turner," Lola replied with a grin.

"Well, what's it for?" Paige asked.

"Many things," Lola said. "Mostly, I like to watch myself havin' sex with beautiful men."

Paige blushed again. "Okay. I don't need to hear any more about your mirror."

"You're as ridiculous about sex as your daddy is about nudity."

"Just with old people havin' sex. No offense."

"I should put a hex on you for that, Paige-Turner," Lola teased. "Sex is as natural as breathin'. And it's fun. Even for *old* people."

"Sorry. Can I tell ya somethin'?" Paige asked.

"Always and anything, sweet girl."

"Justin and I were gonna have sex the night he was…killed. But she killed him before we could."

"I'm sorry, sweetheart," Lola said as she took Paige's hand in hers and gave it a gentle squeeze.

"It was so perfect. He fixed up an old tree house and…"

"Will you let me see as much as you're willin' to let me see?" Lola interrupted.

"Of course. How do I let you in?"

"I could get in without your permission, but I'd never trespass on your private thoughts or memories without your permission."

Paige laughed. "Only when I'm thinkin' about your old lady boobs."

"That thought pertained to me, young lady. Your private thoughts are yours, and I'll never trespass there without your permission."

"You have it," Paige said.

"Just think about that night and I'll see what you experienced," Lola said. "I'll stop when you want me to."

Paige opened her mind and thought about that night. Lola experienced everything through Paige's memory of that night. The tree house, the candles, the cot with green, satin sheets, the song *Feels So Right* playing, the conversation Justin overheard Paige and Lindsey talking about pertaining to that song when they were younger, the florescent, green condom, Justin getting on top of Paige. Then the howl that brought an end to the memory. Garrett told Lola about Justin's injuries and she understood why Paige ended the memory there. She didn't want to relive the rest.

"I'm so sorry, Paige-Turner. That would've been a very special night."

"Yeah," Paige said angrily. "That *bitch* took it and Justin away from me."

"I know it doesn't lessen the pain, but I can tell ya that your first time will be with someone who you love and who loves you too. It'll be very special, too."

"Really?" Paige asked.

"Really."

"Then, if ya can see the future and me with someone I love, we must be able to beat the vampire," Paige said.

Lola hesitated a few seconds. "It doesn't exactly work that way."

"What do ya mean?"

"I can see possible futures, but they're always subject to intervenin' events. Are you familiar with the butterfly effect?"

"I saw the first movie with Daddy," Paige said.

"I haven't seen it, but I know the premise," Lola said. "They deal with someone goin' back in time to change somethin', only to find out that the future they created was worse than what they had before. The same is true for futures. I believe, with all my heart, that we'll defeat the ancient. I believe *this* future I *see* for you will come to be, but anything between now and then could alter this future."

Paige thought for a moment. "I'm okay with that. Not knowin' is okay, too."

"That's a mature outlook, Paige-Turner. Now, would ya like to see what else my mirror can do?"

Paige smiled. "Yes, please."

"Have you ever heard the sayin' that mirrors are windows to the soul?"

"Yep."

"Well, they are," Lola said. "They're also windows to other things as well. Watch."

Paige looked at her reflection in the mirror, and suddenly, Glinda looked back at her. Not the nine-foot-tall Glinda, though. This Glinda was Paige's size.

Beyond a rippled reflection in a pond or stream, Paige had never really seen Glinda before. She'd asked her daddy to take a picture of Glinda with his cell, but he refused, citing the many times cloud pictures had been hacked and released. This had mostly been embarrassing pictures of nude celebrities, but he wouldn't risk it.

Paige raised her right arm and looked at it. It was her human arm, and the mirror Glinda raised her right arm and looked at it, too. Paige threw the covers off and looked at the rest of Glinda. She rolled onto her left side, toward Lola, and saw Glinda's bushy tail. She wagged it and felt it wag in her human body.

"This is *so* cool." Paige exclaimed.

"Wanna see somethin' else?" Lola asked.

"Heck, yeah."

A moment later, Glinda was gone, and Paige saw herself surrounded in a shimmering silver glow.

"That's your aura," Lola told her.

Paige moved her limbs around and watched as the silver glow moved with her. "Is this what you see around people all the time?"

"No," Lola said. "Only when I want to see it, when I *need* to see what kind of person I'm dealin' with. Otherwise, my world would be a confusin' mess of colors."

"Can ya show me your aura in the mirror?"

Lola threw back the covers and an instant later, a shimmering pink glow surrounded her.

That Lola's aura was pink shouldn't have surprised Paige, but she had expected it to be green, like her seeing eye.

"That's beautiful, Lola," Paige said. "But I thought your aura would be green like your eye."

"A seer's aura is never the same color as their seein' eye."

"Why not?"

"Our auras show our special powers; the ones we study and train for. Our seein' eyes are random, but they too have a meanin'. Since mine is green, I have more seein' abilities through totems created usin' nature's greenery."

"Like the green, house shaped leaf in the middle of the totem you hung on your door," Paige said. "That leaf should be dead in the winter, but it's not."

"Exactly. In my care, that leaf will never die. Speakin' of that totem, would ya like to see what my house will look like to someone who comes here with ill intent?"

Excited, Paige said, "Absolutely."

Paige had still been looking in the overhead mirror. When their shimmering auras disappeared, Paige saw Lola's had closed her eyes and her lips moved slightly. She dialed up Glinda's hearing to listen to what Lola said, but no words accompanied her lip's movements. A moment later, Lola's lips stopped moving. She opened her eyes, and the reflection in the mirror changed to a view of the outside of the front of her house.

She hadn't exaggerated the effect of the totem. The front of Lola's house was truly dilapidated. The front porch was caved in as was much of the roof, the front door was gone, the bright, white painted exterior was mostly without paint and mold and rot covered the siding. Tall, dead weeds had sprung up along the house and in the visible yard. Then the vision took a jerky move to the left and showed Lola's garage. A large, dead, pine tree had cratered it in and what was visible of her pristine, 56, Cadillac looked like a rusted and crushed pile of junk.

"What happened when the view jerked left like that?" Paige asked.

"We are viewin' my house through the eyes of an earthen elemental I conjured," Lola told her.

"What's an earthen elemental?" Paige asked.

As Lola explained elemental witch's power to conjure earth, wind, fire, and water elementals, and told her the story, she would tell her daddy later that morning, of how she used a water elemental to destroy the young, arrogant, female vampire, Paige watched in the mirror as the earthen elemental took jerky steps around the exterior of Lola's house to display the full illusion of destruction. When it returned to where it had begun, the view seemed to sink into the ground and disappeared altogether.

Once the elemental disappeared, Paige saw Lola and herself in the mirror. Both of them were naked with the covers still thrown aside from when Paige viewed Glinda, and her aura Lola had showed her. There was no shame in it and neither covered themselves. It felt so natural and good to Paige. She felt free.

"Where'd it go?" Paige asked.

"Back into the ground from which I conjured it. If ya looked upon its origin, ya wouldn't see a single blade of grass out of place. Pretty cool, huh?"

"Very cool," Paige agreed.

"Do ya wanna see one of my favorite mirror abilities?" Lola asked.

"Heck, yeah."

One second Paige saw Lola and herself in the mirror and the next second it was as if the ceiling and roof were gone, and Paige saw the night sky. The almost full, bloated moon was in the western sky, making its way, slowly, to the other side of the world, but its light lit up Lola's bed in a silvery sheen. The stars twinkled down from their faraway places in the galaxy.

Paige's breath was stolen by the sight.

After several seconds, Paige took a deep breath, and turned to Lola. "Can we keep it like this all night?"

"Of course," Lola said with a warm smile. "I sleep under this view every night."

"I love Glinda and what she can do, but I wish I could do some things you do," Paige said.

"You and Glinda are perfect, sweetheart. Now, let's try to get some sleep."

"Okay. Lookin' at this, I don't know if I can, though," Paige said even as a yawn followed the statement.

A few minutes later, Paige was fast asleep. Lola covered her up, so she'd be warm and cozy.

Then she looked up at the celestial night sky, and thought, *If it works, you just might get your wish, Paige-Turner.*

~ * ~

Paige slipped out of Lola's amazing bed and went into the bathroom to freshen up. She had dialed up Glinda's hearing to eavesdrop on the conversation her daddy and Lola engaged in outside. Paige was in the middle of brushing her teeth when Lola brought up giving her daddy a tail and implied how he could use it. She almost gagged and dialed Glinda's hearing as low as it would go. Between the running water, toothbrushing, and walls, it worked. She couldn't hear a further word they said. What she didn't know was Lola had been aware of her eavesdropping and, knowing Paige's aversion to old people having sex, had brought up the tail specifically to end her listening in.

Paige desperately wanted to take a shower, but knew she'd just get dirty again running through the woods and they needed to find Al. The shower would have to wait. She removed the scrunchy from her ponytail and shook out her long, dark brown hair. Finally, because she'd promised to take it easy on her daddy concerning her penchant for being naked in front of him, she pulled Justin's Minion T-shirt from her backpack and put it on.

She was ready. She made her way through Lola's dark living room, opened the door, and stepped out into the chilly morning.

~ * ~

Paige saw her daddy and Lola sitting on the front porch swing and the magical fire keeping the tea warm. Lola took the kettle off, poured some of the tea in a cup, and patted the space between herself and her daddy. Paige took the cup and squeezed in between them. Then she took a big gulp and felt the warmth fill her body.

"G'mornin', sleepyhead," Garrett said.

Paige took another gulp of tea. "G'mornin', Daddy."

"How'd ya sleep?" he asked.

"Lola's bed is amazin'. You wouldn't believe what the mirror over her bed can do."

"Nothin' 'bout Lola surprises me," Garrett said.

Lola grinned. "I'll let you and Mandy use it if you're interested."

"Gross," Paige said with a scowl. "Not as gross as givin' Daddy a tail for…just gross."

"Yeah. I brought that up specifically to keep you from eavesdroppin'," Lola said. "I'm guessin' it worked."

"Oh yeah. I didn't wanna hear any more on that subject."

"Paige has a thing about 'old people' havin' sex," Lola said with air quotes.

"Not old people. Just old people I know," Paige clarified. "Like my parents and you."

"Mandy and I are *not* 'old'," Garrett added with finger quotes, too.

"Maybe a little nudge would help," Lola teased.

"No nudgin'," Paige replied.

"Here's an idea," Garrett began, "How 'bout you *nudge* your butt off the swing so we can go find Al?"

"Okay. Should I just strip here and transform on the porch?" Paige teased her daddy.

"I'd prefer you go around the side of the house and do it," Garrett said.

"See," Paige said and visibly shuttered. "This is how uncomfortable I feel when y'all start talkin' 'bout sex and tails."

Lola grinned. "Y'all both need nudges or therapy."

"No nudges," Paige and Garrett said in unison.

Lola raised her hands in surrender as Paige got up and disappeared around the side of Lola's house. An instant later, Glinda stepped back around the corner. She took two deep breaths, sniffing the air, and immediately transformed back into her human body. She quickly tried to hide behind one of the front porch posts, but the six-by-six porch post did little to cover anything but her center mass.

"What the hell, Paige?" Garrett said as he looked at his boots.

"I'm sorry, Daddy. But I have to tell y'all somethin' important."

"Glinda can talk," Garrett shot back.

"It's hard for me to articulate with her mouth."

"Then try harder to learn how to talk through Glinda," Garrett said.

Lola put a hand on Garrett's knee. "Quit lookin' at your boots and look at your daughter. She covered the parts that make ya *uncomfortable*, and this is clearly important."

Reluctantly, Garrett looked up. Lola was right. Paige had her arms over her breasts and the porch pole covered everything but her bare hips.

"That's not so bad now, is it Garrett?" Lola asked.

"No," Garrett admitted. "I guess not."

"Baby steps, Garrett," Lola said. "You'll get there. Now what's so important that ya almost gave your daddy a stroke, Paige-Turner?"

"When I transformed, I smelled the ancient and Mel immediately. I smelled Al, too. He's about ten miles southwest of here..." Paige began.

"Then, let's go get him," Garrett interrupted.

"There's more, Daddy. It's bad."

"What?" Garrett asked, having completely forgotten Paige was naked behind the post.

"I smelled the ancient and Mel 'bout twenty miles southeast of here, too. There are four dead bodies there."

"Fuck." Garrett shouted.

"That's not all," Paige said. "There was a fifth dead body that left with the ancient and Mel."

"He's got another girl for his cloud," Lola stated the obvious.

"This is gonna escalate outta control before your protection potion is ready," Garrett said.

"Time is not on our side," Lola admitted.

Garrett got up. "Let's go find Al and then ya can take me to the other place."

"I'm sorry I didn't cover up better before transformin' back," Paige said.

Garrett stepped off the porch, and looked at Paige, who was no longer hidden behind the post. "Considerin' everything else. This doesn't really register as a problem for me right now, baby girl."

Paige smiled. She wanted to give her daddy a hug, but remembered Lola saying, "Baby steps." Instead, she transformed into Glinda and dropped to all four legs.

Garrett went to his truck. He grabbed a blanket for Paige to cover herself with when she transformed back and a yellow plastic sheet to cover Al's body with. If Paige was correct, and he knew she had been, he'd need four more yellow plastic sheets. But he'd only brought one for Al's body. He'd deal with the rest later.

Glinda followed Garrett to his truck. After he got the needed items and closed the door, he climbed onto Glinda's muscular back. When he was securely on Glinda's back, she took off at a slow run toward Al's body.

Lola, happy for the effort Garrett made to accept Paige in her natural state, watched them disappear into the woods beside her driveway. Happy as she was for Garrett's breakthrough, she was deeply troubled. Garrett was right; things were escalating quickly. That the ancient had so openly slaughtered four people to get another girl for his cloud was a message. A message to her for having seen him.

Lola extinguished the conjured flame, took the kettle and two cups, and went inside. She needed to consult with Mamma Deupree.

~ * ~

Between Lola's house and where Al's body was, Glinda and Garrett had to cross two roads. The first was a farm to market road and the second was a county road. As they neared the farm to market road, Glinda slowed and then stopped. Garrett saw her pointy ears twitch from left to right. He couldn't hear anything at first. A moment later, he heard the distant rumble of glass-pack mufflers and a few seconds later, an older model pickup truck sped by. Still, Glinda didn't move. Then he heard a louder rumble and a big rig, pulling an empty logging trailer, roared by. An instant later, Glinda, effortlessly, leapt the two-lane road in a single bound and they disappeared into the woods on the other side. At the county road, Glinda didn't slow at all. She leapt it at a slow run. A few moments later, Glinda slowed and stopped.

Garrett understood why she'd stopped and slid off her back. Thanks to Lola's tea, his nuggets, and the rest of him, were nice and warm. After he was off Glinda's back, he held up the blanket. Glinda understood. She stood, turned around, putting her back to him, and an instant later, Glinda was Paige again. Garrett placed the blanket around Paige's shoulders. She grabbed the sides of the blanket and wrapped it around her body before turning around. When she did, Garrett saw she was crying. He pulled her into a tight hug.

"I'm sorry, Paige-Turner."

"He was so scared, Daddy," Paige sobbed. "They did it on purpose. Just like Trevor. I *hate* the ancient and what he turned Mel into. Now there're three of 'em."

"We'll get 'em, sweetheart. I promise ya."

"I can't help for two more days. How bad will it be by then?"

That was the concern. As Garrett had told Lola, things were escalating quickly. That there would be more murders and more young girls turned that night was a certainty.

"We're gonna do all we can before the potion is ready to find 'em." Garrett told her.

"Y'all won't find 'em without Glinda," Paige stated flatly.

Garrett smiled down at her. "Give me a little credit. I found Alexis' den on my own."

Paige smiled a weak smile. "Yeah, ya did."

"Okay. Now…where's Al?"

Paige pointed to Garrett's left. "There's a clearin' about twenty yards that way. He's in the clearin'."

"Stay here. I don't want ya seein' him like this."

Paige nodded.

Garrett turned, made his way through the underbrush, and broke into the clearing. It took him a few seconds to take in the full horror of what he saw. Especially the piece of flesh to the left of Al's body. Al's body laid prone, face up, with his arms and legs spread wide. There were ragged bite marks on the inside of his upper right arm and on the inside of his upper left thigh. It wasn't until he saw the jagged wound on Al's upper left thigh Garrett understood. It was like putting a jigsaw puzzle piece in place because it was the only shape that fit. The piece of flesh to the left of Al's body was part of his penis and one of his testicles. He choked back bile surging up his esophagus.

When Garrett was composed, he set about documenting the scene, which included close-up pictures of the chucks of removed flesh, the savage wounds, and the position of his body. Then he closed Al's fogged over, dead eyes staring, unseeing, at the morning sky. With that done, Garrett took the yellow plastic sheet he had tucked into the back of his jeans and covered Al's body. There was a problem, though. No matter how he positioned the sheet, it wasn't large enough to cover the chunk of flesh that was his private parts. Moving it wasn't an option until after George saw and documented Al's body as well. With no other option available, he removed his Pine View County Sheriff's Department cap and placed it over Al's partial junk. He returned to Paige in the woods.

"Can I see him?" Paige asked.

"I don't think that's a good idea, sweetheart."

"Just his face. It's okay, isn't it?"

"It is. Are ya sure ya wanna see him?"

Paige nodded.

Garrett put his right arm around her small shoulders. "Okay. Just his face."

When they were in the clearing, Paige saw her daddy's hat on the ground to the left of the plastic sheet. She knew what was under it. Thoughts of how the Alpha had removed Justin's privates and thrown them into her face raced through her memory. She felt weak in the knees and had to stop walking before she fell.

Garrett felt her sag and tightened his grip on her shoulders. "Ya don't have to do this."

With pure resolve, Paige straitened. "I need to say goodbye."

"Okay," Garrett said as he ushered Paige past his cap to the end of the sheet where Al's head was.

He let go of Paige, bent down, removed the yellow sheet from Al's head, which revealed his ghostly white face, and stood back up.

Paige, already crying, dropped to her knees, put her hands on Al's cheeks, bent, and kissed him on the forehead. "I'm so sorry, Al. Thank you for takin' such good care of me and Mom. I love you."

As Paige got back up, her knees gave out again. Had her daddy not caught her quickly, and pulled her into a tight hug, she would've ended up sprawled across Al's dead body. She hugged her daddy back and cried into his chest.

Garrett held Paige and felt helpless to ease her pain. All he could do was let her cry, which he did for several minutes.

When the sobs turned into sniffles, Paige said, "I'm okay now, Daddy."

"No," Garrett said while rubbing her back gently. "You're not, but you're the strongest person I know, Paige-Turner. I know you're ready to take me to the other bodies, but I have to mark his position in first. Okay?"

Paige let go of her daddy, backed away a few steps, and used the blanket to clear the tears and snot from her face. "Okay. How in the world are ya gonna do that?"

Garrett took his cellphone from his right chest pocket. "I'll pin our location and send it to Trowa, Ty, and George."

"Smart, Daddy. But isn't Ty off this time of day?"

"Yeah. But Trowa and Ty are the only ones we can trust. They'll need my help to move Al, so I won't send it until I'm back from the other place."

"What about the other people?"

"I'll tell 'em when they get here."

"What about me?"

"After we get back to Lola's, I'll take my truck back to the road next to Al's body so they can find me. You stay at Lola's until I come back. Okay?"

Paige nodded.

As Garrett opened the 'Map' app on his cell, it rang. It was so unexpected it startled him to where he almost dropped his phone. He looked at the phone and saw it was Trowa.

This can't be good, he thought.

Garrett tapped the answer icon and brought the phone to his ear. "What's up?"

"We got two more stolen caskets," Trowa told him.

"Where?"

"Pine View First Baptist and Pine View Presbyterian," Trowa answered.

"Shit." Garrett shouted.

"Deep shit. They belonged to Russ Lomax and Maggie Crawford."

"What the fu... hell. Are they targetin' werewolf victims on purpose?" Garrett wondered aloud.

"That," Trowa said. "Or the ground of fresher graves is just easier to dig."

That hadn't crossed Garrett's mind. It made sense, but so did targeting werewolf victims. After all, Lola and James agreed the ancient vampire was in Pine View County for Paige and Glinda.

"Did ya call someone to pick up the bodies?"

"Yeah. I called Digger first, and he answered. He's sendin' hearses to both churches."

"Okay. I'll need ya later," Garrett said.

"What's up?" Trowa asked.

"I'll fill ya in later," Garrett said and ended the call.

"I'm guessin' ya heard all that," Garrett said to Paige.

Paige nodded.

"Two coffins," Garrett said. "Ya think he only took one new girl for his cloud last night, though?"

Paige nodded again. "Yeah, but he's plannin' on takin' more girls for his cloud. The other one might've been for me."

Garrett shuddered at the thought. "I'm glad ya snuck out last night, but that's your *one* free pass, kiddo. Ya ready to take me to the other place?"

Paige nodded and an instant later, Garrett looked up at Glinda as the blanket fell to the ground. As Garrett collected the blanket, Glinda dropped to all fours. Garrett climbed onto her back and Glinda moved swiftly into the woods.

~ * ~

After taking the teakettle and cups into her kitchen, Lola returned to the dark living room and removed a clay canister from the curio cabinet. It was an oddly shaped, red clay canister with a handle on one side and a top shaped like a funnel. She had work to do before she could summon Mamma Deupree.

Summoning three or more witches was easier than summoning one. This was because, as she explained to Garrett, three or more witches could comprise a coven. The night before, she summoned three and the four of them made a mini coven. Once they linked hands, their forms became more stable. This would not be the case with a private meeting. Mamma would remain a shimmering specter of her corporal body, but that would do.

Lola walked to the middle of her living room, bent over so her face was closer to the floor, and tipped the odd shaped, clay canister forward. A grayish powder, ashes from an Ash tree, flowed out of the funnel shaped top. Once the powder began flowing, Lola moved quickly around the living room and created a pattern on the floor; an incantation hiked her long dress up to her knees to keep it from disturbing the ashes as she worked. When she finished, there was an encircled pentagram on the floor.

The lines of the pentagram and circumference of the circle were perfect. What took Lola less than a minute to create would've taken several people with straightedge tools and string lines hours to replicate.

With the pentagram finished, Lola went to her table, opened the drawer of holding, and pulled out five white candles. She placed one white candle at the five tips of the pentagram, sat cross-legged in the center of the pentagram, snapped her fingers, which lit all five candles immediately, and fell into a trance to summon Mamma. A few seconds later, Mamma's shimmering form appeared in front of Lola. Mamma sat cross-legged on the dirt floor in her Haitian hut, but her shimmering form floated a few inches above Lola's floor.

In a crackling voice sounding near and far, Mamma said, "Why have you summoned me again so soon and why alone?"

"Glinda. Paige came to my house last night after our council," Lola said. "When I returned her home, the ancient was there with the fledglin' he took the previous night. He was there for Paige. Whether he wanted her for his cloud or because he has discovered her identity, I do not know. I saw him and he fled. Then he murdered five people and took one for his cloud. I fear that why he would do this so openly is because I saw him and kept him from takin' Paige."

"You know this how?" Mamma asked.

"Just see," Lola said. "It'll be quicker."

Seers did not intrude in their sister's minds. Not without an invitation. With it given, Mamma's crystal blue seeing eye materialized in the shimmering form and she saw everything that had transpired since their council ended the previous night.

Mamma's crystal blue, seeing eye faded back into the shimmer. "It will not work, sister. It has never worked."

"You don't know her as I do, Mamma."

"I know what you are trying to do has *never* worked," Mamma crackled near and far. "Not even on our own kind."

"She's special," Lola said. "I believe it will."

"If it does not, it could harm her greatly. Maybe even kill her," Mamma told Lola what she already knew.

"It'll work or it won't," Lola said, knowing that challenging Mamma's wisdom on any subject wasn't wise. "I don't believe it will harm her if it doesn't. She's stronger than you know,"

Mamma cackled. "You take a significant risk with someone you love, sister. This is not why you summoned me. I saw your purpose, and this too is dangerous."

"But it can be done?" Lola asked.

"Yes," Mamma crackled near and far. "But not by tonight. You have much love for, and faith in, this child. I do not know her as you do, but I will not bring about her destruction by rushing the potion two days,"

"She *can* handle it, but I won't press the issue further," Lola said. "If you're willin' to reduce the potion by one day, I'll take it."

"Very well," Mamma said as her shimmering hand plucked another rat skull from her necklace and placed on the floor in front of Lola where it materialized.

"Double the brew's content, including your foolish addition, and replace the green flame with a white one. It will be ready tomorrow night."

"Thank you, Mamma," Lola said.

"Do not thank me," Mamma crackled more far than near. "This will, most likely, kill your beloved Paige,"

"It won't," Lola said, but Mamma had already gone.

Frustrated by Mamma's lack of trust, and worried she might be right, Lola extinguished the candle flames with a snap of her fingers, got up, and went to work on the potion right away. When it was simmering over a white flame, Lola put the white candles back into the drawer, took the odd shaped, clay canister and retraced, backwards, the steps she'd taken to create the encircled pentagram. The ashes sucked back up into the canister; not a spec was left behind. She placed the canister back in the curio and went outside for some cool, fresh air. She prayed to the Elements for Paige and Glinda to possess the strength needed to survive the powerful potion.

~ * ~

To get to the next location, Glinda and Garrett had to cross the same two roads they had previously crossed. Both were clear and Glinda leapt them in stride. After these two roads, they came to another farm to market road, which she didn't slow down for either. At Highway Sixty-Nine, Glinda went to one of the several bridges she used and had to wait for light traffic to pass on the southbound side before she leapt under the bridge and again on the northbound side before she leapt into the woods on the south side of the small river that ran under the bridges.

Garrett held on for dear life with every leap and tree dodge Glinda took but felt like he had never been in any real danger of falling off. It was like Glinda had compensated for his weight and center of gravity so the two of them were more like one entity instead of wolf and rider. This made the long ride very enjoyable. Garrett enjoyed the ride so much, he was disappointed when Glinda slowed and then stopped. From her back, he could see above the underbrush, and he saw a house about fifty yards away. He climbed off Glinda's back, held up the blanket again, and draped it over Paige's shoulders an instant later.

"This is the house?" Garrett asked.

After pulling the blanket over her nakedness, Paige turned to face her daddy. "Yeah. I don't know what all happened in there, but it's bad. One body has been burned."

"Burned?" Garrett asked.

"Yeah. It's a sickenin' smell, Daddy."

"Do ya recognize the house?"

Paige shook her head.

"Okay. Wait here."

"Don't worry. I don't wanna see what's in that house," Paige told him.

Garrett made his way through the underbrush to the tree line alongside the yard. Like most houses on the outskirts of the county, it was secluded. There was a road several hundred feet in front of the house, and the front yard didn't have many trees for cover. It wouldn't be good for him to be seen sneaking into a mass-murder house. It might even make him a suspect.

Garrett turned back to where Paige stood. "Any cars comin'?"

Paige dialed up Glinda's hearing to near transforming level and cocked her head from side. "No. It's safe."

Garrett made a quick dash for the front porch. Not high school, QB option quick, but quick enough. The front door was open, so he stepped quietly into the quieter house. He could smell it, too. Burned flesh. It had an almost sweet smell to it, which made his stomach take a turn in his belly.

He walked the short distance from the entry hall into the living room. What he saw was as bad as anything he'd seen the night of the MRB killings. His stomach took another turn, and he puked, but he kept it from erupting from his mouth and swallowed the warm, acidic liquid back down. It burned. Then he bent over and repeated the process two more times. He thought it would never end and was glad it was only sweet and spiced tea that morning. Had he eaten anything, he'd have had to swallow chunks of food with the acidic liquid, and he didn't think he could've managed that. The nausea passed. When it did, he sucked in gasping breaths of air, like a drowning man would do. The smell of barbecued human flesh tainted the air. He gagged, and his eyes watered, but he didn't puke again.

After a few moments, he regained his composure enough to investigate. Unfortunately, stumbling across the carnage by accident wouldn't be plausible. He'd have to wait for a worried friend or family member to find them and call it in. Garrett pitied whoever the unfortunate person would be. He doubted whoever it was could hold back their vomit.

Garrett went from body to body, starting with the teenage boy, who had his throat ripped out, to the dad, who had a fireplace poker through his blackened head and was the source of the sickeningly sweet smell, to the mom, who had a ragged hole in her torso and what looked like a crushed, human heart on the floor beside her, to the little girl with her SpongeBob SquarePants underwear showing, who had two, small puncture wounds high on the inner thigh of her left leg.

Garrett couldn't stand to see her like that. He put on the latex gloves he had in his back pocket and pulled her nightshirt down to cover her underwear. In that moment, he better understood why Paige had put the stuffed Toothless back in Trevor's hand. Some things, even if doing it was, technically, disturbing a crime scene, were the right thing to do.

After giving the little girl a little dignity in death, Garrett looked around the house for some evidence of who was taken. He didn't have to look long. Behind the sofa was a sofa table with an assortment of pictures. All three kids' class pictures were framed, and there was a fairly recent family picture, too. He didn't need to be a cop to pick out the missing family member. The girl in the class picture had long, blonde hair and big, green eyes. She was pretty, but she looked so young. Younger than what James and Lola had surmised was the ancient's taste in cloud members. They also said vampires remove evidence of their fang marks when they kill, as they had done with Trevor and Al. They had left the little girl's puncture marks unmolested. Something had changed the vampire's MO, and Garrett didn't like it. Not one bit.

Garrett took the missing girl's class picture, tucked it under his arm, and made his way to the front door. He peaked out, saw Paige in the woods. She had moved closer.

In a low voice he knew she would hear, said, "Is it safe?"

Paige waved him toward the woods, and he sprinted back to her.

When he was beside her, he showed her the picture and, winded from the quick sprint, huffed, "She's missin'. Do ya know her?"

Paige nodded. "Her name is Megan Williams. She's a freshman."

"Did she skip a few years? She looks like she's about eleven years old."

"No," Paige said. "She and her twin brother, Mitchel, are fourteen or fifteen. We're not friends, so I don't know for sure which. She just looks young for her age."

"Okay. I need to put this back. Is it clear?"

Paige cocked her head and listened. "Yeah. Both ways, if ya don't have a heart attack from all that runnin'."

"You're hilarious," Garrett said before running back to the house and putting the picture back.

He poked his head out again before running back. When Paige waved him on, he ran back to the woods. He was out of shape and decided he needed to start jogging. He'd quit smoking, but was embarrassed by how out of breath the short runs had made him. Garrett had to put his hands on his knees while he caught his breath.

"You gonna be okay, old man?" Paige teased.

"Yeah, smart ass," Garrett huffed. "Must've been the damn cigarettes."

"Or you're just old," Paige teased more.

Garrett stood, felt a little woozy, but said, "And you're not too old for a good, ol' fashioned, spankin', young lady."

"It wouldn't hurt," Paige pointed out.

Garrett gave up. "Okay. How 'bout ya give your old man a ride back to Lola's?"

"Are ya gonna call this in?" Paige asked.

Garrett shook his head. "I can't."

"Why not?"

"Because I'd have no cause to check on 'em."

"So…we just leave 'em there for someone else to find?"

"Unfortunately, yeah," Garrett said. "Someone'll check in on 'em after they don't answer their phones for a while."

"I *heard* you in there, Daddy. You heaved three times, and you're used to this kind of stuff. Think what seein' that will do to someone who cares about 'em?"

"I'm sorry, sweetheart. It has to be this way."

"What about an anonymous call from a burner?" Paige asked.

"Burner? Where'd you learn about burners?"

"From *Breaking Bad*. They use 'em all the time."

"Well, that's TV. Even with a burner, the signal can be triangulated and the call's location discovered."

"Would y'all do that?"

"Us? No. But, when this breaks, the DPS will get involved. An anonymous call would most likely come from the killer, so they would trace the call."

"I could take Glinda way out into the woods, make the call with her voice, destroy the phone, and scatter its parts all over the place."

"They could still trace the point of purchase from the SIM card."

Frustrated, Paige said, "I wish this was a TV show."

"I do, too. It'd be more believable. Now, how 'bout that ride. Can ya help your old man out?"

Paige smiled. "I can do that."

An instant later, Glinda towered over Garrett. She dropped to all fours. Garrett grabbed the blanket and, with some effort, climbed onto Glinda's back, and off they went.

~ * ~

Early that afternoon, after he'd gotten some much needed rest, Dănuţ checked the mailbox in front of the Eternal Rest Funeral Home. He wasn't expecting any first-class mail, but the Saturday edition of the *Pine View Post* was there, and he was interested in that. Not for the news, but for the advertisement he'd placed, which announced the establishment's official opening date of Monday, January 4, 2016. He tucked the paper under his arm and headed back inside.

Once inside, Dănuţ turned to the left and opened double doors leading into the spacious office from which he would deal with grieving loved ones, while pretending to care. The office was tastefully decorated. Different cultures have different expectations where dealing with death is concerned and Dănuţ had studied American culture well before spending his Master's substantial wealth on the funeral home.

The walls were a calming beige with white crown molding and doors. The walls were adorned with comforting pictures—a seascape, a mountain view, a field of flowers, and a waterfall with a rainbow in the mist where the cascading water splashed off rocks that surrounded a crystal blue pond at the bottom of the waterfall. There was a large, mahogany desk in front of a mahogany book shelved wall across from the double-doors, and a leather wingback chair behind the desk. On the desk was a cordless phone in its charging stand, a MacBook Pro, a printer, a dispenser with business cards in it, and a brass lamp with an opaque, green, glass shade. The bookshelves had scattered, leather bound, books and an assortment of knickknacks mixed among the books. There were two leather and wood chairs in front of the desk and a leather sofa along the right-side wall. Along the left-side wall was a mahogany sideboard with brass lamps on each end and a Keurig coffee maker with an assortment of single-use flavors to pick from. Everything grieving people needed to feel more comfortable.

Dănuț pulled back the leather wingback chair, sat, and opened the *Pine View Post* intent on skipping to the adverts, but the headline 'Three-year-old Boy Brutally Murdered Christmas Morning' in large, bold print caught his attention. He read the story.

'Christmas morning turned out to be anything but cheerful for a Pine View County couple, Troy and Penny Henderson. What began as a missing child report turned tragic when their three-year-old son, Trevor Henderson, was found brutally murdered in the woods behind their double-wide trailer house. Sheriff Garrett Lambert could not be reached for comment but, once again, the Sheriff's Department is tightlipped on details of Trevor's untimely demise. This reporter has learned, from an unnamed source, that the little boy's body has at least one large bite wound. This is all too reminiscent of last May's "MRB Massacre." Which begs the question, is it happening again? Will Sheriff Lambert be more forthcoming with this investigation than he was last May. One can only hope.'

Dănuț leaned back in the chair, and ran his bony fingers through his thinning, blond hair. "How did they find the body so soon? The Master will not be happy about this."

He tossed the paper aside, the advert forgotten, powered up the MacBook Pro, clicked on the Safari browser icon, which opened on

Google's website. His fingers hovered above the keyboard. His intent was to locate the seer who had spoiled the Master's plan to take the girl named Paige for his cloud. He figured finding the seer might mitigate the Master's anger over the boy's body being discovered so quickly. What would he search for? With nothing else coming to mind, he typed in 'East Texas Witches.' The results were less than encouraging.

The first search yielded over five million results, which he didn't look through. The first few pages pertained to pagans, who were, mostly, not witches. They were more akin to the druids of old who were earth worshipers and had no supernatural powers.

Dănuț next searched for 'East Texas Seer Witches.' This narrowed the results to about one million but was no more helpful than the previous search. Next, he searched for 'East Texas Palm Readers.' This produced over twenty-eight million results. He had broadened the search, not narrowed it. He tried 'Famous East Texas Witches,' which produced over eleven million results.

Dănuț let out a frustrated growl and leaned back in the chair. He had to think. Dănuț had to be smart. He took several deep, calming breaths, and it came to him. He pulled up the *Pine View Post* website and searched for 'Witch.' No hits. He tried 'Palm Reader.' No hits. He tried 'Seer.' No hits. Frustrated, and about to give up, he typed in 'Healer.' That search produced one hit. Eager, Dănuț clicked on the story. He quickly scanned the story, uninterested in the content, until he saw the name of the healer— Lola Laveau. The story included a picture of the healer, who was a beautiful African American woman with cornrows that had pink and white beads at the end of each braid.

Dănuț printed the picture and reread the article carefully in the hopes it would include her address. It didn't, but it said she lived in northeast Pine View County, though. It wasn't much, but it was a start. He Googled 'Lola Laveau' hoping to find out more about her. There were a few stories, but none of them included her address or phone number. Dănuț was frustrated, but not surprised. Witches were secretive and folks usually found them by word of mouth. If the Master confirmed the healer in the story was the *vrăjitoare* who saw him, Dănuț would spend every waking moment searching for her. He would find her.

~ * ~

Lola was on the front porch swing again and enjoying the crisp, sunny afternoon. She sensed Glinda's approach several moments before she and Garrett emerged from the woods. Glinda stopped at Lola's porch steps; Garrett slid off her back and held up the blanket from behind her. An instant later, Lola looked at Paige's naked body. Garrett quickly draped the blanket over Paige's shoulders, and she wrapped it around herself, concealing her nakedness.

"Well?" Lola asked as they climbed the porch steps and headed for the swing.

After they sat down, Garrett said, "It was bad, Lola. A family of four murdered and a freshman girl who looks eleven years old was taken."

"He is a vile creature, Garrett," Lola said.

"They didn't remove the flesh from the bite on the little girl," Garrett said. "I saw the puncture wounds on her inner thigh."

"I fear this is my fault," Lola said.

"How is it your fault?" Paige asked.

"They remove the flesh to mask their existence, but I saw him," Lola said. "He has no reason to hide now. Which means he'll go old-world, fear and destruction now."

"You're sayin' this'll get worse tonight and tomorrow night?" Garrett asked.

"I'm afraid so," Lola said. "But I have some good news."

"I can use it," Garrett said.

"I summoned Mamma and consulted with her 'bout speedin' up the protection potion."

"And?" Paige asked.

"It'll be ready tomorrow night," Lola told them.

"That is good news," Paige said. "Glinda can start helpin' tomorrow night."

"That still leaves tonight," Garrett reminded them.

"We just have to hunker down and get through it," Lola said.

Angry, Garrett said, "While more people get killed and more

young girls get taken."

"I don't like it either. But we're doin' all we can, Daddy."

"I know. But it still doesn't sit well with me," Garrett said as he got up. "I need to call Ty, Trowa, and George, to get Al's body."

Garrett walked away, but Paige stopped him when she said, "Will ya call Mom, too? I can't."

Garrett turned and saw the tears welling in Paige's emerald, green eyes. "Of course I will, Paige-Turner. Don't you worry 'bout that."

Paige nodded as Lola put her left arm around her small shoulders and pulled her close. Paige buried her face in the crook of Lola's neck.

Garrett turned to leave again, but Lola stopped him when she said, "Tomorrow's Sunday. Y'all goin' to Mass?

"Plannin' on it," Garrett said.

"Good. I think it's time we have another meetin' at your house with our…fellowship," Lola said. "And ya need to invite Father Mike, too."

Garrett thought about it for a moment and nodded. "I think you're right."

Paige looked at her daddy. "He'll understand."

"If he doesn't, I'll nudge him," Lola added.

Garrett smiled. "I love ya both."

"I love you, too," Lola and Paige said in unison.

Lola and Paige watched Garrett get in his truck and drive away.

As the dust settled after his exit, Lola thought, *Love, goodness, and the light will defeat this hate, evil, and darkness.*

Chapter Nine

Sunset on December 26, 2015, in Pine View County, Texas came at five twenty-two p.m. Garrett arrived at his parent's house about thirty minutes before sunset, tired and hungry. Aside from it having been a long day that began before sunrise, securing Al's body had turned out to be much more difficult than expected. First, his body had been more than a mile from the nearest road. Second, Al wasn't fat, but he was a large man and George had been little help. This left all the carrying to Garrett, Ty, and Trowa. They had to stop several times to rest before loading his body into George's County Coroner's van. Garrett hadn't had a bite to eat the entire busy day.

~ * ~

George demanded an explanation when he saw Al's body with the missing flesh, which had been like the Trevor boy's wound.

"Okay, Garrett. Enough of this bullshit," George said. "You keep askin' me to keep cause of death a secret, but ya don't trust me enough to tell me what's really goin' on. Trust goes both ways, my friend. I'm not coverin' for you until ya tell me what's goin' on."

Garrett looked from George to Ty and Trowa, who stood behind George. Trowa shrugged and Ty nodded.

Garrett took a deep breath. "Ya already know about the werewolves last summer."

George nodded.

"This is different," Garrett said.

"This isn't werewolves again?" George asked.

"You saw those bodies," Garrett said. "Does this look like the same thing?"

"No. These wounds aren't as…savage and the Trevor boy's body was completely drained of blood," George said. "I suppose I'll find the same with Al's body, too."

"You will," Garrett confirmed.

Exasperated, George asked, "So, what the fuck is doin' this?"

"This is the work of a vampire," Garrett told him.

"You gotta be shittin' me. Why the fuck are werewolves and vampires hangin' out in Pine View County?"

"Where the werewolves were concerned, Pine View County was just a proximity issue," Garrett said. "You know Alexis, Seth, Dillion, and Cole were SFA students, and we were close enough that they didn't have to shit where they ate."

"The vampire? Why is it here?" George asked.

"Accordin' to two folks who know a lot about this shit, supernatural events, like werewolves, attract more supernatural events, like vampires," Garrett explained.

"Who all knows about this?" George asked.

"Me, Ty, Trowa, Mandy, the two folks I mentioned before, James Huff, a professor at SFA, Lola Laveau, because of Al, Lacy found out last night, and now you," Garrett said, purposefully excluding Paige from the list.

"What about that other SFA professor, Yost?" George said. "She came to the county morgue and inspected the Daniels and Albertson bodies. She doesn't know?"

"She suspects, but I never confirmed it with her. She doesn't know anything 'bout this. You're in an exclusive club, George," Garrett said, purposefully to pump his ego.

"Okay. I'm in. Like I said, trust goes both ways," George said as he nervously adjusted his glasses. "I'll get creative with the cause of death again."

"He had a cold and was mixing cough medicine with alcohol. How 'bout this?" Garrett said. "The combination disoriented him. He went for a walk, got lost, and died of exposure?"

George thought for a moment. "One night in the woods is a stretch for exposure, but, with the other conditions, I can make it work."

Garrett stuck out his hand, which George grabbed. "Thanks, George. It's actually good to have ya in the loop."

He meant it. This would make things easier when the Williams' call came in.

After all that, and Al's body had been loaded and George left, Garrett told Ty and Trowa about what happened at the Williams' house.

"Fuck." Ty shouted.

"He has another girl for his cloud now," Trowa stated the obvious.

"Tonight's gonna be a bloodbath," Ty said.

"I have some good news," Garrett told them.

"What?" Ty asked.

"Lola figured out how to shorten the potion's readiness by a day," Garrett said.

"Glinda will be ready to hunt tomorrow night?" Trowa asked.

"She will," Garrett confirmed.

"She still can't do this alone," Ty pointed out.

"You're right," Garrett said. "She'll need us and one more."

"Who?" Trowa asked.

"Father Mike," Ty answered for Garrett.

"Exactly," Garrett said. "I'm gonna invite him to my house after Mass tomorrow mornin'. I want y'all and James and Lola there, too. Three o'clock work for y'all?"

They nodded.

"Okay. I'll see y'all then," Garrett said and shook hands with both men.

Before they parted ways, Trowa said, "Oh yeah. The preachers at the two churches where the coffins were taken are gonna inform the families. So, ya don't have to worry about that, Chief."

Profoundly relieved, Garrett said, "Thank God for that."

Letting Russ Lomax's daughter know about the coffin theft would be difficult, but doable. Informing Maggie Crawford's mom, Arleen, would've been a nightmare. He'd only visited Arleen twice. Once to tell her that her husband Ben died in a roll-over accident and once to tell her that her daughter Maggie had been killed at the MRB party. Arleen slapped his face at Maggie's funeral. He was glad this news would come from someone else.

"Okay," Garrett said. "Three o'clock tomorrow."

As they were parting ways, Erica Harris' voice crackled over their radios. The Williams family had been discovered by a neighbor who drove by and noticed their front door open. Garrett had hoped for more time and scolded himself for not shutting the front door when he left the house.

Garrett depressed the transmit button on the hip radio he had clipped to his belt. "Ty, Trowa, and I are on our way."

Then he called George, gave him the address, and told him to meet them there.

~ * ~

Garrett, Ty, and Trowa arrived at the Williams' house before George to find a very distraught woman sitting with her back against a tree in the front yard crying hysterically.

Garrett pulled in first. He knew where to go so, Ty and Trowa followed him.

As he got out of his truck, the woman wailed, "They're all dead and Megan's missin'."

"Get a blanket and tend to her, Trowa," Garrett said. "Ty, come with me."

A moment later, Garrett and Ty entered the quiet house.

While in the front hall, Garrett said, "This is bad, Ty. If you're gonna puke, do it outside."

"I've been to war and seen some fucked up shit," Ty reminded him.

"Yeah, okay," Garrett said. "Sometimes I forget that. C'mon."

Ty followed Garrett into the living room and surveyed the carnage. He'd seen a little girl strapped with explosives explode and pulled part of her finger from his leg. Ty'd seen his friend Bobby "Bulldog" Benson decapitated; his other friend, Clint McDonald, dead with a Humvee steering wheel folded like an umbrella and piercing his chest; his corporal, Dirk Burnett, with his legs missing from above the knees, and many other war horrors. He'd never seen a family viscously murdered, though. Ty didn't feel like puking. He felt like crying.

Garrett noticed Ty stood stationary. "You okay, brother?"

Ty shook his head slowly. "Yeah. It's just…"

"I know. A whole family murdered, and one taken."

Garrett got the family picture from the sofa table, and showed it to Ty. "He took her."

"Shit. She looks so young."

"I know. Paige said she a freshman at Pine View High School and fourteen or fifteen years old. The boy is her twin brother."

Ty looked at the boy, who looked older than his twin sister, with the ripped-out throat. "She's still young."

"She is. James and Lola said the ancient likes 'em young."

Ty's eyes drifted to the little girl in the corner. "She the one Megan fed on after bein' turned?"

"Yeah," Garrett said. "And they didn't remove the bite marks."

"Why not?"

"Lola said, since she saw him, he has no reason to hide. He's goin' old-world, fear and intimidation now."

"Then tonight really will be a bloodbath."

"There are three vampires now, and he wants more. Yeah. Tonight will be bad."

"Fuck," Ty growled. "I hate this. I feel so helpless."

Garrett grasped Ty's shoulder. "I know how ya feel, but we need to document the scene now. You want the males or females?"

Ty looked at the dad's blackened, burned head with the poker sticking through it. "I'll take the females."

"Okay. Let's get to it."

Garrett went to the boy and began taking pictures of his body position and the wound.

A moment later, Ty said, "Fuck. Is that her crushed heart on the floor?"

"I think so," Garrett said.

"Wanna trade?" Ty asked.

"No take backs," Garrett said.

Their timing was perfect. Just as they had finished taking the pictures, George showed up.

He walked into the room and looked at the carnage. "What the fuck? This is a completely different MO from the previous two. Is this the vampire or somethin' else?"

"It's the vampire," Garrett said. "You'll find two puncture marks on the little girl's upper left thigh, and she's been bled dry."

"He didn't remove the flesh?" George asked.

"No," Garrett said.

"The MO *is* different?"

"There's somethin' else I need to tell ya, George," Garrett said. "This vampire is collectin' young girls for his cloud."

"What the fuck's a cloud?"

"A cloud is what a group of bats is called, and he's buildin' one. You heard 'bout Melanie Zane goin' missin'?"

George nodded.

"He took her. She's a vampire now," Garrett said. "He took a young girl named Megan Williams from this house last night. She's a vampire now, too."

"Holy fuck," George whispered.

"It's gonna get worse before we find the fucker and kill him," Garrett said.

"Can ya? Can ya kill him, Garrett?" George asked.

"We killed the werewolves," Ty said.

"You still in, George?" Garrett said. "Can we count on ya to help us get through this?"

George was silent, but he nodded.

"Good. We need four body bags," Garrett said. "Have Trowa bring 'em in. You'll have to deal with the bodies later. We'll take care of this."

A few minutes later, Trowa came in carrying the body bags.

He quickly surveyed the scene. "This is fucked."

Garrett and Ty didn't disagree. They went to work immediately. The little girl was the easiest. The mom, dad, and son were not. With the mom and son, they had to handle missing body parts, crushed heart with the mom and the ripped-out throat with the son. Because they had to leave the fireplace poker in place, the dad was the most difficult to fit into a body bag. That and the burnt flesh that peeled off his face when they lifted him. They had to collect that, too.

By the time they had all the bodies loaded in George's van, and the neighbor's statement taken, it was early evening and time to go home.

~ * ~

As Garrett pulled to a stop in front of his parent's house, Mandy came out and wrapped him in a tight hug as soon as he stepped out of his truck. "What took y'all so long? Did Glinda have trouble findin' Al?"

"No. She found him right away. But…crap. I forgot to call Lacy. Anyway, I'll give ya all the details later. The quick version is the vampire took a freshman girl for his cloud and killed the of her family. I spent the rest of the day dealin' with that."

"Oh, Garrett. I'm so sorry," Mandy said and kissed him firmly on the mouth.

After the day he'd had, holding and kissing Mandy felt good. It felt safe.

They were still kissing when Garrett's mom came to the opened front door. "If y'all are hungry, I've got venison chili and sweet cornbread on the table. Or y'all can continue eatin' each other's faces. Up to y'all."

Mid-kiss, Garrett and Mandy began laughing. After that, it was impossible to continue kissing.

Their lips parted and Garrett said, "I am pretty hungry. I haven't eaten all day."

Mandy sighed. "Okay, but I wanna eat your face again later."

Garrett smiled down at Mandy's beautiful face. "Okay. As long as I can eat you a little lower than your face."

Mandy blushed. "You gotta a deal, cowboy."

He squeezed her tight ass with both hands, and they went inside to eat supper.

~ * ~

Dănuț opened the secret door concealing the Master's underground lair at five twenty p.m. and stepped back until he was against the wall. In his hands, he had the picture of Lola Laveau. He watched the minute and second hands on his watch and waited. At five twenty-two, on the dot,

Dănuţ heard his Master's coffin thrown open. An instant later, Dragoş floated into the room and looked down on Dănuţ.

"What is it you are holding?" Dragoş asked, more politely than usual.

Not knowing how the Master would react, Dănuţ moved away from the wall a little. "I think I found the seer."

"Let me see," Dragoş said patiently.

Dănuţ moved a little closer and held up the picture for the Master to see. When Dragoş saw the picture, his lips drew back, exposing all his fangs. He hissed, and the paper the picture had been printed on burst into flames. Dănuţ dropped the burning image to the floor. He didn't dare stomp out the flames, though. If the Master wanted it to burn, it would burn.

As smoke rose between them, Dragoş said, "That is vile *vrăjitoare*. Tell me what you have learned, Dănuţ."

Sheepishly, Dănuţ said, "Her name is Lola Laveau, and she lives in northeast Pine View County. I am sorry, Master. That is all the information I could find today. I will keep searching until I find her for you, Master."

Dragoş smiled a hideous smile. "You did well, Dănuţ. I know you will keep searching until you find her. If you do not, I will feed you to my daughters."

"Yes, Master," Dănuţ said.

"Speaking of my daughters, they are still resting," Dragoş said. "Please awake Agrapina and Antanasia."

"Yes, Master. But…" Dănuţ trailed off.

"But what?" Dragoş hissed.

"The Pine View Post was delivered today. I wanted to make sure the advert announcing the funeral home's grand opening was included…"

"I am growing impatient, Dănuţ. Get to the point," Dragoş interrupted with a growl.

"The boy. Agrapina's first kill. His body was found yesterday morning," Dănuţ said as he took an involuntary step back, away from the Master.

Dragoş' features darkened and his eyes turned into silver slits.

"How could they find him so soon?"

"Perhaps they used dogs. The ones they call bloodhounds," Dănuț mistakenly suggested.

Dragoş was on Dănuț before Dănuț registered movement. He grabbed Dănuț painfully by the top of his head, his clawed fingernails dug into Dănuț's flesh, into his skull. He lifted him effortlessly into the air, so they were blue eyes to silver, slit eyes. Dragoş opened his mouth to its full, deadly extent by unhinging his bottom jaw, and closed it around Dănuț's face.

Dănuț felt the Master's needle-sharp fangs penetrate his skin and thought he would be killed, his face removed in an instant. The Master didn't remove his face. Instead, an instant later, his face was out of the Master's mouth, and he was thrown across the room. Dănuț collided against the white tiled, embalming room wall. The impact broke several of the tiles and several of Dănuț's ribs. He crumpled to the floor in a bloody, broken heap. Dragoş was instantly there; looking down on him through his silver, slit eyes.

"How dare you think a *dog*, a stupid animal, could find one of my kills so quickly," Dragoş growled. "I have been doing this for eight hundred years. I know how to hide a kill so it will not be found for days or weeks."

Dănuț coughed up blood and wheezed, "I am sorry, Master. I did not mean to offend. I thought…"

"What have I told you about thinking, slave?" Dragoş hissed.

Dănuț cried. The tears mixed with the blood on his face from the puncture wounds left by the Master's clawed fingernails and fangs and dripped onto the concrete floor. He coughed up more blood, which splattered on the concrete floor too.

Dragoş reached down for Dănuț, and he braced himself for another bone shattering fling across the embalming room. One that would, most likely, kill him. The Master's grip was, unexpectedly, gentle. Gentle as the Master was, every part of Dănuț hurt as the Master lifted him up and cradled him in his arms like a baby.

Dragoş used one of his deadly thumbnails to slit his right nipple. "Feed, Dănuț. Feed until you are healed."

Dănuţ didn't question the Master's unexpected kindness. He locked his lips around the stiff nipple and drank the sweet, black nectar that was his Master's undead blood. As he fed, he felt his shattered ribs mending and the puncture wounds on his head and face close. In all his years of service, the Master had never let Dănuţ feed so much. Like a beaten dog that still wags its tail at the sight of its abuser because it might receive a pat on the head instead of a kick to its ribs, Dănuţ took the kindness. It never occurred to Dănuţ the Master needed him as much, if not more, than he needed the Master.

When Dănuţ was healed, Dragoş lowered him to the floor. "Clean up that blood before you wake my daughters. I do not need them fighting over your mess."

"Yes, Master."

"I will take two more daughters tonight. Secure another coffin. After you have the coffin, search for the *vrăjitoare*."

"Yes, Master," Dănuţ said and did as he was told.

~ * ~

Lola and Paige spent most of the remaining day outside roaming Lola's property. Paige would've preferred to take the walk naked, but, unlike Lola, who was impervious to temperature, unless she was Glinda, it was too cold. The effects of the tea had worn off, so she wore sneakers, sweatpants, and a SFA hoody.

Lola didn't have a garden, but she walked her property showing Paige which herbs, leaves, berries, and other plants were eatable as she collected some for their supper. Paige knew most of the plants Lola showed her, like the berries, should be dormant in the winter, but Lola's powers kept them in bloom year-round. As the sun sank in the western sky, they went inside.

Once inside, Lola went to the cauldron hovering over the magical, white flame, and looked at the bubbling protection potion. "This is reducin' nicely. You realize that, since I had to double the ingredients, you and Glinda will have to drink twice as much?

"I figured that out on my own," Paige said. "See, I am pretty wise already."

Lola smiled. "For a sixteen-year-old girl, you're pretty wise, but not vampire killin' wise."

"I still think Glinda can take him," Paige said defiantly.

"That, Paige-Turner, is exactly why ya need the potion. You're not wise enough to know better."

"Okay," Paige relented. "I get it. Mind if I get comfortable?"

"Ya don't need to ask," Lola told her.

Paige went into Lola's bedroom, removed the constricting clothing, and, feeling much better, joined Lola in the kitchen to help her prepare supper from the 'earthly offerings,' Lola's words, they had gathered.

Where appetites were concerned, Lola and Paige could not have been more different. Paige had always liked meat but, since becoming Glinda, her taste, need, for meat had increased substantially. Lola was vegan and only ate what the earth provided. When Paige argued the earth also provided plenty of tasty animals to eat, she got an in-depth lecture on the difference between what the earth, meaning ground, and what the Earth, meaning planet, provided. Lola would only eat, or use in her totems, potions, and brews, earthly offerings replenished through natural order. When Paige pointed out there was nothing natural about Lola's ability to keep plants green and blooming year-round, Lola just glared at her. It was an argument Paige couldn't win. She was wise enough to know that.

Lola and Paige had a vegan supper that night, and Paige enjoyed it. Had she known her daddy was enjoying Grandma's venison chili and sweet cornbread at that exact moment, she would have enjoyed it less.

"This is a lot tastier than I thought it'd be," Paige confessed as she brought another fork full of vegetables to her mouth.

"Thank you, Paige. I know you and Glinda require more protein in your diet, but y'all will survive just fine until tomorrow night."

When supper was finished, Paige helped Lola do the dishes and clean up. After that, because Lola didn't have a TV and bad cell reception, Paige was at a loss for something to do. She watched the cauldron hover over the white flame for a time, and she smelled the bubbling content. That was a mistake. It smelled like swamp mud. The thought of drinking it made the vegan supper in her belly knot up.

Lola noticed Paige's boredom and asked if she'd like to meditate with her. Paige had been reluctant, but Lola was persuasive. So, Paige joined Lola on the living room floor to try it. Lola placed a tall, blue candle in front of each of them and lit them with a snap of her fingers on each wick.

"Sit like I'm sittin', close your eyes, and clear your mind," Lola instructed.

The eye closing and sitting parts were easy. Sitting cross-legged with her hands, palms up, on her knees were easy, too. Clearing her mind was another matter altogether. There was so much swirling around in her head. The vampire, Al, Trevor, Mel, Megan, the bodies of Megan's family, and who would be next.

Lola sensed Paige's troubled mind and reached out and took Paige's right hand in her left hand. The instant their skin touched, Lola experienced the turmoil Paige experienced, and eased her mind.

When Paige felt Lola take her hand, she heard Lola's voice in her mind. It reminded her of the first few times she transformed into Glinda and heard an internal voice she thought of as her guide.

Let the past go, Lola's thought came to Paige. *You can't change it. Don't trouble over the future. It hasn't happened yet,*

I'm tryin'.

Let me take this burden from you, Paige.

I don't want to lose these feelin's. I need 'em. Glinda needs 'em.

You won't lose 'em. I'll just take 'em for now so you can relax and regenerate.

Okay. But just for now.

Upon receiving that thought from Paige, Lola siphoned the troubles from Paige's mind. As she did, she felt Paige relax. Soon, Lola took all of Paige's troubles and Paige fell into a deep, meditative trance.

From Paige's perspective, the sensation felt like pouring water out of a bottle until it was empty. Her body felt like an empty vessel. When her mind was empty of the troubled thoughts, Paige felt herself dissolving; felt herself becoming light, like she was floating. At once, she had no sense of being and a sense of being a part of everything. Her eyes were closed, but she could see the universe, as if she were outside of it, beyond creation. Galaxies, stars, and planets were before her.

She breathed deeply but smelled nothing and couldn't feel the intake of air in her lungs. It was like suffocating, but with no sense of panic. Paige didn't need to breathe. She needed nothing. She just was.

Slowly, Paige returned to her conscious mind. The galaxies, stars, and planets zipped past her at light speed, not unlike the special effects in the *Star Wars* and *Star Trek* movies when their spaceships accelerated and the stars fly by in a blur. Then she was back in her body. She felt the floor beneath her and smelled the spice of Lola's living room. She opened her eyes. The entire experience seemed to last only a few minutes, but the tall, blue candle Lola lit when they began had burned almost to the floor.

Paige looked at Lola, who looked at her and smiled. "How long was I...gone?"

"Five hours," Lola told her.

Paige's jaw dropped. She tried to think of something to say, but no words could convey what she wanted to express.

"How do ya feel?" Lola asked.

Paige could sum the question up in one word. "Amazin'."

Lola smiled a loving smile. "Good. I'm glad. You deserve to feel that way."

Paige grabbed Lola and hugged her tightly. "Thank you."

Lola hugged her back. "You're welcome, sweet girl."

Still hugging Lola, Paige said, "I was gone. Outside the universe. Beyond creation. I think that must be where God is. Is that what you experience, too?"

"No, sweetheart. It's different for everyone. For me, I become one with the elements. I am part of the earth, wind, water, and fire. In other words, I'm part of everything earthly."

"What does mine mean?" Paige asked.

"It doesn't have to *mean* anything," Lola said. "But, if I had to guess, I think you *were* with your creator. I think you were shown that even horrible things are insignificant in the big plan. I think you found peace with your place in creation. I think it means that you're the one to bring harmony back to your place in the universe. I think it means that ancient vampire is in trouble."

Paige laughed. "You mean all that?"

"I do. But it's just my interpretation of what ya experienced."

"Yeah. But that's what ya do, right? Interpret things. Like Daddy's recurrin' dream. His…experience."

"Yes," Lola said. "But, like I tol' ya last night, my predictions aren't always correct."

"How many times have you been wrong?"

Lola smiled. "Once."

"What was that about?"

"I never predicted you and Glinda would be in my life."

"I love you, Lola."

"I love you too, Paige-Turner. Now, how 'bout we turn in?"

"Okay. Can we sleep under the stars in your mirror?"

"Of course," Lola said as she stood.

"I was just there, you know," Paige said as she stood, too. "In the stars."

That night, Paige dreamed about being outside of the universe, looking back at creation. As she dreamed, two more girls, one of whom was very dear to her, were taken by the ancient vampire for his cloud.

~ * ~

After supper, Garrett and Mandy cleaned up and were in the kitchen doing the dishes while his folks sat at the kitchen table sipping the last of their sweet tea and talking. In a low voice, but not a whisper because his parents' hearing wasn't what it used to be, Garrett told Mandy more about the day's events while leaving out the gory parts.

An occasional question from his mom, the same questions from that morning, interrupted his conversation with Mandy. She asked where Paige was? He said she was staying with a friend. She wanted to know who. He told her the friend's name was Lola. She asked if Lola was a new friend because she didn't know her. He said she was. She asked why he and Mandy were staying with them. Not that she minded, though. He said their septic system had backed up, and he didn't want to pay weekend rates to have it pumped out. These answers seemed to satiate her curiosity, and the questions stopped.

In the middle of drying a dish, Garett, suddenly, said, "Crap."

"Language," his mom said.

"What?" Mandy asked.

"I still need to call Lacy," Garrett said. "I'm surprised she hasn't called me."

"She probably doesn't want to know," Mandy said. "Call her. I'll finish the dishes."

"Ya sure?"

"Yeah. Even if she doesn't *want* to know, she *needs* to know."

"Okay," Garrett said, and retreated to his childhood bedroom for privacy.

He dialed Lacy's number and steadied himself to deliver the news. She answered on the first ring.

"What took ya so long?" Lacy shouted. "Could y'all not find him?"

"We found him."

"Is he…gone?"

"I'm so sorry, Lacy. Al was a good guy," Garrett said and meant it.

Lacy took a hitching breath. "Where is he?"

"George has him," Garrett said. "He's in the loop now and won't have him long because he knows the true cause of death. He'll probably release him to Digger tomorrow."

Crying, Lacy said, "O-okay. Thank you, Garrett."

"If ya need anything, anything at all, let me know."

"W-what should I tell my folks?" she cried.

"Tell 'em he had too much cough syrup and bourbon, went for a walk, got lost, and died from exposure. That will match up with George's official report."

Lacy sniffed. "Okay. Will ya go with me to Digger's on Monday?"

"Of course. I'll pick ya up. Just give me a time when you're ready."

"Thank you. I hope you and Glinda find that monster and kill it."

"We will," Garrett said, and he meant that, too.

"Okay. Bye, Garrett."

"Bye, Lacy."

After ending the call, Garrett sat down on his bed. The old bed springs squealed in protest at his adult weight. Then he called Lola and James to tell them about the meeting at his house the next day at three o'clock. Lola's cell went straight to voicemail, she was meditating, and he left a voicemail. James answered and happily agreed to come, with some homemade muscadine wine.

A moment after Garrett completed the phone calls, there was a soft knock on the door and Mandy said, "May I come in?"

"Please," Garrett said.

Mandy came in and took a seat on the bed next to Garrett. The springs squealed again. She took his hand in hers and they sat in silence for several minutes.

After a few moments, Mandy said, "Is she okay?"

"No."

"I wouldn't be okay, if it was you."

"She wants me to take her to Digger's Monday."

"Good," Mandy said. "Ya should."

"I love you, Mandy."

"I love you too, Garrett."

They kissed. Their hands roamed. Seconds later, they were lying on the bed with Mandy on top of Garrett.

Mandy broke the kiss and breathlessly said, "Ya think your folks will hear these old bedsprings squeakin' if we make love right now?"

"I don't care," Garrett said.

A moment later, they were coupled with Mandy still on top. Afterwards, they slipped under the covers and snuggled in the small bed. About the time Paige had been viewing the universe from outside creation, Garrett fell into a peaceful sleep.

~ * ~

Dănuţ cleaned his blood from the concrete floor. It was easy to do. The floor slanted to a large drain in the middle of the room. He used a hose to wash the blood away and then went down into the throne room to wake the Master's daughters. They bared their fangs and hissed, but Dănuț was protected, so they could only display their superiority. Then they floated up into the embalming room to join their father. Dănuț had to use the latter. Agrapina and Antanasia clung to each of their father's arms in adoration.

"One coffin and search for the *vrăjitoare*," Dragoș reminded him an instant before he and his daughters dissolved into black mist and wafted away.

"Yes, Master," Dănuț said to the dissipating black mist.

After they were gone, Dănuț loaded the hearse with the tools he needed and left the Eternal Rest Funeral Home. Even though he and the hearse were cloaked in darkness by the Master's power so they wouldn't be seen, going back to one of the previous churches would be unwise. He had Googled 'Pine View, Texas churches' and had a long list to pick from; East Texas was a religious place. His destination that night was Christ Lutheran Church of Pine View, and it wasn't a random choice. Christ Lutheran Church of Pine View was on the northeast side of the town, where Lola Laveau lived. Dănuț arrived at the church about twenty minutes later.

Once there, he drove into the cemetery, got out, and did as he'd done the previous two nights. He looked for a recent grave. He didn't have to look long; the werewolves had made his job much easier. He began digging and because the Master had let him feed freely, he felt empowered and made quick work of it. After clearing dirt from the vault lid, he lifted it and saw an imitation, woodgrain coffin. He easily lifted the coffin from the grave, opened it, and couldn't believe his luck. Another body bag. He dumped what, in life, had been Carla Weaver's body onto the dirt, secured the coffin in the back of the hearse, drove out of the cemetery, collected unconsecrated dirt for the coffin, and headed northeast into the outskirts of Pine View County.

~ * ~

Dragoș and his daughters were mentally connected in whatever form they took. In black mist form, their beings became one, a mixture of the three, which gave him total access to their thoughts, lusts, thirsts, and more. When he saw the vision of loveliness with scarlet hair, big, green eyes, and porcelain skin in Antanasia's mind, he knew he had to have her.

Unlike when he took Agrapina in the deserted, church parking lot and Antanasia in the rural outskirts of Pine View County, the destination Antanasia brought them to for the scarlet beauty was in a Pine View City subdivision with cramped, identical looking houses lining each side of a concrete street. Even though it was early evening, just past six o'clock, and lights were on in every one of the cramped small houses, Dragoş was unconcerned. They materialized, cloaked in darkness, in the girl's front yard.

To Antanasia, Dragoş said, "You must secure an invitation before we can enter."

"I will, Master," Antanasia said with a wicked grin that exposed her needle fangs.

"Very well," Dragoş said as he relinquished the cloaking incantation from Antanasia. "But hide your fangs"

"Yes, Master," Antanasia said.

Dragoş watched her walk to the front door and ring the doorbell. He waited and grinned viscously when the object of his desire opened the door. She was even more lovely in person than in Antanasia's mind and he could smell her untouched youth.

~ * ~

Taylor Shanahan was home babysitting her five-year-old brother, Patrick, that night. Her parents had gone to visit her great grandma who was in an assisted living facility in Nacogdoches. She expected them back soon. When the doorbell rang, she thought, absent mindedly, her parents were home and had forgotten the house key. Had she considered this more, she'd have known that was impossible because their house keys were with their car keys. At fourteen, deep thought wasn't one of her strong points, but she wasn't stupid. That almost saved her life.

~ * ~

Taylor opened the door. "Forget your...? Oh, hey, Megan. What're you doin' here?"

"I was out your way and thought I'd say hey," Antanasia said.

Taylor looked past Megan at the street and not seeing her folks' truck, said, "How'd ya get here?"

"Oh, um. I got ditched at another friend's house, and I need a ride home. Can we come in so I can call my folks?"

Taylor looked closely at Megan in the harsh front porch lights and didn't like what she saw. Megan's skin was white. Too white. It was almost translucent, and she saw black veins and arteries beneath her translucent skin.

Suspicious, Taylor said, "Why not use your cell or call from the other friend's house?"

"I, um, lost my cell and I left my friend's house because we got into a fight. I need to use your phone. Can we come in?"

Taylor shook her head. "No. I'm babysittin' Patrick and I'm not supposed to let anyone in while I'm babysittin.'"

"It's me, Megan. You know me. Just let us in."

Taylor scanned the front yard and street again.

Not seeing anyone else, Taylor said, "You keep sayin' *we* and *us*. Who's with ya?"

"No one," Antanasia almost growled. "Just invite us in."

"I don't think so," Taylor said, and began to close the door.

When Antanasia heard Taylor refuse the invitation and start to close the door, she bared her fangs. "Let us in, you stupid *cunt*."

Antanasia reached past the doorway threshold to push the door back open and grab Taylor. When she did, the skin of her arms breaching the threshold burst into agonizing black flames that smelled of rot. Like rotted meat cooked on a grill. She shrieked in pain and was flung backwards by some unseen force. The black flames went out, but her forearms were blackened and charred.

Dragoş watched, and grew increasingly frustrated, as Antanasia clumsily tried to secure the invitation. When he saw her breach the threshold and her arms burst into black flames, he was mad enough to remove her head. But he didn't have time to deal with her. All he saw was his scarlet prize shutting the door. After losing his chance with the perfection named Paige, he wasn't about to lose another one.

Before Antanasia's black flaming arms were ejected from the house completely, and the door could close, Dragoş was there in all his youthful, princely beauty. Before the scarlet beauty could close the door, Dragoş caught her eye. That was all it took; she was instantly mesmerized.

Taylor saw a deep, crystal, blue eye appear in the small opening between the door and the door frame and all the fright and horror of seeing her friend Megan bare fangs and burst into flames when she reached for her melted away. She stopped closing the door and opened it. When the door was open, Taylor looked at the most beautiful man she'd ever seen. He had a firm chin and high cheekbones. His skin was almost the color of ivory and appeared translucent, but his lips were a deep shade of red, made deeper by the contrast with his flawless ivory skin. The hair falling from under his cowl was long, light brown, and curly. It framed his handsome face perfectly. When he asked if they could come in, she nodded.

Dragoş, Agrapina, and Antanasia, with arms still smoking, entered the Shanahan house. Taylor closed the door and followed them into the living room where Patrick watched a *Shrek* DVD on the TV.

Patrick wasn't mesmerized and Dragoş had no intention of exerting the effort, little as it was, to mesmerize him. What Patrick saw was the ancient, weathered monster with wisps of long, stringy white hair that looked like spun cotton candy. Patrick screamed and tried to run, but Agrapina was quicker and had him clasped in her arms before he took a single, running step. He screamed again.

"My arms, Master," Antanasia said as black tears streamed down her translucent cheeks. "The pain is unbearable."

"Foolish child," Dragoş said in a scolding hiss. "Never cross a threshold without an invitation,"

"I'm sorry, Master, Antanasia said. "I knew you wanted her, and I didn't want her to close the door."

Dragoş stroked her blonde hair. "You will heal when you feed."

"May I have the boy, Master?" she asked.

"No. The boy belongs to the scarlet beauty I am naming Lacrima. You will feed later."

"Yes, Master," she replied.

"Are you not curious as to the meaning of the name I have selected for her?" Dragoş asked.

"Of course, Master," Antanasia said. "I didn't think it was my place to ask."

Dragoş ran a gnarled thumb through the black tears on Antanasia's left cheek, which left a black smear on her translucent skin. "Lacrima is a Romanian girl's name. It means tear. What you did was foolish, but your sacrifice, and her reaction to it, gave me time to mesmerize her before the door closed. I name her in tribute to your tears, my daughter."

"Thank you, Master."

Dragoş looked from Antanasia to Agrapina. "You are my daughters. Do not address me as Master in the future. Address me as Father."

"Yes, Father," the two young vampires replied in unison.

Dragoş smiled his hideous smile. "Now I will create your new sister, Lacrima."

As Dragoş walked toward Taylor to kill and reanimate her, he heard a car drive down the street outside. He paused and waited to be certain. The car slowed and turned into the Shanahan driveway.

Dragoş turned to Antanasia. "You will feed and heal soon. Her adults have returned. When they come in, follow Agrapina's lead."

Agrapina brought Patrick to Dragoş, who put one of his icy hands over the frightened boy's mouth to muffle him. They heard the electric garage door rumble open, and the car pull in. The car's engine died, and the electric garage door rumble back down. A man's and woman's voices could be heard after they shut the garage door. They sounded jovial. There was a jingle of keys, the sound of a lock disengaging on a door that led into the kitchen, and the door swung open. Patrick Sr. and Beth Shanahan stepped into their house; stepped into a nightmare.

Agrapina sprung, in a low but long leap, at the man and pinned him against the kitchen counter. He screamed, but she unhinged her lower jaw, sank her fangs into his carotid artery, and used her lower jaw to crush his larynx and the scream along with it.

Antanasia mimicked Agrapina's move, but less gracefully. She hit the startled woman hard and drove her to the linoleum floor. They slid into the dining room table with a crash that upended the table and sent the four chairs toppling over in all directions. The woman screamed several times before Antanasia unhinged her bottom jaw and fed while crushing her larynx, as Agrapina had done with the man.

Dragoş watched, like a proud father, as his daughters fed and the little boy screamed into his cold, undead hand. He smiled.

Dragoş listened to the man and woman's rapid heartbeats as they slowed. He began to tell Agrapina to stop feeding, but she quit on her own and let the man's last drop of life ooze from one puncture wound. He died the moment she stopped feeding. Antanasia kept feeding, though, and the woman had less blood than the man. Dragoş waited a moment longer to see if she'd stop on her own. When he realized Antanasia would not stop before the woman died, he mentally commanded her to stop. She did, but only just in time. No blood oozed from the woman's puncture wounds. Agrapina had only been a day older than Antanasia, but she was already a much more mature vampire.

When Antanasia stood, with blood covering face, neck, and clothes, she smiled. "My arms are healed, Father."

"Yes," Dragoş said. "Had I not stopped you, you would have fed on dead blood and experienced more pain than any living, or undead, creature has ever experienced. You need to listen to their heartbeat, daughter. You need to be more like Agrapina."

Antanasia glanced quickly at Agrapina, who grinned through the bloody mess that was her face, and begrudgingly said, "Yes, Father."

"Do not pout. It is unbecoming of your superiority over the living. I scold because I do not want to lose you. Now, hold the boy child while I create your new sister."

His words made Antanasia feel better. She came to him, Agrapina followed, and took the boy child from her father. She covered his mouth and watched with anticipation as her father created her and Agrapina's new sister. Agrapina saw Antanasia's creation, but Antanasia hadn't witnessed the miracle of undead birth.

Dragoş approached the scarlet beauty he named Lacrima and, without verbal command, she swept her long, scarlet hair over her left shoulder and tilted her head to the right. He looked at her flawless, porcelain flesh and the clear outline of her carotid artery beating beneath. In eight hundred years of undead existence, Dragoş couldn't remember seeing more perfect flesh. His lips drew back in a horrid smile, which revealed his fangs, and punctured the flesh slowly; he enjoyed the slow penetration and her tight skin around his fangs. The feeling he got from the slow, purposeful penetration was not unlike the feeling a living man received when penetrating a virgin. And he still had the undead act of that experience to look forward to when he tucked her in at dawn.

After slowly penetrating her flawless, tight flesh, he removed his fangs and drank deeply of her virgin blood. Her blood was every bit as tasty as her skin was tight around his fangs. As he drank, he listened to her heartbeats slow. Just before the last beat, he pulled his mouth away and watched one drop ooze out of each puncture would. Not wanting to waste any of her, his long tongue snaked out and licked the two tasty drops. It was time to bring her back. He slit his left nipple and let his black, undead blood flow into her slack mouth.

~ * ~

Even mesmerized, Taylor felt a sudden revulsion when the monster closed his cold, undead lips around her neck. But it was a fleeting sensation. As he drank from her, drank her life away, she realized she was wet between her legs. With each suck he took on her neck, she got wetter. Shortly before she died, she had the absurd thought and wondered if the sensation was what boys felt when girls gave them blowjobs. If it was, she understood why boys were obsessed with getting them. Then everything went white.

In the whiteness, she heard her parents calling her name. Their calls were urgent, but she knew they were at peace. She traveled toward their voices but then a sweet, coppery sensation filled her senses. It was delicious, and she wanted more. She knew her lips had locked on a stiff nipple, and she suckled, greedily, at the sweet nectar like a newborn baby suckles at their mother's breast. As she sucked, the whiteness and her parents' voices faded and then disappeared altogether. She opened her crystal, blue, undead eyes for the first time and looked into the eyes of her beautiful, new father.

~ * ~

Dragoş moaned in ecstasy as his new daughter suckled eagerly at his stiff nipple. She was a greedy child, and Dragoş didn't care. He thought there was something special about the scarlet-haired beauty, but he didn't dare speculate. He'd been disappointed before. Despite that, he hoped.

She opened her crystal, blue, undead eyes and looked at him with such wanting he let her drink past the point of reanimation. He would never let Agrapina and Antanasia know, but Lacrima had quickly become his favorite daughter, which was Agrapina's station moments earlier.

Not wanting to, but needing to, Dragoş pulled her bright red lips from his stiff nipple. A drop of his black blood ran down her chin, but her long tongue snaked out quickly and lapped it up. As he hadn't wanted to waste a single drop of her blood, she didn't want to waste a single drop of his.

The new, fledgling vampire tore her gaze away from Dragoş and looked at her new sisters, and the boy who was her little brother in life. All she saw when she looked at the frightened boy was blood pumping through an animated sack of food. Even without instruction from her father, she made no move to attack him. She was a rare, disciplined, undead child. Dragoş' infatuation with her grew.

"These are your sisters, Agrapina and Antanasia," Dragoş told her. "Your new name is Lacrima, which means tear in my Romanian homeland. The boy child is your first meal."

Lacrima looked from Agrapina to Antanasia to the frightened boy. "Please release him, Antanasia."

Antanasia looked to her father for approval. He nodded. She released him, but the boy didn't move. He just stood there looking, wide eyed, at the creature who had been his big sister.

"Are you mesmerizing the boy, Father?" Agrapina asked.

"No," Dragoş said.

"Then…why is he mesmerized?" Antanasia asked.

Dragoş smiled. "Your new sister, Lacrima, has the boy mesmerized."

"How is that possible, Father?" Agrapina said. "You told me it might take months to learn this skill."

Dragoş' smile broadened. "Every once in a great while, I find a natural vampire. They are rare. In my long, undead existence, she is only my second."

"What does this mean, Father?" Antanasia asked.

"It means, daughters, that Lacrima will be your new teacher in the undead arts," Dragoş told them.

Neither looked happy to hear this, but Dragoş didn't care. He had found a natural vampire. One who would be more help than the other two combined with finding the silver werewolf.

"Feed," Dragoş told Lacrima.

She did, and she didn't need to be told when to stop. As the little boy's heart stopped, Lacrima dropped his dead body to the floor, where he landed in a twisted heap. Unlike her sisters, Lacrima's face and clothes weren't covered in blood. A single trickle ran from the corner of her mouth, but her tongue snaked out and lapped it up. There wasn't even a smear left on her flawless, translucent flesh. Dragoş smiled in approval.

"Come daughters," Dragoş said "We must collect one more daughter for my cloud this night. Thanks to Agrapina's memories, I have selected one who is dear to the girl, Paige."

They came to him. An instant later, the four vampires dissolved into black mist and whisked away on a non-existent breeze. Lindsey Anderson had unwanted company coming.

~ * ~

Dănuţ drove the back roads of northeast Pine View County for hours in search of the troublesome *vrăjitoare*. It was a needle in a haystack search, and he knew it, but the Master had commanded he search for her and search he would.

He stopped at, perhaps, a dozen mailboxes in front of long driveways with concealed houses, the dwelling he thought the *vrăjitoare* might inhabit. But, upon investigation, none of them were hers. He saw several family dwellings, two inhabited by elderly couples, and a few with single inhabitants, but none of them were the *vrăjitoare's* house.

Dănuţ continued searching, but decided he would quit for the night at four o'clock. This would give him time to return to the funeral home and move the new coffin into the Master's throne room for his new daughters.

Dănuţ turned onto County Road Six Seventy-One and drove slowly, looking for something, anything, that might lead him to the seer. He passed two mailboxes on the right, a third on the left and then, after a long stretch of road, a fourth mailbox on the right came into view. It looked like someone took a baseball bat to it and the post it had been mounted on leaned heavily askew. As he passed it, he saw the mailbox was mostly covered in rust, with only a few flakes of deeply faded pink paint on it. He thought pink was an odd color for a mailbox and drove past it.

About a quarter mile after passing the dilapidated mailbox, the image of Lola Laveau flashed in his mind, and he remembered the white and pink beads adorning the ends of the witch's cornrows. Dănuţ slammed on the brakes and brought the hearse to a screeching halt. He backed up to the mailbox, parked the hearse safely off the road. It was cloaked but that wouldn't keep an early riser from plowing into it on the road. He killed the engine, got out, shut the door, and walked back to the mailbox to inspect it closer.

The remaining paint on the battered mailbox was faded pink. There were no numbers or name on it and the flag was missing. Dănuţ grabbed the tilted post and tried to right it, but it was held tight in the skewed position. He found this odd and looked down the driveway that ended at the blacktopped road. The drive was overgrown with tall weeds that looked as though they'd been undisturbed for years. The tree branches on either side of the driveway interlinked above, blocking the moonlight, and gave the appearance that the overgrown driveway disappeared into nothingness. Dănuţ walked into the black hole.

~ * ~

Lola awoke the moment the unwelcomed intruder set foot on her driveway. Paige slept next to her under the mirrored, starry night sky. She didn't wake her, but the night sky vanished from the mirror and was replaced by a view looking out from the front of her house. She waited to see who, or what, came snooping.

~ * ~

Dănuţ, wary of traps a *vrăjitoare* might set, made his way up the dark driveway. More than a minute later, the driveway opened on an overgrown yard, demolished garage, and dilapidated house. He glanced at the crushed garage, saw a rusted car inside, ignored it, and made his way to the house. It was in ruin, but regardless, he felt a need to investigate further.

He put a foot on the bottom step that led to the collapsed front porch. His foot sank through the rotted step with the dry, crunching sound of decayed wood. Undeterred, Dănuţ continued up the steps, checking for secure footing before committing his weight to it, and onto the porch, which had rotted, too. Then he made his way to the missing door and peered in. The ceiling had collapsed, and the floor was missing floorboards in many places. He saw a door on the left had a broken top hinge and tilted into the room it accessed, but the door on the right was intact and closed. He made his way to it and tried the knob. It was stuck but, with a little effort, he turned it, and the door opened on rusted hinges that squealed in protest at the movement. The room was in terrible shape, like the rest of the house, and empty. Satisfied the structure couldn't be the *vrăjitoare's* home, Dănuţ left and returned to the funeral home.

~ * ~

Lola watched in her mirror, as the tall, slender man, who appeared to be in his early fifties, with thinning, blond hair and piercing blue eyes, searched her house. She used her seeing eye to see his aura. It was black with jagged edges. An evil aura. She tried to see into his mind but encountered a wall protecting his thoughts. She pushed harder and broke through, but his thoughts were still guarded. Try as she may, she couldn't discern much. At least, not until he peered into her bedroom, and she could focus on the man instead of his image in the mirror.

Even then, though, information, useful information, had been scarce. She received a fleeting image of the ancient vampire's face very close to his and the vampire opening its grotesquely enormous mouth and engulfing the man's face within it. She could even smell the ancient decay of the vampire's mouth. It repulsed her. Then the image had gone.

That the man was still alive and in her house could lead to only two conclusions. The man was the vampire's familiar, and the vampire was looking for her or Paige. Probably both.

Lola was glad Paige had slept through the intrusion. She didn't want Paige troubled by the event. Worse, Paige might have transformed into Glinda and attacked the man. Lola knew Glinda would kill him. She had also known a vampire and their familiar are mentally connected and that action would give their location away before the protection potion was ready. Lola, once she was sure the man had gone, returned the night sky image to the mirror and closed her eyes. But she didn't sleep.

~ * ~

Lindsey Anderson, Paige's best friend and her late boyfriend's younger sister, was fast asleep in her bed when she heard a rhythmic tapping in her dreams. She was dreaming about summer vacation and going to Lake Nacogdoches with Paige to work on their tans and maybe swim. In the dream, Paige didn't hear the tapping. Lindsey looked around the lake for the source of the noise, but no one was there. This was strange because, earlier in the dream, she and Paige had been checking out all the hot SFA college boys. She looked back at Paige. She was missing, too. The tapping continued. Then the lake view disappeared, like it had been swallowed. A moment later, Lindsey was in complete darkness, and the rhythmic tapping continued. But it was no longer an external sound. It was in her head, tapping on the inside of her skull. She couldn't breathe.

Lindsey forced herself awake and sat up in bed, gasping for breath. She shook her head violently, which caused her blonde hair to fly wildly around her face to shake the nightmare from her mind. It worked, or so she thought.

She sat in her bed for several moments and willed her breathing and heartbeat to slow to a less panicked pace. It was working. Then there was a tap on her bedroom window. It was a light tap, barely audible, but it went off like a gunshot in Lindsey's mind. She jumped and let out a startled scream. The tap came again. This time, it was a little louder.

Lindsey pulled the covers up to her chin and looked at the window. The curtains were closed but the almost full moon was bright, and she saw the silhouette of someone outside her window through the curtains. Her second-floor window. The tap came again; louder than before.

Lindsey stared at the tapping silhouette. It was, or appeared to be, the silhouette of a girl; she saw hair fanning out from the outline's head. The tap came again and with it, a calming thought. It was Paige fucking with her. Paige had been sneaking out since the werewolf problem ended and came to her house often. Lindsey was so convinced it was Paige, had to be Paige, she forgot two important things about those previous occasions. Paige always texted her first and she never floated outside Lindsey's second-floor bedroom window.

Relieved, Lindsey got out of bed and, before opening the curtains, said, "What the fuck, Paige. You scared the shit outta me."

Lindsey opened the window and saw a scarlet-haired girl floating outside. The moment before she was mesmerized, Lindsey recognized her. Not because they were friends. She was a freshman and Lindsey a junior, but because there was only one girl in Pine View High School with hair that color. Her name was Taylor something. Then Taylor something's eyes turned into silver slits and Lindsey thought no more.

"Let us in," Lacrima hissed.

Lindsey did as she was told, and four vampires floated through the window into her room.

Dragoş eyed the girl, who would soon be his fourth daughter. She was young, beautiful, a virgin, and she was close to the prize that had eluded him. She was perfect. The moon streamed through the opened window and lit her with its slivery glow. He decided he would name her Ilinca, which was a Romanian girl's name for moon.

Dragoş approached Lindsey. She moved her blonde hair from her right shoulder and tilted her head to the left. Dragoş sank his fangs into her carotid artery, removed them, and drank her sweet, virgin blood. He drank slowly, taking in all the blood memories she had of the girl named Paige. There were so many of them Dragoş was momentarily overwhelmed, but he sorted them, hoping to find where she might hide or any secrets she might have held in confidence. There were plenty of secrets, but nothing of importance; just ordinary girl secrets about what boys they thought were cute and what girls they thought were bitches. He discerned she thought her best friend was spending the holidays with her father.

Disappointed, Dragoş stopped drinking an instant before Lindsey's heart stopped and her head lulled back. Her dead eyes were open but unseeing. He opened his left nipple with a quick swipe of his jagged thumbnail and let his black blood trickle into her slack mouth.

~ * ~

Lindsey saw the young, beautiful prince approach her and knew what he wanted. What he needed. The pain she felt when his needle-sharp fangs sank into her neck was pleasurable. Erotic, even. As he drank from her, drank her life away, she experienced all the memories of Paige he probed for and, even mesmerized and in ecstasy, she realized she was losing Paige with each exotic drink the prince took. Tears slipped from her dying eyes and trickled down her cold cheeks.

As the last of her lifeblood ebbed away, the darkness that closed in on her vision turned into a blinding, white light, she heard Justin call to her. Then Justin was there, directly in front of her. He shimmered in the blinding light. He grabbed her shimmering arm and begged her to stay. Then a sweet, coppery nectar filled her completely, and the whiteness faded. But Justin stayed, clinging to her arm and begged her to stay.

Just before the whiteness and Justin faded completely, Justin said, "He wants Paige. Don't let him have her."

~ * ~

Dragoş looked down at Ilinca as her crystal, blue, undead eyes fluttered open for the first time. He smiled at her, and she smiled back through lips still locked on, and feeding from his stiff nipple. He let her feed a while longer and then mentally commanded her to stop. She obediently did.

Dragoş smiled at his first three daughters. "This is my new daughter, Ilinca. Ilinca, these are your new sisters, Agrapina, Antanasia, and Lacrima."

As each of their names were spoken, they smiled and nodded at Ilinca.

After the introductions were through, Antanasia said, "Can we feed on and kill the adults now, Father?"

Dragoş shook his head, which caused his long, wispy, white hair to float out from under his cowl. "No. Ilinca will feed from one for strength, but they must live."

"Why must they live, Father?" Agrapina asked.

"Their suffering for their missing daughter will be the girl named Paige's suffering, too," Dragoş said. "She will know what has happened to her best friend, because she knows of me. She will think she is safe while the sun is up. She will come here to grieve with them. I will have Dănuţ keep watch and follow her to wherever she is hiding when she does. If the adult humans are dead, she will have no reason to come here."

"Why is she so important to you, Father?" Agrapina said. "We knew many beautiful girls in life. You can have any of them, Father."

"It is not your place to question me, Agrapina," Dragoş hissed. "If you must know, she fought back against the werewolf that killed Ilinca's former brother, who was also the girl named Paige's boyfriend. She is fearless, and her blood may hold memories that will help me find the silver-haired werewolf."

"Why is the silver-haired werewolf important, Father?" Lacrima asked.

Dragoş sighed, or the unbreathing, undead version of a sigh. "I have such inquisitive daughters. I will make the silver-haired werewolf my new familiar. A werewolf familiar is a vampire's most powerful ally.

It was news of the silver-haired werewolf that brought me from my home in Romania to this…pitiful place."

"If you find the silver-haired werewolf…" Antanasia began.

"*When* I find it," Dragoş corrected her.

"Sorry, Father," Antanasia whispered. "When you find it and make it your familiar, what will become of Dănuţ?"

"I care not what happens to him," Dragoş said casually.

"Can we kill him?" Agrapina asked.

"If you wish," Dănuţ told her.

Agrapina and Antanasia shared a wicked smile. Lacrima and Ilinca, who hadn't had the displeasure of meeting Dănuţ, stood passively by.

"Ilinca, come with me," Dragoş instructed. "You will feed from one of the adult humans to gain strength. You will feed high on their inner thigh from the femoral artery, and you must stop when I command you to stop."

Ilinca nodded and she and Dragoş left, what in life, had been Lindsey's bedroom. Agrapina, Antanasia, and Lacrima waited silently for their father and sister to return. A few minutes later, they did; Ilinca's lips were red with her former father's blood. Dragoş opened his unnatural, long arms with his cape clutched in each hand. Agrapina and Antanasia huddled under his right arm; Lacrima and Ilinca huddled under his left arm. Dragoş closed his cape around them. A moment later, hundreds of vampire bats swarmed around Lindsey's former room. Then, the cloud of vampire bats flew out the window and disappeared into the night.

~ * ~

Dănuţ returned to the funeral home shortly before dawn. He pressed the button on the visor to open the garage door on the left and waited for the door to open. It was dark inside the embalming room, but the hearse's headlights cut through the darkness, and he saw his Master, Agrapina, Antanasia, and two new daughters. One with scarlet hair and one with blonde hair. He pulled the hearse in and pushed the button to close the door. Once it was closed, Dănuţ got out and bowed before his

Master and daughters.

Dragoş ignored the bow. "Let me introduce you to my two new daughters, slave. The scarlet beauty is Lacrima, and the blonde beauty is Ilinca. Ilinca was best friends with the one the *vrăjitoare* is protecting. I left her former adults alive, hoping the girl named Paige will come to their house when she learns her friend is missing. You will spend your days watching the house; watching for the one who eludes me. When she visits, and she will, you will follow her to her hiding place. Unless you found where the *vrăjitoare* lives this night. Understood?"

Dănuţ nodded. "I did not find the seer, Master. But I will wait, watch, follow, and find her."

"Very well. Did you secure a resting place for my fourth daughter?"

"I did, Master."

"Take it to my throne room so that I can tuck in all of my daughters for the day."

"Yes, Master," Dănuţ replied and did as he was told.

After Dănuţ reemerged from the underground lair, Dragoş and his four daughters floated down into the Master's throne room for a good tucking. Dănuţ closed the shelves and table concealing the throne room's entrance, and because he didn't need the hearse for retrieving coffins, got into the black Cadillac Escalade, and drove to Ilinca's former house. He parked down the street, secure because the Master had cloaked him and the Escalade from view and waited.

Her father, the sheriff, arrived, but without his daughter. Dănuţ was disappointed, and about to give up, but the Master had been correct. The girl named Paige came to visit her former best friend's parents. She wasn't alone, though. She arrived with the *vrăjitoare*. When they left, he followed.

Chapter Ten

After the unwelcomed intruder left, Lola laid awake in bed unable to sleep. It had been the barriers in the man's mind that troubled her the most. She'd never encountered barriers of that magnitude before, but she'd never encountered an ancient vampire's familiar before, either. She knew the intruder had been the ancient's current familiar, out to do the dirty work of finding her and Paige. He was cloaked in the same darkness incantation the vampire had been cloaked in when she saw him and Mel at Paige's house. His aura was unique, too. She'd seen plenty of black auras in her day, but none with jagged edges. With no other explanation forthcoming, she decided the mind block and jagged edged aura had to result from feeding on vampire blood for however many years he'd been a familiar, which she thought was quite a few, even decades. With sleep eluding her, Lola slipped out of bed and went into her dark living room. She needed Mamma Deupree's advice again.

Lola, quickly, drew the pentagram, retrieved five white candles from the drawer or holding, placed them at each point of the pentagram, lit all of them with a snap of her fingers, assumed the position on her living room floor, and reached out to Mamma. Within a few seconds, Mamma's shimmering form appeared before her, floating a few inches off the floor.

"This is becoming a routine," Mamma crackled in her heavy French accent. "Perhaps you should put me on speed dial."

"I apologize, Mamma," Lola said with a sigh. "It's just that this…situation is becomin' more tenuous by the minute."

"*Show* me what has happened since we last communed," Mamma said in as soothing a voice that her advanced age would allow.

Lola let Mamma into her mind.

"Yes. Your intuition about why you had such difficulty seeing into the intruder's mind is correct," Mamma said. "Lest you forget, once a human partakes of vampire blood, they have no will of their own. That cursed black blood they drink strengthens them. Physically *and* mentally.

That you could see as much as you did is a testament to your powers, my sister. I doubt any witch in our coven, excluding myself, would have made the progress you did. What you saw is important, though. After all, you have seen the ancient's familiar. He is no longer a stranger to you."

"True. But to no end," Lola said. "Had I not been concerned with Paige's wellbeing, I would've engaged him and perhaps been able to learn more of the ancient's location."

~ * ~

When Lola slipped out of bed, careful as she had been, Paige woke up. Since she had no reason to believe Lola was up for more than some morning tea, she closed her eyes and drifted off to sleep again. Several minutes later, she heard Lola talking with someone. The someone talking back had a thick, French accent and her voice sounded near and far at the same time. She dialed up Glinda's hearing and was astonished to find neither voice sounded any clearer. Curious, Paige slipped out of bed, went to the bedroom door, cracked it slightly, and peaked into the living room. What she saw made her jaw drop.

~ * ~

Mamma's seeing eye darted toward Lola's door an instant before it opened slightly, and Paige peaked out.

"We have an eavesdropper, sister," Mamma said with a crackled laugh.

Lola's seeing eye spun up into her head, so only the white sclera showed. "Really, Paige-Turner? Eavesdroppin'?"

Unapologetically, Paige said, "If I was eavesdroppin', I wouldn't have opened the door on two, seein' witches."

Mamma fell into a fit of crackling laughter that made her suspended body rock back and forth. She laughed until tears ran down the deep wrinkles in her leathery face.

"I see why you're so fond of this child, Lola," Mamma said through crackled laughter. "She certainly *is* fearless. Come, child. Sit with us."

As Paige walked to where Lola sat, naked, on the floor, she felt Mamma seeing her. For the first time in a long time, she felt totally exposed. It wasn't her nakedness that felt exposed. She *was* fearless, so she ignored the sensation and, careful not to disturb the lines of the pentagram, took a seat next to Lola.

"Paige, this is Mamma Deupree," Lola said.

"Yeah," Paige said, but not rudely. "I kinda figured that out."

"By all the Elements, Lola. You were not exaggerating when you described her aura," Mamma said in what passed for awe. "In all my many years, I've never encountered one so pure."

On hearing this, Paige relaxed. It was her aura Mamma looked at so intently.

"It's a pleasure to meet you, Miss Mamma," Paige said.

Mamma smiled a toothless smile. "Miss Mamma. Isn't that sweet."

"It's a manners thing all the kids around here do," Lola said. "She'll call me Lola when her daddy isn't around. When he is, it's Miss Lola."

"Well, child. Your daddy isn't here now. Mamma will be fine."

"Okay, Mamma," Paige waded right in. "What're y'all talkin' 'bout?"

"A little o' this and a little o' that," Mamma crackled as a little of the time she'd spent as a slave in the South peppered her French accent. "Mostly about how the vampire's familiar paid y'all a little visit earlier."

Paige looked at Lola, eyes wide. "What? Why didn't ya wake me up?"

"Because you'd have done somethin' stupid, like transform into Glinda, attack the man, and give away your location before the protection potion is ready," Mamma answered, sounding more southern, instead of Lola.

"I-I-I...wouldn't have. Yes, I would have," Paige admitted, mostly because lying to these two would be impossible.

"This, child, is why the protection potion is so important," Mamma said. "It will give you the wisdom to know when to attack and when to stay hidden. The ancient and his familiar are mentally connected. Had you attacked the familiar, the ancient would have been here in a matter of seconds. As powerful as Lola is, she is no match for the ancient. He would have his prize. A werewolf familiar, and you would be lost to everyone you love and everyone who loves you. You do not want that to happen, do you?"

Paige looked at her knees; her cheeks were flushed. "No, ma'am. I don't want that."

"Good," Mamma said. "You listen to Lola, and I think you might kill the vile creature."

"You're not just sayin' that to make me feel better?" Paige asked Mamma.

"After hearin' 'bout you and seein' your aura, I mean it with all the wisdom my old heart has," Mamma said in an almost pure southern accent. "You must wait until the protection potion is ready, though."

Paige smiled. "Yes, ma'am. I will. Thank ya for helpin' me."

"You're very welcome. Takin' out an ancient vampire does not just help you," Mamma said. "It helps put nature back in harmony, and that is what all elemental witches strive for. Now, if y'all are no longer in need of my counsel, I'll take my leave."

"Go, Mamma," Lola said. "And thank you."

Paige watched in awe as Mamma's shimmering form evaporated without a sound.

"Well, Paige-Turner, after I clean this up, how 'bout I make us some spice tea and we go outside on the porch swing and watch the sun rise?"

"Is it safe to be outside before sunrise?" Paige asked.

"Of course," Lola said. "We could'a been sittin' on the front porch swing when the familiar came snoopin' and he wouldn't have seen us."

Twenty minutes later, they sat on the front porch swing and looked east as a light pink glow announced the approaching morning sun. They were both naked, Lola naturally impervious to the chill in the air and Paige warmed by the spice tea.

Paige was like most teenage girls. Never separated from her from their cellphone. But having the luxury of being naked all the time had curtailed that habit for Paige. At first, she carried it around Lola's house with her. But the reception was so spotty and with no back pocket to keep it in, she relinquished her lifeline to the outside world and left it on the nightstand on her side of Lola's bed, secure knowing, if it did, by chance, ring, Glinda would hear it and she could get to it in time to talk with whoever called. Knowing, too, that it would most likely be Lin or her daddy.

While Lola and Paige watched the sunrise, a call went straight to voicemail. The message was from Mrs. Gloria, Lindsey's mom. She was frantic, talking in incomplete sentences about Lindsey missing and how Mr. Andy was too weak to get out of bed.

~ * ~

Garrett's cellphone blared into life early that morning and woke him and Mandy up. He glanced at the alarm clock beside his childhood bed and saw it was five thirty-one a.m. Then he grabbed his phone and looked at the caller ID. It was Gloria Anderson. A bowling ball sank into the pit of his stomach. He answered the call.

"Garrett. It's Lindsey. She's. Her window," Gloria shouted frantically. "Andy's sick. It's open. The cold. Her window's open. The cold woke me up. Andy can't get. He's weak. I…"

"Gloria. Slow down," Garrett interrupted but the bowling ball got heavier in his gut. "I can't follow what you're sayin'."

Gloria took several deep, unsteady breaths.

"Lindsey's gone. Her window's open and she's gone. Just like Melanie Zane," Gloria said and began to cry.

"What's wrong with Andy?" Garrett asked as calmly as he could manage.

Through hitching sobs, Gloria said, "I-I-I don't know. He-he's white as a sheet and too wea-weak to get out of b-bed."

"I'm on my way."

"Hu-hurry, Garrett," Gloria wailed.

Garrett looked at Mandy. She, too, was white as a sheet, sitting up in bed, with her trembling hands cupped over her mouth. Her chin quivered and tears streamed down her beautiful cheeks.

Through her trembling hands, in an unsteady, muffled voice, Mandy said, "No. Not Lindsey. This'll kill Paige."

Garrett hugged her tightly and kissed the tears on her right cheek. "It's too soon to jump to conclusions."

"You don't believe that," Mandy sobbed. "I see it in your eyes. That monster took Lindsey."

Garrett lowered his gaze, so she couldn't see his eyes. "Yeah. He probably did."

"How are ya gonna tell Paige?"

Garrett shook his head slowly. "I don't know. I have to go. I love you."

"I love you, too."

~ * ~

Once Garrett was outside, and in his patrol SUV, he called Lola. Even though most cellphones didn't get a reliable signal at her house, Lola's always did. It rang several times and just when Garrett was sure it would send him to voicemail, Lola answered.

"Good mornin', Garrett," Lola said in her warm, honey voice.

"It's not. Is Paige with ya right now?" Garrett whispered.

"No," Lola whispered. "She's on the front porch swing."

"Can she hear us?"

On her end of the call, Lola mouthed a wordless incantation. "Not now."

"Are ya sure?" Garrett whispered.

"Yes. Even with Glinda dialed all the way up. I taught her how to control Glinda, but I didn't teach her all my tricks. What's the matter?"

"He got Lindsey."

"By everything holy to you and me. Are ya sure?"

"Pretty damn sure," Garrett said. "Gloria said Lindsey's window was open, and she's gone. She said Andy's white as a sheet and too weak to get outta bed. I'm on my way there now."

"This'll kill Paige."

"I'm aware, Lola. Can ya do that thing you do and tell her in a way that won't crush her?"

"Yes," Lola said. "But only for a while."

"Why only for a while? I don't want her hurtin' this way."

"Well, first, after she drinks the protection potion tonight, the hurt won't be hidden anymore."

"Fuck." Garrett shouted.

"Second, she deserves to grieve properly for her friend," Lola continued in her warm honey voice. "And third, revenge is a powerful motivator. If I had any doubts 'bout Paige's chances against the ancient, I don't have 'em now. She'll be unstoppable."

"Okay. Please save her the pain now," Garrett said. "If ya can help the Andersons too, I'd appreciate it. First, they lose Justin to a fuckin' werewolf and now Lindsey to a fuckin' vampire. That's too much for any parents to bear."

"Of course, I will. Paige and I will meet ya there."

"Thank you, Lola."

"You're most welcome, Garrett."

~ * ~

Lola walked back outside. Paige was swinging lightly; her face a bright orange in the rising morning sun.

She looked at Lola. "Was that Daddy? I thought I heard him whisperin' on the phone to you, but I dialed up Glinda and didn't hear anything else."

"You and your eavesdroppin'," Lola said.

"Well, I thought if it was Daddy, he was callin' for me. Your cell's the only one that gets reliable service out here."

Lola sat down next to Paige. "It was your daddy, and he wants me to tell ya somethin'."

"What?" Paige asked.

"Give me your hands, Paige."

Suspicious, Paige said, "Why?"

"Because I'm askin'."

Paige looked into Lola's seeing eye. She wasn't sure if Lola somehow compelled her to give her hands. But she did. The instant their hands closed together, Paige felt an unnatural calm course through her body. By then, her suspicions were confirmed, but she was powerless to do anything about it, and it felt good. The tea had warmed her body and whatever Lola was doing then warmed her heart.

"Your daddy called to tell me that Lin's missin'," Lola said. "Do ya understand what that means?"

Paige nodded as a single tear crested the bottom lid of her right eye and ran down her cheek. "He has her. She's…one of them now."

Lola nodded, as tears streamed down her cheeks from taking so much of Paige's pain. "I'm takin' this pain from ya now because your daddy asked me to. Tonight, when you and Glinda drink the protection potion, it'll come back. I want you to use it, Paige. Use it to get revenge for Lin and the other girls. Use it to find and kill that vile fucker."

Paige hugged Lola. "I know those are my tears you're cryin'. And I understand what your tellin' me. Daddy's right. I need this to get through today. Thank you, Lola."

Lola held Paige tight. "We need to go see Lin's folks so I can help them, too. Okay?"

"Okay," Paige said as she released the hug, got up, and walked toward the garage where Lola's pink Cadillac was parked.

"Um, Paige," Lola called to her.

Paige spun around, oblivious to the obvious. "What?"

"We need to put some clothes on before we go to the Anderson's."

Paige looked down at her body, as if she had no clue, and saw she was naked. "That's an excellent idea."

Ten minutes later, they were dressed and on the road.

~ * ~

While Garrett was in route to the Andersons, Deputy Danny Stutter's voice came over the radio and made an already bad day worse.

Garrett keyed the shoulder mic. "Garrett here. What's up, Danny?"

"Got another stolen coffin," Danny's voice crackled and hissed over the radio. "This one from Christ Lutheran."

"Who'd it belong to?"

"Carla Weaver. Is this sicko purposefully diggin' up the ones killed by the...ya know?"

"Looks that way?"

"For what?"

"Hell if I know. Have ya called Digger?"

"Ten-four. He's on his way. And the pastor's gonna call Carla's next of kin."

"Okay. Thanks, Danny."

"Any plans on how to catch this sick fuck?" Danny asked.

"I'm workin' on it. And watch your language on the official radio."

"Ten-four. Sorry, Sheriff. I'm out."

A few minutes later, he pulled into the Anderson's driveway and Gloria ran out in her housecoat. Curlers bobbed in her blonde hair and her face was a messy mixture of tears and snot. When Garrett got out of the SUV, Gloria lunged into his arms. Her knees gave out, and she slumped against him. Garrett gathered her in his arms and carried her back into her childless house.

~ * ~

About twenty minutes after Garrett arrived at the Anderson's house, Lola and Paige pulled into the driveway and parked behind Garrett's SUV. Lola was engaged with Paige in a silly argument about who was the better singer. Elvis Presley or Justin Bieber. Elvis was clearly the better singer, but Paige was a stubborn child.

"I met Elvis once," Lola said.

"Bull poop. You did not."

"I did. It was in nineteen-fifty-eight. He was in New Orleans to shoot the movie King Creole. He was interested in voodoo, the occult, and such. So, he and his entourage, the Memphis Mafia, came to the French Quarter one night after shootin' the movie and came into my mamma's shop for a palm readin'. And I did the readin'."

"Seriously?" Paige asked.

"If I'm lyin', I'm dyin'." Lola exclaimed.

"Did ya see he was gonna die young?"

"I did."

"Did ya tell him?"

"Heavens no, chil'," Lola said. "I tol' him he would meet the love of his life in Germany in fifty-nine and that they'd have a beautiful baby girl in sixty-eight. All of which came to be."

"Why didn't ya tell him the bad stuff?"

"Folks don't pay to hear bad readin's. I tol' him the good stuff, and he had a good life for a while."

"You're sweet, Lola."

"I know," Lola said with a big smile.

Had they not been engaged in this conversation, Lola probably would have seen the cloaked Cadillac Escalade parked up the street from Lindsey's house, but they were, and she didn't.

~ * ~

Paige opened the Anderson's front door without knocking. That was her normal entrance, and Lola followed her inside. Garrett and Gloria sat on the sofa; Gloria leaned against Garrett, sobbing heavily. He had an arm around her shoulders and hugged her tightly to him. Gloria, so deep in grief, didn't notice Paige and Lola come in.

When Lola said, "Hi, Gloria. I'm here to help ya."

Gloria looked up.

"How? How can anything help? I lost my boy six months ago and now my daughter," Gloria sobbed.

"She can help ya the same way she helped me, Missus Gloria," Paige said.

Gloria's wet, red eyes drifted to Paige. She hadn't noticed her when addressing the beautiful, African American woman, and sobbed, "Paige. Oh, Paige. They're both gone now."

"May I, Garrett?" Lola said.

Garrett nodded, removed his arm from Gloria's shoulder, and stood. When he did, Gloria slumped into the void left when he got off the couch. He'd seen that exact scene before while at the Henderson's house when Troy got off their sofa to go outside with Garrett to show him where he'd seen the footprints in the frosted grass. His wife, Penny, slumped into the void he left in exactly the same way. History was repeating itself, and he wondered how many more grieving mothers would slump into literal and figurative voids before they killed the ancient vampire.

Lola went to the sofa and sat next to Gloria's head that was pressed into a couch cushion, which muffled her sobs. While hands were preferred, Lola only needed contact to help the grieving. She placed her right hand on Gloria's warm, left cheek and her left hand on the back of her neck. She pulled on the grief. After having lost Justin so recently, Gloria's grief over losing Lindsey was deep and stubborn. Lola pulled some more and felt it give. Then it poured into her like a fully opened faucet. When Lola took enough so Gloria could function, she removed her hands. The whole extraction took less than two seconds. After taking Paige's grief, taking Gloria's grief for both of her lost children affected Lola more than she expected. She slumped back and against the armrest.

Garrett went to Lola instantly and he cradled her head in his strong hands. "Are ya okay?"

Lola's eyes opened slowly.

Lola felt like an emotional truck had hit her, but she said, "I'm okay. Her grief for Justin is as raw as if it just happened, too. I wasn't expectin' to take on both of 'em at once. I'm okay now."

"Ya sure?" Garrett asked, clearly concerned.

"I am," Lola said as she stood up on steady legs. "Paige, honey. Will you sit with Gloria while your daddy and I tend to Andy?"

Paige watched Lola take Mrs. Gloria's grief and knew, firsthand, the feeling.

"Of course," Paige said as she took a seat next to Mrs. Gloria, who had sat back up on the sofa as her daddy and Lola went to the downstairs bedroom where Mr. Andy was in bed, too weak to get up.

When Garrett and Lola entered the darkened bedroom, Andy, in a weak voice little more than a whisper, said, "Gloria?"

"No, Andy. It's me. Garrett. I brought someone to help ya feel better."

The covered lump on the bed moved and Andy's white face, made even more ghostly by the disheveled, graying hair hovering around his balding pate, looked at them with heavy, dim eyes.

Lola approached the bed. "My name is Lola. May I sit?"

Andy nodded slowly.

After Lola was seated, she produced a small, corked vial from pockets she didn't have. "Drink this, Andy. It'll make you feel better."

"What is it?" he whispered.

"It's sort'a, like medicine," Lola told him as she uncorked the vial.

Andy nodded and opened his mouth like a baby bird waiting to be fed. Lola poured the thick, red contents into his mouth. Andy made a face like he'd tasted something bitter, but he swallowed it. The effect wasn't immediate, but it was noticeable. He sat up slowly and color began to return to his ghostly white face. Andy flattened his wild hair with his hands. His eyes cleared and opened wider. He regarded Garrett and the beautiful African American woman who sat on his bed next to him, but he didn't appear surprised to see either of them.

In a stronger voice, but not quite back to normal, Andy said, "Lindsey? Where's Lindsey?"

"That's why we're here, Andy," Garrett said. "To find out."

"I need your help, Andy," Lola said.

"Anything," Andy said in his normal voice. "I'll do anything to help."

"Good," Lola said. "Give me your hands, Andy."

Andy threw the covers off. He was naked but unconcerned and gave his hands to Lola.

When Andy threw the covers off, and Garrett saw he was naked, his impulse was to look away. Obviously, not for the same reason he avoided Paige's naked body; he wanted to look away so as not to violate Andy's privacy. He saw two puncture marks high on Andy's inner left thigh. Right next to his scrotum. The thought of his daughter feeding there made him queasy. That feeling quickly subsided when he realized the creature who fed there wasn't his daughter anymore. Instead of turning away, he watched as Lola did her thing. Unlike Ty, Garrett had never witnessed this procedure.

When Andy's hands were in Lola's, she began rubbing her thumbs

303

on the back of his hands. As she did, Garrett saw the circles get bigger as Lola's thumbs grew longer, too.

"Feel my thumbs, listen to my voice, and look into my right, seein' eye," Lola said in her warm, honey voice.

Andy did, and Garrett saw him get lost in Lola's seeing eye.

"Good, Andy. Now you're driftin' back, back in time. Back before ya woke up this mornin'. Tell me the last time you saw Lindsey."

Hypnotically, Andy said, "She came into our bedroom in the middle of the night. I thought she'd had a bad dream. She's been doin' this since we lost Justin. But..."

"But what?" Lola asked.

"She wasn't alone," Andy said. "A large, shadowy figure was with her."

"See him, Andy," Lola commanded.

Andy's eyes squinted as he looked into Lola's seeing eye, looked back in time. "He's old. Ancient. Too old to be alive. His eyes are silvery slits. He's not human,"

"What happened next, Andy? Does he speak?"

Andy's eyes grew a little larger. "Oh, God. His voice is like wet gravel. He told me to uncover myself. I knew it was wrong 'cause I was naked, but I did. Then..."

"Then what, Andy," Lola said. "Look into my eye and *see* what happened next."

Tears slid down Andy's cheeks. "He told her to feed. To feed high on my inner thigh by my...privates. Lindsey came to me. She, oh God. She used her hand to move my...privates aside. Her hand was cold. Too cold. Then I felt her cold lips and tongue high on my leg. It felt so wrong. My little girl shouldn't kiss me there, but God help me, it felt good, too. Then I felt a sharp pain. She bit me with long, pointed teeth, and she started suckin', hard on the place she bit me. I-I-I can't say what happened next."

In a soothing voice, Lola said, "You can. You're safe, Andy."

More tears spilled down his face. "I-I. God forgive me; I got an erection. By then, I was fallin' into darkness. I thought she'd drink me dry. The inhuman, shadowy creature with silver eyes told her to stop. I could tell she didn't want to, but she did, because he commanded her to."

"Can ya see anything else, Andy?" Lola prodded.

Andy shook his head slowly. "No. I passed out."

Lola released one of Andy's hands, but the trance held. She licked the tips of her middle and index fingers on her left hand, placed the fingers tips on each of the puncture wounds and pressed hard into Andy's flesh. After a few seconds, she removed her fingers, and the puncture marks were gone. Where they had been were two light pink indentions; the color of skin after a scab falls off. Lola pulled the covers up to cover Andy's privates. Then she returned her left hand to Andy's right hand and continued circling it with her long thumb.

"Okay, Andy," Lola said. "Ya did real good. Feel my thumb, listen to my voice, and look into my left eye."

Garrett saw Andy's eyes focus on Lola's normal eye and then he looked down at Lola's thumbs. The circles got smaller. As this happened, her thumbs shrank back to normal size.

"You're comin' back to the here and now," Lola said. "You won't remember any of the things you tol' me. Even though you'll never see Justin and Lin again, you'll know that they loved you and their mom with all their beautiful hearts. And because you know how much they loved y'all, missin' 'em won't hurt as much. Do you understand me?"

Andy nodded.

Lola took her thumbs off Andy's hands.

Andy blinked a few times, as if noticing his surroundings for the first time. "I'm sorry. I can't remember anything after Lindsey went up to bed last night."

Lola smiled. "That's okay, Andy. I bet ya remember somethin' else."

Andy smiled. "Justin and Lindsey loved me and their mom with all their beautiful hearts."

Lola smiled. "That's right, Andy. Now, if y'all will excuse me for a minute or two, I need to talk with Gloria," Lola said as she got up and left Garrett and Andy in the bedroom.

Garrett didn't need to follow Lola to know what she would to do. She would put Gloria's troubled mind at peace, too. Paige would get to witness what he and Ty saw. It was a miracle.

A couple of minutes later, Lola, Paige, and Gloria entered the bedroom. Lola sat Gloria down on the bed next to Andy and they immediately joined hands. They looked at each other. There were tears in their eyes, but they were happier tears. Tears for the love their children had for them and they for their children.

Lola turned to Garrett and Paige. "We can go now."

With that said, Lola turned and left the bedroom. Garrett and Paige followed her out of the house to the driveway.

"What happened in there?" Garrett asked.

"Which happenin'?" Lola asked with a coy smile.

"All of it," Garrett said. "How'd ya calm Gloria? The potion you gave Andy? The trance? How'd ya make his bite marks disappear?"

"What I did for Gloria when we got here, and Paige earlier, was take on their grief to clear their minds," Lola said. "It's useful when someone needs calmin'. But it's temporary. Paige will lose it when she drinks the protection potion tonight. It'll last a day or two for Lin's folks. The potion I gave Andy was to replenish his missin' blood. The thing that used to be Lin drank him almost dry. The trance I put Andy in had two purposes. First, to see through the vampire's mezmery and what really happened. Second, to ease his grief for Justin and Lindsey permanently. I did this for Gloria, too.

"I didn't *take* their grief," Lola explained. "It's there. It'll always be there. As it should be. Their children deserve to be mourned for the rest of Gloria and Andy's lives, but I did permanently ease their pain to make their lives livable, so they can function. As far as the puncture marks on Andy are concerned, after makin' him forget everything I made him remember, it wouldn't do to have two unexplained puncture marks on his leg. So, I took 'em away."

"You're amazin', Lola," Paige said.

"Yes. You are," Garrett echoed.

Lola smiled.

"Oh yeah," Garrett said. "Someone stole another coffin last night from Christ Lutheran. It was Carla Weaver's."

"You know what that means, Garrett," Lola said.

"Yeah. He has another coffin," Garrett replied.

"And?" Lola pressed.

"And what?" Garrett said. "If ya know somethin', tell me."

"You're the sheriff, Garrett," Lola said. "Connect the dots."

Garrett thought for several seconds, trying to "connect the dots." Then it came to him. Whether Lola had helped him connect the dots, or he figured it out on his own, he didn't know. Nor did he care. The implications were troublesome.

"When he took Melanie, he only took one coffin, because that was all he needed," Garrett said. "The next night, two coffins were taken. One for Megan and the other for...Paige. But ya scared him off. That meant he had an extra coffin. One that Lindsey could use. If another coffin was taken last night, he probably took another girl last night, too. He, most likely, has four girls in his cloud now."

"Exactly," Lola said.

"You haven't gotten any calls 'bout another missin' girl," Paige said flatly.

Garrett looked at his watch. It was ten past seven.

"No calls," Garrett said. "Could be nothin'. Another missed opportunity."

"You don't believe that, Garrett," Lola said.

Garrett shook his head. "No. I don't believe that."

"Then what?" Paige asked.

"Then, somewhere in Pine View County, there's another dead family and a missin' daughter," Garrett said. "Just like the Williams family."

"I can find 'em tonight after I take the protection potion," Paige suggested.

"Yeah," Garrett said. "At least we'd know who the fourth vampire girl is. Otherwise, like with the Williams, we'll have to wait until someone finds 'em and calls it in before we do anything."

"What if that doesn't happen for a while?" Paige asked.

"Tomorrow's Monday," Garrett said. "One or both parents will have jobs they don't show up for without callin' in. If they're not found today, someone will find 'em tomorrow."

Paige nodded but said, "I hate this vampire so much."

"We all do," Lola replied.

"Okay. We can't do anything about this unless a call comes in today or Glinda finds 'em tonight," Garrett said. "For now, we need to get on with our day. Paige, you need to come with me so we can talk Father Mike into comin' out to the house this afternoon after Mass. We'll see you at three o'clock, Lola."

"Wouldn't miss the look on Father Mike's face when he sees Glinda for the world," Lola said with a grin.

"Hopefully, it won't come to that," Garrett said.

Lola's grin turned into a warm smile. "Hope all ya want, Garrett. But he'll have to see to believe."

Garrett had nothing to add. Because he knew Lola was right, he just nodded. Then he and Paige got into the SUV and Lola got into her pink Cadillac. Lola backed out first and headed back the way she came. Garrett backed out, headed the other direction, and drove past the cloaked Escalade with Dănuț inside.

~ * ~

Dănuț watched in silent dismay as the girl the Master coveted separated from the *vrăjitoare* and got into the SUV with her father. Worse yet, the girl and the *vrăjitoare* traveled in different directions. He had hoped the girl and the *vrăjitoare* would head to the same destination. To where they were hiding. He had to decide. Follow the girl or follow the *vrăjitoare*. The wrong decision wouldn't be to the Master's liking. Not at all. Because the girl was with her father, he thought she would go to her father's house. The Master already knew the location. He followed the *vrăjitoare*. Dănuț pulled onto the street at what he thought had been a safe distance and followed the *vrăjitoare*. Her bright pink Cadillac made tailing her easy.

~ * ~

Because she was in public, Lola's green, cat-like, seeing eye looked identical to her regular eye. She could still see when her eye was shrouded, but the sight wasn't as clear. Like there was a thin sheet of gauze over it. As she pulled to a stop at the end of Lin's former street, she glanced in the rearview mirror to see Garrett's SUV headed in the other direction. She saw something else, too. The SUV passed a void, a black spot, on the side of the road. Lola casually took her pink, Ray-Ban sunglasses off the visor, put them on, and opened her seeing eye. The void became a black Cadillac Escalade. She couldn't make out who drove it, but she knew. It was the unwelcomed visitor from earlier that morning. Lola waited a moment longer while the driver decided who to follow. When he headed her direction, Lola turned on her right blinker and drove north toward her house.

Lola had no intention of leading the man to her house. She figured he must've had some idea of where she lived, probably from one of the few stories the *Pine View Post* had written about her over the years. Leading him northeast seemed the prudent course of action, though. From a distance, he followed.

About three miles from her house, Lola turned right onto a dirt road with a street sign that read 'Dead End Road.' Underneath the street sign was an arrow pointing down the road with 'Texas Historical Site' written on it. After she'd traveled almost a mile down the dirt road, she saw the Escalade pull in behind her. Lola smiled.

Several miles later, Dead End Road dead ended at a cemetery. The cemetery had a black, wrought-iron fence around it and black, wrought-iron gates that were chained and locked. It was closed to the public on weekends. There was a large arch over the gates attached to two tall posts. The arch was metal and the words 'Not Forgotten Cemetery' were neatly cut from it. To the left was a granite stone with a brass plaque on it explaining why the cemetery was designated as a historical site. Lola didn't need to read it; she knew the place well.

The 'Not Forgotten Cemetery' was the last resting place for many former slaves who the Ku Klux Klan lynched in the years following the Civil War, and free blacks who were born after emancipation and ratification of the Thirteenth Amendment. Their only crime had been the color of their skin. Although the Klan had murdered many of the inhabitants, so had the not so blind, at least for people of color, and the injustice system in Texas through much of the twentieth century. Other inhabitants were family members of those murdered who wanted to be close to their loved ones in death.

Lola got out of her car and walked to the gates. She passed her right hand in front of the padlock, and it popped open. After letting herself in, she locked the gates again and, seeing the Escalade getting closer, hurried into the cemetery. Her destination was a large, white, granite obelisk where several unidentified victims of the racist South's purging of blacks were buried. On each side of the obelisk, 'Unknowns' had been etched into the white granite. Lola slipped behind the monument. She placed her back against the obelisk, pushed, and melted into the solid granite. Became one with the granite. She waited.

~ * ~

Dănuț followed the pink Cadillac northeast, out of town. He was pleased with himself for having gotten so close to the seers' house earlier that morning with nothing more than northeast Pine View County to go on. She was leading him right back to where he'd been looking. When he saw her turn right off the county road they were on, he sped up a little to make sure she didn't turn off it before he got there. When he saw the street sign, 'Dead End Road,' he relaxed and eased onto the dirt road. A dead-end road seemed the perfect location for a *vrăjitoare's* house. He saw her car kicking up dust about a mile ahead of him, and she had no other way out. It was perfect.

Keeping a safe distance, he followed the *vrăjitoare* for several miles. When he saw her brake lights come on, he slowed down as he closed the distance between their vehicles. He saw a clearing, but it wasn't a house. It was a cemetery. Dănuț grinned because he was very comfortable in graveyards. He'd made his living dealing with the dead, and undead, for many decades. He stopped behind the *vrăjitoare's* car and got out. Although it wasn't her house, he was intrigued; especially after reading the historical marker. He figured she had relatives buried there and if he could discover their names, he might trace them back to the *vrăjitoare's* house. After all, homes were passed from one generation to the next.

Thinking himself brilliant, Dănuț entered the Not Forgotten Cemetery.

However, unlike Lola, he had no incantation to open the lock. Instead, he scaled the six-foot wrought-iron fence. He tore his trousers on a spike that tipped each wrought iron bar, but not the skin beneath. He should have seen this as an omen, but he considered himself lucky and ventured into the cemetery in search of the *vrăjitoare*.

Decades of verbal, mental, and physical abuse programmed Dănuț to obey and not think. Of course, occasionally, he thought. This had not been one of those occasions. The Master was obsessed with the girl and the *vrăjitoare*. His decision to follow the seer resulted from that obsession, but it was the wrong decision. Had he thought about it, instead of simply obey, he would have realized the *vrăjitoare* saw through the Master's cloaking incantation. But he didn't. It never occurred to Dănuț she saw him following her, nor that she had laid a trap he had willingly, and excitedly, stepped into.

~ * ~

Lola waited inside the cool granite for several minutes before the tall, slender man with thinning, blond hair walked past the obelisk.

From inside the granite, Lola said, "Hello, again."

Dănuț was so startled, not something he was used to, he jumped sideways, away from the voice. His left calf struck a weathered tombstone hard enough to make him yelp in pain, and he almost toppled over. It was then he realized his colossal error. The *vrăjitoare* had seen him following her. He experienced something else he wasn't used to, except from the Master. Fear.

Trying his best to sound unafraid, but with a waiver in his voice anyway, Dănuț shouted, "Show yourself, bitch witch."

"In due time," Lola said.

Dănuț looked around and couldn't see the cursed *vrăjitoare*. He decided to run. It was his only option. But it was too late.

From inside the cool granite, Lola's lips moved in a silent incantation. It only took a second or two to enact, while Dănuț decided what to do. When the incantation was complete, the well-kept grass around

Dănuț's feet shot up from the ground. The grass turned into sturdy vines, encircled his legs first and then his torso, which secured his arms tightly to his sides. The only part of Dănuț's body that wasn't completely covered in the constricting vines was his face. He struggled to get free, but he was trapped.

In front of Dănuț's startled eyes, Lola stepped out of the granite obelisk and regraded the trapped man with contempt.

"Release me." Dănuț screamed.

"I don't think so," Lola said calmly. "Not until I've *seen* everything I need to know in your blackened mind."

"My Master will kill you for this, bitch witch," Dănuț hissed.

Lola shrugged. "He was gonna *try* to kill me, anyway. Now I have his pet. Soon, I'll know where the beast rests durin' the day. Game over, pet."

~ * ~

In his ornate coffin, his throne, Dragoș opened his undead eyes. Dănuț's destress had disturbed his rest. His eyes turned into silver slits and looked through Dănuț's eyes. What he saw infuriated him. It also concerned him, which was something he hadn't experienced in almost a millennia. He knew the seers' powers well. Dragoș knew, given time, she'd push her way through the protections he'd placed on Dănuț's mind. He knew, once she did, she'd know where his throne room was located. He couldn't let that happen. Dragoș invaded Dănuț's mind.

~ * ~

Lola saw the change in the thin man's demeanor. Suddenly, he relaxed, and his chin slumped to his chest. An instant later, his head shot back up and his blue eyes were silver slits. The ancient took over his familiar's mind.

Lola smiled. "There ya are. You vile fuck."

The thin man's face contorted and, in a voice sounding like wet gravel, growled, "How dare you address me in such a way, *vrăjitoare*. I will destroy you and take the girl named Paige for my cloud. I will do unthinkable things to her perfect, youthful body."

Lola shrugged again and, calmly, said, "I've already seen you in your true form through your pet's mind. You think you're immortal. You're not. You think you're clever. You're not. In fact, I'm disappointed. I would think a vampire of your age would be better at hidin' your pet's thoughts, but your black walls are flimsy. I've already punctured several of your pet's paper-thin walls. You're a pathetically weak fucker."

Lola knew she was playing a dangerous game with the ancient. She was making progress working through the black walls shrouding his familiar's thoughts, but it wasn't as easy as she'd told the ancient it was. She was purposefully taunting him for one of two eventual outcomes. One outcome would be she'd keep the ancient engaged long enough to break through all the black walls shrouding the familiar's thoughts and find out where the ancient's lair was located. The other outcome would end with the ancient killing his familiar. Lola hoped for the former, but the latter outcome would suffice, because, not having a familiar, would weaken the ancient, too.

The slender man's mouth opened incredibly large and the voice that came from his unmoving lips was complete rage. "You vile, *pizda*. I will kill this slave before you have my secrets."

"Go ahead," Lola taunted the ancient vampire. "Losin' your pet will leave ya vulnerable, too. Either way, you're fucked."

"Foolish, *pizda*," Dragoș hissed through Dănuț's open mouth. "Familiars are as plentiful as flies on shit. And I have already selected my next slave. This waste of human flesh means nothing to me."

"You'll never have the silver-haired werewolf as your pet," Lola said as she broke through another black wall that shrouded the thin man's mind.

This took Dragoș by surprise, and he was momentarily speechless. But the satisfied smile on the *vrăjitoare's* face infuriated him and broke his silence.

"What do you know of the silver-haired werewolf?" the ancient hissed.

"A lot," Lola further taunted the ancient vampire. "But you can't penetrate my mind the way I'm penetratin' your pet's mind. So, you'll never know."

"You, *pizda*." the ancient screamed through the slender man's gaping maw.

Lola actually smelled the ancient's rot in the air after the outburst. She was at the last wall shrouding the thin man's thoughts. If she could taunt the ancient for a few more seconds, she'd know everything. She smiled at him.

Dragoş had felt the walls he'd placed around Dănuţ's mind falling. The *vrăjitoare* had lied about how easy it was to break through Dănuţ's defenses, but she had made it to the last wall. He scolded himself as he realized the *vrăjitoare* had taunted him to buy time. That she had played him so easily enraged him. That she knew of his plans for the silver-haired werewolf and claimed to know a lot about it infuriated him.

Lola saw the ancient's rage building in the face of his familiar and realized she was out of time. She pushed, hard, against the last black wall and felt it crumble. Lola was in the familiar's mind, but it was too late. She didn't have time to glean any information before the ancient destroyed the familiar.

With an unholy scream of rage, the slender man's body contorted unnaturally. It looked like he folded in on himself. His body shrank into the vines binding him. Then there was a brilliant burst of blackness and the vines collapsed in on themselves. The blackness obliterated the thin man. Not even his clothing remained. Then Lola heard a loud bang and, when she looked, the Escalade had disappeared without a trace.

Lola hadn't gotten everything she wanted out of the familiar encounter—the ancient's location. It hadn't been a total loss, though. The ancient was without his familiar and this made him vulnerable. If Glinda could find its lair, it would be exposed during the daylight hours. Satisfied, Lola got in her car and drove home. She needed to meditate before the gathering at Garrett's later that day. She smiled as she drove away from the Not Forgotten Cemetery.

~ * ~

The ornate lid to Dragoş' coffin exploded open with such force it dislodged dirt from the earthen ceiling of his underground throne room and rained down in a shower of dust. Dragoş stood bolt upright in his coffin, his arms still folded over his chest, unhinged his bottom jaw, opened his grotesquely enormous mouth to its full limits, and released a primal, rage filled scream. More dirt showered down from the ceiling. Then he threw his arms out to each side, which flung the lids of his daughter's coffins opened.

The explosive sound of their father's coffin lid opening pulled his daughters from their daylight rest. The primal scream of rage made them tremble. Because they were connected to him through their creation, they felt his rage as well as heard it. When their coffin lids, unexpectedly, flew open, they cowered in fear, not daring to even look at him. He screamed again and dirt and dust rained down on their exposed, undead, frightened bodies.

After the two earth shattering screams, Dragoş stood, motionless, and seethed with anger. Losing Dănuţ did not fuel his anger. He cared not for the human who had faithfully served him for decades. He directed his ire at the inferior *vrăjitoare, pizda* who had dared speak to him as if she were his superior. Who had tricked him by taunting him into an exchange to access Dănuţ's mind and his location. It angered him to know he had underestimated the *vrăjitoare*. He wouldn't make that mistake again.

After several moments, Agrapina, his first born whose coffin was next to his on the right, said, demurely, "What has happened, Father?"

Dragoş turned his head and looked down at her through his sliver slit eyes in contempt. Agrapina shrank back from the evil stare in fear.

Lacrima, his third creation, who was a natural vampire and Dragoş' new favorite, whose coffin was next to Agrapina's, said, "Tell us, Father."

Dragoş' deadly stare fell upon Lacrima, but she didn't cower as Agrapina had. Dragoş smiled.

"Dănuţ is dead," Dragoş said through clinched teeth. "The vile, *vrăjitoare* led the fool into a trap and she was penetrating the protections I had placed around his fragile human mind. Had she gotten through, she would have discovered our location. I had to destroy him."

"How will we survive without him?" Antanasia asked.

Dragoş looked at her sharply. "Foolish child. We do not survive because of him. He survived because of me. I will create another familiar soon."

"The silver-haired werewolf?" Agrapina dared to ask.

"Yes," Dragoş hissed.

"We do not know who or where it is," Ilinca said.

Dragoş glared at her, but only briefly. "No. But the *vrăjitoare* does. She told me as much."

"You believe her?" Lacrima asked.

A ghastly smile spread across Dragoş' face. "She knows."

"We do not know where she is, Father," Agrapina said.

Dragoş' features turned dark, his silver eyes squinted, and he roared, *"We will find her."*

His daughters shrank back in fear.

Dragoş calmed. "I had wanted two more for my American cloud. But four will do. Rest, daughters. Tonight, we hunt for the *vrăjitoare*."

With that said, he waved his arms and their coffin lids slammed shut on their startled faces. He slowly descended back into his coffin and the ornate lid gently closed. Before he destroyed Dănuţ, he saw, in his mind, a dilapidated house he had investigated earlier that morning. Something about it didn't seem right. Dragoş closed his silver slit eyes. There was a grotesque smile on his ancient face.

~ * ~

Because Paige and Mandy wanted to go to confession before Mass, they arrived about twenty minutes early. There were two people in the confessional line. Mandy asked Paige if she would like to go before her, but Paige politely declined and hoped no one else would get in line behind her. She thought Fr. Mike might not feel like taking more confessions after hers. No one else got in line behind Paige and she waited for her turn. It didn't take long; apparently the people in front of her, including Mandy, hadn't been sinful of late. Neither had she, but she was about to drop a bomb on Fr. Mike. After Mandy stepped out of the confessional, Paige went in, closed the door, and kneeled.

When the patrician widow slid open, she saw Fr. Mike's dark profile through tightly clustered mesh separating them.

Paige nervously ran her fingers over the silver crucifix hung around her neck on a silver necklace. "Bless me, Father, for I have sinned. My last confession was two weeks ago."

She saw Fr. Mike nod his head through the mesh and continued.

"Since my last confession, I snuck out of my daddy's house, even though I knew I was dishonorin' his rules. I have also had impure thoughts when I think about Justin and what we were about to do before he was murdered. I revealed a secret I've been keepin' from my mom since the night Justin was murdered. I guess I've been livin' a lie with her for all these months. That was wrong. Finally, and I don't think this is a sin, but I'm a werewolf."

Fr. Mike's head turned so he looked at her through the mesh. "You're a what?"

"I'm a werewolf," Paige said. "But she's a good wolf, Father."

"The confessional is no place for games, Paige," Fr. Mike said, somewhat agitated.

"I'm not lyin', Father. My wolf, Glinda, that's what I named her after the good witch in The Wizard of Oz, is good. But she killed another werewolf in self-defense."

"You're confessing to murder?" Fr. Mike whispered.

"No. It wasn't murder," Paige said. "It was self-defense. He was a *terrible* werewolf, and he was gonna kill two of my friends and me."

"Enough of this nonsense, Paige," Fr. Mike said sternly.

"I'm tellin' the truth," Paige implored.

Still agitated, Fr. Mike said, "Do you have any more *actual* sins to confess, Paige?"

"No, Father. This is all I can remember. I am sorry for these and all my sins," Paige concluded her confession.

"For your *actual* sins, pray three Our Fathers and three Hail Mary's after leaving the confessional. Pray the Act of Contrition now."

The prayer was on a card on her side of the confessional, but she recited it from memory, left the confessional, joined her daddy and Mandy on the back pew, knelt, made the sign of the cross, prayed her penance, crossed herself again, and then slid onto the bench between Mandy and her daddy.

Once Paige sat between them, she whispered, "I told Father Mike, but he doesn't believe me."

Garrett and Mandy shared a worried look over Paige's head and then Garrett whispered, "You told him what?"

"That I'm a werewolf," Paige whispered back.

"I'm not sure that was such a good idea, kiddo," Garrett said.

"It's the perfect idea," Paige said. "I told him 'bout it durin' confession. He can't tell anyone. I told him 'bout Glinda killin' *El Lobo,* too. I don't know if he can report me for that or not."

"Paige," Garrett said a little too loudly and several people turned their heads in disapproval.

"He didn't believe me, Daddy. He probably thinks I need phycological help. At least now, he'll be a little more prepared for this afternoon when he comes to the house, and I *show* him Glinda. I think tellin' him now will guarantee he'll come."

"I think she's right, Garrett," Mandy said, taking Paige's side.

"I guess we'll find out soon enough," Garrett said with a shrug.

After that exchange, the three of them sat in silence and waited for Mass to start. Shortly before it did, they were surprised to see Andy and Gloria Anderson walk into the church. They clung to each other but were, otherwise, composed. As they took a seat three pews in front of them, Garrett and Paige marveled at Lola's hypnotic power.

Mass went well but, when Paige walked up with opened palms for communion, Fr. Mike eyed her wearily. Paige wasn't concerned. She took the communion host, said, "Amen," put it in her mouth, made the sign of the cross, returned to her pew, kneeled, and prayed for the Andersons.

After Mass, Garrett, Paige, and Mandy, as well as several others, inspected the pews to make sure the padded kneelers were up, and all the missals and the hymnals were in the wooden shelves on the backs of each pew. Then they waited as the parishioners made their way slowly out of the church, shaking hands and making small talk with Fr. Mike as they left. Andy and Gloria were the last to leave. They regarded Garrett, Paige, and Mandy with weak smiles as they did. It was time to invite Fr. Mike out to their house.

Garrett, followed by Paige and Mandy, approached Fr. Mike, and stuck out his hand. "Good homily, Father."

Fr. Mike took Garrett's hand. "Thank you, Garrett."

He looked at Paige as he shook Garrett's hand.

Paige met his stare and didn't look away.

Their hands parted and Garrett said, "I know ya know 'bout Melanie Zane missin' and Justin's coffin bein' taken. Have ya heard about the three other coffin thefts and three more missin' girls? The murders of Trevor Henderson, Al Sanders, and the Williams family?"

That got Fr. Mike's attention.

He looked at Garrett. "I heard about two other coffin thefts and one other missing girl, Megan Williams. Her family was murdered. I know about the Trevor boy and Al. My condolences, Paige."

He gave her a sincere nod and continued, "When was the fourth coffin taken and who are the other two missing girls?"

"They stole the fourth coffin from Christ Lutheran last night," Garrett said. "It belonged to Carla Weaver, who was killed last May when all the other folks were killed. The other two girls went missin' last night, too. I don't know the identity of one of 'em, yet. The other one was Lindsey Anderson."

Fr. Mike's jaw went slack, and he looked to his left just in time to see Andy and Gloria Anderson's car exiting the church parking lot.

He turned back to Garrett and studied his face for several seconds. "That can't be. They just shook my hand and didn't mention Lindsey missing. I don't believe that's possible."

"I assure you it is," Garrett said. "Gloria called me this mornin' and told me Lindsey was missin'. I went to their house. Lindsey's missin', Father Mike."

"The fourth girl?" Mike said. "If you don't know who she is and she hasn't been reported missing yet, how can you know there's a fourth girl missing?"

"There's a fourth coffin missin' and he only takes as many coffins as he needs," Garrett said.

"Who? Who only takes as many coffins as he needs? And why?"

"I don't know who he is yet, but Paige and a friend of ours, Lola Laveau, have seen him. As to the why, I think ya can help us out on that."

Fr. Mike looked at Paige. "You've *seen* him?"

"I have," Paige replied.

"This isn't more of that nonsense you were saying in the confessional, is it?" Mike asked harshly.

Calmly, Paige said, "No. This is different."

"Different nonsense?" Fr. Mike accused.

Garrett intervened. "We need your help, Father Mike. If ya don't help us, this'll keep happenin'."

Fr. Mike studied Garrett's stern face again. "You're serious, aren't you?"

"*Dead* serious," Garrett stressed. "I'm havin' some folks out to my house this afternoon at three o'clock. We need ya there, Father Mike."

"I should tend to the Andersons. First Justin and now Lindsey. They need spiritual support. Today."

"They've been tended to," Garrett said. "As ya saw, their copin'."

"By whom?" Mike asked.

"Come to my house this afternoon and you'll meet the woman who tended to 'em."

Fr. Mike looked toward Mandy and Paige. They both nodded.

He looked back at Garrett. "I'll be there."

Relieved, Garrett took Fr. Mike's hand again and shook it quickly. "Thank ya, Father Mike. We can't do this without ya. I'll text ya my address and see ya at three o'clock."

"No need to text it to me. I have all my parishioners' addresses in an Excel spreadsheet. I'll see you guys at three o'clock."

As Garrett, Paige, and Mandy walked to his truck, Mandy said, "That could've gone better."

Garrett smiled. "I don't care how it went. I'm just glad he's comin'."

"He won't believe any of this unless he *sees* Glinda," Paige added.

"I know, and I don't care about that either," Garrett told her.

They got in his truck and headed home. It was going to be an

320

interesting afternoon.

~ * ~

Fr. Mike was the last to arrive at Garrett's house, fifteen minutes late. His directions were good but, unlike the others, who had been there before and were familiar with the winding, hilly roads, Fr. Mike drove cautiously and five miles under the speed limit on most stretches of road and ten miles under the speed limit on most curves and some hills.

When he pulled into the driveway, he saw a plethora of vehicles parked out front. He recognized Garrett's patrol SUV and his private black Chevy Silverado, four-by-four, crew cab pickup, Mandy's blue Ford Explorer, and Paige's green Chevy Sonic. The 56, pink Cadillac, blue on silver square-body, older Chevy truck, newer, gray, Ford F-250, four-by-four, crew cab truck, and decked out motorcycle were foreign to him. It looked like an eclectic group of vehicles, and he was interested in meeting the people they belonged to. As he stepped out of his, by comparison, boring, 2002, gold Buick LeSabre, he smelled something cooking on an outdoor grill. It smelled good.

As he made his way to the front door, it opened, and he saw Paige wearing blue jeans, boots, and a brown Pine View County Sheriff Department hoody. Her long, brown hair was pulled back in a ponytail that poked out the strap that adjusted the size of a faded green John Deere baseball cap. He'd never seen her dressed casually, and she looked like the country girl he knew she was. He thought the look suited her well.

"Father Mike," Paige said as she grabbed him by the arm and guided him inside. "We were startin' to think you'd changed your mind."

"Nope," Mike said. "Just being careful on these winding, country roads."

"We'll, c'mon. Everyone's out back. I'll introduce ya to the folks ya don't know. Can ya believe how nice it is outside today?"

"Thank global warming," Mike said.

A couple of seconds later, Paige brought Fr. Mike out onto the back deck where Garrett was busy at the grill. He recognized Deputies Jackson and Raintree, but the short, plump man and beautiful African

American woman were strangers.

"Ya know Mister Ty and Mister Trowa. This is Doctor James Huff from SFA, and this is Miss Lola Laveau, a dear friend. Over there is Doctor James' bulldog, Winston," Paige said as she pointed at each as she introduced them.

Upon hearing his name, Winston raised his large bulldog head. A stringer of drool connected each of his flabby cheeks to a puddle on the wood deck. He looked around then laid his head back into the puddle of drool and closed his droopy eyes.

James got up from the porch table and approached Fr. Mike. Fr. Mike took his limp fish hand in his and shook it. When the shake ended, James didn't produce a carry size tube of hand sanitizer. He had improved on that issue.

"It is a pleasure to meet ya and have ya as part of the fellowship, Father Mike," James said. "We need ya on board more than ya know."

"Thank you, Doctor Huff," Mike said warmly. "I'm not sure of any fellowship or how I can help."

"Please, we're informal. James is fine. You will," James said with a wink.

As James engaged Fr. Mike, in a single blink of her eyes, Lola unmasked her seeing eye to look at his aura. His aura was silver. Nowhere near as pure as Paige's aura, no one else's was, but she knew in that instant he was a good man and he would help. He would need some convincing, but he'd help. Lola got to her feet, but Fr. Mike went to her. Her seeing eye again hidden. They needed to ease him into the supernatural as carefully as possible.

Seeing Lola, and her pink and white beads, pink lipstick, and pink fingernails, Fr. Mike correctly attached her to the pink Cadillac.

He approached her and stuck out his hand. "Nice to meet you, Lola."

"Nice to meet you too, Father," Lola said. "But I'm a hugger."

Lola wrapped him in a tight hug.

Paige saw how uncomfortable Fr. Mike was with the hug and had to choke back a giggle.

He was more surprised than uncomfortable at being so warmly

embraced by a stranger, but he composed himself and patted her awkwardly on the back. Even though he was a committed priest, he wasn't blind. Lola's long, sheer dress left little to the imagination. Even though it had warmed up in the high sixties, her body was incredibly warm. He didn't know it, but he had just experienced his first supernatural event. Lola's elemental witch resistance to temperature.

As they parted, Garrett walked up with a single hamburger patty on a spatula and said to Lola, "Your veggie burger."

Lola grabbed a hamburger bun from a plate on the table and Garrett slid it onto the bottom bun.

Garrett looked up. "Who wants cheese on their *real* hamburgers?"
Every hand shot up.

"Who wants jalapeño cheese on their hamburgers?"

All hands, except Ty, and Trowa's, went down. Garrett was having jalapeño cheese, too. He went back to the grill.

Fr. Mike took a seat at the table next to Mandy. The table was full of hamburger fixings—lettuce, tomatoes, onions, and jalapeños. Condiments, potato chips of different varieties. Two pitchers of tea, which, because he was in Texas, he assumed were sweet tea. A cooler with, which he assumed, contained beer, and a clear jug with an amber colored liquid in it.

Confirming his assumption about the tea, Mandy said, "May I pour ya a class of sweet tea?"

"Yes, please," Mike said and added, "What's in that jug?"

"That is my homemade, muscadine wine, Father Mike," James told him.

"It's delicious," Paige said. "But Daddy only lets me have a little."

Already feeling comfortable in his surroundings, Mike said, "More for the rest of us."

"That's the spirit." James said with a laugh that made his plump cheeks jiggle.

"What's this all about? Why am I here?" Mike asked.

Lola smiled and, in her warm, honey voice, said, "Food before business, Father Tike."

It might have sounded like an innocent mispronunciation of his name, but Fr. Mike was surprised to hear Lola call him this. Tike was his nickname growing up. Anyone other than his parents hadn't called him that since he graduated high school and left it behind when he went to seminary school.

"I'm sorry," Mike said. "Did you just call me Father Tike?"

"Did I?" Lola said with a grin. "I don't think I did."

"Okay. It's just…Tike was my nickname while growing up," Mike said. "Sorry. I must've misheard you."

From the grill, Garrett said, "Grab a plate, some buns, and line up."

A couple of minutes later, everyone sat at the table, eating, and engaged in casual conversation. This was when Fr. Mike found out one of James' academic focuses was the occult. He was very interested in finding out more about James' research. When his assumptions about the cooler were confirmed, Fr. Mike gladly accepted an ice cold Miller Lite from Garrett.

After the meal was over, James grabbed the clear jug. "Who's up for some muscadine wine?"

All hands, including Paige's, shot into the air.

"Okay," Garrett said. "But only half."

"I know," Paige said, somewhat pouty.

James uncorked the jug and poured everyone, except Paige, a healthy portion of the amber liquid.

When he finished, and everyone had their muscadine wine, James said, "What's your toast, Garrett?"

Garrett thought for a moment. "To Father Mike. And hopefully, his help."

The plastic cups came together with a dull thunk and everyone took a drink.

It was Fr. Mike's first taste of James' homemade muscadine wine and he was exceptionally surprised by how delicious it tasted. Sweet on the tongue and the perfect warmth going down.

Fr. Mike took a second sip. "This is amazing, James. You're very talented."

James feigned humility. "Thank ya. But I'm just a novice. There's much better muscadine wine available."

Garrett interrupted the exchange between James and Fr. Mike. "No use puttin' this off any longer. We're here for a reason and that reason is to convince Father Mike to help us stop what's goin' on."

"I don't need convincing," Mike said. "I'm happy to help any way I can, Garrett."

"Ya need to know what you're agreein' to before ya commit, Father Mike," James added.

"Okay. What am I agreeing to?"

"How open-minded are ya with...nonconventional occurrences?" James asked.

"I know this has something to do with the murders, missing girls, and coffin thefts," Mike said. "Garrett told me that much after Mass this morning. I'm not a profiler or criminologist but, I assume, given the circumstances, the perpetrator has a necro fetish and is a sociopath. And probably, a Satanist."

"Actually, that's an appropriate description," James said. "We talked a little 'bout my areas of specialization. The occult, folklore, and mythology. This includes study of folklore 'bout supernatural creatures, like witches, vampires, werewolves, and many other beings."

Recalling Paige's confession, Fr. Mike looked, briefly, in her direction. "If you're asking me whether I believe in these supernatural creatures, the answer is no. I believe in evil, though. Whoever is doing this is, most definitely, evil."

"What if I told ya a vampire was responsible for everything that's happened?" James asked.

Fr. Mike took another sip of the spectacular muscadine wine and regarded Paige again. "I'd say vampires, witches, and werewolves don't exist."

"What if I told ya there was a witch and werewolf sittin' at this table right now?" James asked.

"Enough," Mike said harshly. "I can't breach the sanctity of the confessional, but I can ask what kind of nonsense Paige is being exposed to."

"Let me ease ya into this," Lola said. "I'm a witch. To be specific, I'm an elemental seer. That's how I knew your childhood nickname was

Tike."

Fr. Mike drank the rest of the muscadine wine in one gulp and got up. "I should leave and let you guys indulge in your fantasies."

Mandy grabbed his arm. "Please don't leave, Father. They're tellin' ya the truth."

Fr. Mike shook his head slowly. "I thought you were the only sane person here."

"One more minute, Father," Garrett said. "If you're not convinced, then we'll have to do this without ya and we really need ya for what we're dealin' with. Your turn, Paige-Turner."

As Paige stood, Fr. Mike reluctantly sat back down. He watched as Paige walked over to a shed and went inside.

"Let me guess," Mike said. "Paige is a werewolf, and she's putting on a costume in the shed."

"Not a costume," James said.

Fr. Mike was looking at the shed when Glinda stepped out. His face contorted in horror. He pushed away from the table quickly. Too quickly. One of the chair legs hung up on a slightly raised deck board and he toppled over backwards, which startled Winston into a barking fit.

Fr. Mike tried to scramble to his feet. He had to get away from the madness his mind couldn't comprehend. When he saw an offered hand, he took it. It was Lola's hand. He instantly calmed when their hands touched. With Lola's help, he got to his feet. His legs were a little weak, but they held his weight. He looked at the massive, silver-haired werewolf that was Paige.

"Father Mike," Garrett said, "meet Glinda, Paige's werewolf."

"That's an abomination of God," Mike said flatly.

"No. She's not," Lola said. "And ya know she's not because ya know Paige is in your God's favor. If she wasn't, she couldn't take communion."

Lola's use of "your God's favor" caused Fr. Mike to look at her. He saw her right, cat-like, green, seeing eye for the first time. He took a step back from her.

"I'm not an abomination to your God either," Lola said. "I'm a witch of the light. I have committed my whole life to keepin' harmony in nature. If Glinda unbalanced nature, if she was evil, I'd have to destroy her. She's a force of good. As are you. Y'all both have silver auras. The ancient vampire we're huntin' is pure evil."

"Unlike Glinda, vampires are Satan's creation as a purposeful affront to Christ," James added.

"I-I-I," Mike stammered. "Th-this is too much. How can...? How did this happen?"

~ * ~

Paige kept Glinda in place by the shed as she watched Fr. Mike's reaction to seeing her. She wasn't surprised, but she was disappointed. She knew Lola gave him a nudge when she helped him up. Glinda also knew it was a little nudge. Also, she somehow knew he didn't mean it when he called her an abomination of God. There was no conviction behind his words. It was a programmed response. As her daddy told Fr. Mike the whole truth about the werewolf murders, she walked over to the deck and laid down on the grass. Winston waddled over and snuggled up next to her. Fr. Mike kept casting sidelong glances in her direction, but he listened.

~ * ~

It took almost an hour for Garrett, James, Lola, Ty, Lola, and Trowa to tell Fr. Mike everything that happened during the werewolf attacks and what they knew about the current vampire situation. Everyone was surprised, and delighted, when Lola told them about her encounter with the familiar after leaving the Anderson's house and how vulnerable the ancient was without his daylight protector. They told him about the protection potion for Paige and Glinda that would be ready that night. And they asked him if he would help.

"I'm a warrior for Christ," Mike said. "It's my duty to protect God's children and vanquish evil. I'm in."

Upon hearing this, Glinda raised her massive head and looked at him with her large, green eyes. Fr. Mike got up and approached Glinda.

"I'm sorry I dismissed you this morning, Paige," Mike said as he reached out and placed a hand on her fine, silver fur.

He used his thumb to trace a cross in the fur on her forehead, and above her eyes. "May God bless you in this, and future, endeavors."

When Fr. Mike blessed her, Paige felt a surge of warmth flow through Glinda's body. She'd known Glinda wasn't evil, but that feeling confirmed any lingering doubts she might have had. She stood, towering over Fr. Mike, and hugged him. He hugged her back. After that, she went back to the shed, transformed, got dressed, and joined everyone at the table. Fr. Mike regarded her with a warm smile when she sat down next to him. She ran her fingers over the crucifix and smiled back.

"I still have so many questions," Mike said.

Garrett laughed. "Join the club. I've been dealin' with this since last May and I still have questions."

"I tol' y'all the protection potion will be ready by ten o'clock tonight," Lola said. "Y'all should get to my house a little earlier."

Paige hadn't dialed up Glinda's hearing after transforming and getting dressed in the shed. So, she had missed the start of this discussion.

"Okay. I'll pick up Father Mike, Ty, and Trowa and get there about nine forty-five," Garrett said. "Bring your little holy water sprinkler thingy, Father Mike."

"It's called an aspergillum, and I will," Mike said. "Little holy water sprinkler thingy. Really? I know we haven't studied that in your RCIA classes, but you could Google it on your cellphone."

Garrett's eyes enlarged. Fr. Mike immediately realized, and regretted, what he'd said. Garrett's conversion to Catholicism was to be an Easter surprise for Mandy and Paige.

Mandy looked from Garrett to Fr. Mike back to Garrett. "Your convertin' to Catholicism?"

"Um, yeah," Garrett admitted. "It was *supposed* to be a surprise for you and Paige at Easter Mass before our weddin'."

"Really, Daddy?" Paige asked excitedly.

"Really, Paige-Turner," Garrett said with a smile.

"I'm so sorry, Garrett," Mike apologized. "It just slipped out. In my defense, I've been a little overwhelmed having my world view shattered and reconstructed this past hour."

An instant later, Paige and Mandy, who sat on either side of Fr. Mike, were out of their chairs, around the table. They hugged and rained kisses on Garrett's cheeks.

Mandy stopped kissing Garrett's cheek long enough to say, "Don't apologize, Father Mike. This is a wonderful surprise and I think we need it more now than later."

Paige stopped kissing her daddy's cheek long enough to say, "Ditto, Father Mike."

Garrett wasn't mad at Fr. Mike for letting the secret slip. He was right; they had just changed everything he thought he knew about good and evil. He enjoyed the affection from his two girls, too.

After this went on for a while, Garrett said, "Okay. Okay. I'm glad y'all are happy. But it's startin' to feel like Winston's been droolin' on my face.

"Well," Mandy said in feigned insult.

"Yeah," Paige echoed Mandy's feigned insult.

Winston barked.

"Welcome to the fellowship, Father Mike," James said

"Thank you," Mike said. "Thank all of you for opening my eyes to the real evils around us. I'm proud to stand beside you guys in this battle. And Paige, Glinda is beautiful."

"Thank you, Father Mike."

"It'll be dark soon," Lola said. "We should get all this cleaned up and get home before the sun goes down."

Everyone pitched in and made quick work of the cleanup. Before they parted, James insisted Fr. Mike take what remained of the muscadine wine. He accepted the offering gratefully and headed back to the rectory. Lola and Paige left together. Ty, Trowa, and James went their separate ways, and Garrett and Mandy left for his folk's house.

All of them expected a hunt that night in the hopes of somehow finding the ancient vampire's lair. They didn't know the ancient planned to bring the fight to them.

Chapter Eleven

Sunset on December 27, 2015, in Pine View County, Texas came at five twenty-three p.m. Lola and Paige returned to Lola's house a little after five o'clock. The sun was a big, red ball sinking behind the tall pines on the western horizon. Instead of parking her car in the garage, as she usually did, Lola parked it in her front yard to the left of the porch steps. Having seen the ancient destroy his familiar who had trespassed into her dwelling in the early hours of that morning gave Lola a false sense of security. It wasn't like her to make mistakes, especially with so much at risk, but not parking in the garage would be a bad one.

Lola and Paige made their way into Lola's dark living room.

Lola went to the cauldron that floated over a conjured, white flame, and looked at the potion brewing within. "This is comin' along nicely."

"How can ya tell?" Paige asked.

"I just can. If ya need proof, I'll show you," Lola said and disappeared through the door on the left that led to her dining room and kitchen.

A moment later, Lola returned holding a butter knife. She dipped it into the bubbling brew and withdrew it. The tip was coated in a thick, blackish, foul-smelling liquid. The liquid slid, not dripped, from the knife until only a single drop dangled from the blunt tip of the utensil. Then that drop fell back into the cauldron. The butter knife was as clean as if it had just come out of the dishwasher.

"What's that show?" Paige asked.

"When the potion is ready, it won't stick to anything but you and Glinda," Lola said. "That single drop at the end of the knife was all it clung to, and it did so for only a moment before letting go. That's the portion of the potion not yet ready and it's a tiny portion. By ten o'clock tonight, it'll be ready."

"If it isn't?"

"You doubt my brewin' abilities?"

"No. It's just…" Paige began.

"What's botherin' you, Paige-Turner?"

"Everyone, me included, believes Glinda can kill the ancient," Paige said as she ran a finger over the crucifix. "But how? Do I need a silver-tipped wooden stake, like Doctor James said? Do I need to force him into the daylight?"

Lola smiled her warm smile. "Take a seat."

Lola sat in the high-backed chair, and Paige sat in the chair to her right.

"James is an intelligent and learned man, but he doesn't know everything," Lola said. "Everything he tol' your daddy 'bout killin' werewolves and vampires only applies to humans, not supernatural creatures, such as you and me."

"I don't understand."

"Did *El Lobo* need silver to kill Alexis?"

"No," Paige said with a slight shake of her head. "But he bit her in half."

"He did. But werewolves can regenerate. Had Alexis been able to crawl back to her lower half, she could've healed herself. She couldn't."

Paige thought back to that night and her eyes widened. "Her upper body landed right by me and Daddy. She was dead where she fell. I saw it in her eyes."

"Exactly. Did you need silver to kill *El Lobo*?"

"No," Paige said with a slight look of disgust. "But I tore the top of his head off."

"A grievous wound, to be certain," Lola said and brushed a lock of Paige's hair behind her ear. "But he, too, under different circumstances, could've regenerated. Are ya startin' to understand?"

Paige thought for a moment. "Are ya sayin' that supernatural creatures don't need the things Doctor James talked about to kill each other?"

Lola's smile widened. "That's exactly what I'm sayin'. You understand that's a strength *and* a weakness."

"Meanin' the vampire can kill Glinda without silver or the other things Doctor James said would kill werewolves," Paige reasoned

"Yes," Lola said solemnly. "That, chil', is why this potion is so important, and Mamma's gift so rare."

"Has Mamma ever given her knowledge to anyone else?" Paige asked.

"Only once."

"To who?"

Lola sighed; the memory was a painful one. "To the youngest witch in our coven. Her name was Lucrecia Washington."

Paige noticed the past tense. "Was?"

Lola smiled at Paige, but silent tears trickled down her cheeks. "Lucrecia was a promisin' young seer from Louisiana. In fact, I discovered her, and there was an openin' in our coven. One of my sisters had passed and her replacement, unfortunately, fell with her. Coven witches are not supposed to be in the company of their replacements to keep both of 'em from bein' killed at the same time. That is another story. I introduced Lucrecia to the coven. She passed all the rites of passage and was initiated.

"Several years later, after I had moved to East Texas, a vicious werewolf appeared in Southern Louisiana. This one was nowhere near as prolific a killer as *El Lobo*, but, if it hadn't been stopped, it would have rivaled the Mexican werewolf eventually.

"I offered to help, but Lucrecia was determined to prove herself and battle it alone," Lola continued in a hushed voice. "Mamma agreed, but only if Lucrecia partook of Mamma's wisdom first. Lucrecia agreed and brewed the same potion that's brewin' beside us now. When it was ready, Lucrecia drank the potion, absorbed Mamma's wisdom, and tracked the werewolf down in the Lafourche Parish swamps.

"She was ready. She knew what to do, and she did it. As the werewolf came for her, Lucrecia conjured an elemental created from the thick swamp muck and trapped the werewolf inside. It fought like hell to free itself, but Lucrecia centered her concentration and mirrored every move the enraged werewolf made with the swamp elemental. Unlike vampires and zombies that are undead and don't need to breathe, the werewolf was drownin' inside the elemental. Drownin' 'cause the elemental was a supernatural creature.

"Even with the gift of Mamma's wisdom, Lucrecia got careless,"

Lola said quietly. "She got overconfident. When the werewolf fell, she approached it. She got too close. With its dyin' heartbeat, the werewolf reached out its elemental covered hand and ripped out Lucrecia's throat. They died together, and the gators took their bodies.

"Lucrecia had so much promise and her loss was great to bear," Lola said as more tears leaked from her eyes. "But her sacrifice saved countless lives. For that, we celebrate her to this day in light covens near and far."

"I'm sorry, Lola. But…I don't understand two things."

"What don't ya understand?"

"Well, if it was just Lucrecia and the werewolf, how can y'all know all these details?"

"Once Lucrecia drank the potion, Mamma was with her and could see through Lucrecia's eyes."

"So, Mamma will see through my and Glinda's eyes after we take the potion?"

Lola nodded.

"Then that makes my second question even more important," Paige said. "Why did Lucrecia make the mistake of gettin' too close to the werewolf, and why didn't Mamma warn her?"

"That's two questions," Lola said with a weak smile. "The answer to the first is, and frankly, what we all fear for you, hubris. Over confidence. The answer to your second question is that Mamma was only an observer. The potion gave Lucrecia Mamma's wisdom. That was all Mamma could contribute. Lucrecia's mistake was hers and hers alone. Don't make the same mistake, Paige-Turner."

Paige thought for a moment. "But…how will I know? How will I know if I'm gettin' overconfident and makin' the same mistake?"

"Well, you'll need to trust in Mamma's wisdom. Never doubt it. Follow it no matter what. Unlike Lucrecia, you won't be alone. You'll have me, your daddy, Ty, Trowa, and Father Mike with you."

"Yeah, but *he* won't be alone either," Paige said. "He has four vampires with him. To be honest, I'm not too worried 'bout you and Father Mike. Y'all have power against the ancient. I *am* worried 'bout Daddy, Ty, and Trowa. I *won't* put 'em in danger."

"Nor should you, but I think ya underestimate their strength and resolve. It's born of their love for you, and love is a powerful weapon against hate."

"Maybe, but I'm still worried about 'em," Paige said.

"I know, sweet girl," Lola said as she took Paige's hand in hers. "That makes you and Glinda so special."

"Maybe," Paige said.

"Not maybe. I know. How 'bout we meditate for a bit? That should clear your mind."

"Do we have time?"

"Of course. The time spent meditatin' depends on the length of the candle used. We can still get three hours in. Get comfortable and I'll set it up."

By "get comfortable" Lola meant for Paige to get undressed. Paige was surprised she hadn't already done so; it was usually the first thing she did after entering Lola's house. She went to the bedroom and removed the constricting clothing. When she returned to the living room, Lola's sheer dress hung over the back of the high-backed chair and she sat, naked and cross-legged, on the floor in front of a shorter, lit candle. There was another lit candle in front of where Paige would sit next to Lola. Paige sat next to Lola, assumed the position with her palms up on the knees of her crossed legs, closed her eyes, and melted away. Beyond the universe with her creator, God. Being so close to Him gave her strength and resolve. Mostly, it gave her peace.

~ * ~

As the red ball of sun melted behind the horizon of silhouetted pine trees at five twenty-three p.m., the lid of the ornate coffin opened slowly and Dragoș rose to a standing position with his arms crossed over his chest. The rage he had experienced earlier from the taunting *vrăjitoare* and losing his familiar had dwindled to a seething anger and he concentrated that anger at exploring the dilapidated house Dănuţ had discovered earlier that morning. Dănuţ hadn't been as learned in *vrăjitoare* deception. Dragoș was. The more he reviewed that memory from his dead familiar's mind, the more convinced he was that a powerful incantation cloaked the dwelling. He smiled as he spread out his arms, raised them, and opened the lids of his four daughter's coffins.

His daughters rested peacefully but, when Dragoş said, "Awake," their crystal blue eyes opened, and each rose to a standing position in their coffins.

Dragoş smiled a ghastly smile. "We must feed and then we will find the vile *vrăjitoare* and deal with her."

Somewhat sheepishly, because she felt she had fallen out of her father's favor, Antanasia said, "I know of a family of six who live in a remote area."

"We need sustenance," Dragoş said. "Describe the humans,"

"There are three adults," Antanasia said. "The parents, the woman's brother, and three teenage humans. They live a few miles behind the house this body used to live in."

"Male or female young ones?" Dragoş asked.

"All boys," Antanasia replied.

Dragoş smiled because he would have hated to leave a young beauty behind. Without Dănuţ, he would have no choice; he didn't have another coffin and no one to get it. That the young ones were all male pleased him.

Dragoş looked at Antanasia. "Very good, daughter. They will provide a most excellent meal."

Antanasia smiled, which revealed her deadly fangs.

"Follow me, daughters," Dragoş said as he floated up to the door that concealed his under-ground throne room.

He waved a hand in front of the door, and it silently slid open. He floated into the embalming room.

Lacrima took flight next, followed by Agrapina, Ilinca, and after a struggle, Antanasia followed. They joined their father in the embalming room.

Dragoş waved his hand at one of the garage doors and it rumbled up. Parked outside that door was the hearse. Parked next to it, in front of the other garage door, was the Escalade that Dragoş had retrieved, so as not to leave any evidence that pointed back to the Eternal Rest Funeral

Home, after he destroyed Dănuț to keep his secrets from the *vrăjitoare*.

Dragoş had meant it when he told his daughters Dănuț needed him more than he needed Dănuț. It was true, but it had also been the first time in Dragoş' long, undead existence that he had been without a familiar; excluding a time after he had been created and protected by his Mistress' familiars the same way Dănuț, and his predecessors, had protected his creations.

~ * ~

It was the Fall of 1201, when Dragoş, then a twenty-two-year-old prince, was given the gift of eternal, undead existence. He saw her at a ball thrown by his father, Boian Văduva, the king, to celebrate his twenty-fifth year of rule. She was plump, easily in her fifth decade of life, which was ancient for a woman in those days, and her face was heavily powdered, with ridiculous red rouge on her cheeks, equally ridiculous red rouge on her lips, and an elaborate, powdered wig on her chubby head. She had deep, crystal blue eyes that followed him everywhere he strode. He could not shake her, but she never approached him. She admired his youthful beauty from afar.

That night, long after the celebration had ended, she came to Dragoş in a dream, or so he thought. His room was high on the castle's western wall, and she was floating outside his window. He went to her. Her eyes flashed silver and he couldn't look away. When she asked permission to enter his room, he gave it willingly. She was on him immediately. Her cold lips and tongue caressed his neck. Then he felt a sharp pain as her fangs penetrated the soft flesh of his neck. His world faded to darkness. There was no inviting white light for Dragoş; he was a non-believer in the Christ child and very cruel in life. There were no friendly voices encouraging him to join them, only wicked snarls and pain filled screams in the blackness. The blackness subsided when the sweet, coppery nectar filled his mouth and then his undead body. Dragoş opened his crystal, blue eyes and looked into the face of his creator, his Mistress. He suckled at her ample breast greedily.

When he had been reanimated, his first feeding and kill was his father. Had he not been an undead vampire, his father's death would have made him king. Instead, his Mistress, Cipriana Ardelean, whisked him away to her castle, which was more than a hundred miles east in, what had then been, Transylvania. There he became her sexual plaything and constant nightly companion as they fed on the blood of villagers near and far.

Cipriana never mentioned her creator to Dragoş. Dragoş, who had a taste for young, beautiful girls, could not comprehend why any vampire would create an old companion like Cipriana. She was secretive about much of her past. All Dragoş knew about her was she was over three hundred years old, which put her undead birth, sometime, in the eighth century.

That Cipriana had no Master or Mistress, intrigued Dragoş as he grew tired of her. One morning, after a night of feeding, one hundred and twenty-three years after Cipriana created him, as her repulsively, large body rode his cock, Dragoş, on impulse, reached up and ripped her flabby throat out. Her eyes, that were closed in ecstasy, flew open in surprise and pain as her black blood rained down on Dragoş. She grabbed at the ruins of her throat to quench the bleeding, but the wound was beyond repair. Cipriana slumped on top of Dragoş and with disgust, he threw her large body across the room where it smashed against the thick castle wall with enough force to leave an indent in the large, heavy stones. She sank to the floor in a massive heap and her body withered and aged. Within a few moments, nothing was left but the dust that had been her bones. Dragoş was free.

Her familiar, the third Dragoş knew since becoming her plaything, quickly, and willingly, pledged loyalty to Dragoş and drank of his blood. Dragoş took over Cipriana's castle and began collecting young, beautiful girls for his *nor*. Dragoş' time under Cipriana's control taught him a valuable lesson. Never keep one of his creations long enough for them to grow weary of him and emboldened enough to kill him. From that day forward, Dragoş regularly purged his *nor* members after they had served him for fifty to sixty years, and he always destroyed the older member in front of the younger members of his *nor*. This kept the remaining *nor* members in constant fear and no thoughts of freeing themselves from

Dragoş ever entered their frightened, undead minds.

~ * ~

Dragoş walked out of the embalming room and into the chilly night air. His four daughters dutifully followed him. Once they were outside, Dragoş waved his hand, and the garage door rumbled shut again.

He looked at his four young, beautiful daughters. "Tonight, we fly as a cloud."

An instant later, Dragoş had turned into a large man-bat hybrid with thick, black hair, pointed ears, a flat, hog-like nose, and large, leathery wings. Not surprising to Dragoş, Lacrima, the natural vampire, transformed immediately into a woman-bat hybrid. While her face and head were much like his, Dragoş marveled at her firm breasts that were visible under the thin, scarlet colored hair that covered her human form. Agrapina transformed next, followed by Ilinca. Antanasia struggled but, shortly, transformed, too. Dragoş found them all beautiful.

Without a word, Dragoş flapped his large wings, launched into the night sky, and hovered. There he waited for his cloud to join him, about a hundred feet above them. Lacrima easily followed Dragoş into the night and hovered next to him. Agrapina, closely followed by Ilinca, joined Lacrima and their father. Again, Antanasia was last. She had trouble synchronizing her wings to propel herself upward. After a few failed attempts, she managed and joined her sisters and father where they hovered, waiting for her.

Once she had joined them, she heard her father hiss in her mind, *It is a good thing you are beautiful and provided a destination for our feeding this night or I would destroy you and replace you with a more able daughter.*

I am sorry, Father, Antanasia thought to him.

Dragoş reached out with his clawed, bat-like hand, and stroked her cheek gently. *You will learn, my daughter.*

Antanasia nodded her bat-like head.

After this, Dragoş flapped his enormous wings and flew higher into the sky and in the direction of the girl's body, that had been Antanasia's, former home. His four daughters quickly joined him and flew, instinctively, in the formation of how their coffins were arranged around their father's throne.

~ * ~

Garrett's plan was to pick up Ty first, then swing by and pick up Trowa, and pick up Fr. Mike last before heading to Lola's house. He ran the route in his mind several times and decided, in order to arrive at Lola's at nine thirty, he'd need to leave his parent's house around seven o'clock. It was already after six and he and Mandy were together in his childhood bedroom, sitting on the small twin bed, side by side, holding hands.

"Please be careful tonight, Garrett," Mandy said in a hushed voice.

"I will. And I doubt we'll even see him tonight," Garrett said and gently squeezed her hand. "Once Paige and Glinda have taken the potion, our priority is findin' out who the vampire took last night. After that, if Glinda catches his scent, which she hasn't been able to track yet, we'll see if we can locate his hidin' place. Believe me. We do *not* want to engage this vampire at night. We wanna find where he's hidin' and come for him durin' the day when he's vulnerable. Thanks to Lola destroyin' his familiar, he'll have no one to warn him."

"You make it sound so easy," Mandy replied.

Garrett shook his head. "That is *not* my intent. I don't think anything 'bout this will be easy."

Mandy removed the silver crucifix and chain Paige gave her for Christmas. "I want ya to wear this tonight."

"No. You keep that. Just in case," Garrett told her.

"I'm not the one goin' out tonight," Mandy said. "I want you to wear it."

"Mandy, no. I'll have Father Mike and Glinda with me. I wouldn't feel safe wearin' it knowin' you're unprotected."

"I can't talk ya into wearin' it?"

"Nope," Garrett said. "You put that back around your pretty neck where it belongs."

Mandy reluctantly put the crucifix and chain back on. Garrett leaned in and kissed her softly on the lips. She kissed him back. A few minutes later, the bedsprings in his old bed squeaked rhythmically as they made love. When they were finished, it was time for Garrett to leave.

Garrett got dressed, bent over and kissed Mandy. "I love you."

"I love you, too," Mandy said. "You come home to me tonight."

"Tonight, and every night for the rest of my life," Garrett said with a wink.

He turned to leave but regarded Mandy once more at the bedroom door. Then he closed the door behind him, left his parents' house, got in his truck, and headed for Ty's house. He didn't know it, but the battle he thought would be days in the future, was only hours in front of him.

~ * ~

Dragoş led the way past the house where Antanasia's human once lived and found the house he saw in her mind, deep in the woods a few miles behind it. The cloud circled it several times while Dragoş assessed it. It was perfect. The house was more than a quarter mile off the nearest deserted county road; the lights were on, and he counted four vehicles in front of the house. Dragoş used his inferred vision to look through the house and saw six heat sources inside. Six humans. They would feed well before going for the *vrăjitoare*. Dragoş circled down toward the house; his cloud followed him. They landed in the backyard, outside the glow of the floodlights that lit up most of the yard and transformed back into their human forms. After the change, Dragoş was fully dressed. His young, inexperienced daughters were naked. They would learn.

"Well," Dragoş said with a wicked grin. "All of my daughters are without clothes. Who shall I send to the door to receive an invitation in?"

Antanasia and Lacrima's hands flew into the air simultaneously.

Dragoş eyed them both. "Lacrima will go."

"I know them, Father," Antanasia dared to say. "I think they'll invite me in."

Dragoş' eyes flick her way in a dangerous scowl.

His features softened. "Exactly. They most likely know you are missing. This will put them on guard. Besides, Lacrima has already mastered mezmery. She will go."

Lacrima gave Antanasia a smug look and then walked confidently to the sliding back doors that opened onto a small concrete patio. The blinds were closed. Lacrima knocked on the glass door and waited.

~ * ~

Inside the house, the Porters had just sat down at the dining room table for supper. Chicken fried steak, mashed potatoes with cream gravy, and green beans.

Hal, a big man with a Marine haircut, once a Marine, always a Marine, scooped a healthy portion of mashed potatoes onto his plate when the knock came.

He dropped the spoon, looked at his brother-in-law, also a Marine. "You know the drill."

"Damn right I do," Ashton Wilcox replied.

To his wife, Ashly, Hal said, "Take the boys to the bunker."

"We wanna fight," Trent, Gavin, and Josh Porter said in unison.

"To the bunker with your mom now," Hal growled.

Ashly and her sons left the table and headed toward the bookshelf in the living room that concealed the secret door to their underground bunker.

The Porters, and Ashly's brother, Ashton, were end-of-time survivalists. They had a stash of guns that would make some small countries envious and a store of food and water in the bunker that would last the six of them two years. After hearing about what happened to the Williams family, they were prepared for almost anything.

Hal and Ashton already had Glock 19C, Gen4 handguns strapped to their belts and AR-15 rifles, with thirty round magazines leaned against the dining room wall. They each grabbed one and, per the drill, Ashton headed into the garage that had a side door to flank whoever knocked on the back door.

Hal, with his AR pointed at the sliding back door from the middle of the living room, shouted, "Identify yourself."

The last thing he expected was to hear a female voice, and he let his guard down.

~ * ~

Lacrima heard the angry shout and in a demure voice, said, "My name is Taylor Shanahan. An evil man took me from my home last night and did horrible things to me. I'm naked, cold, and I need help."

Just then, Ashton poked his head and AR around the corner of the house, saw her, and shouted, "Holy shit, Hal. She ain't lyin'. Poor thing ain't got a stitch of clothes on. Let her in."

Ashton let the AR hang from the shoulder strap, took off his shirt, ran to the girl, and wrapped it around her shoulders. "You're safe now, girl."

Hal heard Ashton and used his AR to part the blinds and look out. He saw a pretty, young girl with scarlet hair, standing there. She had Ashton's shirt wrapped around her shoulders, but the shirt was open in the front, and she was definitely naked beneath.

Hal shouldered the AR and opened the door. "Is the evil man lookin' for ya?"

"Yes," Lacrima said. "Please let us in."

Hal began to invite her in, but he caught the plural "us" and didn't think she had referred to herself and Ashton. And there wasn't something right about her skin. But it wasn't her face he looked at; it was her small, firm breasts. Her skin was white, even for a ginger. Too white. Almost translucent. He saw black veins crisscrossing under the skin of her breasts.

Hal took a step back. "Who's with ya?"

"Just me, dipshit," Ashton said. "Let her in."

Hal raised his AR, pointed it over the girl's head, and looked through the night vision scope. He saw them.

Hal started to squeeze off a burst of rounds at the old man and three more naked girls, one of whom was the missing Megan Williams, when Ashton pushed the barrel up. "For fuck's sake, Hal. Let her in."

"She's not…" Hal began.

"Look at me," Lacrima hissed.

Hal did. He could not look away. Her crystal blue eyes flashed silver.

"Invite us in," she hissed.

Startled by the girl's voice and Hal's sudden change in demeanor, Ashton said, "What's goin' on, girl?"

But it was too late.

Hal said, "Y'all are invited."

Before Ashton could register movement, the girl who said her name was Taylor Shanahan pounced on Hal and drove him back into the house. Before Ashton could draw his pistol, another girl, also naked, slammed him against the house and engulfed his entire neck in her incredibly enormous mouth. Agrapina bit and fed.

Inside, Lacrima had the very large Hal pinned to the floor and drank his life blood away.

Dragoş, Antanasia, and Ilinca entered the house. Dragoş sniffed the air, pointed at the bookshelf, flipped his wrist, and sent it flying across the living room.

"Down there," he told Antanasia and Ilinca.

They disappeared down the hidden stairs.

Antanasia led the way. At the bottom of the stairs was a steel door. Antanasia pulled on the door, but it held fast. Ilinca grabbed the door, and they pulled together. The door squealed in its frame and then flew open. Ashly and her three sons were huddled against the back wall and very frightened.

The older boys, Trent and Gavin, recognized them.

Trent said, "Megan? Lin? What're y'all doin'?"

Antanasia pounced on Trent, and Ilinca pounced on Gavin. As they fed, Ashly screamed and Josh ran past the two naked girls who were killing his brothers, up the stairs, and into Dragoş' waiting arms. He clamped his jaws around the frightened boy's throat and fed.

Within a minute, it was done. All his daughters had fed and none of them needed to be told to stop. The two adult males and three young males were dead. Antanasia and Ilinca ascended the stairs to join their sisters and father. All four of his daughter's breasts glistened red with the blood of their kills. They looked delicious. From down the stairs, a woman screamed hysterically. Dragoş descended the dark stairs. A moment later, the woman's screams ended with a gurgling sound.

Dragoş emerged from the dark, hidden doorway and looked at his daughters with a father's pride and a lover's lust.

He smiled a bloody, grotesque smile. "Well done, daughters. Thanks to Antanasia, we have fed well. Now, we must fly to where I believe the *vrăjitoare* lives and destroy her. Transform, my lovely daughters."

All five vampires quickly transformed into bat hybrids, stepped outside, and took flight. They headed for northeast Pine View County. To the dilapidated house that Dănuţ saw. Even in death, he had served his Master well.

~ * ~

Garrett, with Ty and Trowa, pulled into the church parking lot, passed the church, and drove to the back where the rector, Fr. Mike's house was; Ty rode shotgun and Trowa sat behind Garrett. As the truck's headlights illuminated the front of the rectory, a curtain on a window left of the front door moved. Fr. Mike peeked out. His face looked ghostly white in the headlights. For a moment, Garrett thought the priest had changed his mind. Seconds after the curtain dropped back into place, the front door opened, and Fr. Mike emerged from the rectory.

Fr. Mike wore priest clothes. Black trousers, jacket, and shirt with a Roman collar. He had a backpack slung over one shoulder, too. He headed for the driver's side, so Trowa slid over behind Ty on the passenger's side of the truck. Fr. Mike opened the door, tossed the backpack in, climbed in, and shut the door.

Mike said, "I'm really going to a witch's house to watch her give a potion to a werewolf to find and kill a vampire?"

Garrett chuckled. "That 'bout wraps it up."

"This morning, I wasn't even sure demonic possession was real," Mike said. "I thought these were people with mental issues better served by psychologists and psychiatrists than priests. Guess I need to rethink that, too.

"That reminds me," Mike grabbed his backpack and continued. "I brought some things that might be useful."

"The holy water sprinkler thingy?" Garrett asked with a grin.

"The aspergillum? Yes. I brought it," Mike said as he rummaged through the backpack before producing three wooden crosses. "I also brought a blessed cross for each of you."

Garrett and Ty took one but, when Fr. Mike offered the third to Trowa, he said, "No thanks, Father. I'm not a Christian."

"If what James said is true, it doesn't matter," Mike said. "The cross is blessed. Please take it."

Trowa thought for a moment and not wanting to offend Fr. Mike, took the wooden cross.

"Thank you," Mike said.

Trowa nodded.

"Buckle up, Father Mike. We're headed to Lola's," Garrett said as he backed away from the rectory, shifted into drive, and drove out of the church parking lot into the chilly night.

~ * ~

Several minutes after Garrett and company left the rectory, Dragoş and his cloud flew high, and silently, above St. Joseph's Catholic Church on their way northeast. The cloud arrived before Garrett and company did. Dragoş circled high above what appeared to be a house in ruin, and a grotesque smile spread across his hideous features.

"This is the *vrăjitoare's* house," he hissed.

"How can you tell, Father?" Agrapina asked.

"It doesn't look inhabitable, Father," Ilinca added.

"It is a masking incantation put in place by the *vrăjitoare*," Dragoş said confidently.

"How can you be sure, Father?" Antanasia asked.

"Because of the car," Dragoş said.

"It is so rusted and overgrown with weeds that it can't even run, Father," Agrapina said.

"Exactly," Dragoş hissed. "When Dănuţ was here this morning, that car was parked in the destroyed garage."

"How could it…" Antanasia asked.

Dragoş interrupted her small-minded question. "Because it is an incantation. The car, house, and garage are fine. The *vrăjitoare* cast it upon her dwelling to disguise it."

"So, we have her?" Lacrima asked.

"Her and the girl named Paige she has been protecting," Dragoş said with a wicked and widening smile.

"Dănuţ is gone, and we don't have a coffin for her," Antanasia said. "Where would you put another daughter, Father?"

"Perhaps I will kill you, Antanasia, and give her your coffin," Dragoş said with an evil, sidelong look at her. "You are the weakest of my cloud and the least useful."

"I'll improve. I promise I will," Antanasia promised. "Please don't kill me, Father."

Dragoş looked at her, and eyed her perfect, young body. "You bring me pleasure, little one. Perhaps this one can rest with me until I have secured the silver-haired werewolf as my next slave."

Antanasia relaxed a little and when she did, dropped several feet before flapping back up to her sisters and father.

Dragoş shook his head in disapproval. "Follow me. We must be careful. The *vrăjitoare* has likely placed other warding incantations around her house."

Dragoş and his cloud descended slowly, but, as they did, he saw headlights turn off the road in front of the *vrăjitoare's* house and start up her driveway. Dragoş issued a mental command for his daughters to hover in place. They did and watched as a pickup truck pulled up next to the rusted car and stopped.

~ * ~

Lola was pulled from her meditative trance only moments before the candle had burned to the floor and ended it with a sense of danger. Her seeing eye looked up, through her house, and saw the ancient and his cloud floating high above. It was then that she realized her mistake. The ancient had access to his familiar's memories and her car, which was parked in front of her house, but had been in the garage when the familiar visited her earlier that morning. She silently derided herself for being so careless. Then she snapped her fingers, which extinguished the flames on both candles, and brought Paige out of her meditative trance.

Instead of the sensation of rushing through the universe at warp speed that ended her previous meditation, Paige felt a violent pull, and she awoke, on the floor, in Lola's house.

Paige immediately sensed something wasn't right and turned to Lola's startled face. "What's wrong?"

"He's here?"

"Daddy?" Paige asked, knowing it wasn't him.

"No. The ancient and his cloud."

"How…"

"My fault. I stupidly parked my car out front," Lola interrupted her.

"I don't understand," Paige said.

"It doesn't matter. He's here."

"We have to let Daddy and the others know. They're on their way here."

Lola's seeing eye shifted from the ceiling to her front door. "Too late. They're comin' up the driveway now."

"We have to do somethin'." Paige shouted.

"As long as Father Mike is with 'em, he won't attack."

"Are ya sure?"

"Yes. But I'll help. You put somethin' on so your daddy and Father Mike aren't traumatized when they come in."

"Seriously?"

"Yes," Lola said as she got up and headed for the front door. "Seriously. Do as I say, chil'."

~ * ~

Dragoş and his cloud hovered silently, more than a hundred feet above the seemingly condemned house and watched as four men got out of the truck. The moment they were out of the truck, it degraded into a rusted imitation of its former appearance.

"Now, Father?" Agrapina asked, eager to attack.

Dragoş was about to let his daughters attack the four males when he felt the holy man's presence.

He hissed loudly. "No. There is a holy man among them."

"We can take the other three quickly, Father," Antanasia said.

Dragoş considered letting his daughters try, but the *vrăjitoare* appeared on the front porch, looked up at him, and raised her arms. When she did, several earthen elementals sprouted, protectively, around the males and the house.

"No," Dragoş hissed angrily. "We wait."

~ * ~

To Garrett, Ty, Trowa, and Fr. Mike, Lola's house looked normal; they weren't a threat. Garrett parked next to Lola's car and the four of them got out of his truck. An instant later, Lola, naked, rushed out the front door, threw up her arms, and the men were startled, badly, when giant, earthen forms sprang from the surrounding ground.

"He's here," Lola shouted. "Get inside now."

Instead of rushing inside, all four of them followed Lola's seeing eye upward and looked into the night sky for the vampires. They saw nothing.

"*Now.*" Lola screamed.

This time, they listened and rushed past the naked woman as the earthen elementals followed them, protectively, to the porch.

~ * ~

Paige came out of Lola's bedroom, wearing Justin's Minion T-shirt, as her daddy, Ty, Trowa, and Fr. Mike hurried into the house. Lola came in behind them and closed the door. Then she casually walked past the four men, who turned their heads to avoid looking at her nakedness, and slipped her sheer, white dress on.

"What the hell?" Garrett asked.

348

"I apologize for my…sate of undress," Lola said. "Paige and I were meditatin' when the ancient and his cloud arrived and I had no time for modesty, but I insisted Paige put somethin' on while I came to your aid. You're welcome."

All four men looked at Paige.

"Well, thanks for that," Garrett said. "But how did he find y'all and what were those…things that came out of the ground?"

"How he found us doesn't matter now," Lola said. "He has, and we'll have to deal with that. Those *things* are earthen elementals I conjured to protect y'all from attack. The ancient is afraid of Father Mike but he was willin' to sacrifice some of his cloud to kill the rest of y'all. Until I conjured the elementals."

Garrett looked from Lola to Paige. "You okay, sweet girl?"

She was, but she ran to her daddy and wrapped him in a tight hug, anyway. He hugged her back and kissed the top of her head.

"What now?" Mike asked, surprisingly composed.

"Well, I was hopin' to keep Glinda a secret from the ancient a little longer," Lola said. "Worse, he knows Paige is with me, so, if Glinda shows herself, he'll know Paige is the silver-haired werewolf. He covets both. Knowin' they're the same will only increase his desire to have 'em."

"So…we do nothin'?" Ty asked.

"I didn't say that, beautiful man. Before we do anything, Paige and Glinda need to drink the potion."

"Is it ready?" Garrett asked.

"It should be," Lola said. "I'll test it."

"How?" Garrett asked.

"Watch," Paige told her daddy.

Lola picked up the butter knife that was still on the table, dipped the tip into the potion, pulled the knife out, and the thick, blackish, foul-smelling liquid slid cleanly off the knife's blade; not even a tiny drop stuck.

"It's ready," Paige said.

"It is," Lola said. "Ya ready for this, Paige-Turner?"

Paige nodded.

Lola disappeared through the door that led to the dining room and kitchen. Seconds later, she came back with two wine glasses. She placed them on the table. She dismissed the conjured white flame with a wave of her hand. With a flick of her finger, the cauldron floated over to the two wine glasses, tipped and poured some of the thick, disgusting black liquid in one class and the rest in the second glass. The content of each glass was exactly the same, and the cauldron was completely empty and as clean as if it had just been washed. Lola guided the cauldron to the center of the table and it, gently, settled on its surface.

"Gentlemen," Lola said, "Paige will need to get undressed to take the potion."

Without question, all four of them turned around. Paige removed the T-shirt and draped it across the back of the chair next to her.

"When ya drink your half, you'll turn into Glinda without willin' the transformation, but don't worry," Lola told Paige. "The potion is supposed to do that. Then, when Glinda drinks the other half, you'll transform between yourself and Glinda several times as the potion binds to both of y'all. Again, you'll have no control over this. It'll just happen. Once the potion has bound itself inside both of y'all, you'll stop transformin'. Whether ya stop as you or Glinda, I don't know. When it's over, you'll have control again. If ya stop as Glinda, please transform back into yourself immediately."

"Why do I need to transform back into myself?"

"All the pain and anger I took from ya this mornin' over losin' Lin will come floodin' back in," Lola said. "I'd prefer the ancient, who's still floatin' above my house with his cloud, hear your pain and anger instead of Glinda's. Understand?"

"Oh, yeah," Paige said as she picked up one wineglass. "I get it."

"It'll be best if ya pinch your nose and just let it slide quickly down your throat," Lola told her.

Paige pinched her nose, which did little to cut the stench, brought the wineglass to her lips, tipped her head and the wineglass back, and let the foul-smelling and tasting, thick, black liquid slide down her opened throat. It went down easy, like shit through a goose. The next thing Paige knew, she was Glinda and the wineglass she held slipped from her large, clawed hand. Lola caught it and handed the other wine glass to Glinda, who drank it with none of the revulsion Paige had experienced.

The next thing Paige felt was Glinda falling to the floor, but she was herself again before she landed. Then, in a blur that was too quick for Paige to differentiate between being herself or being Glinda, she convulsed on the floor for several moments.

From Lola's perspective, the mass on her floor transformed between beings so quickly that it looked like a blur of silver hair and human flesh. When the convulsions stopped, she looked down at Glinda.

Transform. Lola mentally shouted into Glinda's mind.

After the spasms brought on by the potion binding to herself and Glinda, every muscle in both their bodies, hurt. When it stopped, Paige wasn't entirely sure which form she was in. As Lola said, all the pain and anger of losing Lin to the ancient flooded her emotions. An instant before Glinda let out an ear-piercing howl, Paige heard Lola's mental command, and she transformed back into her human form. What began as a howl ended in a blood-curdling scream of anguish.

The four men heard Paige scream and turned around. The sight of her lying naked in the fetal position on the floor had them turning back around quickly.

Lola dropped to the floor and gathered Paige in her arms. "It's okay, sweetheart. Let it out."

Paige did. She screamed several more times and then sobbed uncontrollably. Lola held her, rocked her, and kissed her tear-stained cheeks repeatedly. Finally, the sobs subsided to a hitching cry, and then sniffled moans of sadness.

"He took Lin, Lola," Paige sniffed.

"I know, chil'. But do you remember what I tol' ya?"

"Yeah. To use the anger to hunt down and kill the fucker. Sorry, Daddy and Father Mike."

"It's okay, sweetheart," Garrett said.

"Understandable," Mike said.

"Look at me, Paige," Lola said.

Paige turned her tear and snot-stained face toward Lola's.

Lola waved a hand over Paige's face, which removed the mess. "See me, Paige."

At first, Paige didn't understand what Lola meant by see her. Mamma's wisdom whispered inside her head. It was like having her werewolf guide all over again. Only this time, she knew who the voice belonged to, and she understood. Paige closed her eyes tightly and then opened them. What she saw was nothing short of amazing.

Lola watched Paige sort through her thoughts and grab onto Mamma's wisdom. Paige closed her eyes and when she opened them again, Lola couldn't believe what she saw. Paige's right eye was no longer green. It was a cat-like, *seeing* eye and as silver as her aura. Lola had told Paige seeing eyes are never the color of the seer's aura, but theirs were.

"What's happenin', Lola?" Paige said. "I can see your aura. Daddy's, Ty's, Trowa's, and Father Mike's, too"

Lola hugged Paige tightly. "It worked. Mamma had doubts, but it worked."

"What worked?" Paige asked.

"One ingredient you put in the potion, and I doubled before I decreased the brewin' time, were tears from my seein' eye," Lola said. "The gift of sight has never been given to another livin' soul; witch, human, or supernatural creature. It's genetic. We're born with it, but I had a feelin' it would take with you and Glinda."

"Why?" Paige asked.

"Because y'all are so special," Lola said with a warm smile. "I keep tellin' ya that. 'Bout time ya believed me."

"I don't know how to use it," Paige said.

"Look up at the ceilin' and listen to Mamma. Since she's a seer too, she can help ya learn to use the sight."

Paige looked up at the ceiling and let Mamma's wisdom wash over her vision. When it did, the ceiling and roof melted away and she saw the ancient and his cloud floating above Lola's house. Even in hybrid bat form, she saw who the girls in his cloud were. Her heart ached for Lin, but she also recognized the fourth member with scarlet colored hair. She didn't know her. They weren't friends, but there had only been one girl in Pine View High School with hair that color. Taylor Shanahan.

"I see 'em, Lola. All of 'em," Paige said with awe and wonder. "The missin' girl is Taylor Shanahan, Daddy."

"Taylor Shanahan?" Garrett said. "Ya sure?"

Paige dialed up Glinda's sense of smell to the point of almost transforming and sniffed the air. She smelled the older death of Taylor's family and the fresh death of several people near Megan's house.

"I'm sure," Paige said. "I can smell her dead family. They also killed several people tonight, near Megan's house, before they came here tonight."

"Shit." Garrett shouted.

"They needed strength before comin' for me and Paige," Lola said. "But they weren't expectin' y'all, and they certainly weren't expectin' Father Mike."

"They are still out there?" Mike asked.

Together, Lola and Paige said, "Yes."

"What do we do?" Garrett asked.

"Well," Lola said, "Paige is gonna put this T-shirt back on so y'all can turn around. Then, we'll figure somethin' out."

Lola grabbed the T-shirt from the chair back and handed it to Paige. They stood and Paige slipped the beloved T-shirt over her head, concealing her nakedness.

"Okay," Paige said. "Y'all can turn around now."

They did and all four of them looked into Paige's cat-like, silver, seeing eye.

"Is this that somethin' extra you were talkin' 'bout, Lola?" Garrett asked.

"It is," Lola said with a warm smile. "What do ya think?"

"Does she have your powers now?" Garrett followed up.

"She has my *sight*," Lola told him.

Paige heard Mamma's wisdom in her head. Lola had told her to follow it and never doubt it, so she followed it. She raised her hand, pointed at the heavy cauldron, and, with a simple flick of her wrist, sent it floating into the air. Paige didn't have Lola or Mamma's practice, though, and almost sent the cauldron through the ceiling. She dropped her wrist, and the cauldron floated back down and landed on the table with a heavy thud.

Lola and all four men watched the cauldron launch into the air and come back down to the table with a heavy thud.

Lola turned to Paige. "How'd ya do that?"

"I did like ya said and listened to Mamma," Paige said with a grin.

In awe, Lola said, "This changes things."

"How?" Garrett asked.

"Well, the potion was supposed to give Paige Mamma's wisdom and, hopefully, my gift of sight. Apparently, she has seer powers along with sight. Sight was a long shot, and I knew it," Lola said. "I had faith. I never imagined she'd have powers, too. They're rare, for sure, but she has 'em. Since she has 'em, she can learn to use 'em."

"How does that help us now?" Ty asked.

Lola took Paige's hand. "Come with me."

They walked out onto the front porch and looked up at the ancient and his cloud.

~ * ~

After the men went inside the *vrăjitoare's* house, Dragoş and his daughters hovered high above it and Dragoş' anger seethed. He had underestimated the seer too often. She had cost him his slave and had preoccupied him while she penetrated the protections around Dănuţ's mind. She had spoken to him with disrespect, no fear, and in a manner of superiority. She had successfully hidden her dwelling from his foolish slave. Now, she had a holy man and a host of protective, earthen elementals surrounding her disguised house.

Dragoş could, easily, destroy several of the elementals, but his young daughters had not the experience to engage the others, which would cause their deaths and his, likely, being buried beneath the elementals, helpless while the seer and her helpers devised a way to destroy him. Yes, he had underestimated the vile *vrăjitoare* greatly.

Just as Dragoş had decided to leave with his cloud, he heard what sounded like the start of a howl but ended in screams. Young female screams. He knew the screams belonged to the girl named Paige, who he desperately wanted for his cloud. Intrigued, because his inclination that the girl was with the seer had been confirmed, Dragoş stayed.

A moment later, the seer and his prize emerged from the decrepit house. Seeing her, so close that he could smell her sex excited Dragoş and his long tongue snaked out and licked his too red lips. He was so excited that he contemplated sending Agrapina, Antanasia, and Ilinca to a certain death with the seer, while he and his other prize, the natural vampire Lacrima, took the girl named Paige. Lacrima and the new daughter he would name Vanda, for the warrior, would be all the cloud he needed to find the silver-haired werewolf. Before he issued the command, he saw his prize look up at him and his cold, black, undead blood boiled. The girl he coveted had a cat-like silver seeing eye.

"NO. This cannot be. What have you done to my prize, *vrăjitoare, pizda?*" Dragoş roared in a wet gravel voice that shook dirt from the protective elementals that stood at attention around the house.

~ * ~

Lola looked up at the ancient and smiled. "I gave her the gift of sight, you vile fuck."

Paige smiled too and followed Lola's lead. "Oh, it be, bitch. I see you, too. You old, ugly piece of shit."

The ancient hissed so loudly that it swept through the surrounding trees like wind. "You have accomplished nothing, *vrăjitoare.* You played your hand too early and now I know. It is my turn to play. I will still have that girl as my eternal, sexual plaything and the silver-haired werewolf as my slave."

"How, fuck-tard?" Lola, purposefully, provoked him. "I took your pet."

It was then that Fr. Mike joined Lola and Paige on the front porch. He held up a large silver cross. He didn't have the gift of sight and couldn't see the vampire cloud, but the cross seemed to know where the evil was. It twisted in his hand. Then, the light of the almost full moon reflected off its shiny surface and its reflection fell upon the ancient vampire forming a lighted cross on his bat-like form.

"Be gone, you foul, spawn of Lucifer." Mike shouted.

The ancient hissed and covered his face to ward off the reflective

355

cross. He screamed in rage so loudly that Lola's house shook. Then he flapped his giant wings and shot up into the night sky so quickly that he was a black blur, even to Lola and Paige's sight. An instant later, the four girls of the ancient's cloud flapped their large wings and shot skyward too.

Paige yelled, "I love you, Lin."

The hybrid bat girl that had been Lin paused and looked back at Paige. With the gift of sight, Paige was sure that the vampire recognized her. She saw it when her silver, slit eyes, briefly, turned crystal blue. Paige saw sadness in her eyes, too. Then she flapped her large wings and disappeared into the dark night.

"Did you see that, Lola?" Paige said.

"I did," Lola said softly and put her arm around Paige's shoulders. "This has surely been a night of wonders. First, your sight and powers. Now Lin."

"What does it mean?"

"Listen to Mamma," Lola replied.

Paige did, and when the answer came, a big, beautiful smile spread across her face. "Could it really be true?"

"What did Mamma's wisdom tell ya?"

"That part of Lin's humanity still lives inside the vampire," Paige said. "She called it a spark. Is that possible?"

"Before tonight, I'd have said it wasn't. I've never heard of it happenin', but I saw what you saw," Lola said. "Recognition and sadness. Part of Lin, her spark, is still alive."

"Can she be saved?"

"You really need to ask yourself these questions," Lola said. "With Mamma's wisdom, you know more than I."

Paige thought about the question and when the answer came, her smile grew bigger.

"It won't be easy, but she can be saved. We can save Lin, Lola." Paige shouted.

Lola smiled. "Let's go inside and tell the rest what's goin' on."

Paige and Fr. Mike followed Lola inside. For the first time since the ancient came to roost in Pine View County, Paige felt optimistic and happy.

~ * ~

Dragoş, suddenly, stopped flying several miles from the meddlesome *vrăjitoare's* house and hovered. His daughters, who had lagged behind, caught up and hovered around him. None of them dared speak; they could feel their father's seething anger and rage.

After several moments, when Dragoş felt composed enough to speak without screaming, he growled, "The *vrăjitoare* thinks she's clever, but she has gained nothing with her paltry meddling. I know where she and the girl named Paige are hiding now, and I know of her elemental powers. I have dealt with many like her over my long existence and have always dispatched them in cruel fashion. I *will* kill her, and I *will* have the girl named Paige in my cloud."

"How, Father?" Agrapina dared to ask.

Without saying a word, Dragoş backhanded Agrapina's bat-like face so hard that she was sent flying. Also, she lost the concentration that she had been using to hover without flapping her wings, and plummeted toward the ground in an uncontrolled, spinning fall. Finally, she righted herself, flapped her wings, and flew back up to her sisters and father. She stopped and hovered out of her father's dangerous reach, though.

"Any more worthless questions?" Dragoş hissed.

His daughters hovered silently around him.

"Good," Dragoş hissed. "I *will* have the girl named Paige in my cloud and the silver-haired werewolf as my slave, eventually. Given the current…circumstances, I think it prudent that we have an interim slave to protect us while we rest during the daylight. I think the optimal prey is one of Agrapina's or Ilinca's former adults."

Agrapina, desperately wanting to gain favor with her father again, said, "The man who was my body's former father is big and strong already. Will he suffice, Father?"

Dragoş smiled at Agrapina. "Yes. I think he will do. I will turn him while the rest of you feed on the woman, and I want my daughters to do so with abandon. Leave a horrific scene for the humans to discover. Let them see the extent of my wrath when provoked."

"Yes, Father," all four daughters replied at the same time as ghastly grins spread across their bat-like faces.

With the decision made, Dragoş took flight to the house that Melanie Zane once lived in, and his daughters followed closely behind.

~ * ~

"What the hell just happened?" Garrett asked when Paige, Lola, and Fr. Mike were back inside.

With a laugh, Lola said, "He's one unhappy vampire right now."

"Yeah," Paige added. "Did ya see his face when he realized I'm a seer now?"

"Was it wise to provoke him like that?" Ty asked.

"Probably not," Lola admitted. "He needed to know Paige had the gift of sight now. So, there was no way around provokin' him."

"Why? Why did he need to know?" Garrett asked angerly. "Doesn't that put Paige in *more* danger?"

"She's been in mortal danger since the ancient first coveted her," Lola calmly said. "Now he knows she has the gift of sight and that he can't take her unaware and mezmery won't work on her. No. She's not in *more* danger. She's in *less* danger. That's why I added my seein' eye tears to the protection potion. That she now has powers of sight and light, she's more formidable than ever."

"So, will he stop tryin' to come for her now?" Garrett asked hopefully.

Lola shook her head, which made the pink and white beads on the ends of her cornrows click together. "No. He still wants her, but, maybe for the first time in his long, undead existence, he's concerned. Concerned about me, Paige, and mostly, Father Mike."

"How'd ya know where he was to reflect the moonlight off the silver cross on him like that, Father Mike?" Paige asked.

Fr. Mike blushed a little. "I didn't. I put my faith in God and He guided my hand."

"Well. It was bad ass," Paige exclaimed then added, "Pardon my language."

Fr. Mike broke into a big grin. "It was bad ass. I *felt* God working through me. I think He's calling me to this work."

"I believe He is," Lola said in her warm, honey voice that even Fr. Mike found slightly enticing and his cheeks blushed a deeper red.

"What now?" Trowa asked.

"Well," Garrett said. "We know who the fourth member of his cloud is now. We still need to wait for the call to come in before we do anything about that. If Glinda's up for it, we can check out the fresh kills we don't know about."

"I'm up for it, and I don't need to transform completely to find 'em," Paige excitedly said. "I already know they're near Megan's old house. East of it. Just get me close and I'll dial up Glinda to find 'em."

"Okay," Garrett said. "But please put some more clothes on and we'll head out."

Paige headed for Lola's bedroom to put on sweatpants, but Lola said, "No. She still might need quick access to Glinda."

"Why do ya think that?" Garrett asked.

"The cloud's in bat form tonight," Lola said. "Unless, at some point, they traveled as mist, Glinda might be able to track 'em back to the ancient's lair. For now, he's still without a familiar, which makes 'em vulnerable."

Reluctantly, and not because he didn't trust the men he was with, it was the idea of Paige having nothing on under the T-shirt, Garrett said, "Okay, but she's ridin' shotgun."

Lola smiled. "That means I get to squeeze into the Manwich in the back seat."

"You're comin'?" Paige and Garrett asked at the same time.

"Of course," Lola said with a sly grin. "It's time I got more involved, and two seers are better than one."

With that settled, the six of them left Lola's house with four of them crammed into the back seat. Garrett drove off toward the Williams' house.

~ * ~

Zack and Kat Zane were asleep in their bed, but it wasn't restful sleep. Lola's message, while they were in her trance, removed most of the pain while they were awake, so they could function. It did little to keep their subconscious minds from visiting their dreams with painful memories of their lost daughter, Melanie. The only thing that kept them functioning during the day was the trance erased the dream memories the moment they awoke, so they couldn't haunt them while awake.

Zack tossed in bed as he dreamed of Melanie being held by some perverted rapist who did vile things to his daughter's body. He could see her in the dream, but she had always been out of reach. He would run toward her, but his feet couldn't gain traction on the dream footing, so he could never get to her.

He could hear her calling for him, "Daddy. Daddy."

Suddenly, he awoke with a start and heard Melanie whisper, "Daddy."

It was as if she'd followed him out of the dream that was already dissolving like mist in the wind. He shook his head, trying to dislodge what was left of the dream, and the whispered "Daddy" came again.

He looked toward the bedroom window that had sheer, white curtains drawn closed across it. Silvery light from the moon lit the curtains like a ghostly, pleated movie screen.

The silhouette of a female body appeared on the dreamlike screen and whispered, "Daddy."

Zack, feeling like he was still in a dream, got out of bed and headed for the window. This time, he could move. When he got to the widow, he opened the curtains and saw Mel outside. That she was naked and floating in the air outside the second-floor window didn't seem strange to him at all. His tortured mind thought he had still been dreaming.

Zack unlocked the window and opened it. "Mel? Is that really you?"

"It is me, Daddy," Agrapina said. "I've been so scared and cold. Can we come in?"

"Of course ya can, baby," Zack said as he opened his arms to embrace his lost daughter.

Agrapina floated through the window and embraced the man who had been her body's father. He hugged her back with his thick, muscular arms.

"You're so cold, Mel," Zack said. "I'll wake up your mom. She'll be so happy to see ya. We'll get ya warmed up and back in your bed."

Then, an enormous shadow blocked the moon's silvery light completely and a monstrous voice that sounded like wet gravel said, "That won't be necessary. My daughters will feed on your mate."

With that said, three forms flew into the room and the girl Zack thought was his daughter slipped out of his powerful embrace and joined the others. Zack looked up into the silver, slit eyes of an ancient monster, and his mind went numb. He was vaguely aware of Kat's screams, but they didn't concern him. When the ancient monster slit his left nipple with a gnarled thumbnail, Zack did as commanded and drank the thick, black blood that oozed from the torn, undead flesh.

~ * ~

Garrett and company drove through the night while Paige sniffed at the air. She had the passenger side window down, which had Ty, Trowa, and Fr. Mike uncomfortably cold in the back seat. Lola was fine and Paige realized, so was she. Like Lola, Paige had become impervious to the cold since drinking the protection potion and gaining seer powers.

Paige used Glinda's enhanced sense of smell to track the source of the recent kills. By her reckoning, they were about halfway to the source, which put them east of Pine View Proper. Suddenly, she sensed the cloud.

Her ears, also dialed to near transformation level, heard Mr. Zack say, "Mel? Is that really you?"

She also heard what had been Mel say, "It is me, Daddy. I've been so scared and cold. Can we come in?"

"Stop the truck." Paige screamed.

Startled, but already slamming on the brakes, Garrett said, "What's happenin'?"

Before the truck came to a complete stop, Paige opened the door, jumped out, and in mid-transformation yelled, "They're at Mel's house."

Glinda hit the ground on all fours and ran into the night, leaving

Justin's Minion T-shit shredded on the side of the road.

Lola climbed into the front seat, vacated by Paige, in the blink of an eye.

She slammed the door shut. "Drive, Garrett. Get to Mel's as quick as ya can."

Garrett hammered the accelerator, fishtailed the truck around in a tire screaming maneuver that filled the air with the stink of burning rubber, and shot down the county road that headed west toward the Zane's house. If the vampires didn't kill them all quickly, he could get to the Zane's house in under five minutes. He prayed that Paige and Glinda would be okay.

~ * ~

Glinda ran through the dense woods at full speed, easily dodging trees, leaping deadfalls, and streams as she went. She heard Mr. Zack say, "Of course ya can, baby," as she cleared the woods and ran in a deep ditch along the road to Mel's neighborhood. As Mr. Zack said, "You're so cold, Mel. I'll wake up your mom. She'll be so happy to see you. We'll get you warmed up and back in your bed," Glinda leapt a six-foot fence with ease and landed on the road a few houses down from Mel's and heard Mrs. Kat scream. She bolted toward Mel's old house.

Then, Mamma's wisdom whispered, *You cannot defeat the entire cloud, but you can scatter them and put the fear of your wolf in the young ones. Rage is your weapon, Glinda.*

At a full run, and with a loud growl, Glinda burst through the front door of the Zane's house. It splintered in her wake. Not bothering with the stairs, she leapt onto the second-floor landing. She skidded to a stop; her dagger claws ripped through the carpet and scared the hardwood beneath. Mr. and Mrs. Zane's closed bedroom door was in front of Glinda. She concentrated and saw through the door and walls. The ancient had Mr. Zack, who fed on his foul blood, while the four other vampires ripped flesh from Mrs. Kat with savage bites. Glinda let out a rage filled growl and leapt, but at the wall, not the door.

~ * ~

Dragoş had the man feeding on his blood; his will and soul were already forfeit. He watched as his delicious daughters savagely ripped chunks of flesh from the screaming woman. Their perfect young bodies were covered in blood. He smiled as he thought of the pleasure it would bring to lick the blood from every inch of their tender skin when they returned to his throne room. His smile grew more dreadful when he thought of making his new slave watch as he did unthinkable things to his former daughter.

This thought was a wicked thought because, unlike vampires who lose all sense of who they were in life, familiars, who are not undead, keep their human memories. The man would know his daughter but be powerless to not see the depravities Dragoş would do with her. When he was feeling especially evil, which was his natural state, he would have Agrapina do things to the man that would scar his mind for however long he kept him, which he hoped wouldn't be long. Just long enough to find the silver-haired werewolf.

Then, as if answering his wish, Dragoş heard a menacing growl, and the house shook as something very large crashed through the front door and landed with another house shuddering impact outside the closed door.

Dragoş smiled a gruesome smile and whispered, "Come to me, my pet."

~ * ~

Glinda smashed through the wall to the right of the door with ease. Sheetrock, insulation, and shattered two by four wall studs burst into the bedroom with the fury of a tornado. Amid the chaos, Glinda stood to her full height of nine feet, the upstairs ceilings were vaulted, and issued a growl that shook the entire house.

The four young vampires shrieked in horror at the sight of the massive werewolf and retreated to their father's side. Before they were all out of reach, Glinda grabbed the nearest vampire by the head with her deadly, clawed hand and squeezed. Antanasia's, always the slowest of the cloud, head caved in like a rotten piece of fruit as black blood sprayed between her werewolf fingers. She fell to the floor and an instant later and disintegrated into a pile of ash. The black muck that was the vampire's head that covered Glinda's hand turned to dust and fell to the floor, too.

~ * ~

Dragoş expected the werewolf to come through the door. With a grin, he cast the man aside and prepared to lock eyes with the werewolf, mesmerize it, and take it as his new, coveted, familiar. His daughters could then dispatch the useless man. His excitement and anticipation quickly turned to confusion when the silver-haired werewolf came through the wall instead. As he beheld the magnificence of the beast, which far exceeded his expectations, excitement returned. Then, as he watched the beast easily dispatch Antanasia, he experienced rage.

"*Look at me, beast.*" Dragoş roared in a voice that equaled the werewolf's growls in intensity.

~ * ~

Glinda heard the ancient's command, but it held no power over her. With the gift of sight, she knew she was immune to his mezmery. She slowly turned her massive head and looked into the ancient's silver, slit eyes with her silver seeing eye. She saw his, and the other vampires', auras.

They were black, and shadowy figures swam in the blackness; their faces twisted visages of horror. Lin's black aura only had one twisted face in it; it was that of a teenage boy who looked, vaguely, familiar. Taylor's black aura had two twisted faces in it; one was a young boy, and the other was a large man. Mel's black aura had four twisted faces in it; Trevor's, Al's, a man's, and a teenage boy who also looked vaguely familiar. Upon seeing the second teenage boy's twisted face, Paige put the puzzle pieces together and realized they were Trent and Gavin Porter. She knew who the fresh kill family was.

The ancient's black aura contained countless multitudes of these apparitions. Their tortured faces swarmed in the blackness like riled wasps. Even without Mamma's wisdom, Glinda knew that the horror, stricken faces in the vampires' auras were the countless tortured souls of his victims.

Beyond the black, tortured auras, Glinda saw something else in the ancient's eyes. Bewilderment and fear.

~ * ~

Dragoş watched as the magnificent, silver-haired werewolf submitted to his command and turned its massive head in his direction. He locked his silver eyed gaze on the werewolf's left, green eye and waited until its head turned completely toward him to lock his eyes on both of its eyes. Then, he would have his prize pet. As the werewolf's other eye came into view, a cat-like, silver seeing eye appeared; Dragoş lost his concentration. He couldn't believe what stood before him. A seer werewolf. It was impossible but there it stood, looking back at him. He knew he'd have no control over the beast, and he felt genuine fear for the first time since he was given the gift of eternal, undead existence.

The werewolf lunged for him. Before it could rip at him with its deadly, clawed hands, or remove his head with its gaping maw of dagger, length fangs, Dragoş wrapped his cloak around his three remaining daughters, his new slave, and dissolve into black mist.

~ * ~

Glinda registered the fear and seeing all the vampires clustered together, next to Mr. Zack, she ignored Mamma's warning about not being able to take out an entire cloud on her own and launched herself at them with her claws and teeth ready to shred all the vampires. As quick as Glinda was, the vampire had been quicker. An instant before her claws sank into their undead flesh, the ancient swirled his cloak around all of them, including Mr. Zack, who she would not injure, and they dissolved into black mist.

Glinda's momentum carried her through the dissipating black mist. She crashed through the wall and window, and landed on her pawed hind feet in the Zane's side yard. She looked up, and with her seeing eye, saw the corporal forms of the vampires and Mr. Zane stretched thin and translucent in the retreating black mist. A low, angry growl rumbled from Glinda's deadly snout.

Then she heard surprised shouts coming from nearby houses as lights turned on in houses up and down the street. Glinda quickly leapt the Zane's back fence, disappeared into the woods, transformed, and waited for her daddy to arrive. She reached out to Lola.

~ * ~

About a mile out from the Zane's house, Karen Parker's voice, the eleven to seven dispatcher, came over the Sheriff Department radios Garrett, Ty, and Trowa, had clipped to their belts.

Garrett, who was still driving at breakneck speed, said, "One of y'all get that."

Trowa was quicker than Ty.

He keyed the mic. "Raintree here. What's up, Karen?"

"A whole lotta somethin' is goin' on at the Zane's house," Karen's voice crackled and hissed through the two-way speaker. "I've gotten, at least a dozen calls in the last few minutes about strange, loud sounds and crashin' noises. The damn phones ringin' again."

"I'm with Sheriff Lambert and we're close," Trowa said into the radio. "We'll take it."

"Thank Christ. Base out," Karen said, and the radio went dead.

"Fuck." Garrett yelled with his knuckles white on the steering wheel.

Lola reached over and put her left hand on Garrett's straining right forearm. "You can slow down. She's okay."

"You better not be doin' any of that nudgin' bullshit right now, Lola," Garrett said through gritted teeth as he kept his foot on the accelerator.

"I'm not," Lola said. "I'm in contact with Paige. She's unharmed in the woods behind the Zane's house."

"Ya sure?"

"I love her too, Garrett. Would I be this calm if she was hurt or in danger?"

Garrett knew then that he hadn't been nudged, and Lola wasn't lying to him. He eased his foot off the accelerator.

"Give me your jacket and let me out," Lola said. "I'll wait with her. Neither of us needs to be seen there. Pick us up on your way out."

"It might take a while."

"We'll be okay."

Garrett stopped, gave Lola his jacket, and let her out. Then he, Ty, Trowa, and Fr. Mike drove into the neighborhood. Lights were on in every house on the street and people huddled together on their front lawns while others gathered on the sidewalks and street. Garrett pulled into the Zane's driveway and as he did, the headlights lit up the ragged hole where the Zane's front door had been. He knew Glinda had made one hell of an entrance.

As the four men got out of Garrett's truck, nearby neighbors shouted over each other about the thunderous sounds they'd heard coming from the house. Oddly, no one asked how he and two deputies had gotten there so quickly or why they had a priest with them. It was the same Pine View blinders most folks wore during the werewolf murders.

Garrett held up his hands, and most of the people fell silent. "Go on back inside and let us do our job."

A badge speaks with authority, and most of the gathered neighbors dispersed and went back inside their houses. Some lagged. When Garrett looked their direction, their heads dropped and they shuffled back inside.

"Impressive," Mike said.

"No less impressive than how folks listen to your homilies," Garrett told Fr. Mike.

"I guess, but everyone listens to you," Mike said. "Only Catholics listen to me."

Garrett looked at the three men. "Y'all ready for this? If I had to guess, it won't be pretty."

Ty, Trowa, and Fr. Mike nodded. The four men entered the dark house through the hole Glinda had made.

~ * ~

Because Paige and Lola were in mental contact, they made their way toward each other in the dark woods and met just outside of the Zane's neighborhood.

Lola handed Paige her daddy's jacket, but she shook her head. "I'm not cold. I'm like you now. I don't feel the cold in human form anymore."

Lola smiled. "Okay. But your daddy won't like it, and Ty, Trowa, and Father Mike will be very uncomfortable if ya get back into the truck naked."

Paige took the jacket. "Okay. But I'm not puttin' it on until they come to get us."

Lola shrugged. "Fine by me. Now, show me what happened."

"How?"

"Open your mind and let me in," Lola said. "I can do it without your permission, but I prefer not to trespass."

Paige let Lola into her mind and Lola saw everything that happened since Paige jumped out of her daddy's truck to when she jumped the Zane's back fence, transformed, and contacted Lola mentally to let her know she was okay.

When she finished showing Lola the events that had transpired, Paige said, "Those tortured faces in their auras are their victims, aren't they?"

"They are. By destroyin' the vampire who was Megan, you released the tortured souls of anyone she's killed."

"Wow. That's kinda cool. Think of how many souls will be released when Glinda takes out the ancient."

"They will certainly flood the afterlife with new arrivals," Lola said.

"I want that evil fucker so bad, Lola," Paige hissed angrily.

"I know ya do, sweet girl," Lola said. "As do I. The ancient is now informed of somethin' he never suspected or expected. Unfortunately, I was hopin' to keep this information from him for a while longer."

"What? What does he know now?"

"I'll give you a hint," Lola said. "He has seen your silver, seein' eye and Glinda's silver, seein' eye."

"Oh, crap."

"Oh, crap is an understatement," Lola said. "He now knows that the two things he covets most, you and Glinda, are the same. After what Glinda just did, a younger, less determined vampire would abandon this quest. The ancient is neither of those things. I'm sure he will be more determined than ever to possess both of you."

"Yeah. But he's even weaker now," Paige said. "You took his familiar, and I took one of his cloud."

"True. But what did you show me Zack doin'?"

Paige made a disgusted face. "He was drinkin' the ancient's black blood. From his *nipple*, like a baby."

"What does that mean?" Lola asked.

"I don't know."

"You know," Lola told her.

Paige sank into Mamma's wisdom for the answer.

When it came to her, Paige said, "Mister Zack is his new familiar."

"Yep."

"I thought he was waitin' for Glinda?"

"He was," Lola said. "When he realized you're a seer now, and that Father Mike is a resolute priest, he couldn't risk goin' without daylight protection."

"So…this is my fault," Paige sniffed.

Lola hugged Paige tightly. "None of this is your fault. Unfortunately, this is the ways of an ancient vampire."

"He's only here because of Glinda."

"That's not your fault, either," Lola said. "You didn't ask for any of this."

Paige knew Lola was right, but she cried anyway. Lola held her close and let her.

~ * ~

As the four men entered the dark house, Garrett, Ty, and Trowa produced small Mag flashlights and turned them on. Fr. Mike felt unprepared by comparison and brandished his silver cross instead. The three beams of light drifted across the splintered remains of the door scattered about the living room.

Ty, who had been there before with Lola on Christmas morning after the Zane's reported Melanie missing and knew the house, said, "The bedrooms are upstairs."

With Garrett in the lead, they made their way up the carpeted stairs single file, with Fr. Mike last in line. At the landing, the flashlight beams drifted across the shredded carpet and deep claw marks on the wood beneath.

"That's not gonna be easy to explain," Trowa said.

Garrett's flashlight illuminated the large hole in the wall beside the bedroom door. "None of this is gonna be easy to explain."

When the four men entered the bedroom, through the door, the flashlight revealed a scene that the bloodiest slasher flick couldn't replicate. What was left of Kat Zane lied on the bed. There were massive bite marks all over her body, most of them so deep they exposed bones. Large chunks of her flesh were flung about the room. The floor, walls, and ceiling were covered in spatter. The bed was a pool of blood and flesh.

Ty sighed. "Son of a bitch."

Then all four men jumped when Kat let out a breath that raddled and gurgled from her lips.

Fr. Mike rushed to the bed, slipped his right hand under her head, to cradle it, and looked into her dim, frightened eyes. She slowly closed them and, with effort, opened them again. That she was alive was impossible to believe, and he knew she didn't have long. He administered Last Rites.

As Fr. Mike rushed to Kat, Garrett pulled his radio and keyed the mic. "I need paramedics at the Zane's ASAP, Karen."

"Got it," Karen said quickly.

Fr. Mike completed the Viaticum, and Kat's dim eyes searched his face. She tried to say something, but blood gurgled from her lips instead of words. Fr. Mike, although not a lip reader, saw that she had tried to say,

"Thank you." Her dim eyes went blank, and her chest settled, never to rise again.

After Kat passed away, Fr. Mike cried. His resolve to do everything in his power, even sacrifice himself if needed, to find and destroy the spawn of Lucifer that poisoned his community grew exponentially. He was on a mission from God. God's warrior.

Ty, who had gone with Fr. Mike to the bed, said, "Cancel the paramedics and call George, Garrett."

"Fuck," Garrett shouted. "Where the hell is Zack?"

To ease Garrett's anguish, Trowa said, "She could not have survived those wounds, Garrett. At least, her holy man was here to help her pass from this life to the next. Since Zack isn't here, he's probably dead, too. Maybe he'll show up later. Take comfort in that."

~ * ~

A dense, black mist seeped in under the left garage door of the Eternal Rest Funeral Home. A moment later, Dragoş, Agrapina, Lacrima, Ilinca, and a very disoriented Zack Zane materialized in the dark embalming room. Zack, who had never experienced the sensation of having his body deconstructed and reassembled on a molecular level, fell to his knees and vomited.

Dragoş kicked the large man hard enough to send him flying across the big room and bellowed, "Clean your mess, slave."

Zack coughed up blood. "Yes, Master."

The effect of turning his daughters into mist to escape the werewolf's wrath had robbed Dragoş of the expected pleasure of licking the blood from every inch of their succulent bodies. The blood left their bodies when their bodies dematerialized into mist. He still eyed them with rage induced sexual excitement. The anger he felt for having to make a hasty retreat, something he hadn't done since he was a young vampire, from the enraged werewolf, was tempered by the new knowledge that the girl named Paige and the silver-haired werewolf were one. His long tongue snaked out and licked his too red lips at the thought of having them. Regardless of the obstacles, he would have them.

"After you've cleaned your mess, undress and come down to my throne room, slave," Dragoş commanded. "You will watch while I sexually ravish your daughter's body. Then, you will experience the pleasures of your daughter's cold, undead flesh and you will enjoy it."

Zack looked at what had been his daughter and felt repulsed because he couldn't resist his evil Master's depraved command.

He swallowed the lump in his throat. "Yes, Master."

Zack watched as the Master and his cloud disappeared behind the concealed door. He cleaned up his vomit, got undressed, and went down into the throne room. The things he witnessed and did that night haunted his tortured mind for the rest of his blessedly brief life as a familiar.

~ * ~

The next two hours were a blur of activity at the Zane house. Trowa taped off the residence with crime scene tape from Garrett's truck. He was always on duty and always prepared. Trowa waited outside to let George in and keep others out; neighbors had congregated in small groups again. Inside, Garrett and Ty documented everything with pictures, which would never be put into the evidence room at the department. They took a sample of the pile of ashes on the bedroom floor, and they collected any, and all, silver hairs they could find, which would never be entered as evidence either.

When George arrived, Garrett told him it was another vampire attack, purposefully leaving out the part Glinda played in the mayhem. Since George was in the loop about everything but Glinda, he was eager to help. When he suggested a cougar as the culprit, Garrett thought it a splendid idea. The Pine View blinders would accept this explanation; even though it did little to explain the structural damage or the large and missing Zack Zane.

~ * ~

After everyone else had left, Garrett and his three companions got in his truck and drove, slowly, out of the subdivision. Almost immediately after leaving the gated community, Paige and Lola emerged from the woods on the left. Garrett stopped. Paige got into the front seat and Lola, gladly, squeezed between Ty and Trowa in the back seat. She spared Fr. Mike the discomfort of squeezing beside hm.

When everyone was in, and the truck in motion again, Garrett said, "It's late and we're all pretty tired. What do ya say we look into the other kills tomorrow, Paige-Turner?"

"It's okay," Paige said. "I know who they were."

Surprised, Garrett said, "Who?"

"They were the Porters," Paige told the four men, who listened intently. "They live a couple of miles behind Megan's house. I saw Trent and Gavin tonight."

"Are they...vampires, too?" Mike asked.

"No," Paige said with a sigh. "They're vampire victims. They're dead."

Then she told them everything that happened at the Zane's house and the conversation she and Lola had in the woods while they waited.

"Well, that explains the pile of ashes," Ty said.

"Why Zack is missin', too," Trowa added.

Garrett was more concerned with Paige's safety, since the ancient now knew she and Glinda were the same possessions. "Then, where will Paige be safe? Do I need to send her away?"

"No," Lola said. "She's still safest with me."

"How?" Garrett asked desperately.

"Paige and I are stronger together," Lola explained. "The ancient knows that. Along with the protective, earthen elementals, I have other powers to use."

Reluctantly, Garrett said, "Okay, but I want y'all checkin' in with me every few hours. If I don't hear from y'all every few hours, I'm comin' with my posse."

"Fair enough," Lola said.

Lola leaned forward and looked at Fr. Mike. "I know you can bless water, but can you bless tears so that they become holy water?"

"Before today, I would've said no," Mike said. "But I'm willing to try."

"Tryin' is all I asked."

"Okay. I'll give it a shot."

"What're you gettin' at?" Garrett asked.

"When you drop me and Paige off at my house, I want Father Mike to bless the tears of our seein' eyes. Don't ask why. It's just a hunch, but one I'd like to try."

"Okay," Garrett and Mike said together.

When they arrived at Lola's house, Fr. Mike did as she asked. Then he got back in Garrett's truck. Lola and Paige watched them drive away. They went inside, got in bed, and slept under the night sky in Lola's mirror.

Chapter Twelve

Monday morning dawned dark and ominous. Paige awoke to find herself alone in Lola's bed. She was lying on her right side and saw the wall with the bathroom and closet doors darker than they should be. Being Glinda gave her an innate sense of time and it was late enough in the morning that the sun should cast a morning glow into the room. She rolled onto her back and looked up into the magical mirror. Low, dark, clouds covered the sky. Flashes of white-hot lightning danced from the clouds and kissed the ground in the distance. Booming thunder rolled over Lola's house seconds after each flash of lightning.

Paige sat up and, using her new seeing power, searched through the walls for Lola. She found her sitting on the front porch swing with a mug in her hand. Beside her, the kettle floated above a conjured blue flame and there was an extra cup on the rail waiting for her. Lola saw Paige looking at her and smiled. Paige slipped out of bed.

By the time Paige joined Lola on the front porch, the extra mug was steaming with her spice tea. Paige took the warm mug and sat down next to Lola. She leaned against Lola, resting her head on Lola's shoulder, and Lola wrapped a warm arm around her shoulders. They sat in silence for a while, watching the storm approach. Soon, rain fell and ran off Lola's roof in sheets of water that gave the world beyond the porch a shimmering appearance.

"Blue Norther," Lola said. "After this passes, it'll be colder than my tit for a few days."

Paige got the reference and laughed. When her Grandma Mary wasn't within earshot, her Grandpa Ray was full of colorful sayings and "colder than a witch's tit" was one he used to describe cold weather.

"Colder than my tit, too," Paige said with a giggle.

"I suppose so," Lola agreed.

They sat in silence a while longer and then Paige said, "What do the aura colors mean? I know about yours and mine, because ya told me.

I saw Daddy's, Ty's, Trowa's, and Father Mike's last night and I don't know what they mean."

"What did you see?" Lola asked.

"Daddy and Ty's were gold, Trowa's was dark brown, and Father Mike's was silver, but not as…shiny as my silver aura."

"That your daddy and Ty have the same color auras is not a coincidence," Lola said. "They share the same traits of bravery, honesty, loyalty, and carin'. They were destined to find each other and become fast friends. Trowa's dark brown aura is not uncommon among his people. It's related to a love of nature and what it offers. I haven't met many Native American seers, but the ones I have shared my green, seein' eye. Father Mike's less shiny, silver aura means he shares your traits of purity. That's how I knew he'd help when he believed in what we're up against."

There was another brief few moments of silence that were broken when Paige said, "You told me a seer's eye and their aura is never the same color, but mine are. What's that mean?"

"I have a theory," Lola said. "Check with Mamma for an answer."

Paige fell into her thoughts and let Mamma's wisdom carry her away. No answer came to her.

When Paige surfaced from her inner thoughts, she said, "Either she doesn't know or she's not sayin'."

"Well, I'm sure she has somethin' to say about it. Maybe she doesn't like the answer. Or maybe she wants ya to figure it out on your own."

"Don't I have enough other stuff to worry about now? What's your theory?"

"I think your and Glinda's seein' strength is the same as your personal strength; purity."

Sarcastically, Paige said, "Gee, thanks. That tells me a lot."

"Don't get sassy with me, chil'," Lola said. "It says a lot to other seers."

"What, then? What does it say?" Paige asked impatiently.

"It says that you're special."

"You keep tellin' me that but I don't know what that means either," Paige said as a bolt of lightning stuck near enough that the world beyond the porch turned blinding white and immediate thunder shook Lola's house.

Not seeming to notice the unnoticeable lightning and thunder, or not caring, Lola said, "Your aura is the purest I've ever seen. You're good to your soul, Paige-Turner. Glinda is a manifestation of your pureness. When I said Mamma might not like the answer, it's because, to my knowledge, and apparently, hers, no seer has ever had a silver, seein' eye. A sliver, seein' eye, must indicate pure sight. The rest of us have some limitations. I'm thinkin' you don't."

"What limitations?"

"Mask your seein' eye so that it looks like your normal eye. Before ya ask how, just think about it."

Paige thought about it, closed her eyes, and when she opened them again, both of her eyes were green.

"Tell me what ya see through your seein' eye," Lola said.

Paige didn't understand why Lola asked her to do this, but she did as Lola asked. She looked through the house, at Lola's pink aura, through the low, angry clouds at the bright sun above, through the porch to the dirt beneath Lola's house, and through the dirt to ancient roots of a tree that had long ago grown there.

When she finished seeing, Paige said, "I don't know what was supposed to happen, but everything looks the same as before."

"Exactly," Lola said. "When I mask my seein' eye, it's like there's a sheet of gauze over my seein' abilities. It's there, but muted. It's like that for all seers, but not for you. I bet there will be other benefits of pure sight. They just haven't been revealed yet."

"Like what?" Paige asked.

"I honestly don't know," Lola admitted. "This is uncharted territory in the history of seers. Are ya curious why I asked Father Mike to bless our seein' eyes?"

"Yeah. I just hadn't gotten 'round to askin' yet."

"When the ancient's familiar stumbled upon my house the other night, his guard was down, and I could penetrate the protections around his mind quick enough to see the ancient's true face through a recent memory," Lola said. "When I encountered him in the cemetery, his guard was up and it was difficult to penetrate the black walls of protection the ancient had placed around his familiar's mind. When the ancient took over his familiar's body, it became even more difficult.

"Tears are just water, and they aren't just for cryin'. They lubricate our eyes," Lola explained. "My hunch is, with the blessed tears coverin' our seein' eyes, we, or maybe just you, will see into the ancient's black mind and find out more about him. Like his name, where he's from and where his lair is. His mind won't just have walls around it, though. He'll have it protected like a bank vault. A black vault. We won't know, unless it doesn't work for me, but, I believe, you can break his vault wide open, easily, with your pure sight. Regardless of the blessin' Father Mike gave us."

"I didn't see anything like that last night when I saw him," Paige said.

"That's 'cause you weren't lookin' for it. Now ya know, and ya will next time. You've got sight mastered. It's natural, but your conjurin' skills need work. You up for some practice?"

Enthusiastic, Paige said, "Heck yeah."

"Okay, then. Let's go inside and start with some small stuff. When the weather clears, we'll see if ya can conjure some elementals."

With that, they went inside. Like most things Paige put her mind to, she was a quick learner.

~ * ~

Garrett arrived at work a little before eight o'clock and was exhausted; it had been a long, late night. The prospects of what the day would bring only added to his tiredness. Today would be the day he, likely, got calls about the Shanahans and Porters not showing up for work.

His intuition was correct concerning the Shanahans. The call came in a little after ten o'clock. Patrick Shanahan didn't show up for work at the CP Sawmill and the owner's, Charles Preston, calls to his home and cell phones went unanswered. It wasn't lost on Garrett that the CP Sawmill had been where Trowa used to park his Airstream trailer, and got bitten and infected by the alpha werewolf, Alexis Jordan. It had also been where the same werewolf killed Deputy Foster Timpson, who didn't believe the werewolf talk. Because he didn't believe, he had refused the clip of silver bullets Mike Middleton had made for every member of the Pine View County Sheriff's Department. When Foster responded to a call from Tracy Beck, who heard animal sounds coming from the sawmill, he became a believer in werewolves. Supernatural events had a way of overlapping as it was with all the stolen coffins having been the final resting place of werewolf victims.

Before the call came in about the Shanahans, Garrett received another call that he'd been expecting and dreading. Pine View was a small town where not much happened. News, big news, was rare. As such, the town's newspaper, the *Pine View Post*, had only come out twice a week— on Saturdays and Wednesdays. Since Trevor Henderson's death happened Christmas day, which had been a Friday, the paper ran the story in the Saturday edition. That didn't mean reporters at the paper hadn't heard about the Williams murders or Melanie Zane and Megan Williams' abductions or about the coffin thefts. When his desk phone rang within a minute of planting his butt in his office chair, he wasn't surprised.

Garrett answered the phone and Erica Harris said, "There's a reporter from the Post wantin' to talk to ya. It's Clair Abbott. Should I tell her you're not in yet?"

Reluctantly, Garrett said, "No. She's probably parked across the street and saw me come in. Go on and put her through."

In the time it took Erica to transfer the call, Garrett wished it was any reporter other than Clair Abbott. She was young, ambitious, and had been a thorn in Garrett's backside during the werewolf episode. He couldn't really blame her. She was doing her job, but he had a particular dislike for her pushiness.

The call transferred and Garrett said, "Mornin', Clair. Ask your questions, but ya already know my answers."

Undeterred, Clair said, "You've had a busy weekend. Two missin' girls. One from a family that was murdered. Four stolen coffins, each from a different church. And your ex-wife's husband's murder, too. Care to comment on any, or all, of these events?"

In a monotone response, that clearly expressed how he felt about talking with Clair, Garrett said, "I can't comment on ongoin' investigations, Clair."

"Does this mean they're all related?" Clair asked in her usual probing manner. "Includin' what happened to Trevor Henderson?"

"I didn't say that," Garrett said, and knew it was a mistake immediately.

"So…" Clair paused briefly before continuing. "Albert Sanders doesn't fit the MO of the other deaths? Was his death different? I heard the Williams' murders were like somethin' Charles Manson's folks did at the Tate house. Blood everywhere."

"No comment," Garrett said dryly and wondered who had leaked crime scene information.

"But the missin' girls, the murders and the coffins are related?"

Irritated with himself more than Clair, Garrett said, "No comment, Clair."

"Why's he stealin' coffins? And always from the people killed last May?"

"No comment."

"These are young girls, Sheriff," Clair continued aggressively. "If there's a sexual predator roamin' the streets of Pine View, our readers have a right to know. And the coffins. Is the suspect a sadist or necrophile?"

"No comment, Clair."

"Are we dealin' with somethin' like what happened at the MRB and the other deaths last summer?" Clair pushed.

"We solved those cases and they're closed," Garrett said.

"That's not a no. To tell ya the truth, Sheriff, I don't believe the official report from those murders."

"That's your prerogative, Clair," Garrett said. "They're solved and closed. Juan Escobar committed those murders, along with a long list of others, and he's dead."

"Does Escobar have a brother?" Clair asked mockingly.

"Not to my knowledge. We done here, Clair?"

"One more question, Sheriff," Clair prodded. "Your daughter, Paige, is in this sadist's preferred age group. Are ya worried 'bout her safety?"

"Nope. Goodbye, Clair," Garrett said and hung up the phone in the middle of another question from the pushy reporter.

After he hung up, Garrett sat there and contemplated the coming shit show when Clair Abbott found out about the two more missing girls, the Shanahan and Porter murders, Kat Zane's murder, and her missing husband Zack. It was a shitty thing to do but, with the Zanes, the simplest explanation would be to blame Kat's death and Melanie missing on Zack. Sometimes Garrett wished he still logged for a living, but never for more than a few seconds.

~ * ~

Even though Paige had clumsily levitated the large cauldron the night before, Lola began with small, unbreakable objects. Her silverware. With each task, Lola had Paige and Glinda perform them separately. Glinda needed to master the powers, too. When they easily removed all the silverware from the drawers and perfectly place them back into their assorted slots, they moved into the living room. There, Lola started by having them remove totems from the walls where they hung and put them back. They made quick and easy work of these tasks, too. Next, Lola had them open the curio cabinet and move the assortment of jars, boxes, and other items around mentally. Each task was supposed to be more difficult as the items became heaver and, as with the items in the cabinet, more delicate, but they performed the tasks with ease. Lola had them levitate the large cauldron Paige had clumsily handled the previous night. Again, they managed the cauldron perfectly and easily. Lola was impressed.

After completing this last task, Lola said, "Y'all are naturals. I don't know why I expected anything less. Y'all excel at everything supernatural. The rain has stopped. Y'all ready to try conjurin' an earthen elemental?"

"Heck, yeah." Paige said enthusiastically.

Once outside, and on the wet grass, Lola said, "To conjure an elemental, ya need to see it in the earth. Construct it in your mind. Then will it to materialize. When it materializes, you'll be able to control it with simple commands, like guard or protect. I'll conjure one first and show ya what to expect."

Lola looked at the ground and within a second, a large earthen elemental grew from the rain-soaked soil. It was mostly made up of dark, muddy dirt, but it had grass on its head and shoulders, like a football player's helmet and shoulder pads. It stood there waiting for a command.

"Now I'll command it to guard us," Lola told Paige.

A second later, the earthen elemental turned, put its back to Lola and Paige, and spread its massive arms in front of them in a defensive posture. Grass roots and a few earthworms hung from the underside of its muddy arms.

"Now I'll dismiss it."

As soon as those words were out of Lola's mouth, the earthen elemental sank back into the ground and there wasn't a trace it had ever been there. Every blade of grass was in place and undisturbed.

"Your turn. First as you and then as Glinda," Lola said.

Paige looked at the ground with her seeing eye and concentrated. It wasn't as easy as the levitating tasks she and Glinda had mastered. Within a few seconds, she saw it in the ground, like it was there the whole time. When she willed it to materialize, it did.

When the earthen elemental stood before her, Paige said, "Holy crap. I did it."

Lola smiled her warm, honey smile. "Ya sure did. Now give it a command."

Paige did. What happened next had her and Lola laughing so hard Paige almost peed herself.

The simple command she sent the elemental had been, 'Dance.'

As soon as Paige sent the mental command, the elemental gyrated its non-existence hips. Then its arms went out to either side and flailed so hard mud flung in all directions. Last, it began stomping its giant legs so hard the ground shook under their feet as it turned in awkward circles.

Still laughing, and with tears running down her beautiful, brown cheeks, Lola said, "Really? Ya told it to dance?"

Laughing every bit as hard as Lola, Paige said, "I thought it'd be funny."

"You succeeded, chil'. Now, please make it stop before I wet myself."

Paige sent a mental command for the elemental to stop, and it did.

"Oh, my word, Paige-Turner," Lola said, still laughing. "Only you, chil'. Only you."

Paige thought for a moment and composed herself. "You told me to make it stop. Couldn't you make it stop?"

Lola shook her head, which made the pink and white beads on the end of her cornrows click together. "No. Only the seer who conjures an elemental can control it."

"That's pretty cool."

"It is. Now dismiss it and try to conjure another one as Glinda."

"Wait," Paige said. "You conjured a lot of these last night. Can I conjure more than one?"

"Of course. Give it a try."

Paige looked down at the ground with her seeing eye. This time, she saw countless multitudes of them. An army of them just waiting to be materialized. She conjured three more, and they sprang from the ground immediately. Having done it once, it was easier the second time.

In awe of what she'd seen in the ground, Paige turned to Lola. "There are more of 'em down there than I can count. Is there a limit to how many a seer can conjure?"

"A seer is only limited in the number of elementals she can conjure, and control, by her power," Lola said. "But conjurin' and controllin' are two different things. A seer might conjure a hundred but only have control of a dozen."

"How many can you conjure and control?"

Lola grinned. "Not to brag but, if I wanted to, we'd be standin' in a crater with hundreds around us and doin' my biddin'."

"Wow," Paige said in awe of Lola's powers.

"You'll learn," Lola said. "Dismiss 'em and let Glinda try."

"I will. But first."

"Don't," Lola laughed, but it was too late.

Paige sent a mental command for the four elementals to dance. The spectacle of four dancing elementals bouncing off each other was funnier than one dancing. Before Paige could dismiss them through tear-filled eyes, warm pee ran down her inner thighs, and she didn't care.

After the dancing elementals were back in the ground, and Lola was, more or less, composed, she saw Paige had peed herself and began laughing again. Lola lost control of her bladder and peed herself, too. This only started Paige laughing again. With both their bladders voided, neither peed again and they regained their senses…eventually.

Lola's stomach cramped from laughing, but she said, "Okay. Try to conjure an earthen elemental as Glinda. But I swear, Paige-Turner. If you make 'em dance again, I'll hex Glinda's ass and she'll drop a turd between your feet."

"You can do that?" Paige asked.

"Wanna find out?"

"No ma'am," Paige said.

"Okay. Do your thing."

Paige transformed into Glinda quickly. The massive, silver-haired werewolf dwarfed Lola. Glinda looked into the ground with her seeing eye and quickly materialized six earthen elementals. They were massive. Where Lola and Paige's elementals were big, but big for a man, Glinda's elementals stood a good foot taller than Glinda, which put them at over ten feet tall.

Not playing around, Glinda sent a command for the elementals to protect her and Lola. They immediately encircled them in an earthen wall. As Glinda, with heightened senses, the earthen smell coming from the elementals was natural and wonderful.

The ancestorial connection meant Glinda and Paige were bonded on a molecular level, unlike regular werewolves that lost their human reason when transformed, and Paige was curious about something. She transformed back into her human body and looked up at the giant elementals surrounding her and Lola.

"Well," Lola said. "That's interestin'. And useful."

"So…that's not normal?" Paige asked.

"It's certainly unprecedented. Elementals, as ya saw, are large. Apparently, they are large in relation to the conjurer. Since ya conjured 'em as Glinda, they took a form large enough to aid her."

"Yeah. That's kinda what Glinda and I thought," Paige said. "I transformed back to see if they'd stay big or shrink with me," Paige said.

"Smart, Paige-Turner. Very smart. That's why I said this could be useful. The question now is, can ya control 'em in your human form?"

"Only one way to find out," Paige said.

Paige concentrated on trying to make the giant elementals walk away, but they didn't move. Undeterred, Paige dialed up Glinda as she concentrated on making the elementals walk away. The elementals remained motionless until Paige dialed up to where she was close to transforming. Then they walked away with ground shaking stomps of their massive, earthen feet. When they had traveled several steps away, Paige sent the guard command again, and they quickly encircled her and Lola.

Lola put an arm around Paige's shoulder. "Yes. This will be very useful, Paige. Very useful."

"Not just because they're bigger, right?" Paige asked.

"Well, men don't like to hear this, but bigger is better," Lola said with a grin. "Bigger means they're more formidable; stronger, and harder to defeat. Like so many other things we've discovered, the ancient vampire hasn't encountered nothin' like this in his long, undead existence. Everything that surprises him works to our benefit."

"That's kinda what I thought."

"Stop bein' modest, chil'. I know ya have Mamma's wisdom to draw from, but ya have natural wisdom, too. Follow your instinct, always."

"Thank you, Lola. I will."

"Okay. Dismiss these…giants and let's try somethin' else."

With a thought from Paige, the giant elementals dissolved back into the ground from which they came.

"As an elemental seer, you can create earth, wind, fire and water elementals," Lola said. "There's not enough water here to create a water elemental. We'd need a stream, river, pond, or any body of water for that. I can create fire to conjure a fire elemental. All we need to create a wind elemental is air and we're surrounded by that."

"How do I conjure an air elemental?"

"Same way ya created the earthen elemental," Lola said. "Look with your seein' eye and you'll find 'em. Then pull 'em outta the air."

"What'll happen?" Paige said. "I get how the earthen elementals can help. They're a physical barrier. You told Daddy how ya used a water elemental to kill that other vampire while I was eavesdroppin'. Before ya brought up givin' him a tail. So gross. I can see how a fire elemental would be useful against a vampire, but a wind elemental?"

"So many questions," Lola chided. "Just do it, chil'."

Paige nodded, looked at the sky with her seeing eye, and saw more wind elementals than she saw earthen elementals. The sky held an infinity of them. Not sure what to expect, Paige focused on one and pulled it into existence. A second later, a whirling mass of air materialized in front of her and Lola.

"What now?" Paige asked over the roar of the wind elemental awaiting commands only a few feet in front of them.

"The best thing 'bout wind elementals are that they're not tethered to the ground," Lola said. "The wind inside that elemental has the power of an F-five tornado. Now, can ya think of how this can be useful to use on flyin' vampires?"

Paige grinned and willed the wind elemental into the sky. It went wherever she willed it to go. She spotted the top of a dead pine tree in the woods encircling Lola's house. It was several hundred yards away, but Paige willed the wind elemental toward it. When it was over the dead tree, Paige willed it lower. What she saw next had been nothing short of amazing.

The wind elemental grabbed the very large, dead pine tree, uprooted it, and turned it to kindling in a matter of seconds. Even though the splintered pieces were sent flying, the wind elemental seemed to absorb the dead tree. When it had finished, the once transparent wind elemental became a whirling brown mass.

Paige dismissed the elemental and the remains of the tree rained down on the woods. From what she could see, what was left of the tree looked like mulch. Not a single large piece fell from the sky.

Beaming, Paige looked at Lola. "Holy crap. That was amazin'. Why haven't ya used this on the ancient?"

"I haven't needed to…yet," Lola said. "He knows we're elemental seers and have power over the elements. He's encountered many elemental seers over his long, vile existence. Encountered all four elementals, too. We have to be strategic in our use of 'em.'"

"But…" Paige began.

"Patience, Paige-Turner. He knows we can use a wind elemental to scatter his cloud. After seein' what your wind elemental did, imagine what Glinda's larger one could do."

Paige thought for a moment. "Glinda could trap him inside one of hers?"

Lola smiled. "That's what I'm thinkin', too. I can scatter his cloud with a few of mine. He's most vulnerable when alone."

"That's when we kill the fucker," Paige shouted.

"Don't get overconfident, chil'," Lola warned. "Just like he's never dealt with the likes of you and Glinda, none of us has ever dealt with a vampire this ancient and powerful. He likely has tricks up his putrid sleeves that we're not prepared for."

Paige's shoulders slumped and, somewhat defeated, said, "Dang, Lola. Every time I think we're makin' progress, ya stomp on it like an earthen elemental."

Lola wrapped Paige in a warm embrace. "We're makin' significant progress, Paige-Turner. Not only do you and Glinda have the gift of sight, thanks to my tears that I added to the potion, y'all have Mamma's wisdom, and against all odds, y'all have all the powers of an elemental seer. I'm just warnin' ya against gettin' overconfident.

"In my heart of hearts, I know we will defeat the…fucker," Lola continued confidently. "But overconfidence could be dangerous. Remember, it's not just us in danger. Your daddy, Ty, Trowa, and to a lesser degree, Father Mike are in danger, too. Everything we do has to be with the forethought about how it could affect them. You already lost your stepdad and there's a chance that we can still save Lin. Let's not get ahead of ourselves. Okay?"

Paige's face was pressed against Lola's firm left breast and Lola's always stiff nipple poked into her cheek. There was nothing awkward about it, though.

Paige nodded and let out a muffled, "Okay."

"That's my girl. How 'bout we head inside and grab some grub?"

Paige nodded, and Lola released her from the warm, comfortable embrace.

Paige looked up at Lola and smiled. "We will kill the ancient fucker."

Lola smiled back. "Yes, we will. But not on an empty stomach and not without a plan. That reminds me. We need to call your daddy before he has kittens. We're supposed to check in with him every couple of hours."

Paige, forgetting she was naked, reached for the back pocket, where she carried her cellphone, and felt her bare butt.

Lola laughed. "It's inside, chil'."

"Yeah," Paige laughed. "I've carried my phone there longer than I've been comfortable naked. I forgot."

Lola put her arm around Paige, and they walked toward her house.

"You wouldn't have made Glinda poop, if she made the earthen elementals dance, would ya?"

Lola laughed. "Oh, yes, I would've. You'd have transformed back with a giant werewolf turd between your feet."

"You'll have to teach me that one," Paige said. "I can think of a few people who I wouldn't mind puttin' a load in their britches."

They were at the front door and Lola said, "Remember, these powers will only last until we destroy the ancient."

As the door closed behind them, Paige thought, *I'm not so sure about that.*

~ * ~

After receiving the call about Patrick Shanahan not showing up for work, Garrett called Ty on his cell. This was a conversation he couldn't have on the radio.

Ty answered before the first ring stopped. He'd been expecting Garrett to call.

"Shanahans or Porters?" Ty said.

"Shanahans," Garrett replied. "But I'm sure we'll get a call about the Porters sometime today. Total shit show."

"Roger that," Ty said.

"I'll call George and have him meet us there. No sirens. I don't want to call attention to our bein' there."

"It's gonna get out," Ty said.

Somewhat defeated, Garrett said, "I know. I just don't want a bunch of people at the scene cranin' their necks to get a look-see."

"Roger that," Ty said. "I'm on my way."

"Me too. Right after I call George," Garrett said and ended the call.

He called George and told him where to meet him and Ty. Thankfully, George didn't ask questions.

His butt wasn't off the seat of his office chair when his cellphone rang. He saw it was Paige. Despite the shit show day ahead of him, he smiled and answered the call.

"Hey, Daddy," Paige said before Garrett could get a word out. "Just checkin' in like ya told me to."

"Hey, Paige-Turner. How's your day goin'?"

"Great," Paige enthusiastically replied. "I created earth and wind elementals."

Having seen Lola's earthen elementals the night before, Garrett didn't need an explanation. "That's great, sweet girl. You're catchin' on fast."

"That's what Miss Lola said, too."

"Well, thanks for checkin' in."

"What's the matter, Daddy?"

"I just got a call about the Shanahans," Garrett said dejectedly. "Ty, George, and I are fixin' to head over there now," he told her.

"Oh. I'm sorry. I love you, Daddy."

"I love you, too. Gotta get gone, Paige-Turner," Garrett said and ended the call.

~ * ~

Zack Zane sat on the concrete floor in a corner of the dark embalming room. His shoulders heaved as he cried uncontrollably. His Master had been true to his word. As instructed, after cleaning up his bloody vomit, he got undressed and descended into his Master's throne room. What he witnessed his Master do to his daughter disturbed his still human mind beyond words. As powerful as he was, he was helpless to make the Master stop engaging in sexually deviant acts with her. Even worse was what the Master had his daughter do with him.

He knew, on some level, the creature who had ravished his body was no longer his daughter. Every part of her young body, on the outside and on the inside, was so cold and dead. Knowing this did little to ease his tortured mind. It was her body. The body of his beautiful daughter. His Master had been correct about something else he said. During 'it,' he *had* enjoyed it. He'd been using the little blue pill to have sex with his wife, Kat, for two years. But he hadn't needed the magic pill with Melanie. His member was rock hard the moment his Master demanded it. When he climaxed inside of what had been his daughter, who the Master had renamed Agrapina, it was so explosive he almost passed out. And he enjoyed it.

The enjoyment ended afterwards, when his Master told him to stop enjoying. Not enjoying it was worse than enjoying it. Not enjoying it brought him back to reality. To reality and what he had done with the creature who had been his Melanie. Had he committed incest? Necrophilia? Or both of the horrendous sexual acts? His tortured mind didn't know. He knew he'd be compelled to engage in these deviant acts repeatedly until his Master did him the favor of killing him. As a Catholic, he was certain what he had become, and what he had done, had earned him a one-way ticket to hell. But hell couldn't be worse than what he was living through. He prayed to God, who he was sure no longer listened, for death to come quickly.

His stomach cramped at the thoughts running through his mind. His crying hitched, and he vomited black blood on the concrete floor between his legs. He knew it would be hours before his Master emerged from his throne room with his daughter and the other two girls, one of whom he knew was Lindsey Anderson. He didn't know who the scarlet-haired girl was, but he got to his feet and mopped up his mess. When he finished, he sat back down and cried again.

~ * ~

Garrett's hopes of not drawing attention to the Shanahan's house evaporated when he pulled his SUV onto the neighborhood street with cramped houses crowded closely together. It was Monday, December 28th. On any other Monday, most folks on the block would be at work or in school. That Monday was between Christmas and New Years. Kids were out of school and despite the rain, judging by the clustered onlookers huddled under umbrellas, many Pine View residents had the time between the two holidays off.

Garrett spotted Ty's SUV parked in the house's driveway; George's van wasn't there yet. The Shanahan's former vehicles must have been parked in the garage, because there was room for Garrett to park in the driveway next to Ty's SUV. He parked and dreading what would come next, got out of his SUV.

As he expected, the onlookers shouted questions at him from all directions. Garrett ignored the questions, and said nothing, but he raised his left hand in a 'back off' motion. Most of the onlookers quieted. The position had power.

Ty met Garrett at the front door and the tears on his cheeks spoke more clearly than any words.

"How bad?" Garrett asked, anyway.

Ty sniffed. "Hell of a mess. Parents and a little boy. He can't be more than five years old, Garrett."

Garrett placed a hand on his best friend's muscular shoulder. "Sometimes I wish I was still loggin' for a livin'."

"Roger that," Ty sniffed as another tear trickled down his handsome face.

"If we were still loggin', we wouldn't be the ones to find and kill this fucker," Garrett said. "Think anyone other than us, and Paige, could've killed the werewolves?"

Ty shook his head slowly. "Nope. The sooner we find this fucker and send him back to hell, the better."

Garrett tightened his grip on Ty's shoulder. "Best let me have a look-see."

Ty moved aside, let Garrett in, and closed the door on the curious neighbors.

As Garrett moved into the silent house, and entered the living room, the first victim he saw was a small, red-haired boy lying on the floor. He approached the boy's body and looked down at him. There were two puncture wounds on his carotid artery. He looked at his fogged over green eyes. Tears leaked from his eyes.

Garrett squatted down and used his fingers to close the boy's eyes. "You're with God now, little man."

As he got up, the boy's eyes slowly opened again. Garrett felt a chill run up his spine.

"Rigor," Ty said. "I saw that happen too many times when I was…over there. If it's any comfort, it looks like he met a less violent end than his folks.

"They're in the kitchen," Ty said and pointed in the kitchen's direction. "Not that any of it will end up in evidence, but I've already documented the scene. Best I can tell, they came home durin' the attack."

Garrett looked toward the kitchen, saw the overturned table, scattered chairs, and the woman's body sprawled on the floor with a ragged wound on her neck. "What makes ya think that?"

"Well, the door to the garage is still partially open and Mister Shanahan still has the car and other keys in his hand," Ty said. "His body is behind the counter on the kitchen floor. Same ragged wound on his neck as on his wife's."

Garrett walked past Ty, into the kitchen, and saw the keys in his hand. "Excellent deduction, Watson."

"I always thought I was Holmes and you were Watson."

Garrett couldn't help but chuckle. "Okay, Holmes. Wrong place and very wrong time."

"Maybe," Ty said.

"Maybe?" Garrett asked.

Ty wiped fresh tears from his cheeks with strong hands. "Would you wanna live if ya came home and found your young son dead and your daughter missin'?"

Garrett considered this briefly. "No. I wouldn't. If I'd lost Paige to the werewolves, I'd have eaten a bullet."

Before Ty could respond, there was a hard knock on the door. Both men jumped.

"That's probably George," Garrett said. "If it's anyone else, use your runnin' back skills to knock 'em on their ass."

Ty smiled in spite of the shit show murders. "Roger that."

A moment later, Ty returned with George Krats who, despite his job as County Coroner, looked a little puny.

"What the fuck, Garrett?" George said. "Ya gotta put a stop to this shit. Soon."

"No shit, George," Garrett shot back, more harshly than he intended. "That's what we're tryin' to do. We're not twiddlin' our fuckin' thumbs."

George shuffled his feet. "I'm sorry. I know y'all are tryin'. But, fuck. Look at this."

"Yeah, well, here's some more bad news," Garrett said. "Another family, the Porters, were killed last night, too. We can't go there until someone reports it. So…we're waitin' for a call."

"Double fuck." George shouted.

"Back your van to the front door, so the neighbors can't see how many bodies we load into it," Garrett instructed. "And for fuck's sake, don't say a word to anyone about how many bodies are in here,"

"Not my first rodeo, Garrett," George spat back.

"I'm sorry. It's just…," Garrett trailed off without finishing the sentence.

"We're all in this together," Ty interjected. "Let's not get aggravated with each other."

Garrett and George shook hands, but they exchanged no words. George did as Garrett requested. A short fifteen minutes later, the three bodies were bagged and loaded in George's van. After George left, Garrett used the keys Mister Shanahan had in his dead hand to lock up the house. He and Ty left to shouted questions from concerned neighbors. Even if Garrett wanted to answer, he didn't. He had no answers for them. Garrett got in the SUV and left the Shanahan's house in the review mirror. As promised, he headed to get Lacy and go with her to see Digger for Al's funeral plans.

~ * ~

Clive Jones had been a nefarious character since Garrett first met him in kindergarten; they were the same age. Back then, he limited his cruelty to putting gum in girls' hair, pulling girls' hair, and pulling chairs out from behind classmates as they were about to sit down. As they got older, Clive took to bullying younger students, and bullying was something Garrett couldn't abide. This had led to several fights between the two of them over the years. Even though Clive had always been much bigger than Garrett, like most bullies, his confidence came from picking on much smaller and weaker kids. Against Garrett, Clive didn't stand a chance. Clive had also been slow and dimwitted, which meant he never learned Garrett would kick his ass every time he witnessed his bullying behavior.

Clive's dimwittedness also resulted in his being held back several years during his K through twelve education. The last run-in with Garrett happened at a MRB party. Garrett had been a senior, and Clive a hulking freshman. When Garrett saw Clive punch his girlfriend, a large and not attractive girl named Maranda Salazar, so hard he knocked her out, he wailed on Clive so hard, if his friends hadn't pulled him off, he might have killed him.

Maranda reported the abuse to the police, and they issued a restraining order on Clive. He received six-month's probation for the assault, too. The restraining order meant Clive could not attend Pine View High School, where the two of them would, by necessity, be near each other. They gave Clive a room in the administrative building to do his schoolwork from and teachers sent his assignments there for him to complete. Clive decided he was done with formal education. Although he had only been a freshman, he was eighteen years old because of the years he'd been held back, and he dropped out of high school.

Clive took a job at a gas station in Pine View, completed his probation, and appeared to be getting his life on track. Then, several pets— dogs, cats, and one goat—in his rural area had been discovered mutilated.

All of them were missing their heads. Of course, Clive had been the natural suspect, but there was no evidence linking him to the brutal crimes. Not until an enterprising deputy sheriff, named Oliver Henry, who would become sheriff one day and hire Garrett, monitored Clive during his free time.

After three days of watching Clive's movements, and on the verge of giving up, he saw Clive disappear into the woods behind his run-down house. Just before Clive entered the woods, he looked back as if to make sure no one was watching. Clive didn't see Oliver, but Oliver saw Clive. After Clive entered the woods, Oliver exited his personal truck and followed Clive. Once Oliver entered in the woods, Clive hadn't been hard to find. Music, AC/DC's *Back in Black* drifted through the woods. Oliver followed the music and found Clive a couple of hundred yards into the woods. He sat in the middle of what could only be described as a macabre shrine. All the missing heads from the mutilated animals, about a dozen, were in a circle around him and the rotting goat's head was propped up against the radio now playing *Thunderstruck*. Oliver pulled his gun and arrested Clive.

Clive had been charged with thirteen counts of cruelty to animals, which was only a Class C misdemeanor. On advice from his court-appointed attorney, Jimmy McGowen, he pled guilty, hoping for some leniency. Clive's past probation for assault, and the judge, a no-nonsense man named Roy Lancaster, had been so repulsed by Clive's cruelty he handed down the harshest sentence he could. Two years of probation. Probation wasn't the harshest punishment Clive would face for the horrific crimes.

Because there were thirteen heads, and one being a goat's head, an unlucky number, and one some people associate with witchcraft or devil worship, town folk branded Clive a Satanist. He wasn't. The number of heads had been an unfortunate coincidence. There'd have been more if Deputy Henry hadn't caught Clive when he did, and Clive just thought the goat's head looked cool.

None of this mattered. The owner of the gas station, Gus Owens, where Clive worked, had two beagles who he loved like family, and he fired Clive the day after he had been arrested for the mutilations. Gus didn't care to wait and see if Clive had done the mutilations. The few people who gave Clive a benefit of doubt, there weren't many, shunned him after he pled guilty. This included Clive's parents. Clive had two younger brothers and his folks were concerned for their safety with him in the house. They kicked him out. Clive became a pariah.

With no home, he lived out of a beat up, 1966 Chevy pickup he bought while working for Gus. With no education or job, Clive resorted to the only activity his dimwitted mind thought left. Burglary. Like with everything else Clive attempted, he hadn't been smart about it. He broke into four houses, over two nights, and stole some valuables. Mostly jewelry, some cash, and two guns. Then, the mental reject tried to sell the jewelry at the only pawnshop in Pine View, called, appropriately, Pine View Pawn. The proprietor of the pawnshop, a man named Richard Newsom, recognized the jewelry from a list the Pine View PD gave him.

Richard made some excuse to go to his office and Clive stupidly waited. Richard called the police and within five minutes, Clive was arrested and in custody. He was processed at the Pine View Police Department, charged with four counts of burglary of residence at nighttime, and transported to the Pine View County Jail for holding until arraignment the next day. Clive had the same court-appointed attorney and appeared before the same judge. Bail was set at fifty thousand dollars, which Clive didn't have. Because of his cruelty to animals' crimes, neither bail bondsmen in Pine View would bond Clive out while he awaited trial for the burglaries.

Clive resided in the Pine View County Jail, also known as the Iron Door Inn by inmates, for four months before his trial date. Once again, Jimmy McGowen was his court-appointed attorney and he, like everyone else who knew of Clive's past indiscretions, despised him. Jimmy was a pet lover, too. Jimmy told Clive to plead guilty and ask for leniency, knowing full well none would be granted. Clive did as his lawyer instructed. This time, Judge Lancaster had Clive by the balls, and he squeezed. Hard.

Burglary of a resident at nighttime, a fourth-degree felony, the least serious felony under Texas law, had a maximum penalty of five-years in a state penitentiary. He sentenced Clive to all five-years without the possibility of parole. Judge Lancaster's only regret was he couldn't hand down a harsher sentence. He knew, if Clive made his way back to Pine View after serving the five-years, he'd see Clive back in his courtroom again.

After serving five-years at the H. H. Coffield Unit, Clive returned to Pine View. He was a changed man, but not in a good way. Before his time in prison, Clive was six-foot, five-inches of dimwitted lard. When he returned, Clive was six-foot, five-inches of dimwitted, well-honed muscle. He looked like he belonged in a professional wrestling ring. His body, even his face, was a roadmap of remarkable prison tattoos with no discernible theme. The facial tattoo was the most impressive and unsettling. Clive's head was shaved, and an extremely talented prison tattoo artist had inked an anatomically correct skull on Clive's head. It gave Clive a ghastly appearance.

Everyone who saw him after he returned, his size and tattoos made Clive hard not to see, and knew of his animal, skull shrine, which had been everyone in Pine View County, was certain the skull tattoo was a gruesome homage to the horrific crimes of his past.

Being who he was, getting a job in Pine View was impossible. Clive got a job as a bouncer at a strip club on the outskirts of Longview called Glitter Galore. The owner of the strip club, Sig Davidson, had no problem with Clive's criminal history or his appearance. Sig found Clive's size and appearance good qualities in a strip club bouncer, and Clive didn't disappoint. He enjoyed showing rowdy customers a very rough exit from Glitter Galore. Several of the strippers did Clive 'favors' for his perceived chivalry. Although Clive enjoyed the favors, in reality, he didn't give a shit about the strippers. What he enjoyed was roughing up the men, and an occasional woman, who misbehaved by touching the strippers in an inappropriate place. A crotch grab or a titty lick.

A strip club, and the type of men who frequented them, wasn't the best company for an ex-convict. It wasn't long before Clive started smoking meth and a short time later, he began selling it to supplement his income. On one of his nights off, Clive rode his Harley out to Knucklehead's Icehouse. He hadn't been there before, but he knew it was a biker drinking hole and he thought he might find a few buyers for the crappy meth he sold. When he got to Knucklehead's, he recognized twin brothers he knew from before he dropped out of high school—Mont and Jack Lee. Clive made two critical mistakes that night. He had still been dimwitted. First, from the Lee brother's appearance, he figured they smoked meth or would know someone who did. Second, they were the only men in the bar who were bigger than him.

Mont and Jack recognized Clive, too. To Clive's demise, they were itching for a reason to kick his ass. The Lees didn't own pets, but they had no affinity for someone who tortured and killed them. When Clive offered to sell them meth, the Lee twins took him out while Dixie Rains, the bartender, called 911.

A very battered, bruised, and bloody Clive was back in the Pine View County Jail within an hour. Judge Lancaster hadn't been surprised when he saw Clive Jones' name on the next morning's arraignment list. Jimmy, the court-appointed attorney, stood next to Clive when his bail was set at one hundred and fifty thousand dollars. Clive spent the next two months in the Pine View County Jail, awaiting his trial date. This time, when Jimmy told him to plead guilty and ask for leniency, Clive fired him and pled innocent. Against Judge Lancaster's advice, Clive insisted on representing himself. Judge Lancaster set the trial date for the following Monday.

The 'trial' lasted less than an hour and the jury returned a guilty verdict within ten minutes. Judge Lancaster sentenced Clive to ten-years in a state penitentiary, without the possibility of parole. Off to the H. H. Coffield Unit, Clive went for the second time. Clive caught a slight break and was released after nine-years because of overcrowding and his crime of selling meth being classified as a 'non-violent' offense.

While serving the second prison sentence, Clive received word his dad had passed away from a heart attack. He shed no tears over his old man's passing. In fact, it brought Clive a measure of happiness. His younger brothers were grown and gone from his childhood home. With his dad dead, he thought his mom would probably let him move back home. When he was released a year early and contacted her, she agreed to let Clive move in.

Clive took odd jobs, mostly day-labor construction projects that paid 'under the table,' where and when he could, and helped his mom around the house. Because of his reputation, the odd jobs were always somewhere other than Pine View. He also stayed out of trouble. This didn't mean Clive hadn't skirted the law from time to time. He did, but his animal torturing, burglarizing, drug using, and drug selling days were behind him.

Growing up in East Texas, Clive loved to deer hunt. As a convicted felon, he wasn't allowed to own a gun. This also meant he couldn't get a hunting license. Neither of these restrictions kept him from deer hunting, though. His dead dad had two rifles in the house, both Remington bolt actions. One was a .308, and the other was a .270. Other than being paid tax free cash for odd jobs, the only other laws Clive broke during the winter months were possession of a firearm, hunting without a license, and poaching. If caught hunting illegally, Clive would end up back in prison. He knew the woods in Pine View County well and eating his mom's fried, venison backstrap, was worth the risk.

It had been the need to kill a deer that had Clive sneaking through the woods, with his dad's .270 slung over his shoulder, on the afternoon of Monday, December 28th, 2015. As he crept through the woods looking for a deer to shoot, the sound of what he thought were dogs fighting caught his attention. Curious, Clive followed the sound to the edge of the woods that opened into someone's backyard.

He was decked out in full military camouflage. Orange camo was for legitimate hunters. Clive went down on his stomach and wiggled through the low underbrush to get a better look. He found the source of the sounds he'd been following. What he initially thought were dogs fighting were two coyotes growling and nipping at each other as they munched on a dead man's body. Clive didn't know it, but he had, inadvertently, found Ashton Wilcox. By extension, the Porter murders, too.

Clive took aim at one coyote and squeezed the trigger. It fell dead. Clive was an excellent shot, but the other coyote hightailed it into the woods before Clive could chamber another round. A third coyote hightailed it out of the opened, sliding back door. Being an excellent shot didn't make him a quick shot. He couldn't get a shot at the fleeing coyote either.

With the coyotes taken care of, Clive got up and walked into the backyard to get a better look. He didn't recognize the dead man, but he saw the Glock strapped to his belt and a nice AR-15 rifle on the ground beside him, the shoulder strap still in place. Clive's impulse was to take the guns and hightail it away like the surviving coyotes had. For a change, reason prevailed over dimwittedness. It was one thing to be caught with a firearm and poaching. That might get him three- to five-years back in prison. If he was caught with a dead man's guns, with his criminal record and reputation, he knew he could end up with a needle in his arm in Huntsville. Texas was serious about the death penalty.

Clive stepped to the side of the dead man, in front of an opened, sliding door, and shouted, "Hello. Anyone in there?"

No response.

Clive shouted, "I'm puttin' my gun down and comin' in to see if anyone needs help."

Clive put his gun down and stepped into the house. Stepped into a nightmare of epic carnage. Despite the vile things he'd done to the animals when he was younger, something he actually grew to regret and be disgusted by, like the folks of Pine View were, he'd never seen people in such a state. He stumbled back outside and vomited in the grass. Then he did the hardest thing he'd ever done. The felon, in full camo and possessing a firearm, that could only be accounted for because he was poaching, took out his cellphone and dialed 911.

A female voice answered. "Nine, one, one. Is this an emergency?"

Clive swallowed hard. "Yes, ma'am. My name is Clive Jones, and I just found several dead people."

"Did you kill these people, Mister Jones?" the woman asked.

"No. God, no. I'm a felon. I have a record. I wouldn't be callin' it in if I did it."

"Okay, Mister Jones. Stay calm and tell me your location."

"Calm?" Clive shouted. "These people have had their throats ripped out. Kids, too. And ya want me to stay clam?"

"Breathe, Mister Jones. Tell me the address."

"I don't know the address. I'm in the backyard," Clive said.

"You're in the backyard?"

"Yes. I know how that sounds, but I didn't do it. I'll explain everything when the cops get here."

"Are you armed, Mister Jones?"

"Yes. I mean, no. I was, but I put my gun down before goin' in the house."

"You entered the residence, Mister Jones?"

"Yes. But just to see if anyone was hurt."

"What made you think someone might be hurt, Mister Jones?"

"There's a dead guy in the backyard and the back door is open," Clive shouted. "Just please send the cops."

"I still need an address, Mister Jones."

"Okay. Okay. I'll run to the end of their driveway and get the address. Please stop callin' me Mister Jones. My name is Clive."

"Okay, Clive. Leave your gun and stay on the phone with me until law enforcement arrives."

"Right. Okay," Clive said as he ran around the house and then down the very long driveway.

When he got to the mailbox, he gave the 911 operator the address, but he didn't know what farm to market or county road the driveway intersected. He heard sirens already approaching.

Out of breath and panting from the long run, Clive said, "Ya knew where I was the whole time. Didn't ya?"

"Yes, Clive. Cellphones have 911 locators on 'em. I just needed ya to stay on the line with me. I need ya to stay on the line with me until the sheriff arrives. You left your firearm behind, correct?"

"Yes. I left it behind," Clive panted. "I would'a stayed on the line with ya without makin' me run half a mile for the address ya already had. I didn't kill these people."

Clive heard an audible click on the line and then the 911 operator said, "That's right. You just torture and kill innocent pets."

"Fuck you," Clive said right before he heard the audible click again.

"Just stay on the line with me, Clive. They're almost at your location."

"You just turned off the recorder to bait me by sayin' I only torture and kill innocent pets."

"I don't know what you're talkin' 'bout, Clive."

Clive saw two Pine View County Sheriff's SUVs approaching fast. "They're here. Fuck ya very much, bitch."

Before he ended the call, he heard the 911 operator laugh and say, "Happy to help."

Clive dropped his cellphone, put his hands in the air, and waited to be arrested for a crime he didn't commit. He could not have been more shocked by the reception his old nemesis, and current Sheriff Garrett Lambert, gave him.

~ * ~

After leaving the Shanahan's and ignoring questions he couldn't answer from the concerned neighbors, Garrett didn't go back to his office. During the previous werewolf attacks, he had gotten very good at skirting the truth with partial, non-explanatory answers to all the questions asked. This situation was different and more difficult. Slain families and missing teenage girls were a new level of depravity requiring a new level of non-committal answers. The only plausible answer was to throw Zack Zane under the speeding bus. After taking Lacy to see Digger, he headed for the only place he could find comfort. To his parent's house where he and Mandy were staying until they handled the vampire situation. He needed some Mandy time and advice.

He called Mandy on the way to let her know he was dropping by. When he pulled up in front of his parent's house, Mandy waited for him on the front porch swing. She got up and greeted him with a tight, warm embrace after he closed the SUV's door. God, she felt and smelled good. Garrett's tension melted away. Holding hands, they walked back to the porch swing and sat down. They spoke no words for several minutes. Just being with her helped Garrett a great deal.

After a few minutes of silence, Mandy said, "That bad?"

Thinking about the little, red-haired boy with the fogged over green eyes that wouldn't stay closed, Garrett nodded as tears leaked from his eyes and ran down his scruffy cheeks.

Mandy shifted on the swing, which caused it to squeak, and kissed the tear on Garrett's left cheek away. "Oh, honey. I'm so sorry you have to deal with all this...crap again."

"Me, too," Garrett said. "But I feel worse for all the people, this...monster's killin' and the girls he's takin'. Despite all her powers, I'm sick over the fact that this monster wants Paige *and* Glinda."

"I know ya do. So do I. I'm worried sick about Paige, too. I also know there's no one else more capable of stoppin' him than you and your posse."

Garrett let out a humorless chuckle. "That's what I told Ty at the Shanahan's house."

"It's true," Mandy said.

Garrett sighed. "I guess, but Lola and James were right when they said dealin' with a vampire would be harder than dealin' with the werewolves. Hell, Glinda can't even track 'em when they turn into mist and drift away."

"True, but you didn't have Glinda durin' the werewolf attacks," Mandy pointed out. "You found Alexis' den usin' good, ol' fashion investigatin'. You're very good at your job, honey. Glinda's one hell of an asset, but don't discount your ability to figure things out on your own."

Everything Mandy had said was true, and Garrett realized he hadn't been using his wits to find the vampire. He'd been leaning on Paige, Glinda and Lola like a three-pronged crutch to do all the work.

Garrett turned his face to look at Mandy; at her stunningly, beautiful, big, blue eyes with white flakes, and with a slight smile, said, "You're right. I've been relyin' on Paige, Glinda and Lola to do all the work. I need to do some good, ol' fashion investigatin' on my own."

Mandy smiled her beautiful smile. "Yes. Please be careful."

Feeling better, he knew Mandy would have that effect on him. Garrett smiled back. "I'll always come home to you, darlin'."

Mandy took his face in her soft hands and kissed him. It was a deep, passionate kiss that made Garrett want to take her inside and make the bed springs on his childhood bed squeak again. Just then, his cellphone rang. Their lips parted and Garrett took his cell out of his chest pocket. It was Paige, checking in again.

Garrett answered. "Hey, pretty girl."

"You sound better," Paige said with relief. "I was worried you'd be even more down after goin' to the Shanahan's."

"I was," Garrett said. "I'm with Mandy now. She made me feel better."

"Gross, Daddy. I don't wanna hear how Mandy made you feel better."

Garett laughed. "We're on the porch swing, smart ass. Just bein' next to her makes me feel better."

"Oh. Okay then. Any word on the Porters?"

"Not yet."

"Okay. Give Mandy a kiss for me. But no tongue."

Garrett laughed again. "I will. I love you, Paige-Turner."

"I love you too, Daddy."

After ending the call, Garrett gave Mandy a peck on the lips. "That's from Paige. She explicitly instructed that the kiss from her not involve tongue action."

Mandy broke into laughter. "That girl is somethin' else."

Laughing too, Garrett said, "Yes, she is. And that somethin' else is a massive, silver-haired, werewolf."

"Not what I meant, but very true."

Somewhat more seriously, Garrett said, "I need your advice on somethin' else. Somethin' that I think I have to do but feel shitty about."

"I'm all ears," Mandy said.

"Durin' the werewolf attacks, I got good at tellin' partial truths to questions asked about 'em," Garrett said. "This is…different. Harder. Unfortunately, the only plausible, untrue answer I can think of to explain these attacks, and missin' girls, is to say Zack Zane is our primary suspect. He's missin', which makes him look guilty. It wouldn't be the first time some guy, a guy no one would suspect of bein' capable of somethin' like this, did somethin' like this. But…it feels so wrong."

Mandy thought for a moment. "Y'all are pretty sure he's the vampire's new familiar?"

"Yeah. We're certain of that."

"And," Mandy continued quietly, "y'all don't see an outcome where Zack lives through this?"

"No," Garrett answered.

"Then ya gotta blame him," Mandy concluded.

Garrett sighed. "Yeah. But blamin' an innocent man, a good man, for all this feels so wrong."

Sympathetically, Mandy said, "Your only other options are to tell the truth, that a vampire is loose in Pine View County, or let it go unsolved."

"Lettin' it go unsolved is an option I've strongly considered," Garrett admitted.

"You'd never get reelected with unsolved crimes like these," Mandy said.

Garrett sighed again. "Honest to God, I don't care about reelection. Someone else can have this damn job."

Mandy squeezed Garrett's hand. "I know ya don't care about bein' reelected, but no one else can do *your* job. Lola and James told us that supernatural events…attract future supernatural events. They were right. What if there's another one after this one? Do ya think someone else as sheriff would be capable of dealin' with it?"

"No," Garrett admitted.

"With all that considered, ya wouldn't be blamin' Zack for personal reasons," Mandy said. "You'd be doin' it because, after the werewolves and somethin' like this, people need closure to feel safe again. Do it for that reason."

Feeling better about the shitty situation, Garrett said, "You're right. Thanks, Mandy."

Mandy smiled. "As long as ya remember that I'm always right, our marriage will be smooth sailin'."

Garrett started to kiss her again when his cell pinged with a text message. He pulled it up and read it. It was from Erica Harris, the seven to three dispatch. Clive Jones had found the Porters. Garrett texted her back to let her know he was on the way and then texted Ty.

"I gotta go, darlin'. Someone found the Porters."

"I'm sorry."

"It was gonna happen, eventually."

"I love you, honey."

"I love you too, darlin'."

Garrett gave her a quick kiss, not the deep, passionate one he'd been about to give her before the text, and left. He watched her get smaller on the porch swing in his review mirror before turning onto the main road, switching on the siren, and flooring the accelerator.

~ * ~

Garrett knew his old classmate, and repeat offender Clive Jones, had made the 911 call. Although Garrett had never seen Clive around town, or the county, after being released from prison either time, he'd been a deputy sheriff when Clive spent time in the Pine View County Jail awaiting trial on the meth selling charges. As he brought his SUV to a stop in front of the skull tattooed Clive, who had his hands in the air, his appearance did not surprise him. The same could not be said for Ty, though.

Garrett stepped out of the SUV. "Ya can put your hands down, Clive. I know ya didn't kill these people."

As Clive slowly lowered his hands, given his past, he distrust of law enforcement, he looked at the sheriff. "Holy shit. Is that you, Garrett?"

Garrett approached Clive and stuck out his hand. "In the flesh. I've been sheriff since Oliver Henry retired a few years ago."

Surprised by the friendly welcome and extended hand, Clive shook Garrett's hand. "Um, congratulations."

When Ty approached, Garrett said, "This is Deputy Ty Jackson."

Ty stuck out his hand, and Clive shook it, too.

"Impressive ink," Ty said as their hands parted.

"Um, thanks," Clive said. "I gotta tell y'all I expected to be in cuffs by now. But y'all didn't even get out with your guns drawn."

"I told ya," Garrett said. "I know ya didn't kill these people."

"You know my past, Garrett. Hell, before I got sent off to prison, *twice*, you used to kick my ass like clockwork. How come you're so sure I ain't the killer?"

"These aren't the first and we already have a suspect we're tryin' to find," Garrett said.

"Holy hell," Clive said. "There's more of what I saw in that house?"

"There are," Garrett confirmed. "Missin' teenage girls, too."

"And people think I'm a sick fuck," Clive said.

"Well, you were a sick fuck," Garrett said. "That's in the past, Clive. I'm gonna need a statement from ya and how ya found the Porters, though."

"Then the cuffs come out," Clive said.

"Not necessarily," Garrett said. "Hop in my SUV and tell me what happened while I drive to their house."

"Okay," Clive said as his shoulders slumped and he headed for the SUV's back door.

"Front seat, Clive," Garrett instructed "You're not in trouble."

Clive smiled a grotesque skull smile and got in the front passenger seat. Garrett got behind the wheel and began down the long driveway as Ty followed. By the time they got to the house, Clive told Garrett how he came across the Porter's house. He told him the truth. That he had his dad's gun and was poaching for venison.

Garrett parked in front of the Porter's house and Ty parked next to him. The three men got out of the SUVs.

"Okay, Clive," Garrett said. "Walk us through what ya saw and did."

"I will, but I don't wanna go back inside that house," Clive said with a skull tattoo grimace. "I seen a lota nasty shit, Garrett. Nothin' like what's inside that house, and I don't wanna see it again."

"You don't have to go back inside the house, Clive."

Clive started toward the side of the house. "Okay. Follow me. The dead guy the coyotes were munchin' on is in the backyard by the opened, slidin' door."

"Munchin' coyotes?" Ty asked Garrett.

"I'll explain in a bit," Garrett said as he and Ty followed Clive.

When they were behind the house, with the dead man and dead coyote in view, Clive pointed at the area of brush flattened by his body.

"That's where I crawled up and shot the coyote. There were two on him and a third ran outta the house, but I couldn't get another shot off quick enough to hit the other two. Bolt-action rifle."

As Clive explained, Garrett and Ty walked over to the dead man to have a look at him. His neck was a mess, but how much of it had been the vampire bite, or the coyotes 'munchin,' neither could tell.

"Damn. He was loaded for bear, Garrett," Ty said. "That's shit I used in the Marines."

Garrett saw the Remington .270 by the back door and pointed at it. "That your daddy's gun, Clive?"

"Yeah," Clive admitted. "Cuff time?"

"I'll make ya a deal ya can't refuse, Clive," Garrett said. "Take your daddy's gun home, hang it up, don't take it outta your mom's house again, no more poachin', and you can go free."

Astonished, Clive said, "Really?"

"Really. If it's venison ya want, I can bring some by your mom's from time to time. If it's huntin' and venison, ya want, drop by my place durin' huntin' season," Garrett said. "Don't bring your daddy's gun with ya, though. If ya get pulled over with it, I can't help ya. I'll let ya use one of my guns to bag a deer and we'll tag it with one of my tags."

More astonished, Clive said, "No shit?"

"No shit, Clive. Oh, and don't talk 'bout what ya saw here."

"I won't," Clive said. "I wanna forget I ever seen it."

"Alright," Garrett said as he stuck out his hand. "Do we have a deal?"

Clive shook Garrett's hand enthusiastically. "Deal, Garrett. Thank you. Most folks, especially cops, ain't very nice to me."

As their hands parted, Garrett said, "The past is the past, Clive. Now take your daddy's gun and get gone."

"You got it," Clive said as he picked up his dad's gun and hightailed into the woods behind the Porter's house.

"A felon with a gun and poachin'," Ty said. "That was damn nice of ya, Garrett."

"Well, we have history and how would arrestin' him help in this situation?" Garrett said. "Then he'd be on the record 'bout what he saw.

Better to let him hunt on my place. That way we don't have to worry 'bout this comin' out later, if he's caught poachin'.'"

"Yeah, I got y'all had history," Ty said. "Everything else ya said makes sense. But I got two questions for ya."

"What?"

"First, how in the hell did you kick that big guy's ass like clockwork? Second, why did ya kick his ass like clockwork?"

Garrett laughed. "He was big back then. Fat, big, and slow. He came back from his first stint in prison, lookin' like that. That's the how. The why was because he was a bully who liked pickin' on smaller kids.

"The last time I kicked his ass was at a MRB party when he punched his girlfriend so hard he knocked her out," Garrett continued as if lost in the memory. "I saw red and might'a killed him if my friends hadn't pulled me off him. The assault on his girlfriend was his first probation and the beginnin' of the end for Clive. I'll tell ya the rest later."

Ty nodded. "If what's inside scared the likes of Clive, I'm not sure I wanna go inside either."

"Yeah, but unlike Clive, we've seen the vampire's aftermath before," Garrett reminded Ty.

"Doesn't make it any easier," Ty said. "Especially with kids. From what Paige said she saw in their black auras, there are three of 'em in there."

"Best we get it over with and call George," Garrett said.

Ty nodded again, and they stepped inside.

Inside, they found a dead man, who had identical firearms as the man outside, and a dead boy on the living room floor. Their throats were shredded. Again, how much of the damage was from the vampire bites or the coyote Clive said ran out of the house was hard to tell.

Ty looked around the living room, the visible dining room with the Porter's last supper on it. "Accordin' to Paige, there should more bodies."

Garrett nudge Ty to get his attention and pointed a slightly ajar bookshelf. "I'm guessin' there's somethin' behind that bookshelf."

Ty pulled it open, and he and Garrett looked down the dark steps.

"Bunker?" Ty asked.

"You saw how armed both of the men were," Garrett said.

"Probably those end-of-times folks like the Lee twins. Bunker makes sense."

Garrett and Ty pulled out their flashlights and slowly descended the steps. At the bottom, they saw the heavy steel bunker door that had been ripped off its hinges.

"Holy shit," Ty said. "That took a hell of a lota strength to pull open."

Garrett didn't respond. He raised his flashlight and illuminated the bunker. They saw a cache of firearms and food that would be the envy of most preppers. They saw three bodies. Two teenage boys and a woman.

"Well, that's everyone," Garrett said.

"You take these three and I'll take the three upstairs," Ty said.

"Who's the sheriff here?"

"You are," Ty said. "But we established earlier that I'm Holmes and you're Watson."

"Okay," Garrett said with a forced chuckle. "Get your ass topside, Holmes."

Ty didn't have to be told twice. He turned and his heavy footsteps ascended the steps to the living room and some sunlight above.

Garrett shone his flashlight against the wall, found a light switch, and flipped it on. Harsh, white, florescent lights turned on and Garrett got a look at the enormity of the bunker. What he and Ty saw with their flashlights had been a tiny fraction of the whole bunker, which, judging by how many lights hung from the concrete ceiling, dwarfed the footprint of the house above. Garrett wasn't there to inventory the bunker; someone else would do this job. His job was to document the dead, which he did.

He tried to text George the address and wasn't surprised to see his cell had no signal. He left the bunker lights on, ascended the steps, and joined Ty, who was outside taking pictures of the first victim they saw. The chilly, fresh air that followed the blue norther felt good.

"Any identification?" Garrett asked as he sent the text to George.

"Yeah," Ty said. "Wallet in his back pocket with his driver's license. His name is Ashton Wilcox."

"Not a Porter."

"Nope."

Garrett took the license and keyed his shoulder mounted mic. "Ten-twenty-seven on one, Ashton Wilcox," included his driver's license number, and continued. "Check any listed next of kin."

Eva Martinez's voice came back with, "Ten-Four. Just give me a sec."

Hearing Eva's voice, who was the three to eleven dispatch, Garrett checked his watch. "Shit. It's after four o'clock, and we have to wait for George to get here. I should'a texted him sooner, but I wanted Clive gone before he got here. By the time we're done here, we won't have much time left before sundown and we don't have a plan for tonight."

Before Ty responded, his cell rang. It was Paige, checking in.

"Hey, sweetheart. How y'all doin'?"

"Good. Are y'all done at the Porter's?"

"Not yet. We're waitin' on George to come and take the bodies."

"When y'all are done, Lola wants you, Mister Ty, Mister Trowa and Father Mike to come out here," Paige said.

"Y'all got a plan?" Garrett asked.

"Not really, but we got some information that might help," Paige said. "We'll need to call Doctor James when y'all get here. Miss Lola thinks he can help get more information, though."

"Okay. I'll gather everyone up and be there as soon as we can."

"Please get here before dark, Daddy."

"I'll do my best, Paige-Turner. I'll do my best. I love you."

"I love you too, Daddy."

As Garrett ended the call, Eva's voice crackled over the radio. "He's clean. No record. For next of kin, I started local. He has a sister in Pine View County named Ashley Wilcox-Porter. Hope that helps."

Garrett keyed the shoulder mic. "Ten-Four. Helps a lot. Thanks, Eva."

"I'm here to help, Sheriff," Eva's voice crackled back.

"Brother-in-law," Ty stated the obvious.

"Yep, and Lola wants us all at her house before sundown."

"They gotta plan?"

"No, but Paige said they have some info that might help. Come on, George," Garrett said impatiently.

"We can speed things up by bringin' the three bodies outta the bunker and all of 'em outside," Ty said.

"Good thinkin', Holmes," Garrett said.

Just as they finished moving the bodies into the backyard, they heard a vehicle coming up the Porter's driveway.

Hoping it was George, and not a concerned neighbor or relative who hadn't been able to reach the Porters all day, Garrett said, "If that's George, have him drive around here. If it's anyone else, use your runnin' back skills and knock 'em on their asses. I'm gonna text Trowa and Father Mike and have Trowa meet us at the church. Then we'll haul ass to Lola's."

"Roger that," Ty said and disappeared around the corner of the house.

Garrett sent the text. He got a ' 👍 ' from Trowa and ' 🙏 ' from Fr. Mike, which he hoped was the priest's version of a 'thumbs up' emoji. A moment later, Ty came back around the corner of the house and George's van drove, slowly, behind him.

George got out of the van and looked at the bodies. "Holy fuck. Six. I'm runnin' outta drawers at the county morgue, Garrett."

"I'm sorry, George," Garrett said. "It is what it is. I don't know what else to tell ya, 'cept we need to bag and load 'em quick. None of us wants to be outside when this fucker starts huntin' again after sundown."

George glanced at the sun that hung low over the surrounding woods. "Okay. Let's get this over with."

Ty's idea of bringing the five bodies outside paid off. That three of the victims were, unfortunately, young, made bagging and loading them easy. Garrett and Ty handled the older boys by themselves, while George handled the young boy by himself. It took two of them to bag and load Ashly and Ashton. Being a big man, it took all three of them to bag and load Hal. All six bodies were bagged and in George's in less than ten minutes.

When George was safely on his way back to the county morgue, Garrett said, "Follow me to the church. You can leave your SUV there."

"I'll be on your ass the whole way," Ty said.

Garrett and Ty got in their SUVs and raced the setting sun to St.

Joseph's Catholic Church.

~ * ~

Paige needed to call her daddy soon, but she had an idea. She wasn't sure if it would work, and she was sure it would be dangerous, but she had a gut feeling she needed to try.

"Can we meditate for a bit?" Paige said. "Not long, though. I need to call Daddy soon."

"Of course we can," Lola said with a warm smile. "I'll get the candles."

Paige took a seat on the living room floor and when Lola placed two shorter blue candles on the floor, she said, "Can I try lightin' my candle the way you light 'em?"

Lola smiled. "I bet ya can. Just hold the wick between your thumb and index finger, concentrate on heat, and snap your fingers."

Paige took the wick of her candle between her thumb and index finger and concentrated on heat. Immediately, she felt heat in her fingertips, but it didn't burn. She snapped her fingers, and the wick caught fire.

"That's so cool." Paige exclaimed.

Lola just smiled. "You really are a natural in all things supernatural, Paige-Turner."

Before Lola could light her candle, Paige, excited by all her new abilities, reached over and lit it for her.

"Showoff," Lala said with a grin.

Paige grinned back. Then they assumed meditative positions.

Paige closed her eyes, cleared her mind, and within seconds, felt herself dissolve into nothingness and everything at the same time. Once again, she was outside the universe, beyond creation with her creator. She was with God again, but her creator wasn't who she wanted to be with. Her plan was to find the vampire's creator.

Her reasoning was simple. If she could meditate to her creator, why couldn't she meditate to the vampire's creator. Paige thought about the souls trapped in the vampires' black auras and felt her perspective shift;

she moved away from her 'place' outside the universe.

As Paige's perspective shifted, she heard the most beautiful voice inside her mind but also everywhere outside the universe, *Fear not, my child. I will be with you.*

Knowing the beautiful voice had been the voice of God, and He would be with her, gave Paige the courage to follow her instinct and search for the vampire's creator. Nothing prepared her for the horrors her destination revealed.

Suddenly, the universe was gone, and Paige became enveloped in darkness. The darkness was blacker than any darkness she'd ever experienced, but somehow, she could see shapes moving in the blackness. They were vile, naked, tortured souls that let off a reddish glow as they swirled around, and through, her. Worse than the darkness and glimpses of the reddish, tortured souls were the sounds. Agonized screams and wails surrounded her; penetrated her. She could hear the snapping sounds of thousands of whips that scourged souls and screams followed. There were also moaning sounds Paige associated with sex. The moans weren't moans of pleasure, though. They were tortured moans. Worse than the screams and wails were the snarls of wicked laughter filling her senses, too. Whatever inflicted the pain surrounding her enjoyed it. It smelled like fire, brimstone and rot. Paige knew she had reached her destination. She had entered hell.

Then the blackness was replaced with reddish-orange glow, and she saw…him. She saw Lucifer, the fallen angel. He was naked and sat on a throne of tortured souls that looked like the agonized visages she'd seen in the vampires' black auras. He was more grotesque than any interpretation she'd ever seen depicting him.

He didn't have a goat's head, cloven feet, or horns. He didn't need those things to be grotesque. Lucifer looked like an enormous man with skin charred black and cracked where, what looked like red lava, blood flowed. He had wings, but they weren't bat wings. They were the boney remains of the angel wings he once had and blackened by the fires swirling around him. His eyes were holes filled with burning embers. When he opened his mouth, Paige saw jagged teeth, as if they'd all been broken, and a long tongue of fire.

"Be gone, Christ child." Lucifer boomed, which made all the other horrors taking place around Paige stop and look her direction.

He can see or sense me. Paige thought.

Lucifer grinned a truly horrific grin and boomed, "Yes. I can see you, Christ child. I will keep you here if you do not leave my domain now."

Paige summoned all the courage she could and shouted, "You can't keep me here. I am a child of Christ. He is with me. Even here, He is with me. He protects me."

Lucifer rose from his tortured soul throne and flapped his bony black wings. When he flapped them, fire filled the gaps between the bony appendages, and he flew toward her at an incredible speed. Paige didn't move. When he was, perhaps, three feet away from her, he slammed into an invisible barrier that, briefly, turned into a blinding white light when he contacted it. He seethed with rage. Paige smiled at him.

"Be gone, Christ child." he roared as fire bellowed from his jagged, toothed mouth and enveloped Paige's protective bubble, which emitted the blinding, white light again.

"No," Paige shouted. "Not until you tell me 'bout the vampire that is after me."

Lucifer chuckled, which caused black smoke to snort from his nostrils. "You cannot compel me, Christ child. Be gone."

Paige thought for a moment and calmly said, "Okay. Maybe I can't compel you, but what about the souls ya have trapped here?"

Lucifer's burning ember eyes widened.

Paige smiled and screamed at the top of her nonextant lungs, "Who created the vampire that is after me? Show yourself."

Lucifer bellowed in rage as the tortured soul of a large, naked woman appeared beside him.

"Are you its creator?" Paige asked.

"Yes," she said, and then screamed in pain as Lucifer raked his long, jagged fingernails down her back.

Paige almost felt sorry for the soul of the woman who, despite Lucifer's tortious reaction to her answer, seemed unable to resist her question. Then she remembered this was the soul of the vampire that created the vampire that took Lin and Mel from her. Not to mention Trevor, Al, and so many others. The sympathy melted away.

Smiling, Paige asked, "What is your name and what is his name?"

"My name is Cipriana Ardelean. His name is Dragoş Văduva," she said and screamed again as the bones from one of Lucifer's wings emerged from her chest in a burst of fire.

"When did you create him?" Paige compelled Cipriana to answer. "How old was he? Where is he from?"

"The year was twelve-hundred and one. He was in his twenty-second season when I created him. We are from Transylvania," Cipriana said with another agonized scream as bones from Lucifer's other wing emerged from her chest in a burst of fire as he ripped her soul in two with a flurry of fire and smoke, but her soul quickly reformed.

Paige felt a tug she couldn't resist. She had more questions, but hell was retreating. Lucifer raised his large, blackened hand and waved. An instant later, she felt the floor beneath her and the fire, brimstone and rot smells were replaced with the spice of Lola's living room.

"By all the Elements," Paige heard Lola say, "what did ya do, chil'?"

Paige felt hot. She opened her eyes and saw her skin blistered and smoking. She could smell her burnt flesh, too. Paige leaned away from Lola and vomited black bile.

"What did ya do, Paige?" Lola urgently asked.

"I went to hell," Paige said before she passed out.

When she came back to consciousness, Lola had her head in her lap, but all her senses were heightened. She was Glinda. She transformed back and looked into Lola's concerned eyes. They locked seeing eyes and Paige showed Lola everything that happened in hell.

"Stupid chil'." Lola said. "Lucky for you, Glinda took over after ya passed out. Without her regenerative abilities, you'd be dead."

Paige sat up, which caused the room to tilt a little. "God was with me while I was in hell, and I knew Glinda would help me when I got back. Easy-peasy."

Lola shook head, which caused her beaded cornrows to click together. "I swear, Paige-Turner. You're gonna give me a heart attack."

"Speakin' of heart attacks," Paige said. "Can we please not tell Daddy I went to hell to get the vampire information?"

"I ought'a tell him just to watch him tan your backside." Lola scolded. "If you were my chil', you'd done been spanked, and good."

"Pretty please, Lola," Paige begged.

Lola hesitated for a moment to make Paige sweat. "Okay, but only if ya promise to never go to hell again."

Paige raised her hand in a boy scout gesture. "I promise. I never wanna see him or that place again."

"Okay. After seein' what ya saw, I believe ya."

"It was so horrible, Lola," Paige said and shuttered. "He was so horrible."

"Good thing ya had help, there and here," Lola said. "To my knowledge, no one has ever been to hell and come back to talk about it. You beat all, Paige-Turner."

"Really?"

"Yes, really. No one but *you* would even think to try it."

"Yeah, but I got pulled out before I could ask Cipriana where he is now."

"She probably wouldn't have known," Lola said. "Everything she tol' ya was stuff that happened before she was destroyed. Now, Lucifer is a different story. This, Dragoş Văduva, is his Earthly henchman. Lucifer would know where he's hidin', but ya couldn't compel him to tell ya."

"No," Paige said defeatedly. "So…all that was for nothin'."

Lola put her warm arm around Paige's healed, cool skin. "That's not the case at all, Paige-Turner. We know his name, who created him, when he was created, and where he's from."

"How does any of that help?"

"Information is power too, chil'," Lola said. "His kind survives on anonymity. The next time he shows his ugly face, and we address him by his name, he'll be more confused than he's been in eight hundred years. Ya know who can use this information to get more information?"

Paige knew who, and she excitedly said, "Doctor James."

"Exactly," Lola said. "Now call your daddy and tell him to come here with Ty, Trowa and Father Mike. Tell 'em to get here before sundown. The ancient knows who all of us are now. At night, there's strength and safety in numbers," Lola told her.

Paige made the call.

~ * ~

Trowa and Fr. Mike were waiting outside the rectory when Garrett and Ty pulled up. Ty parked to the right of Garrett's truck and climbed into the front passenger's seat; Trowa and Fr. Mike climbed into the back seat. Garrett backed out quickly and balled the tires as they hit the asphalt road. The sun had gone from sight. Only an orange glow lit up the western horizon and the almost full moon and stars grew brighter in the purple eastern sky. Time was not on their side.

Chapter Thirteen

Sunset on December 28, 2015, in Pine View County, Texas came at five twenty-three p.m. Zack Zane slept on the embalming room concrete floor, but sleep did not bring him peace. The horrific things he'd seen the Master do to what had been his daughter, and the more horrific things he'd done with what had been his daughter, invaded his dreams like the living nightmare it was. He convulsed on the floor as he slept, like someone suffering an epileptic seizure. He slept until he heard his Master's telepathic command to wake.

Zack sat bolt upright upon hearing the command, but muscles in his arms and legs still spasmed uncontrollably. He willed himself to stand and did. Zack went to the heavy counter and shelf concealing the entrance to his Master's throne room below and easily moved it aside. He backed away as Dragoş, Agrapina, Ilinca, and Lacrima floated up and into the embalming room. Zack averted his gaze from the naked Agrapina, who had been his Melanie in life.

"Look at Agrapina," Dragoş commanded Zack.

Unable to resist the command, Zack did.

"Do you like what you see?" Dragoş asked.

"Yes, Master."

"Shall I have Agrapina ravage your flesh again?" Dragoş said cruelly.

"If that is your wish, Master," Zack said through clinched teeth.

Dragoş laughed his gravely laugh. "Later. Now we must feed and secure my new pet, Vanda. While we are gone, you will sleep and think of new ways to please Agrapina."

"Yes, Master."

"Come, daughters," Dragoş said as he held out his gnarled hands.

Agrapina took Dragoş' right hand, Ilinca his left hand and Lacrima joined hands with Agrapina and Ilinca. A moment later, the four vampires dissolved into a black mist and seeped under the right-side garage door.

They were gone. Zack did as the Master ordered, but this time, his mind wasn't as troubled by the depravities in his dreams. Zack was growing, or devolving, into his master's willing familiar.

~ * ~

It was fully dark by the time Garrett, Ty, Trowa, and Fr. Mike arrived at Lola's house. Their journey after the sunset had been uneventful, though. Garrett parked his SUV next to Lola's pink Cadillac and the four men got out just as Lola opened her front door. They didn't know it, because they had never been a threat and therefore, unable to see the mirage incantation Lola had placed on her property to make it appear dilapidated, but, since the ancient vampire knew where she lived, she had lifted the incantation.

"Come on in, gentlemen," Lola said in her warm, honey voice. "We have important information to share with y'all."

As he walked up the steps, Garrett said, "I'd prefer a plan, but I'll take whatever we can get."

"Well, now I see where Paige gets her impatient nature from," Lola said as she gave Garrett a warm, inviting hug.

She hugged Ty and Trowa as they entered her house. When Fr. Mike extended his hand, Lola brushed it aside and hugged him, too. Despite being a little uncomfortable with the hug, Fr. Mike patted Lola's back awkwardly a few times until she released him. When all four men were inside, Lola looked up at the night sky and, not seeing any sign of the ancient or his cloud, smiled. She closed the door.

"What's this great information y'all got?" Garrett asked.

"Relax, Garrett," Lola said.

Garrett felt the day's tension melt away. "Did ya just nudge me?"

Lola smiled and said, "Just a little. Your tension has your aura in an awful state."

"Damn it, Lola," Garrett said. "We talked about this. If you'd seen the Shanahans and Porters today, you'd be wound tight, too."

Lola shifted her gaze to Ty, and back to Garrett. "Ty's aura isn't in as bad a state as yours, and he was with ya at both families' homes."

Garrett walked over to Paige and wrapped her in a tight hug. "Yeah. Well, the vampire isn't after his daughter."

Paige hugged her daddy tightly. "It's gonna be okay, Daddy."

"I wish I could believe that," Garrett said. "But this fu…bastard is like tryin' to grab smoke."

"Come and sit at the table and we'll tell y'all what we've learned," Lola said as her kitchen door opened and two of her dining room chairs slid into the living room and stopped in front of the dark table.

All of them took a seat around the table, but Fr. Mike, who still wasn't sure how all the supernatural events he'd witnessed configured with his Catholic faith, made the sign of the cross before he sat in one of the, previously, animated chairs. Lola sat in her high-back chair with Paige on her right, Garrett on her left, and Ty directly across from her. Trowa sat on Ty's left and Fr. Mike on Ty's right.

With everyone seated, Lola said, "Garrett, please call James and put him on speaker? He's gonna want to hear this, too."

Garrett took out his phone, placed the call, put it on speaker, and put his phone in the middle of the table. James answered before the second ring.

"Garrett. I've been waitin' to hear from you," James said excitedly. "Please tell me what y'all have been up to."

"I, I mean we, will," Garrett said. "You're on speaker. I'm at Lola's house. She, Paige, Ty, Trowa, and Father Mike are on the call, too."

"Even better," James said. "Tell me everything."

Garrett began, with input from Ty, by telling James about everything that hadn't made it into the newspaper yet. James knew most of it from the local evening news. More accurately, he knew about most of the deaths and missing girls. The Shanahans were mentioned on the local news as a 'crime scene,' but with no details, and the Porters hadn't been mentioned at all. Garrett was so preoccupied with the dogged *Post* reporter, Clair Abbott, and hadn't had time to watch TV, that he forgot about the local evening news.

The Shanahan house was in a neighborhood with lots of curious onlookers. Garrett wasn't surprised to hear it had been mentioned. That no details were available about the Shanahans, and nothing was mentioned about the Porters, meant whoever had been leaking information to the press had gotten no specific information about either set of murders, yet. Garrett took some comfort in that.

He suspected more information would be forthcoming on future broadcasts. Like the news saying goes, 'If it bleeds, it leads.' While there was little bleeding, the vampires saw to that, there had been carnage. To fit these crimes, the press could go with, 'If it's horrific, we will report it.' That was tomorrow's problem. Shitty or not, Garrett was prepared to sacrifice a good man's reputation, Zack Zane, to placate the press.

When Garrett and Ty finished informing James about the physical carnage, Lola and Paige filled him in on all the encounters with the ancient and his cloud. It fascinated him to hear about the vampire's familiar and how Lola had encountered him, twice, and how he had been destroyed. He was especially interested in the black walls protecting the familiar's mind from Lola's intrusion. James had never come across this in any vampire lore, and he made a note of it. He was in awe of how easily Glinda had killed one vampire. James had been fascinated to hear about the vampire victim souls trapped in their black auras. He had read nothing about this in vampire lore either and made another note. It saddened him to hear Zack Zane, the father of the ancient's first cloud member, had become the vampire's new familiar.

After filling James in on all those details, Lola said, "That brings us to today and the new information that Paige and I learned. No one here has heard this yet. Pay close attention, James. I'm countin' on that academic brain of yours to do some research and fill in some gaps."

"I'm all ears and I have a pen and notepad ready to take notes," James said.

Garrett, Ty, Trowa, and Fr. Mike all leaned closer to Lola as she said, "We know his name, the name of his creator, how old he was when he was created, the year he was created, and where he was created."

Together, and talking over each other, Garrett said, "How the hell did y'all get that info?" and James said, "Excellent information. I can work with this. What is it?"

Lola glanced at Paige, then looked at Garrett, and replied, "I found the information through deep meditation."

"It's reliable?" Garrett asked.

With a nod, Lola said, "Very."

"Give me the information." James said.

"His name is Dragoş Văduva. A female vampire named Cipriana Ardelean created him in the year twelve-hundred and one. He was twenty-two years old when he was created. And he is from Transylvania, which is now Romania," Lola told the men.

"Excellent," James said. "Most Excellent. I'll start researchin' his origin tonight."

"Great," Garrett said. "But how does this help us find him?"

"If I may?" Mike said, "I don't know about vampires. In an exorcism, the priest performing the rite must compel the demon to reveal its name to vanquish it."

"Yes. Yes, yes, yes," Ty said. "Knowin' his name may have a similar effect on a vampire."

"It won't," Lola said and dashed Fr. Mike and Ty's enthusiasm.

"Then how *does* it help?" Ty asked.

Before Lola could answer, James said, "This vampire is eight-hundred years old. He likely thrives on the anonymity his age provides. No one remembers the name Dragoş Văduva. If history recorded him at all, which I'll find out tonight, it would just be that he went missin' when he was a young man. Invokin' his name, *and* the name of his creator, will, if nothin' else, catch him off guard. While he's off guard, he'll be vulnerable. How'd I do, Lola?"

The four men looked from the phone to Lola.

She smiled and added, "Very good, James. All I'll add is that Paige and I have a plan if he's momentarily distracted."

The four men looked from Lola to Paige.

"I told ya earlier that I, and Glinda, created earth and wind elementals today, Daddy," Paige said.

"And?" Garrett asked.

"Y'all saw Miss Lola's earthen elementals last night," Paige said. "They're big, but Glinda's are bigger. So, are her wind elementals."

The four men just looked at Paige, but James said, "Are y'all thinkin' of tryin' to trap the vampire in one of Glinda's wind elementals?"

"Yes, we are, James," Lola said with a warm smile on her face. "You certainly are the brightest human bulb in the conversation."

"Well, to be fair," James said with feigned humility. "I have a doctorate, and supernatural folklore is what I specialize in."

"There's more," Lola said. "I can use my wind elementals to scatter his three cloud members. He'll be trapped and isolated."

"What then?" Mike asked.

"Well," Lola said, "if we can keep him trapped in Glinda's wind elemental, and I can scatter his cloud, I can conjure a fire elemental and add it to Glinda's air elemental."

"Excellent. Fire will disable the vampire," James shouted. "He's head will still need to be severed, his heart pierced with a silver tipped steak, his body dismembered, and his body parts exposed to the sun. Will Glinda's air put your fire elemental out, Lola?"

"I don't know," Lola admitted. "We didn't practice that today. We should've, but we didn't,"

"Practice it now," Ty said.

Lola shook her head and the beads in her hair clicked together. "We can't. I scanned the sky for 'em when y'all came in. I didn't see 'em, but we can't be sure *he* wouldn't see somethin' like that in the night sky, from wherever he is tonight. We can't afford to tip him off before we try it."

"What do we do tonight?" Garrett said. "Wait for him to find us?"

"He knows where we are, Garrett," Lola said. "He doesn't have to *find* us, but there's a good chance he'll show up here at some point tonight."

"Or," Paige said, "we go on offense."

"Not if it's dangerous for you and Glinda," Garrett said.

"Everything about this ancient is dangerous for Paige and Glinda," Lola reminded Garrett. "Even waitin' here."

Garrett let out a heavy sigh. "I hate this. What ya got in mind, Paige-Turner?"

"Paige never met the vampire's old familiar and couldn't track him, but she knows Zack," Lola answered Garrett's question. "Glinda might be able to track *him* to the vampire's lair."

Garrett looked at Paige, his pride and joy, the person he loved most in the world. "Is this what ya wanna do, pretty girl?"

Paige nodded. "It is, Daddy."

"Okay then," Garrett told Paige and the others. "As much as I hate it, I'm ridin' Glinda's back with my radio, so I can give y'all directions to where we're goin'."

"Excellent. I'll get busy researchin' what I can find out about Dragoş Văduva and Cipriana Ardelean," James said, and hung up.

Garrett grabbed his phone and put it in his chest pocket. "You're drivin' my SUV, Ty."

With a smile, Lola said, "Will I be ridin' in the back between Trowa and Father Mike?"

"Shotgun." Fr. Mike shouted. "No offense, Lola."

"None taken, Father Mike," Lola said with a warm smile. "Trowa is enough man to keep me happy."

Trowa, who was the only one who hadn't said a word throughout the conversations, blushed.

Garrett stood. "Alright. Let's get gone."

~ * ~

Clive Jones was home and eating supper with his mom, Kelly. She was an excellent cook, and they were enjoying homemade venison stew. Clive mopped up some gravy with buttered cornbread. The TV was on in the living room, which was visible from the small dining room. The evening news was on, but Clive wasn't really listening. All his attention was on the large bowl of venison stew in front of him. When he heard the pretty news lady mention another set of unsolved murders in Pine View, he turned to look at the TV.

The pretty news lady, Clive didn't know her name, reported about a family in Pine View proper named the Shanahans. Clive, dimwitted as he was, knew this hadn't been the family he'd found. He waited to see if she mentioned the Porters. She didn't.

Clive had kept the promise he made with Garrett and had mentioned nothing about the Porters to his mom. He remembered Garrett said they had a suspect, but they hadn't found him yet. Clive reckoned, whoever the suspect was, he wouldn't be hiding out in Pine View, where Garrett, or the Pine View PD, could more easily find him. The suspect would hide, camp, somewhere in the woods. It never crossed his mind the suspect might have fled East Texas after killing the Porters. He was certain the suspect was camped out in the woods. After poaching since he last got out of prison, Clive reckoned few people knew the woods in Pine View County better than he did. Finally, Clive reckoned capturing the suspect, and turning him in, would go a long way in rehabilitating his reputation in Pine View.

That Garrett hadn't mentioned the suspect's name, or even described him, never crossed Clive's dimwitted mind. All Clive thought about was, for once, being the hero, not the villain. Clive mopped up the last of the stew gravy with a large piece of buttered cornbread, stuffed it in his large, skeleton tattooed mouth, and got up from the table, still chewing.

"Where you headin'?" Kelly asked.

Muffled by the mouthful of cornbread, Clive said, "Huntin'."

"You know how I feel 'bout ya huntin' illegally, Clive," Kelly said. "If ya get caught huntin' at night, that's just one more charge the law can tack onto your time back in prison."

Clive swallowed the cornbread. "Don't worry, Mom. This time I'll be helpin' the law."

"By poachin' at night?" Kelly asked.

"I ain't huntin' deer tonight, Mom."

Worried, Kelly said, "What in the world are ya huntin'?"

Clive pointed at the TV. "The guy that's been killin' folks and takin' girls in Pine View."

Kelly laughed. "What makes ya think ya can find him?"

"I know more 'bout this than ya think, Mom."

"How? What'a ya know?"

"Can't say," Clive said.

"Why not?"

"'Cause I made a promise and I mean to keep it."

"Don't be silly. Sit down and watch *Wheel of Fortune* with me,

Clive."

"Can't," Clive said as he pulled his dad's .308, which had a night-vision scope from the gun rack.

"Please don't do this, Clive."

"I gotta, Mom. If I can catch this guy, folks in Pine View might not hate me so much."

"It don't matter what they think," Kelly said.

"Does to me. Gotta go," Clive said as he put on his heavy camo jacket, shouldered the .308, and stepped out into the chilly night air.

~ * ~

After seeping out from under the funeral home garage door as a black mist, Dragoş and his cloud rematerialized, transformed into their human-bat hybrid shapes, and took flight. Without Antanasia's awkwardness, they quickly flew high above Pine View in the freezing air.

Are we going after Vanda now, Father? Lacrima thought to Dragoş.

Not yet, Dragoş thought to his daughters. *We fed well last night, but we need more nourishment before confronting Vanda and the* vrăjitoare,

Are not they both vrăjitoare *now, Father?* Ilinca dared to think.

Ilinca was correct, but the thought made Dragoş seethe with anger. Because he always expressed anger with acts of violence, Dragoş raked his jagged claws across Ilinca's beautiful face. The action left four ragged slashes on Ilinca's left cheek, and black blood oozed from them. Unlike Antanasia, who would have lost concentration and fallen from the sky, Ilinca maintained flight. She kept her thoughts to herself afterward.

After flying in silence for a few moments after Dragoş' attack on Ilinca, Agrapina thought, *I know where we can feed, Father. The man and woman from my first feeding are still alive. Will two adults be enough nourishment, Father?*

An evil grin spread across Dragoş' hideous man-bat hybrid face and he thought to his daughters, *Yes, my first daughter. They will suffice nicely.*

Deftly, Dragoş dropped his right wing, which caused his flight to bank left, and flew toward the trailer house where Agrapina had fed for the first time on a young boy. His daughters, his cloud, fell in behind him as the many lights of Pine View receded and the speckled lights from rural homes in Pine View County came into view.

~ * ~

Once everyone was outside Lola's house, and she had closed the door, put a warding incantation on it, and all entrances to her house, Lola said, "Okay, gentlemen. Turn around while Paige transforms into Glinda."

They did.

Paige, who had shredded her beloved Minion T-shirt, that had belonged to Justin, the night before when she, quickly, and without thought, turned into Glinda to confront the ancient at the Zane's house, wore one of Lola's least revealing dresses. It was big on her, but the only option for quick transformations. Having to remove shoes, socks, pants, shirt, underwear and bra, would take too long. Or she'd have to shred them, too. Paige removed the oversized dress, handed it to Lola, and transformed into Glinda. Lola's porch squeaked loudly under Glinda's substantial weight. Not wanting to put a hole in Lola's porch, Glinda stepped off the porch and onto the still wet grass.

"Y'all can turn around now," Lola told them.

All four men heard the porch squeak in protest under Glinda's weight, but they waited for the okay from Lola before they turned around. When they did, they looked up at the massive, silver-haired werewolf with one emerald green eye and one silver, seeing eye. Fr. Mike was the only one who took an involuntary step back, away from Glinda. He knew there was no evil in Glinda, but the sight of her still unnerved him.

"Can ya smell Mister Zack?" Garrett asked.

Glinda tilted her head back and sniffed the air with her long snout. She turned her massive head in different directions and took in deep breaths. After a few moments, Glinda looked back at Garrett and shook her head.

"Damn it." Garrett shouted.

"Calm down," Lola said to Garrett.

To Glinda, Lola said, "To become a familiar, Zack has drunk the ancient's blood. This will change his physiology, but he's a new familiar. Part of who he was remains. For now, but it's faint. You'll need to be closer to him to smell who he was. Ya need to follow your instinct and search until you're close enough to catch his fadin' scent."

Glinda nodded in agreement.

Garrett said, "This is nothin' more than a wild goose chase. A literal shot in the dark."

Lola smiled and said, "Paige and Glinda have remarkable instincts, Garrett. You know this."

"Yeah. I know that," Garrett said in response. "But it's colder than a witch's tit, no offense, out here and I'm just gonna ride around on Glinda on the off chance she gets close enough to Zack to smell what's left of his...humanness?"

"Trust her, Garrett," Lola said.

Garrett looked up at Glinda. "Do ya think ya can find him?"

Glinda nodded her massive head.

"Okay, then. Let me on your back."

Lola handed Garrett the dress. "You'll need this if Glinda needs to change back into Paige. Unless you're finally comfortable seein' Paige naked."

Garrett took the dress from Lola and replied, "I'm not. I probably never will."

Lola smiled at Garrett.

Glinda went down on all four feet and Garrett climbed onto her broad back.

"No sense in y'all drivin' around unless...until Glinda picks up Zack's scent," Garrett said. "If, when, she does, I'll radio y'all a location. So, stay here 'til I do."

Lola smiled her warm, honey smile. "I'll take good care of 'em *until* ya radio us, Garrett."

Garrett pulled the collar up on his heavy uniform jacket. "Okay, Glinda. Do your thing."

Glinda sniffed the air and took off at a slow run to the south of

Lola's house.

As Garrett and Glinda disappeared into the dark woods, Mike said, "Do you really think Glinda can find Mister Zane?"

"Yes," Trowa spoke for the first time. "She will."

With that said, the three men and Lola went back inside her house.

~ * ~

Clive made his way quickly through the woods, looking for any signs of current or recent camp sites. Despite his size, Clive moved quietly through the underbrush and fallen leaves at a brisk pace. Regular deer hunting with his dad when he was younger, and his more recent poaching activities had taught him how to move quietly. Even in the dark. He used his nose, too, trying to catch the scent of smoke from a campfire. This proved to be inefficient. The first blue norther had blown in, which dropped temperatures below freezing for the first time that winter, and many folks had fires burning in their fireplaces. Undeterred, Clive continued to search.

~ * ~

Glinda moved silently, more silently than Clive, at a slow run through the woods, sniffing the air, trying to catch the human scent of what remained of Zack Zane.

Garrett, although he occasionally complained about the cold, kept, mostly, quiet and let Glinda hunt.

About forty-five minutes into the venture, Garrett said, "What'a say we call it a night and try again tomorrow, Glinda?"

Glinda shook her massive head.

"C'mon, Glinda. It'll be warmer *and* safer to do this tomorrow durin' the day. What if the vampire finds us alone out here?"

Just then, Glinda caught a faint scent of Zack. She didn't burst into a full run immediately, for fear of throwing her daddy off her back, but she picked up her pace in a determined way.

"Ya got somethin'?" Garrett asked.

Glinda nodded her head.

Garrett firmly grabbed her silky silver fur with one hand. "Go."

With his free hand, he pressed the shoulder mounted mic. "Glinda picked up a scent. We're south of Lola's, but Glinda is headin' east now."

Glinda waited until after her daddy had made the radio call and had both hands tightly gripped to her fur before taking off at a dead run.

Ty's voice crackled over the radio. "Roger that. We'll load up and head southeast."

Garrett couldn't respond. He hung on with both hands for dear life, but he, as always, enjoyed the experience of how easily, and deftly, Glinda maneuvered through the trees and leapt deadfalls and streams with ease. Garrett wasn't ready for the sudden stop Glinda made and got thrown from her back. He landed in an awkward roll on the ground with two fistfuls of silver fur.

~ * ~

Troy and Penny Henderson were in their trailer house. They sat on the couch, holding each other close. *Wheel of Fortune* was on the TV. But the TV was muted, and neither had really been watching it. They had buried their three-year-old son, Trevor, that morning. His favorite stuffed toy, Toothless from the movie *How to Train Your Dragon*, had been placed in the tiny coffin with him. What the Hendersons looked at silently was the fake Christmas tree that still had Trevor's unopened gifts beneath it, and a shiny, new, red tricycle with a red bow on the handlebars parked in front of it. A loaded shotgun leaned against the couch on the side where Troy sat. He was ready if whoever had killed Trevor came back. He couldn't know how soon it would happen or how ineffectual a shotgun would be against the monster who killed his son.

Dragoş and his daughters hovered above the Henderson's trailer house. He could feel the despair coming from the child's adults below and he fed on it like mana from hell. Because he thought it cruel irony, he sent Agrapina, who had drunk their young son's life away, down to secure their invitation inside the pitiful excuse of a dwelling.

Agrapina softly landed on the front deck, changed back into her human form, and knocked on the door.

Inside, a man said, "Who's there? I have a gun and I'll fuckin' use it."

"My name wa...is Melanie Zane. I need help." Agrapina said.

"That's the girl who went missin' the night before Trev... Let her in," a woman inside said.

Troy clicked the deadbolt lock open, lowered his shotgun, opened the door, and in a surprised voice, said, "Holy crap. She's naked."

"Then she's freezin', Troy. Let her in," Penny said.

"Can we come in?" Agrapina asked.

Too stunned to catch the plural "we," Troy said, "Of course. Come in before ya die of exposure."

Dragoş, Ilinca, and Lacrima heard the invitation and descended onto the deck immediately.

"What the fuck." Troy yelled as he raised his shotgun, but it was too late.

The four vampires swept into the small living room like a pride of lions on two crippled gazelles.

Agrapina began to sink her fangs into Troy's neck when Dragoş said, "Not so fast, daughter. I think our nourishment should know what happened to their progeny before we take their lives and souls."

Agrapina smiled and hissed, "I was the one who drank the life blood from your little boy. He screamed in fear for his mommy and daddy before I took his life and soul."

Penny, who was being held on the couch by Ilinca and Lacrima, screamed, "Y'all are monsters."

Dragoş, who had still been in man-bat hybrid form, smiled a truly hideous smile, and declared, "We are so much more than that, my dear lady. As you can see, I also give everlasting existence to beautiful young women. I also bring relief to tortured humans such as yourselves. Do you not want to join your progeny? Or would you prefer to remain in this...hovel, missing him for the rest of what, I am sure, would have been long, miserable lives?"

Dragoş hadn't mesmerized the humans. He wanted to enjoy their fear and hate, so it did not surprise him when the man shouted, "Fuck y'all right back to hell," and spit in Agrapina's face.

Dragoş nodded to Agrapina, who immediately sank her fangs into the man's neck. Dragoş took the man's right arm and sank his fangs into his inner upper arm. On the couch, Lacrima sank her fangs into the woman's neck as Ilinca sank her fangs into the woman's inner upper left arm. They fed. As they did, the four ragged slashes on Ilinca's left cheek Dragoş had put there in a fit of anger slowly closed.

~ * ~

When Garrett got up after being thrown from Glinda, he looked and saw Paige standing a few feet away. Even though it was nighttime, the moon was almost full, and Garrett saw more of her than he was comfortable seeing.

Garrett tossed Paige the dress. "What the hell, Paige. Put that on."

Paige caught the dress, and held it in front of her to ease her daddy's discomfort. "No time, Daddy."

"Do ya have Zack's scent or not?"

"I do. But…" Paige began.

"Then transform back and let's go get him," Garrett interrupted.

"No. Listen to me, Daddy," Paige shouted. "The vampires are at the Henderson's. Trevor's parents' house."

"How? Never mind. Transform back, but don't haul ass until I radio Ty and the others."

A second later, Glinda towered over Garrett.

Garrett grabbed the dress, climbed on Glinda's back, and pushed the button on his shoulder mic. "The vampires are at the Henderson's house, Ty. Ya know the way. Get there ASAP."

"Roger that," Ty's voice crackled back.

Garrett grabbed new handfuls of Glinda's silky silver fur and shouted, "Go."

Glinda took off at a dead run, which, for her, was over sixty miles per hour. Garrett held on for dear life and hoped, since Glinda, somehow, knew the vampires were at the Henderson's, they were close.

~ * ~

Dragoş listened closely to the man's heart as it quickly slowed. Two vampires feeding from the same host drained them quickly. He wasn't worried about his daughters, especially since losing Antanasia, who had been a slow learner. Dragoş knew they knew when to stop. He had taught them well.

Just before the man's heart stopped, and he and Agrapina stopped feeding, he sensed, more than heard, the silver-haired werewolf approaching. Approaching quickly.

Dragoş withdrew his fangs and bellowed, "Vanda is coming."

His three daughters stopped feeding as Troy and Penny Henderson died.

~ * ~

About half a mile from the Henderson's house, Glinda stopped.

"C'mon. Let's go." Garrett shouted.

Glinda shook her head.

"You're not goin' in alone." Garrett shouted.

Glinda did the only thing she could without forcefully removing her daddy. She changed back into Paige.

Garrett felt Glinda disappear from beneath him. He landed on his feet and looked down at Paige on her hands and knees. It was awkward, but, at least, he couldn't see any of her girl parts. Until Paige crawled out from between his legs and a second full moon came into view.

Without getting up, Paige looked over her shoulder at him. "Sorry, Daddy. It's too dangerous for you to be on Glinda's back when she does what she has to do."

"Paige…" Garrett protested, but Paige transformed quickly, and Glinda sped away before he could get another word out.

Garrett ran in the direction Glinda went. With his flashlight, it wasn't hard to follow her path. Broken tree limbs and trampled underbrush showed the way.

~ * ~

Glinda cleared the woods surrounding the Henderson's house within thirty seconds. She didn't slow down as she leapt onto the big front porch and crashed through the thin aluminum front door. She saw him in his man-bat hybrid form. He looked ready for her, but Glinda didn't care. As she launched past who had been her friend Melanie, Glinda reached out her massive, and deadly, right hand and ripped her head off. The ancient bellowed as he saw his first daughter destroyed. Glinda did her best to smile with her werewolf snout.

With tremendous force, Glinda collided into the ancient and was more than a little surprised when he didn't crash to the ground beneath her substantial size, strength, and weight. It propelled him back, but only a foot or two as the talons on his man-bat feet dug deeply into the particleboard beneath the thin carpet. It was his turn to smile with a repugnant, man-bat mouth full of bloody, jagged teeth.

Dragoş grabbed Glinda by the throat with impossibly powerful hands, flapped his leathery wings, and lifted her from the floor. As he did this, he sent a mental command to Ilinca and Lacrima, who flew from the couch where the dead woman was still between them, and each grabbed one of Glinda's arms. To her surprise, Glinda *heard* Dragoş' mental command.

The surprise of hearing it caught her so off guard she didn't react quickly enough to stop the two vampires, who she also knew Dragoş had renamed Ilinca, who had been Lin, and Lacrima, who had been Taylor. Somehow, she also knew the vampire she just killed had been Melanie, who Dragoş renamed Agrapina, and the vampire she killed the night before, at the Zane's, was Megan and renamed Antanasia. Glinda was in Dragoş' mind.

Glinda was immobilized. Dragoş laughed a gravely laugh and snarled, "Stupid girl. Did you really think someone as young as you stood a chance against me?"

Even though Paige had gotten pretty good at speaking through Glinda, she didn't like to. She didn't like the way her voice sounded coming out of the werewolf's mouth, but she had to try something. The vampire holding Glinda's, right arm, who, even though was in woman-bat hybrid form, didn't hold that arm as tightly as the one holding her left arm. Glinda knew the one holding her right arm was Lin. She knew because she saw it in Dragoş' mind.

As the ancient brought his deadly mouth toward her neck, through gritted fangs, and with a voice sounding like a menacing growl, Glinda said, "I know who you are, Dragoş Văduva."

Surprised beyond anything he thought imaginable, Dragoş pulled his head back, looked into Glinda's green and silver eyes with his wide, bat-like eyes. "This cannot be. How can you know this?"

Glinda did her best to beam and snarled, "Oh, it be, *bitch*. I met your creator, Cipriana Ardelean, in hell. Where even Lucifer couldn't harm me. Did you really think someone as old as you stood a chance against me?"

Dragoş hissed and tried to bite Glinda's neck again. As his horrid face drew near, Glinda felt the grip on her right arm loosen more. She ripped her arm free, which sent Ilinca flying across the room where she crashed into the Christmas tree and fell to the ground in a daze. Glinda brought her massive, clawed hand down on top of Dragoş' man-bat head, hard. This time he crashed to the ground and released the death grip he had on Glinda's neck as he did.

Glinda quickly threw Lacrima across the room, too. The force behind this movement had been so great that Lacrima smashed through the trailer's back wall and disappeared from sight. Glinda looked down at Dragoş with more savage hatred than she'd ever experienced as a werewolf. His man-bat face had four deep claw marks from the top of his head down to his cheeks. Black blood ran freely from the wounds.

He flapped his giant wings to take flight, but Glinda stomped her left foot down on the vampire's right wing before he could get up and pinned him to the floor. She took great satisfaction when she heard, and felt, bones in the vampire's wing crunch as they broke.

Dragoş looked up at Glinda with measured, savage hatred. Glinda opened her enormous jaws and prepared to put an end to him by squishing his man-bat head between her dagger length fangs like a rotten grape. Just before her jaws closed over his head, Dragoş smiled and dematerialized into a black mist that, quickly, swept out of the hole Lacrima's body had made. Enraged, Glinda howled. She looked at Ilinca, who had gotten to her feet.

Afraid, Ilinca tried to take flight. Suddenly, the massive werewolf disappeared, and Paige stood there. Ilinca paused.

"Lin. I know part of ya, a spark, is still in there. Lola and Father Mike think they can help ya. Don't go." Paige pleaded with her best friend.

Ilinca hesitated a moment longer. A black tear oozed from each of her bat-like eyes. She shook her head, sadly, and flew out of the same hole Lacrima and Dragoş had disappeared through.

Tears came hard. Paige's knees gave out, and she fell to the floor, sobbing for her best friend.

~ * ~

Garrett followed the path as quickly as he could. When he heard the unmistakable sound of Glinda's crashing entrance, he took off at a dead run. In short time, he saw lights through the trees and heard another load crash that made the exterior lights on the trailer house move on its wheeled foundation. A moment later, he was clear of the woods and ran toward the trailer house as fast as he could. In the distance, he heard a siren and knew Ty was close. He heard Glinda howl.

Garrett cleared the front porch steps in one leap and bolted through the hole Glinda made where the front door had been. When he saw Paige crying on the floor, he thought she was hurt. Without a care about her nakedness, he slid to the floor on his knees and wrapped Paige in a tight hug.

"Are ya hurt, sweetheart?"

"No. Not physically," Paige said through hitching sobs. "I saw Lin. I talked to her. I told her we thought we could help her. She left, but she was cryin'. Lin was cryin', Daddy."

Garrett held her tighter and rocked her gently while she cried.

~ * ~

Ty had the accelerator of Garrett's SUV pressed to the floorboard. He drove the curvy and hilly back roads at breakneck speed. The needle of the speedometer drifted between ninety-five and one hundred miles per hour, depending on the curve he took. They were close; less than two miles away. He had to get there. He had to help.

Lola reached over, placed her soft, and warm hand on Ty's forearm. "Ya can slow down now. The vampires are gone, Troy and Penny are dead, Garrett is there and unharmed, and Paige and Glinda are...okay."

Ty slowed the SUV to seventy, which was fifteen miles faster than the posted limit. "Ya hesitated before ya said Paige and Glinda are okay. *Are* they okay?

"Physically, they are unharmed," Lola said. "The pain Paige is experiencin' is emotional. I can help her with that, but I doubt the stubborn chil' will let me."

Ty saw the driveway to the Henderson's house on the left. He slowed and made the turn without kicking up dirt. He trusted Lola. A moment later, the SUV's headlights lit up the front of the trailer house and they saw the hole where the front door had been.

Lola chuckled. "Glinda sure knows how to make an entrance."

Ty parked next to Troy's truck, turned off the siren, and everyone got out.

~ * ~

Dragoş, Ilinca, and Lacrima concealed themselves in the woods behind the human's poor excuse of a home. Dragoş seethed with more rage, confusion, and pain than he'd experienced in eight-hundred years of undead existence. The rage was fueled by having his prize, Vanda, so close to being his, only to lose her again, and by her cockiness. She had called him a bitch. The insolence was unacceptable.

Confusion came knowing Vanda had, impossibly, found out his name and the name of his creator. No one on this plane of existence had uttered his name in over seven-hundred and fifty years. The only place Vanda could have discovered his true identity would have been in hell. How someone so young could have visited hell and lived to talk about it was beyond his substantial comprehension. The source of the pain was obvious. His man-bat face had four deep slashes from the werewolf's deadly claws and his right wing was broken.

Dragoș desperately wanted to go back inside and get Vanda, who, he knew from her crying, was back in human form. He was too injured to do it himself. Unlike werewolves that can regenerate with a transformation, vampires needed to feed to regenerate. After the werewolf had killed Agrapina and rid itself of Ilinca and Lacrima so easily, he didn't trust them to do it alone; he knew the girl could transform back into the silver-haired werewolf instantly. That would mean certain destruction for them.

Dragoș was incapable of affection, but they were fun to play with, so he wanted to keep them around until he secured his prize, Vanda. Finally, he could hear the fast-approaching siren and he knew the vile, older *vrăjitoare* was coming. The holy man, too. He was too weak to confront them.

Trying to hide the confusion and pain, Dragoș said, "Come, my daughters. I must feed to regain my strength."

"Can you fly, Father?" Lacrima asked.

Fighting off the urge to lash out at Lacrima, Dragoș said, "I cannot. The silver-haired beast broke my right wing. We must hunt as mist. When we find sustenance, the two of you must mesmerize my prey before I can feed."

"Yes, Father," Ilinca and Lacrima said together.

Ilinca and Lacrima supported Dragoș as they evaporated into black mist and drifted away through the woods. If Dragoș hadn't been so preoccupied with his own turmoil, he would have sensed Ilinca's treachery of loosening her grip on the werewolf's arm and the hesitation and grief she felt at leaving her former friend. If he had, he'd have been down to one daughter. The beautiful and natural vampire, Lacrima. But he didn't.

~ * ~

Garrett heard the siren turn off and the doors of the SUV open and close. He still held and rocked Paige in his arms. Her deep sobs had dwindled to tears and sniffles.

"Do ya want me to send Lola in, Paige-Turner?"

"Yes, please," Paige sobbed. "Thank you, Daddy."

Garrett got up and dropped the dress on the floor beside Paige. Not that she'd need it with Lola and went outside to meet his friends.

Once outside, Garrett said, "She wants to see you, Lola."

Lola smiled and disappeared into the hole Glinda had made while Ty, Trowa, and Fr. Mike asked questions Garrett couldn't answer.

Lola sat down beside Paige and put her arms around her in a tight hug. "Show me what happened."

Paige felt Lola's mental intrusion and welcomed it. She showed her everything that happened since she left her daddy behind to when the vampire who had been Lin left with black tears on her woman-bat, hybrid face.

When she finished, Paige said, "I'm sorry I used his, and his creator's, names. I know that probably messed up our future plan."

"Nonsense," Lola said. "Invokin' his name is the only reason you're still here and not one of his cloud *and* his familiar. You used your instinct, and ya were right to do so. Always follow your instincts, Paige-Turner."

"He was so strong, Lola. I can't believe how easily he handled Glinda."

"Okay. Let me backtrack a bit," Lola said. "Invokin' his name was the right thing to do. Ya followed your instinct on that. Facin' him alone, when he had three vampires with him, was stupid. I tol' ya, a vampire his age would have some tricks up his vile sleeves, but I wouldn't have believed he was strong enough to withstand the full force of Glinda, either.

"This is where you and Glinda need to be smart," Lola explained. "Don't let rage overpower instinct and reason. But we learned two things that are very important from this encounter, Paige-Turner."

"What's that?" Paige asked.

"First, ya heard his command and knew the names he'd given his cloud members."

"How's that important?"

"Pure sight, Paige-Turner. Ya didn't have to see through the black vault surroundin' his mind like I did. You were in his mind with no trouble at all."

"Okay. But I didn't see anything else," Paige said.

"That's 'cause ya weren't lookin' for anything else. Next time you or Glinda encounter him, but not on your own, ya can see whatever ever ya want to in his mind."

"Like what?"

"Oh, I don't know," Lola said. "How 'bout seein' where his daytime restin' place is, for starters."

"Crap. I should'a done that tonight."

"Ya didn't have time, Paige-Turner," Lola said. "Tonight, ya did what ya had to do to survive. Now I believe ya truly have pure sight."

"That's good to know. But you said we learned *two* important things. What's the second?"

"The second is, as strong as he is, he still needed help from two other vampires to bite ya," Lola said. "That means, one on one, Glinda is stronger than he is."

Paige smiled, but the smile disappeared. "What about Lin?"

"That's good news too, chil'."

"How? She left."

"She had to leave," Lola said. "That ancient still commands her. That she loosened her grip on Glinda's arm, hesitated before leavin', and that she cried is all proof that part of Lin, her spark, is still inside her. Now, more than ever, I believe we can save her."

"If Dragoş still commands her, how do we get her away from him to try?

"We kill his ugly ass, and Taylor Shanahan, first. Once Lin is alone, we can deal with her."

"Ya really think so?"

Lola smiled her warm, honey smile. "I know so. Now put this dress on so we can go outside without givin' the men heart attacks."

Paige put the dress on and followed Lola onto the front porch. Questions came and Paige told them everything that happened.

When she finished, Garrett said, "What now? Do we still go after Zack?"

Lola shook her head, and the beads clicked. "I think Paige and Glinda have been through enough tonight. Best we head back to my place and let her, them, rest."

"Can Glinda find Zack tomorrow?" Ty asked.

"Yeah," Paige said. "She knows his scent now. Daddy was right earlier when he said findin' Mister Zack in the daylight would be safer. Glinda can catch his scent tomorrow."

"What about the Hendersons?" Mike asked.

"Well, that's the worst part 'bout this, Father Mike," Garrett said. "There's no way for us to explain why we're here. We can't say Glinda sniffed out vampires. Just like with the other victims, we'll have to wait for someone to discover their bodies and call it in."

Frustrated, Fr. Mike kicked at a slightly raised board on the deck and announced, "I know they weren't Catholic, but…may I bless them before we leave?"

"Ya can," Lola said. "But it won't do any good. Their souls are trapped in the vampires' auras until we kill 'em."

"I'm going to, anyway," Mike said as he stepped through the hole where the front door had been.

Paige smiled the first genuine smile all night. "Glinda killed Agrapina. Does that mean Trevor's soul is free?"

Lola put her warm arm around Paige's shoulders. "It sure does, chil'."

"Wait," Garrett said. "Who's Agrapina?"

Paige had forgotten to mention the names Dragoş gave his cloud members, so she explained that part of what happened, too.

"So, that means Lin and Taylor Shanahan are the only two cloud members he has left?" Garrett asked.

"Yeah," Paige answered.

"Does that mean he'll try to turn some more young girls to replenish his cloud?" Ty asked.

"He will. But I doubt he'll do it tonight," Lola answered.

"How can you be sure?" Fr. Mike, who had blessed the Hendersons and rejoined the group, asked.

"I'm not sure," Lola said. "But he's weak and confused. In all his years, he's never encountered the likes of our Glinda before."

"He's supernatural, like Glinda," Ty said. "Can't he regenerate like her, too?"

"No," Lola said. "The only way a vampire can regenerate is by feedin'."

"That means he's gonna kill someone tonight," Garrett stated flatly.

"I'm afraid so," Lola said.

Angered by this news, Mike said, "And we can't stop him?"

"No," Lola said. "All we can do tonight is go home and get some rest."

Defeated, Mike said, "He'll take an innocent soul tonight and we can't do anything about it."

"Not tonight," Lola said. "When we kill the ancient vampire, it will flood your heaven with thousands of innocent souls that he has taken over the last eight-hundred years. Take comfort in that, Father Mike."

Fr. Mike nodded. "I guess I'll have to."

The six of them, quietly, no more words needed to be spoken, got in Garrett's SUV. Paige road shotgun and Lola got to squeeze in between Ty and Trowa in the back seat; Fr. Mike sat, cramped, between Ty and the door. They drove away from the Henderson's trailer house to await a call Garrett, Ty, and Trowa knew would come, but dreaded to get.

~ * ~

Clive continued to creep through the woods and look for signs of a fresh camp or a person who shouldn't be there. He came across one deserted camp, but it was large. He saw tent stake hole remains from three tents. The firepit was large and expertly put out with several shovels of dirt, to ensure it wouldn't flare back up and cause a forest fire.

Clive was in prison during the summer of 2011 when a drought had dried the East Texas woods to kindling and several thousands of wooded acres had burned to the ground. As the last days of 2015 ended, the drought had been over for almost four years. But responsible hunters were still careful. Clive moved on from that camp and continued to search.

He was sure he could find the killer and rehabilitate his reputation.

About thirty minutes after he left the camp, Clive's blood ran cold at the sound of a lone, sorrowful howl. It sounded close. Too close. Even though Clive wasn't one of the Pine View folks who still whispered about werewolves doing all the killings the previous summer, the same type of folks who thought he was a devil worshiper, and he wasn't, something about the howl made the hair on the back of his neck and arms tingle. Although dimwitted, after hearing the howl, Clive decided to go home and let the law track down the killer. His mom was right. It didn't matter what the folks in Pine View thought of him.

Clive turned to head home and looked at two beautiful, and very naked, girls. They reminded him of the time he'd worked at Glitter Galore. Instead of their naked flesh being covered in glitter, it was porcelain white, to the point of being almost translucent. Clive couldn't help but smile his skeletal tattoo smile. When the one who had scarlet hair eyes flashed silver, and she told him to drop his gun, he did.

~ * ~

Dragoş, Ilinca, and Lacrima seeped through the thick underbrush in black mist form to find nourishment for Dragoş. They didn't have to look long. To Dragoş' pleasant surprise, they found a large, lone man who would supply more than enough sustenance to fully regenerate him. They transformed back into their human bodies. Dragoş instructed Ilinca and Lacrima to mesmerize the man, have him undress, and bring him to his weakened body. Despite the rage, confusion, and pain Dragoş experienced, he smiled as he watched the perfection of his daughters' naked flesh as they stepped out of the woods and confronted the large man.

Lacrima easily mesmerized the large man's feeble mind, and he dropped his gun when she told him to. He also willingly undressed when she instructed him to do so. Ilinca giggled when the large man was naked, but a quick, mental scolding from Dragoş was all it took to quiet her. Lacrima held out her hand and the large man took it. She led him into the woods where her injured father waited.

Dragoş would have enjoyed lifting Lacrima's mezmery and

feeding off the human's fear, too. But he was too weak to try. When the human was near him, Dragoş sank his fangs into the large human's upper right thigh and drank deeply from the large femoral artery. As he drank the human's life and soul away, his wounds healed.

Ilinca and Lacrima easily held the large man upright when his knees buckled from lack of blood. Just before the human died, Dragoş stopped feeding, and Ilinca and Lacrima released the firm hold they had on him. His large body fell to the ground with a thud, as a final plume of warm air escaped his body, and he died.

~ * ~

Clive felt pain high on his right leg, but he didn't look down to see the source of the pain. His eyes were locked on the crystal, blue eyes of the scarlet-haired beauty who looked into his brown eyes. He felt himself getting weaker, so weak he couldn't stand. The two naked girls held him upright, though. His vision faded. He looked at the scarlet-haired beauty until he could no longer see.

He felt himself drifting from consciousness, but there was no white light or friendly voices calling for Clive. There had only been darkness and sounds the animals had made when he had tortured and killed them all those years ago. When Clive felt their teeth and claws ripping at his soul, he embraced the darkness and pain. Dimwitted as he was, he knew he'd pay for those crimes beyond his time in prison. He'd pay for eternity.

~ * ~

James sat in his study in front of his twenty-seven-inch iMac and reviewed scholarly, folklore articles about, and from, the Twelfth and Thirteenth Centuries, while Winston snored on the couch. He had used his academic credentials to access several data sources not available for public view. It was getting late, and he was getting tired. His eyes blurred occasionally as he tried to decipher some of the older texts. Some were downloadable, others weren't. The ones he could download had been printed and placed in a desktop folder, appropriately named "Dragoş

Văduva." These, he would review later. The articles he couldn't download, he read. Despite being tired, he was in his academic 'groove' and didn't want to stop. At least not until he had some pertinent information he could share with his friends. After all, they were the ones hunting and confronting the ancient vampire at all hours and operating on little sleep, too.

He scrolled through a list of texts and spotted one titled, "Transylvania Royals from the 1100s." No one had mentioned that Dragoş had been born of royalty, but, on a hunch, James opened the document and read it. It was a long article. Transylvania, much like a lot of the world at that time, had been a hodgepodge of fiefdoms with different 'royals' ruling over parts of the entire country. Just when he thought the article was a bust, he read the name Boian Văduva. His eyes cleared, and he read on.

Also, not uncommon then, Boian was married several times. When his first three wives failed to produce a male heir, they were, summarily, executed. These marriages had produced three daughters, one from each wife. His first daughter, born in 1170, had been named Agrapina. She died as an infant, shortly after her mother, Dorina, had been executed. James knew this meant one of two things. Agrapina died of natural causes from childbirth, which wasn't uncommon then, or Boian had her killed. James suspected the latter, which, unfortunately, hadn't uncommon at the time either.

Boian's second wife, Oana, gave birth to a daughter, Ecaterina, in 1173. These two met the same fate as Dorina and Agrapina shortly after the birth. This solidified James' notion the Boian had his first and second daughters killed. Boian's third wife, Luminita, gave birth to a daughter, Sorina, in 1175. While Boian had Luminita had been executed, Sorina lived. James took this change in past behavior as a sign Boian had given up on having a male heir and planned to marry his third daughter to another Transylvanian noble, hoping the union would produce a grandson who would rule over both fiefdoms.

Boian married a fourth time to a woman named Anca, and this union resulted in the birth of a son in 1179, named Dragoş Văduva. James had found proof Dragoş Văduva's existence and the timeline fit perfectly. Dragoş would have been twenty-two years old in the year 1201, when

Cipriana Ardelean claimed to have created the ancient vampire that cane to Pine View County. James read more about the Văduvas.

Boian's third, and only living daughter, Sorina, had been married to Kornid Cel Tradat, a neighboring noble, in 1187. Kornid was forty-seven years old, and Sorina was twelve years old at the time of the union. This hadn't been uncommon either. Unfortunately, Sorina died while giving birth to a still-born son less than a year after the union. Boian's plan for a ruling grandson died with his third daughter and her still-born son. That left Dragoş as Boian's only living heir and the future of his bloodline. James read on to find out more about Dragoş. He didn't have to read long. Dragoş had a reputation.

Dragoş was described as a comely young man, but one with a cruel demeanor. His appearance was described as his having a firm chin, high cheekbones, green eyes, and long, curly, light brown hair. His cruelty was, mostly, directed at females. He used his prince title to take what he wanted, usually from peasant girls in his father's fiefdom. Whether they were willing didn't matter. Also, several peasant girls were found murdered. More precisely, they were found disemboweled. Dragoş had been the suspected culprit of these murders. As the only living, male heir of Boian, no accusations were made. At least not above a whisper.

The Văduva's story ended on the night of Boian's twenty-fifth year of rule. There had been a lively celebration. In the early morning hours following the celebration, Boian died under mysterious circumstances. Dragoş, who would have been king, had never been seen again.

Accusations were made against Kornid. That he had killed Boian and taken Dragoş prisoner to take Boian's fiefdom. The reason behind these suspicions were straightforward. Kornid felt entitled to Boian's lands because Boian's daughter, Sorina, had been too fragile to provide him an heir.

Some skirmishes followed, and Kornid was killed in battle. After Kornid's death, neither fiefdom had a legitimate ruler, and more battles were fought over who would rule either or both.

What happened to the disputed land after Boian's and Kornid's deaths didn't concern James. With the benefit of hindsight, he knew what had really happened to Boian the night of his celebration. Cipriana

Ardelean had attended the celebration, created the undead Dragoş, and Boian had been Dragoş' first kill. That filled in some information on Dragoş, but Cipriana Ardelean remained a mystery, and James did not know when she was created. Determined to find out more about her, James continued to research.

~ * ~

Regenerated by the large man's blood, Dragoş looked at his two remaining daughters, Ilinca and Lacrima. He concluded they were not enough to secure Vanda and deal with the wicked *vrăjitoare*. He needed a third daughter.

"My lovely daughters need a new sister to replace Agrapina," Dragoş said. "Do either of you know someone who can replace her?"

"I do, Father," Lacrima said.

Dragoş smiled. "Take me to her, daughter."

The three transformed into human-bat hybrids and took flight.

~ * ~

The Culpeppers were enjoying a family evening together. Supper had been left over ham, mashed potatoes, and green bean casserole from Christmas dinner. After eating, Don, his wife, Alison, and their fourteen-year-old daughter, Lena, were in the living room watching the Blu-ray, *Frozen*, on TV. Don could have gone without watching it again, but it was Lena's favorite movie and he had a hard time refusing anything his only child wanted.

A fire roared in the fireplace and the only lights on were the twinkling Christmas tree lights giving off a multicolored glow that mixed with the orange flames and the images on the TV. Don sat in his recliner and Alison and Lena sat on the couch together, huddled under a blanket, despite the warmth from the fire and heater. They were both cold natured.

In the middle of the movie's hallmark song, *Let It Go*, there was a knock on the front door. Alison and Lena looked at Don. He knew what they expected, but he wanted to have some fun first.

Don looked back at his wife and daughter. "I'm not missin' this song. One of y'all get the door."

"Daddy." Lena pleaded, playfully.

"I can pause it for ya," Alison said with a smile.

"That's unnecessary," Don said as he lowered the feet of his recliner and got up. "I think I've heard it at least a thousand times."

~ * ~

Dragoş, Ilinca, and Lacrima landed in the front yard of a small, secluded house. Twinkling lights lit the windows and music drifted out from the house. Dragoş didn't bother with transforming back into his human body. Neither did his daughters. Dragoş could smell the innocence of his next daughter inside the house. With Ilinca and Lacrima in his wake, Dragoş walked to the front door and knocked. He heard the humans talking and a moment later, a man answered the door.

Dragoş' bat-like eyes flashed silver. "Invite us in."

Don, who had instantly been under Dragoş' influence, said, "Of course. Y'all are invited in."

Dragoş sent mental commands to his daughters and stepped across the threshold.

"Who is it?" Alison asked.

The question turned into a scream as Dragoş entered the living room.

Following her father's command, Ilinca pushed the man back into the house and sank her fangs into his neck. Mesmerized, he didn't fight back. Lacrima swept past her father, grabbed the woman, effortlessly pulled her over the back of the couch, and pinned her to the floor. She struggled, but to no avail. She screamed in terror, though.

Dragoş didn't bother to mesmerize the girl, who had pushed herself into the far corner of the couch as she screamed; he fed off her fear, too. She was a pretty little thing with long, dark blonde hair and big, brown eyes. He would enjoy tucking her in when they returned to his throne room.

Dragoş grabbed her right shoulder, lifted her from the couch, sank his fangs into her soft, virgin flesh, and drank. Within a few seconds, she stopped screaming and her body went limp in Dragoş' grip. He listened to her strong heart slow and stopped feeding an instant before it stopped. It was time to create his new daughter, a new member of his cloud.

Dragoş slit his left nipple with the thumb claw of his bat-like hand. Black blood ran down his chest. He placed the girl's slack mouth against his bleeding nipple so his blood would fill her mouth. Within seconds, he felt her body reanimate. Her young lips locked on his nipple as she suckled eagerly. Dragoş had long lost count of how many young girls he had fathered, but he never tired of the wonderful suckling sensation their births provided. A moment later, she opened her crystal blue eyes and looked into Dragoş' bat-like eyes with love for her creator.

~ * ~

Lena screamed in horror at the sight of the living monster entering the living room. She screamed again when a second, smaller monster swept into the room and dragged her screaming mom over the back of the couch. She screamed in pain when the bat-like monster grabbed her shoulder, which pierced her tender skin with its clawed fingers. She screamed in pain and fear when his fangs penetrated the sensitive flesh of her neck.

She could hear her mom screaming, but she no longer had the strength to scream. Lena knew she was dying, but death would be a relief to the nightmare her life had become.

She could no longer feel the pain in her shoulder or neck and as her vision turned a blinding white. The fear left her, too. She found comfort in the nothingness of the blinding white. Then she realized the white wasn't nothingness. She heard her grandma, who had passed away two months earlier, call her name. She saw her face in the whiteness. Lena smiled and reached out to touch her grandma's face. As she did, a sweet, coppery taste filled her nothingness. She wanted more of it. As it filled her completely, the whiteness receded. She opened her eyes and looked into the bat-like eyes of her creator. He was beautiful.

~ * ~

Dragoş let his new daughter suckle a while longer; she was a hungry little thing. Then he pulled her greedy lips from his bleeding nipple and looked at the perfection he had created.

He smiled at his new daughter. "Your name is Ruxandra, which means beautiful. I am your father."

Ruxandra smiled, which made her pointed fangs show. "Yes, Father."

To Lacrima, Dragoş said, "Bring your new sister her first feeding."

"Yes, Father," Lacrima said as she roughly yanked the woman to her feet.

Alison thought her voice couldn't handle another scream. She was wrong. One that felt like it ripped her vocal cords apart erupted from her mouth when she saw the porcelain, translucent skin, crystal blue eyes, and pointed fangs on what had, moments ago, been her beautiful daughter, Lena.

"Bring the human to your sister, Ruxandra," Dragoş instructed Lacrima.

When they were face to face, Alison, through tears, said, "Oh, Lena. What did it do to you?"

This comment earned her a backhand from Dragoş, who said, "This is no longer your daughter, woman. She is *my* daughter now. Her name is Ruxandra."

Blood spilled from Alison's lip that was split open from the monster's brutal backhand and the new monster who had been her daughter hissed and lunged for her. Something held her back.

"Patience, Ruxandra," Dragoş whispered.

Still hissing, Ruxandra said, "Yes, Father."

"You must feed slowly and stop when I command you to stop," Dragoş explained.

An impossibly long tongue snaked out from between Ruxandra's fangs. "I understand, Father."

Through sobs, Alison said, "Please, Lena. It's me. Your mom. You don't…"

Alison's words were cut short when Ruxandra unhinged her lower jaw and sank her fangs into the woman's neck. Ruxandra fed until she heard her father's mental command to stop. She did as he instructed, and the woman's body crumpled to the floor when she let go of her. A moment later, Alison breathed her last and her soul became trapped in Ruxandra's unseen black aura.

Dragoş smiled. "Very good, daughter. Now, disrobe and let me look upon your youthful perfection."

Ruxandra did as her father commanded and Dragoş' long tongue snaked out of his man-bat, hybrid mouth as he pondered the fun he would have with her. Ilinca and Lacrima watched their father eye their new sister and imagined the fun they would have with her, too.

"Look at us, Ruxandra," Dragoş said. "Will your body to transform into what you see."

Ilinca and Lacrima expected Ruxandra to struggle with the transformation. They were wrong. Ruxandra didn't manage the transformation as quickly as Lacrima had, but she transformed more quickly than Ilinca, Agrapina, and the always struggling Antanasia.

Dragoş smiled a wicked smile. "Come, my daughters. We will return to my throne room early this night and get...acquainted with my new daughter.

When Dragoş turned and walked out, his three daughters followed. When Dragoş took flight, Ilinca, Lacrima, and Ruxandra took flight behind him. Ruxandra wasn't a natural vampire like Lacrima, but she learned quickly. They flew high above the lights of Pine View and only descended when the Eternal Rest Funeral Home came into view.

~ * ~

As they turned into Lola's driveway, Paige stiffened in her seat. No one, except Lola, noticed. Lola sensed the change in Paige; she didn't see it.

For Paige, the sensation was very similar, too similar, to the connection she shared with Alexis, who was the alpha werewolf that infected her at the MRB party when Justin, and fourteen of her other friends were killed, the previous May. With Alexis, Paige found they were connected, and she saw through her eyes when Alexis was angry, sexually aroused, or, sometimes, unaware.

When it happened with Dragoş, it was very similar. One moment she saw they were turning into Lola's driveway. The next moment, she saw a red front door and Dragoş' hybrid hand knock on it. She heard people, humans in Dragoş' mind, talking from inside the house. They sounded like they were having a good time and it hurt Paige's heart.

Through Dragoş' eyes, she saw a man answer the door and heard, felt, Dragoş say, "Invite us in."

Paige saw the man's face lose all emotion and say, "Of course. Y'all are invited in."

Paige traveled into the house with Dragoş and saw a woman and a younger girl she recognized. When they screamed in horror, Paige pushed back hard and exited Dragoş' revolting mind.

"What is it?" Lola urgently said. "What happened, Paige?"

The four men, who were oblivious to what happened to Paige, looked her way.

Through fresh tears, Paige said, "You were wrong, Lola. Dragoş has gone after another girl for his cloud. I recognized her. Her name is Lena Culpepper. She's just a freshman."

Garrett brought the SUV to a sudden stop that strained seatbelts on everyone who wore one. This excluded Lola, who was already braced.

"How do ya know this, Paige-Turner?" Garrett asked.

"I-I-I was there. I was in his head. Kinda like the connection I had with Alexis after she bit me."

"Are ya out?" Lola asked with a scared edge in her voice. "Did he feel ya in his mind?"

"Yes. No. I mean. Yes, I'm out," Paige said. "I pushed out before he…ya know. And no. I don't think he knew I was there."

"Think hard, chil'," Lola said. "Did he know you were in his mind? If you're not sure, rely on Mamma's wisdom. Do it fast."

Paige closed her eyes, fell into her deep thoughts, and searched for Mamma's wisdom the protection potion gave her. She found her, and she listened.

For Paige, it felt like she listened to Mamma for a long time. For the others, Paige's eyes were only closed for two or three seconds, but it was a long two or three seconds.

Paige opened her eyes. "No. He didn't know I was in his mind."

Lola let out a long breath she'd held. "Thank the Elements."

Fr. Mike disapproved of what Lola said, but he kept his thoughts to himself.

"She also said that invadin' an ancient's mind is very dangerous," Paige said. "That, if he knew, he could…trap me in it. I didn't mean for it to happen. It just…happened."

"Every day I spend with you ages me ten years, Paige-Turner," Lola said.

"I'm sorry. I didn't have control over it."

"I know, chil'," Lola said. "I was wrong earlier when I said ya could use your pure sight to find the ancient's lair. Mamma knows it's dangerous. Ya can't do it again, or let it happen again. We'll have to work on this. Tonight."

"Can ya keep it from happenin' again?" Garrett asked.

Before Lola could answer, Paige said, "But…can't I use this to…"

"No," Lola shouted, which boomed in the truck's cab. "You heard Mamma. If he catches ya in his mind, he could lock ya in. Then, he'd have ya. Don't even think 'bout tryin' to invade his mind."

"But—" Paige began to speak again.

This time Garrett interrupted her. "Absolutely not, Paige-Turner."

"Let me speak, damn it." Paige shouted. "You said I have pure sight, Lola. You said this had never happened before. Mamma said she'd never heard of a seer havin' pure sight, either. He might not be able to trap me."

Calmer, Lola said, "Maybe not. We, *you*, can't risk it. He prizes you and Glinda like he's prized nothin' before. You *cannot* risk handin' y'all over to him. Promise me and your daddy that you won't do anything stupid."

Reluctantly, Paige said, "I promise, but I can't stop it from happenin' like it just did."

"We'll work on that tonight," Lola said again.

"We good on this, Paige-Turner?" Garrett asked.

Paige nodded.

"Pinky promise," Garrett said as he extended his right pinky toward Paige.

Paige hooked her left pinky with her daddy's. "Pinky promise."

With that done, Garrett drove up to Lola's house, stopped, leaned over, and hugged Paige. "I love you, Paige-Turner."

Paige returned the hug. "I love you too, Daddy," and got out of the SUV.

As Lola climbed over Trowa to get out, Garrett said, "Take care of my little girl, Lola."

Lola smiled her warm honey smile. "I will, Garrett. I love her too, ya know."

"I know. But I don't like this one bit."

"I don't either, Garrett," Lola said as she got out of the SUV. "I'll take care of her. I promise."

Trowa closed the door behind Lola. "As my people would say, heap big shit."

Despite the seriousness of everything they were dealing with, the other three men laughed a nervous laugh. Then Garrett turned the SUV around and watched Lola, with her arm around Paige's shoulder, get smaller in the rearview mirror. He hated watching the people he loved get smaller in the rearview mirror.

When Garrett's SUV was out of sight, Lola said, "C'mon, chil'. We got some work to do."

Paige nodded, and they went inside Lola's house.

~ * ~

Dragoș, Ilinca, Lacrima, and Ruxandra landed behind the funeral home in front of the two garage doors. When Dragoș extended his hands, his daughters joined hands. They dissolved into black mist and seeped under the door on the left. Once inside, they rematerialized in human form.

Zack Zane heard his Master's command to ready his throne room when he was on his way home. He did as his Master instructed and dreaded, but less so than he had the night before, what vile things the Master would have him do with his former daughter again. When the Master and his three cloud members materialized in front of him, Agrapina wasn't with him.

"What happened to Mel…Agrapina, Master?"

Dragoş backhanded Zack so hard the large man flew across the embalming room until his back collided with one of the two embalming tables. They were bolted to the concrete floor, which brought Zack to a sudden, and painful, stop. When he hit it, Zack felt several of his ribs break, and black blood sprayed from his mouth onto the concrete floor.

"Agrapina is not your concern, slave," Dragoş hissed.

"Yes, Master," Zack said as more black blood spilled from his mouth.

Dragoş approached Zack, and he was sure another backhand, or worse, would follow.

Dragoş slit his right nipple with his gnarled, yellow thumbnail. "Drink, slave. I cannot have you injured. Not now."

Repulsed, Zack did as he was told. As Dragoş' cold, black blood ran down his throat, he felt his ribs mend. He felt invigorated. Zack felt wonderful. He hated that he enjoyed it.

Dragoş let Zack feed until he sensed his familiar's body had been healed and pulled the large man's mouth away from his bleeding nipple. "Enough, slave. Clean up your mess, undress, and come to my throne room to watch me tuck my new daughter, Ruxandra, in. If I am feeling generous, I may let you enjoy one of my daughters before we rest this day."

It wasn't generosity Dragoş offered. He knew his new familiar was still uncomfortable engaging in sexual acts with his young daughters. Dragoş didn't plan on keeping the human slave any longer than necessary. Any longer than it took to secure Vanda. Until that happened, he would torture his slave physically and mentally.

After Dragoş and his daughters descended into the throne room, Zack did as he was instructed. When his Master had Lacrima couple with him, the deviant acts they engaged in did not repulse him. Part of his mind thought he only enjoyed it because it wasn't Agrapina. Another part of his mind, twisted by his Master, thought he would have enjoyed Agrapina, too. He was changing. He liked what he was becoming.

~ * ~

Lola and Paige sat at her table. Lola sat in her high-backed chair and Paige sat directly across from her. There was a large, blood, red candle in the middle of the table that Lola had lit with a snap of her fingers on the wick.

Lola placed her hands, palms up, on either side of her, toward the two empty chairs. "Put your hands on either side of you as I have mine."

"What are we doin'?" Paige asked.

"I'm callin' a council. Just do as I say, chil'."

Paige mimicked Lola's hand positions and waited to see what would happen next.

In a rhythmic voice, Lola said, "Sisters. I seek your counsel on a matter of grave importance. Come to me with your fearlessness and cleverness in my time of need. Come to me, sisters."

Paige caught her breath when the air on either side of her shimmered in the bright red, candlelight. Shapes materialized in the two empty chairs. The shapes had features, but they weren't corporal. As the two shimmering shapes placed their hands in her and Lola's hand, the shimmering lessened, and their features became more distinct. When they had materialized to the extent they could, they looked like slightly blurred versions of their true appearances and surrounded by their brilliant auras. Paige could feel the weight of their cold, blurred hands in her hands.

The slightly blurred shape holding Paige's right hand had a red aura, looked at her, and in a beautiful Jamaican accent, said, "So, it is true. The girl's seeing eye and aura are the same color."

The slightly blurred shape holding Paige's left hand had a blue aura, looked at her, and in a Hispanic accent, said, "I cannot believe it. Does the girl have pure sight?"

"The girl's name is Paige," Lola said. "Y'all know her name. Use it. And yes. Paige and Glinda have pure sight. That is why I have summoned y'all."

Both slightly blurred heads nodded in agreement.

"The seer to your right is Angelica Freemont," Lola said. "Her red aura indicates fearlessness. The seer to your left is Rosa Chavez. Her blue aura indicates cleverness. You already know the fourth member of my council, Mamma Deupree. Her purple aura indicates wisdom. Her wisdom resides within you, and she may choose to speak through you. If she does, your silver aura will turn a silvery purple. Do not be alarmed if she does."

Paige had no words and simply nodded.

"They have pure sight," Angelica said. "For what purpose do you summon us, sister?"

Before Lola could answer, Paige's aura turned a silvery purple and Mamma's old Haitian voice emanated from Paige's mouth. Paige sat, in astonishment, as Mamma filled Angelica and Rosa in on how Glinda had easily penetrated the ancient's thoughts during the confrontation with him and how Paige saw through his eyes a short time later.

When Mamma finished, Rosa said, "It is true, then. The girl and her wolf have pure sight."

"Yes," Lola said. "As I said a moment ago, they do."

Excited, Angelica said, "She should fucking use it. Get in his mind and fuck with him."

Lola shook her head, which caused the beads click. "Why am I not surprised that you would say this, Angelica. Ya heard Mamma. Dragoş could capture Paige and Glinda in his mind. If he did this, he'd have both his prizes."

"How did you learn his name, sister?" Rosa asked.

Lola glanced at Paige. "Durin' our last meditation, Paige went to hell and compelled the ancient's creator to reveal his name."

Angelica looked at Paige with a mixture of awe and envy. "How the fuck did someone so young and inexperienced go to hell and come back to tell of it?"

"She is reckless," Rosa said. "Something you should understand more than any of us, Angelica."

Frustrated, Paige said, "I was *not* reckless. God was with me, and He protected me. I wouldn't have gone without His protection."

Angelica laughed. "I like you, Paige. But even *I* wouldn't have tried that. You're a fucking badass."

"No seer ever has," Mamma's old voice came out of Paige's mouth.

"The fact that she has perfect sight and has been to hell and back only reinforces my initial thought that she should use her powers to probe Dragoş' mind and fuck with him," Angelica said.

Paige's aura turned a dark, silvery purple color, and Mamma's voice boomed, "No. Lola gathered us to *protect* Paige and Glinda from the ancient's mind."

"Sorry, Angelica," Rosa said. "I'm with Mamma and Lola on this one. It is too dangerous."

"Of course you are," Angelica said angrily.

"Since we agree, sisters," Lola said. "Shall we begin?"

"Begin what?" Paige asked.

"I'm sorry, Paige-Turner," Lola said. "For this, you are a vessel. Close your eyes, open your mind, and let us fill ya."

"But..." Paige began.

"No buts," Lola said sternly. "Open your mind. Lest ya think of doin' otherwise, we'll know and force it open. I advise against this."

Defeated, Paige said, "Okay, but *I* wish had more control over what *I* do with my powers."

"These are *borrowed* powers, chil'," Lola said. "They *aren't* yours. So, ya don't. Now close your eyes and open your mind."

Paige nodded her head, closed her eyes, and opened her mind.

~ * ~

It was after two in the morning and, tired as he was, James still searched through old folklore documents. He abandoned scholarly publications around midnight, for any sign of Cipriana Ardelean's name. On his desk, he had a cup of coffee and a glass of his homemade muscadine wine; he alternated sips from each. Winston continued to snore on the couch.

After finishing a document that provided no information, James leaned back in his chair, which caused it to squeak, stretched, and yawned.

"I don't know how much longer I can do this, Winston."

Winston, who was awakened from the chair's squeak, lifted his large head and looked at James through sleepy, brown eyes.

James laughed. "I'm sorry I woke ya up, Win. Go on back to sleep. I think I can manage a few more documents before I join ya."

Winston laid his sleepy head back on the arm of the couch, which was his favorite sleeping position. James opened another old document and read.

Two documents later, as the clock ticked closer to three, James opened a document titled, "The Scourge of Sighisoara." Since this was a folklore document, not an academic one, it was descriptive of events that took place in Sighisoara in the Eighth Century. James took a gulp of coffee, which was cold by then, and read the document.

The document described events that took place in the year 757. The events were the murders of twenty-three people; seven children, four young women, and twelve young men. The cause of death had been the same for all victims. All had puncture wounds on their neck, inner upper arm, or inner, upper thigh. All were drained of blood. Because it was a folklore document, all the deaths were blamed on a *strigoi*, a vampire.

It provided names for the murdered victims and one of the murdered young men had the surname of Ardelean. This was an important discovery, but the document also told of an older woman who went missing at the same time. Her name was Cipriana Ardelean. Against all odds, James had found proof of Dragoş Văduva's creator.

Cipriana was described as a portly widow and fifty-three years of age at the time she went missing. She hadn't been royalty, but she had married well and late in life; she was thirty-three when she married a man named Dinu Ardelean, twenty-three years older than Cipriana. The union had produced a son named Caturix Ardelean. Caturix, who, although he had only been sixteen years old, was listed as one of the twelve young men murdered during the scourge. James knew Caturix had been Cipriana's first kill after whoever created her, created her.

James downed the rest of the muscadine wine in two gulps, leaned back in his chair, which caused it to squeak again, raised his arms, and shouted, "I found her, Winston."

Winston's large head raised up quickly at the commotion, and he let out a startled bark.

James laughed, got up, and stretched his aching back. "C'mon, Win. Let's go to bed."

Winston barked again, slid off the couch, and followed James to the bedroom.

~ * ~

Paige did not know what was happening to her or how long it took. She had closed her eyes and opened her mind, as Lola had told her to, and felt the intrusion of Lola, Angelica, Rosa, and the ever-present Mamma's thoughts. They weren't discernible thoughts, though. At least not all of them. They were incantations spoken in each of the seers' native language. Even Lola's incantations were a mixture of English and French Cajun that were difficult to interpret.

When the intrusions stopped, and Paige opened her eyes again, she was surprised to see the large, blood, red candle had burned almost to the bottom. Also, Lola and the apparitions of Angelica and Rosa looked exhausted. She could feel Mamma's exhaustion. She felt exhausted, too.

"How long was I…gone?" Paige asked.

"Almost five hours," Lola said, barely above a whisper.

"What did y'all do to me?"

"Ya know how I tol' ya Dragoş' mind has a black vault around it?"

"Yeah,"

"We constructed a white vault around your mind," Lola explained.

Angered, Paige said, "Wait. What? Y'all had no right to alter my mind."

"Calm down, chil'," Lola said soothingly. "Your mind isn't altered. It's protected."

"What if it interferes with my and Glinda's abilities?"

"It won't, Paige-Turner."

"How can y'all be sure?"

"The vault around Dragoş' mind doesn't interfere with his abilities," Lola pointed out. "Your and Glinda's abilities are unaffected.

All we did was protect your thoughts. Now ya can't see into his mind, and he can't see into your mind."

"That's it?" Paige asked.

"Yes," Rosa answered. "You're not the first seer who's needed her mind protected."

"Thank y'all for your help, sisters," Lola said very tiredly. "I know y'all are as exhausted as I am. Please rejoin with your corporal bodies."

Rosa shimmered into nothingness immediately, but Angelica stuck around for a few seconds longer. Paige felt her blurred hand tighten on hers and she looked at the beautiful young seer. When Paige looked at her, Angelica winked at her with her bright yellow, seeing eye. In that wink, Paige saw the fearless Angelica had left, for lack of a better description, an escape hatch Paige could use to bypass the white vault. Paige didn't dare wink back and a moment later, Angelica shimmered into nothingness, too.

Lola stretched. "Ya ready to turn in, Paige-Turner?"

"Yeah. I'm pretty tired from all that."

"It's a difficult, collective incantation to cast. It's for your own good. Ya know that, right?"

Paige smiled. "I do. Thank y'all for protectin' me and Glinda."

"Y'all a very welcome," Lola said as she stood. "I'm just glad it worked"

Paige got to her feet too and smiled. "Me too."

A few minutes later, Lola and Paige were in her bed. Paige looked up at the moonlit, starry night in Lola's magical mirror. As she looked at the magical mirror, her mind probed for the escape hatch Angelica had placed in the white vault surrounding her mind. She smiled when she felt her thoughts slip out through Angelica's escape hatch. Once she'd found it, it was easy to find again. It reminded her of the first tooth she lost and how she liked to poke her tongue through the hole where the tooth had been. Now she had access to dagger length fangs, and she couldn't wait to use them on Dragoş' repulsive head.

Chapter Fourteen

Garrett awoke more refreshed than he thought he would after the previous night's events. His mood diminished when he remembered what he had to do later that day—give a press conference and name Zack Zane as the primary suspect in the murders and missing girls. For a moment, again, he wished he had still been a logger. Then Mandy put her soft, warm hand on his scruffy cheek.

"Thinkin' 'bout last night?" Mandy asked.

"Not really. I don't know what Lola will do to protect Paige and Glinda from sharin' thoughts with Dragoş, but I trust she'll do somethin'."

"So…it's Zack that's got ya troubled?"

"Yeah. I mean…" Garrett began.

"I know ya don't like it, but we talked about this," Mandy said as she caressed Garrett's cheek. "Zack's Dragoş' familiar now. Ya told me that Dragoş took another young girl last night, Lena Culpepper, right?"

Garrett nodded.

"Then don't think about who Zack was. Think about what he is now and how he's helpin' Dragoş; how he *helped* Dragoş take Lena. In that context, Zack *is* the monster you'll make him out to be."

Garrett, who hadn't considered it that way, said, "You're right. You always have a way of puttin' things in perspective."

Mandy smiled. "That's why ya love me."

"That's just one of more reasons I can count why I love you, Mandy Davis."

"Then love me. Now," Mandy said with a coy smile.

A moment later, the bed springs on Garrett's childhood, twin bed squeaked and Zack Zane was the last thing on his mind.

~ * ~

Paige awoke to find herself alone in Lola's bed again. The sky in the enchanted mirror above Lola's bed showed a clear, blue sky, which was the aftermath of the blue norther that blew through the day before. She saw the sun rising on the edge of the mirror's view. She had slept late; later than she had in quite a while, but she felt good. Good and rested.

She knew where she could find Lola—waiting on the front porch with spiced tea. Before joining her, Paige probed for the escape hatch Angelica had secretly placed in the white vault surrounding her mind. She found it quickly and smiled.

When Paige stepped out onto Lola's porch, Lola smiled. "Mornin', sleepyhead."

Paige took the cup of tea and sat on the porch swing beside Lola. "I haven't slept this late since…well, since Glinda came into my life."

"That was a tiresome incantation. For all of us," Lola said. "I only beat ya out of bed by about twenty minutes."

Paige took a sip of the delicious tea. "What's the plan for today?"

"Well, we need to see if Glinda's air elemental puts my fire elemental out. I hadn't considered that until James brought it up," Lola admitted. "I hate when that bookworm thinks of somethin' I didn't. Don't ya tell him I said that, Paige-Turner."

Paige laughed. "I won't."

"Then you and your daddy are gonna look for Zack, now that Glinda knows his scent. If y'all can find that ol' fucker durin' the day, he'll be a lot easier to kill."

"I know I sounded confident about Glinda havin' Mister Zack's scent last night," Paige said. "But what if there's…less of him to smell today and Glinda can't get his scent again?"

"That's a possibility," Lola said. "The longer he's Dragoş' familiar, the less of who he used to be will be there to sniff up."

"I thought that might be the case," Paige said as her shoulders slumped.

Lola wrapped a warm arm around Paige's slumped shoulders and hug her tightly. "You and Glinda have great instincts. Y'all did the right thing by not goin' after Zack last night. Especially since we now know Dragoş took another girl for his cloud. If they'd come back and found you and your daddy there…it wouldn't have ended well for either of y'all.

"All ya can do today is go back to where ya last had his scent and see if Glinda can pick up a hint of who he used to be."

"What if she can't?" Paige asked.

"Well, I gotta feelin' this thing's comin' to a head soon. Whether ya find Zack or don't."

"When?"

"I can't say for certain," Lola said. "That Dragoş created another cloud member last night, when I didn't think he would, tells me he's gettin' ready. Fortifyin' his troupes 'cause he knows he can't take Glinda on with just two helper vampires. If I had to guess, I'd say this ends tonight. Tomorrow night at the latest."

"Are we ready?" Paige asked.

Lola tightened her grip on Paige's shoulder and smiled. "Let's see if that ol' fart, James, is right about Glinda's air elemental puttin' out my fire elemental."

"What about the rest of the stuff he said?"

"What stuff?"

"He said we'd have to behead Dragoş, pierce his heart with a silver tipped steak, dismember him, and expose his remains to daylight."

"James got me on the elementals, but he doesn't know everything," Lola said with a wink of her seeing eye. "He wasn't listenin' very good when we tol' him 'bout Glinda takin' out Megan."

"What doesn't he know?" Paige asked.

Lola laughed her warm honey laugh. "Ya already know this, Paige-Turner. I tol' ya before and you've already killed *two* vampires without all that nonsense."

Paige thought for a moment, and smiled when it came to her. "Supernatural creatures don't need all that stuff to kill other supernatural creatures."

"That's right. But ya gotta remember somethin' very important, Paige-Turner."

"What's that?"

"*When*, not *if*, Dragoş realizes he can't have ya in his cloud and Glinda as his familiar, he'll try to kill Glinda," Lola said.

"He won't need silver to kill her...us."

"That's right," Lola said. "But it ain't gonna come to that. Me, your daddy, Ty, Trowa, and Father Mike won't let that happen."

"You said *when* he realizes he can't have us, not *if*."

"I did. He *will* realize this," Lola said. "Ol' Dragoş has bitten off more than he can chew this time. Pardon the pun. He doesn't know just how much he's bitten off 'cause he's underestimatin' us, too. His arrogance is his greatest weakness. We'll use it to make sure that doesn't happen, Paige-Turner."

"How?"

"Well, we'll figure it out."

"That's comfortin'," Paige said.

"We *will*. First, let's see what happens with Glinda's air and my fire elementals."

"Okay," Paige said as she and Lola stood from the porch swing.

Before they were off the porch, Paige heard her phone ring from inside Lola's house.

"That's your daddy," Lola said. "Best get it."

"I'll be right back," Paige said as she went inside.

~ * ~

The radio clock on Garrett's SUV displayed seven forty-eight as he turned onto the street leading to the Sheriff's Department. George Strait sang *Fool Hearted Memory* on the radio, which Garrett had cranked up to drown out Garrett's pitiful singing voice as he sang along. After the morning with Mandy, he felt pretty good. The feeling and song words died in his mouth when he saw what waited for him in the parking lot. A throng of reporters from East Texas with their tape recorders, microphones, cameras, video cameras, and satellite vans packed the streets and department parking lot.

He had planned to call the press conference at ten o'clock that morning. From the throng of reporters waiting, it was going to happen earlier. He wasn't ready to face them yet or put off questions as he made his way inside the building. Garrett quickly took a left onto a side road that took him to the back of the building. He pulled up next to the covered area where suspects in custody were brought in and processed, got out, and used his key to enter the jail area.

The seven to three shift of deputies were already on patrol, so the only person he encountered was Paula Stamford, the morning shift jailer.

"Good mornin', Sheriff Lambert," Paula said.

"Not by the looks of what's out front," Garrett said.

"Yeah, I saw. There were already a few reporters here when I got to work just before six. I peeked out 'bout ten minutes ago and there's triple the number I saw earlier."

"They know I get to work at eight o'clock. Damn buzzards."

"Oh, yeah," Paula said. "I didn't think of that. Ya gonna talk to 'em?"

"Yeah," Garrett said dejectedly. "I was hopin' to do it 'round ten o'clock. Looks like I'll have to deal with 'em sooner. If for no other reason than to get 'em the hell outta here."

"Ya got any leads?" Paula asked.

"I do. I'm pretty sure Zack Zane is our suspect."

Paula took in an audible, shocked breath. "Melanie's daddy? Ya think he could do these…horrible things? To his own daughter?"

"Well, he's missin' and everything leads me to believe it's him," Garrett said.

"Couldn't he be dead, too? Dead and not found?"

Garrett silently cursed his fool hearted brain for not considering this question, which was sure to be asked by the reporters.

"That's certainly possible, but until I know otherwise, he's our person of interest," Garrett said.

"Wow," Paula said with a shudder. "Not in a million years would I think Zack could do somethin' like this."

"That's the same thing folks thought about Ted Bundy, John Wayne Gacy, Dennis Rader, and a lot of other serial killers," Garrett pointed out.

Paula pondered on this a moment. "True. But Zack Zane? I guess we *really* never know someone like we think we do."

"Nope. Now, if you'll excuse me, I've got the press to deal with and you've got prisoners to feed."

"Okay, Sheriff. Good luck."

Garrett left the jail area and walked past his office to the front desk, where Erica Harris was on duty.

When Erica saw Garrett, she said, "I guess you've seen the mess out front."

"I couldn't miss it," Garrett said. "That's why I parked 'round back. Do me a favor and let 'em know I'll be out in 'bout ten minutes to answer their questions."

"Will do. Good luck."

"Yeah. I'm gonna need it," Garrett said as he turned to go to his office and clear his head for a few minutes.

"Hang on, Sheriff," Erica said. "I forgot to tell ya that Kelly Jones called 'bout half an hour ago to report that Clive went out last night and didn't come home. Here's her number."

Garrett took the sticky note with the number from Erica. "Thanks. Tell the reporters it'll be 'bout twenty minutes before I answer questions."

"Will do."

As Garrett walked to his office, looking at the phone number, he wondered what possibilities Clive missing could open. Clive's reputation aside, Garrett didn't wish him ill will, but Clive Jones would be a much more plausible suspect than Zack Zane. He wouldn't know anything until he talked with Kelly. He shut his office door, sat down behind his desk, picked up the phone, and called Kelly Jones.

Kelly answered before the first ring ended. "Clive? Is that you?"

"No, Missus Jones. This a Sheriff Lambert. I'm returnin' your call. Tell me what's goin' on with Clive."

"He's missin'." Kelly blurted out.

"Yes, ma'am," Garrett said calmly. "I know that. Tell me what he was doin' before we went missin'."

"We were eatin' supper," Kelly said. "I made venison stew and sweet cornbread. Clive's favorite. We had the news on. Clive don't care none 'bout the news. We were waitin' for the *Wheel of Fortune* that comes on after the news. His ears perked up when the news lady said somethin' 'bout the Shanahans bein' kilt.

"After hearin' that, he got up and took his daddy's three-o-eight off the gun shelf," Kelly continued. "I asked him what he was fixin' to do and told him he'd get in a heap of trouble if he got caught poachin' at night. Clive said he weren't huntin' deer, that he was huntin' the guy who kilt those folks and took those girls. I told Clive he didn't know nothin' 'bout what was goin' on, but he told me he knew more than I thought he did. After that, he put on his camo coat and left. I ain't seen him since."

Garrett digested all this information. "Clive knows the woods 'round here pretty good, Missus Jones. I'm sure he'll show up."

"He does," Kelly said. "But he ain't never not come home by mornin'. I'm worried somethin' happened to him, Sheriff. I know he's had his troubles, but he's still my son."

Garrett thought for a moment. "I'm gonna ask ya a hard question, Missus Jones. Do ya think Clive could'a had anything to do with these deaths and missin' girls?"

There was a long pause before Kelly said, "God, I hope not."

Garrett needed more. "Has Clive gone out a lot over the last few days?"

After another long pause, Kelly said, "Yeah. But he's always gone a lot."

"You haven't answered my first question," Garrett reminded Kelly. "Do ya think Clive could'a done these things?"

Kelly sighed. "After what Clive did to those poor animals, I can't say no."

"Yeah," Garrett said. "That's kinda what I was thinkin', too."

Kelly sobbed. "If he did *these* horrible things, he deserves the needle, Sheriff."

Garrett hated what he was doing. Blaming Clive Jones, instead of Zack Zane, would take a load off his conscience. And Garrett knew something Kelly didn't. Dragoş had fed before taking Lena. If Clive was out in the woods, and hadn't come home, Garrett thought there was a pretty good possibility Dragoş had fed on Clive. If that was the case, Clive had already gotten the needle. Two needles in the form of sharp fangs. Of course, naming Clive as the suspect, who might show up unharmed, instead of Zack, who would not show up, was a risk, but one Garrett thought worth taking.

All these thoughts went through Garrett's mind quickly and he said, "I'm sorry, Missus Jones. As of now, Clive's my prime suspect. I'll put out an APB and see if we can find him."

Kelly sobbed again. "Do what ya gotta do, Sheriff. As bad as this sounds, I hope y'all have to kill him. I don't think my heart could take another trial. Not for this."

Although Garrett was pretty sure Clive was already dead, he said, "I hope it doesn't come to that. If he shoots at us, we'll have to shoot back. We don't shoot to wound, Missus Jones."

Kelly sniffed. "I understand. If that happens, I hope he don't hit any of y'all. Clive's a damn good shot, Sheriff."

"We'll be okay. Goodbye, Missus Jones."

Kelly hung up without saying another word.

Garrett hung up the phone, left his office, and headed for the front door and the throng of reporters waiting for him. Before he left the building, he called Paige.

~ * ~

Paige hurried into Lola's house and answered her phone. "Hey, Daddy."

"Hey, sweet girl. How ya feelin' this mornin'?"

"Pretty good," Paige said and smiled even though her daddy couldn't see it. "Lola and her council of seers put a white vault around my mind last night to keep Dragoş from gettin' into mine and me from gettin' into his."

Relieved, Garrett said, "Did it work?"

Not wanting to lie, but needing to keep the escape hatch secret, Paige said, "They said it did."

"That's fantastic news, but that's not why I called."

"What's up?" Paige asked.

"We know Dragoş fed last night to regenerate before takin' Lena," Garrett said. "Do ya think Glinda can sniff out who he fed on to regenerate?"

"Sure," Paige said. "That'd be easy."

"Great. Now, I know this goes against all the rules I have for Glinda's daytime activities but, can ya look now?"

"Really?" Paige said excitedly.

"Yeah, really. But ya gotta be careful. Don't get seen."

"Daddy. Glinda knows how to stay hidden. Why's this so important that ya want Glinda out durin' the day?"

"Because, if I'm right about who Dragoş fed on, I won't have to blame Zack Zane for the murders and missin' girls," Garett said.

"You were gonna do that?"

"It's complicated, Paige-Turner," Garrett said with a sigh. "But, yeah, I was. I'm not now, though. I'm goin' on a strong hunch, and only Glinda can confirm it. If I'm right, the person Dragoş fed on will be close to the Henderson's house. There's no mistakin' who I think it is. If it's him, he'll have a skull tattooed on his head."

"Wow. Okay. Do ya want Glinda to go now?"

"Yes. I'm goin' outside right now to name Clive Jones as our primary suspect in this case. I don't suppose ya can bring your cell with Glinda?"

"No. But, when I find Dragoş' kill, if it's him, I can contact Lola mentally and let her know. She can call ya."

"Great. One last thing."

"What's that?" Paige asked.

"If it's him, can Glinda bury him? Bury him deep?"

"Sure."

"Thanks, sweetheart," Garrett said. "I hate askin' ya to do this, but it's the only way to save Zack's reputation. God, I hope I'm right about this."

"No problem, Daddy. It'll be fun to run Glinda durin' the day."

"Be careful. I love you, Paige-Turner."

"I love you too, Daddy," Paige said and ended the call.

When Paige got back outside, Lola said, "What's up? That was more than a how ya doin' call."

"You weren't listenin' in?" Paige asked.

"I tol' ya I wouldn't do that, chil'."

"Okay," Paige said and then told Lola about the call.

When Paige finished filling her in, Lola said, "That Clive Jones is an evil sonofabitch. Better him than Zack. Best get goin', Paige-Turner. I know Glinda'll find the fresh kill quick as spit. We can practice the elementals when ya get back."

"Okay. I'll contact ya if it's him and you can call Daddy to let him know."

Paige, who was already naked, transformed into Glinda, dropped to all fours, and took off at a dead run towards the Henderson's house. She smelled the Hendersons and instantly caught the scent of the other kill. The other kill wasn't far from the Henderson's house, as her daddy predicted.

~ * ~

Garrett walked out of the Department's front door to a flurry of questions, filming cameras, and photo cameras. He waited a few moments for the ruckus to die down. When it didn't, he raised his hands and patted the air in a gesture indicating he wouldn't speak until some degree of order had been established. It worked and the shouted questions died down.

"Thank y'all for takin' interest in what's been goin' on in Pine View and Pine View County since the disappearance of Melanie Zane on Christmas mornin'," Garrett began. "I assure y'all that these murders and missin' girls are our top priority and we've been workin' 'round the clock to find out who's behind 'em.

"Now," Garrett continued with authority. "Y'all know my standard response to your questions is that I can't comment on ongoin' investigations."

At these words, an angry murmur swelled from the reporters.

Garrett patted the air again, which caused the murmurs to subside. "That said, I can tell y'all we have a suspect in this case."

"Who is it?" at least a dozen reporters shouted, somewhat in unison.

Garrett patted the air again and again, and the reporters quitted. "Our person of interest is Clive Jones."

At hearing this, there were audible inhales from most of the reporters who were familiar with Clive Jones' past.

"For those of y'all who may not be aware of Jones' past, do your jobs, investigate it, and report it," Garrett said. "I don't have time to waste fillin' y'all in on info that's easy to find. For those of y'all who are, and your viewers and readers, what I say next shouldn't have to be said, but I'll say it, anyway. Clive Jones is armed with a high-powered rifle. I confirmed this a few minutes ago with his mom. He's an extremely good shot. Clive Jones is armed and very dangerous.

"Do *not*. I repeat. Do *not* approach or apprehend Mister Jones," Garrett cautioned. "If someone sees him, and he's hard to miss with a skull tattoo coverin' his head, call us or the Pine View PD, dependin' on where he's spotted. Thank y'all. That's all I have to say for now."

Garrett turned as more questions were asked and found himself face-to-face with Clair Abbott from the *Pine View Post*. She had her tape recorder in his face.

"Can you explain the sounds that neighbors have reported hearin' at some of the crime scenes?" Clair asked.

"No comment, Clair."

"What about the destruction at the Zane's house?" Clair persisted. "The front door was busted in."

"Clive's a big boy, Clair. If ya don't know who he is, do your damn homework," Garrett said, irritated with himself for not sticking with no comment.

"So, Clive Jones is some kind of monster?" Clair pushed for a reaction. "That's what my sources are sayin'. That this is the work of a supernatural monster."

Garrett, nicely, but purposefully, pushed past Clair. "Grow up, Clair. Supernatural monsters are in the movies. These crimes are the work of a very deranged and dangerous *man*."

Garrett had the front door open, and began to step back inside, when Clair shouted, "What about Lola Laveau? Isn't she a witch?"

Garrett felt his anger raise. His hands closed into tight fists, and he almost turned around to let Clair have a stern denial. He knew she was baiting him, and his reaction would be exactly what she wanted. The cameras would catch the exchange. Instead, he let the door close behind him and let out an angry breath that sounded like one of Glinda's growls. He wondered if his ancestral werewolf had just made an appearance.

~ * ~

Glinda was on the fresh kill's scent and sped through the thick woods with ease. She jumped deadfalls, streams, a river, and two county roads she knew, from her acute hearing, were void of any vehicles. Glinda easily avoided three people who were deer hunting. She knew they were hunters by the smell of gun oil and bottled coyote urine some hunters used to mask their natural scent.

Before long, Glinda was close to the Henderson's house. The scent of their kills differed from the scent of the close third kill. The Henderson's death reeked of fear, and she hated Dragoş for doing that to them after taking their son. The third kill lacked any hint of fear. She knew what that meant, too. Dragoş had the third kill mesmerized. Despite her mission, a slight smile spread across Glinda's snout. The smile came because she knew why Dragoş had kept the kill mesmerized. He was too weak to confront his prey from the beating Glinda gave him.

Glinda slowed and skirted the Henderson's trailer house around back. From there she followed the scent, which also had gun oil associated with it, a few hundred yards into the thick woods. She found him.

He was an enormous man, naked, his body covered in tattoos, and there were two puncture wounds on his upper right thigh. A skull tattoo covered his bald head. Glinda had found Clive Jones.

Glinda looked around the area and saw Clive's gun and clothes several yards away. They were in a small clearing, which would be a good place to bury Clive and bury him deep. Before she did it, Glinda reached out to Lola and found her. Apparently, the white vault didn't obstruct this power. Lola said it wouldn't, but this relieved her anyway.

I found him. It's Clive Jones. Let Daddy know, Glinda's thought came to Lola.

I will, Lola's thought came.

I'll be back as soon as I bury him.

Okay. Then we'll try our elementals.

Glinda didn't respond. Instead, she began digging large hand-claw chunks of soil from the forest ground. She encountered several roots, some quite large, but her claws cut through them like a hot knife through butter. Within ten minutes, Glinda stood in a hole deeper than she was tall.

She leapt out of the hole, went to the large man, effortlessly picked him up, and returned to the hole. She did not know who Clive Jones was, but, no matter, it didn't feel right to drop him in the hole like garbage. Glinda jumped down into the deep hole and gently placed the man on the dark, damp ground. Then she jumped out and dropped his rifle and clothes into the hole with him. With that done, Glinda filled the hole back in and scattered leaves and twigs over the spot. When she finished, even Glinda couldn't tell the difference in the area where she buried Clive Jones and the surrounding ground. Except for the smell, which even the best cadaver dog wouldn't be able to detect. Glinda was satisfied.

Glinda dropped to all fours, intent on running back to Lola's to practice their elementals, but she hesitated. Since everything about Glinda was enhanced, and she wasn't comfortable probing Angelica's escape hatch to find Dragoş around Lola because she might somehow sense it, Glinda tried to probe Dragoş' mind. After all, it was Lola who told her she had good instincts and to follow them. She did.

She found the escape hatch easily and reached her mind out while she concentrated on Dragoş. After several minutes, when she was about to give up, she sensed a deep darkness. An evil darkness. She pushed harder and felt her mind merge with the evil darkness. Glinda was in Dragoş' head. She knew she was, but there was nothing. No thoughts. Just the evil darkness. She didn't understand how there could be no thoughts in Dragoş' evil mind. It took a moment, but then it came to her. It was daytime and he was resting. That wouldn't do.

Wake up, you fuck, Glinda shouted into the evil darkness.

He did.

Glinda saw through Dragoş' eyes when they opened quickly, but all she saw was the darkness inside his coffin. She felt his rage and confusion. And she loved it.

Dragoş hissed. "Who dares to interrupt my rest?"

To Glinda's surprise and pleasure, she realized Dragoş didn't know the voice was in his head. He thought someone had entered his lair.

Glinda saw through Dragoş' eyes as the lid to his coffin flew open and he stood. Because Dragoş could see in the dark, so could Glinda. She saw earthen walls as he looked around his lair for the source of the voice. Glinda saw four coffins, the ones dug up from different cemeteries, two on each side. She knew three had Lindsey, Taylor, and Lena in them. She knew the fourth was empty and waiting for Paige, but she knew these things because she knew them. Not because she was getting information from Dragoş.

Glinda tried to probe Dragoş' mind. She was through his black vault and should have access to his thoughts, all of them, but his thoughts concentrated on who had spoken to him. She had to scatter his thoughts.

Where are you, fuck nut? Paige thought into Dragoş' mind.

Glinda felt Dragoş' immediate panic as he realized the voice was in his mind, in his black vault, and anger when he realized who had invaded it.

You meddlesome, pizda. Dragoş screamed in his mind.

Glinda laughed and thought, *I'm comin' for ya, bitch.*

Get out. Dragoş screamed in his mind.

Make me, bitch, Glinda thought.

Glinda felt Dragoş push back against her intrusion, but he couldn't force her out. He couldn't remove her from his evil mind.

You can't push me out, Paige thought. *I can live here, if I want. You're a sick fuck and your mind is foul. I'm leavin' now, but only so I can plan how to destroy ya. I'll be back. Back in your black vault whenever I want to. And ya can't stop me, bitch.*

As Glinda pulled out of Dragoş' mind, she heard him roar in anger and saw dirt fall from his earthen lair, from the power of his rage. Instantly, she saw through Glinda's eyes again. Satisfied, she dropped to all fours and ran back to Lola's where, she hoped, Lola wouldn't be able to perceive what she'd done.

~ * ~

Garrett was back in his office when his cellphone rang. It was Lola.

He answered it, but Lola spoke before he could.

"You were right," Lola said. "Glinda found Clive's body. Dragoş fed on him to regenerate."

Garrett sighed with relief. "Thank God. Not that Clive's dead, even he didn't deserve that, but because my hunch was right, and I didn't have to blame Zack for all this."

"You are your daughter's father," Lola said in her warm, honey voice. "Y'all both have good instincts."

"Is she back yet?"

Lola laughed. "She just sent me the message that she found him. Glinda's quick, but she's still gotta bury him before she comes back."

"Yeah. Okay," Garrett said. "I hated havin' to send her to do that. Will ya have her call me when she gets back? I wanna make sure she's okay."

"Of course, I'll have her call ya," Lola assured Garrett. "Remember, she's lived through much worse. If she got through what happened to Justin, she'll get through this. She's one tough girl, Garrett."

"You're right. I still wanna talk with her."

"As ya should. I'll have her call ya as soon as she gets back."

"Thanks, Lola. Thanks for everything."

"You're very welcome, Garrett."

As Garrett hung up with Lola, his desk phone rang. He picked it up and this time, Erica spoke before he could.

"George Krats is on line one. You in?"

"Yep. I'll take it."

Garrett pressed the button for line one. "What's up, George?"

"What's up is that Digger can't take any more bodies, and I can't get an answer at that new funeral home," George said irritably. "These bodies gotta go somewhere."

"Yeah, they do," Garrett said. "Heads up, there will probably be four more bodies today."

"Fuck me." George shouted.

"I met the guy who's runnin' the new funeral home the mornin' Melanie went missin'." Garrett said. "Digger wasn't available, so he came out to pick up Justin's body. He even comped the Andersons a new coffin.

Nice guy, but a little odd. Had a strange, foreign name, too. He told us to call him Dan. I'll look into the new place and get back to ya, George."

George hung up without saying another word.

~ * ~

Zack was pulled from a tortuous half-sleep by Dragoş' mental and verbal rage. He got to his feet quickly, went to the entrance to the Master's throne room, and opened it. Dragoş was on him instantly and threw him across the room, where he collided with a stainless-steel bench. Ribs cracked in an explosion of white-hot pain, and he spit up black blood. Dragoş was in his face again before he could take in a ragged, painful breath.

"She was here," Dragoş shouted in Zack's frightened face.

"Wh-who, Master," Zack stammered in fear. "No one has entered. I assure you, Master."

This earned Zack a painful backhand that split his bottom lip.

Dragoş pointed at his head, and hissed, "She, the silver-haired wolf, was *here*. In *my* head. The *pizda* and her wolf were in *my* head."

"How can I stop that, Master?" Zack wheezed.

Dragoş smiled a hideous smile and hissed, "You cannot. You are useless."

Dragoş considered ridding himself of the useless familiar. Familiars were useful, once trained, as Dănuţ had been, but he'd existed many years without one before. Also, he was certain he would have Vanda and her silver-haired wolf as his familiar soon. That night, in fact.

Dragoş opened his gapping, unhinged mouth to rip the slave's throat out, but he stopped when he heard the phone in the funeral home's office ring.

Dragoş pulled his deadly mouth away. "Is this the first time someone has called?"

"No, Master," Zack said as black blood oozed from his mouth and split lip. "It has rung several times this mornin',"

Dragoş eyes narrowed to slits. "Did you answer it?"

"No, Master."

"You did well by not answering, slave," Dragoş hissed. "I fear this place has been compromised. So, you do not die…today."

"Fortunately, Dănuţ secured a second location in the event this place was compromised," Dragoş continued to hiss. "I have not existed for eight hundred years by being foolish. You must move me, and then my daughters, to the new location now."

"Yes, Master," Zack said eager to please. "Where is the new location, Master?"

Dragoş looked deeply into Zack's wide eyes with his sliver, slit eyes, and imparted the needed information.

"Yes, Master. I know where that is."

"Tonight will be the night I take Vanda," Dragoş said with an evil smile. "That little *pizda* thinks she is clever. I will show her clever. I will show *all* of them that Dragoş Văduva is the oldest of all vampires. The King of vampires. They cannot defeat me. No matter what meddlesome tricks they may play. Guard me with your life, slave."

"Yes, Master," Zack said and coughed black blood.

Dragoş looked at his pitiful slave and slit a nipple. "Feed, slave. I need you strong for what is coming."

Zack eagerly drank his Master's black blood and felt his body mending. By the time Dragoş pulled his face away, Zack felt stronger than he ever had.

"I must wait in my throne room while you bring the hearse inside and load my throne," Dragoş said. "Do not let any sunlight in here until I am safely below. Shut the doors and load my throne into the hearse. Once I am safe in my throne, take me to the new location. Then, come back and bring my three daughters and the fourth coffin to the new location. This will take three trips. Do not fail me, slave."

"I won't, Master," Zack said with resolve.

~ * ~

Garrett couldn't remember the name of Dan's new funeral home, but it wouldn't be hard to find. Until he came to town, Pine View only had one funeral home. Doug "Digger" Stephens' 'Pine View Funeral Parlor.'

A quick internet search provided the name, 'Eternal Rest Funeral Home,' and a phone number. Garrett called the number.

The phone rang four times and then Dan's heavily accented voice said, "You have reached the Eternal Rest Funeral Home. I am not available to answer your call at the moment. Please leave a message with your name, phone number, and the nature of your inquiry. I will return your call at my earliest convenience. Thank you for trusting us to care for your loved ones in this time of need."

Garrett waited for the beep. "Hey, Dan. This is Sheriff Lambert. We met Christmas mornin' at Saint Joseph's Catholic Church when ya helped with the theft of Justin Anderson's coffin. I'm callin' 'cause we've had some…murders over the past few days. I'm sure you've heard 'bout 'em on the news. The other funeral home is overwhelmed. I'm checkin' to see if you can help. I guess ya could use the business, since you're just openin'. Anyway, call me when ya get this."

Garrett left his cell number and ended the call.

After he hung up, Garrett leaned back in his chair and without realizing he was doing it, rubbed the stubble on his chin. He thought about doing some 'good ol' fashion investigatin', as Mandy had put it.

He pondered the timeline of when the vampire problem began, which was, as he told Dan in the message he left Christmas morning and Dan's arrival in Pine View. He hadn't been sure how long before Melanie became Dragoş' first victim that the rebuild on what had been an auto repair body shop, the Eternal Rest Funeral Home, had begun. It had to have been at least two or three months. Had Dan been there, overseeing the remodel, the whole time? Dragoş didn't show until the funeral home was ready to open.

To these thoughts, Garrett added Dan's accent and how strong the slender man, who appeared to be in his early fifties, was. Lola said familiars were strong. Could all of this be coincidence? Maybe. But Garrett's gut told him otherwise. Garrett's gut told him Dan had been Dragoş' familiar. The familiar Lola destroyed before Dragoş took Zack Zane as his new familiar. These thoughts reminded him Lola saw the familiar and could describe him.

Garrett came out of his thoughts and called Lola.

"She's not back yet, Garrett," Lola said. "I tol' ya I'd have her call ya as soon as she is."

"That's not why I'm callin'," Garrett said. "Can you describe Dragoş' familiar?"

"Sure," Lola said. "He was tall, skinny, looked to be in his early fifties, but was probably much older, had thinnin', blond hair, and blue eyes. Why ya wantin' to know what he looked like?"

"Fuck me." Garrett shouted.

"Beg pardon?" Lola said.

"I know who he was. I know who the fucker was."

"Do tell."

"His name was Dannut, or somethin' like that," Garrett said. "He said to call him Dan. He had a foreign accent. I met him on Christmas mornin' when he came out to pick up Justin's body. He worked at the Eternal Rest Funeral Home. Digger's full up and George couldn't get an answer when he called. So, I called, too. Just voicemail. I think that's where Dragoş is hidin'."

Lola thought for a moment. "Ya know, I think you're on to somethin'."

"So...what'a we do?"

"Well, once Glinda gets back, we're gonna see what happens to my fire elemental when I try to put it in her air elemental," Lola said. "If that works, great. If not, at least we have a pretty good idea of where he's roostin'. So, we can confront him durin' day when he's most vulnerable.

"Call everyone and have 'em meet here as soon as they can," Lola concluded.

"Okay," Garrett said and ended the call.

~ * ~

After staying up late researching the origins of Dragoş and Cipriana, James and Winston slept until almost eleven, which was late for James but normal for Winston, who slept about twenty hours a day.

Given the time of day, James couldn't decide whether to have a late breakfast or an early lunch. He rarely ate lunch until around three o'clock. Since he'd never really understood brunch, he settled on eating a late breakfast. He fired up three eggs, two for him and one for Winston, five strips of bacon, three for him and two for Winston, and two pieces of toast, both for him. James also had a glass of orange juice and a cup of coffee; Winston had water in his bowl.

As usual, Winston inhaled his food in a matter of seconds and sat beside the table, hoping for some scraps from James, which he could never refuse giving him. His big, brown eyes were hard to resist. While James ate, he went over his research notes. He didn't think they would be of any use in destroying Dragoş, but proof of his previous life, and of his creator's, Cipriana, interested him, if not anyone else.

While rinsing the dishes, James decided something. He would not sit on the sideline with the vampire, Dragoş, as he had with the werewolves. He had studied and taught supernatural folklore for over twenty years. The werewolves had confirmed what he'd always suspected and hoped. Supernatural creatures of folklore did, in fact, exist. He wanted to see Dragoş with his own eyes.

Being an educated man, he knew, if he told Garrett he wanted to be involved, Garrett would insist he stay out of it. That left only one option. He would drive out to Lola's later that afternoon and be there when Garrett and the others arrived. Unless Garrett actually handcuffed him to Lola's front porch, which didn't seem likely, he'd have to let him take part. After all, leaving him handcuffed to Lola's porch would put him in a very precarious situation.

He made the plan. James smiled when he thought about the look he would get from Garrett.

~ * ~

Lola sat on her porch swing, enjoying the crisp, cloudless day and the fact they had a pretty good idea where Dragoş was hiding, when she sensed Glinda's return. A moment later, the magnificent, silver-haired werewolf bounded out of the woods and up to Lola's porch, where she stopped in the yard and looked at her with her green and silver eyes.

Lola got up, walked to Glinda, and stroked her silky hair. "Don't transform. Let's see what happens when we merge our elementals."

Glinda nodded her massive head, stood, and looked at the sky. As before, when she had been Paige, she saw an unending number of air elementals waiting to be conjured. She concentrated on one and willed it into existence. A moment later, a massive air elemental materialized a few feet in front of her, so close it ruffled her fur and had the beads on Lola's cornrows clicking together wildly. She willed it away until she and Lola were free of its turbulence.

"Very good, Glinda," Lola said with a smile. "As we suspected, it's large enough to trap Dragoş inside it. Now, let's see what happens when I add a fire elemental to it."

Lola bent down and plucked a brown, winter dormant blade of grass from the ground. She rubbed the blade of grass between the thumb and index finger of her right hand. It sparked and caught on fire. Lola cupped the burning blade of grass between her hands, and it instantly became a ball of fire. She willed it to become a fire elemental, opened her hands in a throwing motion, and a fire elemental appeared a few feet away from Glinda's much larger air elemental.

"Okay, Glinda," Lola said. "Let's see what happens when I merge 'em."

Lola willed her fire elemental toward the air elemental. As it got closer, the fire elemental lost shape from the air elemental's swirling wind. Undeterred, Lola forced the fire elemental into the much bigger air elemental. They merged and for a moment, the air elemental became a tornado of fire. Then the fire elemental winked out of existence.

"Damn," Lola shouted. "I hate when James is right."

Glinda transformed into Paige and said, "That sucks. What now."

"Never you mind 'bout that," Lola said. "There's more than one way to skin a vampire. Even without the fire, Glinda should still be able to trap Dragoş in her air elemental while I scatter the other three vampires with mine.

"And your daddy figured out where ol' Dragoş is roostin' durin' the day," Lola said as she looked at Paige. "He's gettin' everyone together to meet here. Then we'll have his ancient ass."

"What?" Paige said. "Daddy knows where Dragoş is hidin'?

How'd he figure it out?"

"Your daddy's a pretty smart guy," Lola said. "Turns out the guy from the new funeral home who came out Christmas mornin' to...ya know, is the familiar who came snoopin' 'round here and Dragoş destroyed before I could penetrate the black walls 'round his mind in the cemetery."

Paige shivered, but not from the cold, which she was immune to. "That's the guy? He was there to get Justin's body. He gave me the heebie-jeebies."

Lola put her arm around Paige and hugged her. "I know why he was there, sweet girl. I just didn't wanna say it. He gave me to heebie-jeebies, too."

"He did not," Paige scoffed. "You're not afraid of anything, Lola."

"You couldn't be more wrong, Paige-Turner," Lola said. "There's plenty that scares me. Dragoş is at the top of the list. But fear is good. Fear keeps ya on your toes and aware. You and Glinda best fear Dragoş, too. Do *not* underestimate him, chil'."

Paige thought about how easily she'd invaded Dragoş' mind. "We won't. I promise."

Lola looked at Paige, as if searching for something. "Okay. All we can do now is wait for the posse. Ya hungry?"

Paige smiled. "Always."

They started toward the house when Lola stopped and held her cellphone out to Paige. "Crap. I promised your daddy you'd call as soon as ya got back. He's worried 'bout ya."

"Okay," Paige said with a smile. "Another minute won't hurt. I'll call him from my cell inside."

"Alright," Lola said. "But, if he asks, ya just got back. I can't believe I forgot to tell ya. Since we don't know when they'll get here, ya best put one of my dresses on."

"Okay. But I'm not puttin' it on 'til I hear 'em comin'," Paige said. "I keep Glinda on high alert these days and I'll know they're comin' from miles away."

Lola smiled at Paige as they walked up the porch steps and went inside.

~ * ~

Garrett sat at his desk. He was frustrated. He'd gotten ahold of Ty and Trowa. They were ready to go as soon as he gave the word. But Fr. Mike was in Tyler at the East Texas Diocese for a meeting. Worse, he told Garrett the soonest he could be at Lola's would be around five o'clock. That left little time to get to the funeral home before dark. If they wanted to catch Dragoş while he rested, and most vulnerable, they'd have to go without him. He started to call Lola and explain the situation when his cell rang. It was Paige.

Garrett answered. "Hey, sweet girl. How ya doin'?"

"I'm okay, Daddy. It was definitely Clive Jones and Glinda buried him very deep."

"Thanks," Garrett said. "I'm sorry I had to ask ya to do that."

"I'm okay," Paige said. "I know that Glinda and I are always part of each other, no matter which form we're in, but Glinda's not bothered by that stuff as much as I would be. I promise."

"As long as you're okay, I'm okay."

"I am. Lola told me ya figured out that creepy guy from the new funeral home was Dragoş' familiar," Paige said. "Good job, Daddy. Now we can get Dragoş while he's restin'."

"Yeah. About that," Garrett said. "Can ya put me on speaker so Lola can hear what I have to tell y'all?"

Paige put her iPhone on speaker. "You're on speaker."

"Slight problem," Garrett began. "I got ahold of everyone. Ty and Trowa are ready to go now. But Father Mike is in Tyler and can't get to your house until around five o'clock. That's too close to sunset for my comfort. Can we do this without him?"

Lola thought for a moment. "We can. Especially since he's restin' and we have surprise on our side. But…we need him if there's any chance of savin' Lin."

"No way," Paige said. "We aren't doin' this today if it means losin' Lin. We know where he is. We can kill him tomorrow."

"He'll come for you and Glinda tonight," Lola said.

"Then we'll kill him tonight," Paige insisted.

"Think about this, Paige-Turner," Garrett said. "He's vulnerable now. If we wait 'til tonight or tomorrow, he'll probably kill more people. He killed *five* people last night. Do ya want that to happen again?"

To Lola, Paige said, "Can we trap Lin and hold her 'til Father Mike can help her?"

"We can try," Lola said. "But there's no way to know if it'll work."

"It's Lin, Daddy. If there's a chance we can save her, we have to try."

"We'll try, sweetheart," Garrett said. "I can promise ya that. But I can't guarantee it. You and Glinda up for goin' now?"

Paige hesitated a moment and, defeatedly, said, "Yeah. I don't want anyone else to be killed by Dragoş or his cloud. If Glinda has to hold Lin down 'til Father Mike gets there, she's doin' it."

"Deal," Garrett said. "I'll call Ty and Trowa and tell 'em to head your way. I love you, Paige-Turner."

"I love you too, Daddy."

Garrett ended the call, called Ty and Trowa, and headed out the back of the jail where he had parked his SUV.

~ * ~

Ty was the first to show up at Lola's house, about fifteen minutes after Garrett told him it was go time. Trowa arrived about five minutes after Ty. And Garrett, who had to drive all the way from the Department, arrived about twenty minutes after Trowa. It was just after one o'clock when all of them got in Garrett's SUV and headed to the Eternal Rest Funeral Home, which was only a thirty-minute drive from Lola's. They had plenty of time.

~ * ~

Zack worked as fast as he could. His Master was safe at the new location, which was the most important task. He had Ilinca and Lacrima's coffins loaded in the back of the two-coffin hearse. The round trip took about forty minutes. He left the Eternal Rest Funeral Home with the precious cargo.

At about the same time Garrett and his posse left Lola's house, Zack arrived at the new location and unloaded Ilinca and Lacrima's coffins. He placed them on either side of his Master's throne and headed back to the funeral home to pick up Ruxandra and the empty coffin.

Zack had left the left garage door open when he departed each time to make transporting his Master's cloud more efficient. When he got to the funeral home, he pulled around back, backed into the opened garage, pushed the button on the visor to shut the door, and got out while the door rattled down. He knew Ruxandra was safe from the sunlight underground in her coffin, but he couldn't chance harming her. If she was harmed, his Master would surely kill him. Unlike the first twenty-four hours after becoming the Master's familiar, when he prayed to a God who no longer listened for a quick death, now, all he wanted was to serve his Master for eternity.

~ * ~

When Garett and company pulled into the Eternal Rest Funeral Home parking lot, there was no sign of the hearse, but a black Cadillac Escalade was parked on the side of the building.

"That wraps it up nicely," Lola said as Garrett stopped the SUV in front of the funeral home's double-door entrance.

"What?" Garrett asked.

"That's the Cadillac Dragoş' familiar was drivin' when he followed me out to the Not Forgotten Cemetery," Lola said.

Garrett looked from Paige in the front seat to Lola, Ty, and Trowa in the back seat. "Y'all ready to do this?"

Everyone nodded and Lola said, "Do not mistake Zack for the man he was. He's all that's standin' between us and Dragoş. After drinkin' Dragoş' foul blood, he'll be extremely powerful. The three of y'all might have to unload all your bullets to take him down."

"Understood," Garrett answered for the three with guns.

As the five of them got out of the SUV, Garrett said, "I'll get the batterin' ram outta the back so we can break down the doors."

Garrett opened the back of the SUV with the key fob, grabbed the battering ram, and the five of them went to the double doors.

"Is this one of them no-knock warrants?" Trowa asked with a chuckle.

"You bet your ass it is," Garrett said as he swung the battering ram back.

"No offense, Garrett," Ty said. "If ya want those doors broke in one swing, best let me do it."

Garrett looked at his muscular friend, nodded, and handed Ty the battering ram.

"Get your guns out," Lola reminded Garrett and Trowa.

They did.

Ty swung the heavy battering ram back and heaved it into the middle of the doors as hard as he could. There was a loud thud as the head of the battering ram contacted the doors. A loud cracking sound followed this as the doors split and swung open; splinters fell from the two top bolt locks where the wooden frame broke on the impact. Ty dropped the battering ram and took out his pistol. The five of them entered the dark and quiet funeral home.

~ * ~

Zack was in the Master's throne room, about to pick up Ruxandra's coffin, when he heard the front doors crash in. He jumped out of the throne room, closed the entrance to keep Ruxandra's hiding place concealed and her safe, and went to kill whoever had dared to enter his Master's abandoned home.

~ * ~

As Paige entered the funeral home, with Glinda dialed up to near transformation, she said, "I smell Mister Zack. But there's not much of him left. Should I transform now?"

"Not yet," Lola said. "Look for Zack. I will, too."

Paige knew exactly what Lola meant by look. She used her silver seeing eye and saw him. He was in an embalming room at the back of the funeral home and headed their way.

"He's comin'." Paige shouted.

"From where?" Ty asked.

"He'll be comin' through the door on the left in about three seconds," Lola said.

The door opened, and a crazed-looking Zack Zane emerged. The front of the clothes he wore were soaked with so much black blood it glistened in the light filtering in through the shattered front doors like old motor oil.

"Stop right there, Zack," Garrett commanded.

"I'm afraid I can't do that, Garrett," Zack said. "I serve my Master and y'all have to go. Now."

Garrett, Ty, and Trowa began shooting. The bullets penetrated Zack's body. Black blood exploded from each bullet hole, but he continued toward them. More bullets struck Zack, and his pace slowed a little. Garrett went for a head shot, but it went wide and ripped Zack's left ear off in a spray of black blood. On he came. Trowa hit Zack's right knee, and he went down in the haze of gun smoke. The shooting stopped.

The air in the funeral home reeked of gunpowder and was so full of smoke from the shots fired that Garrett, Ty, and Trowa couldn't see Zack through it. Paige and Lola saw him, though. He wasn't dead. He got back to his feet and continued toward them through the concealing smoke.

Paige didn't hesitate or bother to remove Lola's dress. She transformed into Glinda, which shredded the dress, pushed past the three men, and with one fluid swipe from her right hand-paw, sent Mister Zack's head flying across the large entrance area of the funeral home. It hit the left side wall with enough force it sank into the sheetrock and stayed there. His head oozed black blood down the wall. His headless body convulsed on the floor as black blood spurted out of his ragged neck until his heart stopped beating. Then it laid still.

"Probably should've done that in the first place," Trowa mused.

"Yep," Ty agreed.

"No time for chitchat, gentlemen," Lola said. "Zack came from the embalmin' room. That's where we'll find Dragoş. And I'm guessin' he heard the shootin'.

"Remember the plan, Glinda," Lola continued sternly. "Trap Dragoş in your air elemental while I deal with his cloud."

Glinda nodded her hunched head. She was taller than the ceiling was high, and turned to the door Zack came through. The others followed in her massive wake.

Once they were in the embalming room, which had been the auto bay of the repair garage and had a high ceiling, Glinda stood to her full, nine-foot height. It was empty, except for two embalming tables, the embalming equipment, and stainless-steel counters and shelves that lined the walls.

"Where is he?" Garrett asked.

Lola looked through the room and saw the hole beneath a counter and shelf to their right. Glinda saw it, too.

Glinda started toward the hidden entrance, but Lola said, "Air elemental, Glinda."

Glinda quickly conjured one and the three men stepped back, away from the living tornado. Then Glinda sent the elemental to the heavy counter and shelf and sent it flying into the hearse. It smashed into the back of the hearse with enough force to blow out all its windows and send it crashing into the closed garage door. The door crumpled outward, and sunlight filtered in from either side. Where the counter and shelf had been a hole in the concrete floor became visible. Glinda started for the hole.

"Wait," Lola shouted to be heard over the freight train sound coming from the elemental. "Send the elemental in first, Glinda. Trap his ass."

Glinda wanted to jump down in the hole, rip Dragoş' head off, and save Lin. As Lola's words sank in, she realized she was operating on rage, which wasn't smart. She did as Lola told her and sent the enormous air elemental down through the hole.

When the air elemental vanished through the hole under the embalming room, the building shook as if a tornado had hit it. Along with the roaring sound of the elemental, there came a crashing sound as the coffins smashed into each other. There was a scream.

"Bring up the elemental." Lola shouted.

Glinda did. As it emerged, the only thing trapped in its whirling winds was Lena Culpepper. She was naked, with translucent skin that had many cuts from the power of the air elemental. Black blood whirled around her small body. Glinda dismissed the elemental and Ruxandra fell to the concrete floor. She was up in a flash. She hissed and bared her pointed fangs. Then she, stupidly, charged at Glinda.

Glinda caught the small vampire by the chest with her dagger claws, pushed in, penetrated her ribs, and closed her hand-paw tightly. Ruxandra's chest erupted in a spray of black blood as Glinda extracted her heart and squeezed it. It popped like a black filled water balloon and Ruxandra's dead body fell to the concrete floor.

Dismayed Dragoş hadn't been caught in the powerful elemental, Glinda threw caution to the wind and jumped into the hole. She was more than dismayed by what she saw in the earthen room she'd seen through Dragoş' eyes only a couple of hours earlier. Except for two empty coffins, the lair was empty.

A moment later, Lola joined Glinda in the earthen lair.

"Where is he?" Lola asked.

Because she didn't enjoy talking through Glinda, and Lola wasn't bothered by her nakedness, Paige transformed. "He was here earlier. I know he was. I saw this...room."

Lola gave Paige a sidelong look. "How do ya know that?"

When Paige didn't immediately answer, Lola said, "What did ya do, chil'?"

"I-I-I kinda invaded Dragoş' mind earlier, when I found Clive's body," Paige confessed. "I figured, since Glinda has enhanced senses, it would work through her. It did. He didn't know I was in his mind. He thought I was...here. I saw this room through his eyes when he looked around for me."

"How?" Lola said. "We put a white vault 'round your mind to keep this from happenin'."

Not wanting to throw Angelica under the bus, Paige lied. "I found a way out, and I wanted to see if I could find him."

"Stupid, stupid, chil'," Lola scolded Paige. "He's gone 'cause ya meddled when ya shouldn't have. We had him, Paige."

Paige averted Lola's condemning gaze. "I know. Daddy found him without my help, and I screwed it all up."

Lola could tell Paige was close to tears.

Instead of scolding her again, which she wanted to do, she put her arm around Paige's shoulders. "Yeah. Ya did. But you're sixteen, and you're a werewolf with pure sight. That's too much power to think ya *wouldn't* screw up."

"What am I gonna tell Daddy?"

"We'll tell him that Dragoş must have sensed we were comin' and left," Lola said. "That's not a lie. We'll just leave out the part 'bout how he sensed it from you."

"Thanks, Lola," Paige said appreciatively. "Do ya think he's gone, gone?"

"No, chil'," Lola said. "Zack moved him and Lin and Taylor somewhere close. Zack was here to take Lena and the empty coffin to his new hidin' place. Makes sense that he'd have a backup hidin' place. I tol' ya not to underestimate him."

"I could…" Paige began.

"Don't ya dare, Paige-Turner," Lola interrupted. "You're not my chil', but I will put ya over my knee and spank your little ass raw if ya do."

"Wouldn't hurt," Paige said.

"You keep forgettin' that supernatural creatures can hurt each other," Lola said with a wink. "I'd set your ass on fire, chil'."

"What's goin' on down there?" Garrett shouted.

"He's gone," Lola said.

"Gone? Gone where?" Garrett shouted.

"We don't know, Daddy."

"How'd he know we were comin'?" Garrett shouted.

"We don't know that either," Lola said.

"Damn it," Garrett shouted. "What now?"

"We'll have to figure somethin' else out," Lola said. "On the bright side, we'll have Father Mike with us tonight."

"Well, hell," Garrett said dejectedly. "C'mon up and let's get outta here."

"Give us a minute, Garrett," Lola said.

"What the hell for?" Garrett said. "We need to get the hell outta here. Someone might've heard that…tornado and come look."

"Okay. We'll come up," Lola said. "But Paige is naked 'cause she shredded my dress when she transformed. There are some girl's clothes down here that might fit her. But we'll come on up."

"Dam it, Paige," Garrett said. "Stop shreddin' your clothes when ya transform. Find somethin' to wear."

Lola and Paige shared a smile before they looked through the clothes that had belonged to Melanie, Taylor, Lena, Megan, and Lin. All the clothes had blood on them, but, at least, it was dried blood. Lin and Melanie's clothes were the best fit. They were the same age and similar in Paige's size. Wearing Melanie's Christmas dress felt too weird. So, Paige wore the nightshirt Lin was wearing when Dragoş took her. It was a little shorter on Paige than on Lin, but it covered what her daddy called 'girl parts.' So, it would work.

A couple of minutes later, Lola and Paige emerged from the hole. Paige looked at what Glinda had done to Lena and felt her stomach turn. Lena's remains had already turned an ashen gray, and her skin was flaking off. She'd be a pile of ash in no time.

"We best get gone," Ty said.

"We need to regroup and figure out what to do tonight," Trowa added.

"Yeah," Garrett said. "But first, we need to hide Zack's body."

"Where?" Ty asked.

Garrett pointed at the hole. "We can drop him in there and put the counter and shelves back over it to hide it."

"Okay," Trowa said.

Lola and Paige waited in the embalming room as Garrett, Ty, and Trowa got Zack's body and head, dropped it in the hole, and with effort, moved the dented counter and shelves from the hearse back in to place over the hole. The counter and shelves were misshapen from hitting the hearse, but it hid the hole, which was what mattered.

All of them felt dejected at not having found and killed Dragoş.

So, they spoke no words as they left the funeral home, got in Garrett's SUV, and pulled out of the Eternal Rest Funeral home.

~ * ~

Dragoş' eyes flew open in the darkness of his throne when he sensed the death of his familiar. Then rage consumed his black mind when he felt the destruction of his newest daughter, Ruxandra.

He wanted nothing more than to leap from his throne and bellow rage at the top of his undead lungs, but the new location, the backup location, unlike his throne room under the funeral home, wasn't impervious to the deadly sunlight. In fact, sunlight filtered in through the partially collapsed roof, rotted wood siding, and broken windows of the barn that once belonged to Dale Wiseman. Although he didn't know it, the old barn had been Alexis Jordan's, the werewolf that began the chain of events that led Dragoş to East Texas in search of the silver-haired werewolf to be his familiar, den.

Dragoş turned his rage inward and waited for sundown. It was only a few hours away. When it came, Dragoş would release living hell on all involved in the killing of his familiar and the destruction of his three daughters, and Vanda would be his. His for eternity.

~ * ~

Garrett and company hadn't made it back to Lola's house when his cell rang. He looked and saw it was Erica Harris.

This can't be good news, he thought.

Garrett answered. "What's up, Erica?"

"I just gotta call," Erica said. "Someone found the Hendersons murdered in their house. I didn't think you'd want this goin' out on the radio. Not with all those folks who like listenin' to scanners. So, I thought it best to call ya."

"Ya mean, scanner listeners like the press?"

"Yes, sir."

"Ya did good. Thanks. I have a stop to make and then I'll head that way," Garrett said and ended the call.

"Hendersons or Culpeppers?" Ty asked.

"Hendersons," Garrett said.

"Ya want Trowa and I to take it?" Ty said. "Give ya a break for a bit."

"Thanks, Ty," Garrett said, "but I need to be there, and y'all shouldn't have to put up with George's bitchin'. That's my job."

"I'll go with ya instead of Ty," Trowa said. "You could use a break too, brother."

"Yeah. I'll take Trowa, Ty," Garrett said. "Get some rest. I gotta feelin' you'll need it for tonight."

"So, will y'all," Ty said. "I can't rest knowin' y'all are workin'."

"Then go home and spend some time with Jasmine and Little D," Garrett said.

"Everybody relax," Lola said. "Ty, you go on home to your beautiful wife and little one. As for the rest of y'all, Miss Lola can brew up some special tea that'll make y'all feel like y'all have gotten twelve hours' sleep before we deal with Dragoş tonight."

"Okay," Ty relented. "Y'all win."

"Do me one favor, though," Garrett said.

"Sure," Ty said. "What'a ya need?"

"Call Father Mike, fill him in on what happened, and ask him to come to Lola's when he leaves Tyler," Garrett said.

"Roger that."

Garrett pulled up in front of Lola's house and Ty, Paige, and Lola got out. Ty headed for his SUV as Lola and Paige headed for the house.

Trowa climbed into the front seat from the back. "Ya ready, Chief?"

"Yeah," Garrett said as he turned the SUV around and headed for the Henderson's house.

~ * ~

Ty called Fr. Mike on his way home and did as Garrett requested. He filled him in on what happened at the funeral home and asked him to get to Lola's as soon as he could. Fr. Mike had questions about what their plan for the night was; Ty didn't have answers. Fr. Mike agreed to come to Lola's as soon as he left Tyler. Ty ended the call as he pulled into his driveway.

He went inside and found Jasmin and Little D asleep on the couch. The TV was on, but the volume was turned down low. Jasmin did this when it was Little D's nap time. *SpongeBob SquarePants* was on, and he and his pals were up to some underwater shenanigans. He didn't want to wake them, so he sat in the recliner where he could watch the two loves of his life sleeping like the angels they were. The recliner squeaked and Jasmin's beautiful avocado eyes fluttered open.

She smiled and whispered, "Hey there, handsome man. What are ya doin' home so early?"

"Gotta work tonight," Ty whispered. "So, Garrett sent me home."

"It's those murders and missin' girls, isn't it?" Jasmine whispered. Ty nodded.

"I saw the noon news," Jasmine whispered. "Garrett said Clive Jones is doin' these horrible things."

"Yeah," Ty whispered. "We thought we had him 'bout an hour ago. But, if he was where he was spotted, he was gone when we got there."

Jasmin, like most Pine View natives her age, knew about Clive's past.

"He's an evil man, Ty. Garrett said he's armed. Please be careful."

"I always am, pretty lady," Ty said with a smile.

Little D's big, sleepy, brown eyes opened. They focused on the TV, and he giggled at something SpongeBob said. Context didn't matter to a three-year-old.

"Hey, little man," Ty said.

Little D's eyes shifted to his daddy, and he shouted, "Daddy's home. Look, Mommy. Daddy's home."

Jasmin laughed. "He is? I don't see him."

Little D giggled and pointed at his daddy. "Silly, Mommy. He's right there."

"Oh. I see him now," Jasmine said and smiled. "Ya better go give him a hug."

Little D jumped off the couch, ran the few feet between the couch and recliner, and launched himself at his daddy. Ty caught him by the waist and propelled him in the air over his head.

Little D spread out his arms and squealed, "I'm flyin', Mommy."

Ty held Little D aloft for a few moments then lowered him onto his chest, and hugged him tightly. "Who's my little man?"

"I am, Daddy," Little D happily squealed. "I'm your little man."

Jasmin watched from the couch and smiled at the two loves of her life.

~ * ~

Garrett and Trowa arrived at the Henderson's and found a very distraught man sitting on the front porch and a late model, red, Ram pickup parked beside the Henderson's vehicles. He got up when Garrett stopped the SUV next to the Ram and he and Trowa stepped out.

The man wobbled on unsteady legs and shouted, "They're dead. Both of 'em are dead."

Garrett approached the man. "Okay. I know you're upset. But I need ya to calm down a bit. Calm down and tell me who ya are and why you're here. My deputy and I will take it from there."

The man took a couple of deep breaths, which seemed to calm him a bit. "My name's Cade Tasker. I work...worked with Troy. He's been off work since what happened to Trevor. I've been checkin' in on him and Penny regularly to see if they needed anything. Ya know, like groceries or anything else. I came out here a while ago and saw the front door broken down," Cade said and shuddered. "So, I went inside to see if they were okay, and...they're not. They're both dead."

"Okay, Mister Tasker," Garrett said. "Did ya touch anything or move anything while you were inside?"

Cade thought for a moment. "No. I don't think I did. Troy's gun is on the floor by him. I thought maybe he and Penny, ya know. Murder, suicide. But there are bite marks on 'em, and there's a hole in the back wall of their trailer, too. What the hell could'a happened, Sheriff?"

"We're gonna try to figure that out, Mister Tasker," Garrett

497

assured Cade.

"Do ya think it's the same person who killed Trevor?" Cade asked.

"I do," Garrett said. "We're lookin' for a man named Clive Jones who we think did all these murders and took those girls."

Cade's eyes went wide. "Really? I was just a kid when he did all that other stuff, but I know who he is."

"Okay. Now listen close, Mister Tasker," Garrett said. "I need ya to go home or back to work, so Deputy Raintree and I can do what we need to do here. You're a material witness, now. So, ya can't talk about any of what ya saw in their house. Do you understand?"

Cade nodded. "Yeah. No details."

"This is important, Mister Tasker," Garrett said sternly. "When we catch Clive, and he goes to trial, you'll be a witness. If ya spread what ya saw in there around, it could impugn your testimony, and Clive might get off on a technicality. We don't want that, do we?"

Cade shook his head. "No, sir. We don't want that. My lips are sealed."

"Good," Garrett said. "Now go on to wherever you're goin' and let us take it from here."

Cade nodded again, got in his truck, and left.

When he left, Trowa said, "Damn. You're good, Garrett. Do ya really think he'll keep his mouth shut?"

"He will, for a while," Garrett said with a halfhearted smile. "When this is over, it won't matter. Most folks'll think he's embellishin' what he saw, anyway."

"What now?"

"I call a very pissed off George and we wait."

"And then?" Trowa said.

Garrett looked at his watch and saw it was almost three o'clock. "We hope that no one discovers the Culpeppers today. As it is, we'll be lucky to finish up here before four o'clock. No time to deal with the Culpeppers before sunset."

Trowa took a seat on the porch steps while Garrett called George. After the call, Garrett joined Trowa on the steps. There was no need to document a murder scene that would never go to trial. They waited in silence.

~ * ~

Lola and Paige rinsed dishes after a late lunch when Paige, who always kept Glinda on high alert mode since Dragoş showed up, heard a truck turn off the road and onto Lola's driveway.

"Someone's comin' up your driveway," Paige said.

Lola looked out the window over the sink, which was on the side of the house, where she couldn't see the driveway, and smiled. "Put some clothes on, Paige-Turner. If I'm not mistaken, that's our friend James Huff's truck."

Paige smiled; she was always happy to see Dr. James. "Ya got anything a little less…see through that I can wear?"

Lola laughed. "No, ma'am. I don't. The men folk'll just have to get comfortable seein' a little more of ya than they'd like. But your boobs ain't near as big as mine. So, at least, they won't poke out like mine."

"Gee," Paige said sarcastically. "Thanks, Lola. Way to make a girl feel good 'bout her boobs."

"Yeah, well," Lola said and smiled. "When you're older and gravity has your once firm boobs hangin' down to your bellybutton, you'll look back on your small boob days fondly."

"Okay," Paige said with a laugh. "That's just gross, Lola."

"Don't say I didn't warn ya," Lola chuckled. "Now go put somethin' on. He's almost here."

Paige heard Dr. James' truck come to a stop in Lola's front yard. She hurried out of the kitchen, through the dining room, through the living room, into Lola's bedroom, and into the closet. Paige had just found the most suitable dress when she heard Dr. James knock on the door. She slipped it over her head and hurried back in the living room as Lola opened the door.

James gave Lola a warm hug and then looked at Paige. He hadn't seen her since she drank the protection potion. He'd heard about the effect it'd had, but seeing it was altogether different.

"Oh, I love your seein' eye," James beamed. "It's beautiful,

Paige."

"Thank you, Doctor James."

"Drop that doctor crap when your daddy's not around and give me a hug," James said.

Paige did, and it felt good to not feel awkward around a man.

~ * ~

"For fuck's sake, Garrett," George said and exhaled harshly. "Do you realize I'm doin' all these postmortem exams myself to keep the true cause of death a secret?"

"Yes, I do, George," Garrett said as he placed a hand on George's shoulder. "I appreciate what you're doin', but there's nothin' that can be done 'bout the people who've already been killed. We are workin' our asses off, day *and* night, to find and kill this fucker. So, cut me a little slack."

"I get it, Garrett," George said. "Believe me, I don't wanna switch jobs with ya. But I'm overwhelmed, and your tellin' me there are two more bodies just waitin' to be discovered and reported. I can't do this much longer."

"Hopefully, ya won't have to," Trowa said.

"Are y'all close to catchin' this…thing?" George asked.

"We were," Garrett assured George. "We missed him by a hair earlier this afternoon."

"Wait," George said. "I thought these things couldn't go out in the daylight?"

"They can't," Garrett said. "He had help from Zack Zane."

George's jaw dropped. His lips moved like a fish out of water, but no words came.

"Oh, yeah. That reminds me," Garrett said. "The reason ya can't get ahold of anyone at the Eternal Rest Funeral Home is because that's where Dragoş, that's his name, was hidin'."

George finally found his voice. "Zack Zane was helpin' the thing that took his daughter? From your news conference, I thought Clive Jones was involved."

"Zack didn't have a choice," Garrett said. "Dragoş turned Zack into his familiar. Before ya ask, familiars are, like, vampire slaves. He had to help Dragoş, and Zack's dead. We killed him earlier when we missed catchin' Dragoş at the funeral home."

"Ya killed Zack?" George asked.

"We had to," Garrett said. "And because he was Dragoş' familiar, it took over twenty bullets to take him down."

"Holy shit," George gasped. "And Clive?"

"Clive's a scapegoat 'cause folks'll believe he's capable of doin' these things," Garrett said. "He's dead, too. But ya don't have to worry 'bout him."

"Do I wanna know why I don't have to worry 'bout him?" George asked.

Garrett shook his head. "Nope. All ya need to know is that he's takin' the fall for all this. He's dead, and ya don't have to deal with his body."

"What about Zack's body?"

"He's taken care of, too," Trowa said.

"I can work with that," George said. "Two fewer bodies to deal with. Just find and kill this thing soon."

"This *thing* is an eight-hundred-year-old vampire named Dragoş Văduva, George," Garrett said. "Since you're dealin' with his victims, ya might as well call it what it is."

George shook his head slowly. "Werewolves and vampires in Pine View County. What's next? Zombies?"

"Don't even *think* it, let alone say *it*," Garrett said. "I'm figurin' out anything's possible at this point."

George raised his hands in an 'I surrender' motion. "Okay. I take it back."

"Okay," Trowa said. "Let's bag 'em, load 'em, and get the hell outta here."

Fifteen minutes later, at four seventeen by the radio clock, Garrett and Trowa followed George's van out of the Henderson's driveway. George turned left, toward Pine View. Garrett and Trowa turned right toward Lola's house.

~ * ~

James, Lola, and Paige sat at Lola's kitchen table, drinking spice tea, as Lola and Paige told him what happened at the funeral home. James was, as always, fascinated to hear about encounters with supernatural creatures. Then James told them everything he'd discovered researching Dragoş and Cipriana's origins. Paige and Lola were fascinated with the story and confirmation of their timeline.

When he finished, James said, "I don't know if that helps y'all but, for me, it's interestin' to know the who, where, and when of it all."

"It can be useful, James," Lola said and smiled warmly. "Dragoş was surprised when Glinda tol' him she knew his and Cipriana's names. Knowin' his father, mother, and sisters' names might have the same affect. Throwin' him off guard again, even for a moment, might just give us the time we need to destroy him."

"I get the who, where, and when, but what about the *why* and *how*?" Paige asked.

"Why and how what?" James asked.

"Well, *why* would a vampire create one as old as Cipriana?" Paige said. "And *why* isn't she still with Dragoş?"

"Vampires, like people, have different…sexual preferences," Lola said. "Whatever vampire created Cipriana must've been attracted to older, portly women. Cipriana must've been attracted to younger, handsome men. We're all too aware of what Dragoş is attracted to. Teenage girls. And, given what James tol' us 'bout Dragoş' behavior before becomin' a vampire, he's stayin' true to his vile nature."

"Okay," Paige said. "I get that, but what happened to Cipriana and Dragoş' creators? *How* are they free of them?"

"They, most likely, killed their creators." James said.

"Then why haven't any of Dragoş' vampires killed him?" Paige said. "How has he existed for eight-hundred years when his and Cipriana's creators are dead?"

"He's shrewd and Cipriana wasn't," Lola said.

"I don't understand," Paige said.

"Cipriana probably kept Dragoş around too long," James explained. "He grew powerful and tired of her. So, he killed her. I'm bettin' Dragoş probably purges his cloud regularly."

"Purges?" Paige said confused.

"He kills his...girls before they are powerful enough, or tired enough of him, to be a threat," Lola answered.

"That's messed up," Paige said.

"No. That's shrewd," Lola said. "That, Paige-Turner, is *why* and *how* Dragoş came to be an independent, eight-hundred-year-old vampire."

"He's probably the oldest vampire ever to exist," James added.

"How can ya know that?" Paige asked.

"Well, I don't *know* for sure, but he's certainly, to my knowledge, the oldest ever documented," James admitted.

"I think you're correct, James," Lola said. "Seers have been dealin' with vampires since the beginnin'. We pass tales down through the generations. None in my council can recall a vampire this old. Not even Mamma Deupree and she's the oldest and wisest seer alive."

"Well, if Dragoş was gonna kill 'em anyway, I don't feel so bad 'bout Glinda killin' Agrapina, Antanasia, and Ruxandra," Paige said.

"Ya got more reasons than that for not feelin' bad 'bout killin' those three, chil'," Lola said. "You saw the trapped souls in the vampires' black auras. By killin' 'em young, ya saved a lot of souls from not meetin' the same fate. Even if Dragoş only keeps his cloud members around for fifty or a hundred years before he kills 'em, think how many innocent souls they could take in that time."

"I know you're right," Paige said sadly. "But Melanie was my friend. Even though I didn't know Megan or Lena well, they were innocent victims, too."

"I know Melanie was your friend," Lola said. "And Megan and Lena *were* innocent victims, but the things Glinda killed weren't them anymore. They were beyond savin'."

"But Lin's not, right?" Paige said hopefully.

"I believe, in my heart, that we can save Lin," Lola said.

Paige smiled and cocked her head. "Someone else is comin'."

Lola, Paige, and James went out on the front porch just in time to see Ty pull up and park next to James' truck.

Ty got out, with a big smile on his handsome face. "Good to see ya, James."

"You too, my friend," James said as the two men bro hugged.

"So, I'm the first one here?" Ty said.

"I was," James corrected Ty. "And I'm goin' with y'all tonight."

"I'm happy to have ya along, but Garrett'll have kittens," Ty said.

"Let him," Lola said.

"Hi, Mister Ty."

Ty looked at Paige, saw through the dress she had on, and looked into her green and silver eyes. "Hey there, Paige-Turner."

Paige wrapped Ty in an awkward for him, hug and kissed his smooth cheek. Unlike her daddy, Ty had always been clean shaven.

When the hug ended, Lola smiled a warm smile at Ty's embarrassment. "I know you two are probably cold. Let's go on back inside. I've still got some special tea to brew. This tea puts Red Bull, Monster, and all those other energy drinks to shame."

They went inside to Lola's kitchen. Paige helped Lola brew the 'special tea' while James filled Ty in on all he'd learned about Dragoş and Cipriana.

He'd have to tell it all again when her daddy and Trowa arrived. And again, when Fr. Mike arrived, but Paige got the feeling James wouldn't mind one bit. He was proud of what he'd discovered and enjoyed talking about it.

As Lola put the kettle over a conjured, orange flame, a regular flame wouldn't work on the kitchen countertop, Paige heard someone else coming.

"Daddy and Trowa are here," Paige said as she hurried out to meet them.

~ * ~

Garrett and Trowa made good time getting back to Lola's, but it could've been better. They got stopped at the only train crossing north of Pine View by a very long and slow-moving freight train. That it was slowing down meant it was stopping in Nacogdoches and dropping off or picking up cars before it headed south for Houston.

When they pulled into Lola's driveway, the radio clock displayed '4:59.'

"I wonder if we beat the priest here?" Trowa said.

Garrett sped down Lola's long driveway and said, "We're fixin' to find out."

As they broke through the woods surrounding Lola's house, Garrett was surprised to see a 1985, blue on sliver Chevy Silverado pickup truck parked beside Ty's department SUV. And Paige came out the front door in a dress that revealed way too much for his comfort.

"What's James doin' here?" Trowa asked.

"I guess we're fixin' to find that out, too," Garrett said.

Garrett parked next to Ty's SUV and Paige wrapped him in a tight hug as soon as he got out.

Garrett hugged her back. "Doesn't Lola have anything less...revealin' for ya to wear?"

Still hugging, Paige said, "Sorry, Daddy. This is all she's got. At least, my boobs don't poke out like hers do."

"Okay," Garrett said. "That's enough talk about boobs."

Paige released the hug as Lola, Ty, and James stepped out onto the porch. Lola had two large thermos bottles in her hands. It was the special tea.

"Really?" Garrett said. "Ya got nothin' else Paige can wear, Lola?"

"Really," Lola said with a sly grin. "That's my normal attire, and ya don't seem to mind me dressin' this way."

Garrett blushed. "Well, you're not my little girl."

Lola smiled at Garrett's embarrassment. "At least her boobs don't poke out like mine."

Garrett raised a hand. "Stop. We've already had the boob talk. No more boob talk."

"She looks lovely," James said.

"Hey, James," Garrett said. "Sorry. I was a little preoccupied."

"James found out some pretty interestin' stuff about Dragoş and Cipriana," Ty said.

"That's good, but ya didn't have to come all the way out here to tell us," Garrett said. "Ya could'a just called."

A smile spread across James' pudgy face. "And miss all the fun? I'm goin' with y'all tonight."

"Like hell, ya are," Garrett said sternly. "I've already got Paige, Lola, Ty, Trowa, and Father Mike to worry about. I'm not addin' you to the list."

"I told y'all," Ty said with a laugh. "He's havin' kittens."

"Like I said, let him," Lola added.

Confused, Garrett said, "Y'all are okay with James comin' along when we face Dragoş and the other two vampires?"

"He's a grown man," Trowa said. "It is his decision. Not ours."

"There's your answer, Garrett," Lola said. "We're perfectly fine with James comin'. And since he knows Dragoş' origin best, he can be an asset."

Defeated, Garrett said, "Okay. Please don't make me regret this, James. You're a good friend. If somethin' happens to ya, I'll never forgive myself."

James walked up to Garrett and bro hugged him. "I love ya, too, Garrett. But ya need to understand somethin'. I've studied supernatural folklore my entire professional career. I chose this area of research 'cause it has fascinated me since I was a little boy, watchin' the old, black and white, Universal, monster movies. I stayed out of the werewolf issue, except for stakin' out Dillion to no end, and I've regretted it since. I have to see Dragoş with my own eyes. I *have* to."

As they parted, Garrett said, "I'm sorry, James. I never considered it from your point of view. I always considered ya an advisor, not a hunter. If it means that much to ya, I'm happy to have ya by my side."

Paige broke the emotional exchange when she said, "Father Mike just turned onto Miss Lola's driveway."

"So, we're almost all here," Ty said. "What now?"

"Yeah," Trowa added as Fr. Mike's car came into view. "We don't know where Dragoş is now."

Paige had an idea. Actually, it was Mamma's idea, but she waited until Fr. Mike joined them.

Fr. Mike parked next to Garrett's SUV and got out. "So, you guys missed him at the funeral home. What now?"

Paige waited a second to see if anyone else had an idea.

When none were forthcoming, Paige said, "We go on offense. But not here. Someplace neutral that gives us the advantage. Someplace most of us know well."

"Like where, sweetheart?" Garrett asked.

Paige grinned. "The MRB."

They met this pronouncement with silence, until Lola said, "Mamma?"

Paige smiled. "Mamma."

Garrett looked at his iPhone. It was five-o-five p.m. He checked the weather app and saw sunset came at five twenty-four. Nineteen minutes wasn't enough time to get to the MRB before dark.

"We can't get there before the sun sets," Garrett told them.

"That's okay," Lola said. "After what we did to Zack and Lena earlier, ol' Dragoş will be operatin' on blind rage when he wakes up."

"That helps us, how?" Mike asked.

"He'll come directly here, and we won't be here," Lola said.

"Then what?" Ty said. "How do we get him to the MRB?"

Lola glanced at Paige. "This little, rhymes with witch, found a way outta the white vault my sisters and I spent almost five hours constructin' last night. She can mislead Dragoş until we're ready."

"Is it safe?" Garrett asked.

"Apparently," Lola replied.

Garrett looked at his cell again. It was five-o-eight. "Then we best get gone. Two SUVs. Me and you, Ty."

"Roger that."

"Wait," James said. "I gotta get my vampire kit."

"Vampire kit?" Garrett asked.

"Yeah," James said as he pulled a leather satchel from his truck and rejoined them. "I'll tell ya 'bout it on the drive to the MRB."

"Do we need vampire kits?" Trowa asked with a grin.

"It's for research," James explained.

"Can we go now?" Garrett asked impatiently.

"Ready," James assured him.

"Okay," Garrett said. "Paige, James and Father Mike with me. Trowa and Lola with Ty."

Lola handed Garrett one thermos. "You, James, and Father Mike need to drink this. Ty and Trowa can drink this one."

"What about you and Paige?" Garrett said.

Lola smiled. "We don't need it."

"Okay. Let's get gone." Garrett shouted.

Paige, James, and Fr. Mike got in Garrett's SUV and Lola and Trowa got in Ty's SUV. A few moments later, they raced the sunset to the MRB. They knew they wouldn't beat sundown to their destination. All they could do was hope Lola had been right about where Dragoş would go first and Paige could mislead him until they were ready.

Chapter Fifteen

Sunset on December 29, 2015, in Pine View County, Texas came at five twenty-four p.m. Garrett, followed by Ty, took the back roads as quickly and as safely as allowed. Paige, who had the thermos with Lola's brew, filled the lid cup with a dark tea that smelled of pine. She handed the full lid to her daddy first. He downed it quickly, grimaced at the taste, and handed the empty lid back to Paige. She repeated this with Dr. James and then Fr. Mike. Both grimaced, but the taste didn't deter Dr. James from talking about everything he'd discovered about Dragoş and Cipriana's origins. Jame's findings enthralled Fr. Mike. Paige could tell her daddy listened to James but wasn't as interested as Fr. Mike. He had other concerns. Her.

A few minutes after drinking Lola's tea, Garrett stiffened in his seat. "Holy crap. That packs a hell of a punch. I feel…great."

A moment later, the tea hit the other two men, who had similar reactions.

"What did y'all put in this tea?" James asked.

Paige smiled. "I could tell ya, but then I'd have to kill ya."

"Ah. Seer trade secret," James said with a chuckle. "I understand. I feel like I could take on Dragoş on my own."

"Don't," Garrett said.

James ignored Garrett and picked up where he left off with the vampires' history, but he talked a little faster and with more enthusiasm.

Only a faint, orangish-red glow of the sun remained on the western horizon, and they were still about ten minutes from the MRB.

~ * ~

Ty, a NASCAR fan, was on Garrett's back bumper like a drafting racecar driver as they sped their way to the MRB. Like Paige had done in Garrett's SUV, Lola handed out lid cups of special tea to Ty and Trowa.

The responses from them were the same as Garrett, James, and Fr. Mike's.

When it hit Ty, he stiffened in his seat. "Wow. You should bottle this and sell it. You'd put those other energy drink companies outta business."

"Hell, yeah," Trowa said. "My people have…medicinal remedies, but we use 'em for relaxin'. With this stuff, the white man never would've removed us from our lands."

Lola smiled, but she watched the sun disappear behind the tall pine trees. She knew Dragoş would awaken soon and come for them. She closed her eyes and sent Paige a message.

Paige felt Lola in her thoughts and heard, *He'll be wakin' up in a few minutes. Can ya get into his mind while he's restin'?*

No problem.

Okay. When he wakes up, tell him somethin' like we're waitin' for him. I think he'll take the bait and go directly to my house.

Then what? Paige thought.

From what ya tol' me earlier, I don't think he can get into the white vault we put around your mind, but don't take any chances. Once he takes the bait, get out.

I will.

Don't mess around, Paige-Turner. I tol' your daddy this was safe. Don't make me regret it.

I won't, Paige's thought came and the mental connection broke.

~ * ~

Garrett noticed Paige fall into a trancelike state and waited for her to come out of it. It didn't take long.

When she did, he asked, "Lola or Dragoş?"

"Lola," Paige said. "She wants me in Dragoş' mind before he wakes up so I can mislead him to her house."

"Please be careful, Paige-Turner."

"I will, Daddy."

Paige closed her eyes, concentrated on Dragoş, and slipped out of Angelica's escape hatch. A moment later, her mind merged with his evil, black one. He had still been resting.

~ * ~

At five twenty-four p.m., Dragoş opened his eyes and opened the ornate lid to his throne. As he stood, Ilinca and Lacrima's coffins opened and they stood, too. Dragoş looked around at the pitiful backup location Dănuţ had secured for him and was disappointed in his previous familiar, but it would have to do until he secured Vanda for his cloud and her silver-haired wolf as his familiar. With the werewolf as his familiar, he could live anywhere he wanted, which was back in Romania. He'd already had enough of America and the disrespectful, challenging *vrăjitoare*, who he would kill, along with the rest of the humans who challenged his claim to Vanda, before he returned home.

~ * ~

Paige was ready to send the mental message as soon as Dragoş was out of his coffin. What she saw, where she saw, through his eyes, momentarily left her speechless; or, in this case, thoughtless.

Paige regained her thoughts and shouted into Dragoş' mind, *Come and get us, you sick fuck. We're ready for ya and ya know where to find us.*

She felt Dragoş' rage erupt as she slipped out of his evil, black mind.

"I know where his new restin' place is." Paige shouted.

"Where?" Garrett asked.

"You won't believe it, Daddy. He's in Alexis' old den."

"Are ya sure?"

Paige rolled her green and sliver eyes. "Yeah. I know that place. His coffins are in *that* barn."

"Does this change anything?" Mike asked.

"Call Lola," James said.

"It changes a lot of things, but I don't need to call Lola to find out," Paige said with a grin. "Mamma told me what we need to do. I just need to call Lola and let her know what's goin' on."

"Do it on speaker so everyone knows how things are changin'," Garrett told her.

Paige nodded and called Lola.

~ * ~

Dragoş eyed his lovely daughters and then heard Vanda's mental intrusion. It enraged him, but it also concerned him she could, so easily, it seemed, penetrate his mind and without his knowledge. The rage overpowered concern, though. He didn't know it, but he took the bait hook, line, and sinker.

"She dares challenge me." Dragoş roared.

The power of his rage caused the dilapidated barn to shake, and dust rained down on him and his daughters, who stepped away from their enraged father.

Dragoş composed himself quickly. "Come, daughters. It is time that we put an end to this…game. Vanda and her wolf will be mine this night, and the *vrăjitoare* will be dead."

"We are without a coffin for Vanda, Father," Ilinca said in a cautious whisper.

"Oh, my lovely daughter," Dragoş said. "You have so much to learn. Vanda will not need a coffin. I secured a coffin for Vanda before I knew she and the wolf were one. She will be a vampire werewolf hybrid, and her wolf will be a day walker. Werewolf familiar by day, vampire daughter by night. She is perfect.

"Come," Dragoş continued with vile grin on his bat-like face. "We must go take Vanda and destroy the humans and *vrăjitoare* who think they can protect her."

Dragoş transformed into a man-bat hybrid; Ilinca and Lacrima did the same. Once outside the barn, they took flight and headed for Lola's house.

~ * ~

When Lola saw Paige was calling her cell, instead of contacting her mentally, she quickly answered. "Did somethin' go wrong?"

"No," Paige said. "It worked perfectly. He'll head to your house, but we have to change our plans."

"Why?"

"This came from Mamma. Put me on speaker."

Lola did.

"I did like ya said and slipped into Dragoş' mind right before he woke up, Miss Lola," Paige began "When he did, and opened his coffin, I saw his new hidden' place. It's the same barn Alexis used as her den. Anyway, Mamma saw it, too," Paige continued quickly. "She said, since Father Mike's with us, we need to go there and desecrate their coffins with holy water and communion hosts. Father Mike has both. Then, they won't have anywhere to rest tomorrow…if we're not successful tonight."

"Okay," Lola said. "But, if we're not successful tonight, Dragoş might have you and Glinda by mornin'. Then what?"

"Well…Glinda's a day walker," Paige said. "So, even if he gets me, Glinda can survive without a coffin durin' the day."

"How do ya know this?" James asked.

"Mamma saw it in his mind while he slept," Paige said. "I didn't, but she did and let me know. That's why he's more determined than ever to have us. Mamma said we're a vampire's…ah, wet dream. Sorry, Daddy and Father Mike. Mamma's thought, not mine."

Trowa laughed. "Still sounds better than a vampire's nocturnal emission. Or, for a vampire, a daytime emission."

Not laughing, Lola said, "Yes, but you'd be his. He'd just have ya dig up some more coffins and protect him."

"But he won't have home soil in his coffin," Paige said. "No matter what else happens tonight, Dragoş is dead in the mornin'."

"She's right," James said. "He has to rest on his home soil."

"This is from Mamma?" Lola said. "Not you messin' around?"

"Yes. I promise."

"She's right about the home soil," James insisted. "This is consistent across most vampire lore."

"Most?" Lola said with a raised eyebrow.

"It's solid lore, Lola," James said.

"I don't like it," Lola said. "But if Mamma and James think it'll work, best do it."

"Turnoff to the MRB is about a half mile up," Garrett said. "Are we doin' this?"

"Yes," Lola relented.

"Do ya want us to follow and help y'all?" Ty asked.

"No," Paige said. "Mamma wants y'all to go to the MRB. We'll meet y'all there when we're done."

"Paige, sweet girl," Lola said. "Dragoş will figure out we're not at my place pretty quick. Can ya keep misdirectin' him?"

"Yeah. I got this. We'll see y'all in a little while," Paige said and ended the call.

Ty backed off Garrett's bumper so he could slow down and make the turnoff to the MRB. They saw brake lights, no blinker, and then Garrett's SUV sped down the side road. Ty hammered the accelerator and flew past the turnoff. They were only about five minutes from the MRB.

"I don't like this," Lola said.

"But ya just said…" Ty began.

"I know what I said, Ty," Lola interrupted him.

"Should we turn around and go with 'em?" Ty asked.

Lola shook her head, the beads clinked together. "No. Not likin' it and doin' somethin' else are different. I have to put my trust in Mamma *and* Paige."

"Okay," Ty said. "MRB it is."

Protect my sweet Paige-Turner, Mamma, Lola thought.

~ * ~

Dragoş and his cloud flew high above the outskirts of Pine View. They were close to their destination and Dragoş' long tongue snaked out of his man-bat face. He licked his too red lips at the thought of the fun he would have with Vanda and her silver-haired wolf.

In all his eight-hundred years, he'd never had a werewolf as his familiar. There were legends of vampires who came before him, and were long dead, who had werewolf familiars. That had been long ago, when werewolves were plentiful in Transylvania. He knew the ritual, too. That was the tricky part. Especially since the *vrăjitoare* had turned his prize into a vile seer, too.

In order to have Vanda in his cloud, and the silver-haired werewolf as his familiar, he needed to make the wolf his familiar *before* he made her transform back into her human form. He couldn't drink werewolf blood, drink her to the point of death, and bring her back as a vampire. This was the only way to have both of them. That the wolf had become a seer too complicated the matter. Mezmery wouldn't work on a seer, but he knew Vanda's seer powers were borrowed, not natural. Dragoş knew if they were borrowed, they could be expelled. He knew if Vanda could find her way into his mind, he could find his way into her mind.

The *vrăjitoare's* house came into view far below them. Dragoş deftly dropped his left wing and spiraled down toward his prize. Ilinca and Lacrima mimicked their father and spiraled down behind him.

Dragoş had been so preoccupied with his thoughts of Vanda, and what he'd do to her perfect flesh, he failed to notice something very important until they were about a hundred feet above the house. Vampires, like other supernatural creatures, can see in the dark, but, unlike most other supernatural creatures, vampires have infrared vision. Infrared vision enables them to see thermal energy; heat living creatures emit. This is used to find prey, or avoid the living, if needed. They also had acute hearing, which was, mostly, used to hear beating hearts. Like bats, they also had sonar abilities. The slightest sound could be used to project an internal image of their surroundings. It, like the infrared vision, could be used to avoid the living too, if needed.

What Dragoş' preoccupied mind had failed to see, until they were almost ready to attack, was there was no thermal energy within the house. If they were there, he should see the heat from their bodies through the structure. He should hear their hearts beating. He saw or heard neither. The house was empty.

Dragoş flapped his powerful wings, shot several hundred feet into the air with the one flap, and let out such a tremendous, angry roar people, for miles around, heard and thought it was thunder in the clear night sky.

Ilinca and Lacrima flew up to their father, but it took many of their wing flaps to match his one tremendous flap. Both stayed out of easy reach of their angry father. Not that the distance would stop Dragoş from instantly killing one, or both, if he wished.

After a few moments, Dragoş contained his anger. It was counterproductive.

"Your future sister, Vanda, is proving to be a troublesome *pizda*," Dragoş hissed. "She misdirected me."

"How, Fath…" Lacrima began.

Dragoş was on her before she completed the words and had his unhinged jaws around her bat-like neck. He bit slowly until his fangs penetrated her flesh.

Lacrima, thinking her father was about to kill her, gasped. "Please forgive me, Father."

Dragoş stayed his anger. He needed her and Ilinca to help secure Vanda and her wolf. He snaked his long, cold tongue around Lacrima's neck, caught the black blood seeping from the puncture wounds, and slid his hand between her legs. She opened them for him willingly. Dragoş traced a clawed nail across her sensual center. Lacrima moaned. He released her, but didn't remove his hand.

With his hand still between her legs, he hissed, "You are fortunate this night, daughter."

"Thank you, Father," Lacrima moaned.

The moan ended in a scream when Dragoş ripped his clawed nail from between her legs with a malicious, upward movement. Tender flesh hung from the clawed nail. Black blood spilled down Lacrima's inner translucent thighs.

"Do not question me again, Lacrima," he hissed.

"I won't, Father," she cried.

"You will heal when you feed from one of Vanda's humans," Dragoş said. "This should be incentive enough to help me find her."

"Yes, Father," Lacrima agreed as black tears leaked from her hybrid eyes.

Dragoş pointed at Ilinca. "Your human knew her well. Where could she be hiding?"

"Perhaps, at her father's house, Father," Ilinca told him.

"We will see. Do not fall behind Lacrima," Dragoş said. "I will not come back for you,"

Dragoş and Ilinca flew off in a southeast direction. Lacrima didn't fall far behind.

~ * ~

Garrett turned down the overgrown driveway leading to the old Wiseman barn. Since it was winter, and the hardwoods had lost their leaves, the entrance didn't look like a living, green mouth as it had the first time he went there and found Cole Duncan's car pushed into the woods. That had also been the day he met Lola, and she told him about the ancestral werewolf in his family. It had been a man named Otis Fletcher from his mother's side of the family. That was the day everything concerning the werewolves had finally fallen into place, and they came up with a plan to defeat them. Garrett hoped the trip to the barn would lead to a successful end to the vampires, too.

Garrett pulled to a stop in front of the barn. "Ya ready, Father Mike?"

"As I'll ever be," Mike said.

Excited, James shouted, "Let's do it."

They all got out of the SUV. Garrett clicked on his Mag flashlight and illuminated the door nearly ready to fall off and opened it. Its bottom hinge squeaked loudly and he stepped inside. Paige followed him in. James followed Paige. Fr. Mike crossed himself and stepped inside last.

Garrett's flashlight beam pointed at the large, ornate, wooden coffin between two regular coffins stolen from different cemeteries since the vampire arrived. He handed the flashlight to Paige, who kept its beam focused on the massive coffin, and heaved the heavy lid open. A powerful stench of mildew and decay spilled out of the opened coffin. Fr. Mike gagged but kept his lunch down.

"What now?" Mike asked.

"Sprinkle holy water on the soil and place a consecrated communion host at the head of the coffin," James answered.

Fr. Mike took a silver, flask-looking bottle, called an aspergillum, from the inner pocket of his coat, removed the lid, and sprinkled the blessed water on the dirt. When the water contacted the orangish dirt, it hissed like water hitting a hot skillet, and foul-smelling smoke erupted from every wet spot.

"That's enough holy water," James said. "Now put the communion host at the head of the coffin."

Fr. Mike handed the holy water to James and removed a pyx from his outside pocket. He opened it, retrieved a communion host from it, closed it, and handed it to James, too.

Fr. Mike held the host up. "The Body of Christ."

Fr. Mike bent, placed the consecrated host on the orangish dirt, and straightened quickly at what happened. The orangish dirt sizzled, putrid smelling smoke erupted from the coffin, and the dirt seemed to deflate as it turned a moldy, greenish gray.

"You killed it," James shouted. "His home soil is a livin' extension of him and ya killed it. Now the other two. But do it fast. Dragoş and his home soil are, likely, connected. So, there's a good chance he knows we destroyed it."

Now that he knew what to do, and it would work, Fr. Mike destroyed the soil in the other two coffins quickly. The only difference between Dragoş' coffin and the other two was the dirt didn't turn as moldy. It hadn't been used as long. He had killed them, too.

~ * ~

Dragoş suddenly stopped in mid-flight. Ilinca flew on for a moment before she realized from her father's angry roar he no longer flew behind her. She turned in time to see Lacrima, who had fallen behind, swerve to keep from colliding with their stationary father and hover several yards away from him. Ilinca flew back and hovered a distance away from her angry father, too.

"What is wrong, Father?" Ilinca asked.

Dragoş seethed with anger and said, in a gravelly voice, "They have desecrated the soil in my throne with blasphemous blessed water and a Eucharist. If mine has been desecrated, yours and Lacrima's surely have been, too."

"How do you know this, Father?" Ilinca dared to ask after what happened to Lacrima when she questioned their father.

"A vampire and their soil are connected," Dragoş hissed in anger. "It becomes a part of us. Bonded to us. You, my daughters, are young and have not yet bonded completely with your home soil."

"Where will we rest?" Ilinca asked.

"My former familiar, Dănuţ, served me well and faithfully," Dragoş said. "He brought more of my home soil for just such an occasion. It is safe back at our previous location, and home soil for the two of you surrounds us. Getting more is not a problem. But, without a familiar to secure a safe place for our coffins, we will have nowhere to rest from the deadly sun when it rises."

"Can we not find some place without sunlight to rest?" Ilinca asked.

"No," Lacrima said. "It is our home soil that gives us strength while we rest. Hiding in a dark place will not save us."

Dragoş smiled at the natural vampire, Lacrima. "Your sister is wise and correct. But our home soil does more than give us strength while we rest. It is an extension of us; it is part of us. Our home soil contains our powers. It regenerates us while we rest.

"This is why it is more important than ever that I secure Vanda and her wolf this night," Dragoş continued with urgency. "If not, we will be destroyed when the sun rises. This means that you were incorrect about Vanda being at her father's house, Ilinca."

"Can we return to our coffins in time to kill them, Father?" Lacrima asked.

Dragoş shook his hybrid face. "The damage is done, and they will have left by now. We fly that way and hopefully find them driving. They cannot have gotten far in this time."

With that said, Dragoş flapped his powerful wings and headed toward their desecrated coffins. Ilinca and Lacrima fell in behind their father, and with so much at stake, Lacrima did not fall behind.

~ * ~

Ty pulled into the MRB drive. Trowa got out, opened the gate that had been replaced since Alexis smashed though it with her truck after realizing Garrett had found her den, and got back in the SUV. With Garrett coming soon, they didn't close the gate behind them. Ty sped down the dirt road. When they got to the MRB, Ty parked his SUV on the right side of the building and out of sight. They got out and Ty and Trowa turned on their Mag flashlights to see in the darkness. Lola didn't need the flashlights to see.

They entered through the missing door and shone their flashlights around the empty building. Ty hadn't been there since the night of the werewolf slaughters, and seeing it again brought back painful memories. He shuddered, which caused the beam of his flashlight to dance across the floor.

"You okay, Ty?" Lola asked.

"Yeah," Ty said as he steadied his hand, and the flashlight beam stopped dancing. "It's just that this place brings back some pretty horrible memories."

"Memories are in the past and cannot be changed," Lola said. "Concentrate on tonight, so we *can* change the future."

"Okay," Ty said. "But I still don't know what we're supposed to do here. What's the plan?"

"Ambush," Trowa said.

"Right," Ty said. "But how?"

Lola looked around. Beyond the flashlight beams she saw a chain with a sign on it at the bottom of some stairs leading to an office. "What, tell, is the Wood Room?"

"Oh, um," Ty said. "That's where high school kids go to…ya know."

Lola laughed. "That is a clever euphemism for the room's purpose. I think we should use it."

Trowa swallowed a lump in his throat. "You don't mean we should…you know?"

Lola laughed again. "No. I don't mean to use it like that. We can use it to ambush Dragoş when he shows up. I can create air elementals to trap his two cloud members while Glinda traps Dragoş in one of hers.

"Besides, Ty's a married man," Lola continued with a wink. "I know he wouldn't stray from his beautiful wife. But you, beautiful Trowa. I will share my body with you anytime. If ya think ya can handle it."

Trowa blushed a deep pink on his coppery cheeks. "If we live through this, I will do my best."

"It's a date," Lola said as she started for the stairs.

Ty looked at Trowa and grinned. Trowa, who had still been blushing, shrugged his shoulders and grinned back. Then they followed Lola up the stairs to the Wood Room.

Lola sent Paige a mental message to check on what Dragoş was doing.

~ * ~

Garrett and the others in his SUV were on the road to the MRB when Paige felt Lola enter her mind with the message. She closed her eyes, let her thoughts slip out of the escape hatch, and concentrated on Dragoş. A moment later, she was in his evil mind, seeing through his eyes, and hearing what he told Ilinca and Lacrima. What she heard worried her.

She pulled her mind out of his mind. "Dragoş has more home soil at the funeral home, but I don't know where it's hidden. He's coming for us. He hopes to catch us on the road."

"So, what the hell do we do?" Garrett said. "Go to the funeral home to find and destroy his extra soil or go to the MRB?"

Paige began to tell him she didn't know what to do when she heard Mamma's very calm voice in her head. "Neither. We head for town."

"What?" Garrett said. "Why?"

"To blend in with other cars and trucks," Paige explained.

"We're in my patrol SUV," Garrett said. "We won't, exactly, blend in."

"Paige is right. Dragoş won't be lookin' for a certain type of car or truck," James said. "Vampires have infrared vision. He'll be lookin' for heat sources *in* the cars and trucks. If we can get around other cars and trucks, we'll be less conspicuous."

"Okay," Garrett said as he slowed and took the next road on the right that led to Pine View proper. "Best let Lola know what's goin' on,"

Paige closed her eyes and contacted Lola.

~ * ~

Lola and Ty sat on the couch that had been the source of so much awkward teenage sex. Trowa, still blushing, sat in the broken office chair. It leaned to one side on a broken leg.

Ty thought back to MRB parties he'd attended while in high school and his and Jasmin's first time on the couch. He smiled without realizing it.

Lola thought about the coming encounter with Dragoş when Paige sent her the urgent message.

"Shit." Lola shouted, which startled Ty and Trowa.

"What?" Ty asked.

"I just got a message from Paige," Lola said. "Dragoş knows they destroyed the soil in his coffin. He has more hidden, somewhere, in the funeral home. She doesn't know where. He's headin' this way to find 'em."

"Are they still comin' here?" Trowa asked.

"No. It's too dangerous," Lola said. "Mamma tol' Paige to have 'em head for town to blend in with other traffic."

"Should we leave?" Ty asked.

"No. That's too dangerous, too," Lola said with a shake of her head, which caused the beads to click together. "They have a head start. Dragoş would certainly see us on the road and attack."

"But...we're safe in here, right?" Trowa asked.

"Not as we are," Lola said, and stood.

"What does that mean?" Ty asked.

"It means vampires see thermal heat," Lola said. "If he flies over the MRB and sees three heat sources, he'll attack us before we're all together and have Glinda with us."

"So, we're fucked if we leave and we're fucked if we stay," Trowa said.

"No," Lola said with a sly grin. "We're not fucked if we stay, but y'all are gonna be freezin' and uncomfortable for a while. Sit on the couch, Trowa. You can't stay in that broken chair. Ya might fall over and crack."

"Crack?" Trowa asked as he complied and took a seat on the couch. "What are ya gonna do to us?"

"I'm gonna freeze y'all, so ya don't give off heat," Lola said.

"Freeze us?" Ty said. "Won't that kill us?"

"No," Lola said. "It's an incantation. It'll put y'all in a cryogenic state. It won't harm y'all. Trust me."

"What about you?" Trowa asked.

"I'm an elemental seer. I can assume the surroundin' temperature at will."

"Then why doesn't Paige do the same thing to Garrett, James, and Father Mike and come to the MRB?" Ty asked.

"Think about that, Ty," Lola said. "With Mamma's help, she could. But Garrett's drivin'. He can't drive while frozen. If she froze Garrett, James, and Father Mike, assume ambient temperature, and drove on out here, Dragoş would be pretty suspicious of a driverless SUV. He's encountered many seers over his long, undead existence. He knows our powers."

"Okay," Ty said, "I trust ya."

"Me, too," Trowa said. "But it won't damage any of our...appendages, will it?"

Lola let out a velvety laugh. "It won't. I got a date with one of your appendages. I wouldn't deny myself that pleasure. Now, both of y'all shut up and let me cast the incantation."

Lola looked at the dust covered desk and found what she needed. An old bolt. She placed it in her left palm.

"What's that for?" Ty asked.

"It's a needed component of the incantation," Lola said. "Some incantations need components and some don't. This one does. This bolt is room temperature, which, thanks to the blue norther yesterday, is eighteen degrees.

"Now, do like I said and shut up," Lola told them. "I'd hate to freeze ya with your mouth open."

Ty closed his mouth.

Lola cupped her hands and let the cold bolt roll to where her hands met. Then she exhaled on the bolt, but the air escaping her lungs wasn't like the plume of vapor regular people breathe out in cold air. It was white and didn't float upward. Her breath targeted the bolt, which turned blue in her hands.

Ty and Trowa saw the white, directional breath leave Lola's lips and then they saw a blue glow emanate from Lola's cupped hands. They saw Lola exhale the white breath again and the blue glow turned into a glowing blue ball about the size of a large cantaloup. After that, she approached Ty.

"You first, Ty."

Ty nodded.

Lola held the glowing blue ball in front of Ty and blew her directional, white breath into his face.

Ty felt the incredible cold hit his face, and then the cold rapidly spread throughout his body. He could see, hear, and breathe, but he couldn't move.

From Trowa's point of view, he saw Lola's white breath go through the blue glow. The breath exiting the blue glow was blue, too. When it hit Ty's face, it turned blue and then his hands, which were the only other part of his skin exposed, turned blue, too.

Finished with Ty, Lola stepped in front of Trowa. "Your turn."

Trowa nodded, and Lola blew through the blue glow. Instantly, Trowa felt the same sensations Ty had.

Lola dismissed the incantation, dropped the bolt, and sat in the broken chair. "I know y'all can hear me. I'll contact Paige and let her know we're safe. Then, we wait."

Ty and Trowa agreed, but they couldn't nod approval. Although they were safe from Dragoş, they were colder than they'd ever been, and they couldn't even shiver.

Lola sent Paige a mental message.

~ * ~

Garrett was near Pine View proper, and several other vehicles were in the area, but not enough for comfort. He needed to get into town to feel safe. They were close.

Paige felt Lola's intrusion and listened carefully.

When Lola finished, she said, "Lola, Ty, and Trowa are safe. She froze 'em so they won't put off heat for Dragoș to see, and she's assumed room temperature. So, he can't see her either."

"She froze 'em?" Garrett asked.

"Yeah," Paige said. "She used an incantation. They're safe. I can do the same to y'all and assume room temperature, too. It's a seer thing, but, if I did, Dragoș might see a driverless SUV and *know* it's us. Lola said he's dealt with many seers and knows our tricks."

"So, how do we get back out to the MRB?" Garrett asked.

"Lola wants me to get back in Dragoș' mind and misdirect him again."

"Be safe," Garrett said.

"I will, Daddy."

Paige closed her eyes, slipped out of the escape hatch, and concentrated on Dragoș. I moment later, she entered his black mind and saw through his eyes.

~ * ~

Dragoș, Ilinca, and Lacrima were getting close to the barn containing their discredited coffins. He scanned a few vehicles on the surrounding roads, but none of them contained what he looked for. Because he knew seers' tricks well, and he knew Vanda had at least two humans with her, her father and the priest, he looked for two or more heat sources, or none. To that point, he'd only seen vehicles with one heat source. Part of him, the angry part, wanted to destroy all the driving humans. He knew that would only waste time, and he didn't have time to waste. His throne had been desecrated, and he had to concentrate on rectifying that first, which meant concentrating on Vanda and Vanda only.

Dragoș banked right and saw a large vehicle with four heat

sources. It was worth investigating. He tucked his large wings back and dove toward the vehicle, with Ilinca and Lacrima close behind. He smiled, but only for a moment.

Not us, fuck-tard, Paige thought in his mind.

Enraged, Dragoş thought, *Enough games, Vanda. I will slaughter every human I encounter unless you face me.*

Paige laughed in his mind and thought, *I'll never be Vanda. I will face ya,* bitch. *Glinda will rip your fuckin' head off, and I know 'bout the extra soil from your homeland at the funeral home. I'm in your head. I know all your twisted secretes. While you go on a killin' spree, we'll be blessin' the rest of your vile dirt with holy water and the Body of Christ. See ya soon, bitch.*

Dragoş pulled out of the deadly dive only a few feet from the vehicle and shot skyward. Ilinca and Lacrima weren't prepared for their father's sudden deviation and slammed into the top of the vehicle, which crushed the roof and sent it swerving off the road and into a ditch.

The humans inside the vehicle, two elderly couples headed into Pine View to play bingo at the VFW hall, screamed in surprise, but, because they were driving forty miles per hour in a sixty-mile zone, were unharmed. Ilinca and Lacrima didn't stay. They flapped their wings and flew up to their father.

Dragoş didn't waste time engaging in talk. He sent his daughters a mental message that Vanda and the priest were going to destroy the rest of his home soil. The three vampires flew towards the funeral home.

Once again, he took the bait, hook, line, and sinker.

~ * ~

Paige stayed in Dragoş' mind long enough to see him abandon the old Chevy Suburban and rocket skyward. She heard Ilinca and Lacrima crash into the Suburban and heard the people inside scream. She hoped they were okay. Then she heard Dragoş' mental message to Ilinca and Lacrima that they needed to protect the rest of his home soil at the funeral home. Misdirecting Dragoş was easy. She smiled and pulled out of his twisted mind.

"Did it work?" Garrett asked.

Paige grinned. "Easy-peasy. He's headed for the funeral home."

"What'a we do now?" James asked.

"Mamma says we need to haul ass, sorry, Daddy, out to the MRB to join up with Lola and the others."

"Then, we haul ass," Garrett said as he flipped two switches on the dashboard, which turned on the roof-top lights and siren.

They had made it to Pine View proper by then, but the lights and siren did their job. Garrett hooked a quick U-turn. The cars and trucks on the other side of the road pulled over and he hammered the accelerator to the floor. The souped-up SUV roared, and the speedometer hit ninety miles an hour in a matter of seconds. The drivers of the cars and trucks in front of them did their civic duty and pulled onto the shoulder to let Garrett pass. In no time, they were back on the mostly deserted back roads on the outskirt of town.

"I need to let Lola know the diversion worked and that we're comin'," Paige said.

"Okay," Garrett said with a white-knuckle grip on the steering wheel.

Paige closed her eyes and reached out to Lola.

~ * ~

Lola felt Paige enter her mind and smiled when she heard what she had to tell her.

Good girl, Lola thought.

It's so easy, Paige thought.

Don't get cocky and don't let your guard down, chil'. Especially with what I'm 'bout to tell ya to do.

What?

We need to know where the rest of his soil is, Lola thought. *Get back in Dragoş' mind and stay there until ya see where his other soil is hidden.*

That's a great idea. I'll do it.

Good. But be careful, Paige-Turner. Just because it's been easy so far, doesn't mean he won't catch on to what you're doin'.

Okay, Paige thought. *I'll be careful. And the way Daddy's drivin', we should be there pretty quick.*

Stay with that ol' fucker as long as ya can. If ya feel him feel you, get out.

I will, Paige's thought and she broke the connection.

"I let Lola know what's goin' on," Paige said. "She's got a job for me to do."

"What job?" Garrett asked.

"She wants me to get back in Dragoş' mind so I can see where the rest of his soil's hidden."

"That's a great idea." James shouted.

"Be careful," Garrett said.

"I always am, Daddy," Paige said with a wink.

Paige closed her eyes, slipped out of the escape hatch, and concentrated on Dragoş. A moment later, she saw through his eyes as he landed behind the funeral home.

~ * ~

Dragoş landed behind the funeral home and saw the crumpled left garage door with the front of the hearse exposed. Seeing the destruction caused by Vanda and her human companions only added to the rage he felt about losing Ruxandra. Losing the slave was a minor setback, but Ruxandra had been fun to play with. He knew, by the extent of the destruction, the silver-haired werewolf had done it. His silver-haired werewolf.

Still in hybrid form, Dragoş went to the garage door, grabbed it, and sent it flying into the night with one powerful motion. He stepped into the embalming room; his daughters followed. He saw the pile of ash that was Ruxandra and the dented counter and shelves covering the entrances to his old throne room. He smelled the rotting corpse of his useless familiar below.

"What is that, Father?" Ilinca asked as she pointed at the pile of ash.

"That is what is left of your sister, Ruxandra," Dragoş hissed. "And what will become of us, if we do not have a safe place to rest when the sun rises."

Dragoş walked through the door Zack came through earlier that day. He saw black blood, bullet holes, and the blood-stained wall beneath a hole in the sheetrock. The image of what happened was all too clear. His slave had withstood a barrage of gunshots, only to be beheaded by the silver-haired werewolf. He would have fun torturing the wolf once she was his.

At the entrance to the funeral home, the office was to Dragoş' right and the showroom for the coffins was to his left. Dragoş turned left and entered the showroom. There were a dozen coffins on display, but Dragoş had only been interested in three. They were the three most expensive coffins in the showroom and therefore, the least likely to interest Pine View's demographics, which Dănuţ had dutifully investigated before commissioning the remodel on the foreclosed, auto body repair shop.

Although least likely to be selected, the price tags were displayed under each coffin. They were priced at thirty thousand dollars each. They were prominently displayed in the center of the back wall. Dragoş went to the top coffin, which was rosewood with gold plated hardware, and lifted the lid. His precious home soil was safe. He quickly opened the two coffins beneath the first one and found none of his precious home soil had been desecrated.

The relief he felt at discovering his soil intact was short-lived, though, because he realized Vanda had deceived him again. He didn't let anger cloud his thoughts.

Are you in my mind, Vanda? Dragoş thought.

If she was, she didn't respond. But Dragoş felt a presence. It was faint but there. He concentrated on isolating the presence. He found it, and he grabbed it.

I have you, pizda, Dragoş thought.

~ * ~

Paige watched as Dragoş made his way through the funeral home to the coffins containing his extra home soil. She had the information she needed and began to withdraw from his black mind, but she enjoyed feeling his rage, so she stayed.

When she heard Dragoş think, *Are you in my mind, Vanda?* she pulled back, but, in an instant, his black vault slammed shut, like a mousetrap, and she was the mouse.

I have you, pizda, Dragoş' victoriously thought.

Fuck you. Paige's panickily thought.

Such foul language, Vanda. You will pay for your insolence.

Paige tried again to pull her thoughts from Dragoş' vile mind, but she couldn't get out.

It is amusing how you try to resist, Dragoş hissed into her mind. *You had your fun leading me around like a dog. Now it is my turn. Let us see what secrets your mind holds.*

She felt panicked beyond anything she'd felt since Alexis' werewolf killed Justin and chased her through the woods while she taunted her.

Paige's scream thought, *NO.*

Dragoş chuckled his gravely chuckle in her mind. *I told you that you were no match for me,* pizda. *Now...let us play.*

Paige felt Dragoş' revolting intrusion into her mind. It felt like she was being raped. Mind raped by an unholy assailant. She pushed and tried to close Angelica's escape hatch. It wouldn't shut.

What was it you told me? Dragoş hissed into her mind. *Aw, yes. You can't push me out. I can live here, if I want. Now, as you Americans say, the shoe is on the other foot. Yes?*

Paige was panic-stricken as she tried, in vain, to escape Dragoş' intrusion. Everything was at stake. If he discovered any of their plans, all would be lost. She could *feel* Dragoş probing her mind, like a snake slithering through her thoughts.

What are you hiding here? Dragoş' thought came into her helpless mind.

Just before he could slither into the part of her mind where their plans were stored, a blinding, purple light filled her head, and she heard Mamma scream, *Be gone from this girl. foul creature.*

Paige felt Dragoş' confusion and then her mind was free of his vile intrusion.

I have closed Angelica's way out of your white vault, Paige, Mamma's thought in Paige's freed mind. *You dabbled too long and almost lost everything. Not just your plans, but your soul. You and Angelica mistake carelessness for fearlessness. They are not the same. I will speak to Angelica about this. I think you have learned a very hard lesson.*

Thank you, Mamma, Paige's thought. *I have learned my lesson. I won't dabble again. I promise.*

Since I am in your mind and know your thoughts, I believe you, Mamma thought. *Even though I do, the white vault is now closed. You could not dabble with that creature again, even if you wanted to.*

With that thought, Mamma vanished, and Paige realized she was being shaken. Shaken roughly. For an instant, she thought Dragoş had her again and fought back. Then she realized it was her daddy, and they weren't moving.

~ * ~

Garrett drove as fast as he could to the MRB. When, suddenly, he noticed Paige go stiff in her seat. Then she convulsed. He braked hard, pulled on the side of the road, and grabbed her. By then, she was foaming at the mouth, and her body had gone ridged.

He shook her. "What's happenin' to her?"

"Has she had seizures before?" Mike asked.

"No." Garrett shouted.

He unbuckled Paige, pulled the top of her rigid body across his lap, and turned her face to the side to keep her from choking. He tried to open her mouth, but her teeth were clenched so tight he'd need the jaws of life to open them.

"Oh, crap." James shouted.

"What?" Garrett shouted as he began to shake Paige's rigid body. "What is it?"

"She was in Dragoş' mind," James said. "He might've found out and trapped her."

Fr. Mike crossed himself and prayed.

A moment later, Paige went limp in Garrett's lap.

"Paige. Paige," Garrett shouted as he continued to shake her now limp body. "Are you okay? Say somethin'."

Paige flailed, but it wasn't convulsions. She was fighting…something.

Garrett pulled her to him and wrapped her in a tight hug. "It's me. You're okay, Paige-Turner."

Paige's green and silver eyes fluttered open.

"Daddy?" Paige said groggily.

"Yes, sweetheart. It's me. What happened?"

"Dragoş figured out I was in his head, and he trapped me."

"I'm gonna kill Lola," Garrett grumbled. "She said it was safe."

"It's not Lola's fault, Daddy," Paige said sounding more like herself. "I saw what I needed to see, but I didn't leave his mind."

"Why the hell didn't you?" Garrett shouted.

"I wanted to feel his rage," Paige said. "I like…liked makin' him angry. It's my fault."

"How'd ya get out?" Garrett asked.

"Did he find out anything about tonight?" James asked

"I prayed. Did that help you escape?" Mike asked.

"Sorry, Father Mike," Paige said with a weak smile. "I'm sure your prayers helped, but Mamma drove Dragoş out of my mind. His extra soil is in three display coffins at the funeral home. He knows I know, so he might move 'em. I screwed up. He doesn't know anything that'll help him. Mamma got me out before he learned anything useful."

"Are ya sure?" James asked.

Paige nodded.

"No more of that shit, Paige-Turner," Garrett said.

"Even if I wanted to, which I don't, I can't get back in his mind and he can't get back in mine," Paige said.

"Are ya sure?" Garrett asked.

"Yeah. Mamma closed the escape hatch I was usin' to get into his head," Paige said as she sat up from her daddy's lap and got back in the seat. "We're cut off from each other."

"Good," Garrett said. "Buckle up. We're still about ten minutes away from the MRB and I'll feel better 'bout all this when we're together."

Once Paige had her seatbelt on, Garrett floored the SUV's accelerator. Gravel sprayed behind them until the back tires squealed on the blacktop road and they sped away into the night.

~ * ~

Once Dragoş had Vanda's mind trapped in his, he had unfettered access to hers. Because he enjoyed pain, he probed the painful memories in Vanda's mind first. He saw and felt her pain when the werewolf killed her mate. Dragoş saw and felt her terror as the werewolf chased her through the woods and taunted her. He saw how the clever girl had plunged her silver chain and crucifix down the werewolf's mouth to get away from it. He felt the pain as the alpha's fang ripped the flesh of her arm, which had created the silver-haired creature he came to claim. Dragoş smiled at the pain in her helpless mind.

Vanda's white vault, not unlike his black one, had layers. The painful memories were easy to access, because they were always on her mind. He had been misled by Vanda twice, which was unacceptable. Dragoş knew, because Vanda had misled him, she and her humans were up to something. He left the lovely, painful memories and delved deeper into her mind.

It didn't take long for Dragoş to discover a particularly, well-guarded area in Vanda's mind. He was there. He had her. In a moment, he would know all Vanda and her humans had planned. Because he had her mind, destroying the humans would be easy. He would have Vanda transform into the silver-haired wolf, kill them all, and come to him where she would be powerless to resist after becoming his familiar and Vanda his prized daughter. Like Paige, who had lingered too long to enjoy his rage, Dragoş lingered too long to enjoy her pain.

As Dragoş prepared to enter Vanda's inner-most thoughts, and control her completely, a blinding purple light exploded in his mind and he heard a crone of a *vrăjitoare* scream, *Be gone from this girl. foul creature.*

He tried to resist the command. Dragoş put all his substantial power into resisting the command, but the *vrăjitoare* was more powerful than any he had encountered. He felt the connection with Vanda dissolve, and he was pushed out of her mind.

Dragoş exploded with rage and tossed the nine display coffins not containing his precious home soil, in the showroom around like they weighed no more than matchboxes. Ilinca and Lacrima tried to take cover, but coffins slammed into them with the force of a large truck and knocked both off their feet. The impact disrupted their concentration, and both turned back into their human forms.

When Dragoş' rage subsided, the nine coffins were in disarray. Some had gone through walls, others were missing lids, and all looked like a wrecking ball had pounded them to crumpled pieces of scrap metal. He saw Ilinca and Lacrima on the floor; both were human in form, naked, and very injured. He couldn't have them weak and injured. Not for what was surely coming.

Dragoş slit each of his nipples with his gnarled thumb nails. Black blood oozed from each.

"Come, my daughters," Dragoş said. "You must feed and regenerate. Your future sister, Vanda, and her troublesome humans, are planning something for this night. I need both of you strong and aware."

"Will our feeding weaken you, Father?" Ilinca said as she took his outstretched hand to stand.

"You are thoughtful to have concern for me, Ilinca," Dragoş said. "I will be fine, and we shall all feed on Vanda's humans shortly."

"Do you know where she is, Father?" Lacrima asked as she took his other hand to stand.

"No," Dragoş hissed. "I do not. But do not worry, daughters. The silver-haired wolf will call for us. Of this, I am certain."

"Why will the silver-haired werewolf call for us?" Ilinca asked.

"Because they think they can destroy me," Dragoş said with a gravely laugh. "They are simple-minded humans. They cannot harm me. Come and feed, daughters."

A moment later, both suckled from his stiff, bleeding nipples. Dragoş smiled with pleasure at the thought of having Vanda, her wolf, and destroying the humans who dared confront him.

Because the crone *vrăjitoare* had severed his connection with Vanda, he was sure she, to protect the girl they knew as Paige, had severed her connection with him, too. That meant the only way Vanda and her humans could confront him would be to have the wolf call for him. No more misleading. They would soon understand why Dragoş was the oldest, and king, of vampires.

Dragoş smiled a gruesome smile on his man-bat face. His long tongue snaked out and licked Lacrima and then Ilinca's cheeks. They looked up at him with their piercing, blue eyes and smiled as his black blood trickled from the corner of their too red lips. They were beautiful.

~ * ~

Lola sat, crooked, in the broken office chair with Ty and Trowa in a frozen state on the couch. She waited to hear from Paige, but the mental message she received came from Mamma.

Dragoş trapped the girl in his mind, Mamma's thought came.

No, Lola's panickily thought. *Is she okay?*

Yes, Mamma thought. *I drove the dreadful creature from her mind. He almost had her and all would have been lost. She would have been lost.*

Thank you, Mamma, Lola thought relieved. *I'm grateful you were with her.*

Did you know Paige was intruding Dragoş' mind?

Yes, Lola reluctantly thought. *But I don't know how she got out of the white vault we put around her mind.*

Angelica, naturally, left her an opening.

I'll ring her pretty neck, Lola angerly thought.

I will deal with Angelica, but you are not without fault, Lola, Mamma scolded. *You knew she was delving where she should not and encouraged it.*

Yes. I did. Lola admitted. *I thought she was safe. I should have known better, Mamma.*

Yes. You should have known better, Mamma thought. *We got lucky...this time. It cannot happen again. I have sealed the white vault. If you had plans to use it again, rethink them.*

Yes, Mamma.

All that matters now is that Paige is safe and will be with you in short time, Mamma thought. *Beware, Lola. Dragoş is a formidable adversary. I believe she and her wolf will prevail. But they must be clear-headed and single-minded to defeat him. I will do my best to help her. You need to keep her from acting irrationally.*

Yes, Mamma. I will, Lola thought, and she felt the connection fade.

Because Ty and Trowa could still see and hear, Lola told them what she had learned from Mamma. They looked at her with blue, expressionless faces.

Shortly after Lola filled Ty and Trowa in on what happened, they heard Garrett's SUV drive up the MRB road. Lola got up and went outside to great them. She prepared to get an earful from Garrett.

~ * ~

Garrett turned onto the dirt road leading to the MRB and was thankful, but not surprised, they had left the gate open. He floored the accelerator, and a trail of dust flew out behind the SUV. In a moment, they were at the MRB. Garrett didn't see Ty's SUV and figured he'd parked around the far side of the building. As he drove past the missing door, he saw Lola come out of it. He pulled around the side of the building and parked next to Ty's SUV.

Paige got out of the SUV and ran to Lola's waiting arms.

Lola wrapped Paige in a tight hug. "Mamma tol' me what happened. I'm so sorry, Paige-Turner."

Garrett was there in an instant and with a stern, accusatory finger pointed directly at Lola's face. "Damn right you're sorry. You said she'd be safe. He almost had her."

Paige freed herself from Lola's comforting hug, turned so her daddy's accusatory finger pointed at her. "I told ya it's not Lola's fault. It's my fault. I stayed too long, and I shouldn't have."

Lola took Paige by the shoulders and turned her so she could look her in the eyes. "Your daddy's right. It is *my* fault. I know Dragoş is

536

dangerous, and I *never* should've encouraged ya to delve into his mind."

Paige stiffened. "Yeah, well. My *delvin'* saved four lives tonight. He was gonna kill four people in the Suburban even though they weren't us. So, it was worth it. No matter what any of y'all think. I know where his extra home soil is. He might try to move it. But where? He knows we desecrated the soil in his coffin at Alexis' den. He can't go there again. Dragoş doesn't have a familiar to help him. My *delvin'* has Dragoş pretty screwed right now."

In spite of everything that had happened, Lola laughed. "My fearless little seer. You really beat all, chil'."

"Paige is right," James said. "It was close, and it was scary. But Paige's intrusions into Dragoş' mind has him at a disadvantage."

Garrett lowered the finger that had lost rigor. "He almost had my little girl."

"As I always say, we can't change the past, but we *can* change the future," Lola said.

"What's the plan?" James asked.

"Let's head on up to the Wood Room and discuss our plans," Lola said as she turned and headed back into the MRB.

They followed her inside.

Paige was directly behind Lola and her daddy was directly behind her as they started up the steps to the Wood Room. Suddenly, all that happened on the night Alexis killed Justin and chased her through the woods, taunting her, flooded her memories and she, inadvertently, shuddered. Then she felt her daddy's muscular hand on her shoulder. It calmed her. She placed her much smaller hand on top of his and squeezed it. He squeezed her shoulder. The terrible memories and shudder subsided.

The strength of a daddy's love is powerful magic, too, Paige thought to herself.

A moment later, they were at what was left of the Wood Room door after a werewolf had broken through it and stepped inside the old office.

Garrett took one look at the blue and unmoving Ty and Trowa. "Holy shit. They really *are* frozen."

"I told ya, Daddy," Paige said. "Vampires see thermal heat. I saw it through Dragoş' eyes when he was gonna attack the people he thought were us. He saw four, orangish-red…people like shapes in the Suburban."

"Very good, Paige-Turner," Lola said with a warm smile. "Since Ty and Trowa are frozen, Dragoş can't see 'em."

"Like Lola, I can assume room temperature," Paige said. "He can't see me either."

"As for you, James, and Father Mike, I'll have to freeze y'all, too," Lola said as she faced the three gawking men.

"Are they…okay?" Mike asked.

"I assure you they're fine," Lola said. "Cold, but they can see and hear us just fine. They just can't move."

"Fascinatin'," James said.

"I gotta know they're okay before I agree to this," Mike said.

"I would never harm y'all," Lola sighed. "But, if you must know, I will show y'all."

Lola turned to the dust covered desk, found a piece of paper, tore off a small corner, rubbed it between her thumb and index finger, it sparked, and caught fire. Lola cupped the burning paper between her hands, and it instantly became a ball of fire.

Paige saw Lola do something similar with a blade of grass to create a fire elemental, but what she did next was new.

Lola walked in front of Ty, bent over, and blew through the ball of fire. The air exiting the fire ball was orange and bathed his face, which turned from blue to his normal color. He blinked his eyes several times.

"Are ya okay?" Garrett asked.

"Yeah," Ty said. "It's not comfortable, but I'm fine."

"Were ya cold?" James asked.

"Yeah," Ty said. "But it's inside cold, not an outside cold, if that makes sense."

"Not really," James said with a chuckle that made his rosy cold cheeks giggle. "But if that's what we gotta do to hide from Dragoş, we have to do it."

"Hold on," Garrett said. "Before ya freeze us, what's the plan?"

"Once y'all are frozen, and Paige and Glinda assume room temperature, Glinda will have to howl to get Dragoş' attention," Lola said.

"He'll be expectin' it."

"Why will he be expectin' it?" Garrett asked.

"Because he knows tonight's the night," Lola said. "The final...showdown between him and Glinda."

"Okay," Ty said. "But won't Glinda's howl get others' attention, too?"

"Yes," Lola said. "But, after what happened last summer, I doubt anyone will investigate. Especially here, at the MRB. Dragoş, like other supernatural creatures, has enhanced hearin'. He'll know it's the silver-haired werewolf he covets and come for her."

"Then what?" Garrett asked.

"Well," Lola said as she turned to Paige. "Glinda, and the rest of us will be invisible to Dragoş' infrared vision. So, to get him in the buildin', Glinda needs to...mark somethin' in here."

Paige caught on. "Wait a sec. By mark, you mean Glinda needs to pee on somethin' in the buildin'."

"See how smart ya are," Lola said with a snicker.

"That's gross," Paige said and crinkled her nose. "I'll do it as long as these guys are frozen and can't see me do it."

"Then what?" Garrett asked.

"Then it gets tricky," Lola said. "Once he's here, Dragoş will be able to see us with his normal vision, but we'll be up here. I'll trap Lin and Taylor in my air elementals and Glinda will trap Dragoş in her larger, stronger air elemental."

"And?" Garrett asked.

"I'll unfreeze y'all," Lola said. "Glinda kills Dragoş and Taylor and with Father Mike's help, we save Lin."

"Just like that?" Garrett said doubtfully. "What if somethin' goes wrong? Do we have a contingency plan if this doesn't work?"

"If this doesn't work, we'll have to rely on Glinda, and Mamma's wisdom in her, to come up with another plan," Lola said.

"I don't like it," Garrett said. "Why don't we just hide until mornin' and let the sun take care of 'em?"

"Because he has extra soil and has a place to rest in the mornin'," James said.

"So, we find him tomorrow and kill him then," Garrett said.

"We can't do it that way, Daddy."

"Why not?"

"Because Lin doesn't have extra soil," Paige said. "Without a place to rest, she'll die, Daddy. I can't let that happen. Not if there's a chance to save her."

"Paige is right, Garrett," James said. "Dragoş is currently without a familiar to secure soil for Lindsey and Taylor. Both of 'em will be destroyed when the sun rises in the mornin'."

Garrett looked at Paige. "I love Lindsey, sweetheart. But I love ya more. I don't wanna lose ya. I *can't* lose ya, Paige-Turner."

"You won't, Daddy," Paige said and hugged him. "Trust me and Glinda. We can do this."

Garrett hugged Paige back and kissed the top of her head. "Okay, sweetheart. Don't make me regret this."

"I won't, Daddy," Paige said and kissed his scruffy cheek.

"Okay, then," Lola said. "Time to refreeze Ty and freeze the rest of y'all. Take a seat on the couch, gentlemen."

Garrett looked at the couch he and his buddies had carried up to the Wood Room when he had been in high school. "That's gonna be a tight fit and uncomfortable."

"Y'all will be too uncomfortable from the cold to notice bein' packed on that couch like sardines," Lola said with a laugh.

"True dat," Ty said.

"Okay," Garrett said with resolve. "Let's do this."

Fr. Mike sat next to Trowa and felt the cold radiating from his blue skin. He crossed himself and said a quick prayer in his mind. Garrett sat next to Ty. It took some work, but James wedged his portly body between Fr. Mike and Garrett. He held tight to his vampire kit. They were ready.

"Can I do it?" Paige asked.

"Sure, ya can," Lola said with a smile.

"Okay," Paige said excitedly. "How?"

Lola bent down and picked up the bolt she had used to freeze Ty and Trowa. "Cup your hands. When I place this bolt in your hands, concentrate on its coldness, and blow the coldness from your mouth on to it. It'll turn blue. Blow on it again and a glowin' blue ball of light will appear in your hands. Then blow through the blue ball of light into each man's face."

"That easy, huh?"

"For you, I have no doubt," Lola said as she handed Paige the bolt. "You're a natural seer. For now."

Paige concentrated on the cold bolt and felt the cold enter her lungs. She took a deep breath and breathed out white air that penetrated the bolt. As Lola said, the bolt turned blue. Paige took another deep breath and blew white air at the bolt again. The cold from the blue bolt emanated out and became a glowing blue ball.

She went to Fr. Mike first, blew through the blue ball and saw blue air exit the other side that bathed his face. His face and exposed hands turned as blue as Trowa's skin. She did the same to Dr. James with the same effect. She skipped her daddy and refroze Ty next.

Paige came back to her daddy, leaned forward, and kissed his scruffy cheek. "We'll be okay. I love you, Daddy."

"You better be," Garrett said as a tear spilled from each of his brown eyes. "I love you too, Paige-Turner,"

Paige blew through the glowing blue ball into her daddy's face and watched it turn blue. Each tear froze on his cheeks.

"What now?" Paige asked.

"Dismiss the cold," Lola said.

Paige did this without even having to think about it. Instantly, the blue glowing ball had gone, and the bolt became a bolt again. She dropped it on the Wood Room floor.

Lola smiled. "Very good. Now ya need to drop your body temperature to the temperature in here."

"How?"

"Vampires aren't the only supernatural creatures with infrared vision," Lola said. "Seers have it, too. Look at your arm with your seein' eye and look for your body's heat. When ya see it, concentrate on absorbin' the surroundin' cold. You'll see the heat in your arm fade from orangish-red to a blueish-black. When all the bright colors are gone, you'll be at room temperature."

Paige held out her right arm, looked at it with her seeing eye, watched as it became an orangish-red glow, like she'd seen through Dragoş' eyes when he began to attack the truck with four people in it. "I see it. That's so cool."

"Yes, it is," Lola said. "Now, concentrate on absorbin' the surroundin' temperature."

Paige did as Lola instructed and saw the heat leave her body as her arm faded from orangish-red to blueish-black.

When all the bright colors were gone, Paige looked at Lola. "Did it work?"

"Perfectly," Lola said. "Your body is eighteen degrees, just like the air in here."

"Will I have to do this again as Glinda?"

"Nope," Lola said. "That's why we had each of you drink the protection potion. Y'all are bonded seers."

"Then why'd we have to do all that practicin' in each form?"

"I was just makin' sure the bondin' was complete," Lola said. "It is."

"This is really cool," Paige said.

"Don't get too used to it," Lola said. "The elemental seeing powers only last until ya kill that vile creature. Now transform into Glinda, pee on somethin' in the buildin', go outside, and howl."

Paige grinned. "Okay. And then we wait."

Paige began to remove the borrowed dress, but Lola cleared her throat. "Perhaps ya should take your dress off out of eyeshot of your daddy and the other men. Remember. Even though they're frozen, they can still hear and see us."

Paige looked at the five frozen men squeezed onto the couch with their eyes open. "I don't care if they see me naked, but I'll be nice and do it downstairs."

Lola laughed. "Naked is fine, but ya draw the line at peein' where they can see?"

"Naked is natural. Peein' is private."

Lola laughed again. "Peein' is as natural as naked. We all pee, chil'."

542

Paige turned to the broken door. "Peein' is different, Lola."

Lola shook her head. The beads on her cornrows clicked together and she watched Paige leave the Wood Room.

Once Paige was downstairs and out of sight, she removed Lola's dress, placed it across the stairway railing, and transformed. Not that she didn't trust Lola, she was curious. She looked at Glinda's long, hairy, powerful arms and saw they were the same blueish-black as her human arms had been.

Glinda looked around the empty building for something to mark. Since she knew they'd want Dragoş, Lin, and Taylor where they could easily see them, she ran to the doors at the other end of the building, turned her backside to it, and emptied Glinda's bladder. A substantial amount of pungent urine splashed onto the walls and concrete floor.

With that done, Glinda stepped outside the MRB, filled her large lungs with air, and let out a howl that shook dust off rafters in the MRB and pierced the chilly night.

~ * ~

Dragoş, Ilinca, and Lacrima flew high above the outskirts of Pine View in no discernible direction. They were many miles from the MRB when Glinda's howl pierced the darkness.

Dragoş smiled an evil smile and stopped his forward momentum. Ilinca and Lacrima, who had heard the wolf's howl too, stopped and hovered next to their father.

Dragoş pointed a gnarled claw. "The wolf is in that direction."

"How will we find it?" Ilinca asked.

"The wolf wants us to find it," Lacrima said.

Dragoş smiled at the natural, scarlet-haired vampire. "Your sister is correct. The wolf wants us to find it."

"Then this is a trap, Father," Ilinca said.

"Of course, it is a trap," Dragoş said "The wolf and its humans continue to underestimate me. There is nothing they can do I cannot overcome. Come, daughters. Let us see what meager trap they have planned."

Dragoş flapped his powerful wings and headed toward the wolf's howl. Ilinca and Lacrima, dutifully, fell in behind their father.

~ * ~

After letting out the howl, Glinda returned to the Wood Room. It wasn't a large room and Glinda had to lie on her belly, sideways, across the front of the couch, to fit. Her enormous head was high enough off the ground to see out of the broken windows to where she had marked the other end of the building. The urine had formed a large wet spot on the concrete floor.

How long before Dragoş gets here? Glinda's thought.

Depends on where he was when he heard you howl and how fast he flies to get here, Lola thought. *I'm guessin' he'll fly pretty fast. So, it shouldn't take long. And you'll probably hear their flappin' wings when they get close.*

Good. I can't wait to kill that fucker and save Lin.

Listen— Lola began.

I am, Glinda interrupted Lola's thought. *I can't hear their wings yet. I'll let ya know when I do.*

I'm not thinkin' 'bout listenin' for their wings, Lola thought. *I wasn't completely honest with your daddy and the others, because your daddy wouldn't like the truth.*

About what? What wouldn't Daddy like?

Dragoş will know this is a trap, Lola thought. *He's dealt with seers before and knows what we can do. Even though your daddy and the others are frozen, and we're room temperature, he'll know we're in here. This is nothin' more than camouflage. All of our hearts are beatin' and he'll be able to hear 'em.*

Then, what the hell are we doin'? Lola, Glinda thought. *Are we settin' ourselves up?*

No. We're not. Our ace in the hole is you, Lola thought. *In all his eight hundred years, Dragoş has never encountered the likes of Glinda. When they get here, you must be clear-headed and single-minded to defeat him. Do not let anger and rage blind you. As much as you'll want to go for Dragoş, you must destroy Taylor first.*

Why?

Dragoş thought he couldn't defeat you with two helper vampires before, Lola thought. *But that was only because Lin, the spark in Lin, made her loosen her grip on your arm, which allowed ya to break free.*

He still only has two helper vampires and Lin is still one of 'em, Glinda thought. *If he wasn't sure then, why will he come now?*

Well, because he has to. He needs ya as his familiar. As much as it hurts me to tell ya this, we can't count on Lin still havin' the spark and helpin' ya again.

Why not? Glinda thought.

For the same reason it got harder for ya to track Zack, Lola thought. *The longer Lin's a vampire, the dimmer her spark will get. If her spark isn't there, Dragoş will have ya. That's why, even though everything inside ya will want to destroy him first, you must destroy Taylor before ya go for him.*

And Lin?

I'll trap her in my air elemental no matter what else happens, and I'll hold her 'til Father Mike can try to save her. I haven't given up on her and I won't. I'm just lettin' ya know things might not go as planned.

Okay, Glinda solemnly thought.

One more thing. And this is very important, Lola thought. *If things go sideways, both of ya need to listen to Mamma. Do not figure out what to do on your own. I keep sayin' y'all have great instincts and y'all do. But y'all cannot outwit Dragoş. Let Mamma's wisdom take control of your actions. Understand?*

Glinda nodded her massive head.

Don't just nod your pretty head. Tell me y'all understand.

We understand. If things go sideways, we'll let Mamma's wisdom guide us.

Okay. I love you, Glinda and Paige-Turner, Lola thought to both entities residing in the silver-haired, beautiful werewolf. *I will not lose y'all to this monster.*

We love you too, Lola.

Their thoughts fell silent for several moments.

Then Glinda's ears perked up at the sound of leathery wings flapping and she thought to Lola, *They're almost here.*

Get ready, Lola thought. *Find your air elemental and be ready to conjure it and trap his ass in it the second ya see him. I'll do the same for Lin and Taylor.*

Glinda looked at the space inside the building with her seeing eye. There weren't as many inside the building as the multitudes available in the open sky. But there were enough. She concentrated on one, caught it, and waited.

~ * ~

As they neared the secluded structure, Dragoş was not surprised to see it was the same structure he and Agrapina had visited the night he created her. The same structure where he had tasted the dried blood on a nail protruding from a piece of wood that belonged to the coveted Vanda from the night she became the coveted, silver-haired werewolf. Things had come full circle. Dragoş smiled a wicked smile as he and his cloud descended.

"I cannot see any heat sources, Father," Ilinca said.

"No," Dragoş said. "The wicked *vrăjitoare* has cloaked their heat; but listen, daughters. Listen and you will hear their beating hearts. She cannot stop their hearts from beating, and the wolf has left a calling. Smell her urine. They are inside."

"I hear their beating hearts, Father." Lacrima said.

"I can hear their beating hearts too, Father," Ilinca said a second after her sister spoke. "But the urine is foul."

"No, Ilinca," Dragoş hissed. "The urine is wonderful. It is the smell of victory."

Dragoş, deftly, lowered his right wing, banked down and to the right, and flew into the structure's missing door. Ilinca and Lacrima followed their father inside.

Dragoş flew to the urine-soaked cement, landed, and turned to face the opening. Ilinca landed to his right and Lacrima to his left. They turned to face the opening, too.

Dragoş roared, in a gravelly voice that almost matched the intensity of Glinda's howl, "I am here. Show yourself, you insolent, *vrăjitoare*. I will kill all of you and take my prize."

~ * ~

Glinda and Lola saw the three vampires fly into the MRB at such a fast speed they appeared as blurred motion. They landed, turned, and Dragoş roared almost immediately after he landed, but it was long enough.

Now. Lola urgently thought.

Glinda brought forth the giant air elemental she had conjured and dropped it on Dragoş. The look of surprise on his face as the massive air elemental swallowed him brought a wicked smile to Glinda's snout.

At the same instant Glinda's elemental swallowed Dragoş, two smaller ones swallowed Lin and Taylor.

Go, Lola thought.

Glinda didn't need to be told. Her muscular hind legs were taught and ready to explode like compressed springs. She sprang through the Wood Room side window, taking a large part of the structure with her, which included part of the top brace securing the Wood Room to a ceiling mount, and landed on the air elemental holding Taylor.

~ * ~

After trapping Lin and Taylor in air elementals, Lola watched Glinda leap through the window and land on Taylor, as planned. But Glinda's mass took part of the Wood Room structure with her and the old office shifted and dropped, dangerously, to the left. She wanted to make sure Glinda didn't go rogue, but the precariousness of the Wood Room's stability meant she needed to unfreeze her friends before the structure fell and they shattered. She hadn't been joking when she told Trowa he couldn't stay in the broken chair because he might fall over and crack.

Lola quickly tore off another piece of paper, conjured fire to unfreeze her friends, but she couldn't play favorites. She needed to unfreeze them in order of importance. She began with Fr. Mike, then Garrett, then Ty, then Trowa, and finally, her dearest friend, James.

When she finished unfreezing them, she didn't dismiss the ball of fire in her cupped hands. The MRB was dark inside. Even though she and Glinda could see in the dark, the men couldn't. She cast another incantation on the fireball and threw it through the destroyed window. An instant later, the MRB's interior was completely lit with an orangish glow.

The sound of the air elementals was deafening in the confined building and the Wood Room shifted and fell a few more feet.

"We have to get outta here before it falls." Lola shouted to be heard over the elementals.

"Where's Paige?" Garrett shouted.

Lola pointed at the destroyed window and shouted, "Killin' Taylor. Now get your asses downstairs. We can't help her if we get crushed when this falls."

This sank in and Garrett bolted out the broken door. His haste almost cost him, at least, broken legs; at worst, a broken neck. Although the Wood Room had shifted and fallen several feet, the stairs were still secured to the side of the MRB. He saw this just in time and jumped up, about three feet, and landed on the top stair.

Everything inside him wanted to run down the stairs to help Paige, if he could. But he stayed put on the top stair to help Fr. Mike and James out of the Wood Room. Lola, Ty, even with his bad ankle, and Trowa didn't need his help.

Not two seconds after Trowa jumped onto the stairs, the Wood Room slid free from whatever held it in place and crashed to the concrete floor with a wood splintering, enormous boom that shook the foundation. Still on the stairs, all of them looked to see what Glinda was doing. Thick dust from the demolished Wood Room filled the air and they, except for Lola, couldn't see what was happening.

They heard the flap of large, leathery wings, followed a yelp of pain from Glinda.

They heard Lola scream, "No."

Then there was another powerful flap of large, leathery wings, which stirred the dust filled building, and a lowed crash that shook the MRB and only the sound of Lola's one air elemental could be heard. When the dust cleared enough for everyone else to see, they saw what had caused

Lola's anguished scream. Taylor was dead and Lin was still trapped in Lola's air elemental, but Glinda and Dragoş were gone. And there was a large hole in the MRB's roof.

~ * ~

The winds inside the elemental were powerful, but not as powerful as Glinda. She forced her head inside the swirling wind and saw Taylor's surprised and scared, wide girl-bat eyes. Glinda opened her deadly mouth and lowered it over her repulsive, hybrid head. She felt Taylor's head frantically turning from side to side as she tried to bite her. Glinda snarled and snapped her jaws shut with an audible crunch. Taylor's head popped like a rotten grape and vile, black blood, bone, brains, tissue, and hair filled Glinda's mouth.

The instant Taylor had been destroyed, the air elemental vanished. It had done its job and returned to its plane of existence.

Glinda looked down at the headless body, which had returned to its human form, and spit the remnants of its head on the concrete floor beside the body. It made a sickening splat sound when it landed and nothing in it, except for one green, human eye, looked like it had been a head, hybrid or otherwise, seconds before.

Then Glinda turned and looked at the trapped Dragoş with her penetrating green and silver eyes. She snarled and bared her deadly fangs at him. He looked scared.

~ * ~

Dragoş had killed more *vrăjitoares* than he could count in his long, undead existence, and dealt with all their futile tricks as well. So, he wasn't surprised, or concerned, when he felt the air elemental surround him. He quickly realized the crucial mistake he'd made when the air elemental enveloped him. He'd never encountered a *vrăjitoare* who had also been a very large and powerful werewolf. He had underestimated the strength of such a formidable creature's air elemental.

He fought against the powerful winds but could not escape. As he fought, he saw the silver-haired wolf behead and kill Lacrima. Dragoş thought it would destroy Ilinca next, in order to take him on alone. He realized he had misjudged the silver-haired wolf again, when it turned its green and silver, seeing eyes on him. The silver-haired wolf bared her deadly fangs. Dragoş couldn't hear the snarl over the sound of the turbulent winds of the massive, and powerful, air elemental he was trapped in. Her intent was perfectly clear. If he didn't escape the elemental in the next few seconds, his eight-hundred-year reign as king of the vampires would end.

~ * ~

Glinda advanced on the trapped Dragoş. Black drool dripped from her lethal snout as she continued to snarl at the vile creature who had caused so much death and pain in a few days. She wasn't sure how best to destroy him. Breaking through Lola's air elemental to kill Taylor hadn't been exactly easy, but she had managed.

Could she break through her own much more powerful air elemental and destroy him, too? Or would she need to dismiss it and pounce on him?

Do not dismiss your elemental, Mamma's wisdom filled her mind. *You have power over the elementals you create. It will open for you while he remains trapped. Reach through it and remove his black heart.*

A gruesome smile spread across Glinda's snout as she reached her deadly hand-paw into the elemental. The swirling winds parted, and Glinda's deadly claws were within an inch of the vampire's man-bat chest.

~ * ~

Dragoş saw the elemental part as the wolf's black, dagger-length claws reach for his chest. His death was imminent. Or was it? Had the silver-haired werewolf made a mistake in its otherwise flawless plan. Dragoş knew if any part of him could escape the elemental, the rest of him could follow. Just before the wolf's claws closed on his chest, Dragoş transformed himself into hundreds of smaller bats and the wolf's claws closed on nothing. One of his smaller bats got ejected from the elemental through the gap the wolf's arm had created.

In an instant, hundreds of smaller bats swarmed out of the elemental. The wolf grabbed and destroyed one, but losing one, small bat amounted to only a flesh wound to the reconstituted vampire who now stood directly behind the silver-haired werewolf. It was his turn to surprise the wolf. He lifted off the concrete floor with a flap of his large wings and attacked.

~ * ~

Glinda watched in confusion as Dragoş' body dematerialized before she could remove his black heart. At first, from the swirling black mass that appeared in the elemental, she thought he'd transformed into black mist again. Her seeing eye quickly realized he wasn't mist. He had transformed into hundreds of smaller bats. She grabbed one and pulverized it, but the rest were escaping her elemental at a blurring speed. A moment later, she heard and felt Dragoş' wings flap behind her. Before she could turn around, she felt the talons of his clawed feet dig deep into each of her shoulders.

The pain was like nothing Glinda had ever experienced. It was a cold, undead pain that radiated from her shoulders and down her arms. Her arms fell, paralyzed, to her sides. It was as if Dragoş' talons contained some supernatural poison.

She couldn't even struggle as Dragoş took flight with another flap of his powerful wings and lifted her substantial weight, effortlessly, off the MRB's cement floor. Then Dragoş burst through the MRB roof. In a matter of seconds, Glinda's paralyzed body was hundreds of feet above the ground.

In any other situation, the view would have been beautiful. As Dragoş took flight away from the MRB, Glinda's mind filled with fear. Fear that she was paralyzed. Fear that he finally had her. And more fear about what he would do with her when they got to where he flew.

~ * ~

Garrett took the steps from what was the Wood Room, four at a time, and skidded to a stop on the concrete floor. Ty and Trowa had matched Garrett's frantic descent and were by his side. Lola joined them next, followed by Fr. Mike, and finally, James joined them. James panted from running down the steps took and, not for the first time, vowed to lose some weight.

"Where is she?" Garrett yelled.

Lola closed her eyes to reach out to Glinda.

"Where the fuck is she?" Garrett yelled.

Lola looked at Garrett. "If you'll shut the hell up, I'll contact her and find out."

Garrett clamped his teeth shut so hard they ground together and the tendons on the sides of his neck bulged. But he nodded.

Lola closed her eyes and reached out for Glinda's mind.

~ * ~

Glinda's vision faded, and she was only vaguely aware of the wind rushing through her silky fur. Even the pain from where Dragoş' talons had pierced her shoulders had gone. She tried to keep her head up but couldn't. Her snout dropped to her chest and her eyes closed. She felt nothing. Even her thoughts were fading to nothingness. Which, because fear filled her thoughts, had been a blessing. Darkness took her.

Deep within the darkness of her mind, she heard Lola's thoughts. They sounded so far away. As if they had a faulty connection, which they did. It took all of Glinda's concentration, but she focused on Lola and the thoughts became clearer.

Glinda. Glinda. Please answer me. Lola's thought came.

I'm here, Glinda weakly thought.

Thank the Elements and your God. Are ya okay?

No. Dragoş took me, Glinda thought but it took all her concentration to do. *He grabbed my shoulders with the talons on his feet. They must have some kind of poison in 'em. I'm completely paralyzed. I can't even open my eyes to tell y'all where he's takin' me.*

Where's Mamma? Lola's franticly thought.

I am here, Mamma's thought came and joined the other two.

Listen, Glinda, Lola thought. *Seers can use the elements to resist poison. Mamma can help ya.*

I am already trying, but the ancient is powerful, Mamma thought.

Mamma, please, Lola panickily thought. *Ya have to save her from him.*

If she can't save me, y'all have to kill me, Lola, Glinda thought more weakly. *I can't be what he'll turn me into. Promise me y'all will do your best to kill me.*

Stop thinkin' like that, Glinda and Paige-Turner, Lola thought. *Y'all have to remain positive for this to work. Y'all need to help Mamma help y'all resist the poison.*

Lola's right, Mamma thought. *You're a* seer *with pure* sight. *I can help, but you need to do your part.*

What can I do? Glinda thought.

Can ya feel the wind? Lola thought.

No.

I can, Mamma thought.

Glinda's mind filled with a faint purple light and a moment later she felt the wind blowing through her silky fur again. The purple light grew in intensity.

I feel it. Glinda excitedly thought.

Good, Lola thought relieved. *Take it in. Let it fill ya and drive out the poison. It'll be like conjurin' an air elemental inside your body.*

I'll try, Glinda thought. *But I can't* see *one to conjure it.*

You don't need to see *it*, Mamma thought. *As an elemental* seer, *it's part of you. Pull it inside.*

Okay, Glinda thought.

Glinda concentrated on the feel of the air ruffling her fur and willed it to enter her body. For a long, horrible moment, she felt nothing but the external air. Then, suddenly, she felt it penetrate her body. It filled her and feeling returned to her paralyzed body. It felt like the air was filling her body and driving the poison out, which is exactly what had happened. She opened her eyes.

It's workin', Glinda excitedly thought. *I can feel and my eyes are open.*

Keep concentrating, Glinda, Mamma thought. *You are not completely rid of the ancient's poison.*

I am, Glinda thought more excitedly. *I can move my fingers.*

Thank the Elements and your God, Lola thought very relieved. *But be careful. Do not let Dragoş know you've regained use of your body. When he lands, he'll release you. Attack him then. He won't expect it.*

I get it, Glinda thought. *Like when Voldemort thought Harry Potter was dead, but he wasn't.*

I do not know what the child is talking about, but the ancient's poison is gone from Glinda's body, Mamma thought.

Mamma's the wisest seer *alive and doesn't know about Harry Potter*, Lola thought with a laugh. *Yes, Glinda. Do it just like Harry, but Dragoş is your Voldemort.*

I will, Glinda thought. *I'll let ya know when I've destroyed the fucker. Take care of Lin.*

I will take care of Lin, Lola thought. *But be careful, Glinda. Do not underestimate Dragoş. He is still dangerous.*

I won't underestimate him again, Glinda thought, and the connection broke.

~ * ~

Lola's eyes fluttered open as she came out of trance-like state needed for such deep mental connections and saw five very anxious men staring at her. Garrett was the most anxious.

"Is she okay?" Garrett asked.

Lola smiled a comforting smile. "Yes. Glinda is okay. She's not out of danger, but she's okay."

"What the hell does that mean?" Garrett shouted. "You were…gone for 'bout five minutes. What happened?"

"It means that Glinda was in trouble, but Mamma helped her," Lola said. "She's not out of danger 'cause she still hasn't destroyed Dragoş. But she has a plan and I'm sure it'll work."

"I fuckin' hate this," Garrett shouted. "We...I should be with her."

"It's better that we're not with her," James said. "If we were with her, Glinda would be distracted by worryin' that Dragoş might use one of us to get her to submit."

"James is right, Garrett," Lola said in her warm, honey voice. "Glinda's best chance to destroy Dragoş is one-on-one combat. She *will* win."

Frustrated, because he knew their arguments had merit, Garrett said, "Okay. But I still don't like it."

"What do we do now?" Ty asked.

Lola pointed at the hybrid who had been Lin and still trapped in her air elemental. "We try to save Lin."

"Wait," James said excitedly as he reached into his vampire kit and pulled out a mirror. "I want to test one of my theories. I might never get this chance again."

"What theory?" Mike asked.

"James thinks the Hollywood notion that vampires don't have a reflection in mirrors is crap," Garrett said. "His theory is that vampires avoid mirrors because they can't hide their true nature in 'em."

"Very good, Garrett," James said as he angled the mirror so he could see the hybrid vampire in it. "If you were in my class, that answer would earn ya an A on a pop-quiz."

Trowa, who stood next to James, saw the hybrid's reflection in the mirror first. "Holy shit. He's right."

James, who saw Lin's human form in the mirror, not the hybrid, an instant later, shouted, "I knew it. See for yourselves."

He handed the mirror to Fr. Mike, who looked. But he glanced away, because Lin was naked, and handed it to Ty.

Ty looked, looked away for the same reason Fr. Mike had, and handed it to Garrett. "James is right. But Lin's naked."

"I don't wanna see that," Garrett said. "She's like a second daughter to me. I'll take y'all at your word. Lola?"

Lola smiled warmly. "I don't need a mirror to see a vampire's true form. Time to save Lin, Father Mike."

"You guys act like I've done this before," Mike said. "No Catholic priest has ever tried to compel a vampire to leave a human host. At least, not that I'm aware of."

"No. But Catholic priests have performed exorcisms," James said. "I'm not sayin' it's the same, but it's not that different. In an exorcism, y'all compel an evil entity to leave a human host. A vampire is an evil entity, too. If Lin's…spark is still there, ya might drive the vampire out of her."

"If I can't?"

"We have a Hail Mary pass we can throw," Lola said with a wink of her seeing eye. "Pardon the pun. But we'll need Paige for that. All ya can do is try, Father Mike."

"Okay," Mike said as he pulled a rosary from his jacket pocket.

The six of them walked to the vampire, who flailed helplessly inside the air elemental, and Fr. Mike prayed the Rosary.

~ * ~

Dragoş flew far from the structure and the troublesome *vrăjitoare* before he spiraled down toward a small clearing in the woods, miles from any signs of life. He hadn't felt Ilinca's destruction. He was sure they would destroy her. The priest was with the *vrăjitoare*. That they hadn't been able to destroy her yet brought a smile to his repugnant, hybrid face. She was fighting back. Dragoş felt a measure of pride in that notion, but losing Ilinca, and even the lovely and natural vampire Lacrima, was a small price to pay for Vanda and the silver-haired werewolf.

Dragoş smiled again at the feel of the wolf's dead weight in his talons. The wolf had been taken by surprise, or didn't know about the paralyzing poison in vampires' talons. Although he hadn't planned on acquiring Vanda and her wolf this way, it would make the process easier. Because the *vrăjitoare* gave Vanda and her wolf seeing powers, mezmery wouldn't work on them, and the crone *vrăjitoare* had severed the mental link he could have used. With the wolf paralyzed, he could force his black blood into its slack mouth to make it his familiar and then force it to transform, drink the girl's virgin blood to the point of death, and reanimate her as Vanda. Then he would take her. Fuck her in the tall grass of the clearing.

When Dragoş was about fifty feet above the clearing, he released the wolf from his talons and watched it fall, helplessly, to the ground. It hit the ground with a resounding thud and rolled, lifelessly, onto its face in a crumpled heap. He didn't have to drop the wolf; he did it because he could, and it brought him pleasure to watch it hit the ground paralyzed unable to brace itself for impact.

Dragoş landed a few feet away from the silver-haired, crumpled heap and hissed, "I told you that you were no match for me and that I would have you and Vanda. It is time to make you and Vanda mine."

~ * ~

Glinda saw, through closed eyelids with her seeing eye, the clearing in the woods and felt Dragoş spiral down to land. She was ready. Or, she thought, she was. She hadn't expected Dragoş releasing her fifty feet above the clearing. She knew the impact wouldn't harm her, but instincts were powerful. It took all her concentration to not brace for impact. Glinda didn't brace and hit the ground hard. She let momentum roll her loose limbs naturally. Glinda ended up face down, which was less than ideal. But it would have to do.

She heard Dragoş land a few feet away from her and give his overconfident speech. Glinda knew he would have to roll her over, so she waited for that to happen. She didn't have to wait long. She felt his repulsive, but strong, icy hand grip her shoulder as he rolled her over onto her back.

Glinda didn't move or open her eyes. She could see him just fine. She watched as Dragoş slit his right nipple with a gnarled thumbnail. Black blood oozed from the wound. It was time.

Glinda's left arm was pinned beneath her, because that's where it ended up when she feigned paralysis as Dragoş rolled her over, but her right arm was free. As Dragoş bent to force his vile, black blood into her slack mouth, Glinda's right arm shot out and she wrapped her immense hand-paw around his thick, man-bat, hybrid neck and pushed him away from her.

Dragoş' man-bat eyes went wide, and he wheezed, through his closing throat, "No. This cannot be."

Through gritted fangs, Glinda growled, "And I keep tellin' ya it can be, *bitch*."

Dragoş hissed and flailed for Glinda's eyes, but she had reach and power on her side. She rolled off her right arm, stood, and held him off the ground at arm's length.

Dragoş did the only thing he could, but it was predictable. He tried to take flight. When he did, Glinda reached out with her left arm, grabbed his right wing, and, with less effort than she expected, ripped the bony appendage from his body. It came off with a spray of black blood and Dragoş screamed in pain through his closing throat.

A gruesome grin spread across Glinda's snout, and she snarled, "I was gonna kill ya quickly in the elemental. Now, I'll have some fun with ya. I never understood the kids who enjoyed pullin' wings and legs off bugs, but I'm startin' to."

Dragoş attempted to puncture Glinda's skin with the talon on his left leg to paralyze her again. Glinda grabbed his ankle, twisted, and pulled. Dragoş' left leg ripped off at the knee with another spray of black blood. A gravely scream tried to erupt from his hybrid mouth. Glinda tossed the useless appendage into the woods and grinned into Dragoş' man-bat eyes; they were filled with pain and fear.

She released Dragoş' neck, and he toppled into the high grass of the clearing. He tried to crawl away; his left wing flapped in a pathetic attempt to take flight. Glinda grabbed his left wing and ripped it off. With her powerful hand off his throat, Dragoş let out a gravely scream that shook the surrounding trees.

"Good thing ya picked a secluded place to take me, *fuck-tard*," Glinda snarled. "If ya hadn't, someone might'a heard that. But it's just you and me. Like ya wanted."

Dragoş rolled over and held up his hands in a defensive posture. Glinda grabbed his left arm in her right hand-claw, twisted it off at the shoulder, and threw it into the woods. He screamed in pain. But that scream paled compared to the one he let out when Glinda crunched through his right arm, below the elbow, with a powerful snap of her deadly jaws. She spit the arm out on Dragoş' chest.

"No, Vanda," Dragoş pleaded. "I beg you. Please stop."

"Her name is Paige, *bitch*." Glinda almost howled.

Glinda had had enough. She placed her right foot on Dragoş' chest and pined what was left of him to the ground. She reached down with both hand-paws, grabbed his head, and with a twist and a jerk, tore it from his neck. Black blood sprayed from his ragged neck on to the tall grass.

She brought his head up to look into his dying eyes. As she watched, Dragoş' eyes blinked several times and the man-bat hybrid face transformed back into one of an ancient man's with long, wispy, white hair. His piercing blue eyes blinked one more time as the black blood flowing from his head slowed to a trickle and stopped. An instant later, Dragoş' head became fine ash that crumbled in her hand-paws. It fell to the ground, and all that was left was his wispy, white hair. The hair turned yellow and brittle, like straw. It too quickly turned to dust and filtered through Glinda's clawed fingers to the ground a moment later.

Glinda dusted off her hand-paws and looked at what was left of Dragoş' body. It had turned to fine ash and sank into the grass. Glinda knew a light breeze would quickly disperse the fine ash and all evidence Dragoş had ever existed would be gone forever. A satisfied grin spread across Glinda's snout.

But there was no time to celebrate. She needed to let Lola know Dragoş was dead and find out if they'd been able to save Lin. As she began to close her eyes, she saw something so amazing it took her breath away.

From the scattered remains of Dragoş' ashes, what was left of his black aura dissipated and thousands of white lights appeared. The white lights quickly took human form and ascended into the night sky. Several lingered and their human forms became more distinct. She saw them. Al, Melanie, Megan, Taylor, and Lena.

They smiled at Glinda, and ascended, too. Tears filled Glinda's eyes as she realized Melanie, Megan, Taylor, and Lena's souls were Dragoş' victims, too. The vampires he had created from their bodies hadn't trapped their souls, after all. They were going to heaven with Al, who was a good man and heaven bound once Dragoş was killed, anyway.

Feeling God's grace, Glinda closed her eyes, concentrated, and reached out to Lola's mind.

Chapter Sixteen

Fr. Mike was apprehensive about approaching the air elemental, trapped vampire. When Lola assured him the elemental would not harm him, no matter how close he got to it, and the vampire could not escape it, he stepped in front of it and prayed the Rosary. He was close enough to the elemental that it blew hair in his eyes, but, other than that, he was unaffected by it. Unfortunately, the vampire seemed unaffected by the praying of the Rosary, too.

After two complete Rosaries, he abandoned the approach and produced a large, silver crucifix from his satchel and held it up in front of the hybrid vampire's wide, and scared, eyes. The crucifix had an effect. The vampire screeched loud enough to be heard over the elemental's roaring winds and cycled from hybrid to human form in violent convulsions. It was too much for Fr. Mike.

"This isn't working," Mike said. "All it's doing is torturing the poor beast."

"That's not a poor beast," Lola said sternly. "It's a vampire and serves Lucifer. Do *not* take pity on it."

"Okay," Mike said. "It's an agent of evil. Nothing I do seems to help bring Lindsey back. I can't truly try to compel the vampire out of her body through the elemental. If you dismiss it, can the other men hold her down?"

Lola shook her head, and the beads clicked together. "No. She'd overpower 'em. Don't underestimate her power, Father Mike."

"Then what?" Mike asked helplessly.

"We need Glinda. She can hold the vampire without help."

Garrett, who paced the concrete floor and anxiously chewing on his fingernails as he worried about Paige, heard Lola mention Glinda. "Have ya heard anything from Glinda yet?"

"No," Lola calmly said. "Not yet, but don't worry. I'm sure she's fine."

"You can't *know* that." Garrett shouted.

"Yes. I can," Lola said. "Glinda and Paige are part of my coven for now. If she were…dead, I'd feel the loss."

"Well, that's comfortin'," Garrett snapped. "She could be near dead, but ya wouldn't know until she actually dies."

"You have to have faith in…" Lola began.

"Faith?" Garrett shouted and pointed at the hybrid vampire screeching in the elemental. "Look what faith did for Lin."

James, who was videoing everything Fr. Mike tried against the vampire on his iPhone, said, "Lola's right, Garrett. Dragoş is no match for Glinda one-on-one."

"Y'all can't *know* that." Garrett shouted.

Ty came up to Garrett, and put a strong, reassuring arm around his shoulders. "Let's go outside for a bit and get away from all this."

Garrett's impulse was to shrug Ty's arm off his shoulders, but he relented. "Okay, but I wanna know as soon as ya know somethin', Lola. Even if it's bad news."

Lola nodded, but as Garrett and Ty turned for the door, she felt Glinda's mental connection, and shouted, "Wait."

As Garrett and Ty turned back, they saw Lola's eyes shut. Garrett held his breath.

I destroyed the fucker, Glinda thought triumphantly. *Nothin' left but ash.*

Are you injured? Lola thought.

Not a scratch on me, Glinda thought with a laugh. *I did the Harry Potter thing. You should'a seen the look on his face when I grabbed him and ripped him apart. I'll give y'all the details when I get back. And… somethin' else happened that I didn't expect.*

What?

When I destroyed him, and his black aura disappeared, all the trapped souls of his victims ascended to heaven like we thought they would, Glinda thought. *I saw Al. I also saw Melanie, Megan, Taylor, and Lena's souls ascend. I thought they would be in hell like Cipriana and hopefully, Dragoş. But they weren't. I'm glad they aren't in hell, but I don't know why they aren't.*

I don't know the answer to that question, Lola thought. *Perhaps Father Mike or James will. For now, I'm proud of you, Glinda. I knew ya could do it.*

How's it going with Lin?

Not good, Lola thought somberly. *We need you. How far away are ya and how fast can ya get here?*

Glinda, who had an innate sense of where she was in relation to where any point of destination was, like built-in GPS, thought back, *I'm forty-seven miles from the MRB. Dragoş wanted a lot of distance between us and y'all. I'll get there as quick as I can.*

Okay, Lola thought. *Hurry back. Your daddy's worried sick about ya.*

On my way, Glinda thought and the connection broke.

Lola smiled before she opened her eyes. "Glinda destroyed Dragoş and is unharmed. She's on her way back, but he took her far from here. It'll take some time before she's back."

An actual cheer echoed through the MRB as all five men let out shouts of victory. Once the adrenaline wore off, Garrett's knees gave out. If Ty hadn't still had his arm around him, Garrett would've crumpled to the MRB's concrete floor. Tears spilled down his scruffy cheeks.

Lola went to Garrett and hugged him. "She's fine, Garrett. I asked if she was injured, and she said she didn't have a scratch on her."

"I was just...she's my little girl," Garrett sobbed on Lola's shoulder.

"I know," Lola said soothingly. "I know."

Garrett felt the tension and apprehension of the last few days ease. "Are ya nudgin' me?"

"Just a little," Lola admitted. "Do ya want me to stop?"

Garrett shook his head. "No. I can't let Paige see me like this when she gets back. Thank you, Lola."

"You're very welcome, Garrett."

Beautiful moment or not, Fr. Mike held the silver crucifix in front of the trapped vampire. It screeched and flailed as it involuntarily transformed from hybrid to human form and back again. Never, in his wildest dreams, did he think he'd pray for a werewolf's help to exorcise a vampire from a young woman. But he did.

~ * ~

Glinda felt euphoric after destroying Dragoş and having done it so easily. She felt even more euphoric, having seen all the tortured souls of his victims ascend to heaven. Especially Al, Melanie, Megan, Taylor, and Lena. But the news about Lin wasn't what she expected. She thought Fr. Mike could help her. And Lola said they needed her. She dropped to all fours and took off as fast as her powerful legs would propel her, and to her surprise, Glinda had a reservoir of untapped speed. She sped through the woods at over eighty miles per hour without tiring.

Trees blurred as she weaved between them. Leaping countless deadfalls, five back roads, three streams, and one river propelled her massive body sixty feet or longer with each powerful jump and she landed, deftly, without slowing. The only problem she encountered was Highway Sixty-Nine. The traffic was too frequent to jump the north and southbound lanes without being seen. She had to take a detour, one costing her precious minutes, to a bridge where the highway crossed the Neches River, several miles south of where she wanted to cross. Within twenty minutes, she sprinted past the pond where the treehouse had been the night the alpha attacked her and Justin. She slowed as she exited the woods on the backside of the MRB, where her daddy and Ty's SUVs were parked. A few seconds later, she loped through the missing door, saw her daddy and friends, and Lin screeching in the air elemental as she, rapidly, transformed from hybrid to human and back repeatedly in front of Fr. Mike's silver crucifix.

~ * ~

When Glinda loped into the MRB, Garrett ran up to her and hugged her enormous head. She had still been on all four legs, or he couldn't have reached her head.

"I was so worried 'bout ya," Garrett said as fresh happy tears spilled from his eyes.

Although she didn't enjoy speaking through Glinda, at least not when it was so effective at scaring Dragoş, she snarled, "I'm okay, Daddy."

Garrett noticed the wounds on Glinda's shoulders where Dragoş had grabbed her with his talons. "I thought ya said she didn't have a scratch, Lola. What the hell do ya consider those bleedin'...holes in her shoulders?"

"Calm down, Garrett," Lola said. "Those were from when Dragoş grabbed her and flew away with her. I'm pretty sure Glinda didn't even think to transform and regenerate before comin' back. She's worried 'bout Lin."

Garrett looked at Glinda, who nodded her head, agreeing with Lola.

"Ya weren't hurt fightin' Dragoş?"

Glinda shook her head.

"If you're satisfied, Garrett, can we get back to tryin' to save Lin?" Lola said.

"Yeah. Okay," Garrett said. "What's the plan?"

"We need to get Lin back to my house," Lola said.

"How in the hell are we gonna do that?" Ty asked.

"Easy. Glinda could penetrate my air elemental to destroy Taylor," Lola said. "Glinda can penetrate the elemental holdin' Lin and restrain her. I'll dismiss my elemental and freeze Lin. Then we can take her back to my house."

"You can freeze undead critters?" Trowa asked.

"Of course," Lola said with a wink.

"What about Glinda?" Garrett said. "If she's holdin' Lindsey, won't she get frozen too?"

"No," Lola said. "You were sittin' next to Father Mike when Paige froze him. Were you affected in any way?"

"No. But..." Garrett began.

"It's a directional incantation, Garrett," Lola said. "It'll only affect the person, or vampire, I direct it at. Any more questions?"

Speechless and embarrassed, Garrett shook his head.

"You never cease to amaze me, Lola," James said. "But why do we need to take her to your house?"

Lola looked at Glinda. "Paige has some meditatin' to do."

Glinda caught on immediately and nodded her head.

At that cryptic exchange, Garrett said, "What's that mean?"

"Best ya don't know beforehand, Garrett," Lola said with a warm smile.

"Is it safe?" Garrett asked.

"She's done it before," Lola said.

"That doesn't exactly answer my question," Garrett said.

"No. It doesn't," Lola said sternly. "It's time that you start trustin' Paige and Glinda and stop doubtin' 'em. Now, give me one of your bullets to use to freeze Lin."

Without questioning, Garrett popped a bullet out of a spare clip on his belt and handed it to Lola.

To Glinda, Lola said, "Ya ready to do this?"

Glinda nodded her head, stood, and walked around behind the air elemental with Lin trapped in it. She pushed her powerful arms into the elemental, wrapped them around Lin, and squeezed her body to hers. As she pulled the struggling vampire to her, it stopped transforming and became stuck in human form.

Lola dismissed the elemental and the sound of its rushing winds was replaced with the unholy screeching of the vampire as it struggled in Glinda's arms. The men, except for James, who had still been videoing everything and found nothing about the female form sexually enticing, turned away from Lin's naked form, but Lola didn't pay attention to them. She blew her white breath on the bullet. It turned blue. She blew again and the glowing blue ball materialized in her palms. She walked up to the flailing vampire and blew through it at its closest, exposed skin, which was its extended left foot, as it kicked at Lola. It instantly turned blue and the blue quickly spread until it choked off a screech as its mouth froze open with her long tongue prominently protruding from between its needle-sharp fangs.

At hearing the screeching stop, the men turned around and saw a bizarre sight. A giant, silver-haired werewolf holding a small, blue vampire. Apparently, seeing Lin naked, but blue and frozen, wasn't as offensive because none of them turned away. She had been frozen in an awkward position. Both her arms were outstretched, her left leg was thrust out, and her head was back with her mouth open and her eyes wide. They stared at the men in a menacing way.

"Where's she gonna fit like that?" Trowa asked.

"In the back seat of Garrett's SUV," Lola said. "I'll ride in the back with her head on my lap. Garrett and Paige will be up front. The rest of y'all will have to ride with Ty. And no speedin'. We're not rushed anymore, and I don't want her to crack."

"Okay," Garrett said. "How do we get her in my SUV?"

"Leave that to me and Glinda," Lola said as she and Glinda, with the blue vampire in her arms, started for the missing MRB door.

Despite Glinda's size and strength, she was extremely dexterous and gentle. After Lola got into the SUV, Glinda delicately maneuvered the awkwardly positioned vampire into the back seat and Lola positioned her head on her lap. The result had Lin on her back with both arms sticking up in the air and the toe of her left foot less than an inch from the SUV's roof.

"This is why your daddy needs to drive slow," Lola said. "If Lin's foot hits the roof too hard, her foot could break off, and I can't fix that."

Glinda nodded, turned, and went back inside the MRB.

When Glinda entered, Garrett said, "Did she fit?"

Glinda nodded and pointed at Lola's dress that had stayed folded on the banister through all the commotion.

Garrett understood. "Everybody out. Glinda's gotta transform back into Paige."

Everyone except James left.

"C'mon, James," Garrett said.

"I'd really love to video her transformation, Garrett," James said with his recording iPhone pointed at Glinda.

"That's my little girl, ya wanna video," Garrett said angrily "She'll be naked."

Before James could mount an appeal, Glinda transformed back into Paige.

"Well shit, Paige," Garrett said as he turned around.

Paige smiled. "Did ya get that, Doctor James?"

"I did," James excitedly said. "Thank ya, Paige."

With his back still turned, Garrett said, "She's sixteen, James. Ya now have a video of a naked sixteen-year-old girl on your phone. Lin is sixteen, too. That makes your video illegal. Better not share that video."

Scandalized, James said, "I would *never* share this video, and it's not illegal. Paige and Lindsey weren't engaged in a lurid act and if anything passes the S in the LAPS test from Miller versus California, this is it."

"The what, in the what, from what?" Garrett asked.

"The Miller versus California Supreme Court case on obscenity," James said. "Look it up. Consider it a homework assignment."

Paige giggled at the exchange between her daddy and Dr. James.

She pulled Lola's see-through dress over her head. "Ya can turn around now, Daddy."

Garrett did and without looking at the dress and Paige's all too exposed body beneath, wrapped her in a tight hug. "Thank God you're okay. I was so worried."

"I'm fine," Paige said. "Now we gotta worry 'bout Lin."

When they got to the SUVs, everyone except James had gotten into Ty's SUV. James got into its back seat while Garrett and Paige got in his.

As they drove past the MRB, Garrett noticed it was still lit with Lola's conjured light. "Will the light ya created go out?"

"Oh," Lola said as she cradled Lin's frozen face in her lap and dismissed the incantation. "Thanks for remindin' me. Done,"

The MRB went dark, and they drove, slowly, to Lola's house. No one bothered to close the gate.

~ * ~

When they got to Lola's house, she said, "Y'all go on inside while Glinda and I bring Lin in."

With the men gone, Paige removed Lola's dress, handed it to her, transformed into Glinda, and helped remove the blue and brittle, frozen vampire from the back seat of the SUV. Glinda carried Lin up the porch steps, which squeaked in protest under her weight, and onto the porch.

Lola stepped in front of Glinda and opened the front door. Glinda had to bend over to get through the seven-foot-tall door, all while making sure she didn't break part of Lin's body off while doing so. A moment later, they were inside Lola's dark living room with the men.

"Lay Lin down on the floor by my curio cabinet, Glinda," Lola said.

Glinda gently put Lin's frozen body on the hardwood floor where Lola told her and returned to Lola's side.

"Okay," Lola said as she turned to face the men. "Time to bring Paige back, gentlemen."

Again, all of them, except James, who was videoing again, turned their backs. This time, Garrett didn't raise a fuss about James' videoing his naked daughter. He knew his earlier response had been a father's impulsive reaction. He also knew James was a man of honor and a good friend. Paige and Glinda's secret, even on video, would be safe with him.

Glinda transformed into Paige and put the dress on. "Okay. Y'all can turn around now."

They did, but their eyes remained locked on Paige's face when they looked her way.

"Now what?" Mike asked.

Lola looked at Paige. "Should I tell 'em, or do you want the pleasure?"

Paige smiled. "I'll tell 'em."

"Prepare yourselves for one *hell* of a story, gentlemen," Lola said with a wry smile as three chairs from her kitchen table slid into the room to accommodate everyone.

After they were all seated, Paige said, "Miss Lola and I weren't…exactly truthful with y'all 'bout how we learned Dragoş Văduva and his creator, Cipriana Ardelean's, names."

"Imagine that," Garrett said sarcastically.

"Then, how did y'all learn their names?" James asked with his usual enthusiasm.

"Well, like Miss Lola said, we used meditation to do it," Paige said and hesitated a moment before continuing. "But I, not Miss Lola, got their names by goin' to hell."

At this, Fr. Mike stiffened. "You're speaking metaphorically, right."

Paige shook her head. "No, Father Mike. I went to hell. I confronted Lucifer. I wasn't able to compel any information from him, but I could summon Dragoş' creator. I could compel information from her. That's how I found out who he was, when he was created, and where he was created. Doctor James did the rest of the work by puttin' the pieces of information I got together."

Fr. Mike crossed himself.

James said, "Fascinatin'."

To Lola, Garrett said, "You let my daughter go to hell?"

"She didn't know, Daddy," Paige said. "I told her after I got back."

"She's a willful, chil'," Lola told Garrett.

"But how?" Mike asked in a whisper.

"Actually," Paige said. "It was pretty easy. When I meditate, I travel outside the universe. Outside of everything. I found God there."

"Did you *see* Him?" Mike asked in awe.

"No," Paige said. "I *felt* Him. Of course, He knew what I had planned. His voice entered my…everything and said, 'Fear not, my child. I will be with you.' That's how I knew I'd be safe in hell. And I was.

"Hell was horrible, beyond anything y'all can imagine," Paige said and shuddered. "Lucifer wasn't happy that I was there. He threatened to keep me there. But I knew God was with me and that he couldn't. When Lucifer tried to attack me, a blindin', white light, *God's* light, stopped him from gettin' me."

Fr. Mike crossed himself again. "Praise God. When this is over, I want you to tell me everything about hell and Lucifer."

Paige nodded. "I will."

"Okay," Garrett said. "My daughter went to hell. At this point, nothin' surprises me anymore. But what's hell got to do with Lindsey and what we do to save her?"

"I gotta go back, Daddy."

Shocked, Garrett said, "Why?"

"Because Lin's trapped there, Daddy," Paige said. "She doesn't belong there, and I gotta bring her back."

"I'm guessin' nothin' I say will stop ya from doin' it," Garrett said.

Paige shook her head. "As long as she's a vampire, her soul is stuck in hell. The only other way to release her soul is to kill her."

"Will God go with you again?" Mike asked.

Paige fell silent for a moment. "I'm countin' on Him comin' with me again. If He does, I'll know that Lin's spark, her Christian soul, is still there and that we can save her."

"If He won't go with you?" Mike asked.

Paige looked over at the frozen vampire who was her best friend, Lin.

Tears spilled from her eyes,. "If He won't come with me, I'll know Lin's spark is gone. I'll come back, transform into Glinda, and destroy her."

Lola put an arm around Paige's slumped shoulders. "Don't fret 'bout what we don't know, Paige-Turner. Stay hopeful and bring Lin back to us."

Paige sniffed and wiped the tears from her cheeks. "Okay, Miss Lola. I will."

"What happens now?" Mike asked.

Lola opened the table drawer, pulled a medium size, blue candle from it, and showed it to Paige. "Long enough to get it done?"

Since she had already done it, and knew how to do it again, Paige said, "Yeah. That should give me enough time."

"How much time is that?" Garrett asked.

"About three hours," Lola told him.

"Three hours?" Garrett said. "She's gonna be in hell for three hours?"

"Three hours for y'all," Paige said. "For me, it'll feel more like a few seconds. Time doesn't really exist where I'm goin'. Not in heaven or in hell. For the souls in hell, every second feels like an eternity of torture. It's awful, and I can't really explain it."

"What do we do for three hours?" James asked.

"Well, if y'all can't keep your traps shut to keep from interruptin' Paige's meditation, you'll have to take your asses outside," Lola said sternly.

"I'm staying and praying, silently, the whole time she's gone," Mike said.

Lola smiled at him. "I kinda figured you'd stay and pray."

"I'm stayin', too," James said.

"There won't be anything for you to see, James," Lola said. "Just Paige sittin' on the floor in a meditative trance."

"I'm stayin' anyway," James said.

Lola looked at Garrett, Ty, and Trowa. "What about y'all? Can y'all keep your mouths shut for three hours?"

Trowa, the one who spoke the least of them, said, "I'll wait outside."

Ty grabbed Garrett by the arm. "I think we should wait outside, too."

Garrett resisted Ty's tug for a moment. "Yeah. I'll wait outside with Ty and Trowa."

Lola handed the blue candle to Paige. "Get ready. I'm gonna get your daddy, Ty, and Trowa somethin' to keep 'em from feelin' the cold. Don't light the candle until they're outside and can't disrupt your concentration."

Paige took the candle and got up. "Okay. I'm ready to do this."

"We can sit in my SUV and run the heater," Garrett said.

"No. I don't want the sound of the motor runnin' to be in the background," Lola said as she walked to the bedroom door wall, removed a totem about the size of a notebook, and handed it to Garrett. "Paige needs natural silence for this to work."

Garrett, who had used a cellphone size totem, with a green leaf in the middle resembling Lola's, green, cat-like, seeing eye that gave her the ability to communicate with him mentally during the werewolf showdown, looked at the larger totem. It, like the previous one, was constructed of small limbs and twigs. But in the middle was a large, orange maple leaf.

Lola passed her hand over the maple leaf, it glowed an orangish-red. "This'll keep y'all warm in the SUV. If y'all talk, whisper, and no music."

Garrett nodded, handed the totem to Trowa, went to Paige, and wrapped her in a tight hug. "Ya know what I'm gonna say, Paige-Turner."

Paige hugged him back. "I'll be careful, Daddy."

Garrett held her tight for a few more moments. "I love you, sweet girl."

"I love you too, Daddy," Paige said as he released her.

Garrett took one last look at Paige when he joined Ty and Trowa at the front door. Then he looked away, and they left. The door closed slowly, though.

"Now what?" James asked.

"Now, you two take a seat, keep your mouths shut, and let Paige meditate," Lola told James and Fr. Mike.

They took two of the kitchen table chairs and sat facing the front of Lola's house, where Paige placed the blue candle on the floor.

We usually do this naked, Paige thought. *I know it wouldn't bother Doctor James, but I don't wanna make Father Mike uncomfortable. Can I mediate in this?*

Lola smiled and thought, *It's best to be free of Earthly constrictions when meditatin'. But you'll be fine in my loose-fittin' dress. You have pure* sight. *I doubt anything would impair your meditation. Ya ready?*

I am, Paige thought as she sat down on the floor.

Paige reached out, snapped her fingers on the candle's wick to light it, assumed the meditative position, and closed her eyes. She cleared her mind and within seconds, felt herself dissolve into nothingness and everything at the same time.

~ * ~

Once again, Paige was outside the universe, beyond creation with her creator. She was with God again and she *felt* His comforting embrace. She knew God knew why she was there and waited for Him to guide her to hell and protect her. Instead of being taken to hell, she was suddenly enveloped in a blinding, but beautiful, white light. And Justin stood before her.

Hey, Paige-Turner, his strong, familiar voice filled her.

Justin, Paige's thought filled the white void. *I miss you so much.*

Don't miss me, Justin's voice filled her. *I'm not gone. I'm here. But I'm with you, too. Always. And I always will be.*

Paige felt tears not there sting eyes not there. *I wanna stay here with you.*

Justin shook his beautiful head and thought, *Ya can't. It's not your time. Save Lin and take her back with you. There's still time.*

Will I see you again? Paige's thought filled the void.

Justin smiled a smile that filled her heart not there with pure joy. *Yes. But not for many, many years of your time on Earth. You will live a long, happy life, Paige-Turner, and I will always be with you.*

I love you, Justin, Paige's thought filled the void.

I love you too, Paige-Turner. Justin's voice filled her. *I have to go now. Save Lin.*

Paige wanted to hug him with arms she didn't have. She couldn't. Justin's form came to her and passed through her. For a moment, she *felt* him and she *smelled* him. She soaked it in, and the bright, beautiful white light vanished.

God? Paige thought into the nothingness.

I am with you, my child, God's beautiful voice filled her.

With that, the universe had gone, and she became enveloped in the horrible darkness again. She saw shapes moving in the darkness; the vile, naked, tortured souls letting off a reddish glow as they swirled around her and through her. The agonized screams and wails surrounded her, penetrated her. As did the tortured moans, snarls, and wicked laughter.

Then the blackness was replaced with a reddish-orange glow, and she saw Lucifer again, sitting on his throne of tortured souls. He saw her. The burning embers in his eye sockets flared.

"You again, Christ child," Lucifer boomed, and all the other horrors taking place around her stopped and looked her direction. "What is it this time? Did you lose your way? Or are you here so that I can torture another of my slaves?"

Paige knew her time was limited, and she needed to find Lin's soul and leave, but she couldn't resist, and shouted, "Dragoş Văduva. Show yourself."

In a flash, the tortured, and blackened, soul of a very young, and handsome, Dragoş appeared in front of her. His eyes burned with pure hatred at her.

"I told you I'd rip your head off," Paige said.

Dragoş' mouth opened to respond, but one of the black bones from Lucifer's wings erupted from his mouth in a flare of fire and ash. Paige hadn't even seen him move from his throne. He was just there. Dragoş screamed.

"Yes," Lucifer hissed as smoke snorted from his nostrils. "You vanquished one of my prize tormentors of God's precious creation. You have had your fun. Be gone, Christ child."

"I'm not finished," Paige said with a smile. "You have a soul that doesn't belong to ya. I'm here to take her back."

Lucifer flung Dragoş' tortured soul across the vast cavern of his domain and bellowed from his jagged, toothed mouth, "Impossible. You cannot have any of my souls. Leave me, Christ child."

"Not without Lindsey Anderson," Paige shouted above Lucifer's rage. "Show yourself."

An instant later, Paige saw Lin's tortured soul appear in front of her. She was naked and her blacked form bore scourge marks from some kind of unimaginable torture. Lava-like blood seeped from the wounds.

"You don't belong here, Lin," Paige said with conviction. "Come with me."

"You cannot have her." Lucifer roared.

Lucifer lifted one of his deadly wings to penetrate Lin's tortured soul. When the pointed and blackened bone struck her, it bounced off an invisible barrier that, briefly, turned into a blinding white light when it made contact. The spark inside Lin glowed.

"No," Lucifer roared as fire bellowed from his horrid mouth and he rained blow after blow on the invisible barrier protecting Lin. "She is mine. You cannot take what is mine. This is not the agreement I made with your God. Once they are mine, they are mine for eternity."

Paige saw the spark in Lin grow. As the spark became a white light, the blackened form she was flaked away, and the wounds healed. Within a few seconds, that didn't exist in the other realms, Lin looked like her

574

normal self again.

"She's not yours," Paige screamed in Lucifer's giant, and seething face. "I'm takin' her back with me. Back to her family and life. In case ya haven't noticed, four of your tortured souls have already escaped you and hell."

For the first time since Paige had encountered Lucifer, rage and hatred were replaced with a look of confusion.

"Impossible." Lucifer roared in rage.

Paige smiled. "When I destroyed Dragoş, I *saw* the souls of Melanie Zane, Megan Williams, Taylor Shanahan, and Lena Culpepper, Dragoş' cloud vampires, ascend to heaven. Their souls didn't stay trapped in hell like Dragoş and Cipriana. They are free of your torture, and Lin is comin' with me. Back to her body."

Lucifer roared in fury at the thought that four souls, his four souls, could have been taken from his domain.

Fire bellowed from his jagged toothed mouth and smoke erupted from his flared nostrils. "Come to me, Dur'zrag."

Paige saw an enormous wolf bound toward Lucifer. It ran on all four legs and had black hair. As it got closer, Paige saw it had burning red eyes, a fiery tongue, and long claws that looked like molten metal. It was much larger than the werewolves Paige had encountered the previous summer, but its eyes were very similar.

"Your job is to guard the gates of hell, Dur'zrag," Lucifer roared. "This...Christ child informed me four souls have escaped my domain. Investigate. If I have lost four souls, you will suffer greatly, Dur'zrag."

The enormous wolf shrank back from Lucifer's words before bounding away.

Lucifer's smoldering hate filled gaze returned to Paige, but she ignored him. Her attention was on Lin.

Paige did not know how bringing Lin back would work, but she was certain it would. More certain of it than anything in her whole life. The form that was Lin, her beautiful friend again, stepped out of hell and into Paige. They were one.

Paige felt a tug she couldn't resist and heard Lucifer bellow in rage, but it was distant. An instant later, she felt the floor beneath her and the fire, brimstone, and rot smells of hell were replaced with the spice smell of Lola's living room.

~ * ~

"Look at her skin," Paige heard Fr. Mike shout. "She's burning up. Is she okay?"

Paige felt hot, like the last time she came back. When she opened her eyes, she saw her skin was blistered and smoking again; Lola's dress smoldered, too. The last time, Paige had vomited black bile on Lola's floor when she came back. She needed to vomit again but knew it wouldn't be the same as the last time. She remembered Lin's soul enter her; become one with her.

Paige quickly crawled over to the frozen, blue form of the vampire, and vomited white light on to it; into it. The white light penetrated the blue form. The blue coloration disappeared, as did the long tongue and fangs. A moment later, Lin coughed a single plume of blackish soot from her mouth and opened her icy-blue eyes. They weren't the piercing blue eyes of a vampire anymore. They were Lin's kind, beautiful icy-blue eyes. Paige collapsed on the floor next to her best friend.

"It worked," Lola shouted with joy. "Paige saved her."

"Praise God." Fr. Mike shouted.

"Fascinatin'." James shouted.

Confused, Lindsey sat up. "Where am I?"

She looked around and saw Fr. Mike, a beautiful African American woman, and a portly man, looking at her. They were all smiling. It had only been then Lindsey realized she was naked. She quickly covered her breasts with one arm and cupped her other hand over her crotch.

"Gentlemen," Lola said.

Both men turned around.

"Hang on, sweetie," Lola said as she got up and turned to her bedroom. "I'll get ya one of my dresses, and another one for Paige. That one's goin' in the trash."

Lindsey noticed a very burned Paige lying beside her. "Paige? Are you okay, Paige?"

Paige rolled over and smiled at Lin with black and blistered lips. "I am now."

Lola came back into the room with two flimsy dresses and tossed one to Lin. "Put that on. She'll be fine as soon as she transforms and back again."

Lindsey caught the dress and slipped it over her head. "Transforms into what? What happened to her?"

"She saved your soul, chil'," Lola said as she removed the smoldering dress from Paige. "Now, get ready to be shocked."

An instant later, Lin saw a massive, silver-haired werewolf appear where Paige had been. She screamed. An instant later, she looked at a very healed Paige again.

Paige sat up, and wrapped Lin in a tight hug. "I knew I'd get ya back. I knew it."

More confused than ever, Lindsey said, "Back from where? What happened? And what the hell did ya just turn into?"

Lola grabbed Paige, pulled her away from Lin, and pushed the dress over her head. "We'll explain everything soon. Right now, her daddy, Ty, and Trowa heard ya scream, and they'll be comin' in...now."

~ * ~

Garrett sat behind the steering wheel, Ty sat shotgun, and Trowa sat in the back seat. Ty placed the totem with the glowing maple leaf on the console between himself and Garrett. Within a few moments, the inside of the SUV was a comfortable seventy-two degrees. The men removed their jackets and sat in silence for several moments.

"I can't believe Paige has been to hell and back," Garrett whispered. "Or that she's goin' again."

"Yeah, I know," Ty whispered. "Do ya think she can bring Lindsey back?"

"She will," Trowa whispered. "Paige is a Yee Naaldlooshii and a medicine woman, a healer. That's one hell of a powerful combination. Lola is right, Garrett. You underestimate Paige and Glinda. She will bring Lindsey's soul back. I do not know how, but she will."

Garrett thought for a moment and whispered, "I guess I underestimate 'em. But, beneath all that she is now, she's still my little girl. And I hate that she keeps havin' to do dangerous things."

"Perhaps they are not near as dangerous for her as ya think," Trowa whispered. "We have not heard of how Glinda destroyed Dragoș, yet. But it appears she had little trouble doin' it, one-on-one, as Lola said. She is powerful. I'll say nothin' else on the subject."

After that, they fell into a tense silence. Except for Trowa, who stretched out on the back seat and fell asleep, almost immediately.

"How can he sleep with all that's goin' on?" Garrett whispered.

"I guess it's because he has the same faith in Paige and Glinda Lola has," Ty whispered.

"I wish I could rest easy like that," Garrett whispered.

"I can't either, and she's not my daughter," Ty whispered. "But I love her like she is."

After that exchange, Garrett and Ty nervously waited for what seemed hours.

Then, after an endless wait, they heard a scream from inside Lola's house.

"I'm goin' in." Garrett shouted as he opened the SUV's door.

Ty and Trowa were close behind Garrett when he opened Lola's front door.

~ * ~

"Perfect timin', gentlemen," Lola said as Garrett, Ty, and Trowa rushed into her living room.

Garrett's eyes went immediately to Paige, who looked unharmed and thrilled. Then he looked at Lindsey, who looked confused but normal. He slid to his knees on the floor and wrapped both of them in a tight hug.

With her face muffled against Garrett's shoulder, Lindsey said, "Can ya tell me what's goin' on, Mister Garrett?"

Garrett loosened the hug and looked at Lindsey. "It's a long story and one that'll be hard for ya to believe."

"Why don't we all sit down and fill Lin on what's been goin' on,"

Lola said as another of her kitchen table chairs slid into the living room.

Lindsey jumped and shrank back from the animated chair, but Paige said, "It's okay, Lin. You're gonna learn a lot tonight."

"Like what you…changed into, Paige?" Lindsey asked.

Paige smiled at her friend. "That and a lot more."

Garrett helped Lin stand; she was a bit wobbly. And they took a seat around Lola's table. Lindsey sat next to Paige and took Paige's hand in hers.

"I believe some introductions are in order," Lola said. "My name is Lola Laveau and I'm an elemental seer."

"A what?" Lindsey asked.

"She's a witch. But a good witch," Paige said with a smile.

"I don't…" Lindsey began.

"Hush," Lola said. "You'll learn everything in due time. I think ya know everyone else here except for Doctor James Huff. He's professor at SFA who specializes in supernatural folklore. He helped us with the werewolves last summer and with the vampires now."

Lindsey's hand tightened on Paige's, and she said, "That's what ya turned into. You're a werewolf?"

Paige smiled. "Yeah. But I'm a good werewolf. Not like the ones that killed all our friends. Her name is Glinda."

"I-I don't understand," Lindsey said. "I knew ya got bit, but I thought that all went away when the other werewolves were killed."

"Ya broke a pinky-promise, Paige-Turner," Garrett said. "Ya weren't supposed to tell anyone."

"It's Lin, Daddy," Paige said with a sly smile. "I tell her everything."

Garrett shook his head.

"It went away for me and Trowa," Ty cut in with the story. "With Paige, it didn't. And like she said, Glinda is a good werewolf."

"Y'all got bit too?" Lindsey asked.

"Yes, yes. They got bit, too," Garrett said irritably. "Their curse lifted when Glinda killed the real alpha. Paige's didn't, for reasons we can discuss later, and Glinda is a good werewolf.

"Right now, we need to know what ya remember 'bout bein' a

vampire," Lola said.

"I was a vampire?" Lindsey asked in disbelief.

"You were," Lola said. "Thanks to Paige-Turner, you're not one anymore. Let's try it this way. What's the last thing ya remember before wakin' up here?"

Lindsey thought for a moment, and a look of awareness filled her face. "I was asleep and dreamin'. Paige and I were at the lake. I heard a tappin' sound. I thought it was in my dream but, when I woke up, I heard it again. Someone was tappin' on my window. I thought it was Paige, 'cause sometimes she sneaks out and comes over, but it wasn't her. It was a girl named Taylor somethin'. I don't know her last name, but she's the only girl at Pine View High School with hair that color. That's the last thing I remember before wakin' up here."

"We'll talk about you sneakin' out later," Garrett said to Paige.

"I only snuck out from Mom's house," Paige offered as a defense. "Never yours, Daddy."

"Will you two hush?" Lola scoffed. "Paige's sneakin' out isn't important at the moment. The girl you saw outside your window was Taylor Shanahan or, as Dragoş called her, Lacrima."

At hearing Dragoş and Lacrima's names, Lindsey shuttered. "I know those names. I don't know how I know 'em, but I do."

"She, you, Agrapina, Antanasia, and Ruxandra were Dragoş' cloud," Lola said. "He called you Ilinca. Does knowin' that bring back any more memories?"

Lindsey's shutter became a tremble, and she quietly said, "Yeah, kinda. But it's all dark. Like a nightmare. Was that real?"

"Yes," Lola said. "You were a vampire in Dragoş' cloud."

"Oh, God," Lindsey blurted out and cried. "I died. I was in hell."

Lola gently nudged Lin to release her suffering. "You were. But Dragoş didn't take all of your soul. Ya still had a spark in ya. Even as a vampire, ya helped Glinda from becomin' Dragoş' familiar. That's how we knew we could save ya. Paige went to hell and brought ya back. You're safe now."

Lindsey looked at Paige. "Is that why your skin was all blistered when I came to? Because ya went to hell to bring me back?"

Paige nodded. "Yep. Me and ol' Lucifer had a good time fightin' over your soul."

"Fascinatin'." James shouted.

Lindsey began crying happy tears, and hugged Paige tightly. "I can't believe ya'd go to hell for me."

Happy tears spilled from Paige's eyes as she hugged Lin back. "Of course I would. You're my best friend. And you're gonna love this. I saw Justin, too."

Startled, Lindsey pushed back. "Justin's in hell."

"No. Of course, not," Paige said. "He's in heaven. I had to go to heaven to get God's help to go to hell and bring ya back. That's why Lucifer couldn't stop me from bringin' ya back. A spark of your Christian soul was still there, and God knew ya didn't belong in hell."

"Is Justin happy?" Lindsey asked.

Paige smiled a smile that was both happy and sad. "He's very happy. And he told me to save ya."

Lindsey stiffened. "Oh, God."

"What?" Lola said. "What else do ya remember?"

"When I was dyin', there was a bright light," Lindsey sniffed. "I saw Justin in it. He begged me to stay with him, but I...couldn't. Just before I left him, he said, 'He wants Paige. Don't let him have her.' Then he vanished, and the darkness was there."

Fr. Mike crossed himself. "Justin was your spark, Lindsey. That's why you helped Glinda when Dragoş almost had her. Justin and God's love for you and Paige are the reason both of you are safe."

Lindsey and Paige looked at each other as fresh tears spilled from their eyes for their love and loss of Justin.

After a moment, Lindsey said, "I know nothin' should surprise me at this point. But what's the deal with your right eye, Paige. Why's it silver with a cat's pupil?"

In disbelief, Lola said, "Look at me, Paige-Turner."

Paige looked at Lola and smiled. Her right, cat-like, silver seeing eye twinkled.

"Can ya still feel Mamma's wisdom?" Lola asked quickly.

Paige searched her inner thoughts for a moment. "Nope. She's gone."

"Are ya sure?"

"I'm sure."

"The protection potion was only supposed to last until the danger was over," Lola pondered out loud. "It's over, and ya still have your seein' eye."

"I got more than that," Paige said as she flipped her right hand and the table levitated a few inches off the floor, which took everyone, except Lola, by surprise.

"If you don't beat all, Paige-Turner," Lola said with a smile. "First ya keep your werewolf powers and now ye keep your elemental, seein' powers."

Paige smiled. "Looks like you're stuck with me."

Lola hugged Paige. "I was already stuck with ya, chil'. But now you're one of my seein' sisters. For good and always."

"I don't understand," Lindsey said.

"Apparently, Paige in now a werewolf *and* a witch," Garrett said. "Now put the damn table down, Paige."

She did.

"Okay. Lin's caught up on most of what really happened," Garrett said. "She, we, can't tell the truth 'bout this any more than we could tell the truth 'bout the werewolves. So, we gotta come up with a plausible explanation for all this."

"Ya got somethin' in mind?" Ty asked.

"I do, but it's complicated," Garrett said. "For it to work, we've got some work ahead of us tonight. And we'll need Glinda."

Paige smiled. "Glinda's always happy to help."

Garrett pulled out his cellphone, pulled up a picture of Clive Jones, and showed it to Lin. "Ya see this man?"

Lindsey nodded. "Yeah. He's scary lookin'."

"Yeah," Garrett said. "He is. He was scary. His name was Clive Jones. For everything I've got planned to work, ya need to tell people he kidnapped ya and kept ya in a coffin at the old Wiseman barn. Can ya do that, Lin?"

Wide eyed, Lindsey nodded.

"That's where Dragoş' and the other two coffins are," Mike said.

"Exactly," Garrett said. "Coffins were stolen and need to be found where Lindsey says Clive held her prisoner. Like I said, we've got a lot to do tonight to make this work. Are y'all ready to listen to what I've got to say?"

Heads nodded.

"Okay," Garrett said. "Here's what we need to do."

His plan was simple, conceptually. Logistically, it was a complicated mess. Lindsey was to stay at Lola's with Fr. Mike and James. That was the simple part. After that, not so much. Garrett, Ty, Trowa, and Paige would go to the Eternal Rest Funeral Home with both SUVs to get the other two coffins from Dragoş' lair. From there, they would take them out to the Wiseman barn and leave them with the other two stolen coffins. Once there, Glinda would have to take Dragoş' coffin deep into the woods and turn it into kindling. After that, his plan got more disturbing.

Luckily, the Culpeppers' bodies hadn't been discovered yet. This meant framing Clive Jones would be easy. All they had to do was have Glinda dig up Clive, his clothes, and his gun. Then, go to the Culpeppers' house and shoot Lena's parents with Clive's gun. Take Clive's body out to the old Wisemen barn. Call in an anonymous tip that someone spotted Clive in the area, have overnight dispatcher Karen Parker call Garrett about the tip, show up, shoot the already dead Clive, and rescue Lindsey.

When he finished, Ty said, "Excellent plan, but there are holes that need fillin'."

"I'm listenin'," Garrett said.

"For starters, how do we explain what happened to the other girls," Ty said. "Also, who makes the anonymous call? Unless one of us has a burner handy, nine-one-one can track any call. Even with a burner, they can triangulate an approximate, call location."

"Not mine," Lola said. "I can make the call. Just tell me when."

"Okay," Ty said. "I don't know how ya have an untraceable cell, but I don't doubt ya. That still leaves the problem of the missin' girls."

"I'm sorry, but this one's on you, Lindsey," Garrett said.

"Me?" Lindsey said and pointed at herself in disbelief. "How am I supposed to explain anything?"

"Unfortunately, you're gonna be questioned by the DPS," Garrett said. "And. since this'll be considered a kidnappin' case when we find ya, the FBI will get involved, too."

Confused, Lindsey said, "What am I supposed to tell 'em?"

"As little as possible," Garrett said. "Be vague. Tell 'em it was mostly a blur of confusion. You can tell 'em ya heard other girls, but Clive kept y'all in the coffins and only took one of y'all out one at a time to feed ya and let y'all…use the bathroom. You can tell 'em that ya knew Melanie Zane, Megan Williams, and Taylor Shanahan were the other girls because y'all could talk with each other from inside the coffins when Clive was gone. Don't mention Lena Culpepper and ya don't know what Clive did with Melanie, Megan, or Taylor. All ya know is that Clive took 'em, at some point, and they didn't come back. Can ya remember all that?"

Lindsey nodded. "Yeah. I can remember all that. But…what happened to the other girls?"

"They were vampires and Glinda killed 'em," Paige said.

Wide eyed, Lindsey said, "Oh."

"That still doesn't explain what happened to the other girls," Fr. Mike pointed out.

"They're ash," Garrett said. "Once the FBI gets involved, they aren't our problem. They'll look and won't find 'em."

"And the postmortem on Clive?" James said. "His been dead longer than this mornin'."

"I can…freshen him up a bit," Lola offered.

"Thanks, I think," Garrett said with a grin. "But George is in on what's goin' on and can fudge the time of death. I think I can get his mom, Kelly, to agree to a quick cremation, too. After all Clive's put her through over the years, she'll want this behind her quick as a duck on a Junebug,"

"Okay," Ty said. "We got a plan. Best get to it."

"Yep. Sorry, Lindsey," Garrett said. "We'll have to come get ya later and take ya out to the barn to complete the plan. And this is very important. To keep ya from havin' to go through some embarrassin' examinations, tell 'em Clive did nothin'…sexual to ya. If all goes well, we'll have ya home to your folks in the mornin'. They'll be very happy to see ya."

"Okay," Lindsey said with resolve. "I can do all that."

Paige hugged Lin tightly. "I'm glad you're back. I love you, Lin."

"I love you too, Paige," Lindsey said.

Garrett dialed a number on his cell. "Hey, Karen. I can't sleep, so I'm out on patrol tonight. If anything comes in about Clive, call me directly. Thanks."

"Don't you think that's a little obvious, Garrett?" Mike said.

"Maybe, but when this is over, no one will give it a second thought," Garrett said. "Folks are kinda blind to things they can't, or won't, comprehend. Before you saw Glinda, did ya believe any of the werewolf talk from last summer?"

Fr. Mike shook his head. "No, I didn't. I get your point."

"We gotta a lot of ground to cover and a lot to do before the sun comes up," Garrett said and stood. "Y'all ready?"

Paige, Ty, and Trowa nodded their heads. With that, they left.

Lola, Lindsey, Fr. Mike, and James heard the SUVs start up and leave.

"You must be hungry, Lin," Lola said in her warm, honey voice. "Would ya like somethin' to eat?"

"Yes, ma'am," Lindsey said. "That be great."

"No, yes ma'ams to me, Lin. Call me Lola."

"Okay, Lola," Lindsey said with a smile. "Thank you."

Lola saw James and Fr. Mike could stand a little grub, too. "I'll make enough for all of us."

The two men stood, and Fr. Mike picked up the chair he sat in to bring it back into Lola's kitchen.

"Don't fret with the chairs," Lola said as all of them animated and slid through the door to her dining room and back to the kitchen table.

"Wow," Lindsey said with awe. "You really are a witch."

"I really am," Lola said with a friendly smile. "And your friend Paige is one now, too."

A few minutes later, James, Fr. Mike, and Lindsey sat at Lola's table while she prepared some food. James questioned Lindsey some more about any memories she might have from being a vampire, but she couldn't answer any of his questions. The time was a dark blur to her.

~ * ~

The plan went, mostly, as Garrett had said it would. The two coffins in Dragoş' lair were pretty dented from Glinda's air elemental that had captured Lena, but that couldn't be helped, and explaining why they were dented wouldn't be a top priority on anyone's question list.

At the Wiseman barn, Glinda had no trouble taking Dragoş' enormous coffin far out into the woods and ripping it to splinters. In fact, Glinda relished in destroying Dragoş' old home. When she was finished, and had spread its splintered remains over several acres, what had been left of it couldn't be recognized as anything more than the natural forest ground cover. Except for the smell, which, over the next few weeks, would throw cadaver dogs, sniffing for remains of the missing girls off. This became a bonus to Garrett's plan he hadn't expected.

After dealing with the coffins, they headed to the Henderson's deserted trailer. Then, they followed Glinda to where she had buried Clive. It didn't take long for Glinda to dig him back up and leap out of the deep hole with his body, clothes, and gun. He wasn't a pretty sight and Garrett, Ty, and Trowa gloved up for the unpleasant job of redressing him. While they were redressing Clive, Glinda dropped the gold coffin Dragoş' coffin into the Clive's body had been in and filled it in. When he was redressed, Glinda carried his body back to where they'd parked and put it in the back of Garrett's SUV.

The next part of Garrett's plan was the most unpleasant of all the tasks on Garrett's list. They drove to the Culpepper's house, and the men went inside; Paige stayed in the SUV for this part. Trowa carried Clive's .308 inside. Once inside, the picture of what happened was all too clear. Lena's dad was just inside the doorway with puncture marks on his throat and her mom was in the living room with similar wounds. They had to decide which of them would have the unpleasant task of shooting the already dead people. Ty offered, but Garrett insisted, since he was sheriff, he should have to do it. Ty insisted, since he'd had war experience, he should do it. While they were arguing, the first gunshot went off. It sounded like a cannon in the confines of the house. Trowa took matters into his own hands and blew a ragged hole through the man's neck where the puncture wounds were. Then he calmly walked past his bewildered friends and did the same to the woman's neck.

Paige heard each of the gunshots and, even though she expected them, tensed in her seat at the sound of both. A few moments later, her daddy, Ty, and Trowa came out of the house. Trowa still had the .308, so it wasn't difficult to conclude who shot them. Once back in the SUVs, they made the long drive back out to the Wiseman barn. Once again, Paige stayed in the SUV while her daddy, Ty, and Trowa carried Clive's body inside.

At the Culpepper's house, Paige didn't want to see what they had to do and didn't look. With Clive, it was different. She used her seeing eye to watch what they did through the old barn's rotting walls. First, they placed the rifle in Clive's dead hands and fired a shot through the front end of the barn. Even with George on their side, Paige knew from TV shows and her daddy, they were making sure Clive had gunshot residue on his hand. Next, Ty and Trowa held the large man's body in an upright position while her daddy shot him. Double tap, center mass. Again, from TV and her daddy, Paige knew they wanted the gunshot trajectory to appear as if Clive had been standing when he was shot. Ty and Trowa let Clive's body slump against the back wall of the barn and left the .308 by his side. The three men came out of the barn and got into the SUVs. It was done. At least, the hard part.

With everything in place, they sped back to Lola's house to carry out the last few steps of Garrett's plan. Bring Lindsey back to the Wiseman barn, have Lola make the anonymous call Clive had been spotted in the area, and rescue Lindsey from a completely staged event.

~ * ~

They got back to Lola's house a little before six in the morning. Lindsey was sound asleep in Lola's bed. Garrett hated to wake her and put her through what the day would bring.

As if reading his mind, which, Garrett realized, she probably had,

Paige said, "I'll wake her up and get her ready, Daddy."

"Thanks, Paige-Turner," Garrett said. "But, if you're in my head, we're gonna have to set up some boundaries."

Paige just smiled and disappeared through Lola's bedroom door.

Once inside the dark bedroom, Paige sat down on the bed next to Lin's sleeping form and shook her shoulder gently. "Time to wake up, sleepyhead."

Lindsey rolled onto her back, opened her eyes, and smiled at Paige. "Did y'all get everything done?"

Paige nodded. "Yep. Now ya gotta go with Daddy, Ty, and Trowa back out to the barn so they can rescue ya."

Lindsey's sleepy eyes looked up at Lola's enchanted mirror. "I love Lola's mirror. It's so beautiful."

"I know, right?" Paige said. "But ya gotta get goin' now."

"Do ya think she'll let me sleep over again?" Lindsey asked through a yawn.

Paige smiled. "I know she'll let *us* sleep over whenever we want to."

"I'd like that," Lindsey said as she got out of bed. "I wanna know everything 'bout Glinda and bein' a seer."

Paige hugged her tightly. "You will. You were a vampire. So, you're part of the supernatural club now."

They headed for the bedroom door, but Lindsey held back. "Did I...kill anyone when I was a vampire?"

"*You* didn't kill anyone," Paige said. "The *thing* Dragoş turned ya into *wasn't* you."

"But the vampire he turned me into killed people," Lindsey said.

"It wasn't *you*, Lin," Paige reassured Lin. "If ya have any doubts, ask Father Mike for communion."

"Okay," Lin said as they exited Lola's bedroom.

When they exited the bedroom, Garrett said, "Ready, Lindsey?"

"Give us a minute, Daddy."

"Okay, but we're burnin'...nightlight," Garrett replied, uncertain if that was a saying.

"Sun rise is at seven eighteen," Lola said, clearly knowing what was about to happen. "This won't take long."

Lindsey hesitantly approached Fr. Mike. "Can I receive communion, Father? I gotta know all of...what I was is gone."

"Of course you can," Mike said as he removed the pyx from his outside pocket.

He removed a communion host and held it up. "The Body of Christ."

Lindsey held out her hands, which trembled a little. Fr. Mike placed the host on them. She brought up to her mouth, said, "Amen," placed it on her tongue, and crossed herself.

Lindsey had received communion since her First Communion when she was eight years old, many times, but she had experienced nothing like she did then. She *felt* the Holy Spirit radiate throughout her body as a warm, white light. In that instant, she knew Christ was with her soul the entire time she'd been...gone. It gave her strength, and she knew, with God's help, she could get through everything expected of her in the hours and days to come.

Lindsey smiled. "I'm ready."

Ready to leave, Garrett said, "Okay. Just me, Lin, Ty, and Trowa on this run."

"I'm goin' with y'all," Paige announced.

"No. You're..." Garrett began.

Lola interrupted him. "When are ya gonna learn, Garrett. Our Paige-Turner is a willful chil'. You're not gonna win this argument. Take her and go. Paige can let me know when it's time to make the anonymous call."

Garrett knew Lola was right. "Okay. Paige and Lin with me. You and Trowa follow us, Ty."

They left to execute the last part of his plan.

~ * ~

Garrett rode up front, by himself, with Paige and Lin in the back seat talking away as if nothing happened.

When they were about twenty minutes away from the Wiseman

barn, Garrett said, "Let Lola know it's time to make the call."

Paige closed her eyes and sent Lola the message.

When Paige opened her eyes, Lindsey said, "Can you communicate with Miss Lola through your mind?"

Paige smiled. "Yeah. It's kinda cool."

Wide eyed, Lindsey said, "That's very cool."

Both girls giggled but, when Garrett's cell rang, they stopped.

Garrett answered. "What's up, Karen?"

"I just got a call. It was untraceable," Karen said. "The caller, I couldn't tell if they were a man or a woman, said they spotted Clive by the old Wiseman barn. Could be a prank, but I thought you'd wanna know."

"Might be a prank," Garrett played along. "But, as luck would have it, I'm not far from there. I'll check it out."

As soon as he hung up with Karen, he called George. Garrett knew the cranky county coroner wouldn't like being woken up so early or having to deal with another body. But his anger might be tempered when he learned this was almost over. They'd still have to deal with the Culpeppers, when their bodies were discovered, but it was finally over.

A very sleepy George answered on the fourth ring. "I really don't wanna know, Garrett."

"There are a couple of loose ends to tie up, but it's over, George."

"Over, over?" George said more alert.

"Over, over," Garrett confirmed. "We destroyed the vampire. All that's left is to pin this on Clive Jones. His body is at the old Wiseman barn. I'm about fifteen minutes out. Do ya know where it is?"

"Yeah."

"How quickly can ya get there?"

"In about thirty minutes, if I hurry."

"Hurry," Garrett said and ended the call.

Garrett looked in the review mirror. "As soon as we're done at the barn, I'll take ya home to your folks, Lindsey."

Lindsey smiled. "Thanks, Mister Garrett."

~ * ~

590

When they pulled up to the Wiseman barn, Garrett said, "You two stay put. No sense in y'all gettin' out."

Paige and Lindsey agreed to stay in the SUV, and Garrett stepped out to talk with Ty and Trowa.

"Lola make the call, okay?" Ty asked.

"Perfect," Garrett affirmed. "I called George. He, predictably, wasn't happy 'bout bein' woken up so early. His mood improved when I told him we destroyed the vampire."

"We?" Trowa asked as a statement.

"I can't tell him Paige is a werewolf and killed him," Garrett said and rubbed a scruffy cheek. "We'll tell him Father Mike got rid of him. He'll be so thankful this is over that he won't ask questions. He's a cranky ol' fucker, but he's covered our asses enough to have my gratitude."

Ty smiled. "True dat."

"Let's tape off the barn and take pictures of everything inside before George gets here," Garrett said. "I'll take the pictures of Clive's body. I wanna make sure they're a little blurry for whoever looks 'em over later. I'll say my hand wasn't too steady after havin' to shoot Clive."

"Smart," Ty said.

"That's why you're the sheriff," Trowa added.

"I don't know how much longer I'll be sherif," Garrett said and shook his head. "Things haven't exactly gone well under my leadership. But that's outta my hands. Let's get this done."

Garrett, Ty, and Trowa made quick work of documenting everything in the barn and taping it off with yellow 'Crime Scene' tape.

When they finished, and stood by Ty's SUV again, Trowa said, "What's the story when he gets here?"

"He'll take one look at Clive and know it's bullshit," Garrett said. "The story is that Karen called me with the anonymous tip. I called y'all for backup, got here, found Clive, he took a shot at me, I killed him, and found Lin alive in one coffin. Even though George'll know it's bullshit, that's the official story that we tell the DPS and FBI when they get involved. George'll back up the story with forensics."

"It's not my shift," Ty pointed out.

"No one will care or question why I called you and Trowa to help me," Garrett said.

"Okay. Okay," Ty said. "I'm just tryin' to make sure we cover our asses on all this shit."

"As long as we keep our in-house story straight, we're fine," Garrett said. "I'll talk with Kelly Jones in a bit and see if Digger can cremate Clive this mornin'."

"And when the DPS and FBI get involved?" Trowa asked.

"Like I said, we stick to our story," Garrett said. "Lindsey sticks to her story. And we let 'em do their thing. They won't find shit to contradict our version of what happened, and this'll pass just like the werewolves did."

Changing the subject, Ty rubbed his hands together briskly. "Get Lola's totem, so we can warm up."

"It's in my SUV, but the maple leaf isn't glowin' anymore," Garett said.

"It served its purpose," Trowa stated.

"Speakin' of servin' a purpose," Ty said, "why do ya think Paige still has elemental, seer powers?"

"Beats the hell outta me," Garrett said with a chuckle. "Because she's Paige."

"Because Paige is special," Trowa said. "She's a natural conduit for the supernatural."

Garrett began to ask Trowa what he meant, but they heard George's van coming toward them on the overgrown dirt drive. A moment later, he pulled into the opening around the barn, parked next to Ty's SUV, and got out.

"Ya made good time, George," Garrett said.

"I wanna get this over with," George said with a stretch. "Show me what ya got and tell me what I need for COD."

"Follow me," Garrett said, and they went inside the barn.

Garrett explained what they'd decided on and George listened.

When Garrett finished, George said, "Looks pretty open and shut to me. I'll test his hands for GSR, dig out the bullets, approximate trajectory, and be done with him."

"Think Digger can cremate him this mornin'?" Garrett asked.

"I can cremate him," George said. "Just get his next of kin's consent. I'm guessin' that won't be hard to do. So, I'll cremate him ASAP, before anyone else starts snoopin' around."

"Hot damn, George," Garrett said. "I didn't know ya had a crematorium. That'd help a lot."

"Course, we do," George said. "We haven't had a John or Jane Doe since I've been workin' here, but we have one, just in case. Now, help me bag this big fella and get him loaded in the van."

They bagged Clive Jones and loaded him into the back of George's van in less than ten minutes.

"I don't suppose y'all can come with me and help me unload him at the morgue?" George asked.

"Ty and Trowa can," Garrett said. "I gotta get Lindsey home to her folks."

"Lindsey Anderson?" an astonished George asked.

"Oh, yeah," Garrett said and pointed at his SUV. "I forgot to tell ya that part. She's alive and well in the back of my SUV with Paige."

"But I thought she was, ya know, one of...them?" George said.

"Nope," Garrett said. "I found her locked in one of those coffins after I took Clive out. At least, that's the official report. Ya good with that?"

George nodded. "Yep. I'm good with that, but one of these days, ya owe me the whole, damn truth 'bout what's been goin' on in *my* county."

Garrett grinned. "Deal. You've earned it."

They shook hands. George got in his van. Ty and Trowa got in Ty's SUV. A moment later, there was nothing left but the sound of their engines and a trail of dust on the overgrown dirt road leading to the Wiseman barn.

Garrett got back in his SUV and looked at Lindsey and Paige in the rearview mirror. "Time to take ya home, Lindsey. Don't forget. Ya gotta tell your folks the same story ya tell everyone else. I'll keep the DPS and FBI away from ya for as long as I can, but they'll question ya, too. Just stick with the story and all this will be over quick as spit."

Lindsey smiled at Garrett's reflection in the rearview mirror. "Yes, sir, Mister Garrett. I know what I gotta tell everyone. I won't let ya down."

Garrett smiled back at the beautiful young woman, who he loved like a second daughter and was no longer a vampire. "Ya couldn't let me down if ya tried, sweetheart."

Garrett put the SUV in drive and followed the diminishing cloud of dust left by George and Ty's vehicles down the overgrown dirt drive.

~ * ~

Thirty minutes later, Garrett pulled to a stop in front of the Anderson's house.

Garrett looked in the rearview mirror. "Y'all aren't really dressed for this, but I doubt your folks will notice when they see ya alive and well, Lindsey."

Paige grinned. "I can give 'em a little nudge, and they won't notice at all."

"Don't you start that nudgin' crap, Paige-Turner," Garrett said sternly but with a grin on his lips.

"What's a nudge?" Lindsey asked.

"I'll explain later," Paige said. "Let's go see your folks. They've been tore up 'bout you missin'. Especially after what happened to Justin."

Lindsey's eyes widened. "OMG. They think I'm dead, too."

"Yep," Garrett said. "Let's go show 'em you're not."

Lindsey bolted out of the SUV, ran to the front door, turned the knob to go inside, and bounced off the locked door.

"I don't have my keys," Lindsey shouted.

Garrett and Paige joined her at the front door, and Garrett gave it three hard knocks. Paige hid her seeing eye by making it look normal. A moment later, they heard the deadbolt click, and an exhausted, sad, and old looking Gloria Anderson opened the door.

"What's the…" Gloria said, but her words choked when she saw Lindsey.

"Hi, Mom," Lindsey said.

Tears instantly streamed down Gloria's face as she grabbed Lindsey and cried, "Lin. Lin. I can't believe it. Are ya okay?"

"I'm fine, Mom," Lindsey said as tears streamed down her cheeks, too. "Mister Garrett saved me from the guy who took me."

Gloria's watery, but happy, eyes looked up at Garrett and she cried, "Thank you, Garrett. Thank ya for bringin' my baby back."

"What's all the racket 'bout?" Andy said from inside the house.

"Lin's home." Gloria shouted.

"Lin?" Andy said in disbelief.

"It's me, Daddy, Lindsey cried out. "I'm home."

A moment later, Andy was in the doorway, crying and hugging Gloria and Lindsey.

"My little girl," Andy cried. "Are ya okay? Where have ya been?"

"I'm fine, Daddy," Lindsey sobbed against her daddy's shoulder.

"Garrett saved her from the guy who took her," Gloria told Andy through sobs and tears.

Andy's watery, happy eyes found Garrett. "Garrett. Thank you. Thank ya for bringin' my little girl back."

Garrett wiped tears from his scruffy cheeks and nodded. He couldn't speak. If he did, he knew he'd be a blubbering mess. He cried and watched the beautiful reunion of his two friends and the daughter they thought they'd lost forever.

Paige sobbed, too.

Garrett put his arm around her shoulders, pulled her close, and whispered, "You made this happen. I'm so proud of you."

"*We* made this happen, Daddy," Paige corrected her daddy. "I couldn't have done any of this without y'all."

After a few more moments of sobbing and holding each other, Andy looked up. "Y'all come on in. Tell us what happened."

They went inside and closed the door. Lindsey sat between her folks on the couch and Paige sat next to Gloria. Garrett took a seat in the recliner.

"What happened to ya?" Andy asked.

Lindsey looked at Garrett, saw him give her a brief nod, and she repeated the story they came up with word for word. Garrett was pleased.

When she finished, Andy said, "He didn't...do anything to ya?"

"No, Daddy," Lindsey assured him. "He didn't touch me like that at all."

"And…the other girls?" Gloria asked.

"I don't know what he did with 'em, Mom," Lindsey said. "All I know is I was the last one left when Mister Garrett showed up and killed him."

"How'd ya find him, Garrett?" Andy asked.

"Luck," Garrett said. "An anonymous call came in that Clive was spotted by the old Wiseman barn. I went to check it out. He took a shot at me, and I took him down. It was only then that I heard knockin' and screamin' from inside one coffin. I opened it and found Lin."

"Oh, my God," Gloria said and clasped chest. "I can't believe he kept y'all in coffins."

"I can," Andy said. "That Clive Jones is…was one sick sonofabitch."

"Can Paige and I go to my room and change?" Lin asked.

It had only been then that Andy and Gloria noticed the almost see-through matching dresses Lindsey and Paige wore. Paige, despite her daddy's warning, gave both of them a little nudge so they wouldn't question why they were dressed the same.

"Of course," Gloria said with a wide smile. "Y'all go on up to your room."

Garrett gave Paige a sideways glance when she and Lindsey got up to go upstairs, but he would not complain about Paige putting something else, not see-through, on.

~ * ~

When they were upstairs, away from her parents, Lindsey said, "What's up with your eye? It looks normal again. Did the powers go away?"

"No," Paige said. "I still have 'em, but I can hide my seein' eye to make it look normal. I almost forgot, but I changed it back to normal when Daddy and I got to your door."

"Show me," Lindsey said.

Paige blinked her eyes several times and changed it from green to the silver, cat-like, seeing eye with each blink. She stopped with her seeing eye visible.

"That's so cool," Lindsey said. "And the werewolf thing. You've been keepin' secrets from me, PT."

"I kinda had to," Paige said and fingered her crucifix. "But no more."

Lindsey looked at, through, the dress Paige wore. "Lola's nice. But her dresses are…not concealin' at all."

Paige laughed. "Yeah. She's a bit of a free spirit. I am too, now. Daddy gets so flustered when he sees me naked."

Shocked, Lindsey said, "You walk around naked in front of your dad?"

Paige laughed. "No. It's not like that. I can't wear clothes when I transform into Glinda. Sometimes I forget and transform back to me in front of him. It really doesn't bother me to be naked in front of him."

"OMG," Lin said scandalized. "You're crazy. I'd die if my daddy, like, walked in on me when I was naked."

Paige shrugged. "It's a werewolf thing. Since naked is natural for Glinda, it's natural for me."

"Wow," Lindsey said. "You've got to tell me everything about Glinda and bein' a witch later."

"I will," Paige said and grinned. "I'll even let you ride Glinda, if ya want."

"Shut up. Seriously?"

"Yeah," Paige said. "Daddy rides me all the time."

Lindsey laughed. "That sounds *so* wrong."

Paige thought about what she said and cracked up, too. They both laughed until they were on the floor in tears.

Garrett killed the laughter when he shouted, "C'mon, Paige. Let's give the Andersons time with Lindsey."

"Be right down, Daddy." Paige shouted back.

"Grab whatever will fit ya," Lindsey said.

Paige and Lindsey both put on sweatpants and hoodies.

"What about shoes?" Lindsey asked as they were about to leave her room. "It's freezin' outside."

"I don't feel cold or heat anymore."

"Seriously?"

"Yep," Paige said as she switched her seeing eye back to normal. "It's an elemental, seer thing,"

"So cool," Lindsey said as she opened her bedroom door.

When they came downstairs, Paige had Lola's two dresses in her arms.

"Remember," Garrett said as Paige joined him by the front door. "I've got Lin's statement, but the DPS and FBI will probably wanna talk with her, too. Y'all can be with her when they do."

Gloria hugged Garrett. "Thank you so much for findin' Lin before that...monster could hurt her."

Then Andy hugged him. "Thank you so much, Garrett. Thank you for bringin' my little girl home."

Paige hugged Lindsey. "I love you so much."

"I love you, too," Lindsey said. "Thanks for bringing me back."

Garrett took their thanks with true modesty and when he and Paige were outside, and out of earshot from Lin's folks, said, "I hate takin' credit for what ya did."

Paige took his big hand in hers. "I told ya. I didn't do this alone. It took *all* of us to kill Dragoş and save Lin."

Garrett squeezed her small hand. "Maybe, but you and Glinda did all the big stuff. Ya know, like killin' Dragoş and goin' to hell to save Lindsey's soul from Lucifer. No big deal, right?"

Paige giggled. "Okay. Those things were pretty bad ass. But you, Mister Ty, and Mister Trowa have had to deal with all the bodies and Mister George. I'll take Dragoş and Lucifer over that any day."

Their hands parted when they got to the SUV and got in.

"I'll give ya this much," Garrett said as he started the SUV. "At least your part in this is over. I've got a hell of a day ahead of me. I'd like to go see Mandy and let her know everything is okay before I go to the department and start on all the paperwork and dealin' with the press. Where do ya want me to take ya? Lola's or Mom's?"

"I wanna go with you and see Mandy."

"Really?"

"Really," Paige said. "I've spent a lot of time with Miss Lola lately and Mom'll be full of questions I don't wanna answer now. Since it's safe now, Mandy and I can go back to your house and relax."

"Okay. Let's go see Mandy. Ya might have to plug your ears for a little while, though," Garrett said with a grin. "I think Mandy will be *very* happy to see me and hear that this is over."

"That's gross, Daddy."

"Yeah, well," Garrett said. "That's how I feel every time you pop up naked in front of me. Before ya tell me naked's natural again, let me remind ya that sex is *more* natural than naked."

"Point taken," Paige said and crinkled her nose. "I guess we'll *both* have to get used to nature, Daddy."

This wasn't the response he expected. He thought Paige was as uncomfortable with his and Mandy's sex life as he was with her nudity. If she wasn't bluffing, he hoped she was, he had just fired the last arrow in his quiver to level the comfort playing ground.

"Buckle up," Garrett reminded her.

"You realize that, even if we got in a wreck and I wasn't wearin' my seatbelt, it wouldn't kill me," Paige reminded him.

"I do, but it's the law," Garrett said. "And what kind of sheriff would I be if I let my daughter ride around without her seatbelt on?"

"Touché," Paige said as she buckled her seatbelt.

Garrett put the SUV in drive and drove away from the Anderson's house. He hadn't been kidding about having sex with Mandy, but not on his childhood bed. He'd wait until they were home.

~ * ~

When they were on the road to his parent's house, Garrett handed his cell to Paige. "Call Mandy and tell her to pack our crap. We're goin' home."

Paige called on speaker and Mandy answered before the first ring finished.

"Garrett," Mandy said anxiously. "Is everything okay? Is Paige okay?"

"I'm fine," Paige said. "Daddy's fine. We killed Dragoş and saved Lin. You're on speaker. Daddy's here."

"Pack everything of ours up," Garrett said. "I'm on my way to get ya and take ya home. Paige wants to stay with you. She can fill ya in on everything that happened."

"So, it's over?" Mandy said. "Really over?"

"Yep," Garrett said. "We'll be there in about fifteen minutes."

"Okay," Mandy said relieved. "I'll hurry and be ready to go home when y'all get here. I love ya both."

"I love you, too." Garrett and Paige said at the same time and ended the call.

Chapter Seventeen

Garrett didn't get to work until almost ten o'clock that morning. After picking Mandy up at his parent's house and bringing her back to their house, his prediction became accurate when a very relieved Mandy stepped into the shower with him. To further slow his progress to work, Mandy had insisted he shave. Garrett wasn't a shaving enthusiast, but, for appearance's sake, usually shaved every other or every third day. She was right, of course. His stubble was turning into one of the metrosexual beards so popular in Hollywood; a place falling into disfavor with him for all the inaccurate supernatural crap they put out. Mandy had pointed out there would be another news conference and he should look his best.

As Garrett stared at his scruffy cheeks, hollow eyes, and gaunt face in the mirror, he'd been running on little sleep and little nutrition; he realized the last time he'd shaved had been Christmas Eve shortly before Midnight Mass. That was December 24th. It was the morning of December 30th. Only five days had passed since he left Melanie alone in the St. Joseph's Catholic Church parking lot after Midnight Mass. Five days and so many lives ruined by Dragoş Văduva. He hadn't kept track of the deaths, but a quick mental calculation put the number at twenty-two.

Regardless of what Paige or anyone else told him, that what happened to Melanie wasn't his fault, he would carry the guilt forever. What if he'd stayed? Would Dragoş have still come for her with them there? If so, would Glinda have been able to destroy him that night without the aid of Lola and her coven members' protection potion? Or would he and Mandy be among the dead and Paige and Glinda relegated to an eternity of service to the ancient vampire? There were so many uncertainties, but he still felt guilty for leaving Melania alone that night.

After shaving and getting dressed in his customary department issued shirt, Wranglers, boots, and brown, felt cowboy hat, he had to look good for the cameras, Garrett left the bedroom with Mandy. He paid for the 'nature' talk he'd had with Paige after leaving the Anderson's. Paige was stretched out on the couch, without a stitch of clothes on, watching a *The Big Bang Theory* rerun on TBS.

He quickly averted his eyes to the front door. "Well played, Paige-Turner."

Mandy laughed at Garrett's discomfort. "What am I missin'?"

"I'll explain when Daddy's gone," Paige said with a grin.

Garrett stepped outside, got in his patrol SUV, and headed into town for what he was certain would be a busy day.

~ * ~

"Well?" Mandy said after Garrett left. "What was that all about?"

Paige sat up on the couch to let Mandy sit. "Ya know how uncomfortable Daddy is with my nudity?"

Mandy laughed. "Uncomfortable is puttin' it mildly. I think traumatized is a better description."

"When we left Lin's house, Daddy said that you'd be thrilled to see him. He was insinuatin' y'all would have sex."

Mandy took a seat on the couch. "Oh, he did. Did he?"

"Yeah," Paige said and leaned against Mandy. "I told him that was gross, and he told me that seein' me naked made him feel the same way. Ya know how I'm always tellin' him naked is natural?"

Mandy nodded.

"He told me sex was *more* natural than naked," Paige said dramatically. "So, I told him we'd just have to get used to nature.

"I know y'all had sex," Paige said apologetically. "I'm sorry for knowin' but, even with Glinda dialed all the way down, I can still... sense it. Anyway, that's why I was like this when y'all came out of the bedroom and he told me it was well played."

"Oh," Mandy said. "I see. No offense, but it's a little disconcertin' that, even with Glinda dialed down, you can still tell when your daddy and I are…together. Y'all are both right, though. Nudity and sex are natural. Ya can't have one without the other. But sex is personal and private."

"I know. Believe me. I don't wanna know, but I can't help it. There's an unmistakable smell associated with sex."

"Okay," Mandy said as she put an arm around Paige's shoulders. "I don't wanna know the details 'bout how sex smells. I wanna know 'bout how y'all destroyed Dragoş and saved Lin from bein' a vampire."

"You're gonna love this," Paige began and told Mandy everything that happened.

When Paige finished, Mandy said, "You went to hell and confronted Lucifer?"

Paige smiled. "*Two* times."

~ * ~

When Garrett turned onto the street leading to the sheriff's department, he once again saw the throng of reporters waiting out front to bombard him with questions. This time, instead of avoiding them by taking the side street to the back jail entrance, he pulled into the front parking lot and parked in his designated spot with a 'Sheriff Parking Only' sign.

As he stepped out of the SUV, video rolled, cameras clicked, microphones and tape recorders were thrust in his face, and questions were shouted.

Garrett paused for a moment. "I have some good news to tell y'all, but I've gotta make a few phone calls first. I'll be back out as soon as I can."

This only excited the reporters, like throwing chum in the water for sharks. Garrett pushed through without saying another word and stepped inside the building. As the door closed behind him, their voices reduced to a muffled blur. He inhaled the familiar smells of the building and let out the breath with a sigh of relief. It was really over.

The electronic buzz of the inner-door unlocking brought him out of the satisfying moment and Erica Harris said, "Mornin', Sheriff."

Garrett smiled and grabbed the door. "Yes. It is, Erica."

A moment later, he was in his office, sitting at his desk, and staring at the phone. Contacting next-of-kin about a deceased family member was the least favorite part of his job and one he made a practice of doing in person. Time didn't allow for the in-person curtesy that morning. Even though it was Clive Jones' death he would report to his mother, Kelly, framing him for all the horrors Dragoş had committed still felt wrong. Other than telling the truth, which wasn't an option, he had no other choice. Feeling shitty about what he had to do, Garrett picked up his office phone and dialed the number on the sticky note still stuck to his desk.

Kelly answered on the first ring. "Clive?"

Garrett cleared his throat. "No, Missus Jones. This is Sheriff Lambert."

Kelly drew in a sharp breath. "Did ya find Clive?"

"Yes, ma'am. I did."

There was a brief pause before Kelly said, "Is he…dead?"

"I'm sorry. Yes, ma'am. He is."

Kelly sobbed. "What happened? Did he do those horrible things?"

Garrett took a shaky breath. "Yes, ma'am. He did. I wanted to let ya know what happened before ya heard it on the news. To the point, I got a call early this mornin' that Clive was spotted by the old Wiseman barn. When I got there, Clive took a shot at me and missed. I know ya said he was a good shot, and I believe ya. Anyway. I shot back and…killed him. Since Clive missed, I think it was suicide by cop."

"Suicide by cop?" Kelly said through sobs. "What's that?"

"It's when a suspect fires on law enforcement and makes us shoot back," Garrett said.

"That's a real thing?"

"Yes, ma'am. Doesn't happen often in places like Pine View County, but it does in big cities."

Kelly took a hitching breath. "Why? Why would Clive, or anyone else, do that?"

"Usually because they're tired of runnin'," Garrett said feeling shitty. "Or, like in Clive's case, they don't wanna go back to prison."

"Oh," Kelly said. "And the girls? Did ya find 'em?"

"Just one. Lindsey Anderson."

"What about the others?"

"We're not sure," Garrett said. "Lindsey doesn't know. I need to tell ya the rest before ya hear it on the news, Missus Jones. The four stolen coffins were in the barn, too. Clive kept the girls in the coffins and only took 'em out one at a time. So, they never saw each other. All Lindsey knows is that, at some point, he took the other girls out and they didn't come back."

"Oh, God," Kelly sobbed. "Coffins? I didn't raise him to be this way, Sheriff. He's just never been right in the head."

"No one's blamin' you, Missus Jones," Garrett told her.

"Yes," Kelly said. "They will. I'm gonna have to move in with my sister in Plano afore someone burns my house down with me in it."

"If ya think that's best, do it," Garrett said. "If ya wanna stay, I'll have my deputies check on ya several times a day until this blows over."

"This'll never blow over, Sheriff. Folks in this town hated him afore. They'll never let this go."

Garrett felt worse than ever about framing Clive. "Yes, ma'am. I understand. And I'm sorry for your loss."

"Are ya, Sheriff?" Kelly almost spit the words.

"Yes, ma'am," Garrett said. "More than you'll ever know."

"What happens to Clive's body?" Kelly asked with a sniff.

"With your permission, I can have him cremated at the County Morgue," Garrett said. "If ya allow that, it won't cost ya anything. If ya go through Pine View Funeral Parlor, they'll charge ya a couple of thousand dollars."

"I don't have that kinda money. Morgue's fine."

"What about his ashes? Do ya want 'em?"

Kelly was silent for a moment. "No. Just promise me you'll dump 'em some place peaceful in the woods. He loved bein' in the woods."

"I will," Garrett said. "Ya have my word."

"Thank you," Kelly said sadly. "I best get packin'. I don't have much to take. Just my clothes and my TV. The rest can burn, just like Clive, when they burn down my house."

"I am *really* sorry, Missus Jones."

Kelly hung up without answering.

Garrett clicked the 'hang up' button on the phone base and made the second call he needed to make. George picked up on the third ring.

"I talked with Kelly Jones," Garrett said when George answered. "Ya can cremate Clive's body."

"I expected as much," George said. "He's already in the oven. What do I do with his ashes? Is Kelly comin' for 'em?"

"No. She's headed out-of-town today. I'll pick 'em up when they're ready."

"You?" George asked.

"Yeah. She wants me to sprinkle 'em somewhere, peaceful, in the woods."

"Okay. I can have 'em bagged later today."

"Thanks, George."

"I'll call ya when they're ready, Garrett," George said and ended the call.

Garrett clicked the 'hang up' button on the phone base again and made the last, and least appealing, of the calls he needed to make. The phone was answered on the second ring.

"Department of Public Safety," a friendly female voice said. "How can I help ya?"

"Mornin'. This is Sheriff Garrett Lambert from Pine View County. Is Trooper Steve Sweeten available?"

"I'll check. Hold on a sec," she said.

There were a few moments of annoying hold music before Steve answered. "Hey, Garrett. With all that's goin' on in your neck of the woods, I was wonderin' when I'd hear from you."

"Yeah," Garrett said. "I was handlin' this in-house, but things changed this mornin' that need your attention. Probably the FBI, too."

"Shit. What happened?"

"I found Clive Jones, from an anonymous call, at the old Wiseman barn," Garrett said. "He took a shot at me, and I took him out. I think it was suicide by cop. Anyway, the four stolen coffins were in the barn, and I found Lindsey Anderson alive and locked in one coffin."

"Fuck me," Steve said in a harsh exhale. "And the other missin' girls?"

"All Lindsey knows is that Clive took 'em out of their coffins, one at a time, and they didn't come back. But, since it's now a kidnappin' case, I knew I had to call ya."

"Yeah," Steve said. "I'll call the FBI office in Dallas, and we'll coordinate on lookin' for the missin' girls. We'll need your official statement on what happened and your service weapon for ballistics, and we'll need to talk with Lindsey Anderson to get her statement, too. Do ya know if there were any sexual assaults involved?"

"Lindsey said he never touched her that way," Garrett said. "He was a sadist, not a rapist. Lindsey's been through a lot, and understandably, she's pretty shook up. I'd appreciate it if y'all took it easy on her and not traumatize her more by submittin' her to rape exam."

"Of course, we'll be easy with her," Steve said. "I can't promise she won't have to have a rape exam, though. Dependin' on what she tells us, we'll make that decision then. I promise ya I'll do my best to keep that from happenin', though."

"Thanks, Steve. And I told her folks they could be with her while she's questioned by y'all."

"Of course," Steve said. "I'll take good care of her and try to keep the FBI in line, too. The good news, for you, is that your part in all this is over."

Garrett chuckled. "You haven't seen all the reporters waitin' for me outside."

"You got the fucker, Garrett," Steve said. "Take your win and tell 'em we'll be takin' over and to direct future questions to us."

"It doesn't feel like a win," Garrett said.

"No," Steve admitted. "Killin' a suspect never does. But ya saved Lindsey's life and the lives of future victims by takin' him out."

"I know. Thanks, Steve."

"I'll see ya later, Garrett," Steve said and ended the call.

~ * ~

Lola sat at her table with a blood, red candle burning in its center. She held her arms out toward the empty chairs on either side of her.

"Sisters. I seek your counsel on a matter of…confusion. Come to me with your wisdom, fearlessness, and cleverness. Come to me, sisters."

The air on either side of Lola shimmered in the bright red candlelight. Shapes materialized in the two empty chairs on either side of

Lola. The shapes had features, but they weren't corporal. As the two shimmering shapes placed their hands in Lola's, a third shimmering shape appeared in the seat across from Lola. This shape held the hands of the other two shimmering shapes. Lola's council was arriving.

As the fourth linked hands with the other three, the shimmering lessened, and their features became more distinct. When they had materialized to the extent they could, they looked like slightly blurred versions of their true appearances surrounded by their brilliant auras.

"What is it this time, Lola?" Angelica asked.

Lola sneered at the apparition of Angelica. "The hole ya left in Paige's white vault almost got her killed."

"I have already dealt with Angelica, Lola," Mamma said.

It was only then Lola noticed Angelica's usually, bright red aura was dimmer, and had a foggy look to it. Mamma had punished her by restricting some of her powers. For a seer, this was a severe punishment.

"My apologies, Angelica," Lola said.

Angelica's apparition sneered back at Lola.

"Glinda has destroyed the Ancient," Rosa said. "Why have you summoned us?"

"Are ya still part of Paige and Glinda, Mamma?" Lola asked.

"No," Mamma's voice crackled. "My wisdom left her the moment Glinda destroyed Dragoş. This is how the protection potion works. You know this, Lola."

"I do," Lola said. "But Paige and Glinda have kept their elemental powers. Seein' eye and all. How is this possible?"

Angelica laughed. "I fucking like this Paige and her wolf."

"This is no laughing matter," Rosa said. "How is this possible, Mamma?"

"I bet it was Lola's seeing tears she added to the protection potion," Angelica said. "Punish her, Mamma."

"All of you hush." Mamma scolded them. "This is truly unprecedented. She kept Glinda because of the ancestral werewolf. To be a seer, a true seer, one must be born from a seer. Our powers are not dormant and do not skip generations. Lola's seeing tears could not have done this."

"Then, how did she…they keep their seeing powers?" Rosa asked.

"Could Paige and Glinda be a natural conduit of all things supernatural?" Lola asked.

"Natural conduits are nothing more than a fucking legend," Angelica said.

"This is not true, my fearless sister," Mamma corrected Angelica. "They are rare. The rarest of all things supernatural. But there have been natural conduits in the past."

"Then, if they *are* a natural conduit, Dragoş couldn't have ruled her, even without our help," Rosa said.

"What does that mean?" Angelica asked.

"It means that, had Dragoş been successful in turning Paige into a vampire, and her wolf into his familiar, he would have had no power over them," Mamma said. "Like with her wolf, she would have had all the powers of a vampire but not be evil."

"So…she could have had werewolf, vampire, and seer powers?" Angelica mused.

"Is there a way to find out if they are a natural conduit?" Lola asked.

"Yes," Mamma said. "I was still with Glinda when she discovered the ancient's hidden home soil. A vampire's home soil is more than a resting place. Their soil regenerates them while they rest because the soil absorbs their powers. It is not only an *extension* of them. Their home soil is *part* of them. This is why they must rest in their home soil. If Paige lays on the ancient's home soil, and is a natural conduit, she *will* absorb his vampire powers."

"Shut the fuck up," Angelica shouted. "You can become a vampire by just lying in their home soil?"

Mamma's spectral form glared at Angelica. "No, child. It would only work for a natural conduit."

"And…Paige and Glinda would be safe?" Lola asked.

"Yes," Mamma said. "If they are not a natural conduit, the soil will not harm them. If they are, they will gain all the powers the ancient had."

"But with no evil, right?" Lola asked for clarification.

"We have all seen her aura and seeing eye," Mamma said. "Paige and Glinda have the purist silver aura I have ever seen. And with their silver, seeing eye, they have pure sight. Nothing can corrupt their pureness."

"Hang on," Angelica said. "You're saying that, if they are a natural conduit, after lying on the ancient's home soil, they really *will* have werewolf, vampire, and seer powers?"

Mamma rolled her old, spectral eyes. "Were you not listening, sister? Yes. That's *exactly* what I am saying."

"Holy shit," Angelica shouted. "They could fly, transform into other creatures, and turn into mist."

"That and more," Mamma said.

"Fuck me," Angelica said. "I want to *be* this girl."

"No," Lola said. "Ya don't. Paige-Turner carries a lot of responsibility with her powers. I don't know if I should even tell her 'bout this."

"You must," Rosa said. "It is not up to us to limit their potential power."

"I agree with Rosa," Angelica said. "What do you think, Mamma?"

Mamma's spectral face looked from Angelica to Lola. "I agree with Rosa and, unbelievably, Angelica on this. It is not our place to limit their potential powers. Tell her and let her decide. Even without my wisdom within her, they are wise for their young age."

"And clever," Rosa said.

"And fearless fuckers." Angelica added.

"I will tell her and let her decide. Thank y'all for your counsel, sisters," Lola said as she released Angelica's spectral hand and their forms shimmered into nothingness.

The candle's red flame extinguished, and Lola sat alone with her thoughts.

~ * ~

Garrett walked out into the throng of reporters and let the dance began. This would be the third time he had to tell the story that morning, and he was tired of repeating it. But it would be the last.

Microphones and recorders were thrust in his face, video rolled, and cameras clicked. Questions came in such a flurry Garrett couldn't discern one from another or who asked them. He let this go on for about thirty seconds before he patted the air with his hands. The shouting stopped.

"I know y'all have questions but let me update y'all on the latest information before y'all start shoutin' over each other again," Garrett began.

"The Department received an anonymous call early this mornin' that Clive Jones was spotted 'round the old Wiseman barn. Despite what many of y'all might think, I've been workin' this case, day *and* night, since it started and was out lookin' for Clive when the call came in. As luck would have it, I was about ten miles from the Wiseman barn when I got the call.

"When I got to the Wiseman barn and went inside, Clive Jones took a shot at me with a rifle. I returned fire and neutralized the suspect."

"Does that mean ya killed him?" Clair Abbott shouted.

"Unfortunately, yes. Clive Jones is dead," Garrett confirmed.

"Why is that unfortunate?" Clair shouted.

"For once, just shut up and let me finish, Clair," Garrett said. "Ya don't see your colleagues in the press interruptin' me. I'll explain everything, if ya let me. *Then* ya can ask questions ya might still have."

Clair showed a rare moment of humility, shrank back into the crowd of reporters, and Garrett continued. "The four stolen coffins were in the Wiseman barn, too. It wasn't until after I neutralized Clive that I heard screams and poundin' from inside one coffin. I opened it and found Lindsey Anderson. She's, understandably, shook up but, otherwise, fine. I took her to her folk's house this mornin'. I'd appreciate it if y'all give 'em some privacy while they work through this.

"Now," Garrett continued with what passed as regret, "the reason I said it's unfortunate I killed Clive is because Melanie Zane, Megan Williams, and Taylor Shanahan are missin' and it would've been nice to question Clive as to their whereabouts. There were four missin' girls and four coffins. Lindsey Anderson confirmed that the other three girls were there. They could communicate with each other through the locked coffins when Clive left, but they never saw each other because Clive would only take one of 'em out of their coffin at a time.

"Lindsey told me durin' the time Clive held 'em captive he took each of the other three girls out and they didn't come back with him. We're operatin' under the assumption that Clive took each of the other three girls into the woods and murdered 'em.

"There are two more things I need to say before I take questions. First, Lindsey insists Clive did not sexually assault her. Y'all know from his past that Clive was cruel. Thankfully, he wasn't a rapist. Second, since this is officially a kidnappin', I have contacted Trooper Steve Sweeten with the DPS and he's contactin' the FBI. So, from here on out, it's their case. Not mine. Questions?"

"Did Clive Jones act alone, or did he have an accomplice?" a reporter from the ABC station out of Tyler asked.

"From everything we know, accordin' to Lindsey, Clive acted alone. For us, the case is closed."

"Will they involve the Pine View Sheriff Department in searching for the missin' girls?" Clair asked.

"Only if the DPS and FBI request our help. Trooper Sweeten told me we finished our job, and they'll take it from here. So, thankfully, y'all can pester him from here on out."

"If the girls weren't molested, what do you think Clive's motive was?" a reporter from the NBC station out of Tyler asked.

"If y'all didn't know 'bout Clive's past when I named him as our primary suspect, I'm sure y'all have done your homework by now," Garrett said. "So, I'll answer your question with a question. Why did Clive mutilate, and kill, those animals a while back? Now, I'll answer it. Clive wasn't right in the head. Instead of prison for those crimes, he should'a gotten psychiatric help. Prison just hardened him. All that said, the only motive I can think of is that Clive moved from terrorizin' and killin' animals to terrorizin' and killin' teenage girls."

"Do you believe Melanie Zane, Megan Williams, and Taylor Shanahan are dead, or could he have moved them to another location?" Clair asked.

"I already told y'all we're operatin' under the assumption that

612

Clive murdered the other girls," Garrett said.

"But why?" Clair persisted. "Couldn't he have moved them to another location?"

"Here's why," Garrett said calmly. "Since Clive was keepin' 'em in the coffins that were stolen, to torture the girls, and no more coffins have been stolen to put the missin' girls in at a different location, my guess is that he killed 'em. But, as I already said, this case is the DPS and FBI's problem now.

"No more questions. I need to do some paperwork and get some needed rest," Garrett said as he turned to the Department's door.

More questions were shouted. Garrett ignored them. He went to his office and filled out Lindsey's witness statement. Next, he filled out his statement of what happened when he confronted Clive. He'd drop by the Anderson's later and have Lindsey sign her statement. Then, he really would be done with the case. He knew the Culpeppers would be reported eventually, but he'd hand that one, along with the .308 rifle Trowa had placed in evidence, over to Steve Sweeten. The Culpeppers were his problem now, too.

~ * ~

Even though Mandy was comfortable with her nudity, Paige put on one of her daddy's T-shirts that fell to her knees after telling Mandy about the events of the morning. They were in the living room watching TV. Actually, they agreed to watch *Jeopardy* and not let her daddy know. He recorded every episode to DVR so they could watch it when he got home. There were several episodes recorded, but he could tell if they watch any of those. Watching it live, to learn the answers for that day's episode, wouldn't be detectable. He'd be surprised when Paige and Mandy got more questions correct and beat him for a change.

Alex was in the middle of reading an answer when Paige felt the tickle of Lola enter her mind.

I need to talk with ya, Paige-Turner, Lola thought.
Okay. What's up?
We should have this discussion in person. Can ya come over?

Is it serious? More trouble?

No more trouble, Lola thought. *But it is serious. Can ya come? Or I could come get ya.*

I can come. My Lil' Dragon is here at Daddy's. I need to get my phone from your house, anyway.

You girls and your phones. It's like an addiction.

A teenage girl without her phone is like a seer without sight, Paige thought.

How soon can ya be here? Lola thought with a laugh.

I'll leave as soon as Jeopardy is over. Mandy and I are cheatin' to beat Daddy when he gets home.

Y'all are so bad, Lola thought, and the connection broke.

"Where were ya?" Mandy said. "You were…gone for a few seconds."

"Sorry. Lola contacted me. She wants me to come over."

"Is everything okay?" Mandy said.

"Yep," Paige said. "I think she's still curious why I kept my seer powers after Glinda took out Dragoș. I was supposed to lose 'em when we destroyed him."

"Why did ya keep 'em?"

"I don't know. I'm guessin' that's what she wants to talk about."

"Are ya goin'?"

"Yeah," Paige said. "My phone is at her house, and I need to get it, anyway. I told her I couldn't come until Jeopardy is over. Rewind it so I can see what I missed. Daddy's gonna be so surprised when we get to this episode."

When *Jeopardy* was over, Paige put on sweatpants, grabbed her keys, hopped into Lil' Dragon, and headed for Lola's house. Lola's cryptic conversation intrigued her, and she couldn't wait to find out what she had to tell her, in person, she wouldn't tell her mentally.

~ * ~

Garrett spent the rest of the morning, and early afternoon, filling out Lindsey's report for her to sign later, and then his report on the encounter he had with Clive Jones. He had just finished when he heard a knock on his opened, office door. He looked up and saw Steve Sweeten and a woman he didn't recognize.

She was attractive and young, perhaps in her early thirties. Her dark brown hair was pulled back in a ponytail, which highlighted her high cheekbones. She had large, blue eyes that seemed to take everything surrounding her in at once. She was dressed in a dark blue pantsuit that highlighted her eyes. Unlike Hillary Clinton, the pantsuit looked good on her. She had to be the FBI agent.

"Bad time?" Steve asked.

"Actually, perfect timin'," Garrett said as he pushed the print button and heard the printer come alive. "I just finished fillin' out Lindsey Anderson's and my statements."

"You filled out Lindsey Anderson's statement?" the woman asked.

"Pardon," Steve said. "This is Mallory Coffey. She's the FBI agent assigned to the case. Special Agent Coffey, this is Sheriff Garrett Lambert."

Garrett stood and extended his hand. Mallory shook it and had a pretty good grip.

"Have a seat," Garrett said as he sat back down.

They did and Mallory said, "I don't understand why you filled out Lindsey Anderson's statement. She should do that, not you."

They were getting off to a rocky start.

"Well, I heard her tell it twice," Garrett said. "Once to me and once to her folks. So, I'm familiar with what she says happened. I'm gonna drop by to have her review it and sign it. If there are any mistakes, she can correct 'em and initial 'em. She's been through a lot, Agent Coffey. I thought I'd save her the trouble of havin' her write it all out again. Y'all are welcome to come with me."

"This is a *highly* irregular procedure," Mallory said angerly. "We *will* come with you. And I'm *Special* Agent."

"Pine View County is rural, and folks are private," Steve said in Garrett's defense. "This isn't all that unusual."

"How certain are you he didn't rape the girl?" Mallory asked.

"She says she wasn't," Garrett answered.

"Oh, well," Mallory almost spit in reply. "I guess that solves that, because a teenage girl wouldn't lie to a man or her parents about being sexually molested."

"Look," Garrett said calmly, "I've known Lindsey her whole life. She and my daughter, Paige, have been best friends since kindergarten. Paige spent some time alone with her this mornin'. Now, *Special* Agent Coffey, why do ya think I had my daughter, Lindsey's best friend, spend some time alone with her?"

Mallory's facial features softened a little. "Because Lindsey would probably tell your daughter if Mister Jones had done anything inappropriate to her."

"Exactly," Garrett said. "Lindsey didn't tell Paige anything of the sort. I'm sure Trooper Sweeten has filled ya in on what Lindsey went through. I think folks in your behavioral unit would call it psychological torture. If Lindsey says she wasn't molested, I think ya should take her at her word, and not further traumatize her by submittin' her to a rape exam."

Mallory thought for a moment. "Okay. But only after I interview her *alone*. If I believe her, I won't make her take a rape exam."

"I told her folks they could be with her durin' questionin'," Garrett said. "But, if that's what ya need to do to keep from puttin' Lindsey through that, I'll make it happen."

Mallory nodded in agreement.

"Ya know I need your gun for ballistics on the slugs removed from Clive," Steve said. "We need the rifle he fired at ya, too."

"Not a problem," Garrett said as he removed his gun from its holster, made sure the chamber was clear, removed the clip, and laid them on his office desk.

"The rifle is in evidence lock up," Garrett said. "I can get that for y'all on the way out."

Steve took Garrett's gun and clip. "I'll get ballistics on this today and have it back to ya tomorrow."

"No rush," Garrett replied.

"We need to see Mister Jones' body, too," Mallory added.

"Yeah," Garrett said. "That *is* a problem. He's already been cremated."

Shocked, Mallory said, "Unacceptable. On whose authority did you destroy *that* evidence?"

"His mother's," Garrett said and had to suppress a grin. "Clive Jones has…had a pretty evil reputation 'round here. Did time for torturin' and killin' animals and for sellin' meth. His mom, Kelly Jones, is so scared how folks 'round here might react to these crimes that she's leavin' town today to go live with her sister in Plano. She wants this over with, and I felt obliged to follow her wishes.

"George Krats is our County Coroner," Garrett continued keeping his dislike of Special Agent Coffey in check. "He tested for GSR, the trajectory of my shots, and removed the slugs before he cremated Clive's body. I assure ya, he's very competent. I have pictures taken at the scene, too. Y'all will just have to work with what ya got."

"I guess this isn't all that *unusual* in Pine View County either," Mallory almost hissed.

"No, ma'am," Garrett said. "It's not. Now, if y'all wanna get gone, I'll get y'all Clive's rifle from our evidence room and we can head over to the Anderson's for a little sit down with Lin."

"Looks like you've left us no other option, Sheriff Lambert," Mallory said.

"Best get gone then," Garrett said as he stood.

Steve and Mallory followed Garrett to the evidence room and took chain of custody of the rifle. Garrett was happy to have it out of his evidence room. They went outside, got in their SUVs, Mallory riding with Steve, and headed for the Anderson's house. Garrett hoped Special Agent Coffey would be a little less abrasive with Lindsey. He was pretty sure she would be.

~ * ~

Paige wasn't surprised to see Lola sitting on her front porch swing when she pulled up and parked Lil' Dragon. As Paige got out of her car, Lola stood and started for the steps. Paige ran to Lola and wrapped her in a warm, tight hug. Lola's hug was equal in intensity and warmth.

Still clinging to Lola, Paige said, "What's so important that ya needed to talk in person?"

"I met with Mamma, Rosa, and Angelica this mornin' to discuss how ya kept your elemental, seer powers after the protection potion ended with Dragoş' destruction."

"And?" Paige asked as the hug broke.

"Come sit with me on the swing and I'll explain everything."

They sat on the swing next to each other, and Lola put her arm around Paige's shoulders. Paige rested her cheek in the crook of Lola's neck. She loved being with Lola the way they were.

"Well, what'd they say?"

"It seems, Paige-Turner, that you're a natural conduit of all things supernatural."

"What's the big deal?" Paige said. "I'm a werewolf and an elemental seer."

"Oh, Paige-Turner. You're much more than that. Weren't ya listenin'? I said you're a natural conduit of *all* things supernatural."

"Is that rare?"

"Extremely," Lola said. "Mammas only heard of a few throughout seer history. And her history goes back well beyond her long life."

"Okay. But I still don't know what it means."

"It means that, even without our help, Dragoş wouldn't have been able to control you and Glinda. Even if he *had* turned y'all."

"I don't understand," Paige said as she raised her head to look at Lola.

Lola smiled. "Oh, chil'. For the record, I didn't think I should tell ya. But Mamma, Rosa, and Angelica said it wasn't up to me to limit your powers."

"Limit my powers how?" Paige asked.

Lola looked at Paige, seeing eye to seeing eye. "You can have werewolf, vampire, and seein' powers."

"How?" Paige said. "I destroyed Dragoş."

"Remember when I tol' ya that Dragoş and his home soil are connected?"

Paige nodded.

"Well, if y'all are a natural conduit, you and Glinda can have vampire powers by lyin' on some of his home soil."

Paige frowned at the thought of lying in the ancient's putrid his soil. "What happens if we're not a natural conduit?"

"Nothin' will happen," Lola said. "Your clothes will get dirty with some fowl soil."

"If I am a natural conduit, I'd have all his powers?"

"Yep," Lola confirmed.

"I could fly?"

"That and a lot more."

"Would doin' this make me evil like he was?" Paige asked.

"No," Lola said and shook her head causing the beads to click. "Your and Glinda's auras are the purest silver Mamma, or any of us, has ever seen. And y'all have pure sight. You'd have the same control over your vampire powers ya have over Glinda and your seein' powers."

"Let's go. I know where his extra soil is."

"Are ya sure ya wanna do this?"

"Heck, yeah," Paige said excitedly.

"Okay," Lola said with a grin. "But your daddy's gonna kill me when he finds out."

"He doesn't need to know ya told me. I can say I learned it from Mamma before her wisdom left me."

Lola shook her head, and the beads clicked. "No, Paige-Turner. If this works, and I'm pretty sure it will, I have to be honest with him 'bout how it happened."

"Ya sure?"

Lola smiled. "I'm sure. If he gets too angry, I'll give him a little nudge."

Paige laughed. "Or I could nudge him."

"My problem, my nudge," Lola said with a laugh.

"Okay. As Daddy would say, let's get gone."

Paige and Lola got into Lil' Dragon and headed for the Eternal Rest Funeral Home.

~ * ~

Garrett parked in front of the Anderson's house and Steve, with Mallory riding shotgun, parked behind him. They all got out.

"If it's okay with you, *Special* Agent Coffey, I'll introduce y'all and tell 'em what's goin' on," Garrett said.

"Of course," Mallory said contemptuously. "It's your quaint little county."

Garrett led the way to the front door and gave it three hard knocks.

From inside, Lindsey's happy voice shouted, "I'll get it."

"If that's Lindsey, she doesn't sound too traumatized to me," Mallory said.

"That's Lindsey," Garrett said. "I guess she's just happy it's over and to be home."

A moment later, the door opened. Lindsey smiled at Garrett, but not at the other two people with him.

"Hey, Lindsey," Garrett said." Remember when I told ya this mornin' that the DPS and FBI would probably take over the investigation since you were kidnapped?"

Lindsey nodded.

"This is Trooper Steve Sweeten with the DPS and *Special* Agent Mallory Coffee with the FBI. I brought your statement for ya to review and sign, and they're gonna ask ya some questions. Okay?"

"You'll need to correct any inaccuracies in Sheriff Lambert's version of your statement, too," Mallory added.

"Who's at the door?" Andy asked.

"It's Mister Garrett, a guy from the DPS and a lady from the FBI," Lindsey said.

"Well, let 'em in," Andy said.

Lindsey smiled. "Come on in."

Once inside, Garrett introduced Steve and Mallory to Andy and Gloria. Everyone shook hands before they got down to business.

"Well, um." Andy said. "I'm afraid our livin' room doesn't have enough sittin' space for everyone."

"I'll get some dinin' room chairs," Gloria said.

"I'll get 'em," Garrett said as he handed Lindsey the statement.

"Thanks, Garrett," Gloria said.

Lindsey took the statement, sat on the couch between her parents, and began reading.

"If Sheriff Lambert got anything wrong, you'll need to correct it and initial the correction," Malloy said as Garrett came back with two chairs.

Garrett placed the two chairs across the coffee table from the couch. Steve and Mallory sat in these, and Garrett plopped down in the recliner.

Lindsey finished reading the statement and looked up. "No corrections. This is exactly what happened to me."

Garrett resisted the urge to tell Special Agent Coffey, "Told ya."

"Are you sure?" Mallory said. "Everything is *exactly* how it happened?"

"I'm sure," Lindsey said. "I told it to Mister Garrett, and he was here when I told my parents. This is *exactly* what happened when Clive took me."

Garrett pulled a pen out of his chest pocket and put it on the coffee table. "Just sign it at the bottom, Lindsey"

"Hold on," Mallory said irritably. "I still need to talk with Lindsey *alone*."

All three Andersons looked at Garrett and Gloria said, "Ya said we could be with Lin when they questioned her, Garrett."

Garrett gave them a wink. "It's okay. *Special* Agent Coffey needs to ask Lindsey some questions that might embarrass her to answer in front of us."

"Nothin' like that happened," Lindsey said.

"I'd still like to talk with you in private, Lindsey," Mallory said.

"Okay," Lindsey said as she stood.

"Use our room," Andy said.

"Okay, Daddy," Lindsey said. "It's this way."

When Lindsey and Special Agent Coffey closed the door to their room, Gloria said, "What's goin' on?"

Garrett began to answer, but Steve said, "The only way we can keep Lindsey from havin' to get a rape exam is if Special Agent Coffey talks with her alone 'bout what happened. She thinks Lindsey wouldn't admit to anything…improper happenin' in front of y'all or us. If she believes Lindsey, she won't have to get the exam."

"You don't think he did…things to Lin, do ya, Garrett?" Andy asked.

Garrett shook his head. "No. I don't. Lindsey would'a told Paige when they were alone earlier. Paige said Lindsey said nothin' like that happened."

"Thank God," Gloria said.

The four of them sat in silence for a few more minutes before Lindsey and Mallory came back into the room.

"Well, *Special* Agent Coffey?" Garrett asked.

"I believe Lindsey," Mallory said. "Mister Jones didn't molest her. As for the other girls, we won't know until we find their bodies."

Good luck with that, Garrett thought.

"Take us to the County Coroner's Office," Mallory said. "Even *without* the body, I still need to speak with him."

Garrett tipped his hat at her, which he was sure would piss her off. "Yes, ma'am. But not until Lindsey signs the statement."

Mallory glared at Garrett while Lindsey signed the flawless statement.

"Thank ya, Lindsey," Garrett said. "We'll leave y'all alone now."

Steve and Mallory were the first out the door. Before Garrett followed them, Lindsey wrapped him in a tight hug.

"Thank ya, Mister Garrett. You and Paige."

"You're very welcome, Lindsey," Garrett said and smiled. "We're all happy to have ya back."

When Garrett was outside and the door was closed, Mallory said, "What did Lindsey just tell you?"

"None of your *damn* business, *Special* Agent Coffey," Garrett snapped.

"Excuse me, Sheriff Lambert," Mallory snapped back. "This is *my* investigation now. So, with all due respect, what she told you is my *damn* business."

"Okay, *Special* Agent Coffey," Garrett said. "Not that it'll help *your* investigation. She thanked me for savin' her life. That's my good deed for the day. What's yours?"

Mallory's face turned red, but she controlled her anger. "My good deed is finding the other missing girls and bringing closure to their families."

"Their families are dead," Garrett said. "But knock yourself out."

"I'll remind you that Mister Zane is missing," Mallory said. "We don't know if he's dead."

"Right," Garrett said. "All the other family members are dead, but Zack's just missin'. They teach y'all that way of thinkin' at Quantico?"

Before Mallory, who looked like she might burst a blood vessel in her face, could respond, Steve said, "Okay. This ain't a pissin' contest. Just take us to see George and then ya won't have to deal with each other again, Garrett."

"Pleasure," Garrett said.

Mallory, who still looked like she was about to explode, said, "*My* pleasure."

With that said, Mallory turned, stormed off to Steve's SUV, and got inside.

"Geez, Garrett," Steve said when Mallory was inside his SUV. "What the hell is goin' on?"

"Sorry," Garrett exhaled. "I haven't slept much since all this started. *Special* Agent Coffey's treatin' me like I'm a retard. I know what the hell I'm doin', Steve."

"I know ya do," Steve said. "Don't worry 'bout her. Worry 'bout me. After we see George, she's my problem, not yours. She's treatin' me the same damn way. Apparently, FBI think their shit doesn't stink."

Garrett laughed. "Better you than me. I'll be glad to be rid of this shit."

With that, Steve and Garrett got into their SUVs and headed to the county morgue. Where Garrett was sure, Special Agent Coffey would rake him, and George, over the coals for having cremated Clive before she could see his body.

~ * ~

Paige parked Lil' Dragon in front of the Eternal Rest Funeral Home. They got out and went inside the deserted, quiet building.

Once inside, Paige turned right. "Dragoş' extra home soil is in those three coffins on the side wall."

Lola looked around at the destruction. "He wasn't happy 'bout you trickin' him into thinkin' you'd already found it."

"Well, all this must've happened after he trapped my mind and Mamma forced him out," Paige said. "I wasn't here to see it, but it wasn't like this before Mamma kicked him out. I'm pretty sure this resulted from Mamma blastin' his ass out of my mind."

"Thank the Elements and your God that Mamma was there to help ya."

"If we're a natural conduit, it wouldn't have mattered anyway, right?" Paige said.

"Yes. But there's only one way to find out."

They walked to the three beautiful, and unharmed coffins. Lola opened the rosewood coffin on top, and she and Paige recoiled from the rotten stench that assaulted their senses.

Paige pinched her nose. "I don't have to do this as myself and as Glinda, do I?"

"No," Lola said. "If y'all are a natural conduit, only one of ya need to lay on the soil. But I don't think Glinda will fit in that coffin."

Paige looked into the coffin and winced. "There are...worms and bugs in the soul."

"Ya don't have to do this, Paige-Turner," Lola said.

"I'm doin' it."

"I thought ya would," Lola said.

"I won't be evil after?"

Lola shook her head, and the beads clicked. "No. If y'all are a natural conduit, you'll get vampire powers and keep your soul. If y'all aren't, you'll just have nasty worm and bug dirt on your clothes. Or ya could do it naked."

Paige shuddered. "No thanks. The less of that that touches my skin, the better I'll feel."

Lola laughed. "I'll help get the worms and bugs outta your hair."

"So gross," Paige said and crinkled her nose. "I forgot about my hair."

"Again. Ya don't have to do this."

"Again. I'm doin' it," Paige said resolutely. "How long will I have to lay on...that before I know if it worked?"

"Not long," Lola said. "If y'all are a natural conduit, you'll feel his vampire powers take hold immediately."

"Here goes nothin' or somethin'," Paige said as she stepped into the coffin.

"Well?" Lola said. "What are ya waitin' for? Lay down."

"Easy for you to say. You're not the one about to lay down in this disgustin' stuff."

Although Lola trusted Mamma, she concentrated on Paige's pure silver aura as she laid down in the coffin. If she saw any change in it as Paige absorbed Dragoş' powers, she was prepared to eject her from it with a powerful levitation incantation.

Paige laid down in the putrid soil and felt the bugs and worms moving beneath her. She shuddered again and waited for something to happen. Lola had said the reaction would be immediate, but, for several seconds, Paige felt nothing. Just when she thought they weren't a natural conduit for all things supernatural, it hit her, and it hit her hard.

Lola watched as Paige lie in the coffin. For several seconds, her aura didn't change. Then, suddenly, it did. But not in any way Lola expected. Paige's aura remained pure silver, but it expanded in size as the vampire powers bonded with her on a molecular level. They were a natural conduit.

It reminded Paige of the first time she transformed into a werewolf. It felt natural and foreign at the same time. But she wasn't as uncertain about the new powers as she'd been with Glinda's the first time. There was no guide, and she didn't need one. She knew all Dragoş' powers and had full control, and Paige felt none of the evil she'd felt in his black mind. There were some new and unexpected powers, though.

Glinda's hearing was more than acute; it was extraordinary. With the vampire powers came a new kind of hearing. Sonar hearing like bats have. Paige closed her eyes and concentrated. Every sound, even Lola's calm heartbeat, reverberated in her sensitive ears and created a detailed image of the room in her mind. The image was in shades of gray, but crystal clear.

Paige opened her eyes to tell Lola about the sonar hearing but became overwhelmed by another new power. In wolf form, Glinda's eyesight was as extraordinary as her hearing. She learned she had infrared vision as an elemental seer the night before. Now she had vampire infrared vision, too. She saw Lola's heat radiating from her body, but there was more to this new sight. Paige could clearly see Lola's beating heart, and her coronary arteries branching off it. She could also see Lola's carotid arteries in her neck, her brachial arteries in her arms, and her femoral arteries in her legs. Paige saw all of Lola's circulatory system, but the most prominent were the vampires' preferred feeding arteries. She knew this from the carnage the vampires left after feeding, but she also knew this instinctively. This information came with her new vampire powers.

Lola sensed something unexpected happened. "What's goin' on Paige?"

"I have sonar hearin' and vampire infrared sight now," Paige said. "It's different than elemental seer infrared vision. More…concentrated on the circulatory system."

Lola smiled. "Of course, ya do. You have all their powers. Even the ability to spout wings and fly. Step out of that nasty coffin, take off your clothes, and will your wings. They will come."

Paige stepped out of the coffin, quickly undressed, and willed vampire wings. She felt them grow from her slender back. She flapped them and her feet left the floor.

"Holy crap," Paige shouted excitedly. "It worked. I can fly."

Lola laughed. "It sure did, Paige-Turner."

"Do I look like those hybrids we saw?" Paige asked while gently flapping her wings and hovering near the ceiling.

"Do ya feel like one of those ugly things?"

"No," Paige said as she looked at her normal arms in front of her.

"You're still your beautiful self, Paige-Turner," Lola said through happy tears and laughter. "What we saw before, in their hybrid form, was their evil nature. Your aura is still pure silver. Y'all are the rarest of rare.

A natural conduit."

Paige ran her tongue, which had grown longer, across her teeth, felt the needle, and sharp fangs on either side of her front teeth. "I have vampire fangs. Does this mean I need to drink blood?"

"Does Glinda need to kill?"

"No."

"There's your answer," Lola said. "You have vampire fangs because ya have vampire powers. But, just like Glinda doesn't *need* to kill, your vampire doesn't *need* to feed."

Paige floated down to the floor, dismissed the wings, and hugged Lola. "Will Glinda have wings, too?"

"Of course," Lola said. "Y'all are bonded. Transform and see for yourself."

Paige willed the transformation and towered over Lola almost immediately. Glinda willed vampire wings and felt them spring from her enormous back.

Lola saw giant, silver-haired wings sprout from Glinda's back and had to duck to keep from being knocked over by one of them.

"Transform back." Lola shouted.

An instant later, Paige stood in front of her with much smaller pink wings protruding from her back. She flapped them and her feet left the floor again.

"Now," Paige laughed while hovering in the air. "How do we tell Daddy?"

"Leave that to me," Lola said. "Get dressed and let's get outta this creepy place."

Paige had already put the T-shirt on and had the sweatpants in her hands, about to lift a leg, when Lola said, "Hang on a sec. I wanna see somethin'."

"What?" Paige asked.

"You have vampire powers now," Lola said. "All of 'em. Since ya got 'em from Dragoş' home soil, I'm sure they came with substantial knowledge. Right?"

Paige nodded. "Yeah. It wasn't like the first time I transformed into Glinda and needed a guide. I just…knew. The sonar hearin' and vampire infrared sight surprised me, but willin' the wings was as natural as knowin' my name. Why are ya askin'?"

"Transform into mist for me," Lola said. "I wanna see somethin'."

Paige dropped the sweatpants and took off the T-shirt, but Lola laughed. "Ya don't have to worry 'bout shreddin' your clothes when ya turn into mist. You'll just…evaporate outta 'em."

"Well, duh," Paige said and crossed her eyes. "I guess I still have a few things to learn."

Paige willed the transformation into mist. From her perspective, it wasn't too different from when she meditated. Suddenly, she felt like nothingness and everything at the same time. She couldn't exactly see or hear the normal way. But she still had sonar hearing and infrared sight. She was acutely aware of her surroundings. She knew where everything in the room, including Lola was. She willed her form to move and slid, if that was the right word, around Lola's ankles. When she did this, she could feel Lola as if she was part of her. It was pretty cool.

From Lola's perspective, Paige simply dematerialized in front of her. The T-shirt floated down into a mist of pure silver, not black like Dragoş'. The mist had Paige and Glinda's silver aura around it. In silver mist form, it was difficult to tell where the mist ended, and the aura began. She watched as mist encircled her legs and felt Paige's presence invade her body. It was wonderful.

"If ya can hear me, come on back," Lola said.

Paige couldn't hear her, but she sensed Lola's request and transformed back into her body.

"Did ya see what ya expected?" Paige asked.

Lola smiled. "I did. Your mist is pure silver. What did it feel like?"

Paige considered how to put it in words for a moment. "It felt like nothingness, but I had total awareness. I couldn't see or hear normally, but still had infrared sight and sonar hearing. So, I knew everything that was goin' on around me, but I didn't hear ya ask me to come back. My mist was around ya, part of ya, and I sensed ya askin' me to come back. Does that make sense?"

"Yes," Lola said. "I get that feelin' when I'm meditatin'."

"Yeah," Paige said. "Me too. It was like that but, unlike when I meditate, I didn't leave this plane. I was here."

"You and Glinda beat all. A true conduit. I still can't believe it. Are ya gonna name your vampire?"

"Maybe. I'll have to think about it. But this mist thing'll make sneakin' out a lot easier."

Lola shook her head, and the beads clicked. "So much power for a sixteen-year-old girl. A better use of the mist would be dissolvin' into it and then transformin' into Glinda to save your daddy the trauma of seein' ya naked."

Paige shrugged her shoulders. "Yeah. I can to that, too."

Lola laughed. "You're so bad sometimes, Paige-Turner. Now go on and get dressed so we can leave this creepy-ass place."

Paige got dressed and a few minutes later, they were in Lil' Dragon and headed back to Lola's. Paige had never felt better.

~ * ~

"Unacceptable," Mallory barked at George.

"Don't jump on George," Garrett said. "I told ya Kelly Jones wanted it done quickly, and I told George to cremate Clive this mornin'."

"I don't like how you run your county, Sheriff Lambert," Mallory said matter-of-factly.

"I don't give a shit what ya think, *Special* Agent Coffey," Garrett said and felt the tendons on his neck strain. "Ya got the postmortems on all the victims. Ya got the slugs I shot Clive with and my service pistol to match ballistics with. Ya got the GSR results and Clive's rifle. George did an excellent job of notin' the wound trajectories and takin' pictures of the wounds with those...sticks in 'em. Ya got Clive's fingernail clippin's. And ya got the pictures I took of Clive's body at the Wiseman barn. What else do ya need?"

"His body would have been nice," Mallory shot back. "Instead of a box of fucking ashes. And your pictures are...shit. They're blurry as hell."

"Well, excuse the hell outta me," Garrett almost growled. "I'd just been shot at, killed a man who I'd rather have questioned, and found

Lindsey locked in a fuckin' coffin. And my hands were a little shaky. I guess that's everyday shit for you *special* FBI agents."

Steve stepped between Garrett and Mallory. "Everyone take a deep breath and calm down. It would've been nice to have his body for more forensics, Garrett. But we have enough to work with, Special Agent Coffey."

"I also checked his mouth and penis for vaginal fluid," George said, needing to feel useful. "I didn't find any."

"Well, that's helpful," Steve said. "It backs up Lindsey Anderson's statement that he wasn't sexually molestin' the girls. As Garrett put it earlier, when we were talkin' on the phone, Clive was a sadist, not a rapist."

"We don't *know* that," Mallory said. "Lindsey has no recollection of time from when she was inside the coffin. She can't pinpoint when Mister Jones took the other girls and didn't come back with them. He could have raped all three before he killed them and cleaned up afterwards."

"Not to, specifically, contradict your statement, Special Agent Coffey," George said. "But Clive wasn't much on washin'. It's only been five days since Melanie Zane went missin', and Clive's body was filthy. I doubt he'd washed since all this started."

"Speculation, Mister Krats," Mallory said.

"I think we're done here," Steve said. "Where to next, Special Agent Coffey?"

"I guess we are," Mallory said, patting her sidearm. "I'd like to see the Wiseman barn where Mister Jones held the girls. Hopefully, Sheriff Andy Griffith, I mean, Deputy Barney Fife, didn't fuck it up too much."

"That's uncalled for, Special Agent Coffey," Steve said. "Garrett's one of the best sheriffs I've ever worked with."

"It's okay, Steve," Garrett said with a grin. "Might be her...time."

"How *dare* you *patronize* me with your *sexist* remarks," Mallory shouted.

"Typical bully," Garrett said. "Ya can dish the Deputy Fife shit out, but ya can't take it. Ol' Clive was a bully, too. Liked to pick on little kids. Even knocked his girlfriend out at a MRB party. I beat the livin' shit outta him for that. Do I come across as a sexist, *Special* Agent Coffey?"

"Or, maybe, it's 'cause I haven't slept much in the last five days," Garrett continued angerly. "Maybe it 'cause Clive came after my daughter, Paige, too. I'm sure, if you've done your homework on this, ya know Clive killed Albert Sanders, my ex-wife's husband, and Paige's stepdad, too. Luckily, she was at my house that night. Or maybe it's 'cause you've been a real bitch toward me since Steve introduced us."

Mallory's face turned red with rage, but she didn't respond.

Garrett ignored Mallory. "Do ya know where the Wiseman barn is, Steve? Or do I need to take y'all out there?"

"I can find it, Garrett," Steve said. "I think the sooner you two are done with each other, the better."

George picked up the box of Clive's ashes and handed them to Garrett. "Here ya go. I'd like to knock off a little early. I haven't gotten much sleep over the last few days either."

As calmly as she could manage, Mallory said, "Why are *you* taking custody of Mister Jones' ashes? His mother should do that."

"I told ya she's scared and leavin' for her sister's today," Garrett said. "She's got packin' to do. So, I offered to bring Clive's ashes to her."

"Well, aren't you just a knight in shining armor," Mallory

"Yes, ma'am. I try to be," Garrett said and turned to leave.

Right on cue, as if it couldn't have been planned better, Eva Martinez's voice crackled over his radio. "I just got a call, Sheriff Lambert. Don and Alison Culpepper are dead. Shot in the neck, the caller thinks. Their fourteen-year-old daughter, Lena, is missin', too."

Garrett looked back at Steve and Mallory. "Mine or yours?"

"Mine," Mallory said.

Garrett keyed his shoulder mounted mic. "Give me the address. But the DPS and FBI are takin' this one."

Eva's voice crackled back with the address.

Garrett watched Mallory put the address in her iPhone. "Got it? Or do ya need Eva to repeat it?"

"I've got it," Mallory said more friendly. "Thank you."

Garrett keyed the mic again. "Got it, Eva. Thanks."

"You're welcome, Sheriff," Eva's voice crackled back.

"It won't be pretty," Garrett said. "None of the scenes have been."

"Thanks, Garrett," Steve said. "We'll manage."

Mallory's face had gone from red to a pale white. Garrett wondered if the young FBI agent had ever worked on an actual homicide. By the look on her face, he thought not. Bitch or not, he actually felt sorry for her.

~ * ~

Paige and Lola were back at Lola's house. Paige was trying out her new powers. Specifically, flying. As soon as she got out of Lil' Dragon, she stripped, willed the vampire wings, and took flight. But not too high. She couldn't risk someone seeing her from the road in front of Lola's house, but there were plenty of trees for cover, so she soared as high and fast as she could. It was the most amazing sensation. Lola watched her from the ground. She clapped and laughed at the sight of Paige, literally, stretching her wings.

Paige made a daredevil dive toward the ground. She intended to swoop back up only inches from the ground. But she heard her phone ring from inside her car. Instead of swooping back up into the sky, she deftly landed on her feet beside her car.

Paige, with the beautiful wings still jutting from her back, answered the phone. "Hi, Daddy."

"Hey, Paige-Turner. I need your, I mean Glinda's, help with somethin'. Are ya busy?"

Paige dismissed the wings. "I'm not busy. How can Glinda help?"

"I promised Clive's mom I'd sprinkle his ashes somewhere in the woods," Garrett said. "Somewhere pretty. I figured Glinda would know someplace like that."

"Oh, yeah," Paige said. "There are several places like that."

"Great. I'll drop by the house and pick ya up."

"I'm not home. I'm at Lola's."

"Lola's? I thought ya wanted to spend the day with Mandy?"

"I did, but my phone was at Lola's. So, I came here to get it."

Garrett laughed. "God forbid ya go without your phone for a whole day."

"That was Lola's reaction, too," Paige giggled. "But here I am. If I hadn't come out here to get it, I couldn't have answered your call. So, you're welcome."

"Okay. Ya win. I can be there in about twenty minutes."

"I'll be ready," Paige said and ended the call.

When the call ended, Lola said, "Ya want me tell him 'bout the vampire powers now or later?"

"Later. Later's always better with Daddy."

Lola laughed. "Later it is. Best get dressed."

"He's twenty minutes away," Paige said as the wings materialized. "I've still got some time to play."

~ * ~

Garrett pulled to a stop and parked his SUV next to Paige's Lil' Dragon. He saw Paige and Lola on the porch swing as he came into the clearing, and Paige and Lola were already heading down the steps as he got out.

Paige flung her arms around his neck. "I'm so glad this is over and Lin's safe."

Garrett hugged her tightly. "Me too, Paige-Turner. Me too."

"Your aura's a bit…dirty, Garrett," Lola said. "Rough mornin'?"

"The FBI agent they sent down to look for the missin' girls was a handful," Garrett said. "And the Culpeppers have, finally, been discovered."

Paige let go of his neck. "Do ya have to go there after we sprinkle Clive's ashes?"

"No. Thank God," Garrett said. "The only good thing 'bout today is that, from here on out, it's the DPS and FBI's problem. Believe me, the FBI *special* agent doesn't want me involved at all. She really hates me."

"Good," Paige said. "Not that she hates you, but that ya don't have to deal with anymore of this."

"If she knew even half the truth of what we've been up against, she'd change her mind 'bout ya, Garrett," Lola added.

"I don't care what she thinks 'bout me. I'm just glad my part in this is *over*."

Paige looked at the box in her daddy's hands. "There's a really pretty spot close to here where we can put his ashes. If you're ready, Glinda can take ya."

"I'm ready," Garrett said, and turned around for Paige to undress and transform.

Watch this, Paige thought to Lola.

Lola did. In the blink of an eye, Paige dematerialized into silver mist. Her clothes hadn't even fluttered to the ground before the mist rematerialized and Glinda towered over her.

"Okay," Lola said. "Ya can turn around now, Garrett."

Surprised, Garrett turned around and looked up at Glinda. "That was damn quick."

"That's our Paige-Turner," Lola said with a wink. "Always full of surprises."

Glinda went down on all fours and Garrett climbed onto her broad back.

"Take it easy on your old man, Glinda. I gotta hold on to Clive's ashes with one hand, and for a change, we're not in a hurry."

Glinda nodded her enormous head and took off at a gentle lope. Lola watched them go.

~ * ~

It was cold, but Garrett enjoyed the briskness on his face as Glinda made her way through the dense woods. Sun broke through the leafless hardwood trees and shafts of white light peppered the forest undergrowth. They passed several deer that looked up, briefly, and then went back to foraging for acorns. They knew Glinda wasn't a threat.

Garrett wished the ride wouldn't end. But Paige had said the spot wasn't far from Lola's and Glinda slowed to a walk. A few seconds later, they broke through the underbrush into a small clearing. It was perfect.

A small stream was to Garrett's left. There was about a three-foot drop the stream flowed over. Where the water collected had eroded a small pond about the size of a residential swimming pool before flowing off to the right. Unlike most streams in rivers in East Texas, with sandy bottoms making the water mud brown, this little stream flowed over limestone, so the water was crystal clear.

"This is perfect, Glinda," Garrett said as he slid off her back.

Once he was off her back, Glinda went behind a tree.

"Where ya goin'?"

"Sorry, Daddy," Paige said. "I don't want to be Glinda for this. I know he was an evil man once, but he wasn't anymore when Dragoş killed him. Glinda could tell whatever evil had him when he was younger was gone. He deserved better than this."

"Yeah. He did. But this place is beautiful, sweetheart. Ya picked a pretty spot for him to rest."

"Thanks, Daddy," Paige said. "I love it here. I come here as Glinda as often as I can and transform back. I even swim in the pool."

Garrett thought about what Paige had said about Clive not being bad anymore and looked at the box of his ashes. "Ya wanna come out and help me spread his ashes?"

"Really? Ya don't mind?"

"Oh, I mind," Garrett said with a chuckle. "It's not like I haven't seen ya in your birthday suit before. I guess I gotta get used to this. You're not gonna change, so I gotta change. But let's not make it a regular thing, and only around me, your mom, Mandy, and Lola. But only with me when it's just us. Okay?"

"Okay," Paige said as she stepped out from behind the tree. "Thank you, Daddy."

"C'mon," Garrett said as he opened the box and took the plastic bag containing Clive's ashes out. "Let's get this over with."

Paige stepped up next to him and looked at the bag. "Hard to believe that's all that's left of him. He was a *big* guy."

"Yeah," Garrett said as he opened the bag. "Ashes to ashes and dust to dust. Dig in."

"Shouldn't we say somethin' 'bout him first?"

Garrett cleared his throat. "I'm sorry things worked out for ya like this, Clive. I'm sorry ya gotta take the blame for all this, too. If it's any consolation, your death served a good purpose. And your mom will be safe and happy livin' with your aunt in Plano."

Paige crossed herself. "Amen."

Garrett did the same.

After the short, impromptu service, Garrett and Paige took turns grabbing handfuls of Clive's ashes and sprinkling them in the pond. When it was down to less than a handful, Garrett emptied the rest into the pond. They watched as the ashes swirled around in the pond's circular current before being carried out the other side of the stream.

"Where do ya think he'll end up?" Paige asked as the last of Clive's ashes trickled away downstream.

"I'm sure this stream enters a river somewhere," Garrett said. "From there, my guess is, the Gulf of Mexico."

"So, eventually, he'll be part of all the water on Earth," Paige said.

"I guess he will," Garrett said. "That's a nice thought, Paige-Turner. Now, bring back Glinda. I've had 'bout as much of this I can take."

Paige laughed, but it turned into a snarl an instant later as Glinda came into form.

"Thank you," Garrett said.

Glinda went down on all fours. Garrett climbed onto her back, grabbed two handfuls of her silky silver hair. He had the crushed box and plastic bag held tight in his right armpit.

"Run, Glinda," Garrett shouted.

Glinda did. It was cold. But wonderful.

~ * ~

Lola sat on the porch swing, waiting for Glinda and Garrett to return. She sensed Glinda only a second or two before she burst out of the woods at a fast run. Garrett held on for dear life but had a smile on his face a belt sander couldn't remove. With his cowboy hat on, it looked like the world's strangest rodeo event. Werewolf back riding.

Glinda slowed as they got to her house and Garrett shouted, "That never gets old."

When Glinda stopped by Lil' Dragon, Garrett slid off her back and to Lola's surprise, Glinda transformed back into Paige right in front of Garrett. She waited for his reaction and was surprised again.

"Dam it, Paige," Garrett said. "What did I just tell ya?"

"You said I could be naked in front of you, Mom, Mandy, and Miss Lola," Paige said genuinely confused.

"What did I say right *after* that?"

Paige thought for a moment. "Oh, yeah. Ya said I could only be naked in front of you when it was just us."

"Is this just us?"

"No, sir. Miss Lola's here."

"Listen and think, Paige-Turner."

"Yes, sir. I'm sorry, Daddy."

What surprised Lola about the exchange between Garrett and Paige was his aura. He wasn't mad, and he wasn't embarrassed to see her naked. Garrett was frustrated, but a normal frustration any parent has with a child who disobeys. Lola was happy to see he'd finally gotten over the embarrassment he had with Paige's natural form.

When Garrett turned and went to his SUV to put the box and bag from Clive's ashes in it, Paige gave Lola a crooked, guilty grin. Lola laughed. She couldn't help herself.

Paige got dressed quickly. She only had the T-shirt and sweatpants to put on. She was covered when Garrett came back from his SUV.

"Remember the celebration we had last summer after we got rid of the werewolves?" Garrett asked Lola.

"Of course I do," Lola said.

"Feel like celebratin' again?" Garrett said.

"Heck, yeah." Paige shouted.

"Tomorrow night's New Year's Eve," Garrett said. "I can't think of a better way of kickin' twenty-fifteen in the ass than all of us gettin' together at my house. I just wish it wasn't so damn cold out so we could celebrate on my back deck again."

"That's a wonderful idea, Garrett," Lola said. "And don't worry 'bout the cold. I'll bring some of my special tea. No one will feel cold, and we can celebrate outside."

"That'd be great, Lola," Garrett said. "Oh, yeah. Anyway, I

thought we could invite a couple of more people to this one."

"Who?" Paige asked.

"Well, your mom knows about Glinda now. So, we can invite her. And George Krats has been coverin' my ass since the werewolves. I think he deserves to know the truth."

"And Lin," Paige added.

"Ya really think her folks'll let her outta their sight after all this?" Garrett asked.

Paige grinned. "They will if I ask 'em."

"Ya mean if ya nudge 'em," Garrett said.

"Well, yeah," Paige said. "What's the harm? Lin's safe now. She saw Glinda at Lola's house after I brought her back from hell. She deserves to know everything."

"Why the hell not?" Garrett said.

Paige hugged him. "Thank you, Daddy. I'll drop by their house when we leave here and meet ya at home. We got some Jeopardy episodes to catch up on."

"That's right," Garrett said. "We do. No cheatin'. Can she nudge an answer from me?"

"No," Lola said with a laugh. "It doesn't work like that."

"Did ya nudge me to make me more comfortable with you bein' naked, Paige?"

"No, Daddy. I swear I didn't."

"Is she tellin' me the truth, Lola?"

"She is," Lola said. "I can see the change in your aura. If she'd nudged ya, it'd be temporary. Have ya changed your mind?"

"No," Garrett admitted.

"See," Paige said. "No nudge."

"Just when I got used to Glinda's powers, now I gotta get used to your seein' powers," Garrett said, as his aura bubbled with frustration.

You don't know the half of it, Lola thought.

No. He doesn't, Paige thought.

I wasn't thinkin' that to you, chil'.

I know, Paige thought, and grinned.

I will light your little ass up, Paige-Turner.

Paige just grinned.

Hang back a minute after your daddy leaves. I need to tell ya somethin'.

Okay.

"I don't even wanna know what you two are thinkin' 'bout," Garrett said. "I'll pick up some pizzas and fireworks and see ya at home, Paige-Turner."

"I'll be quick."

"Don't speed," Garrett said as he opened the door to his SUV and got inside.

"I won't," Paige said before he closed the door.

Once he was headed out of Lola's driveway, Paige said, "What's up?"

"Zack Zane's what's up," Lola said.

"What about him?"

"Did ya notice your daddy didn't have his gun?"

"Yeah. So?"

"He shot Clive with his gun," Lola said. "The DPS and FBI have it to match the bullets in Clive with the bullets from your daddy's gun."

"Ballistics. I know 'bout that stuff."

"Zack's body has some of your daddy's bullets in it, too."

"Oh, crap," Paige said.

"Exactly. Here's what ya need to do tonight after your daddy and Mandy go to sleep," Lola said and explained her plan.

When Lola finished, Paige said, "Easy-peasy. Especially with my new vampire powers."

"Ya still need to be careful," Lola told her.

"I'm always careful," Paige said with a grin.

"I will light your little ass on fire, chil'."

Paige smiled. "I'll be careful. How 'bout a hug instead of lightin' my ass on fire?"

Lola hugged her tightly. "I love you so much, Paige-Turner."

Paige hugged her back and took in her cinnamon scent. "I love you very much too, Lola."

"Let me know when it's done."

"I will," Paige said. "I'll see ya tomorrow night at Daddy's."

"Yes, ya will," Lola said and smiled warmly. "There are gonna be some very surprised folks there when I tell 'em 'bout you bein' a natural conduit, and ya show 'em, your vampire powers. Hell, James might wet himself."

They both laughed at that thought.

They released each other. Paige got in Lil' Dragon and drove away. Lola watched her go and marveled at the fact the girl she loved most in the world was a natural conduit.

What were the odds? One in over seven billion people currently living on the planet, Lola reckoned. She went inside to summon her sisters to let them know.

~ * ~

Paige snuggled in her bed and thought about the day's events. She couldn't believe all that happened in the last twenty-four hours. Dragoş was gone, Lin was safe, she had vampire powers, her daddy finally accepted her natural self, Lin was coming to the party and so was everyone else, the pizza had been great, and she and Mandy had beat her daddy on the *Jeopardy* episode they cheated on.

She had Glinda dialed up to listen to their breathing and heartbeats to tell when they were asleep. Unfortunately, she had to dial Glinda way back when they had sex again, but the vampire part of her heard their frantic heartbeats during the act and she didn't know how, or couldn't, dial that back. She'd need to practice. Especially since she heard their climax in their heartbeats. She almost puked in her mouth.

That had been earlier. They had gone to sleep, and Lola had a job for her to do. Paige dissolved into silver mist, slipped under her bedroom door and then under the front door. Sneaking out had never been easier.

Once she was outside, she took her human form, willed the wings, and flapped up into the beautiful night sky. She took a few minutes to enjoy her new freedom by looping and barrel rolling. Then she flapped her powerful wings and headed for her destination. She marveled at how fast she could fly. She could fly faster than Glinda could run.

A few minutes later, she softly landed behind the Eternal Rest Funeral home. There was room for her body to fit between the hearse and garage opening; the door was gone. She thought, correctly, Dragoş had removed the door in anger. Enjoying her new powers, she dissolved into silver mist again and slipped inside the embalming room. From there, she slipped under the crumpled counter and shelves into Dragoş' old lair. When she rematerialized, Glinda's large body filled the earthen cavern. Zack's crumpled body was under the hole in the concrete floor above. Glinda went to work.

First, she dug a deep hole and dropped Zack's body into it. She didn't need to bury him. Lola had told her what to do next. Glinda looked deep into the ground with her seeing eye and conjured giant earthen elementals from the depths. As they materialized and filled the cavern, Glinda willed wings and hovered upward. When she got to the hole, she dismissed the wings, flipped the counter and shelf out of her way, and climbed out. She continued to look down into the cavern and conjure earthen elementals until the cavern filled in. Zack's body had been buried at least thirty feet beneath the funeral home. It would never be found. But she wasn't done.

Glinda put the counter and shelves back in place and tore the back of the hearse open. She grabbed some silky material from the inside with her razor-sharp claws, rubbed it together until it sparked and caught fire. Then she conjured a massive fire elemental. It hovered over the concrete floor, awaiting instructions.

The message Glinda sent it was simple, *You are not dismissed until this structure, and everything in it is ash or melted.*

The fire elemental grew in intensity. Glinda grabbed the hearse and easily flung it into the embalming room. She wouldn't have believed it possible, but Glinda was stronger than ever. She had the vampire's strength, too. It crashed into the embalming tables and the fire elemental engulfed it.

Glinda went out the missing garage door and used her pure sight to locate the door. She grabbed it and flung it inside the fire engulfed embalming room. Glinda willed her wings, which were massive to match Glinda size, and with one powerful flap, launched about five-hundred feet into the night sky. She flapped again to put more distance between herself and the ground. She hovered and watched the fire elemental do what she conjured it to do.

After about twenty minutes, Glinda heard sirens approaching in the distance. From a thousand feet up, their flashing lights looked like toys. They got to the funeral home a few minutes later, but their water was no match for the fire elemental.

After about forty minutes, the fire winked out. Glinda used her seeing eye to inspect what was left of the funeral home. It had been flattened. The metal structures inside, counters, shelves, and coffins, were molten blobs of running red rivers that quickly hardened as the firefighters continued to douse what was left of the structure with water. The metal counter and shelf above the hole in the concrete melted and then solidified, which created a permanent cap to Dragoş' old lair. Satisfied, Glinda turned and flew home.

With Glinda's much larger and powerful wings, she was home in under a minute. She landed, softly, in the front yard, dissolved into silver mist, and slid her way back into her bedroom. She rematerialized, climbed into bed, and smiled.

~ * ~

Lola was in bed, but wide-awake, waiting to hear from Paige. She looked into the enchanted mirror at the beautiful night sky and imagined Paige, or Glinda, flying high above.

It's done, Paige's thought came.

Any trouble?

Easy-peasy. Just like I said.

Good night, Paige-Turner.

Goodnight, Lola. Paige thought, and the connection broke.

Lola closed her eyes and smiled. Within a few minutes, she was fast asleep, and the smile stayed on her beautiful face.

Chapter Eighteen

Sunset on December 31, 2015, in Pine View County, Texas came at five twenty-five p.m. For a change, sunset didn't bring with it the horrors of nightfall the previous five nights had brought. And Garrett, Paige, and Mandy had a busy morning getting ready for the celebration party scheduled to start at three o'clock. For starters, since they were a family of meat eaters, Mandy went to the Pine View Grocery to pick up veggie-burgers for Lola, paper plates, plastic knives and forks, red solo cups, and charcoal for the grill. Winter wasn't grilling season, and they were out of grilling supplies. Garrett braved the cold and cleaned the grill. Paige helped him clean the grill, but the cold didn't bother her. Everyone was in a jovial mood and before they knew it, it was two o'clock and time for Paige to pick up Lin.

"Remember. Only nudge 'em if ya have to," Garrett told her as they walked to Lil' Dragon.

"I know," Paige said. "I nudged 'em a little yesterday when I asked. Since Lola said nudges are temporary, I might have to nudge 'em again. Only if I have to, though."

"Okay. Drive safe."

"I will, Daddy," Paige said as she got in Lil' Dragon.

Garrett watched to make sure she put on her seatbelt. She did. He watched her drive out of the driveway and turn left toward Lindsey's house. He sighed in relief. All was right with the world, again.

~ * ~

Paige made good time getting to Lin's house and parked in the driveway at two twenty-two by the clock on her radio. Unfortunately, even though her daddy had asked the press to give the Andersons privacy, there were several reporters parked on the street in front of their house. She got out and made her way to the front door as they shouted questions at her.

She ignored them and knocked on the front door. Lindsey must have been watching for her because, before her hand knock on the door, Lin opened it. More questions erupted from the reporters at the sight of Lindsey.

"Come in. Quick," Lindsey said and yanked Paige inside and shut the door on the reporters' questions.

"When did that start?" Paige asked.

"Not long after ya left yesterday after askin' my folks if I could come to your house today."

"Daddy asked 'em to leave y'all alone," Paige said. "Have ya talked with 'em?"

"Hell, no," Lindsey said. "They're just a bunch of buzzards."

"Have your folks changed their mind 'bout lettin' ya come to my house?"

"Not exactly."

"What's that mean?"

"They wanna come, too," Lindsey told her.

Paige grinned. "I can fix that."

"Really? How?"

"I'm a seer now, like Lola," Paige said. "I can give 'em what's called a nudge. It'll change their minds."

"That's so cool," Lindsey said. "It'll come in handy at school. You can nudge teachers into givin' me better grades."

"Or I could nudge you into studyin' more," Paige said with a laugh.

"Ha. Ha. We'll talk 'bout this later. Nudge my folks so we can get outta here. I'm tired of bein' stuck inside."

"We'll have to go through the reporters."

"Fuck 'em," Lindsey said with a grin.

As if on cue, Mr. and Mrs. Anderson came out of their bedroom dressed to go with Paige and Lin. Paige felt bad about what she had to do, but they couldn't come and learn the truth about everything that happened since the previous May when she was bitten and the alpha bitch killed Justin.

"Hey there, Paige," Andrew said. "Gloria and I talked about it, and we'd like to come to the party, too. Is that okay?"

"Of course, it's okay. I think y'all would be bored, though," Paige said as she gently nudged both of them. "We're just gonna sit around and talk 'bout stuff y'all wouldn't be interested in."

Andrew paused for a moment. "Ya know what? I think you're right. We'll just stay home and watch TV."

"Yeah," Gloria said. "Y'all have fun."

Lindsey smiled. "Okay. Bye Mom and Dad. I love y'all."

Both girls giggled as Lindsey shut the front door, and the reporters began shouting questions at her. They ignored them, got in Lil' Dragon, and drove away.

~ * ~

When Paige pulled back into her daddy's driveway, she saw Trowa's beat up, 1972 Ford F-150 pickup and Lola's 1956 pink Cadillac.

"Whose pink Cadillac is that?" Lindsey asked.

"Guess?"

Lindsey smiled. "Lola's. She has pink fingernails and those pink and white beads in her hair."

"Yep. Trowa's already here, too. Did ya notice that the top's down on Lola's car?"

"Yeah," Lindsey said. "It's too cold to have the top down."

"We don't feel cold or heat," Paige told Lindsey.

"Shut up. You've *really* gotta tell me 'bout all your powers."

"I will," Paige said as she parked Lil' Dragon next to her daddy's personal truck. "You'll find out some cool stuff later today. Also, Lola brewed a special tea, so y'all won't feel the cold either."

As they got out of Paige's car, a 1985 Chevy Silverado pulled into the driveway.

"That's Doctor James. Ya met him at Lola's when I brought ya back."

"I remember him," Lindsey said.

"I hope he brought Winston."

"Who's Winston?" Lindsey asked as James parked next to Trowa's truck.

"C'mon," Paige said as she walked towards James' truck. "We'll see if Winston's with him. You'll love Winston."

James stepped down from the truck. "Hello, Paige and Lin. Is it okay if I call ya Lin?"

"Yes, sir," Lindsey said.

"Did ya bring Winston?" Paige asked.

Before James answered, Winston jumped, fell out of his truck. Even though it was cold, Winston's long tongue hung out of his lower, jutting jaw and he was panting.

Paige fell to her knees and held out her arms. "Winston."

Winston's brown eyes found Paige. His nubby tail wagged, and he waddled to her as fast as his pudgy body allowed.

Lindsey fell to her knees next to Paige. "OMG. He's so cute."

Paige grabbed Winston, hugged him tightly, and giggled as Winston's long, wet tongue licked her neck. Then, true to his nature, he began humping her leg.

James laughed. "That's my boy. He's a lover, not a fighter."

Paige handed Winston to Lindsey, and she giggled as he licked her neck and humped her leg enthusiastically.

"Did ya bring your homemade muscadine wine?" Paige asked.

James reached into his truck and pulled out two large, one-gallon jugs of the amber liquid. "I brought plenty."

Lindsey looked up. "What's muscadine wine?"

"It's delicious," Paige said. "Daddy lets me have a little. I'll make sure he lets ya have some, too."

James laughed; his belly heaved. "Usin' you seer powers for the good of everyone already, I see."

"Just a little," Paige said with a grin.

As Lindsey got up, Winston still attached to her leg, two more vehicles pulled into the driveway. The first was Paige's mom in her 2015 black Chevy Traverse and the second was Ty's 2012 gray four-door Ford, F-250 pickup truck. Jasmine and Little D were with him.

Paige ran to her mom's Traverse and hugged her as soon as she stepped out.

"Hey, Mom."

"Hey, sweetheart," Lacy said and hugged her tightly. "So, this is really over?"

"It is. We'll tell ya all about it later."

"And...Glinda killed the vampire?"

"Glinda did," Paige said. "But not without everyone else's help."

Ty got out of his truck with Little D in his arms, and Jasmine got out, too.

James walked up to Ty. "Hello, my friend. This must be Little D and your beautiful wife Jasmine."

Jasmine hugged James. "It's nice to meet ya, James. Ty's told me a lot about ya."

James laughed, but he couldn't hug her back with the jugs of muscadine wine in his hands. "It's nice to meet y'all, too. I owe ya a hug when I put this wine down."

Paige and Lindsey came over to Ty, who handed Little D to Paige. "This is Paige. Can ya tell her 'Hi?'"

Little D giggled. "Hi, Paige."

"Hi there, Little D. This is my friend Lin."

Little D reached out and grabbed some of Lindsey's blonde hair in his pudgy hand. "Hi, Lin."

Lin kissed his chubby cheek. "Hey, Little D. You're a cutie."

"I'm a cutie." Little D squealed.

Everyone, including Little D, began laughing, and the last two members of their expanding fellowship pulled into the driveway. The driveway was full, so Fr. Mike pulled his 2002 gold Buick LeSabre off the left side of it and George pulled his 2008 red Ram, extra cab, Dakota truck off the right side of it. They got out and joined the others. Ty made introductions where needed.

When the introductions done, Paige said, "I smell meat on the grill. Let's go 'round back. Daddy, Mandy, Lola, and Trowa are on the deck."

"I don't smell anything," Lacy said.

James laughed. "It's a Glinda thing. She can smell stuff long before the rest of us."

"Who's Glinda?" George asked Ty.

Ty chuckled. "You'll meet her in a little while. Hope ya brought some extra undies."

"Extra undies?" George asked as the others headed toward the side of Garrett's house.

"Ya wanted to know everything," Ty said as he put a muscular arm around George's rounded shoulder and began walking him toward the back of Garrett's house. "You're gonna learn a lot tonight."

~ * ~

As everyone converged on the deck, handshakes, hugs, and kisses were exchanged and Garrett introduced George to Lola. To Garrett, Mandy, and Paige's surprise, Lacy gave Mandy a big hug and kissed her on the cheek. If that hatchet had finally been buried, it would be a wonderful night.

Lola passed around the special tea. It smelled like rose water. After everyone had downed their tea, jackets came off and everyone felt warm and comfortable.

The group self-segregated, with the men drinking beer and helping Garrett at the grill and the women, except for Paige and Lindsey, who were on the deck playing with Winston, getting the table ready with plates, cups, buns, condiments ready. It wasn't long before Garrett announced the grub was ready and everyone loaded their plates and began eating.

There was small talk as they ate and the sun set. It was like everyone knew the story of what happened with Dragoş couldn't, properly, be told until after it was dark. After all, that's when the best horror stories are told.

When the food was finished, the women cleaned the table and Garrett, with the help of the other men, started a fire in his outdoor fire pit. It wasn't for warmth; it was for atmosphere for when the stories began. All was ready.

James placed the two jugs on the table. "Who's up for some of my homemade muscadine wine?"

All hands went up.

"Ya know the rule, Paige," Garrett said. "I'm not sure it's my place to let Lindsey have any."

"Please, Daddy," Paige said with her best pouty face. "It's just a little. No one will know, and she *was* a vampire. I think she's earned a taste."

Startled, Lacy said, "She was a what?"

"You're in for a shitload of shockin' news tonight," Trowa said. "Sorry, little missus."

Garrett thought for a moment, while the other banter took place. "Why not. But just two small cups like you, Paige."

"Did ya nudge him?" Lindsey whispered to Paige.

"No," Paige whispered. "I didn't have to. That was all Daddy."

James filled red, solo cups for the adults and Garrett poured Paige and Lindsey's portions.

"First toast is yours, Garrett," Lola said.

Garrett raised his cup. "May Dragoş burn in hell where he belongs."

Cups clunked together with hardy, "Here, heres," and, "Amens" from the fellowship and everyone took a drink.

For those who hadn't had the pleasure of tasting James' homemade, muscadine wine, George, Lacy, Jasmine, and Lindsey, compliments followed. James blushed but took the compliments with pride.

Trowa was the first to finish his wine. He was used to stronger Wild Turkey and poured some more for himself. Then the others followed Trowa with refills and a stern warning from Garrett to Paige and Lindsey their second, small, amount would be their last.

When everyone happily sipped their second cup, George said, "Well? Are ya finally gonna tell me the whole truth, and nothin' but the truth, 'bout what's be goin' on in Pine View County since last May?"

"Yep," Garrett said. "It's a collective story and everyone who already knows the truth will chime in with their own recollection. That's the only way the whole truth can be told. So, George, Lacy, Jasmine, and Lindsey, get ready for some pretty unbelievable information and an…incredible sight."

The complete story, starting with Russ Lomax's death, to how Paige went to hell to save Lindsey, took almost two hours to tell. There were more than a few questions, which were answered by whoever could best answer them. Jasmine was shocked to learn a werewolf had bitten Ty and he almost became one.

The story stopped, with Paige saving Lindsey. Lola and Paige had more to add and were about to when James asked the perfect question to open the conversation.

"I'm still curious 'bout one thing," James said. "How did Paige keep her seein' powers? From everything I've read on the topic, and what you've told me, Lola, she should've lost 'em when she destroyed Dragoş. Isn't that how the protection potion was *supposed* to work?"

"I'm glad ya asked, James," Lola said. "That's exactly how the protection potion was *supposed* to work."

"Well?" James said. "What happened? Why does she still have 'em?"

Lola glanced at Paige and then back at everyone who looked at her. "Our story isn't quite finished. There's more that I need to tell y'all 'bout our Paige-Turner."

"Why do I get the feelin' I'm not gonna like this?" Garrett said.

"Ya probably won't like it," Lola said in her warm, honey voice. "But it's done and can't be undone. And as y'all can see, Paige is fine."

"What *did* you do?" Garrett said sternly.

"I *did* it, Daddy," Paige said. "Lola told me 'bout it and *I* decided to do it. For the record, Lola was the only one in her council who thought I shouldn't know."

"Know what?" Garrett asked impatiently.

"This is gonna be good." James said as he rubbed his pudgy hands together in anticipation.

"I met with my council of seers to consult with 'em 'bout why Paige's seein' powers didn't leave when she destroyed Dragoş," Lola said. "Mamma said that Paige and Glinda would have to be a natural conduit of all things supernatural for 'em to keep their powers."

"I've heard tale of natural conduits in my research," James said. "But they're just that, tales. I didn't believe it was true."

Trowa cleared his throat. "I mentioned Paige might be a natural conduit while we were waitin' for George at the Wiseman barn."

"Ya did?" Garrett said.

"Yes," Trowa said. "Native American culture speaks of those who can channel all supernatural entities. Paige is obviously a natural conduit."

"Fascinatin'," James said. "I've never delved deeply into Native American lore. May we talk more about your peoples' lore later?"

Trowa nodded.

Lola smiled at Trowa, which made his coppery cheeks blush. "Our friend of the Cato Tribe can teach you much, James. While true, this is *extremely* rare. Mamma only knows of a few throughout seer history. If I had to guess, I'd say Paige and Glinda are the only natural conduit alive."

"So, she kept her seein' powers," Garrett said. "We already knew that. What's the part I won't like?"

"Yes. They kept their seein' powers," Lola said. "Since they are a natural conduit, they can also have vampire powers, too."

James drained his cup of wine and leaned forward. "Y'all destroyed Dragoş. How can they get vampire powers now?"

"As you well know, James, a vampire and their home soil are connected," Lola told him.

James clapped his pudgy hands together and shouted, "Of course."

"Of course, what?" Garrett asked, not wanting to know the answer.

"Paige and Glinda could get vampire powers from Dragoş' home soil," James excitedly said. "But how?"

"By lyin' in it," Lola told them.

Garrett looked at Paige. "Ya didn't?"

"I did," Paige said.

"*Why*, Paige?" Garrett asked.

"Did it work?" James asked at the same time.

"Why?" Paige said. "Because Dragoş had a *lot* of power. I wanted that power. Yes, it worked, Doctor James."

"Is her soul safe?" Mike asked.

Paige fingered the silver crucifix on the silver necklace around her neck. "Yes. Just like with werewolves, vampires avoid silver. *Especially* crucifixes. I couldn't wear this if my soul was…compromised."

"I've seen their auras when in vampire form," Lola said. "It's still the purest silver I've ever seen. Her soul is fine, Father Mike."

"So, let me get this right," Mandy said. "Paige is a werewolf, vampire, and seer now?"

"Actually, I can be all three at the same time," Paige told the astonished faces around the table.

"Great," Garrett shouted in frustration. "Just great."

"I knew ya wouldn't be happy 'bout this, Daddy. Think how much more useful we can be in the future, now."

"For what?" Garrett asked.

"Like James and I tol' y'all last time we had one of these celebrations," Lola said. "After the werewolves were takin' care of, trouble begets more trouble. Pine View County has a *stain* on it. That's what brought Dragoș here."

"We've dealt with werewolves and vampires," Garrett said irritably. "It's unlikely that Frankenstein or the Mummy will show up. What's left for my werewolf, vampire, seer, daughter to deal with?"

James glanced at Lola. "There are more evil, supernatural monsters out there than werewolves and vampires, Garrett."

"Just like Dragoș, they'll be drawn here," Lola said. "It's even more likely now that both werewolves and vampires have *stained* Pine View County."

Garrett threw up his arms in defeat. "Great. So, this'll never end?"

"This could be the end, Garrett," James said.

"But not likely," Lola added.

"No," James agreed. "It's not likely. Especially after werewolves *and* vampires have been here."

"The point is, Daddy, Glinda and I will be more useful than ever, if somethin' else happens."

"I don't like this," Lacy said.

"Me either," Mandy agreed.

"Well," Paige said. "It's done."

"And it *can't* be undone," Lola said. "So, y'all best get used to it."

Paige grinned. "Y'all wanna see what we can do now?"

"Yes," James shouted.

Paige stood and said, "Okay. I'll turn into Glinda first. Then I'll show y'all the cool new stuff."

When Paige didn't walk away, Garrett said, "Shed. Unless ya

wanna shred your clothes?"

"I don't need the shed to not shred 'em transformin' into Glinda anymore, Daddy," Paige said as she willed her body to dematerialize.

Everyone, except Lola, gasped as Paige vanished and her clothes fluttered down into a silver mist.

"See," Lola said. "The evil werewolves were black, and Glinda is silver. The evil vampire's mist was black and Paige's vampire mist is silver. Her soul is pure."

"Wonderful," James shouted

An instant later, Glinda sprang up from the silver mist.

Jasmine and George, who had never seen Glinda before, gasped again.

Little D giggled and held up his hands toward Glinda. "Big doggy."

Glinda reached down and gently picked up Little D. Jasmine, held him back for a moment, but let her have him.

Glinda brought Little D up in front of her face. He giggled again, grabbed her enormous nose, squeezed it, and squealed, "Big doggy."

Glinda giggled, too. But it sounded like a low growl.

Jasmine gasped a third time, but Ty said, "He's safe. Glinda would never hurt him. Hell, she'd be the safest babysitter he could ever have."

Glinda nodded and handed Little D back to Jasmine.

"Well?" James shouted. "Show us more."

Glinda, not wanting to accidentally hurt anyone, stepped off the deck a few feet and willed her vampire wings. Giant, silver-haired wings sprang from her back.

"Most excellent," James shouted.

"Holy crap," the usually quiet Trowa said.

"Can she actually fly?" Garrett asked.

Glinda knew a powerful flap would blow everyone over and launch her high into the night sky. She flapped them softly and hovered a few feet off the ground.

James pulled out his iPhone and began recording. "Has there ever been a...mixture of these powers before, Lola?"

"Not to my knowledge," Lola said.

Glinda landed, went down on all fours, and walked up to Garrett. "Is she? Does she want me to ride her?"

Glinda nodded.

"Garrett?" Mandy asked.

He smiled. "Hell, yeah."

Garrett climbed on Glinda's back. He put his knees under her giant wings and grabbed onto her silky hair. Glinda walked away from the deck, flapped her wings a little harder, and took off from the ground.

Garrett watched as they cleared the top of his house and then the top of the trees around his house. When they were clear of obstructions, Glinda flapped harder and took flight higher over the woods. Garrett had experienced nothing as thrilling in his life. He saw his parent's house far below them and then they flew higher and all of Pine View County came in to view below them.

~ * ~

James stopped recording when Glinda and Garrett were out of sight. "This is incredible. It's the highlight of my academic career. Hell, it's the highlight of my life."

"Yes," Lola said. "Too bad ya can't *ever* mention it."

"I know," James said with a head shake that caused his cheeks to jiggle. "I know I can't. Knowin' this magnificent…creature exists is enough."

"That *creature* is my daughter," Lacy said.

"I didn't mean to offend ya, Lacy," James said apologetically. "But she, they are supernatural creatures. There's no other word for what Paige is."

"How 'bout wereampeer?" Ty asked with a chuckle.

"Were-a-what?" Trowa asked.

"Wereampeer. Were from werewolf, amp from vampire, and eer from seer," Ty explained.

James laughed. "Perfect. She's a wereampeer."

"I like it," Lola said.

"Me, too," Lacy, Mandy, Jasmine, and Lindsey said at the same time.

"Father Mike? George? Trowa?" Lola asked the men.

"There's nothin' in any of my peoples' language for this combination," Trowa said. "Natural conduit, yes. But not what she's become. Wereampeer works for me."

"I don't care," George said.

"I'll stick with Paige," Mike said.

Lola's seeing eye looked skyward, and she said, "They're comin' back."

A few second later, Glinda flew over the roof, banked left, and softly landed.

Garrett slid off her back and shouted, "That was amazin'."

Lola grabbed Paige's clothes from the deck, walked over, and handed them to Glinda. Glinda took them and went into the shed. About a minute later, Paige walked out and joined everyone on the deck.

"Ty came up with the perfect name for what ya are now," Lola said.

"What?" Paige asked.

"You're a wereampeer," Ty said.

Paige considered it for a minute and smiled. "I like it."

James picked up the jug with the last of his wine in it. "A toast to the wereampeer."

"Can Lin and I have some more?" Paige said.

"I don't think so," Garrett said. "Ya still have to drive Lin home."

Paige smiled. "News flash, Daddy. I can't get drunk. My metabolism won't allow it."

"That still leaves Lin," Garrett said. "I can't send her home with liquor on her breath."

"Can Lin spend the night?" Paige asked

"Can I, Mister Garrett?" Lindsey said. "Please let me spend the night."

"Okay," Garrett relented. "But only if her folks agree."

Paige grinned. "They will, if *I* ask."

Garrett smiled and shook his head. "You're gonna be more trouble than ever."

"Thanks, Daddy."

"Thanks, Mister Garrett."

James emptied the first jug into Paige and Lindsey's cups. It was a little more than they had the previous two times, but he didn't think it mattered.

"There's still somethin' I don't understand 'bout when Glinda destroyed Dragoş," Paige said. "I've already told Miss Lola, and she's not sure either. I thought Father Mike or Doctor James might know, though."

"What?" Mike asked.

"Do tell," James said.

"When Glinda destroyed Dragoş, he was in several pieces," Paige began.

"Several pieces?" Garrett asked.

"Yeah. Glinda kinda ripped off his wings, one leg, one arm, bit off the other arm, and then ripped his head off," Paige said. "Anyway, his black aura spread out across the clearin' like all his pieces were connected. When he finally turned to ashes, his aura disappeared and thousands of white lights, like fireflies, rose, took on human forms, and ascended to heaven."

"Praise God," Mike said.

"We expected this to happen, Paige," James said. "What's got ya confused?"

"Well, five forms stayed and came up to Glinda," Paige said. "One was Al, Mom."

Lacy teared up. "Did he look happy?"

"Very," Paige said with a warm smile. "He smiled at me before he ascended."

Lacy began crying happy tears, and Mandy put an arm around her shoulders.

"Who were the other four?" Mike asked.

"Melanie, Megan, Taylor, and Lena," Paige said. "This is what I don't understand. From everything we *thought* we knew, once they became vampires, their souls were damned. Just like how Dragoş and Cipriana's souls were in hell when I went there to find Dragoş' creator and to save Lin. Her soul was in hell, too.

"Lucifer was surprised to find out their souls were no longer in hell when I told him," Paige continued with a grin. "He said that wasn't the deal he made with God. I'm glad their souls aren't in hell. They ascended, too. But...how did they escape? Lin's soul was still there."

"Lindsey was still a vampire when ya went to hell to save her," James said. "That's why her soul was there."

"Okay," Paige said. "But how did the others get free of hell? They were vampires when Glinda destroyed them, just like Dragoş and Cipriana."

Fr. Mike thought for a moment. "They were innocent young women when Dragoş took them. From what James found out about Dragoş before Cipriana created him, he was already evil."

"Dragoş had a taste for innocent, young women," James said. "They were his...fetish, for lack of a better word."

"So, y'all think that, because they were innocent when Dragoş took 'em, their souls were pure and Lucifer couldn't keep 'em?" Paige asked.

"Exactly," James said. "Dragoş has been doin' this, creatin' clouds of young women, for eight hundred years. My guess is that Lucifer lost a lot more than four souls when ya destroyed Dragoş."

"I think my learned friend is correct, Paige," Mike said. "When Glinda destroyed Dragoş, it freed all his innocent creations from hell. Praise God."

Paige looked at Lola. "What do ya think? Does that sound possible?"

Lola smiled warmly. "I think it's very possible. Ol' Lucifer is probably still tryin' to find out how many souls Glinda freed from his domain."

Paige smiled. "I hope he's pissed."

This brought chuckles and laughs from everyone and an, "Amen," from Fr. Mike.

"There's still somethin' I don't understand," Paige said.

"What?" James asked.

"I didn't see Mister Clive's soul escape from Dragoş' aura when I destroyed him," Paige said. "I know he did some bad things when he was younger, but Glinda didn't sense any evil in him. So...why didn't he ascend, too?"

"I was curious about Mister Jones after Garrett named him as the primary suspect and did a little research on him," Mike said. "The things he did when he was a young man were evil."

"But we know God forgives sins," Paige said.

"Yes," Mike said. "But only to those who confess and ask for forgiveness. So, even if Mister Jones grew to regret his former actions, his only salvation was in asking God for forgiveness. I don't think he was a practicing Christian of any faith."

"Still," Paige said sadly. "It's a shame he's stuck in hell."

"Don't even think about it, Paige-Turner," Lola said.

"Think about what?"

"Goin' to hell to save him."

"I won't," Paige earnestly said. "I promise, Miss Lola."

Lola scrutinized Paige with her seeing eye. "She tellin' the truth."

Garrett let out a sigh. "How 'bout we set off the fireworks I got?"

Everyone agreed this was a good idea, and they spent the next thirty minutes watching the fireworks go off. Little D clapped his pudgy hands and squealed with excitement at every display and boom. Winston hid under the patio table.

The highlight of the firework show came when Paige transformed into Glinda, sprouted wings, flew high into the night sky, and lit, with a snap of her deadly, werewolf fingers, a Roman Candle. The multicolored shooting balls of fire could be seen for miles. Those who saw it from a distance did not know who, or what, was behind the magnificent display.

After the fireworks were finished, and Paige back in human form, James said, "Well, the muscadine wine is almost gone. How 'bout a last toast, Garrett?"

Garrett raised his cup. "To good friends, freed souls, puttin' the current troubles behind us, and to the *wereampeer*."

All eleven cups came together with a loud clunk. And they were trouble free. For a while...

Epilogue

January 1st, 2016 dawned a new day and new year. While the Dragoş nightmare was behind them, sorrow of the aftermath was not. Garrett's initial mental calculation of the number of people killed since Dragoş' arrival of twenty-two had been wrong. Counting Clive, who had been a victim too, the actual number of dead was twenty-four in Pine View County. He had no way of knowing about Dragoş' victims on the voyage or at the Houston Ship Channel.

This included Albert "Al" Sanders, Lacy's fourth husband and Paige's stepdad. His funeral was held on January 2nd, 2016. Trevor Henderson had already been put to rest, but his parents' funeral, and those of all the other victims, were held over the next few days. Garrett, Paige, and Mandy attended as many as time and scheduling allowed.

The Pine View County blinders, like the aftermath of the previous werewolf situation, were on. That Clive Jones had committed the horrible acts had been, universally, accepted. These deaths were much easier to explain because, unlike the werewolves, who many survivors saw and talked about, Dragoş had only been seen by his victims. They, except for Lindsey, who didn't remember her time as a vampire, were all dead.

After the services he attended, Garrett took the congratulations, handshakes, and pats on the back with all the grace he could muster. It was difficult, though. To his way of thinking, all he'd done was frame an innocent man. Glinda had killed Dragoş and saved Lindsey. No matter how many times Paige told him it was a group effort, he knew Paige and to an extent, Lola, had done the heavy lifting.

No services were held for Melanie Zane, Megan Williams, Taylor Shanahan, or Lena Culpepper, as hope they would be found alive remained optimistic among those who were prone to optimism. Most people, though, had accepted the brutal truth that they had been killed by Clive Jones, but hoped their bodies would be recovered and properly buried remained. The same sentiment was shared for Zack Zane.

~ * ~

An investigation into the fire that reduced the Eternal Rest Funeral Home to blackened, cracked concrete, ash, and pooled metal was launched by the Pine View County Fire Commissioner, a man named Ronald Guillory. Since the foreigner who had purchased the establishment, the insurance, the licenses required for construction listed his name as Dănuţ Roşca, had interacted with very few and not been seen since the structure burned, arson was suspected. The investigation had found no accelerants and Dănuţ Roşca had not filed an insurance claim to collect on the one-million-dollar policy. Nor had they found his remains in what was left of the structure.

To further frustrate the investigation, the fire had been so intense that locating a natural cause, like faulty wiring or leaking gas, had been impossible. The fire had simply covered its own origin by being too intense. Another complication came from the firefighters who had responded to the fire. All of them, to a man, swore the fire was 'unnatural' and wasn't deterred by the water they pumped into it. Some even described it as a 'living beast' with 'arm and leg like appendages,' and the fire just winked out when the 'living beast' finished destroying the structure. Ronald chalked these reports up to fatigue and the fact the fire had simply run out of fuel. There wasn't anything left to burn.

Since all that was left after the fire had been the blackened, cracked, concrete slab, and melted metal that had pooled and hardened afterwards, Ronald's only option was to list the cause of the fire as 'unknown' on his paperwork and wait to see if Dănuţ Roşca showed up to collect the insurance. If he did, Ronald would have questions for the man, but Dănuţ Roşca did not show his face in Pine View County again. After two months, Ronald filed his report and put the Eternal Rest Funeral Home fire behind him.

~ * ~

Trooper Steve Sweeten and Special Agent Mallory Coffey's investigation continued for several weeks after Clive Jones' death. Steve had been politely sidelined after a few days into the investigation as Mallory brought more FBI agents to Pine View County to take over the investigation herself. For Steve, this had not been a disappointing development. Although he kept a more professional relationship with Special Agent Coffey than Garrett had, he hadn't lied to Garrett when he told him Mallory treated him with contempt, too.

To Mallory, who came from Augusta, Maine and graduated at the top of her class from Quantico, the local law enforcement were incompetent, backwoods, rubes who couldn't find their dicks with a flashlight in the middle of a sunny day. All her training and resources did nothing to answer the questions she had or the desire to find Melanie Zane, Megan Williams, Taylor Shanahan, Lena Culpepper's, or Zack Zane's bodies.

She believed Clive Jones had committed the crimes, and he acted alone. Regardless of Lindsey Anderson's statement, she didn't believe there wasn't a sexual component to Clive's behavior. From his past behavior, torturing and killing animals, Clive met the FBI's profile of an eventual serial killer, and the evidence supported this conclusion. But she couldn't reconcile Clive's selected victims, attractive teenage girls, without sexual activity. It made little sense to her.

The only way to prove otherwise would be to find the missing girls' remains and find them quickly, before the elements and decomposition destroyed evidence of semen in, on, or near their remains. Mallory dismissed Trooper Sweeten and brought the full force of FBI resources to the investigation. Helicopters, specialized agents, and the best cadaver dogs searched every inch of Pine View County, as well as surrounding counties, for almost a month. They searched for bodies, clothing, burned areas, and everything else associated with the girls. The cadaver dogs 'hit' a few areas, but, to Mallory's disappointment and growing frustration, all the hits turned out to be dead wildlife. The cadaver dogs were trained to hit only on human remains. It was as if they were getting frustrated, too, and they found nothing. It was as if the Clive had made the girls vanish completely.

When, after twenty-seven days had passed without developments, Mallory's supervisor, Special Agent in Charge Darrel Boykin, told her to call off the search. An argument ensued. It had been an intense argument, which wasn't wise on Mallory's part. Darrel didn't take the argument personally. He'd seen this behavior before. Special Agent Coffey had become obsessed and suffered from burnout. But Mallory's insubordination couldn't stand without repercussions.

Within a week of being removed from the Clive Jones investigation, Mallory was transferred to the FBI office in Missoula, Montana. The Missoula office had a reputation of being one of the least active FBI offices in the country. If she were lucky, Mallory might get to investigate some drug trafficking, but the Canadian border wasn't a hotbed for this activity. This activity was much more common in Texas, where drugs came in from Mexico every day.

Her specialty was sex crimes, including sex trafficking. Montana wasn't a hotbed of this activity either. One kidnapping case she had volunteered to lead because she thought solving it would be easy and get her a promotion, not a demotion, had ruined her future.

Mallory had said she wanted to find the bodies to bring closure to the families Sheriff Lambert had, correctly, pointed out were all dead. What she really wanted, craved, was closure for herself. She *needed* to prove Clive Jones was a sexual predator and a sadist. That had been her downfall.

A week after Special Agent Coffey was removed from the Clive Jones case, Special Agent in Charge Boykin called an end to the search. The investigation would remain open, but all FBI personnel were removed from Pine View County.

Trooper Sweeten and Sheriff Lambert were asked to report anything related to the missing girls, and Zack Zane, to the FBI. Steve thought, after the FBI's extensive search, this was unlikely. Garrett knew it would never happen, but both agreed and parted with Special Agent in Charge Boykin on good terms. Unlike Mallory, Darrel was likable. Within two days, the FBI had gone, and Pine View County returned to normal.

~ * ~

A week after the FBI left East Texas, a special vigil was held for Melanie and Zack Zane, Megan Williams, Taylor Shanahan, and Lena Culpepper at City Hall. The vigil took place after the sun went down. Everyone, including all of Pine View County and people from surrounding counties, were given candles. Once they were lit, downtown Pine View glowed bright orange as various pastors of the missing girls' faith, and Fr. Mike for Melanie and Zack Zane, offered prayers for their safe return or their departed souls.

Since he knew the truth of what happened to all the missing people, this proved a somber task for Fr. Mike. Especially since he knew none of them would return. He offered sincere prayers for their safe return anyway and for the repose of their souls. It was his job, and he prayed God would take pity on their souls because they were victims. These prayers were silent and repeated several times a day, every day.

~ * ~

After the tumult of Dragoş' aftermath died down, Mandy and Paige remained busy. They had a wedding to plan. It was early February by then and the wedding date had been set for Saturday, April 30th. It would be a small wedding, held at St. Joseph's Catholic Church and officiated by Fr. Mike. Paige would be Mandy's maid of honor and Ty would be Garrett's best man. They would be the only ones standing with Garrett and Mandy. Although Little D was a little young to be the ring boy, the task was given to him. Although Lindsey was a little on the old side to be the flower girl, the task was given to her.

A small wedding didn't mean less stress for Mandy and Paige. They still had to pick a wedding dress for Mandy, a tuxedo for Garrett, a color and dress for Paige, and a tuxedo for Ty that matched Paige's dress. As for the color of Paige's dress, that was easy. It would be green. That meant Ty's tuxedo would have a green bowtie and vest. They narrowed Mandy's gown down to two choices, but when she tried each of them on, the choice was obvious to both of them. It was a contemporary design. No veil or train for Paige to manage. It was a beautiful, white, off the shoulder, long sleeve, crosshatch lace gown that highlighted Mandy's figure perfectly. Garrett's tuxedo vest would match the crosshatch lace design and his bowtie would be white.

With that done, they shifted planning to the cakes and reception. Garrett's groom cake was easy. It would be in the shape of his six-sided badge and decorated to resemble his Pine View County Sheriff badge. The wedding cake wasn't difficult either. It would be a simple, two-tier, yellow cake, with white icing and icing flowers on top. The reception proved pretty easy to plan as well. They rented the Knights of Columbus Hall in Pine View, catered barbecue, with all the fixings, lots of sweet tea and because it was a Catholic wedding, a sixteen-gallon keg of Miller Lite beer.

Because it was required, Mandy and Garrett attended Pre-Cana wedding classes taught by Fr. Mike. There were six classes they had to attend. Initially, Mandy was concerned, since Garrett wasn't Catholic, getting married in the church might be a problem. It wouldn't have been an issue. But Fr. Mike had let it slip Garrett was becoming a Catholic at the Easter Sunday Mass, which was before their wedding.

~ * ~

Time passed, and Easter Sunday came quickly. It was on March 27th. Garrett shaved and put on his best suit. Mandy and Paige were pleasantly surprised to see him all dressed up. He shaved before Mass, but his best Wranglers, dress boots, a button-down shirt, and sometimes, a sport coat were his usual Mass attire. For this occasion, he wore a suit and tie.

"Well, look at my handsome man," Mandy said when she saw him.

"You look really nice, Daddy," Paige added.

Garrett actually blushed. "What? It's Easter Sunday. I'm gettin' confirmed and receivin' first communion today. I think a guy should get dressed up for a day like this."

Mandy kissed him on the lips, which left some of her lipstick on them. "Of course ya can. This is a big day for you. We're just not used to seein' ya all dressed up."

"Yeah," Paige said. "Ya look good, Daddy. Ya should do this more often."

"Maybe I will," Garrett said as Mandy straitened his tie.

"I'd like that," Mandy said as she used her thumb to remove lipstick from his lips.

"Okay," Garrett said. "Enough fussin'. Let's get gone before the church fills up."

Paige and Mandy shared surprised, and happy, smiles as Garrett ushered them out the door and to his truck. They got in and left.

~ * ~

They arrived at the church early enough to park close and even found the right front pew empty. They sat in the pew and waited for Mass to start.

Mass went as it usually did until it was time for communion. At this point, Fr. Mike made an announcement.

"Brothers and sister in Christ," Mike said with a wide smile. "It is my pleasure to announce that we have a new parishioner who is joining the Catholic faith today."

Everyone except Garrett, Mandy, and Paige looked around to see if there was a new face in the crowd.

Fr. Mike laughed. "I should have been a little clearer in my announcement. Our new parishioner is someone all of you know well. He has completed the Rite of Christian Initiation for Adults and will be received into our faith through confirmation and first communion. Garrett Lambert, will you please join me at the altar?"

Before Garrett could move, Mandy and Paige, who threw their arms around him and showered his face with kisses, almost tackled him. Even though they knew, both of them cried happy tears, and the rest of the congregation clapped enthusiastically.

"Okay," Garrett chuckled. "Don't kill me before I convert."

Paige and Mandy let him go.

"I love you so much, Garrett."

"I love you so much, Daddy."

"I love y'all, too. How much lipstick did y'all have on my face?"

People within earshot of Garrett's comment laughed.

"A lot," Mandy said as she removed a tissue from her purse and cleaned his face.

"No rush, Mandy," Mike said. "God will wait."

Laughter joined the applause at this comment.

A moment later, on weak legs, Garrett joined Fr. Mike on the altar.

Fr. Mike confirmed Garrett first and then it was time for his first communion.

Fr. Mike removed a Eucharist from the chalice and held it up. "The Body of Christ."

"Amen," Garrett said.

Fr. Mike placed the Eucharist in Garrett's cupped hands.

Garrett took it and said, "Amen."

Garrett brought it to his mouth and received the sacrament. Then he crossed himself, as was the custom.

The congregation, silent through the ceremony, erupted in applause. Garrett gave them an embarrassed wave and quickly returned to the pew, where Mandy and Paige covered his face in kisses again before exiting the pew to receive communion. Everyone who passed the pew on their way to communion offered their hands for shaking, pats on the back, and some ladies added to the lipstick on his cheeks with hugs and kisses.

When Mass ended, Fr. Mike said, "We are having a celebration to welcome Garrett into the Catholic faith in the Fellowship Hall. If you can attend, please do. Cake and punch will be served."

Garrett did not know a celebration was planned, and it took him by surprise. All he wanted to do was go home, but he appreciated Fr. Mike's celebration and he, Mandy, Paige, and just about everyone who had attended Mass made their way to the Fellowship Hall after Mass.

On the way to the Fellowship Hall, Garrett said, "I wish Father Mike hadn't thrown a celebration."

"*He* didn't," Paige said. "*We* did."

"Y'all did this?"

"Of course," Mandy said. "It's a special day, and we wanted to celebrate it."

"Father Mike thought it was a great idea, too," Paige added.

"Well, it wasn't necessary," Garrett said. "But thank y'all."

Once inside the Fellowship Hall, Garrett received more congratulatory handshakes, slaps on the back, and hugs and kisses from those who attended. When the celebration was over, they returned home.

~ * ~

Another big event occurred before the wedding. Paige's birthday. On Sunday, April 10th, 2016, Paige turned seventeen years old. It was a small party with Lindsey, Garrett, Mandy, Lacy, Ty, Jasmin, Little D, Lola, Trowa, James, and Fr. Mike attending. No one was surprised when Paige transformed her hand in to Glinda's hand-paw and used her dagger-length claws to cut the chocolate cake.

With Paige's birthday, Garrett dreaded the nightmare, *experience*, that accompanied each of her birthdays since the first one he had when Paige was two years old. This time, a seventeen-year-old Monster-Paige would rip her way out of Lacy's tortured dead body and leave with the larger werewolf who, Lola explained, had been him through the ancestorial werewolf he and Paige inherited from his mother's side of the family.

When the experience failed to invade his subconscious dreams, Garrett consulted Lola. She smiled, and in her warm honey voice explained, since Paige tamed her ancestorial werewolf, the shared experience no longer threatened either of them. Therefore, the experience would no longer visit his dreams. Garrett, who never fully understood the depth of Lola's knowledge, accepted her explanation. He was happy to have that tortured part of his life behind him.

~ * ~

More time passed and Saturday, April 30th, 2016, came. It was their wedding day. St. Joseph's Catholic Church is small, and accommodations were lacking. Garrett, Ty, and Little D had to use the 'Cry Room' to get prepared, while Mandy, Paige, and Lindsey used the vestry where Fr. Mike changed before Mass into his liturgical vestments.

Frustrated, Garrett yanked the bowtie he'd been trying to tie off. "Why couldn't Mandy have gotten us clip-on bow ties?"

Ty laughed. "Maybe 'cause ya left all the weddin' plannin' to her and Paige and told 'em you'd wear whatever they picked out for ya to wear."

"Thanks for pointin' out the obvious," Garrett said frustratedly. "But that doesn't help me tie this damn thing properly."

"Not all of us have spent our whole lives in Pine View," Ty said with a smile. "Some of us have traveled the world and have culture."

"Oh, really?" Garrett said. "Ya got culture in the Middle East?"

Ty grinned, took the bowtie from Garrett, and began tying it. "Don't be stupid. Jasmin showed me how to tie one this mornin'."

"Don't be stupid," Little D squealed and giggled.

When Ty finished, Garrett looked in the mirror at the perfectly tied bowtie. "You two are hilarious."

"What's hilours mean, Daddy?" Little D said.

"It means Mister Garrett thinks we're funny," Ty said and picked up Little D.

Little D giggled and squealed, "We are funny, Daddy."

~ * ~

In the other room, where the ladies were getting ready, things were much more orderly, but no less nervous. Paige and Lindsey were putting on the finishing touches of Mandy's makeup and primping her dirty blonde hair, which was up, to highlight her slender neck and the off-shoulder wedding dress. She had, of course, her engagement ring on and the silver necklace and crucifix Paige gave her for Christmas. It matched the one Paige wore.

When they were finished, Mandy said, "How do I look?"

"Beautiful," Paige and Lindsey answered at the same time.

Mandy turned, looked at herself in the tall mirror on the back of the door, and smiled. "I *really* do. Y'all did a great job with my hair and makeup. Thank y'all *so* much."

"You're always beautiful, Mandy," Paige said. "We just spiffed ya up for your special day."

Mandy smiled warmly. "Thank you, Paige-Turner. Can ya believe, in about an hour, I'll, officially, be your stepmom?"

Paige smiled and tucked a strand of Mandy's dirty blonde hair behind her right ear. "I've thought of ya that for a while already. I couldn't ask for a better one."

"Thank you, sweetheart," Mandy said. "Now stop talkin' like that or you'll make me cry and y'all will have to redo my makeup."

"Okay," Paige said. "I might start cryin', too."

"And me," Lindsey added.

Mandy had a thought, covered her mouth, and giggled like a schoolgirl.

"What's funny?" Paige asked.

"I was just thinkin' 'bout your daddy tryin' to tie his bowtie," Mandy giggled through her cupped hands. "It's gonna give him a fit."

"Should I check on him?" Paige asked.

"You don't need to," Mandy said more composed. "Jasmin showed Ty how to do it this mornin' so he could help your daddy."

"Sneaky," Paige said with a smile.

"Should I let Father Mike know he can come in now and get ready for the weddin' Mass?" Lindsey asked.

"Of course," Mandy said. "I keep thinkin' 'bout this as *my* day. I'm afraid my manners are secondary."

"It is *your* day," Paige said as Lindsey opened the door for Fr. Mike to come in.

~ * ~

Garrett paced anxiously back and forth in front of the Cry Room window. Through it, he saw their limited guests had all arrived.

"Why's it takin' so long for Mandy to get ready?" Garrett said nervously.

Ty laughed. "Think about how long it takes women to get ready to go out for supper. Now, multiply that by, at least, a hundred for her weddin' day."

"You're right," Garrett said. "I always think about Brad Paisley's song, Waitin' on a Woman, while I'm waitin' for Mandy to get dressed when we're goin' out. I'll relax."

At that moment, Fr. Mike opened the Cry Room door. "It's time to start, gentlemen."

Garrett gave Ty a nervous look.

"Ya got this, brother," Ty said.

"You guys remember what to do and when from the rehearsal last night?" Mike asked.

"Yes, sir," Garrett said as Ty picked up Little D and they headed out the door.

Outside the door, in the narthex, Garrett almost ran into Tommie Davis, Mandy's dad, as he headed into the room Mandy was in to walk her up the aisle in a few moments.

He smiled. "Take care of my little girl, Garrett."

"I will," Garrett said. "I guess, no matter how old they get, they're always our little girls."

"Yep," Tommie said. "Now get outta here so we can get this started."

"Yes, sir."

A few seconds later, Garrett stood on the right side of the altar. Deputy Danny Stutter, one usher, had seated his mom and dad in the front right pew and they smiled at him. Behind them sat Lola, Trowa, James, George, and Lacy. Lacy smiled at him, too. Behind them were some of his friends, which included Al and Gloria Anderson, Becky Middleton, and Steve Sweeten, off duty deputies, and off duty dispatchers.

On the left side of the aisle, Mandy's family and friend's side, her mom, Edith Davis, was seated by Deputy Austin Turner, the second usher, in the front pew. She smiled at Garrett, too. Behind her were Mandy's friends, most of whom Garrett knew. Pine View was a small town. In all, there were about forty people in attendance.

A moment later, Fr. Mike appeared at the back of the church, closed the inside doors, walked up to the altar, and turned to face the wedding party. "Please rise."

Everyone stood as one of the back doors opened and Ty, with Little D in one arm, and his other arm looped with Paige's arm, walked up the aisle. At the altar, they parted. Paige went left and stood off to the side to leave room for Mandy. Ty went right and stood next to Garrett.

After positioning herself on the left side, Paige ran her fingers over the silver crucifix hung around her neck. This wasn't a subconscious action, as it had been in the past. She was fully aware she did it and did it because it brought her great comfort. All the evil of the past, and what she became from it, hadn't corrupted her soul. God was still with her. Paige smiled.

On the other side of the aisle, Ty whispered, "Keep a knee bent so ya don't pass out."

"Okay," Garrett said as he bent his right knee slightly.

One of the back doors opened again, and Lindsey, with a basket of flower peddles, stepped through.

Karen Parker, the overnight dispatch who played piano, began playing *Here Comes the Bride*. Deputies Danny Stutter and Austin Turner opened both back doors, and Mandy and her dad appeared at the back of the church.

Garrett was awe-struck by how beautiful Mandy looked and felt his left knee buckle.

Ty hooked a firm hand under Garrett's left arm for support and whispered, "Easy there, Garrett."

Garrett regained his footing as Lindsey started down the aisle, sprinkling the flower petals in front of Mandy and her dad. At the altar, Lindsey went left and stood beside Paige. Tommie shook Garrett's hand, sat next to Edith. Mandy stepped up to the altar and faced Garrett.

"God, you're beautiful," Garrett whispered.

Mandy smiled. "So are you. Please don't make me cry…yet."

Fr. Mike began the Mass and the marriage liturgical rite.

For Garrett, Mass never seemed to drag on and fly by at the same time. Before he knew it, it was time for the vows. Garrett repeated the vows Fr. Mike ask him to repeat.

Fr. Mike asked him, "Do you, Garrett Lee Lambert, take Amanda Lee Davis as your lawful wife, to have and to hold from this day forward, for better, for worse, for richer, for poorer, in sickness and health, to love and cherish until death do you part."

"I do," Garrett said.

He took Mandy's wedding ring from the heart-shaped pillow Little D held up and slipped it on her delicate finger.

Then it was Mandy's turn to repeat and take the vow.

Fr. Mike asked her, "Do you, Amanda Lee Davis, take Garrett Lee Lambert as your lawful husband to have and to hold from this day forward, for better, for worse, for richer, for poorer, in sickness and health, to love and cherish until death do you part."

"I do," Mandy said.

She took Garrett's wedding ring from the heart-shaped pillow Little D held up and slipped it on his thick finger.

"By the power vested in me, in the name of the Father, Son, and Holy Spirit, I now pronounce you husband and wife," Fr. Mike said. "You may kiss your wife, Garrett."

Garrett and Mandy had tears streaming down their cheeks as they kissed for the first time as husband and wife.

The guests applauded and Trowa let out a whistle easily heard over the clapping.

"Mass is over," Fr. Mike announced. "Go in peace with Christ."

The Catholics in attendance, Mandy's side, responded with, "Thanks be to God."

"The reception is being held at the Knights of Columbus Hall in Pine View," Fr. Mike said. "I'm sure all of you know how to get there."

Mandy and Garrett led the procession out of the church, and everyone headed to the KC Hall.

~ * ~

At the reception, their first dance as husband and wife was Tracy Byrd's, *The Keeper of the Stars*.

When it came time to cut the cake, there were no dirty tricks. Neither tried to push cake into the other's face. Ty gave a heartfelt, and touching, best man toast. The guests ate and drank, some to excess in both areas, but not Garrett and Mandy. Aside from champagne after Ty's toast, they abstained. Neither wanted to forget a moment of the day, and they still had to drive to Dallas that night to catch their flight out of Dallas Love Field the next morning. It wasn't a non-stop flight. They'd have to board another plane in Atlanta, Georgia that would take them to London, where they would start their European Honeymoon, the next day. And Garrett's parents had insisted on reserving them a luxury villa at the Four Seasons Resort. Everything was perfect.

Paige and Lindsey took turns dancing with Little D and the dancefloor was full of other people enjoying the music being played by a hired DJ. James dancing with Lola, who wore a modest dress, was a sight to behold. Especially since they were dancing to The Eagles' *Hotel California*. James' belly jiggled in ways Paige had never seen before and she couldn't help but laugh.

Shortly before five o'clock, Garrett and Mandy slipped away to change into more comfortable clothing for the drive to Dallas. Paige would stay with her mom while they were on their honeymoon, but she agreed to take Mandy's wedding dress to her daddy's house after the reception. Ty was to return the rented tuxedos.

Before they left, Mandy tossed her bouquet over her shoulder, and Paige caught it.

"No time soon, Paige-Turner," Garrett told her.

Paige blushed, and the guests laughed.

While the reception was going on, Ty, Trowa, and the other deputies slipped out and 'decorated' Garrett's truck. It was a sight to behold with condoms attached to everything they could be attached to, white shoe polish sayings on all but the front windshield, and Miller Lite cans tied to the back bumper.

Garrett and Mandy took it in good humor; Mandy even managed to slingshot one condom directly into Ty's surprised face, which brought a roar of laughter. The Miller Lite cans were appropriate, but Garrett insisted the cans be removed so he wouldn't get a ticket for littering as they fell off on the almost three-hour drive to Dallas.

Just before they left, Garrett and Mandy pulled Paige aside to talk with her.

"We're gonna be gone two weeks," Garrett said. "Are ya gonna be okay?"

"I'll be okay, Daddy."

"Ya sure?" Garrett pressed. "When we planned all this, we didn't think 'bout when we'd be on our honeymoon."

Paige knew what her daddy referred to. They'd be gone on May 8th, the one-year anniversary of the MRB Massacre. The one-year anniversary of her boyfriend's, Justin's, death.

Paige smiled. "I'll be okay, Daddy. Now I *know* he's always with me."

Garrett knew what Paige referred to. She saw Justin in heaven and spoke with him.

Garrett smiled back at Paige. "Okay. But try not to get in trouble while we're gone."

"I'll try, Daddy."

"That's not, exactly, the answer I wanted."

"I'll try, Daddy," Paige said. "But ya know, I don't look for trouble. It finds me."

"If any finds ya, ignore it until we get back," Garrett told her.

"Jeez," Paige said with a smile. "I'm a wereampeer, now. Ya think I can't handle myself?"

"What your daddy's doin' a poor job of sayin' is, be careful," Mandy said.

"I will. I promise…Mom."

Tears leaked from Mandy's eyes. "Are ya really gonna call me mom?"

"Yeah," Paige said as tears filled her eyes. "If it's okay with you? And as long as Mom doesn't know."

Mandy wrapped Paige in a tight hug. "Of course it is. I couldn't wish for a better daughter, Paige-Turner. It'll be our secret."

"I love you, Mom."

"I love you too, sweet girl," Mandy said as they parted.

Garrett grabbed Paige, lifted her off her feet, and hugged her tightly. "I love you, Paige-Turner."

"I love you too, Daddy," Paige said and planted a kiss on his smooth, for a change, cheek.

Garrett put her down. "This'll be the longest I've ever gone without seein' ya."

Paige grinned. "I could fly over and join y'all."

Garrett and Mandy knew Paige wasn't talking about flying on a plane.

"Stay put," Garrett said. "Right here in Pine View County."

"I will."

"We'll use that Facebook video thing to call ya as much as possible," Mandy said.

"Y'all better." Paige said.

After that, Garrett and Mandy got in Garrett's truck and drove off into the twilight. Paige watched until her daddy's truck turned right toward Highway Sixty-Nine, Dallas, Atlanta, London, and other stops in Europe. She couldn't remember ever being happier.

~ * ~

Paige, her daddy, and Mandy used Facebook's video messenger to talk almost every day while they were on their honeymoon. They had recognizable landmarks, like Buckingham Palace and the Eiffel Tower, behind them as they chatted. Paige was happy for them, but also a little jealous. She promised herself she'd see those sights in person someday. Either on her own honeymoon or with Lin. Either scenario was fine with her, just as long as she got to go.

Garrett and Mandy's return flight was scheduled to land at Dallas Love Field at eight eighteen a.m. on Saturday, May 14, and they had invited Paige to spend the weekend with them. She couldn't wait and she had it all planned out.

They would have to go through customs in Atlanta, Georgia, when changing flights on the way back. So, Paige figured, allowing time to get their luggage, they'd be home between noon and one o'clock. She'd have the house decorated and pizzas waiting. She knew they might feel the effects of jetlag, but hoped they'd sleep on the planes and have enough energy to tell her all about everything they'd seen and done, minus the sex, and show her countless pictures and videos they'd taken on their cellphones.

It was Thursday, May 12th. Paige couldn't believe a year had passed since the werewolf killings and five months since the vampire killings. All was right in Pine View County. She ate supper with her mom, who had truly grown affectionate for Mandy, no one knew, but Lola had nudged the change, and once Lacy got over her initial dislike of Mandy, the affection became real, went upstairs, and did her homework.

At ten twelve p.m., Paige got in bed to go to sleep. She had an exam in Government class the next day. It was her last exam before finals, and she was ready for it. So was Lin. Paige had used her new powers to nudge Lin to study more, and it worked. Lin aced her exams, and her teachers were pleased with her grades. Lin suspected Paige had nudged her, but she didn't care because making good grades was gratifying.

With all this on her mind, Paige thought she'd toss and turn for hours before falling asleep. She was wrong. Within ten minutes of resting her head on the pillow, Paige fell fast asleep.

~ * ~

Lola got into bed shortly after Paige, at ten forty-one p.m. She lay on her back and looked up at the enchanted mirror. The waxing, crescent moon hovered high in the sky, surrounded by a multitude of sparkling stars. There wasn't a cloud in the ink black, night sky and the celestial view was beautiful. Lola smiled, closed her eyes, and fell asleep.

~ * ~

Paige was, suddenly, pulled from a beautiful dream by an unfamiliar, and unknown, force. In the dream, she'd been hovering high above the Eiffel Tower with a beautiful, full moon in the night sky. The unfamiliar force spoke a language she didn't understand; it was a female's voice. It reverberated in her head like it couldn't find a way out. She shook her head, but it wouldn't leave. She looked at her alarm clock. It was, exactly, three o'clock in the morning. She tried to reach out to Lola, but the intruder blocked her from doing so. The instant her alarm clock turned to three-o-one, the voice vanished.

Lola. Paige's mind screamed when the intrusion left her.

I'm here, Paige-Turner, Lola thought.

Did ya...hear that?

Yes, Lola thought. *I think every light witch within a hundred miles heard it.*

So...it could be a hundred miles from us?

No. It was close. I believe the Pine View stain has attracted another evil force.

What? Paige thought. *What was that?*

It is the witchin' hour and a Friday the thirteenth, Paige-Turner. That was someone embracin' dark powers.

I thought the witchin' hour was midnight?

No, Lola thought. *As James would say, that's more Hollywood bullshit. The witchin' hour is twelve hours after your Christ died on the cross at three o'clock in the afternoon. So, the witchin' hour is at three o'clock in the mornin'.*

What does Friday the thirteenth have to do with it?

Probably nothin'. But it's believed to be an unlucky day. So, a dark coven would find it an ideal day to embrace dark powers.

What language was that? Paige thought.

That was Aramaic. The language used by your Christ when he walked the Earth over two thousand years ago.

Did ya understand what it was sayin'?

No, Lola thought. *But I have trapped the message and will consult with Mamma immediately.*

What does all this mean, Lola?

It means that we have at least one witch who has embraced the dark powers.

At least one? Paige thought. *There could be more?*

Yes. With a message that strong, I believe we have a coven of dark witches in Pine View County.

Is that bad?

Very, Lola thought. *You let me worry 'bout this for now. Your daddy and Mandy are returnin' tomorrow. Enjoy their homecomin'. I'll let ya know what I learn from Mamma tomorrow. Go back to sleep, Paige-Turner.*

I can't just...turn this off, Lola.

Ya can and ya must. There is nothin' we can do until I learn more.

Okay. I'll try, Paige thought.

Goodnight, Paige-Turner, Lola thought with a hidden nudge and the connection broke.

Paige didn't think, after hearing a dark coven was in Pine View County, or the voice in her head she couldn't repel, she could go back to sleep. There was too much to worry about, but her eyelids felt heavy, and she couldn't keep them open. She knew Lola had nudged her to fall asleep. As a seer, she had the power to resist Lola's nudge but decided not to. Lola was right. She couldn't do anything about the recent development until Mamma interpreted the incantation. Paige embraced sleep, but her beautiful dream had gone. Instead, she dreamed about being back in hell with Lucifer, and God wasn't there to protect her.

~ * ~

A black candle flickered in the darkness, deep in the woods of Pine View County. Its bright light illuminated a dead cat with its innards removed, a blood-stained, bone-handled dagger, and the pages of an ancient, black, leather-bound, opened tome. On the left-side leaf was an inverted pentagram with the face of a horned beast in the middle. On the right-side leaf were words in Aramaic runes. It was the old language. All the pages in the tome were written with a quill dipped in human blood. The blood of Christians sacrificed to Lucifer and penned by dark monks in His service.

Although it was written in Aramaic runes, the tomb was not from the time of Christ. Books didn't exist then, just scrolls. This book was, roughly, a thousand years old. The incantations, though, were passed down in Aramaic, since the crucifixion of Christ for those who practiced dark powers and worshiped the Antichrist. That tome was the oldest known to exist. It had been passed down from the original author through generations of his bloodline.

When the incantation that invaded Paige's and Lola's minds ended, the dead cat's head moved. It raised unsteadily and opened its eyes. Its eyes were white, no irises or pupils, unseeing eyes. It blinked several times and stood on wobbly legs with its pool of innards on the ground beneath it, attached by a single strand of intestine. Its mouth opened and it let out what sounded like a scream.

The bone-handle dagger came down in a fluid motion and severed the screaming cat's head. The scream ended as its body and head fell to the ground. Its body was motionless, but its white, unseeing eyes continued to blink. Its mouth had still been open in a silent scream and its rough, pink tongue licked blood it couldn't taste from its whiskers.

Five sets of hands dug in the moist, black soil until the hole was big enough to bury the cat. Its body, entrails, and head were placed in the hole. The cat's white, unseeing eyes blinked up at the five people until the moist, dark soil covered it.

Unseen by the five people, the cat's eyes continued to blink, or try to blink, as dirt covered its eyes and scratched painfully each time it tried to close its lids. Dirt filled its opened, un-screaming mouth and caked its rough, pink tongue. Its reanimated head would remain in that painful state for eternity. Or, until someone broke the blood, sacrificial curse.

A female's hand closed the tome. The worn, black leather cover was embossed with Aramaic runes inked in the blood of sacrificed Christians. The title of the tome was, ܟܬܒܘܬܐ ܟܫܝܦܘܬܐ. In English, the words translated to *Dark Craft*.

"It has begun," a young woman said as the black candle snuffed out and darkness enveloped the dark coven.

Also by the Author
at
Rogue Phoenix Press

The Pack
Pine View County Trilogy
Book Two

Prologue

A lazy quarter moon hovered over the Gulf of Mexico. High, thin clouds passed in front of the moon, causing its light to flicker off the calm, dark waters below. Small waves broke with milky-green foam and gently lapped at the shores of South Padre Island, Texas. At the far south end of the island, in Isla Blanca Park, a lone figure stood on the beach at the water's edge and looked out across the Gulf at the moon's reflection on the water.

Aside from the sounds of the waves and the soft rustle of wind blowing through the fronds of scattered palm trees, the sounds of partying college students engaged in many acts of debauchery filled the night air. It was Saturday, March 14, 2015, which had been the kick-off week for Spring Break in Texas. Over the next few weeks, tens of thousands of party eager college students would invade the small resort island, hoping to get drunk, get high, and get laid. This created the perfect conditions for an entrepreneurial individual—the demand for drugs had been there, someone needed to provide the supply. Alexis Jordan planned to be that someone.

~ * ~

Spring Break came toward the end of Alexis' second year at

Stephen F. Austin State University in Nacogdoches, Texas. She pursued a Bachelor of Science degree in Business Administration. Not that she had an affinity for business, per se, but she lacked interest in anything more focused.

"The important thing," her dad would say, "is that you get a degree."

Those imprinted words shaped Alexis' plan—get a degree. She wasn't a bad student, but she didn't try to be a good student. In the spirit of 'getting a degree,' she put the least amount of effort into that outcome as possible. This resulted in Alexis being a B and C student.

By most measures, Alexis was an attractive young woman. She had long blonde hair and big blue eyes. Alexis was meticulous about health, vegetarian, not vegan, and fitness. She spent more time working out in the recreation center than she did in the library, and it showed. Attractiveness ended at her outward appearance, though.

On the inside, egotistical, vengeful, and uncaring best described Alexis. Since she had money, looks, and a deceivingly good-natured personality, usually when she wanted something from someone, girls wanted to be around her, as well as boys who wanted to be inside her. Even though Alexis didn't lack acquaintances, she was a Tri-Delt, to party with on Thursday nights at the Flashback and Frogs bars, she didn't have any real friends and that suited her just fine. Friends meant caring about someone else and she couldn't be bothered with that.

Alexis had a boyfriend, though. His name was Seth Daniels, and he was in the Theta Chi fraternity. They met at a Greek Mixer in the fall of 2014. It wasn't love at first sight, or even love after six months. He had been attractive—six feet tall, one-hundred eighty-five pounds of finely honed muscles, with dark brown hair and smoky brown eyes. Most importantly, for Alexis' standards in dateable men, he came from a wealthy, Dallas family.

At first, Alexis thought of Seth as nothing more than a living, breathing sex object. When she'd allow him to touch her, she loved making him beg, the sex was satisfactory. He came more than she did, but Alexis was used to this in lovers. She had toys to make up for his 'shortcomings' in bed. Seth also provided a way to supplement her allowance, she willingly let Seth spend money on her. No begging required there. To her surprise, she missed his company over the four-week Winter Break. Despite her predilection not to, she cared for Seth.

They would spend Spring Break apart, too. Alexis begged Seth, which was something she rarely did, to come to South Padre Island with her, but he stood fast on plans to go skiing on Powderhorn Mountain in Colorado with several of his fraternity brothers. This angered Alexis so much she almost broke up with him. She didn't, because she wasn't sure Seth would approve of her entrepreneurial Spring Break plans—he didn't complain about the money his parents 'allowed' him to have. Besides, she would make him pay for choosing a week with his frat brothers skiing, over a week with her in skimpy bikinis on the beach, by withholding sex. After all, she could go longer without sex than he could. If she found herself particularly horny before Seth suffered enough, she'd never had a problem getting boys into bed. If she were feeling vengeful, she'd have sex with one of Seth's ski-buddy frat brothers.

Bros before hos my sweet, tight ass, Alexis thought as Seth kissed her goodbye the last day of class before Spring Break started.

~ * ~

On her way from Stephen F. Austin State University to South Padre Island, Alexis stopped off at her dad's house in Houston for one night. It had been on the way, and she scored 'daughter points' for doing so. The daughter points would pay off in the future in the way of more purchasing power on her dad's credit card. Alexis had another reason for 'dropping by' and spending one night in Houston—her dad's safe.

Her dad, Alex Jordan, was a wealthy man. Not Bill Gates, billionaire rich, but he was worth around fifty million. He made his millions in real estate—rode the housing bubble through 2008 and got out just before the bubble popped. Since that time, he made his money off the misery of others by purchasing underwater, foreclosed properties for pennies on the dollar and reselling them for a nice profit.

Alexis had no compunctions with the way her dad made money. She believed in making money any way she could, short of selling her body. Her dad's millions made her life much easier, too. She drove a silver, 2013, Mercedes-Benz CLS Coupe, her high school graduation present, and had a Chase Visa with a twenty thousand dollar limit her dad paid off each month. He would complain if Alexis spent more than a couple of thousand dollars in a month—he 'allowed' her to spend five-hundred dollars a week, but he kept the limit high 'in case of an emergency.' So, Alexis didn't have a problem with over-spending, often buying jewelry, expensive clothing, and more shoes than she could count in an afternoon. As is often the case with spoiled, rich offspring, enough wasn't enough for Alexis.

Alexis knew her dad kept a 'chunk of change' in his home safe for occasions when he needed quick cash for an evaporating deal. She planned to 'borrow' what she needed, purchase drugs in Mexico, sell them for a nice profit to spring breakers, and replace the money she borrowed from her dad on the way back to Nacogdoches. She even knew the safe combination—the month, day, and year of her birthday, 08081995. It was like he wanted her to borrow the money.

After her dad fell asleep, Alexis went into his home office. She didn't need to sneak—the house was huge, and her dad was sleeping many rooms away. Once inside his office, she pushed the wood panel in the wall behind his desk that concealed the safe, it slid aside. She punched the combination into the keypad and waited. A second or two later, the safe's red light switched to green. Alexis opened it.

Chunk of change, my ass, Alexis thought as she looked at the stacks of bundled cash.

Although tempted to take as much as she could carry, she'd already agreed on an amount with her 'associate' in Brownsville, Texas. She knew she could trust the associate because she had the same arrangement with him the previous Spring Break, but on a much smaller scale—five thousand dollars. That deal netted her three thousand dollars. With the same markup, Alexis stood to net thirty thousand dollars this time.

Using her head, Alexis removed bundles of cash from the back of the safe. When she'd removed the agreed upon fifty thousand dollars, ten thousand for her associate and forty thousand for the Ecstasy, she couldn't tell, at a glance, any cash was missing. Satisfied, she started to close the safe. Just because she could, she took another five-thousand-dollar bundle—her dad would see her Spring Break spending on the credit card statement, and she didn't want him bitching at her if she splurged. He wouldn't see the extra five thousand dollars on the credit card statement, and she would replace it with her profits when she returned. At least, that had been the plan.

Alexis shut the safe and went to sleep with visions of bundled cash dancing through her dreams. In the morning, she kissed her dad goodbye, loaded her heavier by fifty-five thousand dollars bags into the back seat of her CLS Coup, and headed for South Padre Island.

As Alexis pulled into Isla Blanca Park, the clock on her dashboard read two thirty-seven a.m. She was supposed to meet Carlos Garza at two thirty and he wasn't a man who liked to be kept waiting.

Not wanting to call unwanted attention to herself but, also, not wanting to keep Carlos waiting any longer than necessary, Alexis set her cruise-control at five miles over the speed limit and merged south on to the Channel View Loop. When the Loop curved east toward the Gulf of Mexico, Alexis slowed down and looked for the horseshoe offshoot road on the right that would lead to her and Carlos' meeting spot.

After pulling into the offshoot road, Alexis parked her car next to Carlos' crappy, old Chevy pickup. He was still there. She locked her car, and headed across the sand to where Carlos was supposed to be waiting.

~ * ~

Alexis crested a high dune and spotted Carlos standing on the beach looking out at the calm Gulf waters. Alexis stopped well short of the water's edge—she'd dressed for the beach in a black bikini top, white shorts, and black sandals, but they were five-hundred-dollar Fendi Isabel sandals, and she wasn't about to get them wet.

Instead of joining Carlos at the water's edge, Alexis shouted, "Hey, Carlos. Sorry I'm late. Best laid plans and all that shit."

Carlos turned and walked toward Alexis.

When he was close enough to not shout, he said, with a heavy Mexican accent, "Jou make me wait while jou party?"

Alexis laughed. "Cut the Tex-Mex, gang-banger accent shit, Carlos. I wasn't partying. It was a long drive from Houston. I took a nap, and I overslept."

Carlos smiled and, in a perfect Texas drawl with no hint of his

Mexican heritage, said, "All right, all right. Ya know, I don't like waitin'. Time is money, *amiga.*"

~ * ~

Alexis considered Carlos Garza a bit of an enigma. He looked like the stereotypical gangbanger. His body was covered in tattoos, which included a tear under his left eye. Whether Carlos ever killed someone, which is what that tattoo signified in gangs, Alexis didn't know. He had a hangman's noose around his neck, pistols on his forearms, spider webs on his shoulders with nasty looking black widow spiders with human skulls for heads hanging by a thread of webbing on his biceps, a beautiful wooden cross on his back with the cross member going from shoulder to shoulder, the top going up the back of his neck, and the base going to the small of his back, and an equally beautiful depiction of a praying Virgin Mary that covered his entire chest and stomach. Those were just the tattoos Alexis had seen.

Continuing with the gang-banger theme, Carlos had a shaved head, a long, black, braided goatee that hung to the middle of his chest, and a gold upper grill that twinkled when he smiled. He always dressed in very baggy jeans that were prevented from sliding off his ass by a thick, black, leather belt with his name in silver letters on the back, tight, sleeveless, white, 'wife beater' T-shirts, beautifully engraved silver-tipped, with turquoise inlays, black, cowboy boots, and a very large, black, leather wallet that was attached to his belt by a larger than necessary, chrome-plated chain.

Although Carlos looked like a gangbanger, he chose to remain unaffiliated in the United States. To Carlos, being affiliated meant inviting unwanted attention. His contacts were in Matamoros, Mexico, which was just across the border from Brownsville, Texas, where he was born and raised.

His contact, the *Cartel del Golfo*, the Gulf Cartel or CDG for short, afforded him security and why state-side gang members left him alone. The CDG had been one of the oldest organized crime cartels in Mexico. It started by smuggling alcohol into the United States during Prohibition and shifted to drug trafficking in the 1970's. Carlos used this connection to facilitate drug trafficking in South Texas.

By all outward appearances, and his chosen profession, Carlos appeared to be a poor, uneducated thug who fell into drug trafficking because he didn't have options. This had been where the 'enigma' came into play. Alexis knew the other side of Carlos Garza. He wasn't any of those things. Carlos came from a well-to-do, well-respected, ranching family. His father served six terms in the Texas House of Representatives.

Carlos had a good education, too. He graduated from St. Joseph Academy with honors and received a Bachelor of Science degree in Criminal Justice from Texas A&M Corpus Christi. The irony of Carlos' college degree was not lost on Alexis. Not a victim of circumstance, Carlos trafficked drugs because it was profitable and because he enjoyed it.

~ * ~

"Speakin' of money," Carlos continued, "ya got it?"

Alexis nodded. "Yeah. Fifty thousand, like we agreed. Ten K for you and forty for the X."

Carlos stroked his goatee, he did this often. "Okay, *amiga*. This is different than last year. I could do four thousand outta my supply. The guy I found doesn't deal Ecstasy…he's a cocaine dude, but he got what ya needed. Your forty-K will get ya two thousand pills…that's twenty bucks a pop. You should be able to sell 'em for thirty-five or forty bucks a hit. That's decent profit, *chica*."

Alexis grinned. "Yes, it is. How do we do this?"

Carlos stroked his goatee again. "That's the tricky part. Homeland Security and Border Patrol are thick. I got a spot just west of Hidalgo where we can cross. He'll meet us there."

Alexis wasn't exactly eager to cross the Rio Grande River and sneak into Mexico to get the Ecstasy, but Carlos insisted. He said he didn't mind getting 'pinched' with cocaine or marijuana, but his 'street cred' as a drug trafficker would take a serious hit if he were caught smuggling Ecstasy without a 'pretty *puta*' to blame it on. Alexis agreed to go.

Alexis took this information in. "What's your guy's name?"

Carlos smiled; his gold grill sparkled in the moonlight. "His name is Juan Escobar, but he goes by *El Lobo*."

"He goes by The Wolf?"

"Yeah," Carlos laughed, "I hear he's one *loco cabrón*."

Alexis started walking back to her car but, upon hearing this, she turned back to Carlos. "You *hear* he's a crazy bastard? You haven't done business with him before?"

Carlos flashed his gold grill again. "It's cool, *chica*. He comes highly recommended."

Alexis shook her head. "I don't know, Carlos. This sounds like a bad idea."

The smile dropped off Carlos' face, which made him look dangerous. "Don't waste my time, *puta*. Ya back out now, fine. I get my dime, regardless. Now…are we gonna do this or are you gonna drive your sweet ass back to SFA broke?"

Against her better judgment, but not wanting to abandon an opportunity to make thirty thousand quick dollars, Alexis nodded.

The gold grill grin instantly reappeared on Carlos' face. "Don't worry, *chica*, these tattoo *pistolas* aren't the only ones I'm packin'. If the big, bad wolf causes trouble, I'll put 'em down."

As Alexis and Carlos walked back to their vehicles, Carlos said, "Follow me into Hidalgo. You can leave your car at the Walmart and ride with me the rest of the way."

Alexis didn't like the idea of leaving her CLS Coupe at a Walmart or of riding with Carlos in his piece of shit truck. She knew he could afford nicer transportation and didn't understand why he continued to drive the rusty old truck.

"I don't wanna leave my car in a Walmart parkin' lot. Some Mexican might steal it. Can't we go together in my car?"

Carlos grinned at the Mexican remark. "I'm not comin' back here afterward; more business elsewhere. Your car'll be safe at the Walmart. Park it under a light. Besides, your car can't drive where we're goin'."

By the time Carlos had finished explaining why Alexis couldn't bring her car all the way into Mexico, they were back at their vehicles.

Reluctantly, Alexis nodded. "Yeah, okay. But if someone steals my fuckin' car, I'm taking your shitty truck back to South Padre."

Carlos smiled, and moonlight sparkled off his gold grill again. "My shitty truck's worth more than your import, but…okay, *chica*. Ya gotta deal."

Alexis found Carlos' statement more than a little odd, considering his truck was an ancient, rusted pile of shit, but she nodded. They got into their vehicles and headed west for Hidalgo.

About the Author
leewpayne@me.com

Lee W. Payne has a BS, MA, and Ph.D. in Political Science. He is a Professor of Political Science at Stephen F. Austin State University, where he has taught since 2006. Lee is well published in peer-reviewed academic journals and textbooks but has always enjoyed storytelling. *The Cloud* is his second novel and the second of three novels in the subtitled Pine View County Trilogy. Lee lives in Nacogdoches, Texas with his English Bulldog, Tank.

VISIT OUR WEBSITE
FOR THE FULL INVENTORY
OF QUALITY BOOKS:
http://www.roguephoenixpress.com

Rogue Phoenix Press
Representing Excellence in Publishing
Quality trade paperbacks and downloads

in multiple formats,

in genres ranging from historical to contemporary romance,
mystery and science fiction.

Visit the website then bookmark it.

We add new titles each month!

www.ingramcontent.com/pod-product-compliance
Lightning Source LLC
Chambersburg PA
CBHW050118030726
47505CB00007B/1922